THE MARKER CHRONICLES

THE FIRST TRILOGY

DANIELLE DEVOR

CITY OWL
PRESS

This book is a work of fiction. Names, characters, places, and incidents either are products of the author's imagination or are used fictitiously. Any resemblance to actual events or locales or persons, living or dead, is entirely coincidental and not intended by the author.

THE MARKER CHRONICLES
The First Trilogy: Books 1 - 3

CITY OWL PRESS
www.cityowlpress.com

Cover Design by Tina Moss. All stock photos licensed appropriately.

Edited by Tina Moss.

For information on subsidiary rights, please contact the publisher at info@cityowlpress.com.

Hardcover Edition ISBN: 978-1-944728-47-2

Digital Edition ISBN: 978-1-944728-46-5

Printed in the United States of America

By Danielle DeVor

SORROW'S POINT
SORROW'S EDGE
SORROW'S TURN

THE MARKER CHRONICLES: THE FIRST TRILOGY

TAIL OF THE DEVIL
THE DEVIL'S LIEGE

CONSTRUCTING MARCUS

DANCING WITH A DEAD HORSE

STRANGE DARKNESS

Short Stories
THE CASE
CRABS
REFLECTION
THE DARKEST DREAM
LOVE ME TO DEATH
EMMY'S PUPPY
DAWN
THE SHROUD
PAPAP'S TEETH
DUST

Anthologies
THE DARK DOZEN
Love Potion #9

Praise for the Works of Danielle DeVor

Named Examiner's Women in Horror: 93 Horror Authors You Need to Read Right Now

"Defrocked priest Jimmy Holiday's narrative voice is a strong blend of insightful, self-deprecating, and sincere."
- *Publisher's Weekly*

"SORROW'S POINT was probably one of the most terrifying books I've ever read. The book is a page-turner, but definitely not for the faint of heart. There were a few chilling scenes that will leave me with nightmares for weeks."
- *Heather Wood, Book Chatter*

"DeVor weaves a clever plot and brings the reader a huge mixture of emotions such as fear, anxiety, wonderment and complete shock."
- *Romance Thriller Author, Lilian Roberts*

'SORROW'S POINT is a great horror story read. For me, this harkens back to the books of my youth, where the mystery and the horror were the main characters."
- *Paranormal Mystery Author, Rebecca Trogner*

"Move over, Stephen King. Danielle DeVor is on her way!"
- *YA Paranormal Romance Author, Katie O'Sullivan*

"SORROW'S POINT by Danielle DeVor is a new take on *The Exorcist* and for me a much better read. The author has invoked pure spine-tingling flesh-crawling terror from every chilling page."
- *Fantasy and Horror Author, Simon Okill*

"The thing I love most about Danielle DeVor's work is that she never takes the easy road. Her imagination seems boundless. Sure, there's horror, demons, ghosts, and a myriad of other spooky goings-on. But I've noticed that she likes to mess with her characters. A lot. And the reader is better for it. And speaking of roads, the entourage is now headed for Tombstone, Arizona, in SORROW'S EDGE, where more ungodly things are brewing. Good luck, Jimmy!"

- *Horror Thriller Author, Steven Ramirez*

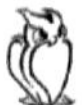

For my father, the real-life Jimmy Holiday.

Good thing you never had to battle a demon,

they wouldn't stand a chance.

- Danielle

Book One of the Marker Chronicles

Sorrow's Point

Danielle DeVor

City Owl Press

SORROW'S POINT (Book 1)

Not All Exorcists are Equal....One is Marked

When defrocked ex-priest, Jimmy Holiday, agrees to help an old friend with his sick daughter, he doesn't expect the horrors that await him. Blackmoor, his friend's new residence, rests upon the outskirts of the town of Sorrow's Point. The mansion's history of magic, mayhem, and death makes it almost a living thing – a haunted mansion straight out of a Stephen King novel. Jimmy must decide if the young girl, Lucy, is only ill, or if the haunting of the house and her apparent possession are real.

After the house appears to affect him as well with colors of magic dancing before his eyes, rooms warded by a witch, and a ring of power in his voice, Jimmy is met by a transient who tells him he has "the Mark." Whatever being "marked" means, Jimmy doesn't care. All he wants to do is help Lucy. But, helping Lucy means performing an exorcism.

Chapter One

The Devil's Brood

1950

WHAT WAS LEFT of O'Dell's hair blew in the wind like the last strands of cotton candy left in the machine. But it was too damn hot to have the windows up. With the sun beating down and the extra weight he'd put on over the last few years, the drive up the hill to Blackmoor turned hotter than an inferno. This year it'd been a hard summer. He'd lost count of the amount of times he had to yell at kids for messing with the fire hydrants.

He adjusted his uniform, pulling at the hem of his shirt. The stiff fabric clung to his skin like nothing else. In this heat, he'd rather be home in his cotton undershirt, sitting on the back porch and drinking a beer. But work came first.

O'Dell parked the cruiser in the drive and looked up at the monstrosity before him. Damn thing was massive—about double the size of a football field. Three levels to it. Way too huge for any normal family, but then, the Blacks were anything but normal. To him, the house seemed like *Moby Dick*: massive, vengeful and misunderstood. He grabbed his hanky and wiped the sweat off the back of his neck.

"Just what I need, Black breathing down my neck. To hell with you, Doris."

He closed the car door as he stretched the kinks out of his neck and took in his surroundings. No birds or any little creatures stirred. No sound could be heard other than the ragged snorts of his own breath. Goosebumps traveled up his arms. He walked the stone steps to the front door and pressed the button. The doorbell peeled in some tinkling tune O'Dell couldn't name.

He waited.

No one came to the door.

Failing at the entrance, he wandered around. The place was so big it took a while to find the back. By the time he got there, his breath tore out of him and the air felt like twenty pounds in his lungs.

"Goddamn humidity."

He stood in some sort of garden area. Flowers bloomed in beds arranged strategically about the back of the house, like something you'd see in an art book. A stone patio graced the top of the steps. He hobbled up them, still panting. The porch was large enough to host a "quiet" party of three hundred people. Yes, the Blacks were a whole different breed.

He knocked on the back door. Still no answer.

Then, he heard it, a noise at last, a thump from inside the kitchen. He peered in the side window.

It was too much for his brain to process. Flashes blinked in rapid succession as if his mind could only handle it in pieces. Red ran over the walls like a sprayed Jackson Pollock painting. It covered the doorway and dripped from the top as bright as cherry syrup. On the kitchen sink rested a dish drainer. Long black hair pooled around the severed head of Mrs. Black. The blood dripping from the neck stump had matted the hair to the counter.

O'Dell turned away from the windows and puked. Nothing like this ever happened in Sorrow's Point. The most he usually dealt with was a stupid kid shoplifting from the five and dime. He flew off the patio to the front of the house in record time. His sides ached and his head swam. Nausea beat at his gut. Fumbling with the driver's side door of his cruiser, he jerked it open, hopped inside, and pulled out his radio.

"Jesus Fucking Christ!" He wiped his mouth with the back of his hand and pressed the button on the receiver. "Mable?"

"What?" Mable answered, the receiver crackling.

"I need goddamn backup at Blackmoor!"

"What? Oh God. Sorry, Walt. I'll make the call."

O'Dell released his radio and waited. The sour-sweet smell of the vomit on his shoes turned his stomach. He forced the bile back down his throat.

One at a time, the deputies arrived. For a town the size of Sorrow's

Point, two deputies was all the town could afford. O'Dell's fist tightened on the handle as he got out of his car.

"Sheriff, what's going on?" Deputy Jones asked.

Boy was a young one, fresh out of the academy. O'Dell hoped he'd be able to pull his weight. He took a deep breath. "It's bad, Jake. Real bad."

Jones glanced over at the other deputy, Parker, and then turned back to the sheriff. "I've never seen you this messed up, Sheriff. You okay?"

The sweat dripped from O'Dell's head in rivulets. He glanced at his reflection in the side mirror of his cruiser. His face flushed bright red. Before this case was done, he'd need more blood pressure pills. He threw his hat into the dirt. "No, I'm not fucking okay. Black has gone and killed his whole family!" He poked Jones in the chest. "I want you to go get that sumbitch. Cuff his ass and get him in the car. You hear me?"

Jones swallowed. O'Dell watched his Adam's apple bob. Then the deputy motioned for his partner.

"Go round back," O'Dell said.

#

Jones crept around the side of the massive home. He looked this way and that like they had taught him in the academy. This was the first time something serious had gone down in Sorrow's Point. He set his jaw, bound and determined to do the best damn job he could.

The sheriff's footprints pressed into the tall grass, making it easy for him to know where to look. They led him to the back of the house and stopped as soon as they reached the stone patio. Something smelled sour-sweet. Flies would be swarming along soon. He walked up the steps and across to the door. The aroma grew stronger, but he didn't notice anything else out of the ordinary. Suddenly, his foot slid and he almost fell. His eyes drifted to the patio. A pile of puke, almost the same color as the stone, coated the bottom of his boot. "Great."

Backing up a step, he wiped the sole on the stone as best he could. Then, he sidestepped the puddle and peered in the window. Black sat at a butcher block table, facing the window. His dark hair stood up from his head in all directions. Eyebrows arched like the Devil's own. The deep red blood covered him from head to toe. He took another bite out of the small human leg he held in his large hands, grinding his teeth through the raw flesh.

"Oh shit." Jones shook, unable to release his death grip on the windowsill. The world shifted.

Jones peered down the smoking barrel of his gun, following the path through the broken window. He hadn't meant for the gun to go off. He didn't even remember reaching for his weapon. Black's chin slumped against his chest, the back of his head gone. Bits of gray matter stuck to the wall behind him. Black's fingers relaxed. The leg fell to the floor.

Chapter Two

Things to Start With

Present

HERE I WAS, sleeping in my bed, warm and relaxed, when the phone rang. To a lot of people, a phone call is a mundane thing, an everyday occurrence that, for the most part, has no bearing on daily life. But this phone call, it was something else entirely.

I glanced at the clock—3:00 a.m., the true witching hour. I grimaced. That was the last thing I needed to be thinking about. I blinked the sleep from my eyes and groaned. The phone rang again. *Are you kidding me?* I reached for it.

"Jimmy?" the voice asked.

I wiped my hand over my face to try to wake up. *Who in the hell is this?* I threw the covers off my legs and rose. Then, turned and dangled them over the side of the bed. It hit me. I recognized this voice. Someone from my past, someone I hadn't heard from in years. The voice, after all this time, seemed somehow unchanged. "Will?"

His breath hissed into the phone. "I'm sorry for calling so late."

Why was he apologizing? I wasn't sure. The deed had already been done. I'd be lucky to get back to sleep at all.

He coughed. "It's about Lucy."

A buzzing started in my brain and drifted over my body like a swarm of locusts. I had better shit to do with my time—like sleep. He was calling, waking me up, for someone I didn't even know? "Lucy who?"

"Lucy," his pause weighted the air, "my daughter."

Someone sucked all the oxygen out of my lungs with a shop-vac. I bent at the waist, doubled over. A long time ago, Will and I had been great friends. I hadn't spoken to him in who knew how long. It had been before I'd entered seminary for sure. Still though, I didn't even know he was married, but then, maybe he wasn't. Stuff wasn't all that cut and dry these days. "I," starting awkwardly, I took a breath to center and tried again, "I didn't know you had a daughter, Will."

"Aw, hell." A thud reverberated over the line. "Shit. Has it been that long?"

I rolled my eyes. *Yes, you idiot, it's been years.* "Yes, it's been that long."

"Well damn, but ah," he said and honked his nose as he blew it into the phone. "I have a question."

One or many, I wondered, but said simply, "Okay."

"My daughter needs help, and I don't know what to do."

Not a question. I wiped my eyes with the back of my hand, trying to rub the sleep out of them. "What's going on, Will?"

He took a deep breath then hit me with the two ton question he had failed to speak earlier. "Do you still believe?"

My brows wrinkled together. A common habit. My mother used to comment on it all the time. It irritated the hell out of me. But this shit with Will wasn't making any sense. "What are you talking about?"

"God. I'm talking about God."

Oh Christ. I hadn't been asked that question for a long time. Ten years at least. And, then, it hadn't been a very happy occasion. "Yes, I still believe."

Another shaking breath told me this wasn't going to go well. "Can I meet you somewhere?"

I sat up straighter. Somehow, I had a feeling this could easily turn into one of those stories I would tell at the local bar so people could laugh over drinks. "Now?"

"Please, Jimmy. I know this is a lot to ask, but I'm desperate."

I rolled my head to stare at the ceiling. My breath escaped out of my lungs in a hiss. My shoulders slumped. Any chance at sleep disappeared. I was going to kick myself, but I couldn't avoid the inevitable. "Where are you?"

"Sitting in your driveway."

I snatched the phone away from my mouth. "Are you shitting me?"

I jumped up and pulled back the curtain next to the bed. Sure enough, a green Toyota 4Runner that had seen better days sat idle in the driveway. I waved, let the curtain fall, and hung up the phone.

Damn creepy. My insides churned like I'd walked off a roller coaster. Something was wrong about this whole situation. Someone I hadn't talked to in over fifteen years randomly showing up at my house in the middle of the night?

I dropped the phone on my bed. "Hell." Bed looked good right now, going downstairs didn't. I left my room, stumbling. When I hit the bottom step, I turned on the hallway light. It bathed the room in a harsh yellow glow that stung my eyes. As I opened the front door, he stood there, blonde hair mussed, face white, hands shaking. What had happened to him?

"Come in," I said.

He stepped over the threshold and the wooden floor popped. We both jumped.

"Don't worry about it. It's an old house." It still left me uneasy. That floor had never popped there before. The over-active imagination I had wanted to cue in the creepy music.

He hobbled in and headed straight to my living room. Narrowly avoiding my pile of books, he plopped in my old brown recliner. I shuffled my feet on the brown shag carpet, dreading this conversation. I sat opposite him on the sofa.

"I'm scared, Jimmy." He blurted it out with nothing to back it up.

I shook my head. "I'm not trying to be cruel here, but what's that got to do with me?"

He leaned forward in the chair and looked me in the eyes. "I need a priest."

"Okay." I sighed. I should have known. This was going to be so much fun. "But I'm not a priest, Will."

He stared at me. "Why not?"

Oh, God. Where in the hell did I start? "Look, it's not that easy of a story."

"I'd like to know," Will said.

Fine. Not like it was a secret, so what the hell. I was too tired to refuse and it all started tumbling out of my mouth like teeth that had been busted out by a prizefighter. "My mother always said we were related to Doc Holliday, so maybe, somehow, I was trying to live up to the importance or something. But since our names weren't even spelled the same, I kind of doubted it."

Will waved a hand at me to continue.

I sighed, liking this less and less. Looking into my old friend's eyes snapped something inside me. It felt wrong and irritating and my blood pressure rose. The whole sordid affair came pouring out of me. I wondered idly how long I had kept it down. "My folks were both alcoholics. I don't know if you knew that, but it's true. Dad was a nice drunk. Mom always had these grandiose ideas." I scratched my arm and stared at the floor.

"I remember her. She kind of always had her nose in the air," Will said.

"Then you know exactly what I'm talking about," I replied. "Anyway, growing up wasn't exactly cushy. I probably don't react the same way as regular people. In a roundabout way, that's how I ended up becoming a priest. Church was the one place I felt relaxed. My mom was always bickering at my dad about this or that. Sometimes, I wonder if she drove him to drink, but I know better. There was a darker story beneath all of that."

Suddenly, a loud crash interrupted my sad tale as the noise echoed against the side of the house.

"What the fuck was that?"

Will and I jumped. I ran out the front door and around the yard. My garbage cans were knocked over. I could just barely make out a striped tail as the animal ran away.

"Dammit."

I was breathing hard, like I'd just run a marathon. Too much stress and not enough sleep. I glanced at Will.

"Well, that was interesting," he said.

My look turned to glares. It wasn't interesting. It was a pain in my ass. "You aren't funny."

His face paled. "I wasn't meaning to be."

I ignored him and went back inside. I just wanted this over and done with and him out of my house. But it was ironic that my house had been normal and fine before he'd arrived. Now, odd little shit kept happening—the popping floor, the trashcans crashing—and I was getting close to ripping my hair out.

When Will came back into the house, he seemed almost energized. Excited, maybe. He sat in the recliner. “Okay. I want to finish hearing this.”

I had been hoping he forgot, but whatever. If telling him got him gone, so be it. “When I was fourteen, Father O’Malley asked if I’d thought about becoming a priest. All it took was that question and I figured it was the thing to do. As soon as I graduated from high school, I entered the seminary and that was that.”

“And I went off to college.”

I hummed my ascent. “It’s been a long time.”

He paused as if formulating words. “So I get the start, but why aren’t you a priest anymore?”

It wasn’t any of his damn business, and frankly, he was a bit too nosy. But if I didn’t get it all out, I’d have to talk about it sometime to someone. He was as good as any. “I was fine until I finished seminary and continued ‘going out amongst the people.’ That’s when I met Tabby. She didn’t go to the church I was assigned. She didn’t go to church at all. I would see her, long red hair blowing in the wind, walking past my church every day. Finally, one day I spoke to her. From that first word, I was done for. The church no longer held me. It was the beginning of the end.”

I remembered it all like it was only a few minutes ago. Hell, I even remembered the smell of her. “I fell for her fast. Ironically, we didn’t even have a physical relationship at that point. But a parishioner noticed I was spending a lot of time with a pretty young lady. I guess she figured that since Tabby was pretty and I was young, she needed to say something.” I clenched my fists together then released them. Thinking about it still made me want to punch something. “I hadn’t turned my back on my vows then, but the parishioner used poetic license and contacted my superiors. I was pissed—not only at the little old biddy who lied, but at my superiors for believing her instead of me. They wanted me to change dioceses and get away from Tabby as fast as possible. I had had enough. When I refused to stop seeing Tabby and wouldn’t move, they defrocked me.”

“Jesus,” Will said. “And here I thought something like a church would be above shit like that.”

I stretched my fingers, aching to clench them again. "It's that free will thing. Some people are assholes. At any rate, I had a hell of a debt to pay off. When you leave the church—whether you're kicked out or you quit, you have to pay the church back for your education. Tabby and I tried to stick together, but it wasn't working. Eventually, we parted ways. I got a degree in Graphic Design, began working professionally, and minus my irritation about the past, I've been pretty happy ever since." I ran a hand through my hair. "My life in a nutshell."

"It doesn't change things, Jimmy," he said, his eyes capturing mine, searching. "I still need a priest."

My heart started pounding in my chest for no good reason. I'd never had a panic attack as far as I knew, and none of this was cause for one. I focused back on Will. "And I can't help you."

A haunted, sunken look circled his pupils. What caused it, I had no idea, but it was unsettling to see him that unhinged. "I know," he said. "But *they* won't listen to me, and Lucy needs one."

This was beyond catch up with Jimmy. "Why do you think Lucy needs a priest?"

Will wiggled out of his coat and laid it on the floor beside the recliner. His arms were scratched so badly, like he'd recently tangled with a lion.

"See what she did to me?" His eyes grew wider than I thought possible. I was afraid they were going to fall out of his head. "She's possessed."

I sat back. This was way beyond me. You don't randomly hear someone talk about possession every day. Nor see injuries to rival an ill-fated hunter's. "Why do you say that?"

His face turned serious, lines forming across his forehead. "Because she is."

Only I would get someone off their rocker looking for an exorcist at three-o-clock in the morning. For the person to be someone I knew, an old friend, made it all the more strange. The weirdness was stacking up. "Are you sure? Have you thought about taking her to a psychiatrist?"

His hands clenched the armrests of the chair hard enough that his knuckles turned white. With his face growing redder than an apple, his eyes seemed to bulge from their sockets. "She was in a fucking hospital for two weeks!" He jumped out of the chair and began pacing across my floor. "They did nothing for her, and they wouldn't after she almost gouged out a nurse's eye."

Normal took a nose dive off a cliff and I was in a basket. "How old is Lucy?"

He stopped midstride. "Six."

I peered at him, trying to discern the truth in his words. "You're telling me a six-year-old almost gouged out a nurse's eye?"

"Yes." He dropped into the recliner again.

"Will, that could be a bunch of things—"

"We haven't talked about the cat."

The more I heard, the more I wondered if it was Will who needed the psychiatrist.

He stared at me, but more so, he stared through me, lost in his thoughts. I didn't know what to do. Even when I was a priest, I never had anything like this happen. And then you add in the vibe he'd brought with him…a sick, twisted energy. Like poltergeist shadowing the room.

It was going to be a long night.

I rose from the couch and headed to the kitchen. It was too damn late, and I needed some caffeine. My kitchen was a galley style that hadn't been updated since the seventies, but I liked it. Green refrigerators rocked, no matter what anyone else tried to tell me. And the energy didn't follow me there.

I pulled out the coffee maker and got it started. Then I went back into the living room. Will hadn't changed positions.

He whipped his head around, fast and sharp. "Can we turn on some more lights?"

I glanced around. The hallway light provided enough for me to see fine. I couldn't read in it, but it wasn't uncomfortably dark—at least not to me. Maybe the darkness he felt was creeping up on him. Maybe it was something more. I switched on the lamp.

"I can't stand the dark." He scrubbed a hand over his face. "I know you think I'm crazy."

Yeah, he seemed crazy all right, but I wasn't about to tell him that. "You seem scared."

He nodded. "I feel safe here."

I shrugged. I had no idea if I could do anything to help him. And some of the stuff he was saying, and feeling, he'd brought with him. How worse off was he at home? "Will, I need to know what's going on. The whole story."

"I know." He took a deep breath. "I wish I'd never gone to Sorrow's Point."

Chapter Three

Sorrow's Point

WILL WRUNG HIS hands over and over before speaking again. The additional light seemed to help, but his brows continued to furrow as if he struggled to find the words. This was not the Will I'd known. The one I'd known had been kind of a bad ass. After a time, he spoke, "Before I saw the house, I saw the town."

There was a pause, almost like a heartbeat. A single one you hear right before someone takes their last breath. Chills ran up my arms.

I opted for a distraction, a typical sarcastic moment to lighten the mood. "You have to admit, Sorrow's Point is a great name for a town."

"Oh, it gets better than the name." He smiled briefly, but it didn't reach his eyes. Last I remembered, he had bright pale blue eyes. They were much darker now.

"Sorrow's Point is like any other small town," he said. "Everyone knows everybody else's business, the police chief has doubled as the town librarian on more than one occasion, and nothing ever happens there—at least that's what they tell you."

He stared into his palms. His nails were scraggly; he'd clearly been biting them. I didn't know if he was expecting to see blood like Lady Macbeth, but he focused on his hands a little too much.

"It has no Starbucks," he continued on. "No Wal-Mart, and only one fast food restaurant. There's a small elementary school, and the middle school and high school exist comfortably in the same building. Looking at the town, you feel transported back in time." He paused, glancing from his hands and turned to me. "Is the coffee done yet?"

"Dunno, I'll check." Grabbing a couple of mugs from the dish rack, I checked the coffeemaker. When it finished making gurgling sounds, I poured Will and myself a cup. "You take anything in it?" I asked him, sticking my head out of the kitchen so he could hear me.

"Black is fine," he said.

His jumpiness had me nervous. The energy was floating through the air, almost crackling. I could feel it on my skin, a festering malignancy

I stepped back into the kitchen. And then, a coldness struck me. The window over the sink lay wide open, the curtains blowing in the cool breeze. I froze. There was no memory of opening it, and if it had been open very long, I would have felt the cold before now. I shivered. I had enough to worry about. But if this type of crap kept happening after Will left, I was going to need an exorcist.

I clutched the mugs and made my way back into the living room. Maybe caffeine would help us both. Shit, at this point, I was willing to try almost anything. I didn't dare tell Will about the kitchen. He was already unhinged enough as it was. And that was the reason I didn't mention what had happened with the damn window. No need to add to his delusions or whatever they were.

Will had finally gotten comfortable, having taken his shoes off and placing them next to his coat on the floor. I handed him a mug and sat back on the couch.

He took a sip of his coffee and set the mug on the table next to the recliner. "Where was I?"

"The town," I said. I found myself looking off into the shadows left by the places the light didn't reach. Almost as if I was waiting for monsters to come out of the closet.

He nodded. "Sorrow's Point is located among the Blue Ridge Mountains of Virginia. At one time, coal was big business, but now, its main income comes from the hikers passing through the Appalachian Trail." He took another sip, the mug shaking in his hands. "When I first saw it, I thought it was the perfect little town. But like all small towns, there are secrets, hidden away like Aunt Marge's Christmas present. I never really thought about how dangerous secrets can be, but as I found out, in Sorrow's Point, the secrets can kill you."

"Jesus, Will. Do you have any idea how crazy you sound?" I scrunched my brows. He seemed to be trying to distance himself from anything that caused him pain. He focused on the town's history, the smallness and quaintness, the secrets, anything but his problem. From the clear exhaustion and hurt radiating from him like a halo, I wasn't sure it was working very well. Already I'd gotten in way over my head.

He grinned at me. "You don't sound like a priest."

I couldn't help laughing. I'd heard that before. "How is a priest supposed to sound? Granted, I probably shouldn't have taken the Lord's name in vain, but that's a minor sin. Plus, it says nowhere in the Bible that you can't cuss. The church created those rules over time. Not God."

"That's why I came to see you. You're the only one I know crazy enough to believe me."

"And why is that?"

"Well," he tapped his chin idly, "because you had all that stuff happen."

I blinked. I hadn't thought about *that stuff* in a while, but I knew right away what he meant. "You mean my sister's death?"

He had the sense to look chagrined. "Yes."

I didn't like being reminded of it. And it showed just how clueless the man really was. Candy's death was not something I talked about, back then or now. But I rationalized that he was here not for himself, but for his kid. He wasn't thinking straight. I needed to keep that in mind. "And your daughter?"

"Lucy." He dug into his pants pocket, pulling out his wallet. Then he flipped through it and held it out to me.

I took it reluctantly. Seeing the girl would only get me in this mess deeper. *Too late.*

The wallet was made of nice leather, but it had worn around the edges. He obviously used it a lot. The photo in the plastic envelope was of a beautiful girl. Blond hair, blue eyes—your typical little doll. Honestly, she was too pretty to have come from Will. At one time, my sister had had a crush on him; I never could understand why. His mouth was too big for his face, but I guess she liked his dirty blond hair. Blonds were rare where I grew up. But beyond his hair and his mouth, Will had some nose. It was so big that when we were kids, he got teased because he had to turn a pop can sideways before he could drink out of it. I handed back the wallet. "How'd you end up with her?"

He laughed. "She takes after her mother." Then his eyes seemed to change. They darkened while the pupils contracted and the lids drooped. He pulled out his cell phone, fiddling with it for a few seconds. Nothing could have prepared me for what I saw on that small screen.

"This is Lucy, this morning," he said.

The blond hair hung limp around her face. The blood vessels around the whites of her eyes appeared burst from pressure. Her skin had a strange yellow cast, almost like the color of an old bruise. Her face had thinned from the wallet photo. She looked…sunken. The basic facial features remained, but I could hardly tell it was the same little girl. My body grew cold again, like it had in the kitchen. This time, though, there was nothing to make a draft. The only window in the living room was the large picture one. It didn't open. I rubbed my arms. "What the hell happened?"

He clasped the phone like a lifeline. "The house."

My brows rose. I tried to think if any abuse could cause what I saw, but I came up short. The blood in her eyes occurred from some sort of internal pressure. Punches to the face could have caused intense bruising outside the eye and around the socket, but that wasn't what I saw in the picture. Scratches littered her face too, but they were thin, as if caused by her own fingernails. I was dumbfounded. What did he expect me to do? My body gradually warmed up again, but I'd had just about all the oddness I could take for one evening.

"Are you going to help her?" he asked.

Help her? She needed a doctor, not an ex-priest. "Will," I said. "How can I help her?"

"You know what to do." He sat motionless in that chair. Nothing, no part of his body moved. He didn't even blink.

I stood up and turned away from him. I couldn't face him to say the next part. I wasn't even sure he'd listen to reason. "She needs a doctor."

"Goddammit!" He grabbed me from behind and spun me around. His face burned red with intensity. His grip on my shoulder was so tight it hurt. "She's had a doctor! She's had twenty fucking doctors. She's been to internists, psychiatrists, PCP's, neurologists, and they all keep passing the buck."

I reached over and peeled his fingers from my shoulder. I wanted to beat the shit out of him for grabbing me and maybe knock some sense into him, but the man had clear stability issues. If something didn't give soon, he was going to have a nervous breakdown. "What do they all say?"

He threw himself into the recliner, the rage dissipating with his spirits. I had let the air out of his basketball. "The shrinks aren't sure what she has, maybe a split personality, or schizophrenia. I took her out of the last hospital because the quacks were considering electroshock therapy. ECT on a six-year-old! Jesus Christ." He put his head in his hands.

"Okay, I get it." I held up my hands and sunk into the sofa. "But what makes you think she's possessed?"

His voice came out in nothing but a whisper, yet the words had more impact that a five alarm fire, "Because she's not my little girl anymore."

Chapter Four

Tabby: Part 1

SOMETIMES, BEING A girl kind of sucked, especially when the mornings came too early. "Shit." I glanced at the window. The sun began to creep above the skyline. My insides churned like I'd eaten something that didn't sit right. The clock on the nightstand read six. A welcome relief. Class was hours away. I still had time to rest.

I rolled over and stared at the wall. It didn't matter how hard I tried, I couldn't shake the feeling in my stomach. It wasn't butterflies, and it sure as hell wasn't happy memories. It was more like a cramp, but those weren't quite due yet. I closed my eyes and tried to go back to sleep, but my brain wouldn't stop cycling around in my head.

"Screw it." I sat up, shook out my hair, threw back the covers, and got out of bed.

Scratching the sleep out of my eyes, I focused on the wall. What the hell was I going to do with this much time on my hands? I popped my back and stood. Reaching for an elastic off my nightstand, I pulled my hair up into a loose bun. Class wasn't until eleven, so I had time to work on my grading, but I would rather sleep than grade papers. Being a Ph.D. student stunk sometimes. Then again, it was better than working at McDonald's, trying to scrape my life together.

I strolled the hallway as my cat, Isaac, brushed against my legs. He was a Siamese with unusual habits. My mother had found him as a stray. A rare find to see a purebred wandering around with nowhere else to go. When I first saw him, he reminded me of Isaac Newton. Why, I didn't know.

I walked across the living room, turned on the lamp, and sat on the futon. Isaac trotted over and rubbed his fang on the back of my hand. I glanced around, trying to figure out what had me so uneasy, but I didn't see anything. The acid churned like I'd eaten a whole pizza. The only sound in the apartment was the ticking of the clock that hung above my television. I wiped my eyes again. It was too early.

I headed for the kitchen. Eyeing Isaac's empty bowl, I pulled the bag of food from under the counter and filled it up. Then I ambled over to the sink so I could get a glass of water. The sensation hit me like a brick. As soon as I had the glass in my hand, I spun around. *Dead.* Every plant on my table was dead. All the flowers had fallen off, and they drooped over their pots, brown with rot. Yet they'd been fine the night before.

Bad omen. There had been no reason for plants like those to die. I was descended from a long line of witches, and when plants died, it meant evil things were afoot. Sometimes, even the demonic. Until I knew what was going on, those plants were getting the hell out of my house. I seized a garbage bag from the pantry, loaded them all in, and unlocked the door to the deck. I put the plants out. When I left to go to class, I'd make use of the dumpster.

Thinking about the stench made me want to gag. I had a weak stomach anyway and this omen, or whatever-the-hell, wasn't going to make things any better. I walked back in the house and paused. I sniffed, but I only smelled my normal apartment scent—buttercream candles mixing with the Chinese food I'd had the night before. Nothing seemed out of the ordinary. Heading over to the altar, I clutched a sage bunch and lit it. It was best to do the cleansing now before anything else happened. From the looks of things, I was going to need all the help I could get.

Chapter Five

Timmy

AFTER I'D GONE to my room to call my boss and get him to give me a leave of absence—not exactly an easy call—I headed back to Will. Without knowing how long this whole mess was going to play out, I'd figured it was probably the safest course of action. The stairs creaked as I descended. Will looked up from the recliner. I put up a hand before he could say anything. "Just a second."

Crossing the living room, I headed for the bookcase. Books upon books were crammed into every space. I began pulling some off the middle shelf. Last I remembered, I'd put the religion stuff on that shelf, but other tomes had long since been shuffled around. Finally, after moving about ten of them, I found my copy of the Roman Ritual. It had been buried underneath a Stephen King novel and a book of Thai cuisine. I snatched it, stacked the others so that they wouldn't fall on my feet, and shuffled over to my desk. I snagged a notepad and a pen, and then sat at the sofa.

"What are you doing?" Will asked.

I stared at his face. His eyes didn't appear to be hiding anything. "What is it you want for Lucy?"

"I want her to get better. She needs an exorcism."

I could understand having a child so sick that you no longer know what to do about it, but exorcism? What would drive him to even think about calling in a priest, let alone think his daughter was possessed? I kept my questions to myself. "If you're going to get an exorcism, you first have to convince me she's possessed. Then I have to look into the process."

His brows drew together. "You don't know how to do it?"

I chuckled. It never failed. Ever since the movie, *The Exorcist*, people thought that every Catholic priest could walk right up to anyone who seemed possessed and drive the demons out of them. Somehow, they never got that the story of *The Exorcist* was one of an exorcism gone awry. The priest died, and his assistant somehow got the demon to possess him and leave the little girl; then he promptly threw himself out the window. Not your rosy picture. "No, I don't know a thing about exorcism."

"Didn't you go to school to be a priest?" he asked.

"Yes." I resisted the eye roll. "Let me let you in on a little fact, Will. The church likes to sweep exorcism under the rug. In the past, there were many people who were thought to be possessed, but really had psychiatric disorders."

His face had turned red and his eyes bulged ever so slightly.

"I'm not saying that it can't happen, Will. I've just never seen it. More importantly, the only ones who really know a thing about exorcism are exorcists. The Vatican even has a school."

He glared at me, but his eyes pleaded. "Will you come with me to Sorrow's Point?"

I had a feeling this was coming. It had been the whole reason I'd asked for the time off. It didn't take a rocket scientist to figure out I was going to have to embark on this colossal mess of a journey. I knew where it was leading Will, but I had no idea what was in store for me. I grinned at him. I don't know why, but I did. "Thought you'd never ask."

He returned the smile.

I stretched my back. "Look, let's get some sleep. We can get our stuff together when we get up, and then we can try to figure out how to help Lucy."

He nodded.

"You can take the couch if you like."

He moved to the sofa and put his cell phone on the coffee table.

I brought him an extra blanket from the hall closet while he arranged the pillows, then crossed toward the lamp.

"Leave it on, please."

I dropped my hand from the switch and went upstairs, leaving the hall light on as well. It unnerved me to think he was afraid of the dark. The Will I'd known had been fearless; this new Will was…different.

#

The trip to Sorrow's Point was solemn and blessedly uneventful, but once we entered the sleepy town, I instantly knew what he was talking about. A strange heavy stillness laid over everything like a suffocating blanket. Homes lined the main street and had porch boxes with flowers in them; the whole effect reminded me of a wig trying to cover up a bald head. Even with the sun shining, the insides of the houses appeared too dark. The town looked nice, but there was something about it you couldn't put your finger on. A wrongness needing to rest. I didn't like it.

Will stopped the car. We were on a road that looked like it led to nowhere. Trees hovered over the road, an unnerving archway. The pavement was well maintained, but wet, as if from a recent rain.

"This is it," he said. "I'll understand if you want to back out now."

I glanced at him. "If I wasn't going to help, I would never have gotten in the car."

He nodded. "You can stay at the bed and breakfast or you can stay with us. It's your choice."

I wouldn't be able to live with it if there was something I could do for that kid. I'd stay at the house. So be it. "If I'm going to investigate this, really investigate it, then I need to be around her."

The path had a gentle grade to the left, and I found myself leaning in the car. He turned into a driveway I never would have seen unless I was looking for it. I would have expected a massive gate, proclaiming the house's existence, but there was none. It was almost as if the house wanted you to find it. My gut told me something was wrong about all of this. Granted, I sort of already knew that, but my prehistoric senses were kicking in now. I didn't have a lump, I had a lead weight. And sensing intelligence from an inanimate object factored right up there with possible possession. Creepy as hell.

When he pulled up in front of the house, I wasn't prepared for the sight. I kept expecting the grandmother from *Flowers in the Attic* to be staring at me through a tall window with her piercing gaze, but only curtains showed from the panes of the house. This was one of those mansions where the windows looked like eyes.

Will led me through the front door. It was even crazier inside than out. So much mahogany pervaded everything that my head swam a little. Mahogany staircase. Mahogany paneling. As far as I could see, everything was mahogany but the black and white checked marble floor. If this was the foyer, what the hell did the rest of the house look like?

"Tor, he's here," Will called.

Soon, a woman with the blondest hair I'd ever seen appeared from the back hall. I could see what Will meant when he said Lucy took after her mother. Her pale hair had a sparkle to it, and she had Elizabeth Taylor eyes. They couldn't be called anything but violet. She was slender and walked with class. Yes, there was no doubt about it. Will had married into a lot of money.

I held out my hand. "Jimmy Holiday."

She placed her palm gently in mine and shook. "Victoria Andersen. You may call me Tor. Mr. Holiday, I thank you for coming."

I glanced around the entryway. The massive mahogany staircase leading to the second floor was carved with intricate cupids and flowers. Old world craftsmanship. The checkered marble floor was even decked out in a diamond pattern. I was way out of place. "I don't know if I'll be any help, but I'll try."

She inclined her head. Unlike Will, she didn't seem to be so obsessed with everything. She wasn't jittery; she didn't have that wild look in her eyes that Will did. She was there, a normal mom that cared for her daughter. I couldn't fault that.

I followed them through the back hall. Will pointed out the living room, a powder room, and finally, led me to what could only be called "The Library." Mahogany overwhelmed the room once again. Here it was bookcases, wood panels, desks, and tables. Blue Persian carpets with a floral motif covered the floors. The room was roughly the size of the ground floor of a townhouse. Two large windows let in natural light. In various places, leather couches and chairs allowed for intimate conversation. A massive wooden desk centered the room as the main focal point.

"I think you'll be most comfortable here. You can't hear the noises quite so much in this part of the house," he said.

"What noises?" I asked, although I really did want to know. If there was some sort of tapping sound, a tree could be close to the house accounting for it. I'd have to check if that was the case.

He nodded. "You'll see."

I held back a retort. Being cryptic led to lies and I had no time for liars. It was one of my major pet peeves. Here apparently was a very sick little girl. One parent seemed to be hell bent on an age old ritual, and the other seemed to tolerate her husband. I was walking in a field of landmines already.

After Will had me put my bag on one of the couches, I followed him into the kitchen. Tor stood at the stove cooking. I didn't ask what it was, but I could tell it was Italian by the smell–some garlic, a bit of basil. Scents I could handle.

"Have a seat, Jim," she said, motioning toward the kitchen table.

It was one of those fancy glass tables with polished silver toned metal legs. The chairs matched with plush grey velvet cushions. I prayed to God that I wouldn't make a mess.

"We won't talk about any of this until tomorrow morning. The night is bad enough. I don't need it to be worse." Her hands gripped the counter as if struggling for composure. "Please don't make it worse."

I paused. She was much more stoic than Will. She didn't wear her emotions on her sleeve, and I could tell it hurt her to display these feelings in front of a stranger. She was used to an entirely different life, and either Will or something weird with her daughter, had turned that life upside down. I kind of felt sorry for her. Yet I wasn't sure why talking about it now would make any difference. Still, it was her house.

"That's fine," I said. "I'm here to help."

Apparently satisfied, her body visibly relaxed. She finished making dinner and served it to us, saying nothing. It was a quiet meal. Some sort of chicken with a red sauce and garlic bread. I couldn't complain. It had been a long time since I had a home cooked meal.

As she finished cleaning up, the sounds began: strange knocking in the walls, and something scurrying in the ceiling.

"We've had exterminators, carpenters, plumbers and engineers over here." Will waved his hand around the room. "They all say everything is normal, but they aren't here at night."

While not necessarily the sign of possession, the noises made my spine tingle. Knocking I could explain by bad pipes, but scurrying, not so much. "You don't have a pet?"

"Not," Tor played with a pendant at her neck, her mouth drooping into a frown, "Not now."

"And these happen every night?"

Will nodded. "Sometimes, and then for no reason at all, the noises stop. That's when other things start. It's hard to sleep."

Right now, it sounded like regular haunted house stuff, not demonic possession. But I'd yet to see Lucy. "When did the noises begin?"

Tor cleared her throat and sat at the table. "Let's not talk now. Talking about it gives it power."

That's when I heard the growl. It wasn't an animal per se, but it was odd, almost choppy. Completely unlike anything I had ever heard before.

"See," Tor said, letting go of her necklace. "Let's relax. I've already given Lucy her medicine."

"What about her dinner?" I asked.

Tor sighed. "She's been tube fed for about two months. At first, we had a nurse coming in everyday to check things, but that got too hard. The tube feeding, it's easier, and with her teeth, eating certain things is too difficult for her."

I wanted to know what had happened to her teeth, but I figured it would all come out in time. I was afraid for the little girl, and there was no doubt in my mind that *something* was going on.

After dinner and a blatant refusal of my request to see Lucy tonight, I went to bed. I made myself comfortable on the library sofa facing the door. For me, it felt safer to be able to see who was coming. Tor had given me a large afghan, and I had it draped over me. If it wasn't for the noises, I would have been at ease. But the strange sounds continued all night long in fits and starts. I would be deep asleep, relaxed, and then an odd noise would take over—a noise that even my subconscious couldn't ignore. Something was off about the house. I wasn't certain what, but I was going to find out.

"Yeah sure," I said aloud to the empty air. "Jimmy Holiday, old time cowboy coming to the rescue of a little damsel in distress." I snorted, sounding like an idiot. Finally, about five, the sounds stopped. Relief wasn't the word for it. I rolled over and drifted off. Then the dream began.

Wandering in a great forest, I put my hand in front of my face to orient the direction, but it was hard to see. The fog was so thick I could only make out the ground right in front of me. The trees, I only saw when I was right on top of them. It was like a forest of evergreens without the smell of pine. In fact, I couldn't smell anything.

Then I heard it, the strange choppy growl. I froze in place, not knowing if the sound was in front or behind me. Sweat trickled down my back, the fear turning my skin sticky.

"I don't think you want to go that way, mister." I heard a child's voice say.

"Why not?" I asked.

"Cause the soul eater lives there." Fingers grasped my shoulder.

I jerked awake.

Will pulled his hand back as if I'd shocked him. "You okay, Jimmy?"

I sat up, blinked the sleep out of my eyes, and took stock of the room. There was nothing out of place. Will stood over me. "Jesus Christ."

Will scratched at his head. "Guess I should have mentioned the dreams."

My jaw dropped. How could he keep that from me? I already told him it was important to tell me everything. It would have been nice to know that strange dreams had been happening to him. Then again, why would he assume that I would have one? Why would I have one? This already wasn't going well. "That's it," I said. "I told you that I've got to know everything. If you keep something from me one more time, I'm going home." Unreasonable? Maybe. But I was not letting it go. The dream still haunted me.

Will stepped back, his eyelids drooping. "Jimmy, don't. I'm sorry. I was hoping you would sleep. I didn't know if the dreams affected just me and Tor or not."

I wasn't sure if I bought his explanation, but it would have to do. "All right. Today, I want the whole story, but first, I want a shower. Then I want some breakfast. After that, we are going to talk."

#

I got my shower in Will and Tor's master bathroom. It was as crazy opulent as the rest of the house. Pink marble took over everything except for the gold faucets. Heat floated from the floor. I supposed that when it got really cold, having heated floors would come in handy, but what was the use of marble if it didn't act like marble?

I stood awkwardly in the bathroom, uncomfortable using the damn thing. It was too fancy for my taste. After the quickest shower ever, I wiped the stall and hung the towel on the rack to dry.

When I was finished with everything, I went downstairs to breakfast. It took me a couple of wrong turns, but eventually, I was able to find the kitchen again. Tor and Will were sitting at the table. Will was eating a muffin. Tor looked exhausted.

"Hello, Jim," Tor said. "I wasn't up to cooking this morning. I hope coffee and muffins are okay."

I smiled. "Lady, my usual breakfast is coffee and whatever I can scrape together. Believe me, muffins are fine."

She beamed. "What's the plan?"

Will grabbed her hand. "If he is going to help, he has to know everything, Tor. Otherwise, I don't know what else to do."

"But the last time—"

"What do you mean, the last time?" I asked. I couldn't not ask. Another lie of omission would have me hitting the roof. It was not instilling confidence in Will as far as I was concerned. So what if I hadn't brought my car? I was sure I could find a ride out of town one way or another. My thoughts were spinning.

Will sighed. "I went to the local priest first. It was he who recommended she go to the hospital."

I tapped my fingers on the table. "And this was the hospital that wanted to do shock treatments?"

"Yes," Tor said.

I was glad I didn't jump to conclusions and yell at him again, but Will needed to handle this better. There was no way the church would believe anything about the house, about Lucy, if he continued keeping secrets or omitting events, even if unintentionally. It all had to come out.

"I mean it this time, Will," I said. "No more secrets. You have no idea how difficult it is to prove possession to the church."

He stared me dead in the eyes. I knew mine had grown dark. They always did when I was angry, but they were a help. When my pupils enlarged and the irises went dark, people shut up and began to listen to what I had to say. My mother thought it was something magical. I had a more realistic view—my blue eyes looked darker when I held my head a certain way. I did this when I was angry. It gave a hell of an effect, one that had a logical explanation. That's what I had to do with Lucy, rule out all logical explanations surrounding her. If I had none, she was probably possessed. The chances of me finding no logical explanations for anything were very slim, and I was banking on science.

"What do you need?" Tor asked.

Now here was someone who had some sense. "Just my things. We can do this wherever you want." I got up from the table. "Give me a minute." I shuffled down the hall and into the library. Digging through my bag, I retrieved my notebook, a pen, and my Roman Ritual.

"I have a question," Tor said when I walked back into the room.

"Okay." I sat at the table and placed everything on top of it.

"If you think she's possessed… is there a chance you could do it?"

My brows pinched together. "Do what?"

"The exorcism."

Here we go again. I tried not to groan. It amazed me how little people understood about the Catholic Church. Technically, anyone could do an exorcism, whether it worked or not was another story. Not that exorcisms by priests always worked. The way I understood it was that in order to be an exorcist, you had to be pure of heart and mind. While I tried to be a good person, *pure* certainly wasn't a word I could call myself. But I guess it all depended on perception. I definitely wasn't pure of mind, but perhaps being pure of heart mattered more. That was really up to God. "If you want a church sanctioned exorcism, they will appoint an exorcist. I can assure you, I will not be on that list."

"Why not?" she asked.

I smiled then. "Because I'm not a priest. Not anymore."

"What if the church doesn't believe?" she asked.

"Well, I guess we'll figure that out if and when it happens." I arranged my things and turned to the section on exorcism in the Ritual. A list of things "proved" possession. I was supposed to disprove it. "So where shall we begin?"

Chapter Six

The Story

"WELL," WILL SAID, "I already told you about the town, but when Tor saw the house in person, she fell for it." He fingered his coffee mug and turned toward his wife. "I'll admit I was being a bit of an ass."

"When aren't you a bit of an ass?" Tor inched away from him. Definitely a place of conflict. That could possibly explain their bad dreams. My own, I didn't want to think about.

"What Will is trying to say is that I had already talked to Momma about the house. He wasn't real happy about it, but I didn't care. The house was to be my Christmas present."

I raised an eyebrow. "Who gets a house for Christmas?"

Will snorted. "The girl from Miracle on 34th Street and my wife."

Tor's eyes flashed. If Will wasn't careful, she was going to kill him.

I scratched my ear. "Anyways, so you got the house. What was it like?"

"Pretty much what you see now," Will said. "The furniture came with the house, and except for Lucy's bedroom and ours, the living room, and this table, we kept things as they were."

"The furniture was too lovely to get rid of," Tor said.

I nodded. From the tone in her voice, I could tell there was more to it than that. I really didn't care about the furniture, not if it didn't affect Lucy.

Will cleared his throat. "So we moved in roughly two weeks after closing. Lucy alternated between fear of living in a new place and bursting with energy."

"It got a little strange when we were unpacking." Tor stared into her coffee cup like it was a crystal ball about to give her a vision. "There is a huge attic. That's where we put the furniture we weren't going to use from Lucy's room. Lucy and I were looking around the attic while the movers were transferring furniture. She found this large old mirror. It was the strangest thing, oval with a tarnished gilt silver frame. The type you used to hang in a hallway. It would have been lovely with a little work, and if the looking glass hadn't been painted black."

Mirrors. Didn't it figure? There were old legends about mirrors. They were supposed to be doorways to other worlds. Something about the silver backing was meant to keep evil things from crossing over from the other side. What one painted in black meant, I had no idea. "That's a little unusual, isn't it?"

"Stranger is the fact that Lucy loved the mirror. She even begged me to allow her to put it in her room." She smoothed her hair back with her hand. "Needless to say, I refused. Everything was fine for a few weeks after that, and then Lucy started acting up. Sometimes, she was very mean. Not the Lucy we knew at all."

I was writing all of this as quickly as I could. It reminded me of taking notes in seminary, and like seminary, my scribbling was never fast enough. "So then what happened?"

She sighed. "We had a cat since it was a kitten—Miss Pretty. Lucy had picked her out." Tor got up from the table, took away our coffee mugs, and the muffins. She replaced it all with a soda for each of us.

I could see the strain in her face. Some memories will do that to you—the ones that make you look much older. I had one or two.

"I had left Lucy out back while I was in here doing dishes. She liked to play in the backyard." Her voice started to quiver.

I really hoped she wasn't going to cry. I hated crying. It was one of my bigger obstacles toward priesthood. Tears made me feel all uncomfortable and skitchy. I could understand it when someone died or something really horrible happened. But there were some people that cried over everything.

"I could look out the window and see her." She pointed to the window left of the table above the sink. "Lucy was supposed to stay where I could see her."

She sat, gripping her soda can so hard I was afraid it was going to explode. Her knuckles went white.

"Then I heard a growl. It was not Lucy's cry. The voice was different. It came from Miss Pretty." She swallowed hard. "I ran outside, over by the hedge. Lucy was standing there poking Miss Pretty with a stick. I asked her what she was doing. She didn't answer me. That was when I noticed that Miss Pretty wasn't moving and—"

She collapsed into sobs, her head lying on her crossed arms on the table. Will stroked her hair, and she sat up some and leaned on him. Her body heaved. It was a tenderness I didn't expect from them both given the way they'd acted earlier. I had a feeling that this back and forth could be affecting Lucy. Exactly how, I couldn't be sure, but a child could fake being sick because her parents were having problems. Then again, Lucy had killed a cat. Killing an animal was the sign of deep seeded mental problems. In my opinion, the priest had been right to refer them to a psychiatrist.

"Tor called me on my cell," Will said. "I'd gone to the store…can't remember why." His body stiffened. "Lucy had gouged out the cat's eyes, Jimmy. I…we didn't know what to do. Lucy seemed nonchalant about it. We knew she needed help, but we didn't know where to begin."

I squeezed my pen, scribbling questions marks on the paper. "That could be a lot of things—a brain tumor or even thyroid problems can cause mood changes, what they used to call multiple personality disorder—"

"That's what I thought at first too." He opened his soda and took a drink. "I buried Miss Pretty. Tor took Lucy upstairs and cleaned her up. She didn't speak to either one of us. When I asked Lucy why she hurt Miss Pretty, all I could get out of her was, 'Mr. Black showed me how.'"

I didn't know who the hell Mr. Black was, but the story rang oddly around in my head. I had that suffocating feeling again, the one I'd gotten when we drove through Sorrow's Point. "Any idea who Mr. Black is?"

Will nodded. "That's just it. There are two Mr. Blacks connected to this house. One long dead since the fifties, the other, well we bought the house from him."

I chewed at the inside of my cheek. It was a bad habit, but it helped me think. My dentist was going to squawk over it. I really didn't care. "So did you research the Black family?"

"At first I thought that the realtor was pulling a fast one or something, but after reading more about the house, that's when I started thinking Lucy might be possessed." Will cracked his knuckles and gently pushed Tor off him. She settled herself and wiped the rest of her tears away with a napkin.

"The house we're in actually has a name," he said. "It's called Blackmoor Hall. Black both because that was Archibald Black's surname, and for the black seam of coal running through the grounds. Moor because the land reminded him of the moors of Scotland, his homeland."

"And you found this out where?" As far as I knew, he played with an Ouija board to get the information.

Will smirked. "The public library. The town is actually really proud of Blackmoor Hall, despite its dark history. Believe me, I wish we would have known about it before we bought it, but I guess it just happened that way."

"Or you could have used Google." I tried not to snark, but it was hard. Did I feel sorry for Lucy? Hell, yes. Did I feel sorry for Will about the house? Not so much. Sometimes it paid to do your homework.

"It's not on Google," Will said.

I arched a brow at him. "What do you mean? Everything is on the net these days."

Will shook his head. "Not the Blackmoor articles. The library hasn't gotten around to digitizing their microfiche library. At least that's the official line."

That explained it somewhat. "And the Black family?"

He chuckled. "Oh, they're on Google. General information about how the Black brothers made their fortunes in coal. The truth behind Archibald Black's death isn't online though."

"Interesting and odd," I said.

Will's shoulders hunched. "If Lucy wasn't involved, I'd probably write about it. As it is, I wouldn't have heard about it if I hadn't spoken to the librarian. When she found out I was the new owner of the 'Black House,' she said she couldn't keep the truth from me. She wasn't having that on her conscience."

Tor jumped up, went to a cabinet near her stove, and grabbed a cookbook. She began to flip through it. All of this really did freak her out. She was skittish like a rabbit. Maybe she had a reason to be scared.

"What I'm about to tell you is what keeps me up at night," Will said.

"Besides the noises?" I cocked my head.

"Yes, besides the noises. At any rate, when I went into the library, I approached the front desk and asked the girl where I could find information about Blackmoor." He sighed. "It was like what you see in a movie. The whole library grew quiet. I kid you not. Then this little old lady walked over to me from behind the desk and told me to follow her. We went behind the circulation area and into a glass windowed room. She closed the door behind us."

His eyes glazed over with a faraway look as he took a drink of his soda. "She was a trip, telling me how the collection was delicate and that I could only touch the items while wearing gloves. I thought it was a little overkill, to be honest."

"Maybe we should call her for help?" Partially, I was joking, but I also had memories of grumpy old librarians when I was in school. Some of them, I'm sure, could scare a demon.

Will glared at me. "That's not funny."

"I didn't mean it to be. She knows all this town history; she might be able to help."

He exhaled a rough breath. "Anyways, I searched the room. She asked for my name, and I told her. She stared at me for several minutes, and then asked me if I had any children. I told her I had a daughter. Then she put her hand on her chest and went over to this wooden cabinet and opened it with a key. What she pulled out wasn't what I expected." He sucked in air. "It was a huge book filled with aging newsprint that was enclosed in some sort of acid free plastic. She motioned for me to sit at the desk, and I did. She put that book in front of me and flipped the pages until roughly the middle."

Will wiped at his mouth with the back of his hand.

"'Read 'til it stops talking about the Blacks,' she said. She gave me the impression that 'newcomers' aren't supposed to know this old history. She left the book with me anyway and exited the room."

I waited for him to continue as he seemed to gather his thoughts.

"The first headline that jumped out at me was, 'Cannibal or Misunderstood Millionaire?' It went like that for pages after pages of text about Archibald Black and his obsession with the dark arts, his other misdeeds, and most of all, the events that led to his death."

"Wait a minute." I set my pen aside and stretched my fingers. I heard a crack. I was going to be lucky if I could even open my hands tomorrow.

"You okay?" Tor asked.

I nodded. "Cramp."

After a few minutes, the cramp abated. It had been too long since I'd written like that. I didn't want it on the computer though. Last thing I needed was to accidentally leak it and ruin Will's reputation. Not that computer work would really save my hands. Arthritis was arthritis. I was doomed. "Go on."

Will cleared his throat and took another drink. "Archibald Black didn't die under normal circumstances. According to the articles, there had been screams coming from the house all afternoon the day he died. Finally, a neighbor phoned the police. They knocked on the door, but no one answered it. After looking around the house, one of the men heard an odd thumping. They broke into the home and found Mr. Black sitting at the kitchen table, ripping the flesh from his six-year-old daughter's dismembered leg with his teeth. A young deputy, who had recently joined the force saw the scene and fired his weapon. His aim was true, hitting Black in the head. Black didn't drop the leg until he slumped over—dead."

He stared at me. "I practically ran out of there, Jimmy."

I tapped my pen on my teeth. "Doesn't it seem kind of bizarre and hokey that a random librarian would have these things no one else has, like there's some type of conspiracy?" If I didn't ask, I wouldn't be able to live with myself. It sounded too fantastic and too easy to be true.

Will said nothing, staring at the table.

The Blacks and their history provided him with an outlet for his denial about what was might be really wrong with Lucy. I hoped that wasn't the case, but I couldn't ignore the possibility. Then it hit me, what did Will do? It didn't seem like Will was the type of person to live off his wife's money, but this Will wasn't the same one I'd known for years. Why did he have the time to fret and worry about all of this? "What is it you do, Will?"

He looked me in the eye—hard, almost as if he was expecting a fight. "I'm a columnist."

That surprised me. Journalists were supposed to back up sources.

Wouldn't he himself think this whole thing with the librarian was odd and convenient? It made no sense to me, other than the denial. More and more, that seemed to be possible rather than something supernatural going on.

"Don't feel bad," Tor said. "I thought it was stupid too. Until I explored the attic better."

I glanced at her. "What are you talking about?"

She smiled, but it was a cold smile. "It'd be easier to show you."

Without giving me a chance to respond, she jumped up from the table so fast I had to scramble to catch up to her. She led me to the dining room with its silk wallpaper and old landscape scenes. The massive mahogany table in the middle was large enough to seat twelve. Crossing the room, she opened a door and revealed a long set of steep spiral stairs.

"It's up there," she said, pointing at the staircase.

"You're not coming?"

She paused. "I've already seen as much as I care to."

It felt like a challenge. Was I really brave enough to go up there? Yes. I climbed the stairs. It was kind of claustrophobic, spiraling around upwards into the darkness. By the time I reached the top, I was seriously out of breath. "I need to walk more. This is ridiculous."

At the top of the stairs, another door was painted black and not as well cared for as the rest of the house. The paint cracked and flaked. I expected to have trouble with it, but it slid open easily.

I took a breath and peered inside.

Chapter Seven

Revelations

1950

THE MAN STOOD in the room, his room of power. In here, no one could touch him, feel him, or challenge him. In here, he was God.

He opened his hands and spoke the words the demon had told him the last time. Golden fire floated between his fingertips. It smelled hot and sulfuric, but his hands remained unharmed, as the dark one said they would be.

He picked up the small rodent from its cage. It squealed and struggled, trying to bite him. He let the fire travel over the animal. The creature burned. Its skin melted. Its eyeballs burst from the heat. He dropped the smoldering body to the table and grinned. His hands were still unharmed. The flames danced between his fingertips.

A sound broke his concentration, a child's laughter. The fire disappeared from between his hands.

Black threw open the door to his special room and walked over to the attic window. He peered into the yard. There they were: his wife, his daughter. The stupid cow was supposed to keep the spawn quiet when he was in his room working. That was the first rule he'd set when she asked him for a child.

He opened the window and yelled to her, "Glenna, are you forgetting something?"

His wife put her hand over her mouth and let the spawn back into the house. It was time he was rougher with her. Through pain, she would know his power, and learn to respect him. They both would learn.

Ritual

Present

I WENT THROUGH the door, expecting a place caked in dust, but it wasn't. In fact, it was amazingly clean. Even the sheets covering the old furniture appeared spotless. I wandered around. The attic had an oak floor. With its plastered walls, it could have been used for other things than storage. Oak encompassed everything up here, and it was surprisingly light. The rest of the house was so dark because of all the mahogany. Windows lit up both sides of the attic. I breathed deeper and easier, standing in such a sunlit room.

Then, toward the back of the attic, a door stood out. This door, like the one leading to the stairs, was painted black but freshly done. I thought it was another staircase, but when I opened it, a foul pungent aroma hit me. Darkness invaded the room, even with the uncovered windows. Black paint coated the plastered walls. One large bookcase, which held a treasure trove of old books and silver goblets, took up a section. There were wooden wands with crystals attached to the ends by gilded wire and little wooden boxes with the names of herbs and minerals on them—all things that I recognized as having to do with magic.

The air felt heavy and something invisible pressed me down. While I saw nothing disturbing, the darkness and the cold were enough for me to know things had happened there that weren't natural. This wasn't melodrama. This was real, and it scared the ever loving shit out of me.

When I turned to leave, I spied the mirror Tor had described earlier. It was propped up against some boxes on the floor. She mentioned the glass of it had been painted black. She'd neglected to mention the scratches in the paint that looked suspiciously like those from a child's fingernails. I wrestled the mirror into my arms, closed the door to that room, and made my way back downstairs.

I found them waiting for me in the kitchen. When Tor saw me, she screamed.

Will jumped up and grabbed a hold of her.

"What?" I asked.

Tor made a strange sound like a low keen. "I don't like looking at that—thing," she said, pointing at the mirror.

I sat at the table and leaned the mirror against the chair next to me. "Why not?"

Will let go of Tor, and then walked over to the table and sat across from me. "We found it like that after Lucy killed Miss Pretty."

Tor began pulling things out of the pantry.

"Did you look at the back of the mirror?" Will asked.

"No." I shook my head. "It didn't occur to me."

Will snatched the thing and flipped it around so I could see. There was an old label on the back. The ink had faded to an odd brown color.

Cavētis Tēctus Prōdiora

"It's Latin," I said.

Will seemed a little more uneasy than before. "Do you know what it means?"

I nodded. "Loosely, it means 'beware the hidden betrayer.'"

He set the mirror on the floor. "On a mirror, what does that mean?"

Tor dragged a few pots out of cabinets and began chopping vegetables, ignoring the rest of us.

I turned back to Will. "I don't know. Not yet. Do you know if the house has been exorcised before?"

Will swallowed hard. "I have no idea."

Tor coughed then looked down her nose at me. "Can we get that *thing* out of here, please?"

Will grabbed the mirror and took it out of the room. While he did so, something was buzzing at the back of my head, the properties of mirrors, how the ancients thought your soul could be trapped in one. Something about this house wasn't right.

When Will came back, Tor and I were sitting in silence at the table. She'd gotten whatever she was making simmering. She didn't say anything to me, so I did the same.

"What happened after the cat died?" I asked Will.

He clasped his hands together. "I knew it wasn't normal for a kid to kill their pet, especially not like that. Tor…she didn't want to think about it."

Tor's eyes snapped toward him. "Well, who wants to think their little girl—"

He took her hand. "I wasn't judging you. I was telling Jimmy how it happened."

He turned to me. "We started with the pediatrician. It was horrible, Lucy fought and screamed. We sent her for tests at the hospital. MRI, CAT scans, anything that would show a reason for her mood changes. The tests turned out normal. That was when we began the parade of psychiatrists. They thought so many things, different psychoses, schizophrenia, delusional disorder, one even thought she was on hallucinogens! Christ, could you imagine? They had no idea. I've already told you about the last hospital."

I nodded. "But what makes you think she's possessed, really? I mean there are tons of disorders out there that most people don't know about."

"Jimmy, it's the things she says. She says things that she couldn't know. I don't know how to explain it."

There was too much to absorb. It was time for me to get away. "Ever think about revisiting the librarian?"

#

When we got to the library, I was struck by how small it was. A simple two story building that looked like it had been designed in the sixties. It was covered in light colored concrete and some sort of tan stone decorative plaster. It was a squat and ugly rectangular building, but serviceable.

It had that usual library smell too—books and heat.

Will stepped up to the desk and motioned to an elderly lady who was doing something with a stack of books at the back. She had an older style bob cut like a gray Doris Day. She was stocky, but not fat.

Not exactly my standard views of a librarian.

She looked up. "Mr. Andersen," she said. "How can I help you?"

He grinned. "I need to look at the papers again. And my friend and I have some questions."

She glanced at Will again and then at me. Her eyes narrowed. I was expecting her to throw us out, but she motioned to us and unlocked the glass door behind the circulation desk. Will entered first, I followed, and she locked the door behind us.

"Questions?" she asked. Her spine was rigid, straightening her posture like an arrow. Apparently, Will had told a state secret.

Will nodded. "My daughter…she seems to be affected by the house." He pointed at me. "My friend Jimmy is trying to help us. He used to be a priest."

Her eyes widened. I was kind of used to the reaction, being built more like a linebacker than a priest.

"You aren't one of *those* priests, are you?" she asked in a snooty tone.

I knew what she was referring to, the molestation scandals. "No, Ma'am, I left because of a very mundane reason." There was no way in hell I was giving her my life story. It wasn't any of her business, and where did she get off accusing me like that?

She wanted more, I could tell, but she didn't press any further.

"I want to see the papers that Will told me about, but I have a question. Do you know if the house was ever exorcised?"

There was a spark of life in her eyes. She motioned for us to sit at the table. Her demeanor changed on a dime. It was almost as if by mentioning the exorcism, she took me seriously and found me worthy of knowing what she knew. She leaned over and spoke so quietly it was hard to hear her.

"They did a lot of things after the murders. Priests, ministers, and all types were brought in. Nothing seemed to help. Until they found a spiritualist."

Now, I was intrigued. What would a spiritualist do that a priest couldn't? "Why are these papers here instead of the regular part of the library?"

She sat back in her chair and laughed. "Right after it happened the people of the time burned everything. They thought it was contagious or something. The papers here are the only ones we know of that are left. I wanted to get them digitized, but the director refused. I think they hope these papers will come up missing one day, but they'll be here as long as I am."

I nodded.

"Now, back to the Black House. I'm not saying witchcraft was used or any such thing, but the rumors I heard was that the spiritualist didn't try to get rid of him like the rest. Instead she trapped him."

A cold chill traveled straight through me. Goosebumps appeared on my skin. Mirrors. Silver. The scratched black paint. "Trapped him in what?"

"They never said."

She pulled out the papers for me to read. Will left the room with the librarian, and I dove into the articles. After a moment, my vision began to fade.

The Style of Pain

1950

BLACK STOMPED DOWN the massive wooden steps of the front hall. He checked his appearance in the mirror. His suit was impeccable, black, made of fine wool and tailored to him. He straightened his tie and turned around.

"Be quiet for daddy, honey," he heard his wife whisper. A normal person wouldn't have been able to hear her, but he had powers normal people did not.

He smiled and headed toward them. The kitchen was where she belonged, but by tonight, she'd learn what it meant to cross him.

Black paused in the doorway. His wife was fluttering around, trying to please him. Trying to get back in his good graces. If she wasn't so stupid, she'd realize that if she'd play by the rules, she wouldn't have to do anything extra to please him.

He coughed.

She froze. Slowly, she turned around to face him. Her eyes wide and her mouth gaping, but she didn't make a sound. He liked that.

"Come take your medicine, Glenna," he said.

Her lips began to tremble. "What…what about the baby?"

He smirked. "The baby will be waiting for you when you get back."

She swallowed hard, wiped her hands on her apron, bowed her head, and followed him out the door.

#

He kept the room in the basement; the dark room, the punishment room, her personal Hell. Glenna knew it well, too well. Each time she'd displeased her husband, she'd been brought to this room. Each time after, she hadn't been able to function for weeks. Each time, the more pain she experienced, the happier he seemed.

She stepped out of her clothes without a word and glanced at her husband. He motioned to the wall. She gulped. The wall was the worst of all. She tried to gather her resolve as she slunk to the wall, legs shaking, and placed her hands in position.

In no time at all, he fastened her wrists to the cuffs attached to the cement. She could feel his breath on the back of her neck.

She wanted to beg him, plead with him not to hurt her, but she knew better. It was best to keep quiet. Begging made him hurt her much worse.

A whoosh and a smack.

Her body shook with pain. She could feel the searing burn across her back, the blood dripping down her legs.

Whoosh. Smack.

This time, she cried out. She couldn't hold it back. Her stomach roiled.

He laughed.

Whoosh. Smack.

Her whole world went dark, black.

Chapter Ten

trouble

WHEN WE RETURNED to the house, I didn't know what to do. The vision I'd had of the Blacks haunted me. I rubbed my temples as if I could somehow erase the nightmare. I wasn't like my ex, Tabby. I wasn't supernatural in the slightest. Now, I'd had dreams and visions connected to this damn house. The last one wouldn't leave me alone. It danced before my eyes as I had read the article in the library, overtaking my mind, and playing with me like a puppet. Worse, I still didn't know why Will thought I could help Lucy. Maybe it was the priest thing, but they'd already tried one, and that priest did the same thing I would have done…recommend a psychiatrist.

Even if the visions meant something supernatural, what could I do? If Mr. Black's ghost was trapped here, that would account for some of the weird things going on. God, my head ached and I was getting myself nowhere with all of the speculation.

I fisted my hands at my sides, determined to ignore the throbbing in my skull. I needed to get back to the basics. Will asked me to help Lucy. I needed to see her.

Will parked the car in the front drive rather than the back of the house where the garage was. I guess it was for my benefit, but I didn't ask. We came in the front door and took off our coats. Will hung them on the antique coat rack beside the door. "You wanna meet Lucy?"

"Yes," I said. I was trying to look at meeting Lucy like being introduced to any other child, but that picture of Lucy from Will's phone kept coming to mind. That picture….that picture stuck with me.

Will led me up the main stairway, and when we entered the hall, the cold hit me. I tried to remember the location of the attic in relation to Lucy's bedroom, but I wasn't sure. If the attic sat above Lucy's, there might be some bleed over. I sure as hell wouldn't want my daughter sleeping below a room that had once held black magic.

We stopped at the first door to the left. Will knocked and then opened it. "Hi Lucy."

I walked in behind him and spotted her. The picture on the phone failed to capture reality. A smell so foul, I had to force myself not to gag, permeated the air. It was the scent of rotting flesh and over ripe fruit. Yet I saw nothing that would account for it. On the off-white painted walls, nail holes faintly showed where pictures once hung. No toys cluttered the floors, nothing that made me think of anything but institutional.

"Lucy," Will said, "this is Jimmy. I knew him when I was a kid."

Lucy directed her horrid eyes toward me. Seeing the whites so full of blood turned my stomach. A slow rage bubbled inside me, urging me to hurt whatever had done that to her. I stared at those eyes carefully, scrutinizing the details. Definitely not contacts. It didn't hurt to be sure.

"Hi, Lucy," I said.

She snarled in a voice much too deep for a child. "What do you want, Priest?"

Even if she was very smart, her voice couldn't sound like that. You could tell from the tone and articulation of the words that you were not talking to a little girl, you were talking to something else. Still, I wondered. Did Will tell her I used to be a priest? I wasn't dressed as one. She'd have no reason to call me that. If he hadn't said anything, a six-year-old psychic was as scary to me as a possessed little girl. A little girl who could know things would be a hard child to raise, and difficult to keep people from exploiting her talent.

Suddenly, there was a noise, similar to great claws digging into the plaster and running across the ceiling. I followed the track of the invisible thing with my eyes. There were no marks on the ceiling.

I returned my focus to the little girl in the bed. "I'm here to check on you, Lucy. Your dad asked me to come."

A choppy growl burst from her throat. No. It wasn't quite a growl at all, but laughter.

Goosebumps rose on the skin of my arms, and I was glad I was wearing a long sleeved shirt. That way, she couldn't see.

Will cleared his throat. "We'll leave you to your rest, Lucy."

She smiled at me, bearing her rotten and broken teeth. "Don't you want to spend more time with me. Get to *know* me?"

I swallowed. Hard. "Of course I do, Lucy. But your dad is right. You need your rest."

She chuckled like a demon extra on an old heavy metal album. Then, picked up her hand and waved.

We had been dismissed.

As we were leaving, the ties on the bed caught my attention. When he closed the door behind us, I stopped. "How do you know if she needs something?"

"Baby monitor."

We headed downstairs and met up with Tor in the kitchen. She was pulling the pot pie out of the oven.

"I'm going to be here a while." I strummed my fingers along the counter, trying to figure out how to say this. "Something's odd about this house. And Lucy isn't well. Does any nursing staff come to see her?"

Tor took a drink from a glass. "We used to have a nurse when Lucy was more docile, but since she attacked the nurse and the priest, we figured we'd better not risk it."

"How do you handle it all? Lucy's tube feeding, her medication?"

"I had the nurses at our local hospital teach me what to do. I can do it as good as they can now. If Lucy needs something more, we take her to the doctor right away."

"So, why exactly did you start tube feeding her?" My head started pounding again. There was too much going on with Lucy and the house and everything. If it wasn't for the fact my folks were alcoholics, I'd consider taking a drink.

Tor sighed. "You've seen her teeth?"

I nodded.

"She chewed on the walls, the bars on her bed. She chewed on everything until she broke all her teeth."

I swiped a hand through my hair and tried to focus. Then, I arranged my notes, and asked, "How would you describe Lucy's speaking voice?"

"Like any little girl's, I guess," Will said. "We have some home movies if you'd like to see how she used to be."

"That would be helpful." I paused, unsure what to ask next. It was difficult trying to figure out what information the church would want, and the hammer continuously pounding at my brain didn't help matters. "Tell me about what happened with the first priest."

Will's eyes turned distant. "It was before she was in the hospital, like I told you." He stared into the flower arrangement on the kitchen table. It appeared to be silk, some lilies, but not a cheap arrangement. "We were at our wit's end. No doctors were able to help her. Then, after talking to my mother on the phone one afternoon, she mentioned going to the church. Now, she didn't recommend exorcism, understand."

"So what did she say?"

"She reminded me that priests were also counselors, and maybe it wouldn't hurt to try. It wasn't bad advice, but not the right choice for Lucy." He wiped his face with his hands. "We'd finished with yet another round of doctors. None of them could tell us anything, they all kept saying psychiatry, even though Lucy had had three psychiatric diagnoses at this point. So I called the only Catholic Church here. It's a Roman Catholic church." He paused, as if waiting for me to do or say something. When I didn't, he pressed on.

"I called the church and was put through to Father John. He's a pretty young priest, honestly, in his early thirties. I explained I was having trouble getting a diagnosis for Lucy, that we'd exhausted medical options, and thought the church might be able to help. We made arrangements for him to stop by that afternoon. We hadn't started tying her hands yet. The self-mutilation was still pretty mild." He sighed.

I waited for him to continue and wrote *self-mutilation* in my notes.

"When Father John got here," Will said, "Lucy seemed anxious. Father pulled up a chair in her room and sat beside her bed. He'd barely asked a question before she jumped up and snatched him by the throat. She'd moved so fast we couldn't stop her. Somehow, her little body had too much strength. It took both Tor and I to get Lucy off him. After that, we started restraining her when there were visitors." His head hung limp from his body, as if he couldn't deal with the weight of it any longer.

"Father John recommended the hospital. I don't really blame him.

He probably didn't know what the hospital would do to Lucy."

"When did the subject of exorcism come up?" I asked.

"After the attack, I asked Father John about it before he left. He said he didn't believe in exorcism or demonic possession."

Another hurdle with the church. Demonic possession had been underplayed so much, many priests didn't believe in it anymore. I heard a small amount about it in seminary, but everyone treated it almost like a joke. While I imagined most people who believed themselves possessed were either full of it or insane, I also kept an open mind. Too many things science hadn't quite figured out yet. "I know you're desperate, but again, why exorcism?"

He slumped in the chair. "We've tried everything else. If it doesn't work, I'm afraid I'll lose her."

Tor patted Will on the shoulder.

I let what he'd told me percolate around my brain and I needed to do some checking. "Okay, I've got it all for now. I'm going to go into the library and do some research. Let me know if you need anything."

#

When I reached the library, I sat at the huge desk, arranged my notes and opened my copy of the Roman Ritual to the section on exorcism. I had a set of twenty-one instructions that needed to be met before I could do anything. I already knew an exorcism needed to be approved by the bishop, so I skipped that and the part about the chosen priest needing to be schooled in exorcism. I rolled my eyes. "Fail there."

Section three contained useful information. First, I needed to exhaust all possibilities of something physical causing Lucy's condition. Second, Lucy needed to speak or understand languages she could have no way of knowing. Third, she needed to demonstrate knowledge of hidden things. Finally, she needed to exhibit strength beyond her age and condition. This was going to take a while.

I flipped through the rest of the section, which dealt with carrying out the exorcism itself. It didn't apply to me. But a nagging feeling wouldn't leave me alone. It dug into my brain like the blade from a madman's skull saw. I tried to push it aside. I wanted to ignore that room in the attic. I wanted to ignore the mirror. And above all, I wanted to ignore Lucy. Her abnormal face, her bloodied eyes haunted my waking dreams. And then, the still unanswered question. How did she know I had been a priest?

I left the library and went down the hall in search of Will. I found him in the massively white living room. The mahogany paneling either had been taken out of the room, or was never present to begin with. Everything in here read white, ultra-modern, clean. This, I could tell, was Will's room.

"Hey, Will," I said. "Can I see one of those home movies?"

Will's eyes darkened, but he said, "Sure."

He popped a DVD in the player as I sat on the couch. "This is last Christmas."

The screen filled with a beautiful Christmas scene, a large tree with multicolored lights topped with a golden angel. A cream-colored wall provided the perfect neutral backdrop to highlight the tree. Surrounding the bottom of it were numerous presents, some big, some small, but all ornately wrapped.

"Tor likes wrapping presents," Will said.

I grinned at him. "I can tell."

A giggle like a bell added to the coziness. Lucy appeared on the screen. Her blond hair was messy, but from sleep, not illness. She wore a red plaid nightgown.

"Daddy!" she said with another tinkling giggle. "I wanna open presents."

Will chuckled behind the camera.

Tor came into view. "I don't know why you have to film everything. I'm not even dressed."

"Oh come on, Tor. I like to preserve things," Will said, off screen.

"Well, at least let your daughter open her presents."

The rest of the video revealed more of the same. Lucy unwrapped all her gifts, complete squeals of delight at everything. A solid black cat played amongst the torn paper around the floor.

This was not the same Lucy as the one upstairs, and for the first time, I let myself really believe, deep down that something supernatural had taken Lucy.

Will stepped out of the room when the movie ended. I could hear him in the hallway. I stayed where I was to let him have his privacy.

Women never seemed to understand that about men, I mused as I let the screen turn to snow. A lot of men cried in private. It wasn't so much about being ashamed, more about being protectors and showing weakness was never a good idea. Granted, dumb prehistoric bullshit, but one of the few instincts the human race had left.

Of course this train of thought got me thinking about the last time I'd cried—when Tabby and I broke up. Even though it'd been mutual, I knew I'd been a dumbass and if I'd paid more attention, we'd probably still be together. Even now, I couldn't imagine a girl more perfect for me. She taught me to live and be comfortable in my own skin.

The irony, and what would have made the church a lot harder on me if they had known, was that Tabby was a witch. Not the ride on the broom sort of witch, mind you, but a goddess fearing pagan. Of course, there really wasn't any fear about it—except her magic scared the crap out of me. Maybe it was I who was goddess fearing and not Tabby?

My superiors would have branded her damned, but I knew better. She was one of the kindest people I had ever met. She tried her best to live a good life. I didn't care that she was different. I didn't understand the logic of the church. How could someone so kind and caring be damned? I never believed God as vengeful. Odd for a priest, maybe, but a few of us didn't feel the same way as the church.

I watched the snow drift on the screen, lost in my thoughts. If this all went to hell, I could call Tabby. She did have a lot more experience than I did with supernatural stuff. Not every day an ex-priest has a witch to call on. Maybe there was something at work, getting me involved with Lucy. Maybe there wasn't and I was getting dragged into this craziness by my idiotic brain. Either way, if things got out of hand, calling Tabby would be a good move. She would give me a kick in the ass if I needed it. Maybe she might even be able to help.

I sought out Will and Tor in the kitchen to tell them this change of plans. "How would the both of you feel about me bringing in a friend who might be able to help?"

"What sort of friend?" Tor asked, her gaze never leaving the cans she was arranging.

"My ex-girlfriend. She might be useful."

Tor snapped her eyes toward me. "And how would your ex-girlfriend help?"

I took a deep breath. "Because she's battled a demon once before."

It got so quiet you could hear a bat's whiskers twitch.

Then Tor straightened and put some cans in the pantry. "You really think she can help Lucy?"

I shrugged. "I think she can try."

AS I HOPPED into my car, I almost expected it not to start because of all the weird stuff that had been happening. Even though I had dumped the ruined plants in the dumpster, I still didn't feel safe. Something was not right, but I couldn't put my finger on it. Cueing up my iPod, I cranked the volume on the car stereo. It was a Type O Negative day.

It probably was weird to have specific days set aside for music, but I'd always done it. If I didn't play the right music, things didn't work out. Almost like a transmission that was missing enough tines on the gears to sound off but could still shift. The beats rained in perfect rhythm to stave off the bad luck. Most people familiar with the band would feel their music was downright morbid, but when I looked underneath, it was all sarcasm and message. When I felt upset, it was the perfect thing to deaden the bad things in my head. I hated that I would never hear Peter's dark voice again. I drummed my fingers on the steering wheel. *Rest in peace, Peter Steele, wherever you are.*

Suddenly, I heard an upbeat beat in the background, completely counterpoint to the song.

"Oh shit, the phone."

I snatched my purse from the backseat while keeping my eyes on the road. The car swerved slightly. I rooted around with my hand. Locating the handle of my purse, I grabbed it and threw it onto the front passenger seat. I finally retrieved the phone.

"Yeah," I said.

"Tabby?"

Holy shit, it was *him*. The *him* that got away. The *him* I'd corrupted. My defrocked priest, Jimmy Holiday.

Taking a deep breath, I steadied my nerves and said, "Why, Jimmy. I thought you'd disappeared."

He laughed. "Nah, just stuck in a cubicle for way too long. You still witchy?"

I snorted. "Um, yeah. I was born a witch. I don't think that's going to change anytime soon."

"Good," he paused, "you wanna come to Virginia?"

What the hell? Maybe this was the wrongness I'd been sensing. Things were pretty bad if Jimmy Holiday was asking a witch for help. When we were dating, he avoided my work like the plague. Now he was asking for my help? My gut clenched. It hit me—whatever was happening with Jimmy had to be what caused my plants to die. There was a badness he had gotten himself involved in. I sensed it. If he wasn't careful, something this bad could kill him. "What's going on, Jimmy?"

He coughed. Classic stalling. "You got any experience with possession?"

My body went cold. I pulled into my space at the college. "Why?"

"I'm here in a town called Sorrow's Point." He chuckled. "I know, great name for a town." A lengthy silence ensued and for a moment I thought he'd hung up. "Anyway, I'm here trying to save a little girl."

"You didn't go all priesty on me again, did you?"

"Nope. Guy I knew from back home contacted me because I used to be a priest. He thinks his daughter is possessed. I'm…," the air felt heavier and his breathing turned deeper over the line, "I'm starting to think it's possible."

Right then. Not your every day, average call at all. "How old is the little girl?"

"Six."

It was all I needed to hear. "Where in Virginia?"

Chapter Twelve

Acquaintance

I SET MY PHONE on the table. "She's on her way." My heart beat harder. I needed to keep my head on straight. "She has to drive from Morgantown."

"Morgantown?" Will asked.

I nodded. "Morgantown, West Virginia. It's where she lives now. She'll probably be here in five or six hours. She said she'd be in touch."

He stretched his arms overhead. "Good. We can use all the help we can get."

"Besides," I played with my soda can, letting the aluminum crackle in my fist, "if an exorcism is granted, they recommend a female be present." I glanced sideways at Tor. "I'm not sure you want to see your daughter's exorcism."

Her quick intake of breath and her hand flying against her mouth told me all I needed to know.

"I don't think I can take much more as it is," she said.

"It's settled then." I eyed Will, not certain if I should even ask. The state of him didn't bode well, but he was Lucy's father. "Do you want to be present?"

He paused. "I'd like to try."

Would he really be able to do it? I didn't know, but it was his choice to make. Anyway, the exorcism depended on the church. My job was to collect information and get proof. I gripped my notes. I had no proof toward anything, yet. I needed to get some soon, one way or the other.

Chapter Thirteen

Tabby: Part 3

AS SOON AS "Die With Me" came on the radio, I got all teary-eyed. Dammit. This was *our* song. Figured, Jimmy would throw himself into my life again just when I got my shit together. I wiped the tears away with my hand and refocused on the road ahead. Then I flipped to the next song on my iPod. No sense in getting myself all upset over nothing.

It was Jimmy's fault we'd broken up. But, if I was honest with myself, it was as much mine. I wanted him to be something he wasn't. I wanted to change him—my first mistake. I should have counted myself lucky for having a guy willing to upend his whole life for me. He would have taken a bullet for me if I'd needed him to, but that was also the problem. There were plenty of times when I could take care of myself. Jimmy tended to forget that.

And now, here I was rushing back into his life. Completely voluntarily. I needed my head examined.

Jimmy owed me for this. My Ph. D. was now on hold. Isaac was staying with a friend. I took a leave of absence. I knew Jimmy was only calling me because he had to. I couldn't imagine how the family must feel with their girl in such a state that the father became desperate enough to believe she was possessed. With the dead plants, the feeling in my gut, and the fact I was now on my way to Virginia, it didn't look good. At least I knew what all the omens were about.

I wished Jimmy had been calling me because he wanted to, not because he needed my witchy expertise, but I didn't want to get my hopes up.

I looked at the dashboard clock, a little after six. Time to get something to eat. Each time a roadside sign appeared, I hoped it was a food sign, but none came. First came gas, then came attractions, and finally, food.

An Olive Garden. Perfect. I turned off at the exit. The way I saw it, food with garlic was a necessity. Garlic had cleansing properties, and from what Jimmy described, I was going to need them.

Chapter Fourteen

Timmy

AFTER DINNER, WE settled in the living room, Will in the chair, Tor and I on the sofa. Tor arranged it so I was sitting between them. We sat there, silent. I got the feeling they didn't entertain often, and that they almost never used the living room for other people besides Will.

"Does anyone sit with Lucy at night?" I asked.

Tor's expression was guarded. "Not usually. When the sounds start, she's asleep. When I look in on her, her eyes are closed and her breathing is steady. She's the only person able to rest through the noises."

Something about her words made me doubt Lucy was sleeping. Will played with his watch, twisting it around on his wrist as far as he could get it to go, then he'd twist it back. His wrist was turning red from the metal rubbing across his skin.

"She sleeps," Will said. "I checked to see if she was faking once, but she wasn't. She was fast asleep."

With all the supernatural stuff involved, it didn't seem plausible for her to be able to sleep through it. But I let it go. "So, whatever this is, it is causing havoc not only with Lucy, but throughout the house."

"I guess so," Tor said. "I mean, it's scary." She ran her fingers through the fringe on a pillow. It was some sort of mottled velvet with sparkles in the fabric.

"Well," I said. "Maybe Tabby will be able to help."

Granted, I hadn't done much except witness Lucy's oddities. Tor and Will hadn't been lying about their daughter's transformation. But I needed another set of eyes I could rely on. I could only read the Roman Ritual so many times. Tabby had always been good in unusual situations because of her ghost hunting. Plus, maybe she could be a buffer between my brain and my doubts.

"I hope so," Tor said. She looked away quickly, but not before I saw the tears forming in her eyes.

#

It was a long wait for Tabby to get there. Almost as soon as night fell, the noises started. Because it was winter, night fell pretty early, around six. It got me thinking again. Would a six-year-old really be asleep at six p.m.?

Suddenly, it sounded like something ripped a giant hole in the roof. I jerked and stared up at the ceiling. Of course, there was no sign of any damage.

"Have you ever tried waking Lucy up while the noises are going on?" I asked.

Will's eyes narrowed.

I waved my hand. "I'm not trying to say you haven't done anything, Will. I'm trying to figure it out. That's why you brought me here."

Will's face softened. "I'm sorry, Jimmy. I'm so used to getting ready to fight with doctors and everyone else."

"It's okay. But have you ever tried to wake Lucy up once the noises have started?"

"No."

"Let's see what happens then, huh?" There was no refusal. I took my chance before they changed their minds.

I felt like a fourteen-year-old dared to go into a haunted house. Will said he was too afraid to do it, and Tor didn't want to, so I climbed the stairs to Lucy's room alone. Somehow I wasn't freaked out. Not really. I mean, she was tied down for Christ's sake. It wasn't like she could hurt me. So far, I hadn't seen anything to make me want to run out of there screaming, and the only thing supernatural I'd experienced was that room. My dream could possibly be explained by other means, and the noises I was currently listening to, well…we'd soon see.

When I got to Lucy's door, I paused to see if I could hear anything coming from her room. Nothing. I knocked and opened it. Again, the smell hit me. It was stronger this time. I had to suppress the urge to gag. I reached over and felt along the wall. As soon as my palm landed on the switch, I flipped it. Lucy laid there in her bed, but her eyes were not closed.

She smiled at me like a snake getting ready to strike. "What do you want, Priest?"

Something small scrabbled across the floor. I couldn't see it, but I heard its claws.

"Nothing, Lucy," I said. "I came to check on you. Are you feeling okay?"

She laughed rough and broken. The sound seemed to travel to the ceiling and out through the rest of the house. "You like to feel things in this house, strange things, don't you?"

I nodded. "There's a lot strange here."

"You like to feel other things, don't you, Priest? You can feel me if you want." She raised her hips in a suggestive manner, not at all befitting her age.

I wanted to back up against the wall. This was so fucking wrong. "No, Lucy. Don't do that again."

She giggled and flopped her hips back on the bed.

"Go to sleep. I wanted to make sure you're all right."

She grinned again with her broken teeth and licked her lips in a way that made my skin crawl. "I'll be fine if you untie my hands. I'll be really fine then."

I backed away from the bed. This was sick in so many ways. What had happened to my sister wasn't far from my mind. There was no way Lucy could know about that of course, but it didn't help the way I felt. Chills danced along my skin like a colony of ants after a soda can. "Not going to happen. Why don't you try to rest?"

I had to be careful of what I said. I didn't need to give her anything she could use against me. It was too easy for people to accuse priests of molestation with all the cases out there. When I had been one, I had been overly careful that nothing I did or said could lead anyone to that conclusion. And well, me being defrocked meant that people assumed it had been because of that versus anything normal. Thanks media.

"I'll rest better when you are a part of me," she winked.

My body stiffened. The way she'd said it, that part wasn't sexual. She was implying more. Like my soul. I coughed and stepped out into the doorway, turned off the light and closed the door. I was torn with what to tell Will and Tor. Part of me wanted Lucy examined for possible sexual abuse, part of me wanted to investigate further. Sexual abuse didn't feel right somehow, not as an answer, but I couldn't ignore the fact that Lucy shouldn't be sexual at six. She also shouldn't even know what she knew about sex at six.

I couldn't withhold anything from her parents. I didn't want to tell them, but I knew I had no choice.

I took the steps slowly, one at a time, half steps if I could, trying to figure out how to approach this. My mind rebelled at the thought. I found them in the living room where I'd left them. Without any lead up or any chance to think, I stumbled into it. "Lucy wasn't asleep."

Will sat up in the chair. His eyes widened in surprise. "She wasn't?"

I crossed the room and sat on the couch. "No."

"The noises never stopped," Tor said, almost accusingly. She put her hand over her mouth and made a sound similar to a squeal.

I tapped my chin with my fingers, opting for a different tactic. "This incident at Lucy's daycare, you never said what it was."

Will sighed. "A male caretaker molested some kids. We had Lucy checked. He didn't touch her."

"Are you sure?" If I had hackles, they'd have risen now.

"The doctors said she hadn't been touched," Tor said.

"And you asked her?" I turned my head and stared at them both.

"She said no." Will wrung his hands together.

I sat back in on the sofa. The puzzle pieces started to fall into place. "She definitely needs some psychiatric help, possessed or not."

"Why?" Tor asked.

I groaned. "Because she came on to me. That and the way she spoke to me. It wasn't normal." Hearsay, even eyewitness testimony like what I'd experienced upstairs wouldn't cut it. We needed more. "We need to start videotaping conversations with her."

"What? Why?" Will set his soda on the coffee table, almost dropping it.

"The things we're looking for, they're going to come out in what she says and does while we're with her. Recording everything is our best recourse in documentation when we go to the church."

The doorbell rang, interrupting all conversation. One word escaped my lips, "Tabby."

#

I walked into the hallway in time to see Will let Tabby inside. She looked as I remembered, with her long red hair twirled up on the back of her head. Her pale skin flushed pink from the cold, and her green eyes were glassy with circles under them.

"Jimmy," she called as she ran over and hugged me. She smelled of something flowery as she always had.

I sniffed her. "I missed you, Tabby-cat."

"I missed you too."

The choppy laughter rattled the ceiling.

Tabby jumped back. "What the fuck was that?"

"Oh," I let loose a sarcastic laugh, although the hairs on my arms stood on end. "That's Lucy saying Hello."

"You're kidding, right?"

I shook my head. "Nope." I glanced past Tabby and saw Tor and Will standing there, watching. I coughed. "I'm sorry, Will, Tor, this is Tabby."

Tabby glanced at the ceiling for a moment then she squared her shoulders, came over, and shook their hands.

Will picked up Tabby's suitcase. It was one of those older models without wheels. As far as I knew, she'd always had it. It was a faded olive green with a hard case.

"If you don't mind," Will said. "You can share the library with Jimmy."

Tabby looked at me, a question in her eyes. "When do I get to see her?"

"Tomorrow. The activity is worse at night," I said. I turned to Will, waiting for him to say something, but he didn't. "The noises are quieter in the library."

"Lucy's noises?" she asked.

I nodded. We followed Will into the library.

"This is some place, huh?" she asked me.

"You haven't seen the half of it."

We set Tabby's suitcase next to the other sofa—the one that wasn't facing the door.

"Did you eat?" Tor asked Tabby from the doorway.

Tabby turned and smiled. "Yeah, I stopped on the way."

Tor nodded. "Are you tired?"

"Not yet, I'm not," Tabby said.

But she'd lied. The darkness under her eyes really stood out against her pale skin. I said nothing.

Tor ushered us all into the kitchen. "I'm making hot chocolate," she said. "Then, I think Tabby needs to know why she's here."

Chapter Fifteen

Investigations

I WOKE UP WITH a particular smell in my nose, the aroma of sunshine and quiet. I'm sure people would think me strange I say I can smell quiet, but I can. For me, it smells like Tabby's perfume and the scent of her hair.

Catching Tabby up to things last night didn't take long. Once we were done, the tiredness had really started to set in. Noises or not, she fell asleep quickly. She was still sleeping now, her arm tucked under her head. She always looked so innocent in the mornings. I didn't realize how much I'd missed her. No, that was the lie I told myself to make our breakup easier. I missed her from the moment she left me. I missed her goodness, and her reactions to my boneheaded stunts. I wasn't being sappy, at least I didn't think so. I couldn't shake the feeling I was stupid for screwing things up with her.

I couldn't even say there was any one event that ended it. Yet what I'd figured out over the years was I didn't appreciate her enough and I was an idiot. She was better off without me. I knew that. It was hard to admit to it sometimes.

After a bit, her eyes popped open, and she stared at me. "What are you looking at?"

I snorted. "You."

She rolled her eyes. "I should punch you or something."

I shook my head. "Nope. No punching allowed. Why don't we leave all the negative stuff in the past, huh? At least until we get this under control."

She sat up and brushed her hair out of her way. "I don't think this is something you can control."

She was right. "Probably not. Truce?"

A minute passed without a word, her staring at me all the while. "All right. Though, I have to point out I'm not even mad at you right now."

"Okay. I'll shut up then."

"Good idea." She snorted. "So what do we do now?"

I felt my face grow red. Good one, Jimmy. Real Smooth. "First, I want you to check out that room upstairs, and then see what you think about the mirror up there. I also think it would be a good idea for you to meet Lucy in person, and tell me your impressions."

Tabby nodded and headed for the bathroom. Soon as she was done with her shower, I rushed through mine. When I finished, I stood in the doorway and watched her for a minute. She was sitting on the bed, waiting.

"You ready?" she asked.

I shrugged. Time to try the "let's clear the air" thing again. Better this time. "I wanted to say I'm sorry."

"For what?"

"Everything."

"It isn't that easy, and you know it," she sighed, "but it's nice to hear you say it."

If it all was easy, I would have dragged her back home like a caveman a long time ago. Too bad it wasn't that simple. "So, we good?"

She snorted. "Jesus, Jimmy. I guess. What more do you want from me?"

"Truth?"

She nodded.

"Everything."

Her eyes went wide, but she didn't reply, just motioned with her hand toward the door. We dropped off our things in the library then headed to the kitchen.

Tor was leaning with her back against the stove. Bags hung under her eyes that hadn't been there the day before.

"How's Lucy?" I asked.

She looked at me, her nose red. "I think she needs a doctor."

It didn't take me by surprise given Lucy's condition. "Do you need Tabby and I to do anything?"

Tor sniffled. "Go ahead and do what you'd planned. Will is

readying Lucy so we can take her to the emergency room."

"What do you think is wrong?" Tabby asked.

"I don't know what it is," Tor said.

#

Tor went outside to get the car while Will raced upstairs to get Lucy. I waited by the front door to hold it open so they could get her into the car easier.

"Do you think she's going to be okay?" Tabby asked.

I shrugged "I have no idea. She isn't well."

Will came downstairs carrying Lucy bundled up, almost like a mummy. As they passed, I caught a glimpse of one of her eyes watching me. She never made a sound except for breathing heavily.

Tabby and I observed from the doorway as they got Lucy into the car.

"What happened to her eyes?" Tabby asked.

"I don't know." Heck, life would be a lot easier if I did know.

Tabby and I returned to the library and sat on our respective sofas.

"Jesus Christ," Tabby said. "What a mess."

I chuckled uncomfortably. "You're telling me? I really don't know what's going on. I wish I did."

She paused for a moment. "Tell me about this room."

"Freakiest place I've been in a while, that's for sure."

"How so?" she asked.

"I think you need to see it. I doubt my descriptions will do it justice."

Her brow rose.

"No, really. Get your witchy stuff and let's see what you can do."

Tabby laughed. "My witchy stuff? You never change, do you?"

As we made our way through the house, an oppressive sensation took hold of me. My windpipe narrowed, an invisible force grabbing onto it and squeezing. I cleared my throat. "It's up here."

Tabby followed me up the staircase into the attic. When she stepped in, she looked like a little kid dying to explore. We wandered along, Tabby peering under sheets, until we reached the other side of the house. I didn't have to tell her where the room was. She walked straight to it…and froze, literally in front of the door, almost as if a string had pulled her there and had gotten stuck.

"I see what you mean," she said.

I let her do her thing. She pulled out a bundle of sage from her bag and lit it. Then, she opened the door to the room. She paused again when she stepped over the threshold. A gust of cool wind blew, making her hair fly around her face. She began chanting and moving the sage around. At first, it seemed like nothing was happening, but then her sage stopped burning. No smoke, nothing. It just stopped.

"I've never had that happen before."

I scratched my head. "Maybe it's trying to keep you from cleansing it."

Tabby pulled a lighter out of her pocket and tried to relight the sage, but it wouldn't catch. When she flicked the lighter, the fire would appear, but as soon as it got near the sage, the flame would go out again. She growled.

"All right," she said, staring out of the room. "If it doesn't want me cleansing it. I'll do something else."

Tabby stepped out of the room and closed the door. Then, she started walking toward the other side of the house, so I grabbed her by the shoulder.

"Did you see the mirror?" I asked, pointing at it.

"Oh my God," she said.

"What?" I asked.

She crouched and turned it over. "Do you know what this is?"

I tried not to be stupid. "Well, it's a mirror…"

She swatted me on the leg with her hand.

"Ow."

Ignoring my distress, she continued, "It's much more than that. It's an old mirror. It's silver backed."

"So?"

"So!" She stood up. "So! You see the black paint?"

"Yeah."

"This mirror was a receptacle."

I leaned over and inspected the mirror again. "What do you mean?"

"Spirits, demons, whatever can be trapped in a mirror, but they can only be trapped in a silver backed mirror."

"Why does it matter?"

Tabby put her hands on her hips. "Because silver has purifying properties, that's why. It is an ancient thing because it's an element. Silver has been used to fight evil for a long time. Only a very powerful witch could have done this."

I really had no idea what she was talking about. "You mean like a spiritualist?"

"No, I mean a witch." Tabby cocked her head at me. "Who told you about a spiritualist?"

"You won't believe me," I said.

"Out with it." She tapped her foot, clearly willing to wait until I caved.

"The town librarian."

1950

O'DELL STOOD IN the foyer of Blackmoor. He hated being there, hated the feeling of the whole damn place. Ever since Jones had killed Black, reports of strange things going on in the house came to his office near daily. The Black brother wanted to sell the house, but wouldn't step foot in the place. He left it all up to O'Dell. Living in a small town, O'Dell never minded wearing many hats. Running the library was easy, being sheriff was his passion, but trying to get this place ready to be sold…that was a nightmare. The young Mr. Black had made it perfectly clear, if he didn't get the house presentable—meaning get rid of the evil inside it—he was done. If O'Dell didn't take care of this, he knew he'd be out of a job…all of them.

Finally, he saw a black Ford pull into the drive. She was the last resort. The minister couldn't do anything about the feel of the house. The priest had tried to exorcise whatever evil resided inside, but had a heart attack during the ritual. Another priest died trying to fix the damn thing. It had taken some time, but he'd found Eldora Williams, the most revered spiritualist in the country. She'd helped police from all over on a variety of cases—murders mostly. If she couldn't help, he didn't know what the hell to do.

He'd tried to get the other Black to burn the place to the ground, but Black wouldn't have it. O'Dell sighed. "If I can't fix it, let him live in the fucking thing."

Mrs. Williams got out of her car. Dressed in a large black mink coat with a hat to match, she opened the trunk of her car and pulled out a large black satchel.

He opened the front door of the house and waited.

She smiled at him, adjusted her hold on her bag, and came through the doorway. But, as soon as she crossed the threshold, she froze.

"A powerful spirit you've got here," she said in a voice that sounded like a croak.

O'Dell coughed. "Ma'am, I need you to move so I can close the door."

She looked at him, a puzzled expression on her face. Finally, she stepped aside.

He closed the door. Sniffing, she began walking toward the staircase.

"Wait, ma'am. Can I take your coat?"

She ignored him and headed up the stairs.

"Damn woman," he mumbled, but followed her. She didn't stop until she entered a bedroom in the east wing. The Blacks hadn't used it in years, the furniture covered in dusty sheets.

Mrs. Williams sniffed again then glanced upwards. "What's up there?"

O'Dell cleared his throat. "Attic. I think there's a storage room up there too."

She nodded. "Take me to it."

"We've got to go back down to reach the staircase to it." He took a deep breath. "You sure I can't take your coat?"

She shook her head and said again, "Take me to it."

O'Dell led her through the house and to the steps that led to the attic. Once they got up, she practically knocked him over and darted toward the extra room.

Pointing at the door to the storage room, she whispered, "That's the heart."

His brow furrowed. "The heart of what?"

"Of the house, of course."

O'Dell watched her grab all types of things from her bag: candles and bottles of oils in enough colors to make his head swim, dried flowers and sticks of things he couldn't recognize, and even a few old iron nails. He'd never seen anything like it. With all of that in her arms, she entered that storage room. He stayed outside, staring anywhere but that room. No need to get involved more than he already had. The bumps and growls coming from inside only reiterated the fact that he'd made the right choice.

"Mr. O'Dell!" she screamed. "Go in my bag and bring me the mirror."

He raised his eyebrows, but said nothing. Grasping the large oval looking glass out of her bag, he crept over to the door. He took a deep breath, his heart pounding in his chest—*lub dub, lub dub*. He jerked the doorknob.

A huge black cloud filled the room, glowing with an eerie purplish brightness. The smell of the black formless fog drifted toward him. He gagged.

"Mr. O'Dell!"

He swung around and saw Mrs. Williams motioning to him. He handed her the mirror and could have sworn that out of the black mass eyes stared at him.

Backing out of the room, he closed the door behind him. He didn't care what she did, as long as she took care of that *thing*.

Present

TABBY LET LOOSE an uneasy laugh. “Nothing here is normal, is it?”

“And think, you haven’t even met Lucy yet.”

“I know, Jimmy. I know.” Tabby shook herself. “Okay, this is what we’re going to do. If, and I mean if, Lucy is possessed, then we can recapture the demon in the mirror. If she isn’t, we’ll simply seal up this room and put the damn thing inside.”

“Seal the room, you mean with wax?” I asked.

“Basically, and wards.”

I could imagine how much of a mess that would be if and when we got the church involved. “Let’s wait and see if Lucy meets the requirements for exorcism. That’s what her dad wants anyway.”

Tabby smiled. “All right, let the church decide, but here’s a good question for you. What if the church washes its hands of the whole thing and Lucy really is possessed?”

She brought up a good point. The church would probably have notes from the local priest about his recommendation to the psychiatric hospital. If she really was possessed, the church would look at everything harder, and the church was anything but infallible.

“I guess if the church wants no part of it, we’ll have to try ourselves—if Lucy’s possessed.”

“Isn’t that dangerous?” she asked.

“Well, I figure we probably will be about on the same playing field. I mean, most of the priests who are the diocese exorcist in areas over here have never even performed an exorcism. It’s a title in name only, at least that’s what I read online.” I paused for a minute, thinking. “So the way I see it, if they've never done an exorcism before and neither have we, then it's about the same odds." I ran my hands over my arms. It was cold near the room.

"You know," she said. "It's almost like an old joke, an exorcist and a witch walk into a bar…"

I chucked her lightly on the shoulder. "Shut up. Besides, I'm not an exorcist."

Tabby laughed at me. "Jimmy, I think from the moment you heard about all this, you've wanted to do it. Maybe you were meant to do this."

"And if it all goes bad?"

"Maybe that's meant to happen too."

I sighed. "I can't see how it's meant to happen for a little girl to die."

She frowned. "Jimmy, kids die every day, and this little girl is sick. It could happen."

I can't explain the feeling I got then. Some mix between trepidation and empowerment. "Then it's up to us to make sure it doesn't happen."

Tabby looked at me skeptically, but she said nothing, almost as if she wanted to avoid a fight. "Now what?"

I shrugged. "I guess we can go back downstairs and wait for news. I don't know what else to do."

Tabby grabbed another item from her bag. She began writing all types of symbols on the door to the attic room with a piece of chalk. Her hand moved so furiously that I could see sweat running off her neck.

"There," she said. "That should help."

"What is it?"

She put the chalk back in her bag. "I warded this door to keep anything else from coming from the portal in that room."

"I thought we were waiting to see if Lucy really was possessed or not."

She snickered. "If the crap coming from that portal is what's causing Lucy's illness, I've solved your problem for you. If she's possessed, then what I did probably didn't do any good at all."

"Is the portal why the room felt so weird?"

Tabby smirked at me. "Yes, Jimmy."

She was being so condescending, but I didn't mind. When we were first together, she tried to teach me, but I wouldn't have any part of it. She had the right to lord it over me now.

"So," I said. "Do you think the original owner, Archibald Black, was possessed?"

Tabby stood and tapped her chin idly. "Well, it's possible, but there's also the possibility that his spirit's the one doing the possessing."

#

Later that evening, after Tabby and I made the most of delivery pizza, Will stormed into the kitchen through the back door.

"Jimmy, I'm sorry. I didn't know it was going to take this long." He threw his keys on the table so hard I was afraid the glass was going to break. He flung his coat on the floor.

I stood up, rushed over to him, and clutched him by the shoulders. "What the hell happened?"

He roared. I let him go and stepped back.

"I'll tell you what fucking happened, goddamn doctors." Sinking into a chair at the table, he seemed to collapse. I found him a soda in the refrigerator and set it in front of him.

"I'm tired of it," he said. "No more."

"All right, Will." I opened the pop tab and placed it back in front of him.

"I spent six-fucking-hours at the police station, wanna know why?"

It was Tabby who asked. "Why?"

He slammed his fist into the table. My empty soda fell over with a clang. "They, somebody, thought I was abusing my own daughter. Fuck!"

"Calm down," Tabby said. "You're going to hurt yourself." She placed her hand on his arm. That's all it took. Tabby was full of special gifts, and her ability to calm people was one of them. All it took was a touch, and Will's whole body visibly relaxed.

"Now why did they think Lucy was abused?" she asked.

Will took a sip of his soda. "Her eyes. It finally took Tor getting her PCP to fax over a note explaining the reason her eyes are the way they are." He wiped his hands over his face. "I guess some nursing student reported Lucy looked abused, and called the cops. The doctors didn't even know about it until I was already dragged to the station. Turns out it's severe oxygen failure, and those fuckers…" He collapsed into sobs.

"Is she going to be all right?" I asked.

Tabby handed him a napkin.

He swiped at his eyes. "For now, I think. They gave her a few things, got things going again. She's going to have to be on dialysis for a while."

I nodded. "So her kidneys too?"

"Yeah."

How much sicker could she get? "And her breathing's better?"

"Fluid in her chest, they had to do a chest tap to release the fluid."

"Jesus Christ," I said.

"Yeah." He wiped his eyes again with the napkin. "I don't want my little girl to die."

#

It was strange to go to sleep without a sound at all. At home, I was used to the cars passing by on the street next to my house, but with Lucy gone the sounds had ceased. The only noise I heard now was of the old house settling. Tabby and I stayed up late into the night talking—she on her couch, I on mine, but even she finally drifted off. I wasn't used to so much damn quiet. The last time I'd slept like this was when I was in seminary, and that drudged up some memories I'd rather forget.

My mind couldn't stop bowling over the same facts and events. I couldn't fault the hospital staff for questioning Will. Even I had wondered at first. Perhaps, for safety's sake, Will needed to put a security camera in Lucy's room so that she was monitored at all times. Then, if she did something to hurt herself, it would be recorded and Will would have something to back himself up with.

Plus, if there was an exorcism, the church would want video documentation anyways. It was standard practice now. I remembered hearing about a case in seminary where a priest was arrested for abusing the girl during the course of an exorcism. Now, I didn't know what the priest did, but if the movies were any indication, trauma was something that the possessed did to themselves. It could look like abuse, sure, but it was probably self-inflicted.

At last, my mind stopped spinning and I drifted off.

"Jimmy, wake up. I'm bored." Tabby woke me a little after eight.

From past experience I knew it was pointless to argue with her. She always had this unspoken rule—if she was up and couldn't sleep, those around her couldn't either. This impulse was one of the reasons we broke up in the first place. I still remembered times when I had a big project due the next day and she'd wake me up at three or four. Of course, after that, I couldn't get back to sleep. It was one of those things that got worse as time went on.

"Tabby, why do you have to do that?" I asked.

She shot me an obnoxious grin. "Cause it's fun to devil you."

I ran my hands through my hair. "You know, Tabby, there are times I really miss you, but not right now."

"Oh, come on, you know you love me," she said, batting her eyelashes at me.

I stared at her. "That's the problem. I do."

My utterance had a reaction from Tabby I wasn't anticipating. She kind of shivered then left the room. I didn't mean to unsettle her, and honestly, I hadn't meant to let that slip. We knew each other too well—knew what buttons to push. But it wasn't the buttons, we'd left a lot of things unresolved. I had to wonder if I was inviting more trouble by having her come. I hadn't thought about it before, but now, I knew I might have made a mistake.

Tabby went to shower while I searched out Will. An idea had hit me upside the head like a battering ram. I found him staring into his coffee mug in the kitchen. "We need to talk."

Will picked up his head, searching my face as if lost. "About what?"

"There's something that's been bothering me about the night you came to my house," I stared at him, pointedly. "Something you said."

"About Lucy?" he asked.

"Yes."

"Okay." He wiped his upper lip.

"You told me the hospital wanted her gone after she almost gouged out a nurse's eye, but you said that you took her out of there when they were going to try shock treatment. So which is it, Will?" I drank my coffee, watching his face. "If she tried to gouge out a nurse's eye, wouldn't there be charges? Or at least a complaint from the nurse?"

He sat still, very still. "And if the nurse didn't press charges?"

"What do you mean?" My eyes narrowed.

"Lucy did try to gouge out the nurse's eye, but luckily only scratched the cornea before others pulled her away." He took a deep breath. "So we made a deal. Lucy's so young." His grip tightened on the mug. "Tor and I paid for the nurse's hospital bills. Luckily, her eye fully recovered. It was after the attack that the hospital considered ECT."

The answer satisfied my question, but it did nothing to ease my mind. Lucy could be psychotic. Odd cases happened where children killed. She could grow up to be a monster. That thought almost made possession preferable. "What if an exorcism isn't granted? Will, what are you going to do then?"

"I don't know," he said. "I honestly don't know."

#

Tabby appeared soon after Will left for the hospital. She didn't speak to me for a long time. She sat in her chair at the table. I sat in mine. The only break in the silence was the kicking on and off of the fan in the refrigerator. Finally, around noon, she asked me to join her outside. I didn't question it. I followed her, wandering around the grounds.

Underneath the snow, you could see the outlines of the hedges bordering each garden. Snow covered statues and fountains dotted the grounds. If it wasn't for the history of the house, I would say it was a stunning place, but somehow, beauty and evil didn't go hand in hand in my mind.

Outside, the house seemed normal, but I knew what lurked in the attic. Tabby froze at the edge of the woods surrounding the property.

"What's wrong, Tabby?" I asked.

"This isn't good."

I walked up to her. "What isn't good?"

"This," she pointed at my feet, "is a ley line."

"What?"

She smacked her head with her hand. "I forget how clueless you can be sometimes. A ley line is a power source, kind of like a grid, but a magical one. They're also doorways."

"To what?"

"To let things go, and to let things in."

I rolled my eyes. "I hate it when you talk in riddles."

She huffed. "Someone who can do magic can tap into the power source in the ley line and use it for magical purposes. Supposedly, very powerful practitioners can actually travel by way of them, but I've never seen anyone that strong. The bad side is the danger in ley lines. Dark beings can use them as doorways into our world."

"So what does this mean?"

She put her hands on her hips. "It means that Mr. Black was probably a very accomplished practitioner with a penchant for the dark side. Darth Vadar to your Han Solo."

I laughed. "If I'm Han Solo, who's Luke Skywalker?"

"Whoever can send this damn thing back from where it came from."

"Do you think it jumped the line? Or did Black invite it in?" It was an honest question. I didn't have a clue.

"Right now," she said, "I don't know. But when Lucy comes back, we can ask it."

I shook my head. "Nope, bad idea. Demons are liars. We can ask it its name. We can ask it when it will leave, but we cannot ask it anything else."

"Why not?"

"Because the rules say so."

She snorted. "Jimmy Holiday, since when are you ever the sort to do anything by the rules?"

I smiled. "Never."

"Exactly my point."

#

Later that day, Will called to let us know Lucy was coming home. "The doctors figure since the worst is over and we have her feeding tube equipment here, we can probably manage her at home. I don't know if she was weak, or if she wanted back here, but she didn't act out or cause anything weird this time. Her organ failure has stopped. It happened suddenly." He paused. "So much of what's going on with Lucy is odd. They think that it's probably all right for her to leave the hospital since she appears to be stable. Honestly, I don't think they know what to think."

When Lucy came home, the house darkened. The walls and floors almost rippled for a moment and then righted. It was hard to explain, but without her, it felt like a normal house. With her, it was oppressive.

As Will came in with Lucy, there were no theatrics. She was bundled in a sheet with only her face peering out. Her yellowed skin and bloody eyes remained the same. She stared at me—hard—as Will passed by. She did nothing to prevent him from taking her back to her room.

With Lucy in bed, we sat at the kitchen table. None of us really said anything. It was tense and difficult when everyone felt awkward. None of us wanted to chit chat. We were waiting for something to happen. Finally, Will wandered in a few minutes later, a bleeding scratch on his hand.

"Got you, did she?" I asked.

"She always does when she's not restrained. I'm surprised she waited as long as she did."

"Maybe she didn't want to be restrained," Tabby said.

I glanced at her. "Maybe so."

After dinner, I figured it was time I brought up my idea. I wasn't sure if they'd go for it, but it was worth a shot. "Ever thought about installing a security camera?"

"You brought up something like that once before, didn't you?" Will asked.

"Yeah, for the exorcism."

"Well, we have a security system," Tor said.

"No." I threw up my hands. "I mean in Lucy's room."

Will looked at me, puzzled. "What are you talking about?"

"Think about it. If you record her, you have proof the injuries she causes are self-inflicted, then you'll be able to quell any accusations that might come up. Plus, the church, if they grant an exorcism, will want everything documented. These days, they use video."

Will tapped his fingers against his coffee mug. "It's something to think about."

"But what about Lucy's privacy?" Tor asked.

"She's six, what privacy does she need?" Will countered.

"What about when I bathe her?" she asked. "I sure don't want to record that."

"Well," I said. "You could cover the camera with a cloth. That way you'll have the audio portion proving that nothing bad happened, and you'll still be able to bathe her without invading Lucy's privacy."

Tabby smiled at me.

"That might work," Will said. "I'll call around tomorrow and see what I can do."

Chapter Eighteen

Belief

THE SILENCE HAD to end sometime, I guess. Round about eight the noises started. At first, it was so quiet I barely noticed. Then sharp rapping came from inside the walls. Patters of little feet ran across the ceiling, interspersed with that same choppy laughter.

The antics kind of amused me in a weird way. I mean, come on, it was screwing with us. I should have been afraid. I wasn't. Of course, it wasn't funny at all with Lucy's life at stake, but there was a kind of perverse humor in it.

"I guess Lucy got out of her funk," I said, staring up at the library ceiling.

Tabby followed the sounds with her eyes as they traveled around the room. "It's amazing that all of this is coming from one little girl."

"Or a little girl who so happens to have spirits attached to her."

Will and Tor had gone to bed early. Their movements had been slow and their eyes drooped. Toward the end, Will could hardly keep his head up. So, it fell to Tabby and I to be the witnesses of Lucy's nightly antics.

After Tabby got tired of staring at the ceiling, she turned to me. "Do you think Lucy is in there somewhere, asleep?"

I shrugged. "Probably. Little as I know about it, from what I understand, when the demon is forward, the possessed is in a trance-like state. They don't even know what's going on. That is, people who are really possessed. People who aren't are just terrific liars."

"How much research have you done?" she asked.

"Tons. Every night you haven't been here, before I went to sleep, I surfed the net for information."

"Shame we can't wake Lucy up," Tabby said.

I smiled. "That's exactly what the rite of exorcism is supposed to do. It 'wakes up' the possessed and drives the demon out. Hopefully, to Hell."

"And if there is no Hell?" she asked.

I shrugged. "I guess that's what your mirror is for."

I slipped off my shoes and socks and stretched out on the sofa, propping my feet up on the coffee table.

"Are you ever afraid?" she asked.

"Sure," I said. "Wouldn't be human otherwise." The truth is, I'd been scared many times, mostly by losing people I cared about—Tabby included. "Are you scared?"

She nodded. "You know me. I don't touch the dark, never did. And this thing… it's nasty. It was bad enough I dealt with that demon as a kid."

"How did that happen?"

She sighed. "When I was about ten, a couple of friends and I were playing with an old Ouija board in the house. You know, usual sleepover type of thing." She rubbed her hands up and down her arms. "Like idiots, we'd waited until three. Since my mother had always told me three was the 'real' witching hour, I shared that with my friends. We figured we'd have the best luck contacting a spirit then."

Tabby scratched her leg and looked at her feet. "At first, nothing happened." She glanced up at me. "Then, the planchette began to move. We got spooked, so we pulled our hands away, but the planchette kept moving. It went faster and faster in a circular pattern around the board. And then, it stopped dead with the pointy part right at me."

She swallowed. I could tell that even now, it had terrified her.

"I felt something grab me and a bad odor filled the room. Things began to look almost brown—like I was looking through a dusty fog. I took a deep breath. Then, I heard voices. They were telling me all types of weird things. Some of them whispered to me to do violent things. I stood up and began calling the corners." A chill fell over the library as she spoke. "I hate to think what would have happened if my mother hadn't trained me in the arts."

"What happened to the thing?" I asked.

"I said some incantations for protection, and it disappeared. Luckily for me, it must have been a very weak demon, but I've never touched an Ouija board since."

"I don't blame you." I had heard the story before, but it was good to ask her to tell it again. Some of the things seemed similar to Lucy's situation. I put my hands behind my head. "Look at it this way. If we get the church involved, we probably won't even be active participants. They'd view us unworthy, I imagine, with me being defrocked and you being a witch."

She scratched her head. ""'But that's what scares me. I have a bad feeling about all of this."

"What type of bad feeling?" I asked.

"That the church will refuse. Then, who's left to help Lucy? Me and you, and neither one of us know diddly squat about exorcism."

"At least you have experience with demons."

Tabby rolled her eyes. "One demon, and it was a weak one. Nothing like what's going on here."

I pulled my copy of the Roman Ritual from my bag. "I don't know if it matters, to be honest. In the early church, any Christian could do an exorcism. In the ritual, it clearly states that the exorcist must be pure in thought and intention. For both of us, all we want is for Lucy to be okay. To hell with the extra baggage. How much purer of a mindset can you get?"

"Is that even a word?"

"What?" I asked.

"Purer."

I chuckled. "I have no idea."

#

As we went to sleep, the noises of the house stayed with me a long time. Yet the scratching and pitter patter didn't bother me so much anymore. Will had said the sounds kept him and Tor up, but I didn't understand how that could be when I was getting used to them and I'd only been here a few days. Maybe they heard different sounds upstairs. Maybe the thing spoke to them through the baby monitor. I really didn't know. I fell asleep, figuring I would have more time to think about it tomorrow. Then, at about three, I heard it.

"Jimmy," it whispered.

I jerked awake and surveyed the room. Nothing. Whoever or whatever it was, it had spoken near my ear. Not creepy, just a loud whisper. But the notion that something tried to break through unsettled me.

I didn't bother going back to sleep.

The rest of the night the house was eerily silent. Even the settling noises of the house disappeared.

The next morning, I flailed when I woke. What I was dreaming, I couldn't remember. At some point, I must have fallen back to sleep. I uncurled my legs and groaned at the stiffness. Then, I felt something—a piece of paper clutched in my hand. I opened it. In a child's handwriting it said:

Liberaté mē

Liberate me. When does a six-year-old learn Latin? And how in the hell was she able to do this?

I stood up, walked out of the library, and headed straight to Lucy's room. It appeared almost normal. The early morning sunlight drifted in from the window. Lucy slept, at least I think she did. Her restraints were fastened to her wrists. The covers arranged around her comfortably. This was so far beyond what I knew how to manage. The impossible made possible. Granted, I'd read about people choking up nails during the course of an exorcism, things like that. But this wasn't part of an exorcism. This was from a dream. Now I had another mystery to solve.

Who wrote the note? And if it was Lucy, how in the hell did she do it? She'd been restrained at all times. Nothing about this made sense anymore, and I was starting to wonder if my mind was slowly cracking.

I left Lucy's room and headed back downstairs to the library. Tabby was sitting up on her sofa.

"Where were you?" she asked.

"I had a note," I said, but as I raised my hand to show it to her, the note was gone. Not in my hand. Not on the floor. Not on the sofa. I searched everywhere; it was nowhere. I ran out of the room and retraced my steps. Even in Lucy's room. The note had vanished.

I took the stairs easier this time around. No sense in rushing. Either I'd had the most vivid dream of my entire life, or someone was messing with me.

When I got back to the library, Tabby was standing inside the doorway. Her lips bent in a frown and her eyes searched my face. "Are you okay?"

I shrugged. "I have no idea."

"What's wrong?"

I sat on my sofa. "Either Lucy tried to contact me in a dream, by writing a note—in Latin no less—or someone here is playing a hell of a joke."

Tabby furrowed her brow and walked over to me. "That doesn't make any sense."

"Yeah. I know."

"Jimmy?" I heard Tor call from the hallway. I ran out. Tabby followed right behind me.

"What's wrong?" I asked.

Her face was strained. "Lucy… she…" she pointed upstairs.

I ran upstairs, Tabby following close behind. Lucy's back arched so far she was raising herself off the bed. Her eyes rolled back in her head so only the whites showed.

"Shit." I ran over to release the restraints. "Tabby, hurry, come help me!"

Tabby ran over and blocked her side of the bed to prevent Lucy from falling out. Tor watched from the doorway, her face lined with stress and the strain of it all. Lucy's back bowed so far I prayed she didn't hurt herself.

"Tor, has Lucy ever had a seizure before?" I asked.

She nodded. "Once in the mental hospital. They thought it might have been brought on by the medication."

I let go of the breath I'd been holding. "She's had CAT scans, right?"

Tor sighed. "She's had so many tests, but I know both the CAT scan and the MRI came out clear."

"Okay," I said.

Suddenly, Lucy completely relaxed. She focused those horrid eyes on me.

"Good morning, Priest," she said.

I grinned at her, as best I could. "Good morning, Lucy. You gave us quite a scare."

She opened her mouth to reveal her crooked grin and decrepit teeth. I realized then Lucy had spoken to me without her mouth. I took a step backwards. This was so very wrong. Her lips hadn't moved…at all. The sound had come from somewhere else.

I swallowed hard, stepped closer to her, and reattached the restraints to the bed. "Try to get some rest, Lucy. You might have to go back to the doctor."

She laughed a sound out of a horror film, all deep and wrong.

It wasn't until we were all downstairs and in the kitchen once more that I realized one of our party was missing. "Where's Will?"

Tor sighed. "He left early this morning to get some new prescriptions filled for Lucy. She's out of one of her morning medications."

Will had left early. He could have been the one to pull the note thing on me, but what would he accomplish by doing it? True, he could be insane enough to think it could help make me believe Lucy was possessed, not that I needed much convincing at this point. But it still didn't make any sense, which meant I still had no explanation for what had happened. "I think Lucy needs to be checked out again," I said. "Grand mal seizures aren't something to play around with."

Tor tucked her face in her hands. "When's it ever going to stop, Jimmy? When's my little girl going to be okay?"

I shook my head. "I don't know, Tor. I don't."

Chapter Nineteen

Medicine

GETTING LUCY INTO the car was no easy feat. Tor had called the doctor, and he wanted to see Lucy right away. All of Lucy's IV's and her feeding tube had to be unhooked. Then, Tor changed her nightgown and even before we took her out, Tabby had to be ready near the front door with the back door of her car open.

Will had come back just in time for Tor to explain what we were doing. He decided to go ahead and head out two hours to Costco for a video camera. I didn't mind helping Tor, I truly didn't, but there was part of me that wondered if Will should have been the one going to the doctor while Tabby and I tried to find a video camera. I envied him.

"Why the back seat?" I asked Tor as she carried Lucy downstairs.

"Because," she said, "if Lucy's upfront, she'll grab the wheel."

I nodded. "What about a car seat?"

Tor swallowed hard. "We stopped trying to get her in one. I'll deal with it if we get pulled over."

Lucy kept strangely silent. I don't know if she wanted to go for a car ride or if she wanted to see the doctor, but she said nothing.

During the drive, everything seemed calm…until we passed a church.

"Malenki Bog," Lucy said.

I spun around in the front seat to stare at her. Tor glanced at me, her eyes wide. The air inside the car grew cold. Goosebumps broke out along my skin.

"What did you say, Lucy?" I asked.

Tor stared at her daughter.

"Yevo Nyet."

"What honey?" Tor asked.

It was my luck. It figured, Lucy started speaking in different languages when I had no way to document her. I wished I knew what she was saying. It sounded like Russian.

Tabby kept glancing in the rear view mirror as she drove. Her mouth gaped open like a fish.

Then Lucy laughed, her head laying against her mother's chest. There was a pause as her head hung lower, her lips pulled into a frown. "Mnye ploho."

Frost started to form on the inside of the car windows.

Tabby pulled into the parking lot at the doctor's office, located in a small shopping center. The building was red brick with white wooden accents. The sign had federal style swirls on the top and bottom and read, "Wilbur Sine, MD."

"Wait here," Tor said. "It'll be easier. If I need anything, I'll call."

In this light, Lucy was nothing scary, just a little girl far too sick for her age. Her skin was pale, yet slightly yellow. Deep scratches surrounded her cheeks and forehead, most of which had healed. Her face appeared practically branded with lines of scars.

"Well, what do you think of that?" Tabby asked as Tor and Lucy disappeared into the doctor's office.

I sighed and rubbed my hands together. "I'm pissed cause we had nothing to record her with. And I wish we could prove somehow what happened here." I pointed at the moisture in the inside of the windshield. "But I don't know if the language stuff would have been proof anyway."

"How come?"

I tapped my fingers on the dashboard. "Will's mother is Russian. I remember that from way back when. She could have taught Lucy some words."

Tabby stared at me. "I don't know, Jimmy. Her accent was too good. It was like a native speaker. I mean, my roommate took Russian in college. She used to practice in our doom room. I know what Russian is supposed to sound like, and she had it down cold. Didn't you say on the video you watched that Lucy sounded like a normal six-year-old?"

"Yeah."

"So," Tabby said. "How in the hell is a kid whose main language is

English, and whose parents only speak English, able to deal with consonant clusters?"

I sighed. "It doesn't matter anyway. We didn't get it recorded."

"I really can't believe this. Finally, something happens that could be used, and you don't have your shit together to do much of anything."

"What do you mean?" I asked.

"You have a cell phone. I assume it takes video."

I chuckled at her. "Yeah, and cell phone videos are such reliable evidence."

She blinked. "They can be."

"Would you believe a cell phone video of a supposed possession?"

I didn't get an answer. She leaned back in her seat and stared out the window.

There was nothing I could do. I knew the church wouldn't see it as proof. Lucy had to do something like speak biblical Greek for them to take the case seriously. Russian, would have been great, that is if Lucy didn't have a Russian grandmother.

It was disappointing. It wasn't that I thought I knew better, but it seemed like every time I got an idea, something was laughing at me, seriously wanting me to fail. If I knew what Lucy had said, it might have given me some clue as to where to turn, but I had no idea what she'd said. I really wished I spoke Russian.

#

About an hour later, Tor came out carrying Lucy. Lucy appeared to be sedated by the way she hung limply in Tor's arms.

"What did the doctor say?" Tabby asked.

Tor sighed. "That he would send in the paperwork for her to have another CAT scan. And if happens again, I'm supposed to take her to the emergency room. Thank God for good health insurance."

Tabby's hands tightened on the wheel and she never met my gaze as she drove. Still pissed. I guessed because I pointed out again something that she didn't want to face—that according to the church and many other people, we were unreliable sources. It wasn't my fault the church was so thorough. If the world was perfect, we wouldn't even be here.

When we got back, I helped Tor get Lucy into the house while

Tabby parked her car around back. Hopefully, she'd calm soon. I was going to need her help.

"Hey, Tor?" I asked, sitting at the kitchen table.

"Yes, Jimmy?"

"Did Lucy's grandmother teach her any Russian?"

Tor turned around. "Honestly, Will's mother hasn't spoken Russian in so long, she's probably rusty. I'm almost positive she's taught Lucy nothing."

I nodded. "Just making sure."

She leaned her back against the counter. "What do you think, Jimmy, really?"

I'd been waiting for this question. I wasn't sure if I had the answer she wanted. "The truth is, I do think there's a spirit haunting Lucy. Whether it's a full possession, I don't know. But then, I wasn't supposed to know. When I was a priest, I was a regular parish priest, nothing special."

Her eyes teared up, but she said nothing.

Tabby came in through the back door, closing it quietly behind her, and ignoring me completely.

#

Finally, a little after five, Will showed up. He clumped into the house through the back door with bags and boxes, completely out of breath.

"What took so long?" Tor asked.

I jumped up from the table and helped Will with some of the packages. After we got everything into some sort of cohesive arrangement on the floor, Will threw himself into a kitchen chair.

"Costco didn't have the camera system. I ended up going to four different stores in order to get everything we need, and made a side trip to an AV repair place for instructions on how to set up the whole mess."

"Is it going to be hard?" I asked.

Will shrugged. "It's not supposed to be, but you know how those things always work out."

"Well, there are four of us. Maybe it really won't be so bad."

"I hope not."

Tor sighed. "Do I even want to know how much all this cost?"

"Probably not," Will said, an odd look in his eye.

Tor got up, served him a bowl of cabbage soup, and sat back at the table. She said nothing more.

Apparently, their distress was coming from more than one direction. I didn't want to pry, but it was hard hearing all of this. I was too close. Now I knew about their marital problems, and a hint of financial problems. I hoped the longer I stayed, they would realize they were letting me know things I shouldn't know, but somehow that seemed unlikely. Sometimes, I wondered if they forgot Tabby and I were even there.

Will ate in silence, but Tor and Will's body language spoke for them. Although they sat next to each other, they made sure not to touch. It was strange to watch, and I didn't want to, but something unwritten compelled me to anyway.

"Jimmy?" Will asked when Tor started doing the dishes.

"Yeah?"

"Want to help me get this set up?"

I got up from the table. Tabby followed. I figured she finally got tired of trying to stay mad at me. We dragged the boxes and bags upstairs. Lucy was eerily quiet. Not even a peep of the noises could be heard.

Once we got to her door, Will knocked and opened it. "Lucy, honey? We are going to hook up this stuff, and then we'll let you rest."

We all stepped into the room. Lucy watched us, her eyes following us around the room. Her face was still yellow and the scarring made her look like she was wrinkled in odd places. Being restrained allowed the scratches to heal, but the scars were still dark against her skin.

"Why not say what you mean, father?" Lucy gaped at him. "You are putting cameras in here to watch me, to see what I'll do."

Will paused. I could tell he was torn between knowing his daughter was only six-years-old and this thing making her speak years older than she was.

"Yes, Lucy," he said. "We need to watch you."

"Why, want some kiddy fuckers to see me, daddy?"

Will's shoulders slumped. "Why don't you rest now?"

Lucy laughed, quietly and an octave lower.

It was bad. Really bad. If I had any doubts, I just heard more than enough to know she truly was possessed. Six-year-olds didn't talk like that.

It took over two hours to get the system running. When it was time to place the camera in the bracket and attach the cables, I volunteered to climb the ladder. Will was exhausted from the traveling he'd done all day, and Tabby, well, I didn't want her to deal with it.

"Tabby," I said. "Hold the camera, and I'll let you know when I'm ready for it."

She nodded. "It's under control, Jimmy."

"Okay, turn it on. Let's see if it works," I said.

As the wiring all went into place, something pushed me. I clutched the ladder—hard. Tabby screamed. The ladder tipped and swayed back and forth across the floor. I was caught on an insane teeter totter whose focus was to throw me off.

"Lucy, stop!" Will stood frozen in the middle of the floor, his body straining against invisible forces that held him motionless.

The ladder stopped moving.

"But, Daddy," it said, no longer Lucy. "I was having fun."

I got off the ladder, one wrung at a time. Lucy grinned at me. It was one of the scariest smiles I'd ever seen. Her bloody red eyes narrowed, and her lips pulled up too far on either side of her mouth, almost like a dog's mouth without a snout. At first the pupils of her eyes appeared to turn elliptical, like a snake's, but when I blinked, her eyes rounded, human again. Bloody, but human. Her mouth, however, did not change.

"Father Holiday and I are good friends, aren't we?" she asked.

"If that's what you want to call it," I countered.

Then she laughed again. We left the room.

"Did you get all that?" Tabby asked.

Will grinned. "It might have scared the shit out of Jimmy, but yeah, I think I did."

He took a look at the DVR and made sure the green light indicating it was recording was still on. "Let's go see."

Chapter Twenty

Getting Stronger

TABBY AND I headed for the living room while Will went to the kitchen to check on Tor. My stomach roiled, still unsettled by Lucy's attack. Tabby, however, seemed unaffected. Then again, she didn't tend to show things outwardly. And since the threat was now gone, she had no reason to freak out. Knocking me off a ladder wouldn't have killed me, not from that height, so I was left wondering if the demon wanted to scare me.

Will entered alone.

"Where's Tor?" Tabby asked.

He coughed. "Tor says she's scared enough. She doesn't want to see it."

I nodded.

Will attached his laptop to the TV. While the video loaded, I peered over at Tabby. She seemed thoughtful.

The footage picked up as the ladder was teetering back and forth. I suppose that for the beginning of the attack, the machine must have been booting up.

I glanced over at Will. He stood in the doorway. "I think this is going to work."

Will smiled, but it was a sad smile. "It better for what I paid for it. What now?"

"Now that we have the video, starting tomorrow, Tabby and I are going to spend more time with Lucy. If I can get the proof we need, I'll contact the church."

"That's it?" Will asked.

"That's all we can do."

#

I got an odd feeling in the middle of my sleep. I wasn't sure what was going on, but something felt awry, and not quite of this world. My eyes snapped open. I stared at the clock. Once again, I awoke at three. I glanced over at Tabby. She was still asleep, but her body tossed restlessly. Standing behind Tabby's sofa was an immense black hooded figure—at least seven feet tall. I couldn't see its face, but red eyes peered out from underneath the hood. Skeletal hands, no flesh on them at all, reached out.

My body froze, not only from fear, but the freezing air in the room. I didn't know if it had come through the ley line or if it had broken Tabby's wards on the room upstairs. Hell, maybe it was the physical manifestation of the thing possessing Lucy. I did know one thing for certain—I didn't want this thing hurting Tabby.

"The lord is my shepherd," I began.

The thing snarled. I couldn't see its face because of the hood, but something told me I didn't want to. It swung its hand at me. It didn't connect, but an invisible force did. A giant burst of energy seized hold of me and threw me into a chair across the room. The chair collapsed underneath me.

"Holy shit!"

My whole body hummed with pain, but I didn't have time for it. Hell, I didn't have time to breathe. I hobbled off the broken chair, knelt on my knees, and closed my eyes. I prayed to God to keep Tabby safe, prayed to send this thing back to where it came from.

A breath later, I opened my eyes. It hadn't moved. Anger outweighed fear, coursing in my blood, and pumping adrenaline through my veins. I turned my head up toward it. "Listen, you overgrown bag of bones. I didn't invite you here, and I sure as hell know Will and Victoria didn't invite you either, so get the fuck out of this house! Your invitation is revoked!"

I panted. One breath. Two. The thing disappeared with a loud bang. The room trembled. I hobbled over to Tabby and shook her awake.

She punched me in the eye.

"Damn it." That's what I needed, a black eye to match my other bruises. "What the hell was that for?"

"You lived with me for four years, Jimmy Holiday. You know better than to touch me to wake me." She sat up and rubbed her hand.

This was turning out to be a helluva night. Not only was I beaten up by a hooded demonic force, but I'd been punched in the eye by my ex-girlfriend. What was next, a house falling on me? Adrenaline raced through me. I knew I'd come down from it, but not now, not yet. I had to hold on to whatever strength remained in me.

"In case you're interested, a shadow person thing tried to eat your soul," I said, huffing.

"What?"

"You heard me." I took a moment to get my breath back. This had moved from bizarre to seriously screwed up. I mean shit, a skeletal demon figure? What the hell? Something inside me knew the answer. "A soul sucker."

Glancing around the room, her gaze zeroed on the broken chair. "It did that?"

I nodded.

"Jesus Christ."

"Nope," I shook my head, trying to lighten the mood. "Not Jesus. Jimmy Fucking Holiday."

She stared at me like I'd grown about fourteen heads.

"You got anything to say?" I asked.

She raised her eyebrows, a smirk breaking across her lips. "You know you've given yourself at least ten years in Purgatory."

"Who told you about Purgatory?" I asked.

She lay back on the sofa and closed her eyes. After a moment, she opened one eye. "Purgatorians."

I got on my own couch and hunkered down. "Go to sleep."

She threw a pillow at me. "You go to sleep. I'm trying to rest."

"I'll shut up now."

"You do that."

#

Last night sucked. No bones about it. Everything that was happening had one thing in common—Lucy. Our moods were affected, the weird happenings like the note and the hooded beast thing, all of it was connected. And how did I know the hooded thing was a soul sucker? I'd never seen one. Hell, I only heard about them from that dream. It was like I'd been caught between two worlds.

My bruises ached. At least nothing was broken, but I still felt like shit. I sat at the table, waiting for the others to make their appearance. I sure as hell wasn't going to go see Lucy alone, but I wasn't sure if I wanted Tabby to go or not. Not after what happened last night. I rubbed my jaw where Tabby had punched me. It hurt.

Tabby wandered in and plunked down next to me. "Done sulking yet?"

"No, I'll have you know, I'm not done sulking yet." I crossed my arms.

She rolled her eyes at me. "My God, you are such a big baby. Wanna grow up a little so we can get things done here?"

I picked up my shirt, revealing the bruises that had appeared overnight.

She stared at my body. "Damn."

"Yeah, and your soul swallower threw me when I prayed at him."

"What made it stop?" she asked.

I smiled. "I cussed at it."

Her features twisted, as if she couldn't decide if she was amused or confused. "What?"

I nodded. "Yup, I cussed at it."

"That doesn't make any sense. You don't make any sense, Jimmy. No sense at all."

"I know," I said. "But if I made sense, I wouldn't be as interesting."

"True, very true." She wiped her hands on her jeans. "So, what are we doing?"

"We get the proof we need for Lucy's exorcism like before," I said. "That's my priority." I thought about it for a moment. "Maybe you and I will start sleeping in shifts."

She grabbed my hand and turned it palm up, looking at the various bruises that dotted me. "God, I'm sorry, Jimmy. I didn't realize it was this bad. I kind of hoped you were kidding, or it was a dream. Are you okay?"

I nodded. "Yeah, just bruised. The biggest problem is that we don't know enough about this thing messing with Lucy. I don't know if it's leaving Lucy at times to cause havoc or if it is bringing other things in."

"If it's bringing other things in, how do we stop it?" Tabby asked. "I mean, I warded that room upstairs."

Everything else was nuts about this place, maybe someone or something had damaged Tabby's spellwork. "Maybe we should check upstairs to make sure."

Something had happened. The black figure should not have gotten in. I doubted if a shadow person was what was attacking Lucy, but there was so much about paranormal junk I didn't know.

As soon as Tabby and I opened the door to the attic, we could smell something foul. Gone was the lackadaisical tour; we headed straight for the attic room. The symbols Tabby had made with the chalk were burnt black and looked as if a great claw had scratched through each one. The door to the attic room lay wide open.

Tabby snorted. "Guess we know how it's getting in."

"So what do we do?" I asked.

She shrugged. "I guess we'll leave this room alone. I don't have anything else."

"Nothing?"

She shook her head. "Nope."

I blinked. "You're serious."

"Completely. If I knew of anything else to do, I would come out with it. It's not like I can make things the way we want them."

"All right, let's figure out then how the hell to help Lucy." I wiped the back of my neck with my hand. "Jesus Christ."

Never in a million years did I ever think I would be dealing with something like this. I wanted to say that it felt like it was too hard, that I wanted to give up, but that wasn't true. Maybe Lucy would speak to me if I made her mad. I needed her speaking something other than Russian. The church could find a reason to reject the Russian. If I could get Lucy speaking Latin or Greek, now that would be real proof.

"Before we start, I want you to hide this from me." I turned to Tabby, taking a breath, and handing her my phone.

"Why?" She took the phone from me, staring at it.

"I have an idea. Just do it, please." I counted my breaths as she left, calming my heart and steadying my nerves. When she returned a few minutes later, I asked, "You didn't eat anything, did you?"

"No, what's up?"

I exhaled, slowly. "Because, before something like this, it's best to fast—like you do with your witchy stuff."

"Why?"

"Demons do gross things. I don't want to go into detail, but they do things that will make it hard not to vomit if they so choose. I think also there's something about fasting that helps you keep your head clear."

She raised an eyebrow.

"I know. It sounds like a bunch of bullshit. I know your stuff has reasons for fasting. I imagine they're somewhat similar. I'm trying to get used to it all. If it helps, I never thought I would have to fend off a soul sucker."

She paused, thinking. "What about our strength if this takes a long time?"

"If what takes a long time? All we're doing is talking to Lucy today," I said.

We made our way to Lucy's room. When we got to the hallway, I stopped. "If we do end up doing an exorcism, I can guarantee it will take a long time. But you can take breaks. Usually, an exorcism session only lasts a couple of hours."

"How do you know that?" she asked.

"The internet."

"Boy, are we in trouble." Tabby stepped back and let me knock on Lucy's door.

I took a deep breath.

"Lucy?" I said as I opened the door and entered the room. It was still full of that foul odor. At the doorway, the room felt normal, but closer to Lucy's bed, it was so cold I could see my breath. "Good morning, Lucy."

Lucy glanced at Tabby and cocked her head to the side. "Who's the cunt?"

I nodded toward Tabby. "Just a friend. We'd like to ask you some questions."

Lucy let forth a strange gurgling growl.

"What is your name?" I asked Lucy.

She rolled her bloody eyes. "It is whatever you think it is."

I could tread no further with that type of question. To do so would be doing an exorcism on our own, and I wasn't going there.

"How are you feeling today?" Tabby asked.

"Ahh," Lucy said. "What a kind bitch. I'm doing well, dearie. Did you like your present?"

"What present?" Tabby asked.

Lucy grinned, revealing her broken teeth.

"Your visitor." Lucy let forth that broken laugh.

"Now Lucy, I have a question," I said.

"And what is that, Priest?"

"I've misplaced my cell phone, do you know where it is?" I asked.

"And why should I help you?" she snarled.

"It's up to you," I said. "I thought I would ask in case you knew."

Lucy smiled again then focused her eyes on Tabby. "Why don't you ask her, she's the one you told to hide it from you."

And there it was, at last, proof. "Please, Lucy. Think of it like a game."

Lucy's eyes rolled back in her head and she farted so long I thought she would hurt something. The smell that issued forth fouled the air so much my eyes watered and the back of my throat burned.

"A game, eh? Well, maybe you should check the kitchen. Victoria's pantry under the dried pasta."

We left her then and there. I closed the door behind me. Tabby handed me her phone and I turned on the video feature so we could have documentation of our finding the lost object. My hands shook. I took a deep breath and steadied myself. A shaky cam video wasn't going to do anyone any good.

As we got to the stairs, Tabby stopped. "Why does Tor like the kitchen so much?"

I shrugged. It didn't take a rocket scientist to see Tor used food like other people would use drugs—to cope.

Tabby sighed. "No really? Black died in the kitchen. Will told her that when he told you the story, right?"

She did have a point. There was no weird feeling in the kitchen minus the heaviness that always pervaded the home at Lucy's presence. "Probably before that. She didn't seem shocked when Will told me the story."

"Then why doesn't the kitchen scare the shit out of her?" Tabby asked.

"Maybe because it doesn't feel spooky. I don't know."

"She seems to react easily to everything else, it seems strange." Tabby leaned back.

I really didn't know what to say. Tor's penchant for the dramatic had irritated me more than once. Knowing she was hanging out in a room where someone died should have had some sort of effect.

When we reached the kitchen, Tor and Will looked at us oddly. I suppose we did look weird: me leading, holding the phone in front of me, and Tabby bringing up the rear.

I opened the door to the pantry and turned on the light. Like everything else to do with the kitchen, it was arranged immaculately, except for the bags of pasta. I held the phone forward and moved the bags aside. There was my phone all right, but dented and with a busted screen.

I picked it up and pressed the power button. Nothing happened.

"I didn't do that, Jimmy," Tabby said.

"I know."

I stopped the recording on Tabby's phone and handed it to her. Then, I set my ruined phone on the table.

"Lucy did this." I pointed to the cracked screen.

Will glanced up at me as if he were looking over the top of a pair of glasses, even though he wasn't wearing any. Then, he shook himself. "Wait what?"

I nodded. "Somehow, she did it. One of the things I need to prove for someone being possessed is that they know the location of lost objects so I had Tabby hide my phone from me. How, I don't know, but Lucy knew Tabby hid it, and somehow she broke it."

"Well, Jimmy," Tor swallowed hard, "we'll get you another phone."

"It's insured. It's just strange. It didn't have to break it." The corner of my mouth crept into a smirk. "I guess there is no doubt, this thing really doesn't like me."

Tabby chuckled. "Of course not, Jimmy. You were a priest. There isn't anything in that book of yours that says you have to be an active priest to perform an exorcism, is there?"

"No, but the exorcist is supposed to be approved by the bishop, so I hardly think a bishop would grant permission for a defrocked priest to perform an exorcism."

"Well then," Tabby said, waving her arms with a flourish. "No matter what, you are a threat, Jimmy Holiday. You could possibly cast it out."

Both Will and Tor became excited then. They sat higher in their seats, their legs shaking and their eyes sparkling with energy.

"Then there's no reason to wait for the church," Tor said.

I held up my hands. "Oh, hell no. We are not doing that. You forget, I know about as much about this as you do. We are getting the church involved."

"Why?" Tabby stared at me, eyes flashing.

I held up my hand. "No, Tabby. Don't get riled. I mean, what do you know about exorcism?"

"Not much."

"That means you know as much as I do, or almost. You've seen the movies. All I have on you is this one little book."

She snorted. "Well, if the word of God is only a book, the Salem witches should never have had a thing to worry about then."

"Let's not talk about it anymore. I'm hungry. I'm tired, and I want to go get a new phone."

Tor jumped up from her chair and pulled a package of Danish out of the pantry.

"Did you get what you needed from Lucy this morning?" Will asked.

I nodded. "One part of it. There are still three more things on the list, but it's a step forward."

Will nodded. "Yeah, it is."

#

After we finished eating, Will followed me into the library to get rid of the broken chair. The pieces had ended up near the fireplace. The legs snapped from the base in pointed, splintered ends. I rubbed my ribs.

"What other things do you need to prove?" he asked, eyeing the chair.

"I'd rather not say," I said. "Honestly, that way if I'm asked if Lucy could have been influenced, then I can say without a doubt that there is no way she could have been coached."

"But, don't you trust me?" His eyes looked wounded—round and a little too wide.

I ran my hands through my hair. "Will, it's not about trust. It isn't. Everything with the church is about perception. What they will look at is not only if Lucy's possessed, but if it gets out, how it will look in terms of the perception of the church."

"I thought the church was about helping people," Will said.

I chuckled. "Oh they are, but they are about politics too. I should know."

Will said nothing more. He and I took the broken pieces of the chair into the basement and stacked them next to that week's garbage.

I stood up straight and stretched my back. Then, I noticed something unusual. For the most part, "haunted houses" are creepiest in the basement. Here, the basement was quiet and warm. It didn't feel threatening at all. The one weird thing was on the far wall. A couple of metal rings attached to the concrete with brackets. In the back of my mind, I remembered the crack of a whip. Black and his wife. It happened here. But still, the basement felt safe somehow. I couldn't explain it.

I kept my thoughts to myself. I already had Will jumping from one conclusion to the next. It was hard to tell how he would feel if he knew what I was thinking.

We left the basement and headed to the kitchen.

"Jimmy," Tor said. "I *am* going to get you a new phone. My daughter broke it, it's only right."

"Tor, honestly, it's okay. I already told you, I have insurance."

Will came up from behind me and patted Tor on the shoulder. He turned toward me. "You might as well give it up, Jimmy. When Tor sets her mind to something, that's it."

Tor grinned. She ambled over to the sink, put her hands in the soapy water and began to wash dishes. "Will is going to take you wherever you need to go to get a new phone."

"Are the two of you going to be okay while we're gone?" I asked.

Tabby laughed. "We'll be fine. Tor and I already decided we won't leave each other alone the rest of the day. There's too much that's strange here. Plus, this is bath day for Lucy, and I'm sure Tor could use some help."

I nodded. "Be careful."

#

Will ushered me into the 4Runner soon after. Some things didn't add up about Will and Tor. The car was a prime example. Why did they have a mansion, but an old car? It made no sense at all.

Will pulled the car out of the driveway as we headed for the main road. "We got about an hour drive."

"Is everything an hour from here?" I asked.

Will laughed. "No, there's a Wal-Mart about a half an hour away. Not much else, but at least there's a Wal-Mart."

"Do you think you would have liked living in Sorrow's Point if this hadn't happened to Lucy?"

Will inclined his head in thought as he drove. "I think so. It was out of the way, away from danger, or so we believed. It seemed like a decent town to raise a kid in, ya know? We haven't been able to do most of what we planned."

"What do you mean?" I asked. There it was again. The denial. He'd either forgotten or pushed out of his mind what small town living had been like for us.

"In D.C., we took the metro most places. We used the car rarely. Here, we need a car all the time." He scratched his hand. "We were going to get a new car after we moved, but I haven't bothered. Lucy takes up so much time."

All his hopes had dried with Lucy's illness. He was broken—a shell of the man he once was.

"When Lucy gets better, are you going to sell the house?"

Will sighed. "No way we can. This house had been on the market for over ten years."

"Isn't there something about nondisclosure of a murder? You might be able to get out of it… probably," I said.

"If we'd known, it likely wouldn't have mattered. Tor still would have wanted the house. Hell, the Black family paid for a caretaker to keep up the grounds and make any repairs as needed. No way we could afford that. If we sell the house, it would probably take forever. So we'll be staying there."

Not what I wanted to hear. "Will, if that thing got Lucy to let it out once, what's to say it won't happen again?"

Will grasped the steering wheel so tight his knuckles turned white. "I don't know what to do, Jimmy. If Tor and I give up the house, we'll have to go live with Tor's mother. Mom and Dad died one right after the other not long after we moved into this house. Asking Mom about Lucy was one of the last conversations I had with her. There literally isn't anywhere else for us to go."

"You could stay with me." It flew out of my mouth before I could stop it. I couldn't imagine what that would be like. A nightmare most likely.

"That's really nice, Jimmy, but I couldn't do that to you." Will moaned. "Besides, I can't see Tor surviving in that kitchen of yours."

I laughed. "Yeah, somehow I don't think she'd find my retro fridge groovy."

Will smiled sadly. "You know something?"

"What?"

"Lucy would love it."

Chapter Twenty-One

Development

"TABBY, WANT TO help me give Lucy a bath?" Tor asked.

I looked up from the eBook I was reading on my phone. "Sure. I can do that."

Jimmy and Will had been gone for a while. And I had no qualms about making myself useful. Better that than sitting around.

I followed Tor up to Lucy's room. The stench wasn't as strong as the last time I'd been up there, but it still smelled pretty bad. Almost like the pee smell in nursing homes. My nose wrinkled.

"Lucy, time for your bath," Tor said, opening the door.

I followed behind. Lucy sat in her bed quietly. Tor walked out of the room and through another door.

Lucy smirked at me. The child-like part of me wanted to stick my tongue out at her, but I didn't. This was a possessed kid. Who knew what she would do?

When Tor came back in, Lucy let her undo the bindings. Tor picked her up and carried her into the adjoining bathroom.

"Could you get some towels?" Tor asked me.

I followed them both and grabbed some from the shelf in the bathroom. Then I set them on top of the toilet while Tor set Lucy into the bathtub.

"Water okay?" Tor asked Lucy.

She nodded.

I let my eyes wander while Tor bathed Lucy. Leaning against the wall, I poised, ready in case Tor needed anything. But so far, she had everything under control.

My eyes closed, just for a moment, and Tor screamed.

My lids jerked open and my gaze flew in the direction of the bath. A woman's razor arched through the air and landed on Tor's arm for what had to be the second go. It slid down, cutting her skin to ribbons.

Lucy laughed in a choppy growl like it was the funniest thing she had ever seen.

"Oh. My. God."

Lucy's gazed landed on me as sharp as the blade. The razor rose up from Tor's arm and started for me. My knees wanted to go weak, but I focused and grounded my energy.

"Hail, Guardians of the Watchtower! Protect us from evil. Protect us from this servant of darkness!" I put my essence into the words, but Lucy only laughed. The razor dropped to the floor.

I clutched a towel from the stack, wrapped it tightly around Tor's arm, and dragged her out of the room.

"We need to get you some help," I said.

"I'll be okay. We can't leave Lucy."

My thoughts spun, but I couldn't argue with her. The child—possessed or not— couldn't be left alone. "Shit."

#

Finally, back in Sorrow's Point, my phone had been replaced with something far fancier. I didn't bother trying to stop Will. He seemed to want to do something to make it all up to me. I still felt guilty though. If they were having financial problems, I didn't want to add to it, and a fancy phone was an expenditure that didn't make sense.

We left the car in the front drive, walked up the huge stone steps and entered through the door. Will paused for a moment in front of me. I heard nothing. He stepped forward and I followed as he headed toward the kitchen. It was a hell of a sight. Bloody rags covered the table. Tabby held a towel to Tor's arm.

"What the hell happened?" I asked.

"Tor was giving Lucy a bath in the tub. She seemed so complacent. Tor thought it would be okay. It was…until Lucy used the razor," Tabby said.

"Shit," Will said. "Are you okay, Tor?"

She nodded. "I think I need stitches."

"I'll take her to the hospital," Tabby said, "you two check on Lucy."

I searched the room. "And where's Lucy?"

Tabby stared at me, her eyes wide. "She's still in the bathtub."

Will and I ran out of the kitchen toward the staircase and dashed upstairs. He darted into Lucy's bedroom with me following close at his heels. Bits of blood coated the bathroom; some spattered on the wall, while the rest sprayed the bathtub and Lucy. Where the blood dots hadn't landed, the blood smeared as if Lucy had been rubbing it on her body. She sat in the tub, playing with toys as if nothing was going on.

Will snatched Lucy out of the tub while I held the door open. After Will got Lucy dressed and into bed, we strapped her in. I ran back into the bathroom and rummaged through cupboards until I found a clean wash cloth. I wetted it in the sink and walked back into Lucy's room. I handed it to Will. He managed to get most of the blood off Lucy.

We left her alone and went back into the bathroom and cleaned up the blood.

"Where did Lucy get the razor?" I asked after Will had closed the door to Lucy's room and we headed downstairs.

He stopped in the middle of the staircase. "I don't know. There shouldn't have been a razor in her room. Tor shaves in our bathroom."

I wobbled a little where I was perched above Will on the stairs. "That's strange."

Will nodded. "She has to be getting out of the restraints somehow. So far, she hasn't left her bed on camera."

"Does Lucy know where Tor keeps her razors?" I asked.

"Probably," Will said. "Lucy used to beg to take a bath with her mommy."

I nodded. "She could be telekinetic."

Will stopped at the bottom of the stairs. "What?"

"You know, telekinesis. It's the ability to move objects with your mind. If she isn't getting out of bed, she's bringing things to her, or using something else or someone else to get what she wants."

"How?"

I sighed. "Tabby said your house is built near a ley line—a direct power source that magical entities can use as a doorway to other worlds. This house, especially that room upstairs, is kind of a conduit for that line. I think Lucy is using the house to bring things in to help her."

"Could this line be where this thing came from to begin with?"

I shrugged. "It's possible. I think old man Black messed with a lot of things he shouldn't have. I believe he got himself possessed, and ate his family. Then, this thing kept causing problems, so the town stepped in and brought in the experts to bind it to that mirror. Apparently, it wasn't bound enough because it could still speak to Lucy, and got her to let it out."

"How do you know that?" Will asked.

"I don't. It's my current hypothesis. We should know for sure after the exorcism."

#

Three hours later, Tabby and Tor shuffled into the house. An ace bandage covered Tor's arm with a support board strapped to it.

"What'd they say?" I asked.

Tor sat in the chair opposite from me. "They gave me a tetanus shot, and I have to go back in two weeks to get the stitches out. Thank God it was a disposable razor. It didn't cut too deep, but bled a lot. And it hurts like hell." She smiled sadly. "Guess I won't be cooking for a while."

I patted Tor on the shoulder. "It's okay. We'll survive. Tabby can cook, and so can I. Get some rest. Will and I'll head to the grocery store."

Will dropped me off at the market while he went to the pharmacy to get Tor's prescription filled. As I wandered the aisles, my thoughts drifted back to Tor and the attack.

Was the demon putting a spell over Will and Tor? The constant attacks had to be doing more to them than what they were showing me. One minute, Tor was all upset and squealing at the thought of something Lucy had done. The next, after she'd been directly attacked, she seemed almost passive. Will alternated between being irritated at Tor and pushing toward exorcism to sitting around and doing nothing. None of it made sense except the demon. It had to be affecting their psyche.

I hopped into the car as soon as Will pulled up in front of the market. It was weird. His face was a blank mask. He was so nonchalant about it all, not concerned about Tor; of course, maybe I was looking too far into it. Maybe that's how it is when you fall out of love with someone. I didn't know a thing about that.

"Are you afraid to die?" Will asked me as we left the parking lot.

I peered at him out of the corner of my eye. "Not really, no."

"Why not?" Will asked. "What if this is all there is? What if the only thing left is nothing?"

I laughed a little. He must be in denial. There was no other excuse for it. "Will, your daughter is possessed, right?"

"Yes."

"Then you're contradicting yourself. How can you believe there is nothing out there after we die if you're afraid of demons?" I paused for a moment to let it all sink in. "There's a line from an old movie that puts it as plain as I could ever say it, 'If you are afraid of dying, you will see devils trying to take your life away, but if you have made your peace, the devils are really angels, taking you to heaven.'"

"What movie is that from?" he asked.

"*Jacob's Ladder.*"

"Isn't that a scary movie? I mean, you were all priestly when that came out. Was that allowed?" Will asked.

I rolled my eyes. "There's nothing out there that says a priest can't watch a scary movie. Is it looked down on if you watch *Harry Potter*? Yes, but you aren't punished for it. *The Exorcist* is a little different though. It's banned by the church."

"Aren't the *Harry Potter* books banned too?" he asked.

I chuckled. "No. The pope at the time declared them evil, but they aren't banned."

"Tell me, how does that make sense?"

I snickered. "It doesn't."

Why he chose to bring all that up, I had no idea, but then, I reminded myself that I knew little of his religious upbringing.

"How long do you think Lucy's exorcism will take?" he asked.

I turned toward him. He seemed shakier than usual. "I don't know. It depends on how powerful the demon is."

Will wiped his mouth with his hand. He was so nervous he was sweating. "Can… can the sins of a parent cause a child to be possessed?"

So that was it? He'd done something and was afraid what he'd done had caused Lucy's possession? His whole demeanor was caused by simple guilt. It would be a good idea to keep all that in mind.

"It depends on the sin, Will," I said. "If you'd say, hurt someone or beat them up, then no, you couldn't have caused Lucy's possession."

Will swallowed.

I reached over and decreased the heat in the car.

"What is an example of a parent's sin that could cause the possession of a child?" he asked.

I took a deep breath. "About the only thing would be if you participated in a black mass and promised her soul to the devil."

"Jesus Christ, do people do that?"

I nodded. "Very evil people, yes."

Will sighed. His knuckles gripped tighter on the dashboard. "What about adultery?"

There it was, the admission I'd been waiting for. It accounted for Will's attitude, it accounted for the tension between Will and Tor. What it didn't account for was anything to do with Lucy. At least, it had nothing to do with Lucy being possessed.

I rubbed my chin with my fingers. "No, adultery doesn't cause a child to be possessed. Adultery will cause you to spend some years in purgatory to atone for your sins, but it doesn't cause demonic possession."

I thought about it. If Lucy were older, it could be conceivably possible Lucy could try to make believe something was wrong to get back at her parents for their problems, but possession was something that didn't make a lot of sense in that scenario. Especially with all the supernatural shit going on with Lucy.

When it came down to it, what I felt didn't matter all that much.

"So, anything I did, didn't cause Lucy to be like this?" Will asked.

"Not to my knowledge. The way I see it is you stumbled on a house Tor felt drawn to, possibly because it's so damn huge. Unfortunately, this house had a hidden past your real estate agent should have told you about before you bought it. Then, something drew Lucy to the mirror. Even Tor admitted that." I glanced at Will. He was nodding. "I figure Lucy wanted to know if the glass was black all the way through, or if it was covered up, so she inadvertently released the thing, whatever it is and wherever it originally came from."

Tears began to well up in Will's eyes. "I love my little girl, Jimmy. I don't want her to die."

"I know, Will. I know."

We pulled into the driveway of the house. I felt drained, but I thought it was worth it. Will had gotten something huge off his chest. Honestly, he could use some therapy, and I'm sure Tor needed the same. Lucy needed a lot of things. I wished I could give her the help she needed.

We stopped and unloaded everything from the car. Will paused and stared up at the sky.

"Looks like it might snow," he said.

"Maybe."

#

After dinner, Tabby and I washed dishes and Tor directed us where and how to put things away. I would like to have said it was because we were trusted, but I really think it's because Tor felt so bad. Her face blanched white and the corners of her mouth pursed.

"I think I'm going to go to bed," Tor said.

Tabby turned from the sink. "Are you all right?"

Tor nodded. "Just hurting. I think I want to lie down for a while. Get all that stuff as best you can. I don't care anymore."

We watched her go in silence.

"That's not good," Tabby said.

"No, it's not, and after what I learned this afternoon, I'm not surprised."

"Can you tell me about it?" she asked.

I shook my head. "It was never specified for me not to tell anyone else, but the subject matter alone makes it something I'd rather not talk about."

Tabby nodded. "I think I can figure it out."

"This is a very unhappy family."

"Yeah. Too unhappy."

I found Will in the living room soon after. He was sitting alone, staring off into space. I knocked on the door jamb, Tabby close at my heels. "Mind if we come in?"

Will looked up. "Sure."

Tabby and I sat on the sofa. Will was nursing a beer. I could see the condensation dripping off the can and onto the coaster.

"Tor went to bed," Tabby said.

I rubbed my hand across the pile on the fabric of the sofa. "She said she was hurting, so she was going to go lay down."

"I still can't believe Lucy did that to her," he said.

I believed Lucy did it. She'd almost knocked me off the ladder, brought in a soul sucker to come after Tabby, and I got hurt by the same creature. I had no trouble believing Lucy was capable of anything.

Will's eyes narrowed. He must have figured my thoughts by his expression.

"It's not that I don't believe she actually did it," he said. "It's that I find it hard to believe this is the same Lucy I've known for six years."

"That's the point, Will. Demons like to change the most beautiful things into the most profane. I suppose, in a way, they do these things because they aren't worthy of God's love. If they make us like them, maybe they think God will no longer love us."

Tabby's eyebrows furrowed. "Is it really so simple?"

I shrugged. "Probably not, but it's how I've always understood it. I might be right, but my theories don't mean much at all."

"And if you're wrong?" Will asked.

I took a breath. "Then I'm wrong. I wasn't made perfect, and God doesn't expect us to be perfect. Otherwise, there would be no reason for purgatory."

"You should be a theologist," Tabby said.

I scratched my arm. "It wouldn't be the life for me. I like to help people. If I were a theologian, I would spend most of my time studying the word of God. I did that in seminary. God and I have a certain understanding. I believe in Him. I love Him, and I generally try to be a good person."

"And what does God get?" Tabby asked.

I grinned. I couldn't help it. I didn't know what she was asking for, but I answered her as truthfully as I could. "He gets amused."

#

Oddly enough, I woke refreshed the next morning, even though I'd not had a lot of sleep. Tabby agreed to try to ward the room today, so we wouldn't have to sleep in shifts again. Yet even with the off and on two hour spurts I felt better than I had in a while. Maybe it was having a plan, or maybe it was I was so damn tired. Either way, I knew it would be best to work with Lucy well rested and energetic.

"Sleep okay?" I asked as Tabby returned from her shower.

She put her stuff in her bag. "It was quiet. Almost too quiet, if you know what I mean. I can't help but wonder if this is the calm before something worse happens."

I nodded. "Do you need anything for your ward thingy?"

Tabby chuffed me on the arm. "I haven't even had a chance to look, Mr. Smartypants. You're lucky I know you so well, otherwise I would have no idea what the hell you're talking about." She motioned with her hand toward the library door. "Go get your bath. We'll tackle this after."

"Yes, Ma'am."

When I came into the library after my bath, I saw one hell of a mess. "Um, what's this?" I motioned toward the herbs scattered all over the floor. They were sort of arranged in piles. One appeared to be basil, but there was a pile of brown stuff with stems too, a pile of slightly brownish purple stuff, and a lot of piles of green powder.

Tabby grinned. "I'm in luck. Tor had enough for me to do this."

"Did you ask her if you could use them?" I said with a raised eyebrow.

She looked like she wanted to hurt me—bad. "Yes, you idiot. I didn't come out of a cave you know."

"How long is this going to take?"

"As long as it takes. Right now. I'm organizing and figuring this out."

I nodded.

"Why don't you go in the kitchen with Tor? I know you haven't had breakfast, and you'll give Tor something to do."

"Have you had breakfast?" I asked.

"I wanted to fast before I did this. Now go!" She stood up and pushed me toward the door.

Not wanting to irritate her any further, I went. I didn't like leaving Tabby alone, but she hadn't given me a choice. I wanted to help her, I really did, but I guess my questions and reactions were more irritating than helpful.

I wandered into the kitchen. Tor was sitting at the table looking completely dejected. "You okay?"

She looked up. "Will and I had a fight. He left about two hours ago."

I sat across from her at the table. "Need to talk about it?"

"Will confessed," Tor scratched her good arm, "about his affair. Somehow he expected me to give in, to tell him it was all right. Goddamn it, it isn't all right."

"Can you forgive him?" I asked.

"Right now, I can tell you I don't want to. Do I need to? Probably, but I feel betrayed."

"Well, if you went by the church, they don't believe in divorce, but some things about the church need updating. I'm not saying you should divorce Will, I'm saying you should explore every option."

She stared at me. "What would you do?"

"Honestly?"

She nodded.

Given what I'd seen my parents go through, staying together for the kids alone didn't work. In fact, it turned everybody miserable. Granted, neither Tor nor Will were alcoholics, but it would still be a disaster. Lucy would grow up in a home that appeared normal, but was anything but. I'd been there. I lived it. It sucked.

"I can't say I would definitely do this because what we think we'll do and what we end up doing are usually nothing alike. I think I couldn't stand that betrayal. I would get out as soon as I could."

"Even if you had kids?" she asked.

"Especially then. I lived in a house where my parents didn't love each other. Each year got worse instead of better. If I didn't have the church to escape to, I would probably, at the very least, be a drug addict. Most likely, I'd be dead by now."

"Hmm….I have a lot to think about," she said, wiping at her eyes. She cast a sad smile. "Want some breakfast? My arm isn't hurting as badly as I thought it would."

I smiled. "Whatever you want to make."

#

After breakfast, Tor went outside. I crept back near the library.

Tabby was drawing symbols in the air and stirring a mixture in a small iron pot. I didn't have any idea what she was doing, but it was interesting.

I heard a noise, something with great claws scrambling up the wooden steps to the upper level. I turned my head, but of course there was nothing there. Out of the corner of my eye, I managed to catch a flash of green where Tabby was working. For a small moment, the green that appeared shifted into a symbol. As I looked toward Tabby, I saw nothing but her drawing in the air. This time, I could tell what she was drawing was, in fact, the symbol I had seen.

I allowed Tabby to believe as she believed, but there was a strong part of me that didn't take it seriously. For whatever reason, and maybe it was my church training, it was hard for me to believe in magic unless it had to do with black magic. Technically, you could call transubstantiation a type of magic ritual, but the church didn't view it that way. Doing so would get you branded a heretic. Then again, I was already considered something less than dirt by the church. It couldn't get much worse.

But with Tabby, I always knew she was anything but. She was a good egg, and I believed, without a doubt, she would never do anything evil to another living soul. That knowledge still didn't erase the fact that I now knew Tabby's witchy stuff was real. It turned my stomach sour, but there was also something comforting about being able to see it. In *knowing* it was there. Her power didn't need faith for it to work. What I thought was blasphemy, wasn't it?

I turned my head to the side again. This time more than one symbol appeared. Each had its own color: mostly reds, oranges, blues, greens and yellows. Beautiful to look at, but not something I'd seen before. I wondered if it was only Tabby's magic I could see, or if something had changed within me.

As soon as Tabby finished, she glanced up and noticed me. She blushed. "How long were you standing there?"

I grinned. "You would probably say too long, but it was long enough for me."

"Long enough for what?"

"For me to figure things out."

Chapter Twenty-Two

Cocoon

AFTER EVERYTHING WAS put to rights in the library and the herbs were swept up from the floor, I said, "Tor's had a bad morning."

Tabby furrowed her brow and wiped the sweat from her upper lip. "What do you mean?"

"Remember how I told you things were bad yesterday?"

Tabby set her bag on the sofa.

"Well," I said, "Will fessed up to Tor. We're either already in the middle of World War III or waiting for it to start."

Tabby tapped her chin with her fingers. "Do you think that's why things were calm last night?"

"I dunno."

Tabby brushed her hair off her forehead. "So what's on the agenda?"

"Today, we see if Lucy will speak to us, *really* speak to us."

Tabby waved a hand toward the door. "Lead the way."

I grabbed my notebook and a felt tipped marker. I hadn't forgotten what Lucy had done to her mother with a razor blade, and I wasn't about to take any chances.

After we left the library, I paused at the bottom of the stairs and took a deep breath.

"Okay," I said more to center my resolve than to Tabby, "here we go."

I began ascending, Tabby followed. There were no sounds, just the creaking of us walking the stairs. The old wood groaned with every step. How did this house look when Black had it? Granted the furniture was Black's, but somehow I imagined the house looked darker, more sinister when he lived there. I was speculating too much again, letting the *special something* of the house distract me from the real issues. It didn't matter what the house was like when Black had it except for maybe the attic room, but the house, at this point, had nothing to do with Lucy at all. Mr. Black, however, I think had a lot to do with Lucy.

As soon as I reached the top and turned toward Lucy's wing, the laughter started. Then she began to sing, "Where oh were has my little priest gone? Where oh where can he be!"

The lights winked out of my vision. Darkness. I was blind. I heard nothing. The void intensified like I'd been transported to a space of nothingness. I was alone. I'd completely disappeared.

Demon tricks are many, I thought. *It wants fear. You need to relax.*

Tabby's hands on my arm hit me first. I opened my eyes. Things returned to normal.

"Jimmy?" she asked. "Are you okay?"

Her fingers squeezed. I smiled at her, but inside spiders crawled under my skin. "Yep."

"What happened?"

"Lucy playing a trick." I reached for the wall to orient my body to the surroundings. "Nothing more."

Tabby's eyes darkened and she stared at me for what seemed like forever. "Are you sure?"

I nodded. "Come on. I think Lucy's a bit bored."

"Are you sure this is a good idea?" she asked, trying to keep up with me as I started down the hallway.

"It doesn't matter if it's good or not," I said. "It's the only option we have."

Tabby ran in front of me and stopped, putting her hands on her hips. "What are you blathering about? There are always options."

I shook my head. "Not for Lucy there aren't. Time's running out, Tabby. You've seen her. She isn't well. I don't know if the possession is causing her health to fail, but I know this little girl is dying. There isn't time for me to be chicken shit."

She paused then nodded grimly.

"All right," I said. "Let's go."

When we got to Lucy's door, it was so cold I could see the puffs of my breath. "She's getting stronger."

Tabby stared into my eyes, a wild look in the depths of her pupils.

Hell, I was scared. Lucy was something I hadn't faced before. She was creepy as sin, and I think she knew it. She seemed to get a charge by making people feel uncomfortable, not like a six-year-old at all. She once was a normal kid, and now she wasn't.

I reached toward the door, but as soon as I touched the knob, I jerked my hand away.

"What's wrong?" Tabby asked.

"It's cold. Ice cold." I used the hem of my shirt and opened it.

Lucy was in her bed, grinning like a Cheshire cat. "So you've come to visit me, Priest?"

"Yes, Lucy," I said. "Tabby and I thought that we would sit with you for a while and visit. I'm sure you're bored."

Lucy chuckled like a woodpecker hammering at a tree. "Oh, I find things to keep me entertained. A little chaos here, a little thanatos there."

Thanatos, classical Greek for death. No way at all Lucy could have learned about it.

"What is it about thanatos you like, Lucy?" I wanted to show that she understood. I could only hope she'd comply.

Lucy fixed those ugly, bloody eyes on me. "Thanatos, dear Father Holiday, is the point to everything. Through thanatos, I get what I want, and each time I experience death, I get to go after another soul. Through that I am reborn."

I nodded. "Does thanatos liberate you?"

It cackled. "Liberaté me. Liberaté me!"

My brain flashed back to the note I received during my dream. Shame I couldn't have used that before. Okay, we had Greek and Latin, what was next?

"Du bist interessant, Vater Holiday," Lucy said.

I paused. Holy crap, now she was speaking German. This was proof. No doubt.

"Thank you, Lucy," I said.

"Nechevo," she answered.

Good God. Greek, Latin, German, and Russian in the space of five minutes. It would be difficult for the church to deny this.

I tapped my fingers on the footboard of Lucy's bed. "We'll go now, Lucy," I said. "You need your rest."

She smiled.

Tabby and I left the room as nonchalantly as possible. I was glad we kept our cool. Never a good idea to give the demon any emotional ammo. I waited until we were downstairs in the kitchen before I exploded. "I can't believe it!"

"Shh," Tabby held her finger in front of my mouth.

"Shit, sorry. I never expected that. Four languages she has no way of knowing. I feel so damn…I don't know…lucky."

Tabby stared at me, her eyes haunted and far away. "Why should you feel lucky?"

I must have sounded like a cross between a madman and an idiot. "I meant I can't believe how this has turned out. We couldn't have better luck for Lucy. The church is going to have a hard time ignoring this evidence."

"I don't know, Jimmy," Tabby said. "Is it enough?"

It hit me then—what she meant. I was so excited by Lucy's capacity for language I was missing the point. The church, depending on their mood, would do what they liked. We had another piece of the puzzle that would make it hard for them to ignore. Hard, but not impossible.

#

That evening, Will camped out in the living room. We weren't given the full explanation about what happened, but I imagine it was going to take some time for Tor to forgive Will, if she decided to do so at all.

Tabby and I left Will alone and got ourselves arranged in the library for the night. Part of me felt like I should feel guilty for not asking Will to share the library with us, but for me, it was nice to have a break from everything.

Round about three—God I was getting tired of that number—Tabby and I woke to a loud booming noise. I jerked my head up. The doorway to the library glowed green and a huge dark figure loomed in the doorway. Every few seconds, it would raise a massive hand and strike at the open space of the doorway. He looked like a cross between a mountain troll and a Mack truck, all organic yet cybernetic. With each strike, the boom intensified.

I stared at Tabby. "What the hell is that?"

She stared at me, eyes wide. "I have no idea." Pulling the blanket back from her legs, she sat up, still staring at the doorway. "If the wards hold…"

The thing kept pounding. The symbols vibrated each time the creature beat against the wards. With every boom, I wanted to back away, but I stayed where I was. There was only so far I could go.

"Why do they glow green like that?" I asked.

Her lips pulled into a frown. "What are you talking about?"

Tabby sat on her knees, staring over the back of the couch at the thing.

"The wards, they glow green each time that thing decides to bounce a hand off them." I didn't have to turn my head now to see the wards pulsate.

She cocked her head and stared at me. "Um, Jimmy?"

"Yeah?"

"That's not normal."

I slumped back onto my sofa. "What do you mean?"

She took a deep breath. "When I drew them, *I* couldn't even see them." She moved over and pointed to the main symbol, or at least its general area. "Draw it for me."

I ripped a piece of paper from my notebook and traced it as best I could. I held it out to her when I was finished.

Tabby's mouth dropped open. "Jimmy," she said. "Could you do this before?"

I shook my head. "It started today when you were warding the doorway."

She leaned closer. "Wow."

"Wow what?"

She shook herself and then paused, thinking. "You've been given a gift of sorts." She rubbed her hands up and down her arms as if trying to get rid of a chill. "Can you see other things?"

I shrugged. "Not as far as I know of." I peered around the room. "I mean, I haven't tried."

"Just…let me know if you see other things, okay?" she asked.

I nodded and swallowed hard.

Finally, the thing stopped. Nothing he could do would let him pass Tabby's wards. Thank God. He stood there for a moment, staring at us. Then with a crack he disappeared.

Chapter Twenty-Three

Revelation

"PRIEST," IT WHISPERED in my ear.

I woke up, frantically checking the library, and saw nothing. No creatures, no demons, nothing went bump in the night. Tabby was fine, resting. The blanket pulled up to her chin. The entrance to the library looked the same, normal. Nothing there.

"Priest," the voice whispered again.

I shot up and put my elbows on my knees. Was it a trap? Lucy doing something to get me to leave the library? I focused my hearing, but there was no sound. If Lucy was in medical distress, the alarms on her equipment would be going off.

"Priest," it said again.

"What," I said sharply. I thought I heard what sounded like the giggle of a little girl, but it was faint.

"Come and play with me," the voice said.

I scowled. "No, I don't think so."

It was quiet for a moment, and then the banging on the wards began again. Tabby jumped awake.

"What is it this time?" she asked.

"Absolutely nothing," I said, and I didn't lie.

She glanced around the room. "Where's the noise coming from?"

I shrugged. "Lucy. There's nothing attacking the wards that I can see. I'm going to guess our Lucy is a mimic."

Her face went blank. "That's kind of interesting, but scary."

I nodded. "It means we're really going to have to be on our toes. If she can impersonate a noise, you know she can mimic any one of us."

"And the library is the only safe place in the house."

I scratched my head. "You could ward other places."

Tabby's face scrunched. "We saw how well that worked when I warded the room upstairs. We're lucky the wards worked here."

I sighed. She was right. For some reason the library worked. Maybe, simply, because this was not a place in the house the badness crept in. "I don't know what else to do. If we could find out exactly what that thing wants, we'd be a step closer."

Tabby ran her hands through her hair. "You told me yourself that demons are tricky."

"Yeah, so?"

She took a frustrated breath. "Don't forget what it told you. It wants Lucy's soul, but it wants more too."

"Of course it wants more, it's a demon."

Tabby rolled her eyes at me. "It's more than that, Jimmy. It's like she's affecting your brain somehow. You aren't usually this easy to jump to conclusions, and this thing with you being able to see magic…it's scary."

I stared at her. "What are we going to do about it?"

"I'm fine," she said. "You need to keep yourself in check. I don't know what's going on, but honestly, I don't like it."

I threw my hands in the air. "Dammit, Tabby, what do I need to do, huh? You know all this weird shit. I know about graphic design, saying Mass, and keeping my house from falling apart."

"Shh," Tabby put her finger over her mouth.

"Oh come on, if they didn't wake up with all the booming, I hardly think my voice is going to wake them."

"Jimmy, God you can be such an ass. Did you notice how tired Tor was? Maybe she hears the noises, and then can't sleep. I don't know, but I think Will and Tor hear it. Maybe subconsciously, they're glad it has new people to pick on, even if they're still getting hurt."

I couldn't deny that. It had been stronger here from the beginning. Maybe I'd been dead wrong about the whole thing.

"Okay, what can I do to keep my head straight?"

Tabby grinned. "I'll go out tomorrow and get you a piece of jewelry to wear. Then I'll spell it for clarity, so that anytime you wear it, which will be all the time, it will keep your brain from getting muddled."

"Okay."

"Now, can we go back to sleep, please?" she asked.

#

After breakfast the next morning, Tabby left to get something so she could make the clarity charm for me. Will was out doing yard work, trying desperately to get Tor's approval. I offered to help, but Will gave me that look that said, "I need to do this alone, otherwise it won't matter."

Tor came in not long after Will left the house. Her arm was still wrapped, but she seemed to be in less pain than the day before.

She sat at the table beside me and stared out the window. "Tomorrow, I think I'll make bread. I could use some comfort food."

"Feeling better?" I asked.

She nodded then turned her heard toward me, staring at me in a strange way.

"Something is bothering you," she said.

"A lot of things are bothering me."

Wrapping her hands around her coffee cup, she said, "Like what?"

I settled back into my chair. This looked like it was going to take a while. "Was Lucy baptized?"

She glanced into her coffee. "Yes, at my family's church. I have the pictures somewhere. She wore my great-grandmother's christening gown."

I smiled. At least I now had another question answered. "Before you left D.C., did Lucy act upset?"

Tor stared out the window. "Not strange exactly, but alternating between clingy and withdrawn. One minute, she'd be crawling all over me or Will, the next she wanted to be left alone."

I had to tread carefully here. This was already a family in crisis. Things were bad enough without my interfering, but I needed the answers. Lucy's life might depend on something that Tor or Will would view insignificant.

I took a deep breath. "Any chance Lucy could have known about Will?"

At first, she seemed puzzled. Then her eyes darkened as she realized what I was asking. "It's possible, but I don't know how she could have."

"I guess we'll have to ask Will then," I said.

Tor snorted. "Asking Will about anything is pointless, haven't you figured that out yet?" She pushed her coffee cup away. "Now, I have a question for you. Will told me that he'd told you about the affair the day before he told me, is that true?"

I nodded. "He told me on the way back from getting my new phone. He was worried that his transgression caused Lucy's possession."

"Did it?" she asked.

"No. Plenty of kids have parents who split up and have affairs, and most of them are never possessed. No, I don't think what Will did had anything to do with it."

She sighed. "Why Lucy then?"

I rubbed my face with my hand. "That's the question, isn't it? Is it as simple as her being the one to scratch the black paint on the mirror? Is it as simple as Lucy being a very sensitive child? I don't know. That's one of the hardest things about possession. It forces us to see what is good turned into something foul."

Tor narrowed her eyes at me. "You're very astute, you know that?"

I chuckled. "I wouldn't say that. More like for my first job, I was trained to listen, think and see how people's actions affect those around them."

"What about the molesters?" she asked.

It always came to this. The fucking perverts had forever changed the view of what was once a trusted position and I hated them for it. "Like anything else," I said. "It only takes a few bad apples to spoil the bunch. There are good priests out there. Sadly, every priest now has to fight that stigma and the molesters usually don't get enough punishment."

"What do you think should happen to them?"

The rage I felt made the acid in my stomach boil. This was going into an area I wasn't crazy to talk about. It was too close to home. "They should be killed. Molesters are broken people. Studies have been done, even castration doesn't stop them. A lot of people will argue that a molester's victims get to move on with their lives, so it isn't that bad of a crime. Bullshit."

"Priests aren't supposed to advocate killing, are they?"

I grinned. "I don't have to worry about that anymore."

"Don't you think condemning someone to death is a little harsh?"

I stared at her. She'd never been there. "People like to think that it's easy to recover from things, rape and molestation in particular. That's far from the truth. You think about your sins, whether you believe in God or not. Your body suffers, sometimes surgery is needed to repair things. And people say the molesters have rights? What about the rights of the victims?"

"You really feel powerfully about this. Were you molested?"

I grunted. "No, my sister was."

"How is she now?" Tor asked.

I looked her in the eye. "She's dead. Killed herself when the police let the bastard walk because there wasn't enough evidence."

"How did your parents cope?"

"They didn't. They both drank. My father drank himself to death."

"What about your mother?"

"She lives in a small apartment in a retirement community. She goes to AA, tries to keep straight."

Tor leaned back in her chair. "I had no idea."

"Neither does anyone else. That's what I meant about actions affecting others. The man that raped and molested my sister destroyed her life and broke my family. Ironically, the church was more understanding than anyone else."

"And your view on the church protecting molesters?"

"When I felt safe at church was long before any of that went public. Now I'm disappointed. Kind of glad I left."

"It's a scary world we live in." Tor hugged herself.

"And I don't see it getting better anytime soon."

#

Tabby returned a little after Tor got Will ushered up to their bathroom to get cleaned up. She came through the library door, thumping her arm against the doorframe. "Dammit." Her eyes were sparkling. She rubbed her arm and closed the massive doors behind her. "I found the perfect thing."

A huge part of me wished those doors could lock even though I knew a mere lock wouldn't keep the evil out.

Tabby put the bag on the coffee table in between our sofas. "Ready to see it now?"

I nodded. She pulled a small box out of the bag and handed it to me. It was a black velvet ring box. I stared at her with a raised eyebrow then focused my attention on the box. I opened it, not sure what to expect. There, nestled in ivory silk, was a man's ring. It wasn't an engagement ring or anything, just a ring. Somehow calling it simply a ring, however, didn't fit either. It was a larger man's ring with a Celtic cross in the center. The metal was either white gold or platinum, I wasn't sure which. The cross was bedecked in diamonds and emeralds. It was a beautiful thing, but too much.

"I can't accept this, Tabby," I said.

She smiled back at me. "You don't have a choice, Jimmy Holiday. That's the one that spoke to me when I was looking. Besides, you'd be surprised at how much I paid for it."

I scratched my arm, already feeling the goosebumps rising. No, I probably didn't want to know. I asked anyway. "How much?"

"Uh, uh. No, you don't. Let's say that flea markets are sometimes very good things, and the lady that sold me the ring wasn't sure if the diamonds were real or not."

I sighed. No use arguing. I was stuck. "As long as it didn't cost you much."

"Not much at all." She dug in her bags and placed some candles of various colors on the table. "Now do you want to be here while I work?"

"I'd like to be." And it was true. I wanted to be around her.

"All right then. Give me a piece of your hair and relax. This will take a while."

I plucked a hair out of my head like she asked and handed her both the hair and the ring box. She took her time. Once she began working, I saw colors again. I was getting used to it now. But one thing did cross my mind as I watched Tabby work. What if the colors were the result of whatever Lucy was doing? If I put the ring on that Tabby was fixing for me, would the colors stop?

After she finished, Tabby handed me the ring. I put it on my ring finger and it fit perfectly. The logical part of my mind told me it was coincidence, but my gut told me otherwise. I wasn't the same man. I kind of liked it.

Chapter Twenty-Four

Chrysalis

A HUGE CRASH vibrated along the ceiling. Tabby and I ran upstairs. I heard Will whimpering from Lucy's room. Tor ran down the hall ahead of me. When she reached the door, she jerked it open.

Lucy stood on her bed, the torn restraints hanging from her wrists. Will slumped in the far corner of the room away from Lucy, blood spilling over his face from a gash in his forehead. With his eyes closed and breathing labored, he appeared half dead.

I shouted to Tabby, "Help Will."

Walking over to the foot of Lucy's bed, I stared up at her. Bile collected in my throat, but I pushed the fear aside. It wasn't important. "What did you do?"

She stood over me like a demonic archangel. The light from the window shined in, molding to give her wings constructed from shadows. Her bloody eyes glowed red. Her hands curved into claws. "I gave him the punishment he wanted."

Tabby and Tor crouched next to Will, Tabby checking his pulse.

My heart began to pound faster. I turned all my attention on Lucy. "Uh huh. How did you break the restraints?"

She stared at me with her narrowed bloody eyes. "It's not like they were very strong."

I wasn't about to argue with her, but the restraints were made of canvas, not something easy to break. I had to be savvy about this, but I didn't know what to do. We needed to get Will out of there without any more damage. I did what I always did when I was at a loss. I winged it.

"All right, Lucy. Are you going to cooperate?"

She let herself fall to the bed and cackled. Her body bounced several times before settling. The *wings* disappeared. "Depends on what you mean by cooperate, Priest."

I snatched a receipt from my pants and grabbed the felt marker from my shirt pocket. I scribbled a list on it. Then I walked over to Tabby and handed it to her. "Take this and get me some supplies." It was worth a shot. Maybe Lucy wouldn't know what was on the list if I didn't make it obvious. "Don't look at the list until you leave the house."

Tabby nodded and ran out of the room. Tor held a towel to Will's head. I nodded at her.

"Are you sure?" She asked me.

"Yes. Go. Help Will."

Will woke up and helped her hold the towel to his head. She eased him to his feet and ushered him out of the room. I closed the door behind them.

I turned back to Lucy.

"You going to fuck me now, Priest?"

I swallowed. This wasn't going to be easy. Not mentally. Not physically. This was going to suck. "No, I'm going to sit here to make sure you don't hurt yourself. You've sent your dad to the hospital, someone has to watch you."

She rolled her eyes in the back of her head and a strange gelatinous substance started coming out of her mouth. It drifted toward the ceiling like smoke badly re-created with CGI. It almost looked plastic.

I'd only seen anything like it in old photographs from the séance craze in the early part of the century.

"The ectoplasm doesn't scare me, Lucy." The sweat on the back of my neck, however, told the truth.

The paranormal blob disappeared and Lucy focused her sickly gaze on me once more. She sat up—her lower body not moving at all. "What does scare you, Priest?"

I smirked at her. "It would be kind of stupid for me to tell you, wouldn't it?"

Shooting me a devilish grin, she said, "I'll find out eventually, so you might as well tell me."

"Hmm....how old are you, really?" I asked. "Lucy's six, but I know you're much older than that."

She rolled her eyes again. "I don't think it matters much, do you?"

"What are you afraid of, Lucy?"

Her smiled widened, her jagged teeth poking out at a painful angle. "I am afraid of nothing. I am oblivion."

I was treading into dangerous territory here, but I had to keep her distracted until Tabby got back. If I asked questions that were normally part of an exorcism, did that put me in the middle of doing one? I had no idea. I was left there alone, grasping at straws.

"You should rest, Lucy. I'm sure you'll want to play more tricks this evening."

She stood back up, but her body did nothing to make it happen. It felt like a video feed had skipped forward, but I was watching her myself, not on a DVD or through a lens. If it wasn't for the fact I was so focused, I think I would have pissed myself.

"If you would stay out of that *room*, I could play lots of tricks." Her voice boomed a thick bass.

"I'm not a big fan of your tricks, Lucy." Shivers were dancing up my spine.

She laughed darkly. "You are no fun at all."

I heard footsteps pounding up the stairs. Soon after, Tabby opened the door and thrust a bag at me.

"No," I said. "You need to do that part. I'll hold her."

I tackled Lucy on the bed. She bucked beneath me; her hands scratching at any exposed skin. "Keep still, Lucy."

"Fuck you!"

She threw me across the room. Tabby screamed. My body slammed into the wall. I saw stars. My back hurt, but getting Lucy restrained was more important. I pushed myself to get off the floor, took a deep breath and pounced. Throwing Lucy on the bed, I began to pray. Tabby stooped onto the floor, attaching chains.

"The Lord is my shepherd…"

The clinks of the chains echoed through me. Lucy's guttural groans added to the macabre symphony.

"He maketh me to lie down…"

The more I prayed, the stiller she felt.

"Yeah though I walk through the valley of death, I will fear no evil."

By the time the prayer ended, Lucy was outfitted with padded handcuffs from a sex shop and various dog chains fastened to the metal of the hospital bed.

"Okay, it's done," Tabby said.

I rose and stopped my prayers…at least aloud.

"I'll see you dead, Priest."

I stared at her, zeroing in on the thing inside Lucy. I couldn't see it, but I felt it there and to it I spoke. "I'll see you in Hell first."

Tabby pushed me out the door and closed it behind us. She ran her hands over me as if looking for something,

"You're okay?"

"Gonna hurt worse tomorrow, but yeah. Just more bruises." I followed her down the hall. Lucy had been secured as humanely as possible. Didn't make me feel any better.

"Where on earth did you find the handcuffs?" I asked as we descended the stairs.

Tabby snorted. "Tor had them. Apparently, she likes things a little naughty in the bedroom."

"I didn't need to know that."

"Hey, you were the one who asked."

When we got to the kitchen, Tabby tossed the paper bag into the garbage. I leaned against the center island and popped my neck. The pain started to kick in as my adrenaline wore off.

"Tor take Will to the hospital?" I asked.

Tabby nodded. "He needed stitches."

"Well, when he gets here, we can look at the footage."

Tabby sighed and ran her hands over her face. "Can we contact the church now, please?"

Her voice shook. I'd never seen her this upset.

"Yes, tomorrow." I reached over and took hold of her hand. It felt right.

#

Tor and Will came home hours later. Will had a bandage across his forehead. His body slumped, tired and bruised, but otherwise unharmed.

"What did the doctor say?" Tabby asked.

"That I had a heck of a bump. I don't have a concussion at least."

Will held an ice pack to his head.

"That's good," I said.

"Did you watch the video?"

I shook my head. "We didn't stop the recording, and I'm glad we didn't. A lot happened after you left."

Will ate some steak Tor set in front of him then wiped his mouth with a napkin. "I don't know how many more injuries we can take. As it is, the hospital is asking questions. I mean, how are all of us getting hurt this close together? None of this would happen normally. But at least since it's us getting hurt, and not Lucy, they aren't doing anything. Not yet."

I nodded. "I'm getting the church involved tomorrow."

"What about the rest of the evidence?" Tor asked.

"After what happened this afternoon, we've got all the evidence we need. It's not going to be easy for them to ignore it."

After he and Tor finished eating, he ushered Tabby, Tor, and I into the living room. We settled around the TV while Will setup the playback on the security system's DVR.

For a while, everything was calm on the feed. Then Will said something about needing Lucy to be nicer to her mother and Lucy exploded. She rose from the bed like Nosferatu rising from his coffin. Stiff as a board, she simply elevated into a standing position on the bed, the restrains ripping from her wrists and ankles. Will stared at her, his mouth gaping.

"You do not give me orders," Lucy said, and struck Will so hard he flew across the room, hitting his head on the windowsill. His body collapsed into the corner.

Next, it showed us coming in and everything Tabby and I went through getting Lucy restrained again. One thing was different. While I was holding her down, my body blocked her face from the camera. Then, somehow, the DVR showed a close-up of Lucy's mangled face. She grinned into the camera.

"Jesus Christ!" I jumped.

The feed went back to normal a moment later, showing Tabby and I with Lucy in our last exchange.

"That was…disturbing." Tabby rubbed her hands along her arms in rapid strokes.

I took a deep breath. "I think we all better sleep in the library tonight."

Tabby swallowed. "That's probably a good idea."

We all hunkered in the library with the lights on. It wasn't safe enough for us to sleep in different parts of the house whether I needed a break or not. It was hard to get that image of Lucy smiling at the camera out of my head. My stomach felt like butterflies were tap-dancing inside it.

Tabby and I kept our sofas. Tor took over a sofa that was placed in front of the windows and Will deposited himself in a chair he moved from the other side of the room.

"I think we should take bathroom breaks together," Tabby said.

"That's not a bad idea," I massaged a particularly sore spot along my shoulder, "and a lot cleaner than my idea."

"And that was?" Will asked.

I grinned at him. "A really big bucket."

Tabby hit me with her pillow. "You know, honestly, we should try to all use the bathroom early. Then there will be no one out of this room late tonight."

Everyone went quiet then. I stared at them all in turn. They were trying so hard not to show they were afraid, but I could still see it. Each time the house settled, the level of fear rose with it. I didn't care about the house. Unless it decided to fall on me, it was pretty damn harmless. Lucy-demon-thing, however, was not. I'd learned that the hard way. We all had.

I did my best to not freak out. Enough fear flooded this room and there was no need to make things worse. Demons fed on fear, and I had a feeling that with what happened with Lucy earlier, and the amount of fear hanging around the room, we were in for a hell of a night.

Tor coughed nervously. "Is it wrong to be scared of my own daughter?"

"No, not wrong," Tabby said. "There are plenty of parents who are afraid of their kids, most though, just have severe behavioral problems. I think with having a possessed child, you have the right to be afraid."

"Try to keep calm," I said. "Demons feed on fear, and the more agitated you become, the stronger you'll make it."

"What are you telling me, Jimmy?" Tor asked.

"I'm telling you that if you can, don't think about your daughter tonight. Everyone needs to stay calm and I want us all to stay in this room. I don't care what noise Lucy makes. The only reason to leave this room is if the alarm on one of her monitors goes off—anything else, do not listen. It is very tricky, this demon."

"When do you think we should get everything?" Will asked.

"Before the noises start."

#

As I expected, things started up about three. Tabby, Tor, and Will had settled into an uneasy slumber. I stayed awake. I couldn't sleep and I couldn't explain it. I could feel it in my gut that something was going to happen.

The pounding began. It started out softly, but gradually grew louder and louder, until I could see something was trying to break Tabby's wards. It was invisible, but each time it started the assault, the wards glowed brighter. At times, they seemed to stretch, almost as if they were about to break. Then the pounding stopped. I looked around. Tor and Will had their blankets tucked underneath their chins. Tabby was sitting up on her sofa. Like me, she seemed to be getting used to this.

A little girl's giggle broke the momentary silence. Tor threw off the blanket.

"Stay still," I said.

The giggle happened again.

She stood up. "If Lucy's okay…"

"Lucy is not okay," I snapped. "This thing plays tricks. It tries anything to get you to leave the confines of this room."

The pounding started again, more vigorously than before. This time, when it stopped, a figure appeared in the doorway of the library—a figure of a little girl with pretty golden hair.

"Mommy?" it said hesitantly.

Tor started for the door, but I snagged her before she reached it.

"It's a trick, dammit!" I shouted at her. "Lucy is upstairs in her room chained to her bed. This thing," I pointed to it, "is a cruel trick."

The little girl disappeared. Tor whimpered.

"Come out, Mommy. I swear I'll be good," the thing said. I couldn't see it, but I could feel it was there, hiding itself.

Tor begged me with silent pleas.

"No."

"What does it want?" she asked.

I stared at her. "Your soul, and I don't think it's above killing to get what it wants."

The little girl appeared in the doorway again, crying. "You don't love me anymore, Mommy."

I kept hold of Tor.

"My baby," she wailed.

I shook her this time as Will and Tabby stared at the figure. "That is not Lucy, Tor. It's an apparition. It's fake."

She struggled and tried to break free of my arms. I glanced over at Will for help. He sat frozen in his chair.

"My sweet Lucy," Tor cried.

I shook her harder. "That is not your baby!"

It pressed its head against the film of the wards.

"These wards only keep out things that mean harm," I said, trying to get her to see sense. "Why else can all of us move freely, and it can't come in?"

The Lucy thing snarled; its face became an exact replica of the Lucy upstairs.

"You can stay there all night, I don't care." She smiled with her broken teeth. "I could always start a fire, you know?"

I laughed. "No you won't. If you destroy this house, you destroy the connection to that ley line."

It giggled. "You are too smart for your own good, Priest."

Then it disappeared.

"Is everything okay now?" Will asked.

"Hell if I know. Tabby and I have had nights that nothing happened. There have been nights with only noises." I ran a hand through my hair. "Then there are nights where the bad things come out. So is this all tonight? I don't know."

Tor and Will searched my face expectantly.

I stared back at them. The weight of the world rested on my shoulders. They had put me on a pedestal. I didn't like it. "Why are you looking to me to save you?"

"Because you're a priest," Tor said.

I sighed. "I'm not a priest. I quit, remember?"

Tabby put a hand on my shoulder. "What if God's rules and the church's rules are two different things?"

I had no answer to that.

#

I watched the night fly by staring out the window. It was calm, but a normal calm. All I saw were trees. Nothing freaky going on outside. Snow covered the ground and ice glinted from the branches. It looked like a Bob Ross winter landscape. I expected more, held my breath for more. Like a ticking bomb waiting to go off, I knew more would come. Maybe Lucy knew the real fight was coming too? Hopefully, I could get someone from the church here soon. If I couldn't, I didn't know how much more we could take. I was exhausted, but sleep wouldn't come.

Tabby's chest rose and fell with every breath. Her sleep was a comfort to me. I knew it wasn't normal. Yet whenever I felt stressed out, watching someone breathe helped relax me. Maybe breathing was a normal function that helped me to focus. Or maybe it grounded me because I knew my sister stopped breathing a long time ago.

I missed Candy. She'd been my protector for so many years; the one who bandaged my knees when they were bloody, and nursed me when I was sick. I hadn't been right since her death. Suicide sucked. I peered back out the window and stared into the night. No one who hadn't been through it could quite understand the feeling of loss when someone killed themselves. When someone who committed suicide died, most people assume it would be the same as when anyone else died. Sadness would encompass you for a while, and then over time, the pain wouldn't hurt the same way anymore. The difference was, when someone committed suicide—they *decided* to die. They made the honest choice to stop living and the rest, those that cared about them, were left wondering what they could have done to keep the one they loved from killing themselves.

"Jimmy?" Tabby asked. "Are you okay?"

I turned around. Something must have woken her up. "Yeah, why?"

"You're crying."

I wiped my hand across my cheek, moisture coated my skin.

"What's wrong?" she asked.

"I was thinking about my sister. That's all. I still miss her, even after all these years."

"How old was she when she died?"

"Eighteen," I focused on the melted snow dripping across the windowpane. "She was eighteen."

Tabby and I watched the sunrise. I could see why Tor chose the house then. The sunlight danced over the ice on the tree branches. So pretty. The evil of the house didn't match up with the land around it. Black must have made the house the way it was. The land itself wasn't bad. It couldn't be, not to have mornings like this.

Tor woke up not long after the sun finished rising. "That was awful."

"Calm in comparison to some nights," I said.

She nodded. "Do you think it's okay to leave the room now?"

"Probably. Most of the stuff during the day seems to be confined to direct contact with Lucy. I don't know if she's saving her strength for the night, or if some of the things helping her with her tricks are nocturnal."

Tor stretched. "Well then, I'm making omelets for breakfast. Come along, you can pick out what you want."

After we ate, I accompanied Tor to Lucy's room. I was no longer going to let anyone move around the house alone. It wasn't safe—except for the library, where last time I looked, Will was snoring.

When we got to her room, we found Lucy asleep. Her chained arms lay beside her on the bed.

I helped Tor refill Lucy's feeding tube and change the glucose drip on her IV.

We said nothing to each other the entire time. Tor had tears in her eyes when we were leaving, but I paused inside the door. On the other side of the wood, deep scratches had been forced in the grain. They were gouges like someone made them with massive claws. I snapped a picture with my cell phone.

Tor cocked her brow at me in question, but I shook my head. We left the room and closed the door behind us.

"What did you do?" she asked.

"Wait until we get back downstairs."

When we reached the kitchen, I pulled out my phone and showed Tor.

Her hand went over her mouth. Her eyes were wide with alarm. "What caused that?"

I shrugged. "Whatever did it, didn't hurt Lucy. We have other things to worry about."

"Why'd you take the picture then?"

"More proof."

Tabby came in, breaking up our debate. "Will's still asleep."

"Where were you?" I asked.

"Bathroom."

"I thought we agreed we wouldn't go anywhere without anyone else."

Tabby rolled her eyes. "I had to pee, and Will is in there snoring. I couldn't wait, so I went to the bathroom."

With things the way they were, I couldn't help but feel like she took an unnecessary risk.

"So wake up Will," Tor said. "We have things to do. We'll get our showers," she turned to me, "then you are free to do whatever you need to do."

"All right," I said. "Let's get started."

Chapter Twenty-Five

Pain is a State of Mind

IT DIDN'T TAKE too long, not really. Will was sitting in his chair. The blanket had fallen to his waist, but he slept on, snoring lightly.

"Will," I shook his shoulder.

His eyes snapped open.

While he stretched and got settled, I turned on my laptop and browsed for a few minutes. My search landed on the local directory. "What's the name of the Catholic church?"

Will rubbed his eyes. "St. Mary's."

I Googled it and wrote a few numbers. Starting with the first, I counted three rings before it was answered.

"St. Mary's," the voice said.

"Hello." I leaned back on the sofa. "My name is Jimmy Holiday and I could use some help. I need to talk to the priest."

He paused for a moment. "You're speaking to him. I'm Father John. What can I do for you, Mr. Holiday?"

"I'm calling on behalf of a friend. Will Andersen?"

The man coughed. "Yes. How is his daughter?"

"Not doing so well, the treatment at the hospital didn't work."

I could hear him rustling papers. "That's a shame," he said. "Perhaps I can help find another hospital—"

"No, Father. I…," This would be the toughest part, "I really think you need to see Lucy. I don't think she's mentally ill."

He cleared his throat, then a snide tone overtook his calm demeanor. "And what do you think is wrong with her?"

My eyes narrowed. "Maybe you should know that I used to be a priest."

"Really?" I could tell I'd gotten his attention.

"Yes, but that's a story for another day, I'm afraid."

"Maybe today is the day," he said. "Now really, why are you no longer a priest?"

He was starting to annoy me, but if I didn't clarify, he'd assume the worst. "Quite simply, I fell for a girl."

He snorted. "And you defiled your profession—"

Pompous ass. No way, was I letting that slide. "Actually, I did not. My vow of celibacy was true until I left the priesthood, but I think that's enough about me. I want to talk about Lucy."

"All right," he sighed. "Let's talk about Lucy."

"I think she's possessed."

He coughed. "Honestly, Mr. Holiday, you had me going there for a minute."

I let him get the giggle out of his system, before hitting him with the proof. "What six-year-old do you know can speak: Russian, German, Biblical Greek and Latin?"

"What?" he asked. The distinctive sound of sputtering on a drink echoed over the line.

"She displays every sign. I have it all on video."

"Good God." A book slammed shut.

"We need your help."

He coughed again. "I know nothing about exorcism."

"Father, even I know that each diocese is supposed to have its own exorcist. Contact the bishop, and get back to me."

He took my number and promised to get me some word as soon as possible. All I needed was for them to come and investigate, and that was exactly what they would do next. I knew the church too well, much too well.

When the good Father called me back, Tabby and I were sitting at the kitchen table watching Tor pour over several cookbooks. Her therapeutic cooking had hit overdrive since the events from last night.

"Yes, Father." I sat stiffly, ready to fight with him if I needed.

"When do you think it would be convenient for me to visit Lucy and look at the evidence?" His voice shook with the smallest quiver. Had his superior reamed him or was he simply scared?

"Hold on one moment," I said.

I placed my hand over the mouthpiece and spoke to Tor, "Father wants to know when he can come and see Lucy."

"As soon as possible. Whenever he likes." She shivered.

"Anytime would be fine, Father."

The good Father was quiet. "Are precautions in place?"

I chuckled. "Are you asking if she's restrained? Then yes, in fact recently we had to enhance the way she was restrained. You'll see why in what we have to show you."

He clicked his tongue against his teeth. "Is this afternoon too soon?"

"No, Father. The family wishes for someone to help Lucy as soon as possible. This afternoon will work perfectly."

"I'll be by after one."

"Do you remember how to get here?" I tapped my pencil along the table.

"Mr. Holiday, everyone knows how to get to Blackmoor."

Then he hung up. I dropped my phone a little too hard on the table.

"What's wrong, Jimmy?" Tabby asked.

"He called it Blackmoor. The only other person I've heard call this house that is the local librarian. The name's been used in horror films a lot."

"But not when this house was built," she said.

I stared at her. "Good point. At any rate, he's supposed to be here at one. Where's Will?"

Tor shrugged. "He hasn't left the library. I guess he's going to sleep the day away."

"I'll be glad when I can sleep again."

Neither one of them said anything about that. Unfortunately, just because the priest was coming today didn't mean anything would happen now. We knew we still had nights ahead like last night. But how many?

#

When the priest arrived, we'd all been standing, looking out the front window like a bunch of kids waiting for Santa. It would have been funny if the situation wasn't so dire. Tor had the front door open before the man even reached the walkway.

"Father, welcome," she said. "We're so glad you've come back."

He patted her on the shoulder and allowed her to lead him inside. He was younger than I expected him to be. Not too much older than me. Grey barely flecked his black hair. He was dressed in black with a brown canvas coat.

"Do you want to see Lucy first?" I asked as Will took his coat.

He nodded. "That would probably be best. I take it you're the friend?"

"That's right."

He glanced between me and Tabby for a moment. "Interesting. Very interesting." After his scrutiny, he turned to Tor and Will. "It is best if I see her now. That way, when I ask my questions of her, I am not already biased."

I stayed out of it then. No reason for me to do anything but wait downstairs with Tabby. We heard enough anyway.

"Is he going to believe her?" Tabby asked.

"Believe it or not, this is part of it. The possessed say foul things, do foul things. You've seen the old movies."

She nodded.

"While some of the effects are fantastic, they are pretty realistic. In fact, *The Exorcist* had several priests on staff as consultants."

"Really?"

"Yup. One of them even wrote a book about possession after the movie—"

A thud from upstairs interrupted our conversation. We waited a breath to see if we could hear anything else. Nothing. I searched the ceiling then glanced at Tabby. "I hope he wasn't stupid enough to unhook her restraints."

The priest ran down the stairs. He stopped when he saw us. "Is she always like that?"

I raised a brow at him. "Pretty much. Sometimes she's very violent though."

He nodded. "She threw her father. I don't know how."

"What do you mean?" Tabby asked.

"She threw him against the wall without even touching him."

"So the restraints are still in place?" I asked.

"Oh, yes," he said. "There's little doubt in my mind she's possessed, but I have to see the signs."

Will and Tor came downstairs with Will holding a towel to his nose.

"Want me to help?" Tabby asked Will.

He shook his head.

"You sure?" I asked. When he nodded, I added, "The Father wants to watch the videos."

Will held up his finger for me to wait. He and Tor headed toward the kitchen. We were quiet for several minutes, waiting. When they returned, Will had tape on his nose and it had stopped bleeding.

"She broke my nose," Will said, leading us into the living room. Tabby walked with Tor back to the kitchen. I knew Tor didn't want to see it again, but I had a feeling Tabby was kind of glad she had Tor as an excuse to get out of watching it a second time.

Will cued the DVR to the proper file. As the video showed the peculiar situation, Father John gasped at Lucy's language prowess. The rest, he watched in silence.

"This is very bad," he said when we'd watched all there was.

"When do we hear if she gets an exorcism?" Will asked.

"Sometime soon," the priest said. "I have to let the bishop see the evidence. After that, I should have some sort of answer for you."

Will gave Father John copies of the files on discs. "Call anytime. We don't care what time it is. Lucy needs help."

The priest scratched his head. "I'll do the best I can."

With that, he left, scurrying out of the house like a mouse. The man was deeply scared, but would it be enough?

Chapter Twenty-Six

The Call

I WAS HEADING to the kitchen to get something to drink when my phone rang. I about jumped out of my skin. I scrambled for it, trying to dig it out of my pocket. Almost dropping it twice, I somehow managed to answer it before it went to voicemail. "Hello."

"Mr. Holiday, I'm calling, well, I have some bad news," the voice said. It sounded like the priest.

"Father?" I asked.

He coughed. "Yes, and please, call me John."

I shuffled into the kitchen. The conversation Tabby, Tor, and Will were having ceased.

"Okay, John. Is it all right if I put you on speaker phone?" I sat in the empty chair at the table.

"Yes, that's fine."

I hit the button. "What's going on?"

"The news I have, it isn't good."

I waited for him to say something else. He didn't. "What's the bad news, John?"

He cleared his throat through the phone. "Well, the exorcism's been granted."

Tor gasped then clasped her hands over her mouth.

"That doesn't sound like bad news," I said.

"No. I'm sorry." He paused. "It's been granted, but it's going to be a while before it happens."

"But why?" Tor asked in a voice that was not unlike a squeak.

I heard him sigh. "Right now, in America, we only have about twenty-three exorcists. There's supposed to be one for each diocese, but we don't have them."

"Uh huh," I said. "And how does this affect Lucy's exorcism?"

"There's a waiting list," he paused as if not wanting to say the rest, "I'm afraid the earliest Lucy will get her exorcism will be in about six months."

"She won't last that long!" Tor started to cry.

"Mrs. Andersen, please," Father John said. "I'm doing everything in my power to change that. Times are that hard."

"Is there any way you could do the exorcism yourself, Father?" I asked.

"No, Mr. Holiday. I'm afraid I don't have the training."

I hit the table with my hand. It cracked. This paper pusher was standing in the way. A little girl's life was at stake for crying out loud. "What do you propose we do for six months?"

"Well, if you could take her to Rome—"

"Father, can you imagine Lucy on a plane? She'd attack everyone in sight."

"It was a thought," he said. "In Rome, all you need to do is make an appointment with an exorcist. It's almost like going to the doctor."

"None of that does Lucy any good." I hit myself on the leg. Better to add another bruise than to completely destroy the table.

Will was holding Tor with her head lying on his shoulder. It was the most comforting I'd seen them toward each other.

"Well, Mr. Holiday. You could check with other religions."

"Other religions? Like what?" I asked.

"I believe the Jews have their own form of exorcism. I don't know how well it works."

My mind jumbled and a red haze swam before me, but I didn't know what else to do. Father John had tried, I guess. It wasn't his fault the best he could do was put Lucy on a waiting list, as ridiculous as that sounded.

"Well, keep her on the list," I said. "Maybe God will work a miracle."

"Maybe so," he said.

I hung up the phone. They all were staring at me.

"What?" I asked.

It was Will who first spoke. "You have to do it."

"I have to do what?"

"You have to do the exorcism." He reached over and wiped tears away from Tor's eyes. "You know Lucy won't make it six months. Hell, I don't even know if she'll make it one month."

I knew it was true. There was no avoiding it now. The demon was doing something to Lucy, something I couldn't quite understand, but whatever it was, it was making her sick. If I didn't intervene, she could die. The demon could make sure of it.

"I'm not even a priest."

Tor pleaded with me between tears. "The church said that. I don't know anyone with as good a heart as you have, Jimmy. Please, save my little girl."

What was I going to say to that? Free will could really be a bitch sometimes. I wished I could be told what to do, but it never worked out that way. I wasn't that lucky.

"All right, Tor. I'll do my best," I said, hoping I hadn't made the worst mistake of my life.

#

I went out the back door and around the house to the driveway. God, I needed a break. Tabby followed for some reason. I leaned against her car. "What do you think would happen if I up and left?"

Tabby stared at me and crossed her arms. "To you or to Lucy?"

"Both, I guess."

She sighed. "Jimmy, you've seen Lucy as much as I have. She's not well. Modern medicine is holding off what seems to be the inevitable. What happens if her organs fail again?"

I rubbed my arms. Leave it to stupid me to go outside without my coat with snow on the ground. "Yeah, that isn't something I want to think about."

Fire leapt into Tabby's eyes. Her face flushed. "That's great, Jimmy. If you don't do this, if you didn't try, do you really think you could live with yourself by going back on your word? Let alone if you walked away and later found out Lucy died, waiting for that exorcism."

"What if I make things worse, Tabby? I know nothing about doing this."

Tabby snatched my shoulder and jerked me off her car. "You know what?"

"What?"

"Neither did the first exorcists. They laid their hands on the possessed and spoke to the demons until they got tired. Possession has to do with strength of will. You told me that. Your will has to be stronger than the demon's."

"It's a shame Lucy's 'will' isn't strong enough to protect her." I wasn't this girl's father. Why should it be my responsibility? My insides rebelled. I knew I was being a prick, but I didn't like being cornered without options or a way out. How the hell had I gotten myself into this?

Tabby cocked her head. "Not everyone can be you, Jimmy. Believe it or not, you're unique."

"I don't know how…" I tried to find another solution, anything. "So I have to do this thing?"

She nodded. "Yep."

"And you'll help?"

"If I can."

I sighed. "All right then, sounds like I better study the ritual. Try to think of spells you can cast on Lucy and her room for light, health, and honesty. Who knows, it might help."

"Any spells you'd like me to cast for you?" she asked.

"Yeah. Luck. It looks like I'm going to need it."

We went back inside and sat at the table. Tor was futzing at the counter, making God knows what. Will sat across from me, nursing a cup of coffee.

"Is there anything I can do to help?" he asked.

I thought for a moment. What I needed him to do and what he was capable of were two different things.

"Honestly, I don't know," I said. "I'm going to need vestments and the rest. Tabby knows what she needs. Mostly, I need something that no one can help me with."

"And what's that?"

"Bravery, hope, strength, luck. Take your pick." I ran my hands through my hair. "I can't promise this is going to turn out okay, Will. I don't know what to do. I don't want Lucy's death on my hands."

Will let out a breath slowly. He seemed old and tired, as if he'd aged twenty years since it all began. "You know, Jimmy, without you, Lucy would have no chance at all." He pushed his coffee cup off to the side and clasped his hands together. "Okay, you don't know what you're doing, but more important is that you care about that. You care about making Lucy worse."

I sighed. He believed in me too much. "I don't want you to put me on a pedestal or anything. I want you to understand. Once I start this, I don't know what's going to happen. I don't know what Lucy is going to do. I know there's a camera, but I don't want you to blame me if something goes wrong."

"Jimmy," he fisted his hands on the table, "Tor and I have talked about this. Lucy has no other choice. If she dies anyway," he swallowed hard, "well, at least we did all we could, including having you try to get this thing out of her."

"And what if you change your mind? What's going to happen then?"

Will clasped my shoulder. I stared at him.

"We will never blame you, Jimmy. Never."

I jerked away. "You say that now, but people never know how they're going to react."

Will stared at me. "I'm going to be in the room, Jimmy. I'm going to help. How can I blame you if I'm in there doing the same work?"

I had no response to that. He wasn't exactly reliable. I couldn't help but think this was going to be one huge fiasco.

#

Tabby and I set ourselves up in the library early that night, before the others came to bed. Too much to do. I didn't know if I should study the ritual until I had it memorized, or if I should wing it. I swallowed hot water for the umpteenth time. I didn't have the church backing me up. I didn't have the knowledge. Now I wished I had gone to school to be an exorcist.

I tapped my pencil against my lips, staring at a blank piece of notebook paper.

"Are you going to need holy water?" Tabby asked.

I looked up. She was amazingly astute at times. "Actually, yeah. I do need some."

"Does it have to be your type of holy water, or can it be any type?"

I thought for a bit. It wasn't like I was going to be doing this by the book. "Honestly, I don't know. I mean, you always hear about it the Catholic way with the holy water I'm used to, but I have no reason to believe it wouldn't work with any other type. Why?"

She smiled. "Well, you can't get holy water from Father John 'cause he'll suspect. Isn't there something where you can't make holy water now?"

I nodded. "Because I'm not a priest, I can't make 'Catholic holy water.' I'm not supposed to be saying any rituals or masses at all."

"I can make holy water," she said.

I stared at her. It seemed lately Tabby was the answer to everything, but there was still so much about her I didn't understand. "How can you make holy water?"

"Witches and the Voudou do it all the time to cleanse areas and to fight bad things."

I tapped my pencil against the side of my chin. "What do you need to make it?"

"Prayers, rose petals, and vodka."

I dropped the pencil and about swallowed my tongue. "You put vodka in holy water?"

Tabby laughed. "In Voudou, vodka is an offering to Papa Legba."

My mouth froze in a straight line.

"Okay, okay," she said. "Papa Legba is the gatekeeper. Kind of like the equivalent to St. Peter, as far as I understand it."

"So why are you making an offering to this Papa guy?"

She chuckled. "You are so…," she put her hands on her hips when she stood up, "you, Jimmy Holiday. We want the gatekeeper to keep things from coming through the gate, so we put an offering to him in the water."

"Why the rose petals?"

She rolled her eyes at me. "Because, as you well know, roses are related to God. I think there was an old story about roses being the thorns in the crown Jesus wore during the crucifixion or something like that."

"I thought witches didn't believe in Jesus or didn't like Him."

She grinned. "I think we all worship the same being, Jimmy. I don't think the Supreme Being is male or female. I think it is what it is."

"Okay, so, do you have what you need?" I asked.

"Nope. I need rose petals—fresh rose petals, and vodka."

I sighed and settled back into the sofa. "I wish Tor and Will weren't counting on me so much."

"They count on you because they don't have anyone else they can count on."

"Doesn't make it any easier. It's not good, Tab."

She nodded. "No matter what, you have to figure out what you're going to do."

It was more like how I was going to do this. I was stumbling blindly through a field of thorny bushes. "You know my set of instructions equates to like a half-hour worth of prayer?"

"Seriously?" she asked.

"Yeah. I get a half-hour of instruction for something that is going to take weeks probably to deal with, maybe years."

Tabby gasped. "Years?"

"Yes. In Rome, people go to exorcists for years. It's not like how it is in the movies."

"I wish there was another option," she said.

"So do I." I gritted my teeth. "It's going to be dangerous, Tabby. If you want to back out, I'll understand."

"Jimmy, don't go all, 'I'm the man and you don't have to do anything cause I'm here to protect you' on me. I'm here because I chose to be. You need help. Maybe this is the way it's supposed to be?"

"Maybe," I said.

Tabby and I tried to relax. I stopped pouring over everything. The only thing I seemed to be doing was going crazy.

Tor came into the library carrying a chocolate layer cake.

"What on earth is this?" I asked her.

Will stood sheepishly behind Tor.

"I wanted to give you something, something to thank you," Tor said.

God help me. There was nothing worse than someone making a dessert at a time like this. All I wanted to do was swallow a few Rolaids, not eat a piece of chocolate cake likely to give me a headache.

"How thoughtful," Tabby said to Tor when she saw it.

Tor set the cake on the coffee table. Will grabbed a couple of chairs and brought them over, placing them on either end. Then he put plates, napkins and silverware on the table. Soon Tor had large chucks cut for each of us.

I swallowed bile. I hadn't even eaten dinner, and I didn't want cake, but it was one of those situations where you couldn't refuse. I smiled and choked down my piece. Setting the plate aside as easily as I could, I tried not to jostle. I could only hope my stomach would hold out. Outside it was getting dark.

"When are you going to start?" Will asked.

"Sure as hell isn't going to be tonight." I was trying not to puke. "I feel safer during the day. Besides, Tabby needs to get some supplies before we begin."

Tor's fingers began to shake a bit. Will took her hands to steady them.

This was getting harder and harder. The last thing I needed was to see how badly it was affecting them. If I was selfish, I would have had Tabby try to ward another room, but I couldn't do that.

Tabby looked a little green. The sugar influx hadn't done her any favors either.

Slowly, I sat up on the sofa. "Tor," I said. "As usual you've outdone yourself, but I can't eat stuff like this anymore."

Tor looked like I'd stomped her pet hamster. "I'm sorry, Jimmy. I didn't know you wouldn't like it."

I didn't have the stomach for sensitive anymore. I held up my hand. "That's why I didn't want to say anything. It's not your cooking, it's my stomach. I'm so nervous I'm about to puke, and now I got a slab of chocolate lying in there like a disgruntled wildebeest. It's my stomach, not your food."

Tor relaxed, but looked sheepish. "I cook when I'm nervous."

I raised my eyebrow.

She laughed. "No, I meant to say I cook *more* when I'm nervous."

"Well, I don't care if you cook things for us, but while we are doing this and preparing for it, I'm not going to be able to eat much."

"Why are we always talking about food?" Tabby asked. "I mean, we've got major shit going on, and we're sitting here talking about making food and eating or not eating."

I laughed. "Tabby, I think food is what we've focused on because

Tor cooks. Truth be told, we're all trying to avoid the pink elephant in the room as much as possible."

"Well, fuck the food," Tabby jumped from the sofa and walked over to one of the huge windows. "I'm scared, dammit, and it's not okay."

I got up and put my hand on Tabby's shoulder. "You know, it's okay to be scared. I'm scared. Tor and Will are scared. But you know who is the most scared?"

Tabby turned to me. "Who?"

I smiled sadly. "Lucy. She's scared to death. She sees what this thing is doing to her parents. All she wants is to have things go back to normal."

I heard a sob behind me. I turned around to see Tor's head buried in her hands and her chest heaving. I glanced back to Tabby. "You okay?"

"Yeah, I think it caught up with me."

#

Hours later, I reclined on the couch, still awake. It was one of those quiet nights, the ones that really scared the crap out of me because I knew it was building up and saving power for what was next.

I passed the hours reading the Roman Ritual. There was some comfort in reading the prayers, but it left me with a lot of doubts too. The ritual was short, too short. I don't know how the priests before me had managed to do what they did. Being a regular priest was easy. Being an exorcist wasn't. Jesus himself simply laid his hands on the possessed and told the demons to get lost—I wished I was that powerful, but I was just a man.

I drifted off to sleep.

Soon I was standing in the middle of a misty room. I'm not sure if it was a room or an expanse of mist with no walls. I stepped forward and heard a child's laughter, but nothing could be seen in the mist. Then, as if she appeared there, Lucy stood in front of me. The real Lucy. I could feel it was her.

I felt no fear, no nothing. Calm swept over me.

"Hi, Mr. Holiday," she said in a small voice.

I crouched. "Hello, Lucy."

She smiled shyly in the way little girls are apt to do. "He says for me to tell you that no matter what happens, it was meant to be."

It sounded odd coming from her mouth. She didn't sound like a six-year-old, but not in the demonic way. This was different. "He who?"

She grinned broader. "You know."

I shook my head and she returned it with a knowing look. Then she wandered off into the mist.

"Lucy, don't go," I called after her.

Very faintly, I heard her sing. "Jesus loves the little children…"

I jerked awake. The only sound to be heard was the ticking of the clock in the hallway.

Chapter Twenty-Seven

Beginnings

THE NEXT MORNING, Tabby and I traveled to find her supplies for the exorcism. It took about thirty miles to locate the place Tabby had seen on the internet—some sort of special new age store. I didn't mind. If it helped Lucy, what did I care? The items I needed for the exorcism — the vestments and everything else — had appeared on my sofa in the library. I didn't question how they got there. I knew I hadn't somehow packed them in my bag and then forgot. I hadn't had any of the garb in my possession since I'd left the priesthood. Was it divine intervention or something else? I had no one to ask. The only person who had been with me in the house had been Will and he definitely didn't have access to the garb. This one, I took on faith.

Tabby pulled into the parking lot of the store called "Pyewackett." I didn't ask.

I fiddled with my shirt and stared off into space as Tabby went in to gather her supplies. I was trying to gear up for what I had to do later. It wasn't as cold so I didn't bother turning the car back on.

Rap! Rap! Rap!

An old man with long greasy white hair stood beside the car, dressed in a caftan. He looked like something right out of the sixties.

I rolled down the window a bit. "Can I help you?"

The man shot me a cool grin. "You got the mark."

I blinked. What the hell? "What?"

The man pointed at me. "*You* got the mark."

I patted my body and gazed over every exposed piece of skin, but saw nothing. "The mark of what?" The guy wasn't playing with a full deck. His grin, I was sure, couldn't get any wider, but somehow it did.

"You know, *the mark*." The man gestured with his fingers like he was going to say "oogie boogie." "You can see the colors no one else sees. You witness the writing in the air no one feels, and you hear the noises others fear to hear. You got the mark."

I raised an eyebrow. "How do you know I have, 'the mark?'

He grinned again. "We markers know other markers."

I sighed. This kook was pretty damn different. Now how he knew I could do any of that, I had no idea. And this mark thing made no sense. "What do 'markers' do?"

He stared at me, his smile dropping into a stoic mask. "You'll see."

With that, he raced away as if the Devil were on his heels.

I jumped out of the car, trying to follow him. Running around the building, I kept trying to catch up, but something seemed to stop me. When I got to the back, I searched everywhere. He should have been there. He wasn't.

I ambled to the car, catching my breath. As if I didn't have enough on my plate, now I had psychos telling me I was part of some weird secret society. I wanted to chalk it all up to a ration of bullshit, but I couldn't do that. There was no way he could have known about what I could see. No plausible explanation for that at all.

A piece of paper stuck out from under Tabby's windshield wiper. It read, "Jesus Saves."

"This is getting ridiculous," I mumbled.

I climbed inside and slumped in the passenger's seat. Soon Tabby came out with a large bag.

"Got everything you need?" I asked.

"I think so."

I didn't bother telling her anything about what had happened. It was all too unbelievable. And I had much more important things to worry about—like the soul of a little girl.

"Do you smell something?" Tabby asked.

I sniffed, there was a foul odor. "Yeah, it doesn't smell good."

Tabby got back out of the car and walked around to the front of it. "Sweet Cartwheeling Jesus!"

I rolled down my window. "What?"

"Somebody shit in front of my car! How did you not notice?" She stared at me, her eyes darkening.

I jumped out. "It must have happened when I was gone."

She shot me a glare. "Gone? Where were you?"

I sighed. "I guess I wasn't paying attention. There was this guy… I don't know."

Tabby grumbled and buckled into the driver's seat. "You really are ridiculous sometimes, you know that?"

I kept quiet. Now was not the time to explain about the man, and there was a part of me, a pretty large part, that knew it was possible he'd taken a dump in front of the car. How had I missed the smell?

We rode back to the house in silence. I wanted to tell Tabby the truth, but it was bad enough I was distracted by the whole thing. I didn't need her distracted too.

"Hungry?" she asked.

"Yeah, kinda."

She seemed relaxed, her anger gone. "No offense to Tor, but I'm getting tired of gourmet food."

I snickered. "So what are we getting?"

"Grease. Something with lots of grease."

#

When we pulled into the drive of the house after our grease filled meal, I gripped her arm gently.

"What?" she asked.

"How long will it take you to make the holy water?"

She cast a lopsided smile at me. "How long did it take you to make holy water?"

I shrugged. "I dunno. A few minutes anyway. The prayers took more time."

"Same here, except I have to crush the rose petals and add vodka."

"Vodka. If the church could see me now."

Tabby snorted. "It could be worse."

I couldn't imagine it getting any worse. "How so?"

She hopped out of the car and snatched her bag. I followed.

"I could be telling you to piss on a coconut and kick it out the front door yelling, 'Get the fuck out of my house!'"

I stared.

She grinned. "See?"

When we came in, Tor was sitting at the kitchen table, coffee cup at her side, reading the Bible. Of all the people I would have expected to be reading the Bible, Tor wasn't it.

"Where's Will?" I asked.

She glanced up from the book. "Getting drunk in the library."

Tabby set her bag on the table. I stayed where I was—right near the counter.

"Did something happen?" Tabby asked.

Tor wiped at her eye. "We went to fix up Lucy's feeding tube."

I left the protection of the counter and stepped forward. "Okay."

"Lucy was levitating."

"What? How?" Tabby asked.

"I could see underneath her body when I changed the bag for her feeding tube. She…she was levitating as far as the chains would let her."

I nodded. "So why is Will getting drunk?"

Tor slammed her Bible shut. I winced.

"Because he's an asshole! 'Can't take it,' he said." She pushed the book across the table. "Am I the only one that sees that there's a huge problem if he's supposed to help with the exorcism?"

I sat in the chair beside her. Tabby started unloading her bag to make the holy water.

"If he's drunk, he's not going in that room," I said. "He'll be vulnerable, and that sets him up for possession. I'm not taking that chance."

"That means I have to do it," Tor said. "Damn him."

I shook my head. "You don't have to be there. I'm doing the exorcism now. Tabby is going to be there. If you want to see, you can watch the monitor on the security system."

Her shoulders slumped. "Thank God." She got up, gripped her Bible, and stowed it in a drawer in the center island.

"Do you have a large pot I can use?" Tabby asked, holding up the roses. "Making holy water."

Tor pulled a large stock pot out of the pantry. "This okay?"

It was the biggest damn stock pot I'd ever seen, something meant for restaurant use.

"That's perfect." Tabby's eyes widened with excited energy.

Tor handed it to Tabby and turned to me. "Why aren't you making the holy water?"

I smiled. "I'm not a priest."

Tor sighed. "I'm going to pretend that makes sense."

She sat in her chair while Tabby got to work. It went pretty quickly, at least the mixing of water, vodka, and rose petals. Then the prayers began. Tor watched, seeming fascinated. I was interested too, but for a different reason. With each prayer or spell she recited, I saw a layer of color appear on the holy water then slowly fade away. It brought me back to this *mark* thing. I couldn't ignore it. When Tabby stopped her ritual, I decided I needed to talk.

"Have you ever been to that store before?" I asked her.

Tabby raised her eyebrow at me. "Why?"

"While you were inside, this old guy with long hair spoke to me."

Tabby giggled. "What?"

"Never mind," I said.

"Okay, weird old guy, check," she said. "Keep going."

"He talked about things. Stuff with magic." I sighed. "He said, and I quote, 'You have the mark.'"

She pursed her lips together. "What mark?"

"That's just it, I don't know."

"Jimmy, after all of this is over, I think you need a nice holiday."

I slumped in my chair. "I don't even know why I bother."

Tabby patted me on the head. "Be a good little exorcist and get ready."

#

Climbing the steps to Lucy's room as an exorcist was far different than before. It was like the mere thought of what I was about to do was so oppressive I could hardly breathe.

I reached into my pants' pocket. Yes, my rosary was there. In my other side, there was a flask of holy water—it was the best I'd been able to do under the circumstances. Over the top of my regular clothes, I wore the vestments and the purple stole. Like a kid dressed up for Halloween. When the clothes appeared, I hadn't put much thought into it. And no one at the house even had access to a church to get them. I chalked it up to someone, maybe the real Lucy, trying to help me.

I looked ridiculous, hell I felt ridiculous. Here I was, wearing a suit coat borrowed from Will, a white T-shirt, and a pair of jeans. Over this I wore a collar and a purple stole. I felt like a clown.

Strange growls seemed to float along the walls as Tabby and I walked. I paused in the middle of the staircase.

"What's wrong?" Tabby asked.

"I'm supposed to confess before the exorcism."

"Does it have to be to a priest?"

I laughed a little. "We're not exactly doing this by the book anyway."

She nodded. "Okay, what do you have to confess?"

I sighed. "I've had impure thoughts about you. I've been angry with Will because of his weaknesses, I've been short of patience with Tor, and I have wanted to run from this."

She smirked then forced the smile away. "Is that all?"

"Yes."

"Okay, you've confessed. Let's go."

I took a deep breath and started back up the stairs. The sounds continued. Then, a smell so foul I gagged met us on the landing. It was sulfuric and had an undertone of rotten meat.

"What is that?" Tabby asked.

"The smell of the demon." I'd been so sure when we started the climb. "It does these things to show us its power. It wants us to doubt our abilities."

"Don't listen to it," she said.

"I won't. Neither should you."

When we got to her door, I stopped and turned to Tabby. "Bow your head."

She stared at me, but didn't question it. I closed my eyes.

"Saint Michael, the Archangel, defend us in battle; be our defense against the wickedness and snares of the devil. May God rebuke him, we humbly pray; and do thou, O Prince of the heavenly host, by the power of God, thrust into Hell Satan and the other evil spirits who prowl about the world for the ruin of souls. Amen."

"Amen," Tabby said quietly.

I took a deep breath then turned and opened the door to Lucy's room. She was levitating against the chains.

"Hello, Priest," Lucy said.

Tabby and I stepped inside. It was cold enough to see our breath, and yet, Lucy was covered in sweat.

"Hello, Lucy," I said.

"Lucy isn't here anymore, Mr. Holiday," it said. "But you already knew that."

Tabby and I sat on the floor around the bed.

"I don't know if Lucy is in there or not, but I have faith that she is."

It cackled. "Poiba Toohnyet sgoloveh."

I shook my head. "I don't speak Russian."

It grinned. Its bloody eyes seemed to glow. "Shall I translate for you?"

"Yes."

"A fish rots from the head down. God is dead, we are in power now."

I grunted. "Lies, demon. All you can do is tell lies."

It laughed again. "I have more truth than you know."

I began to pray. "Our Father who—"

It thrashed against the bed. "Fuck you! Fuck you!"

"Art in Heaven. Hallowed be thy name! Thy Kingdom come! Thy will be done on Earth as it is in Heaven!"

It snarled and spat at Tabby. A blood clot landed on her face. She grimaced, but wiped it away with a tissue.

"Give us this day our daily bread. And forgive us our trespasses as we forgive those who trespass against us. Lead us not into temptation, but deliver us from Evil. Amen."

Lucy flopped around on the bed. Her eyes rolled into the back of her head. Her mouth hung open. And then, diarrhea began spilling from her mouth onto the floor.

"Is that possible?" Tabby asked.

"Normally no, but this is the demon."

It laughed. "Your sister said to tell you, 'Hello.'"

I froze then whispered, "How is she?" Stupid. I shouldn't have asked, but it slipped out. Dammit. I needed to be more careful.

It smirked, poor Lucy's brown teeth rotted to black. "She's hanging around."

There was no way Lucy could have known my sister hanged herself, no way in hell. The demon struck low and hard. I refused to be swayed from saving Lucy.

"What is your name?" I asked it with as much force as I could muster into the question.

It let loose a horrendous howl of laughter. "You didn't think it would be that easy, did you?"

The feces disappeared. It had all been a parlor trick. "Cheap tactic."

Lucy's eyes snapped toward me as if it knew exactly what I was thinking. "You don't want to get me angry now, do you?"

I changed courses. "Is Mr. Black around?"

It smiled again. "He's around. She's around. We're all around."

Tabby waved for my attention and pointed to the Roman Ritual.

I had lost my place. I didn't know what I was doing. I was in way over my head. I got up and placed a hand on Lucy's forehead.

"I exorcise you, Most Unclean Spirit!"

It cackled at me again. "You are pathetic."

"What is your name?" I couldn't give into it. Tabby put her hand on my shoulder.

I stared down the demon, willing it to do what I wished.

Lucy turned her head toward me. "I am the one who has control. I am the one who feeds, feeds on the flesh and the blood of the life while you are the one who bleeds."

I threw holy water across the demon in the shape of the cross. Blisters appeared on Lucy's skin where the water hit. There was a sound so strange, I didn't know what it was at first. Then I identified it and my heart sunk. It was the sound of a child crying.

I glared at the demon inside the child. "What is your name?"

"I want my mommy!" It wailed.

I'd been waiting for this trick. Too soon, too easy. I crept closer to the bed. "What is your name?"

It tried to punch me, but I wasn't close enough.

"What's wrong?" I purposefully antagonized it. "Used too much energy?"

It growled so loud it shook the house. "Lucy goosy likes to eat pussy." It grinned at me with the sweetest of smiles. The bloody eyes and the black teeth spoiled that effect.

"When are you going to stop playing this game, Black?"

It stared at me.

"I'm not stupid you know," I said. "You are the flesh eater, you are the one who likes to make people bleed."

"Oh you silly thing," it said. "I was in Mr. Black. His soul is long gone."

"How am I to believe that, if you haven't given me your name?"

"Tricky, tricky." Then it closed its eyes and pretended to sleep.

Tabby and I left the room.

"Round one over, I guess," I said.

"What do we do next time?" Tabby asked.

"Same damn thing. That's what an exorcism is, a battle of wills between the demonic and the exorcist."

"So what do we do now?" she asked.

"Prepare for round two."

Chapter Twenty-Eight

Take Two

AFTER A BREAK, Tabby and I headed upstairs again. No foul smell permeated the air this time. I opened the door and switched on the overhead light. Lucy was sitting up in bed. She watched us come into the room with those awful eyes of hers. The blood overtook all the white, leaving dark black pupils and circles of red.

"Good evening, Lucy," I said.

"Where am I, Jimmy?" she asked, but it wasn't Lucy's voice, and it wasn't the demon's.

"Who are you?"

Lucy buried her head in her hands. "How could you? You let him do this to me. Why?"

Then I knew. The damn demon was copying again. It was pretending to be my sister. While that sank a cold, hard pit in my gut, it bothered me more that the demon was resorting to using tricks again. It was old and redundant. And it pissed me off.

"Candy is dead, Lucy," I blinked away the tears that were already forming.

It smiled. "But she's with us, Priest. She's always been with us. Suicide is a direct trip to Hell."

I stepped backward. The blood drained from my face and my palms started to sweat.

It laughed.

I motioned for Tabby to sit. She did. I followed. We took position at the end of the bed on the floor, facing Lucy. It was time for the real fight to begin.

"One, God does not punish the mentally ill. Two, give it up. You are more original than that."

"But you can't be sure," she said in a sing-song voice.

"Candy has been gone for almost twenty years. The Candy I knew was dead before she killed herself."

"If you let us take you, you could see her again."

"I can see her anytime I want. She's here," I patted my chest."I remember her."

"And you," it turned to Tabby, "don't you think God is overjoyed an itchy witch is trying to chase me out. Evil can't move evil."

"I'm not evil," she said.

It cackled. "You know the words, 'Thou shalt not suffer a witch to live!'"

Tabby's eyes narrowed. "Too bad that was a poor translation. The original text doesn't say that at all. That passage talks about charlatans who charge money. They want to bilk people out of their riches by proclaiming to know the future or do spells for them to make them wealthy. It doesn't apply to me."

"Oh really?" It moved the index finger of her right hand around. An image appeared, hovering over her head. "Itchy witchy thinks she's smart. She thinks she's good at heart, but her heart is marred by the devil's lie, making her sure to die." As she said the riddle, a little Tabby replica walked across the bed until a large hand squashed her to nothing.

"That isn't scary," Tabby stood stoically.

I was proud of her.

"Not scary?" The hooded figure appeared, looming over her.

Tabby jerked away and backed up. It floated across the floor toward her.

I rose and blocked its path. "Back."

It paused.

"Back," I said. I held my hand high. A beam of green light shot out of my palm and wound around the dark figure like a rope. It surprised the hell out of me, but I kept going. I had to protect Tabby. I had to save Lucy. I couldn't stop. "You will do no more bidding for the thing that lives inside Lucy. Back!"

The figure rippled and disappeared.

"Jimmy, what the hell?" Tabby asked.

"I'm…" I stared at my hand where the light had radiated only moments ago. The man in the parking lot, his words came to my mind. It was true. "I'm a marker."

It squealed like a pig.

I had the upper hand. Time to use the advantage. "What is your name?"

It flopped on the bed and rolled around.

Tabby took me by the shoulder. "We need to talk later."

It sat back up. "Talk now, I won't bite."

I sighed, no longer afraid. Strength flowed through me like water. "You know, you're a little pedantic."

It flung me across the room without touching me. My head hit the wall, the pain crushing. My sight dimmed.

"You stop that!" Tabby snatched a pouch from her pocket. "You evil--" She threw holy water on it.

It screamed.

I sat up, my head swimming. It was attempting to fling Tabby like it'd done to me, but somehow Tabby remained rooted to her spot. I could see red light bouncing off her. I focused on it and attempted to stretch my power toward her.

"No!" Tabby yelled.

I stopped.

"Don't link with her mind, it will get you," Tabby said.

While Tabby's attention focused on me, it threw Lucy's IV pole at Tabby, hitting her in the head.

Tabby cried out. A gash opened on her forehead. Blood ran into her eyes. She fell over unconscious.

I jumped up and sprung over to Tabby. She went still. I felt for a pulse, grateful to find one, but the fear rose in me like prickling pins. I had to push it down.

I glared at the demon. "You son of a bitch!"

It smiled. "Not nice words for a priest."

I stood up and smacked it across the face. "I'm not a priest!"

The whole room shook. It felt as if the earth shifted and then righted itself again. I fell and covered Tabby's body with my own.

Someone knocked at the door.

"Don't come in, whatever you do, don't come in."

They ignored me. Will came bursting into the room, staring at Lucy.

"I came to take Tabby to the Emergency Room. I saw everything on the monitor."

The shaking ceased.

It let us leave the room with Tabby. After Will and I got Tabby into the car, I went back in with Tor and helped her clean up Lucy's broken IV and fix the feeding tube for the night. The entire time, it watched me with a huge grin on its face.

Before we left the room, it said, "You're all alone now, Priest."

I shut the door.

Chapter Twenty-Nine

Solution

1950

"IT'S HAPPENED BEFORE, you know?" the demon said.

The old priest stood up straighter, his wizened hands hanging loosely at his sides. "What is it you are referring to?"

The darkness of the room drifted into one corner. The bookcase behind was visible now, and the silver objects glowed with a faint blue light. "Many have tried and failed, Priest."

The old priest reached into the breast pocket of his coat and pulled out a flask of holy water.

"Do you really think that will hurt me?" it asked.

The priest threw the water on the darkness in the corner of the room. Wind began to blow, tossing books from the shelves.

The priest searched the room—and then, a hand landed on his shoulder. He whipped around. Mr. Black's ruined face stared at him. "You didn't think it would be that easy, now did you?"

The priest swallowed. "This will not scare me. There is nothing frightening about the dead."

The broken face smiled at him. "And the undead?"

The black mass surrounded the priest and covered him. The pain was massive, like a large pole rammed down his throat. He didn't even have time to scream.

The priest's body slumped to the floor. The visage of Black disappeared. The darkness disintegrated. The laughter ceased.

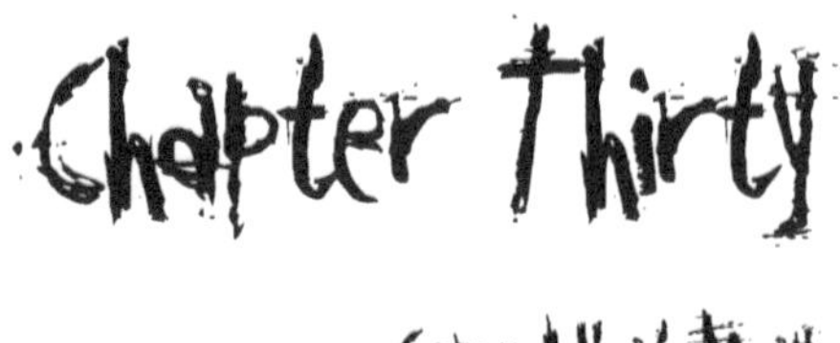

Chapter Thirty

Come What May

TOR AND I sat in the kitchen. She couldn't stop moving around. When she'd gotten up and wiped the counter for the fourth time, I couldn't take it anymore.

"Stop," I said. "You're making me nervous."

She plopped down at the table. "I'm so sorry about Tabby."

I nodded. "She'll be okay. Will called and told me she came to on the way to the hospital. If they don't release her tonight, they will tomorrow."

"I didn't mean for anyone to get hurt," she said.

"It could be worse. At least she wasn't seriously injured." I was beyond thankful that the thing inside Lucy hadn't killed her. I had had about enough of all of this. Things had changed. It had hurt someone I loved.

I pulled out my phone and checked for a text from Tabby, but there was nothing.

Tor sighed. "My Lucy's going to die, isn't she?"

I grabbed Tor's hand. "Stop talking like that. We know nothing. I'm doing what I can. If it doesn't work, you can wait for the church's exorcist."

Tor covered her mouth with her hand and cried out. "I don't think she'll last that long."

"When is her next CAT scan?"

"I canceled it. I can't risk anyone else getting hurt."

#

When Will came back with Tabby in tow, I jumped up and hugged her. I couldn't help myself.

Tabby coughed. "I need to breathe sometime."

I let her loose and chuckled.

"She's supposed to stay awake for the next twenty-four hours to make sure she doesn't have a concussion. The tests were inconclusive," Will said.

"That won't be a problem." I pointed my finger at Tabby. "No more exorcism for you."

Tabby jumped up. We had to grab her as she almost fell.

"Dammit, Tabby," I said. "You got hurt. Enough already."

"But don't you need witnesses?"

I put my hand on her shoulder. "I have the camera. All three of you can watch the feed. That's three witnesses."

"No more tonight," she said.

"No, not tonight. I'm going to keep you up for twenty-four hours. Lucy can wait."

Tabby looked me in the eyes. "I hope so."

We all hunkered in the library for the night.

Tabby sat on the sofa. "What do you think is going to happen tonight?"

I scratched my head and finished chewing. "I don't know."

Will and Tor were listening, but they had sequestered themselves to the other side of the library playing chess. I glanced over. Even though they looked like they were playing, I could tell that they were listening to the conversation—no one had made a move.

"What are you going to do?" Tabby asked.

I shrugged. "The best I can, I guess. I mean, it's not like I can do anything else."

"Well, tomorrow we'll—"

"No," I glared at Tabby. "You are not going back in with it. I don't care if I have to drag Will in there whining like a baby. You are not going."

Tabby shook her head. "How else are you to trap the demon, genius?"

She had a point. I was flying by the seat of my pants. The only thing I seemed to know how to do was piss the demon off. I hadn't gotten it to do anything, let alone tell us its name.

"I could always move the site of the exorcism," I said. The energy in the room increased and seemed to crackle around us.

"What are you talking about?" Tabby asked.

"I could move the exorcism into the attic."

It seemed like time stopped. I could hear nothing, no wind outside, no ticking of the clock, I couldn't even hear them breathe.

"What?" I asked.

Tabby stared at me. "That's either the stupidest thing you've ever said, or you are a freaking genius."

I sighed. "The way I figure it, if I manage to get it out of Lucy, then it will jump the ley line and get the hell out of here."

"What if Lucy brings other things in?"

"That hasn't stopped it in her room. I don't see what difference that would make in the attic. Anyways, I can do the green ball thing."

Tabby stared at me like there was something wrong with me. "What green ball thing?"

I pointed. "Up in Lucy's room, the hooded thing. You didn't see it?"

"Oh, I saw the hooded thing all right. I saw you yell at it until it left. I saw no green ball thing."

I scrunched in my chair. "That must be my marker stuff."

Tabby sighed at me. "I think you are losing your mind, I really do."

"Tabby, when was I ever sane?" I chuckled.

She grinned. "Good point."

"The marker stuff. Even I don't know what it is exactly. That old guy—the one that probably shit in front of your car, talked about the things I'd been doing lately."

She raised an eyebrow. "What things?"

"Seeing the colors of your magic."

#

Will and Tor went to sleep sometime before eleven. Tabby and I sat on her sofa, reading. I looked up now and again to make sure she was still awake. So far, there had been no problems. She seemed okay, and I was thankful for that.

Finally, Tabby caught me staring at her. She peered out over the top of her book. "Are you really going to do it?"

"Yeah," I said. "I think it's reached the point of no return. Even if

I quit now, the demon knows us and would try to come after us someday."

"How are you going to do it this time? Are you still going to use the Roman Ritual?"

"No. It doesn't seem to be working too well for me. I can't do parts of it and I don't feel right wearing the vestments. You kind of need those to do it the Catholic way."

"Why don't you feel comfortable?" She set her book on the coffee table.

"Once you give up the priesthood, you can't wear the uniform. Think about a cop who is no longer a cop. They aren't supposed to wear the uniform. It's against the law, considered impersonating a police officer."

Tabby tapped her chin. "Well, maybe you need a different ritual."

"And where am I going to find that?"

"You don't have to. We're going to write one." She leaned over and dug around in her bag. She came up with a notebook and pen.

I sat up, my book dropped to my lap. "We are?"

"We are. To do magic you don't need a special outfit," she said. "A lot of people work skyclad."

I raised an eyebrow. "Is that what I think it is?"

Tabby smiled.

"I am not doing an exorcism nude."

She laughed. "I don't expect you to. Clean clothes will do."

"All right, what else?"

"Evidence of the four corners. North, south, east, and west. Earth, air, fire, and water."

"I don't know about this."

She snorted. "It's better than your plan of winging it."

I felt sheepish as hell. She'd nailed me. I had nothing left. I was intending to yell at the demon. "Okay, I'll trust you."

#

When it was my turn to sleep, it didn't take long to crash. The dream began as a scene. I was in the kitchen of Blackmoor. The cabinets were wooden with crisscrossed slats over the glass so you could see the china inside. In the center of the room, a large rectangular table stretched the length of the kitchen. There was no center island. A baby sat in an old fashioned wooden high chair.

A pretty brunette was running around the kitchen, fixing something. She stopped, almost like she sensed me. Bruises circled both of her eyes. She was as thin as a corpse and the severe black dress she wore did nothing to take away that impression. Holding her finger to her lips, she whispered, "Shhh. It will hear you."

Spinning wildly, she finally centered on me. Her walk was in fits and starts—like she would appear at different points as she moved forward. She pointed toward the ceiling.

"Don't take her there."

"Why?" I asked.

"You know."

I jerked awake. "Jesus Christ."

#

When I woke up a second time, Tor and Tabby were sitting on the sofa, watching me sleep.

I rose. "What time is it?"

"About six," Tor said.

I got up, went over to the chair where Will was sleeping and kicked his foot.

His eyes popped open.

"Come on, bucky. We've got work to do."

He sat up, wiped the sleep out of his eyes and stood.

"Let's go," I said.

We made a stop at the garage so Will could get some tools. Then we headed upstairs. Lucy's room was cold, but there were no foul smells, no sounds. Lucy appeared to be sleeping. Will and I dismantled the camera system. She never woke. We left the room and closed the door.

"That was uneventful," Will said.

I hit him on the arm. "Don't jinx us."

We headed toward the attic, flipping on lights as we went. The covered furniture inside looked like an army of ghosts. Of course the bulb was burned out to the little room. I took a deep breath and opened the door to what was going to become my battlefield. This time, instead of magical artifacts scattered around the room, I saw projectiles Lucy could throw at me. "I need a big box."

"Why?" Will asked.

I pointed around the room. "Too much stuff."

Will set the camera equipment aside, grabbed a box, upended it, and dumped the contents onto the floor.

After that box and two others, we had all of the crap out of the room.

Sweat dripped off my brow. Will wasn't in much better shape.

"Let's do this," I said.

We hooked up the camera, and after a few trips downstairs, we got the wireless feed working properly.

"Fuck, I need more sleep."

Will stared at me. "You don't have to do this today, you know?"

"Yeah, I do. I don't want to drag it out any longer than it needs to be."

"You could take a nap," he said.

I chuckled. "No need. If I don't make it, I'll get all the sleep I'll ever need."

As I walked to the library, I remembered I had used my last set of clean clothes the day before. When I entered the room, I found my clothing out of my bag, clean, and folded on my sofa. They must have done them while Will and I were getting the camera fixed. "Thank God for women."

I changed clothes, grasped the items Tabby had set out for me—a bottle of holy water, a feather, a candle, and a rock. I put the pages of the ritual we had written in my pocket. I yawned. I didn't know what to make of that dream. Could that have been Mrs. Black? The one who'd been eaten. Warning me away from the room was kind of sweet in a way for a ghost, but I had no choice anymore.

I knelt in front of the window. "Heavenly Father, give me the strength to do this. If someone has to die, let it be me. Lucy has a whole life to live."

And then, I heard a whisper. "It will be all right, Mr. Holiday."

The voice, the whisper, it was the same I had heard days before. It was the voice of Lucy—her true voice.

I took a deep breath and left the room. After this, if I survived it, I was going to need therapy.

"Got any hooks we can screw into the floor?" I asked.

After a trip to the garage again, we had our supplies. "Where do you want it?"

I pointed to the far corner. We screwed the latch to the floor. The steel end flipped up so that the chains could be passed through it.

I grabbed the mirror from outside the room and put it inside the door.

"Ready to get Lucy?" Will asked.

"As ready as we'll ever be," I said.

We got into Lucy's room as she was waking. When her father walked to the side of her bed, her eyes went wide.

"What are you doing?" it asked.

I smiled. "We are taking you where you want to go."

"And where is that, Priest?"

I smiled. "To the room in the attic."

It visibly relaxed. "You'll have to take the chains off the bed to do that."

I nodded. "Yes, but remember if you do anything to either one of us, you can't make it to the attic room."

Its eyes narrowed then relaxed. "As you wish."

Chapter Thirty-One

Sweet Release

I UNDID THE chains from Lucy's handcuffs. They clinked in a way that sounded final. It wasn't a usual sound, more like an old iron gate being closed. Will detached Lucy's feeding tube, took her in his arms, and walked out. I followed behind with the chains. Lucy kept her word. She was completely docile, allowing Will to carry her without any problems. When we entered the attic, Will let me go first. I attached the chains to the latch screwed to the floor. I doubled them up so Lucy couldn't get too far. We set Lucy on the floor while I attached her handcuffs to the chains.

Will stepped away.

"Do you want to stay?" I asked. His face turned pasty white and dripped with sweat.

Will shook his head. "How long do you think this will take?"

"I don't know. About an hour or two."

The demon's laughter encompassed the room.

"All right." He left, closing the door behind him.

I stared up at the camera. The green light was on, indicating it was recording. This was it. The nervousness in my stomach made my guts rumble. I turned to peer at the demon inside Lucy. It was sitting up, smiling sweetly—or what it considered sweet. It looked damn freaky to me like a lion about to pounce on an antelope.

"Why do you like this room so much?" I asked.

It snarled at me. "It is a place of power."

My heart began thumping in my chest. I could feel the vibration through my sternum. I took a deep breath and pulled the items out of my pocket.

The room was bright. The early morning sun shone through the dormer windows. At least, due to the sun, I could tell where east was. I set up my magic circle with salt the way Tabby had told me to do, doing my best to make a semi-correct circle on the floor with me in the middle.

Numerous clawing sounds skittered around the walls. The scratching echoed. I paused. The circle was not complete yet, and the theatrics were already beginning. For a moment, I wondered if there was more than one demon in Lucy, and then I remembered—Lucy was a mimic.

"You don't think that circle will save you, do you?" it asked.

I stared at it. Again, it was smiling. I finished the circle, ignoring it. I set the items where the four corners should be and began calling the corners in the clockwise fashion.

It rolled its eyes at me. "You're doing it wrong. Widdershins is most powerful."

I shook my head. This demon was trying to get me to do evil. Tabby had explained to me that counter-clockwise was the way of black magic.

"Who are you?" I asked.

It smiled. "You know my name. It's in your book."

I sat in the middle of the circle, and brushed the excess salt off my hands. "Which book?"

It snarled. "Your religion."

This thing was so entrenched in Lucy, it couldn't even say anything holy—anything to do with God. "Okay, you mean the Bible?"

It spat a gob of bloody phlegm at me. The mucus didn't reach. It bounced off the invisible shield of the circle, except it wasn't invisible to me; it glowed a pale blue.

My heart hammered hard in my chest. *Lub Dub. Lub Dub. Lub Dub.* The electricity rose in the room. I had to begin.

"Hail to the guardians. Guardians of light, strength, hope and peace. Hear my call."

It snarled. The room shook with a massive rumbling. "This is boring."

The floorboards groaned.

I paused. When nothing else happened, I continued, "By the power of three times three, save this little girl. Send her soul back to her, back to the light. Expel the dark one. Bind him, hold him, keep him from others for a thousand years."

It growled. The walls creaked and rattled. My bottle of holy water fell over. The sunlight had dimmed. Almost like darkness was taking over the room. The sun was trying to come through, but the blackness canceled it out. It got darker and darker until the only light that could be seen was from the four candles in the circle.

"Bind me!" it screamed.

Wind blasted around the room like a tornado. The force pulled at me, but so far it didn't move me.

It held its hands over its head. The light flickered in the room, jumping back and forth from the complete darkness to the sunlight and back again. The demon's face clenched. The skin stretched over the cheeks so tightly I thought it might tear. It grimaced hard. The teeth broke further and a few fragments fell out of its mouth.

The gusts picked up. I toppled over and the force of the winds pushed me across the floor until I slammed into the barrier of the magic circle. My head swam, my mouth dried, and my skin felt like it was going to be ripped from my body. I don't know why the wind could come into the magic circle, but the demon and I were separated by it.

Then the child became the demon. The skin rippled as if something was underneath it. When the rippling stopped, its skin appeared scaled. It snarled and the breath came out like green steam. The smell that radiated from it was like a cross between curdled milk and charred human flesh. The pupils of its eyes elongated—the eyes of a viper.

I forced myself to stand against the wind, but it was too strong.

"No one will bind me. No one will bind Asmodeus!"

The plaster of the ceiling cracked and bent. The howling of the wind deafened me. It stood up, somehow not bothered by the wind at all. Its hair didn't even move. Its mouth opened as if it was laughing, but I could hear nothing but the wind.

I forced my foot through the salt, breaking the circle. I paused, keeping my footing. The wind forced my feet to scuff along the floor until I slammed against the wall. I searched around for the mirror. Then I saw it being forced across the floor by the brutal gales. I gathered what will I had and thrust my hand out against the force and managed to grab it. "Leave her!"

Asmodeus snarled and began to levitate. "This cunt is mine."

The squalls blew harder until I was pressed into the wall with such force I could barely breathe. I held on to the mirror as best as I could. Something invisible pried my fingers away from it—one by one. And then, the blasts ripped the mirror from my grasp.

The wind stopped. I stepped away from the wall. The demon held the mirror in Lucy's small hands.

My heart pounded fast and hard like a beat machine turned up to the highest speed. A great booming vibrated around the room. Lucy gagged and coughed. Three iron nails fell from her mouth, covered in bloody mucus. It smiled then looked at me. "Shall I gut you, Priest? Dig these little hands in deep?"

I stood there. My feet planted to the floor. I stared it in the bloody eyes. "You won't be gutting me or anyone else."

It laughed, deep and rough. It echoed in my brain and I bent over, the pain of the echo resounding like an explosion. I fought the pain and stood again, forcing myself to push it aside. I held up my hand and made the sign of the cross. "Leave her, you foul being. You denizen of the deep, teller of lies, face of many. You are not welcome here!"

It howled with laughter. "All said to me before. Can't you come up with anything original?"

I wasn't sure how much longer I could take it. It was pulling me toward something dark. The tentacles of such evil reached inside me. "Lead me not into temptation…"

"Oh you'll get more than temptation when I'm done with you. Your sister knows all about that."

I rose up taller. Sweat ran down the back of my neck. I closed my eyes, centering my focus. When I opened my eyes again, something had shifted. My heart calmed. My mind cleared. The world seemed to have stilled.

"Leave her!" The ripples of the force of my scream beat through the air in vivid colors and streams.

It dropped the mirror. The glass shattered across the floor.

"Leave this world for your own. Leave the world of light. Leave this pure child of God!"

"Fucking priests!" it said.

A shard of glass streamed from the frame of the mirror.

I jumped and pressed my back into the wall. I threw my hands over my face, expecting the glass to come flying at me.

The demon would kill me. I knew it.

I heard a loud thump and a bump.

I lowered my hands. Lucy fell to the floor. The shard of glass had been driven through her left eye. Blood spread around her body in a pool. She was dead. The demon had arranged it all.

"Stupid, stupid priest. The girl is ours!" Asmodeus' voice echoed throughout the air.

I howled in rage—my voice sending light, white light around the room. Everywhere my voice reached, the darkness seemed to run from it. Impulsively, I felt my legs travel toward Lucy's body. I made the sign of the cross on her forehead with my finger.

Bang.

The room returned to normal. The darkness had faded.

"It's over, Jimmy," the whispering voice spoke to me. "You've done well."

I glanced around the room. There was no one there. "But she died!"

A hand rested on my shoulder that I could not see.

"Her soul is marked. You marked her. As long as her soul is marked, the Devil cannot do anything with it."

I gazed at my shoulder. Depressions appeared in my shirt where invisible fingers touched me. "But what will happen to Lucy?"

"She'll stay with you until I can reclaim her. I've needed another marker for a long time."

My mouth hung open. "Are you God?"

I heard a soft chuckle. "No, his servant like you. I take care of the gates."

"Peter?" I asked, but then the light in the room dimmed.

I collapsed. My legs no longer wanted to support me. I had lost, but I hadn't failed. It didn't make it any better.

Without thinking, I turned back to Lucy, mentally preparing for the sight of her dead body. My eyelids flicked closed. I needed another second, or two, or three. A soft sound invaded my mind. Some whistling noise like…breathing! I snapped my eyes open. Lucy's chest began rising and falling.

"Will!" I jumped up and ripped open the door. "Goddammit Will, call nine-one-one!"

I hit the alarm button on the recording device outside the door. Then I ran back into the room, took off my shirt, and wrapped it around Lucy's head. I had to slow the bleeding.

I heard a giggle then spun around. A beautiful Lucy stood in the corner. "I'm okay, silly."

I swallowed hard and spied the flashing lights outside the window a few minutes later. Would they believe how it happened at all?

Chapter Thirty-Two

The Sweet Sound of Silence

THE FOOTSTEPS POUNDED up the stairs. Lucy was still breathing, but the other Lucy, the perfect one, stood over in the corner dancing. Every so often she would wave at me.

"Mr. Holiday?" I glanced at the doorway, a uniformed officer stood at the entry. "I'm Sheriff Bedecki."

"Where are the emergency people? She's bleeding too much."

The sheriff nodded. "I had to make sure nothing crazy was going on." He picked up his walkie-talkie and spoke into it. "Bring 'em on up. Scene's safe."

As soon as the EMT's got there, I left Lucy to them. She had a better chance to survive—even if her soul was separated from her body. They put her on a stretcher after they stabilized her as best as they could and took her out of the room.

A tingling sensation burned across my right wrist. When I looked down, an odd tattoo of a cross encircled with seven words in a language I could not read ringed around it. My fingers touched it reverently. "The mark."

After the EMTs disappeared with Lucy, the sheriff stared me in the eyes—hard. "You do that to her?"

"No sir," I said, unflinching, "the demon did."

"Uh huh. How did the 'demon' do it?"

I coughed. "It would be easier if you watched the feed."

"You have video?" He cocked his head to the side. "Okay. Where is it?"

"In the device outside the door."

I led the sheriff to the recording device. Lucy's spirit hovered around, watching everything. I didn't want her to see the scene of her death again, but I had no way of telling her that. It wouldn't be good to have the sheriff see me talking to thin air.

#

After Tor was off to the hospital with Lucy's body, the sheriff took the rest of us to the station for questioning. It was a small station, a nondescript grey block building. The sign was in good condition and the building had been repainted.

It was the first time I'd been questioned by the police. They ushered me into an empty grey room with a long table and a few cheap chairs. A camera rested in the corner of the ceiling not unlike the one we used with Lucy.

I sat waiting for around two hours before the sheriff came in.

Lucy's spirit kept wandering the room, exploring things. Luckily, she didn't try to make me laugh or anything.

"Mr. Holiday," the sheriff said. His bloodshot eyes searched my face.

"Yes, sir."

He sat in one of the chairs near me. "Explain to me how an ex-priest ends up performing an exorcism."

I sighed. "Will asked me. At first, I wasn't even sure she was possessed. When it became clear she was, we contacted Father John."

The sheriff motioned for me to go on.

"The church sanctioned the exorcism, but couldn't get an exorcist here for six months. In this country, the few exorcists are in high demand. With Lucy's health the way it was, she couldn't wait six months. So Will and Tor asked me to exorcise Lucy."

The sheriff leaned back in his chair. "That video's the damnedest thing I've ever seen. Weird crap over the years at Blackmoor."

I nodded.

"Got an AV guy from the appliance repair shop to look at it. He confirmed it wasn't tampered with." He sighed. "My grandpa was the one who found old Black, you know?"

I stared at him. "No, I didn't know that."

He nodded. "That's a bad house. Should be burned to the ground."

"At this point, the Andersens will probably agree with you."

"Gotta ask you to stick around. Least for a while."

"That's fine. Any motels around here?" I couldn't go back to that house. Not now.

"Got a Day's Inn out on seventy-seven."

"That's where I plan to be."

He reached into his pocket and handed me a card. "Call me when you have the particulars."

"Will do."

Lucy didn't wake up, at least her body didn't. It was comatose in the hospital for an indeterminate amount of time. What I'd come to think of as the real Lucy was with me. Sometimes it was hard not to laugh at her antics. The doctors said she was in a persistent vegetative state. After about a month, Sheriff Bedecki told me I could go home.

Will and Tor paid for my hotel room. Why they did it, I didn't know. It was like they wanted to repay me somehow, but couldn't stand to be around me. I didn't blame them.

They stayed at the hotel too. I don't know what they planned to do about Blackmoor. I never asked. We kept our conversations light.

When I left, all I got was a simple nod from Will.

#

Four months later…

I was trying to get everything ready for Tabby to move in. We decided we were going to give it another go. At least I'd finally found some freelance graphic design work. I lost my job in the month it took me waiting around to see if I was going to be charged with anything connected to what I'd come to think of as *the incident.*

Lucy was still with me. I hadn't broken that part to Tabby yet. I hoped she wouldn't hold it against me.

I'd finished cleaning the house. Tabby was set to arrive tomorrow with the U-Haul. It was about eight, and I was tired.

"You're going to get a phone call," Lucy said, pushing a magazine in the middle of the coffee table.

"When?"

"Three," she said in a sing-song voice.

Dread licked up my spine. "Not again."

Lucy nodded. "Yup."

"You going to help me?" I asked.
She smiled her bright smile, teeth perfect, eyes dancing. "You bet!"

THE END

Book Two of the Marker Chronicles

Sorrow's Edge

Danielle DeVor

CITY OWL
PRESS

SORROW'S EDGE (Book 2)

Uncovering The Truth…Will Take An Exorcist

Jimmy Holiday, defrocked priest turned exorcist, is trying to get his life in order. With his on-again off-again witchy girlfriend moving in, the spirit of the little girl from his last exorcism hanging around, and a secret organization of exorcists hounding him, Jimmy equals stressed.

When a stranger calls in the middle of the night asking for help with a possession, Jimmy is about to land in a mess of trouble. Especially since the man on the phone claims to have gotten his number from Jimmy's old mentor. Too bad his mentor has been dead for years.

After a mysterious silver flask arrives at his doorstep, Jimmy is left with two options: either ignore the newest enigma the universe has tossed him, or listen to Lucy and travel to Arizona to solve the mystery before all hell breaks loose…again.

Chapter One

It's All Coming Back to Me Now

I GOT THE phone call at three. Just as Lucy said I would. I was really starting to hate the true "witching hour." I needed sleep, dammit.

I let the phone ring a few times, hoping that whoever was on the other end would just hang up. I wasn't that lucky. I dragged my tired-ass body up, grabbed my phone off the nightstand, and swiped the screen.

"Mr. Holiday?" the man asked when I grunted into the phone.

"You realize it's 3:00 AM, right?" My head hit the pillow. I did not want to be doing this right now.

The man sighed. "It couldn't be helped. We need you."

I twitched. Who the hell was this guy anyway? Kind of presumptuous to call somebody at random this late at night when you'd never met the person on the other end. Apparently, manners weren't his strong point.

I glanced around the room. The lamp in the corner was on. The light glowed just enough to keep my mind at ease. I'd gotten into the habit of sleeping with a light on ever since Sorrow's Point. Yeah, it was irrational, but hey, I was trying to keep the beasties at bay. From the dim light, I could see Lucy sitting on the floor in front of the TV. I, just barely, made out the program through her. Her hair was as pale as usual and so blond it seemed almost white. She wore the same white nightgown she always did.

"How did you get my number?" I had to know. I mean, I doubted Will would suggest me to someone else. Things hadn't exactly ended on a positive note.

"You came highly recommended."

That was news to me. A very small group of people even knew I did something besides graphic design. "By who?"

"That's not important right now. You're needed. That's what should matter."

I sat up. Not important to him, maybe, but it sure as shit was important to me. I squeezed the phone so hard my knuckles began to ache. If I broke it, this asshole was going to owe me another phone. "Listen. I'm not about to traipse around and do whatever the hell it is you want me to when you won't tell me who you are or who told you about me."

"O'Malley said you'd be difficult."

I froze. Father O'Malley had been the one who allowed me to see the church as a vocation when I was a kid. But there was one problem. He'd been dead since before I left the church. I didn't care where he got the information. That was a low blow. I clenched my teeth.

"I'm going to hang up now. I'd appreciate it if you didn't call here again—"

"No, wait!"

The desperation in his voice was the only thing that kept me from hanging up the phone. "All right. I'm listening."

"O'Malley told me about you in a dream. When I woke up, your phone number was scrawled on my hand."

Yeah, I knew that kind of weird. I had firsthand experience with it. Having a dead person talk to him in a dream wasn't that different from a disembodied soul speaking to me in a nightmare. Yeah, my life was *really* interesting. Though I'd never drawn on myself in my sleep. That was a new one. "Who is it who needs an exorcism?"

The guy hung up. I literally heard the phone hitting the cradle. Who used an old phone like that anymore? I almost threw my cell phone against the wall. I mean, what the hell? Wake me up in the middle of the night for what?

I scratched the sleep out of my eyes and glanced over at Lucy. "Don't you ever sleep?"

She stared at me and grinned. Her blue eyes almost sparkled. "I don't have to."

I shook my head. Of course a kid would think it great to not sleep. I, on the other hand needed my rest—strange phone calls or not. And if someone else called, I'd probably be facing a murder charge.

"Do you think Tabby will like me?" Lucy asked. She stayed dressed in this little white frilly nightgown. I wasn't sure if it was her favorite or if there was something else at work keeping her dressed that way. When I'd done her exorcism, she sure wasn't in frills.

Now that was the question, wasn't it? I'd been toying with the idea of not telling Tabby about my ghostly child, but it appeared that was no longer an option. And with my luck, Tabby would eventually see her, freak out, and the whole thing would be blown out of proportion.

"I'm sure she will…" I hoped that was true. "After she gets used to the idea."

Lucy stared at me for a bit. I could tell she wasn't buying it. Best I start remembering there was more to her than to a regular six-year-old.

"It will all work out," I told her. "Eventually." Part of that was me trying to convince myself. There was only so much oddness a normal person could take, and I figured I was probably getting close to the threshold.

"Uh-huh," Lucy said, back to watching the TV. How she could just sit in front of the TV for hours on end, I didn't know. It was almost like she became somehow hypnotized by it.

I laid my head back on the pillow. Hopefully, I could go back to sleep. Hopefully, I could stop worrying about that odd phone call. Hopefully…who was I kidding? I was seriously screwed. Again.

#

By the time the sun was stabbing into my eyes like pins into a suicidal pincushion, I'd gotten maybe four hours of sleep. Leave it to Lucy to put a voice to my fears. My best option was to tell Tabby outright, and while I knew she was used to unusual things, how could I be sure this wouldn't be so far out of left field she'd think I was insane? She probably already thought me nuts, but that was beside the point.

I got out of bed and crawled into the shower. The heat and the steam felt good. I needed to relax more, but it wasn't like my life lent itself to a lot of relaxation. My shoulders were so tense they hurt every time I tried to move my head. I ran my hands over my hair, getting the last of the soap out.

I needed a hobby. Something calming, like fishing. Too bad it was too cold. And, then, I wasn't the most patient person in the world.

Yeah, no fishing.

"Jimmy?" Lucy asked through the door.

I turned off the shower so I could hear her better. "What?"

"The phone's ringing."

I swiped a towel off the rack, wrapped it around my waist, and headed toward the door. Out of the corner of my eye, a brown disembodied head passed through the mirror. I left the bathroom and held the towel around my middle in a death grip. No sense in giving Lucy an eyeful. Yeah, she was a spirit, but she was alive too—long story. I wasn't about to take any more of her innocence away when the demon took most of it. Of course, I went through all of that and the phone had already stopped ringing. I picked it up—no notification of voicemail. Then I glanced at the missed calls. I was almost afraid Mr. Creepy had called again. But no, it was Tabby.

I called her number and waited, starting to hang up when she answered at last.

"What the hell are you doing?" she asked.

I was glad she couldn't see my eyeroll. If she could, I probably would have been socked in the arm. "Um. Getting a shower?"

She made a grunting noise like she was trying to move something heavy. I could imagine her pushing her long red hair out of the way while she tried to get a handle on the boxes. I loved her hair.

"Did anything strange happen last night?"

How did she know? Sometimes her insight was just creepy. "Yeah. There was a phone call."

"Another one?" A little hint of sarcasm in her voice. I wasn't sure if she was annoyed with me, the situation, or packing.

"Maybe. It's kind of complicated." Well, as complicated as *Attack of the Killer Tomatoes*, but whatever.

"Everything is always complicated with you, Jimmy. When I get there, I'll be expecting details. But is this something you want to do again?"

Good question. Heck, I wasn't even sure if the phone call had been a stupid prank. "I'm not sure if I have a choice."

"I thought God was all about free will, and all that?"

For normal people, he was. I gave some of that away when I became a priest, and some of the stuff I swore to I still kind of believed in. "To a point, yeah. But we could talk theology for hours."

"True."

"How much longer till you get here?" I asked. Having her here was going to be a change, but I viewed it as something good.

She sighed. "Who the hell knows? I've got so much stuff here."

If I hadn't needed to get my house moved around for her to put her stuff in here, I would have been up there to help. "Okay, okay. I'll stop pestering you."

She snickered. "If I didn't want to be pestered, I wouldn't have called you."

I grinned. She liked my bugging her. "I miss you."

"I miss you, too," she replied.

Too bad her witchiness wasn't strong enough for her to wave her hand and make her packing do it by itself. But then, real magic didn't work that way. "I'll let you go. Get back to packing."

"Okay. Be good."

I snorted. "Always." That was a lie. I played being good really well, but I was way too ornery to do what I was supposed to and leave it at that.

#

During the rest of the morning, I finished straightening up the house. No sense in letting Tabby freak out about the state of the place. I wasn't the type of guy to live in a pigsty, but I had some clutter too. The clutter had to go, for the time being at least. I mean, Tabby needed more than a path to move her things into the house. My books needed to be picked up from the floor. After rearranging things, I'd even managed to make room in the living room for her to add some bookcases. Between the both of us, we had a lot of books.

Lucy stayed in front of the TV, mostly to stay out of the way, I think. I didn't know if things passing through her hurt her; she'd never said. Of course, she'd been quiet all day. She hadn't spoken to me since I'd refused to let her watch a horror film.

"What are you doing?" I had asked.

She had turned around. "This is so fake."

Some scary thing was ripping out a guy's stomach on the TV. Spirit or not, she was six. I knew her dad wouldn't want her watching that stuff.

I snatched the remote off the coffee table and turned off the TV.

"Hey!" she said.

"Hey, nothing. I don't have permission from your dad for you to be watching something like this." I wasn't exactly sure, if I had a kid, if I'd want them watching something like that at her age either.

She glared at me. "I've seen worse anyway."

Damn. It was hard. She was this sweet kid. I couldn't deny that she'd seen and experienced worse. If I could, I'd take it all away. "I hope you can put that behind you one day."

Her gaze fixed on me. "I'd rather have him where I can see him."

I was unable to argue with that.

As I was walking into the kitchen later, I suddenly noticed all of the light in the house had grown dimmer, almost as if something was blocking out the sun. I went to the front door, opened it, and peered outward. The sky was clear yet darker somehow. Almost like something big, yet not totally opaque, obstructed part of the sun. I didn't want to think about omens, but if I'd paid attention to some signs with Lucy, maybe things would have turned out better.

The darkened sky with no clouds was a hell of a clue, but of what? Usually, it meant a storm was coming, but there weren't any storm clouds I could see. Definitely strange.

"Are you seeing this, Lucy?" I knew she could hear me. It didn't seem to matter how far away; she always heard me. I peered up at the sky, probably doing a damn good meerkat impression.

"You need to listen," she said from behind me.

To what? I was looking at stuff, not hearing anything. I turned around. "Lucy, the only thing you were talking about was some dumb horror movie."

She nodded. "And you didn't listen."

I closed the door and crouched down in front of her. Maybe I should start paying better attention. "What did that movie have to do with this?" I pointed at the sky.

She shrugged. "Doesn't matter now. He's coming." Then she disappeared.

"Who's coming?" I asked, hoping she wouldn't ignore me. She didn't answer. Not good.

The doorbell rang.

#

I'd like to say the doorbell ring connected to someone who could help with all of this, but no dice. It was the postman delivering a package. I probably should have thought about its arrival more intensely, but I was too worried about the dark sky and Lucy than the package.

I opened the door, staring for a minute. I'd begun to sweat. My palms were damp, and my heart was trying to tap dance. I don't know what I was expecting. Maybe some tall guy in black who could take over and save the day. But no, the guy shoved the box toward me. I took it. He left. There was nothing strange about it.

The box was square, about fourteen by fourteen and six inches tall. It wasn't real heavy, but I could tell there was something in it. I held the box up to my ear. No ticking. Not that I knew anyone who would send me a bomb, but hey, you couldn't be too careful.

I lowered the box, closed the door, and wandered into the living room in a daze. I felt like I hadn't slept for about four days. Something had wiped me out.

"What's that?" Lucy asked. The sunlight from the window was passing slightly through her. It cast a shadow on the floor that was sort of a shadow and sort of not.

I glanced up. "I have no idea."

After walking into the kitchen to get some scissors, I leaned against the counter and studied the package— regular brown shipping box with clear packing tape and no name on the return address. Just an address in Tombstone, Arizona. I didn't know anyone in Arizona, and to be honest, it didn't give me a happy feeling getting something from a place called Tombstone. I'd had enough of this omen shit. I didn't need to be hit over the head with a cinder block, for God's sake. I wasn't that stupid.

I took a deep breath and sliced through the tape. Nothing happened. No explosion. That was promising.

"Is that a good idea?" Lucy stood in the doorway to the kitchen now. Kind of disconcerting to have a kid that you could never hear walk around the house. I was always thinking she was up to something just because she was quiet.

I shrugged. "We won't know unless I open it."

"That's what the girl thought when she opened that box in that movie."

I set the scissors on the counter. "What have you been watching when I go to sleep at night?" I vaguely remembered seeing a trailer for a movie like that. Something about a possession. She didn't need to watch that type of stuff. How in the hell did you get a therapist for a spirit?

"Stuff."

I rolled my eyes. Yeah. Stuff. Great. That left me feeling really relaxed about the whole thing. Right.

I opened the flaps on the box and took a deep breath. Something was wrapped and taped in bubble wrap. I picked up the scissors again and cut through the tape. Nestled amongst the plastic wrap lay a silver flask, the initials J.H.H. were etched into the side. I searched through the packing, but there was no note, no nothing. Okay, why did someone send me this?

"Is it okay?" Lucy asked.

"I guess so. No strange smells or anything." Just a silver flask. Nothing odd I could detect about it. Except that I was sent it, but that was beside the point.

She crept over to look at it. I held it down to her level. After a minute, she shrugged and sauntered out of the room.

"Okay. Guess it isn't dangerous," I said to no one.

The lack of danger had me nervous. Who had sent it, and more importantly, why? I had a sinking suspicion that phone call wasn't a prank after all.

Chapter Two

Time Is On My Side

THE CLOCK ON the microwave read a quarter to eleven, but I was hungry enough for lunch. Part of me wanted to offer Lucy a sandwich or something, but she couldn't eat. No kid should ever be deprived of chocolate. Or Easter. Or birthdays. Jesus, I was starting to depress myself.

I knew if Tabby didn't get her chocolate fix, she'd be a force to reckon with. Maybe it was a good thing Lucy didn't appear to get hungry. No sense in tempting fate, though. I was worried about Tabby's impending arrival, but it paled in comparison to the strange shit. I'd rather have Tabby around when all this crap happened. At least she could help me make sense of it. But I'd better make sure the house was stocked up.

I took out a pan, fried myself an egg, and made a sandwich. It would have been better with bacon, but I was out. Another reason to hit the grocery store. Bacon was a staple.

I went into the living room and plopped onto the sofa. It was an old brown thing I'd picked up ages ago. All of my furniture was old, but it was me. Lucy was watching some dog show on the Animal Channel. That, at least, I could approve of. Dogs were safe. Little kids liked them. I could relax.

"When can I go home?" she asked me suddenly.

I froze, my sandwich poised in mid-air. Crap. I had no idea how to answer her. "I don't know. It's up to God, I guess."

Lucy nodded and turned back to the TV. I wished I could do more for her besides give her a place to hang out, but there wasn't anything else I could think of. It wasn't like I was all that smart or knew what I was doing. If I could make a magic carpet to carry her soul back to her body, I would. Hell, if I could somehow manage to make her body whole and nothing wrong with it, I would. Where were the medi-wizards when you needed them?

I picked up my phone and called Tabby. I needed to hear her voice. I needed some point of normalcy. After a bit, she picked up.

"What's up?" she asked.

What was left of my sandwich stared at me from the plate. I wasn't all that hungry anymore. "You leave yet?"

She snorted. "Uh. No. I thought I told you I'd call you when I left."

Dammit. I couldn't just come out and say that things were hard. I was at a loss. If I did that, I'd have to explain Lucy. "Yeah, but weird shit keeps happening."

I heard her rustling things in the background. "Just wait 'til I get there, okay? It's not like it's going to take me forever."

"Six hours." For now, that felt like a lifetime. I knew I was being ridiculous, but I needed her.

"It's not that long," she replied.

"I just didn't want you to drive at night." Bad things were out at night. Things I couldn't control.

She chuckled. "No, you're scared and you don't want to admit it."

Yeah, she had me. She was so damn smart. Hard to hide anything from her.

"So," she said. "Let me finish packing and maybe I'll actually get there tonight."

"Okay." It had to do. She was going to handle things her way, and nothing I said was going to make her change her mind.

She laughed again and hung up. I was starting to wonder when I was going to get my balls back.

I'd run out of things to keep me occupied. The house was more spotless than it had ever been, the refrigerator and pantry were stocked with food—I'd made sure to include tons of chocolate—and I'd made room for Tabby's things in the bedroom. I was even prepared to haul some of my shit out to the garage if needed.

Sharing a bed with her again would be strange. I missed her smell and her heat next to me. But there was the small problem of Lucy. Most parents did their thing when their kid went to sleep. With Lucy never sleeping, I was going to be a celibate man for a while. I'd have a hard time explaining that to Tabby. I didn't even want to think about it. Stranger still that I was kind of sticking to the old priestly ways. Though, I had to admit, it was no longer by choice. The usual advantage of being with Tabby was gone, at least while Lucy was with us.

About eleven at night, my doorbell rang. I'd been getting ready to shut up the house for the evening and go upstairs to sleep. I glanced at Lucy. She shrugged.

Staring through the peephole, I flung the door open. Holy shit.

"I was starting to think you'd leave me out there all night," Tabby said.

I picked up the bag she had in her hand. I couldn't stop myself from grinning like an idiot. She was here. "I thought you said you weren't traveling at night."

I let her enter the house and then I shut and locked the door behind her. It was such a relief to have her here. Safe.

"You sounded so odd on the phone that I figured I'd better get it over with."

"Where's Isaac?" I asked. He was this goofy cat who would rub his eye teeth on your hands if he liked you. I missed his fang-bumps.

"At Mom's. I dropped him off on my way down."

That explained it. "Are you hungry?"

"I'm more tired than anything." She took off her jacket and threw it on the sofa. I'd pick it up in the morning.

I wanted to kiss her and hold her for a while, but we weren't quite that close yet. We'd been taking everything slow this time. Probably for the best, with how badly I had botched things up before. Maybe I'd been too young, or maybe I'd been too green just leaving the priesthood. Having a relationship with her wasn't sunbeams and rainbows. Somehow, I never connected marriage counseling and me having a relationship with the fact that bonds weren't something like at the end of a sappy movie. Real people had problems. I just hadn't expected one of them to be me.

"I'm going to bed," she said. Bed, yeah, I could do that. Eventually.

"Okay. I'll be up later."

I don't know why I didn't follow her upstairs. Being chickenshit probably. But I needed a moment to pull myself together. To get centered so I wouldn't do or say the wrong thing. I guessed the talk about Lucy would have to wait until tomorrow.

Lucy stood near the TV looking at me. I waited until Tabby went upstairs. "I'll tell her tomorrow."

Lucy glared, and then sat back down in front of the TV. I was messing it all up with her too.

"You're going to rot your brain," I chided her.

"I don't have a brain, remember?"

Shit.

I went upstairs after that. Me staying down there irritating her wasn't going to solve anything. I knew the conversation with Tabby about Lucy was going to be a disaster. Just like everything else lately.

I headed to my bedroom. The white walls seemed accusatory, my bed representing the judge's bench. Tabby was pulling up her hair into a ponytail.

"Who were you talking to?" she asked.

Oh, shit. I did not want to do this now. I wiped my eyes with my hand. "I'll tell you tomorrow."

Tabby turned around and put her hands on her hips. "Tell me what tomorrow?"

I took a deep breath. "Please." I could tell the big fight was coming and I was stepping right into the pile of shit in the middle of it. "You're tired."

She rolled her eyes. "No, now I'm pissed off."

I hunkered down on the bed. When was I going to learn? I wanted to protect her too much, maybe. "This was not how I wanted this to go."

"You think?"

It was like all the old hurt, pain, and fuckup we'd had before Lucy was crawling up out of the rock it had been hiding under. All of my righteousness, all of my opinions between right and wrong that Tabby had to beat out of me, resurfaced. I remembered some of the stupid crap I used to say. I was such an idiot. No sense in putting it off. Tabby needed to know. "Lucy's still here."

"What?"

I sighed. "Lucy never left." How else do you explain to someone that a spirit had been following you around for about four months? My only strong point was that she wasn't going to think I was crazy, at least I hoped not.

"What the fuck are you talking about?"

Yup. There it was. "Lucy's soul."

Tabby froze. "You can't be serious."

It was time I put it all out there. The time for hiding was over. I needed to start treating her like the strong person she was instead of the little girl I wanted to protect. "When I did the exorcism…she was separated somehow from her body. Then, Peter came—"

"Peter who? Who's Peter?"

I stared up at her. "The Pearly Gates?" Crap. Any moment now, she'd be grabbing her cell and calling the guys in the white coats to cart me off. Did they even wear white coats anymore?

"You're shitting me." Her hands dropped down to her sides.

"Nope."

"She's here?" A hint of interest. Maybe this wasn't going to be that bad after all.

"Downstairs, watching TV." At least she was when I had left her down there. She could be doing who knew what by now. I found it hard to believe she spent all her time watching TV when I wasn't around. But what could she be doing instead? That was kind of a scary thought.

"Can I see her?"

"I don't know." And I didn't. So far, no one had noticed her when I went to the grocery store, but that didn't mean that there would never be someone who could see her. Tabby would be a good candidate with her witchiness, but I really didn't know.

Before I could stop her, Tabby rushed past me and down the stairs. She was going so fast I was afraid she was going to fall. The stairs were a little narrow, and I'd fallen down them a couple of times myself. I tried to follow as close behind her as I could without taking a header. This was going to be either okay, or completely shitty.

I followed Tabby to the living room. The only thing left on was the TV. Usually, Lucy went upstairs to bed with me, so I turned that TV on for her, but she'd stayed downstairs. Probably because of Tabby. I couldn't say whether Tabby would mind or not. That remained to be seen. Lucy looked at us like we were on Mars.

"Lucy?" Tabby asked. I watched her turn her head back and forth in front of the TV.

"Hi," Lucy said quietly.

Tabby slowly turned her head just slightly toward Lucy's voice. Then, she froze. "I can see you now."

I leaned against the wall. Okay, no freaking out. This was going better than I'd thought.

"Is it okay I'm here?" Lucy asked. Her eyes were on the verge of spilling tears. If she did cry, where would the water go? If there was water? I was so confused. The strangeness meter had upped its ante.

Tabby nodded. "Just let me know if you're around. I wouldn't want to trip over you."

Lucy smiled. Her tears stopped. "You should be okay. Jimmy hasn't killed me yet."

I snickered. I couldn't help it. My mind had just completely split in two. I was no longer losing my mind. I'd lost it.

"He is goofy, isn't he?" Tabby asked Lucy.

Lucy's whole demeanor seemed brighter. Happier, somehow.

"Uh-huh. Very goofy," Lucy replied.

That was it. I was officially outnumbered by two females. God help me.

#

Nothing else happened. I slept like the dead. No dreams. No strange noises. It was almost like I had my own little happy family. I knew better. Hell was on its way, and there was nothing I could do about it. The omens hadn't been about Tabby coming; they had been about something else. Something I didn't want to deal with, but would probably have no choice about. Lucy stayed downstairs though. Maybe she felt we needed some alone time.

The next morning, I woke to the smell of bacon sizzling. I sniffed and opened my eyes, making sure I wasn't crazy. Nope, I could hear someone rattling around in my kitchen. Looks like I didn't have to feed myself this morning. I got up and wandered downstairs. I found them at the tiny kitchen table. Lucy was smiling—a nice thing to witness.

"I see you finally woke up," Tabby said.

Awake was kind of a misnomer. Moving around was probably a

better way to put it. I shrugged. "You make a man bacon, and he'll come."

She rolled her eyes.

"Morning, Lucy," I said and glanced down at her. She grinned smugly. Maybe having Tabby here and knowing about Lucy would be good for the kid. Prior to Tabby, Lucy just followed me around or watched TV. It could be the female thing. The mother figure. What was I talking about? I knew nothing about psychology.

"Is there anything I can help with?" I needed to make an effort. I couldn't exactly stand around and do nothing.

Tabby shook her head. "Why don't you install yourself at the dining room table? I'll be there in a minute."

I knew better than to ignore her. I was lucky enough she was making me breakfast. It felt awkward being nudged out of my own kitchen. I went into my "dining room." Really, it was just extra space that was technically part of the living room. The important part was that it fit the old table.

"Are you okay?" Lucy asked.

I was starting to think that, now that Tabby was here, Lucy was more in tune with emotions. Weird. I gave her a smile. "Yeah. Sure. I'm okay."

"You don't look okay," she said.

She seemed a little sad. I pulled out the chair next to me and patted the seat. She sat.

"I'm fine. Just getting used to having more people in the house." It was true. I'd been by myself for a while. And I was having to get used to Lucy taking part of Tabby's attention away from me. Yeah, it was juvenile, but with my family, you had to fight for any attention you got. It took Lucy being here for me to realize I was still carrying that around with me.

Lucy nodded. "You're gonna have to learn to deal with it."

I snorted. I couldn't help it. It sounded so funny coming from her. "Why do you say that?"

She stared up at me, her eyes wide. "You don't think I'm going to be the only one, do you?"

I froze. Oh, shit. I did not want to be the guy everyone thought was crazy because I spent all my time talking to dead people. Later, there would be these movies about my life that would actually be mostly false, but everyone would think was the gospel truth. Yay, me.

Suddenly, Tabby came in with a big platter of bacon and eggs. Food. Thank God.

"What are you guys talking about?" she asked.

I leaned back in the chair. "Stuff even I'm not ready to deal with."

Tabby snorted. "You might as well get with it. I don't think you have a choice."

I snatched a piece of bacon and bit into it. The salty goodness made things a little better. Not much, but some. "Probably not."

"You are going to have to deal with this sometime," Tabby said, after she wiped her mouth with a paper towel.

"Can we let my bacon settle, please?" I didn't want to be having this conversation. I wanted to sit back and reminisce about my bacon time. Stupid, yes. But I wasn't exactly considered intelligent most of the time.

"Nope. Whether we talk about this now or not, your bacon is going to have to adjust. I have a full U-Haul sitting outside."

Oh yeah. Crap. I'd forgotten about that. The pack horse must do his duty. I downed the rest of my coffee. "When do you want to get started?"

"As soon as possible. If I don't turn that thing in before closing time, I'll have to pay for another day."

I saluted her. "Yes, ma'am."

"Smartass."

#

In all truthfulness, it wasn't that bad. Tabby had a lot of her furniture in storage. At some point, I supposed, we could figure out what of my crap we were keeping. But for now, my things would do. The hardest part wasn't the little bit of furniture or the books. Yeah, they were heavy as hell, but that wasn't what was unusual. When I began hauling in boxes that had Tabby's witch stuff, there was a sort of glow around them. I knew her magic had color, but I had thought it came from her. Either the magic came from the books, or these books had been used so often that Tabby's magic had imbued them.

"Aren't you done yet?" Tabby asked from the front door.

I'd been huffing and puffing boxes around for what seemed like hours. I was only one person. I needed a team of minions. "With what?"

"You've been standing there, holding that box, for about five minutes."

Oops. Okay. Having a complete blank-out wasn't good. Plus, my back was going to hate me for it. "Sorry." I hauled my ass into the house and set the box down beside the door. I stood up, popped my back, and stared at her.

"How much more is left in the truck?" Tabby asked.

"Just your bookcases."

After we got the truck dropped off at the U-Haul place, Tabby and I went home, got cleaned up, and I threw a frozen pizza into the oven. I knew I didn't feel like going out. My back ached and I wanted to just take it easy.

"Jimmy?" Lucy was standing in front of me.

"What's up?"

The kid seemed paler than usual, if that was possible. She was shaking.

"I'm scared," she said.

Oh, shit. Lucy saying she was scared was not a good sign. In fact, it scared the crap out of me. It was something like Tabby saying she didn't like chocolate. This was not cool. "Scared of what?"

"I have a bad feeling."

Okay. Bad feeling. Check. I wished I could hug the kid. Jesus. A bad feeling coming from her meant something was seriously wrong. But what? I couldn't imagine God giving her soul to the devil. I suspected it had something to do with that darn phone call.

"What's the feeling about?" I asked.

She wrapped her arms around herself. "I don't know yet."

Great. I figured I needed to put it out there. Maybe I was wrong, just maybe. "Are we going to Arizona?"

Lucy glanced up at me, her eyes wet. "You need to go."

Needing to go and wanting to go were two different things. Needing meant there would be consequences I couldn't deal with if I didn't go. It figured. If I had any luck at all, it was bad.

"Does it have anything to do with that flask?" I'm not even sure why I brought that up. Something was linking it all together in my brain.

She shrugged and left the room.

I blinked. Seriously? Sometimes I wished she could communicate better, but it wasn't her fault. She was only six, after all.

It was going to be interesting to break it to Tabby that we were going to have to haul ass to Arizona. I knew she was exhausted and it would be better to wait, but Lucy's bad feeling had me nervous. Did I want to go to Arizona? No. I wanted to stay home and get settled and try to find a job. Plus, I didn't want to be responsible if there was something big and bad that was able to take Lucy from me. Or do something bad to someone else. It wasn't like I was experienced at this. Doing one exorcism did not make me an expert, and I didn't know enough about the whole process. I had no idea how I could make heads or tails of any of this; there was too much that was unnatural. I'd tried searching online for "marker" and all I got were Sharpie advertisements. It wasn't like Lucy was walking around with a black check mark on her forehead.

"Is everything okay?" Tabby asked when she came into the kitchen.

"No," I said. The beeper on the oven went off. I got a pot holder out of the drawer and got the pizza out of the oven.

She sat down at the table. "Okay?"

"Lucy is scared." I waited for that to sink in. The last time Lucy had been scared was when the demon had her in his grip, and she still hadn't talked about it to me.

"Okay. So she's scared. She's six." Tabby leaned back in her chair.

I picked up the pizza cutter and attacked the darn thing. Sometimes Tabby made stuff hard. If she would just think for a minute, it would be clear. "This isn't what you think it is. Lucy spends a lot of time watching scary movies, for God's sake. If she's scared, it's bad."

"Did she say what she was afraid of?"

I gnashed my teeth together. I loved Tabby, I did, but sometimes she made me practice my patience. I shook my head. "She said she had a bad feeling about Arizona."

"And what's in Arizona?"

Now, that was a question I could answer. Sort of. I shrugged. "It's where the flask came from."

Tabby glared at me. "What flask?"

Ah ha! My turn to be irritating. "The one I got in the mail the other day."

"Someone sent you a flask in the mail?"

"Yeah, I guess." It sounded stupid. I knew that. But it wasn't. It was a sign of stuff to come.

"Who?"

I rolled my eyes. "I don't know. There wasn't a name on the return address." If I'd have known who sent me the damn thing, I would have Googled them and I wouldn't be freaking out like this.

"Jesus, Jimmy. The weirdest shit happens to you. Did you open it?"

"What? The package?" Why wouldn't I open a package addressed to me? I guessed if I were someone important like the president, I'd have a minion to open it for me. That way, if it had a bomb or something, they'd be blown to smithereens and not me.

"No, doofus. The flask."

I paused. I hadn't even thought about it. I'd been so relieved there was nothing scary in the box I took it at face value. "No…"

"Where is it?"

I pointed to the box on the floor next to the garbage can where I'd left it.

She grabbed it from its spot. After sifting through it, she glanced up at me. "Did you throw anything away?"

"No. There wasn't a note or anything." All there had been was that bubble wrap.

Tabby shook the flask. A faint sloshing sound came from it. "If this is blood, I'm going to shit myself."

"You won't be alone." I didn't want it to be anything gross or creepy. I had had enough of that with Lucy. Please, God, let it be something normal.

She unscrewed the cap and held it up to her nose. Then, she jerked back. "Jesus Christ!"

"What?" I had a moment of terror, afraid her nose was melting off her face or something.

She stared at me and rubbed her nose. "Worst rot-gut whiskey I've ever smelled."

I did my best not to laugh. "Who would send me bad whiskey?"

"You're asking the wrong questions. More like, who would send you a flask with these initials?"

Now, she had me confused. What did the initials have to do with anything? "Why?"

"I think this might have belonged to Doc Holliday." She turned the flask over in her hand studying the etching more closely.

"Nah."

She nodded. "Yeah. See, the silver has a faint bluish tint to it. Not like today's silver."

"Couldn't that be faked?" Not that I knew much about silver. Most of what I knew had come from Tabby, and that was all about the magical properties of the stuff, not antiques.

"No. The silvering process is different today. The engraving could be more recent, but I doubt it."

Heh, its being old didn't exactly instill confidence. "Why?"

"Because why would someone send you a fake flask to get you to come to Arizona? It doesn't make sense."

"Nothing makes sense." A hang-up phone call about a sort of exorcism and a box from Arizona that had an old flask in it had nothing to connect the two, as far as I could tell.

"That's the damn truth, but there's something here. Lucy's feeling notwithstanding."

Of course there was. "Fuck me."

"When are we going to Arizona?"

"When I can get a flight, I guess." I was so not looking forward to this trip. I could imagine running around and asking people on the street if they'd heard of Father O'Malley. I'd be in an institution before the day was out.

"What are you going to use to pay for it?" she asked.

Yeah. That had been the thing I'd been keeping in the back of my head for a long time, trying to ignore it. I wasn't all that far off from being broke. My steady job had gone bye-bye. After Lucy's body was put in the hospital, and all the loose ends were tied up, I didn't have a good enough excuse. I thought I'd probably be able to pick up another job, but the bottom had fallen out of the market for graphic design as badly as everything else. My unemployment was going to run out in a couple of months, and even then, it wasn't enough to pay for everything. My savings were shot.

I served us both up a piece of pizza. "Guess we aren't going to Arizona."

Tabby drummed her fingers on the table. "I do have a credit card."

I grabbed her hand. "No. We aren't going to do that. You don't have a job. I can't have you ruining your credit." I wasn't about to let her go into debt for me when it had to stand on something this flimsy. It wasn't worth the risk.

"What are we going to do?" she asked.

"I don't know."

#

If I said I slept, I'd be lying. I didn't want to do badly by Lucy, but I couldn't make myself financially destitute either. If I were a more religious man, I'd probably decide to take the "God provides" frame of mind. But even as a priest, I was more realistic than that. God gave me a brain. It was up to me to know how to use it.

If I had to go get a job at McDonald's, I would. I had Tabby to think of now. Sure, she'd probably get a job, but I wasn't about to put the whole monkey on her shoulders. I wasn't that type of guy.

If only my "profession" gave me a stipend or something. Yeah. Great wishful thinking there, Jimmy.

"Jimmy?"

I woke up, never remembering having fallen asleep. Tabby was standing over me. I glanced at the clock. A little after seven. "What?"

"Did you go somewhere last night?"

I searched the room; nothing was out of place. What was she talking about? "No…I came up to bed when you did, remember?"

"You have to see this."

She took me by the hand. I threw back the covers, got out of bed, and followed her downstairs. She was moving so fast that I missed a step and somehow didn't go down.

"Sorry," she mumbled.

I caught up to her in the dining room. She paused in front of the table.

"What?" I asked.

"Look." She pointed at the table. On it was an iPad. I didn't own one.

"What the fuck?"

"I don't know. It was sitting here this morning when I came down to make breakfast."

I knew there wasn't a magical iPad fairy. Something was up. "Did you ask Lucy?"

"She's been strangely quiet this morning."

Hmm. Usually, that meant the kid was involved, but I knew it wasn't the case here. Lucy was a spirit. Yeah, she could go through doors, but there was no way she could make a tablet pass through a wall. This hadn't been the first time something had appeared at random. When I had to get the demon away from Lucy, the vestments I needed to do the exorcism had somehow appeared in my suitcase. I hadn't packed them, and Tabby hadn't been with me when I brought my suitcase to Sorrow's Point.

I picked it up and pressed the "on" button. Maybe I could find out who the damn thing belonged to. Burglars took stuff out of your house; they didn't leave it. When it powered up, a video suddenly began.

A guy was sitting at an ornate gold desk. The walls in the background were this odd color of yellow.

"Mr. Holiday," the man said.

The dude on the screen appeared to be this old priest, dressed in white robes. He was not unlike my old mentor with bright white hair, but this guy had an Italian accent.

Tabby stared over my shoulder.

"Welcome to the Order of Markers. Fate works in mysterious ways and all that."

My eyebrows rose. "Yeah, no kidding," I said aloud. More like I wanted to know who broke into my house. Why couldn't they have knocked on the door, said, "Hey dude, we want to help," and handed me the sweet iPad. But no, I had a random technological device sitting on my dining room table.

"Eventually, you will need to come to Rome for your official training, But for now, your services are needed. We apologize for not introducing ourselves earlier."

He pulled up the robe on his right arm and displayed the inside of his wrist. He had a mark too. It was hard to see, but I could swear it was exactly like mine.

"Sometimes it takes a while before we know another mark has made itself known. I'm sure you've been alerted to your next project, so I'll keep this brief. If you haven't noticed, there should be a credit card taped to the underside of the device you are holding. Think of it as your corporate account. Use it for anything to do with your work."

I glanced at Tabby. She stared back at me. Maybe wishes really did come true. But I was feeling uneasy about all of this.

"On the device, you will find forms to fill out so we know where to deposit your salary. Welcome to the church…again." He chuckled and the screen loaded up the normal home screen I'd seen on these devices at the mall. Like he said, there were a few files that seemed like the documentation I needed to fill out. I turned the thing upside down and sure enough, there was a credit card.

I pushed the *too good to the true* thoughts from my mind. This was something I'd needed. I wasn't going to mess it up. "Guess I don't have to look for a job after all."

"Fuck, Jimmy. This isn't right." Her eyes practically popped out of her skull.

Part of me wanted to chuckle. I'd never seen Tabby this freaked before—minus the demon, that was. It was kind of cute. Finally, she readjusted herself and glared at me.

"What are you?" she asked.

A rhinoceros? Yeah, it was a good thing she couldn't read my mind. I'd be so dead. "A marker, I guess."

"It's like you've just entered the mafia or something."

I couldn't argue about it. She was right. "I kind of have. Think about it. Secret organization who gets their funds via secretive means in order to accomplish various agendas and be a front for the big boss."

She blinked. "I think you just described the church."

I patted her on the head. "It will be okay."

"You sure about that?"

Mr. Roboto

YEAH, I KNEW Tabby had a point. I should probably have been more concerned with the fact that someone had broken into my house to deliver an iPad. It wasn't like that was any sort of normal church behavior, but I knew there were other forces at work here too. And the Big Guy never did things subtly, not as far as the records went. I mean, who would notice if suddenly all the crumbs in the house were gone? God needed more blatant shows of his power.

The guy on the video had a mark, and he was also a priest. Part of me wanted to trust him because of that. But I knew better. Not all priests were good. And I'm sure my no longer being a priest had some in the Order grumbling. With that swanky desk and all, there was a lot of money involved, and money made people mean.

All of this didn't make me nearly as uncomfortable as Lucy and her bad feeling.

"Jimmy?" Tabby broke into my thoughts.

"What?"

"What are you doing?"

I glanced around. Nothing was out of the ordinary. "I'm thinking."

"Yes. Think away. You know about all of this strange crap going on. What are we doing? Are we going to stay here and unpack, or are we going to go on your bizarre quest?"

Good question. But with this credit card, I was tempted to go for it. I'd never been to Arizona, and the worst thing that could happen if I found nothing was that Tabby and I would have a vacation. Even I chuckled over that. No way was it going to be that easy.

Her phone rang. "Yeah, Mom?"

That couldn't be good. Tabby didn't exactly get along with her mom. On the best of days, it was strained. The woman wasn't quite sane, which made things worse.

"He's never done that before," Tabby said. She tapped the table with her fingernails. "Okay. Okay. We'll come get him."

She hung up. "We have to go to Huntington to pick up Isaac."

"Why? What's wrong?"

"He bit Mom."

I snorted and she glared at me again. I stopped myself from telling her I didn't blame the cat, but I also knew better than to let that out of my mouth. It was better for me to stay neutral. "Is she okay?"

"Yeah. She just can't keep Isaac anymore."

"I'll go get the keys."

#

We were quiet in the car. Not much to say. We had to drop everything because Tabby's mother was a pain in my backside. There were times that I wished Tabby would wipe her hands of her mother, but that was the funny thing about love. Sometimes you loved people who treated you like crap.

Lucy "sat" in the back seat. I knew now not to ignore little things, and animals sometimes could see and sense things humans couldn't. But I'd be crazy if I didn't worry. Lucy, after all, had killed her own cat when the demon, Asmodeus, was taking control of her. While she hadn't been violent in her spirit form before, the possibility was there.

"Hey, Tab? Want to get some lunch before we go get Isaac?" I asked.

Tabby rolled her eyes at me. "Isaac needs to be away from Mom. Besides, I'm sure he'd want a hamburger too."

"Oh, yes, anything for the cat."

Lucy giggled.

Tabby's mother's house was an old ranch-style thing with fake brick on the outside and a big window near the front door. It was once red brick, but had faded to a more orange color. The windowsills needed painting and the front walk had weeds growing up through the cracks in the pavement. The weeds were trimmed though; I had to give her mother that.

"Will you look at this?" Tabby's mother said as soon as she opened the door. She was holding her arm at an odd angle.

Instead of inviting us inside, she stuck her hand in Tabby's face. I could faintly see a red mark. There was so much I wanted to say, but I bit my tongue.

"Yes, Mom. I see. That's why we're here." Tabby sighed.

When she finally let us into her home, it was normal. Actually, it was cleaner than my house. The front door opened into the living room with a blue couch, matching recliner, and a TV. One picture hung on the wall. It must have been taken when Tabby was in high school. She was pretty even then.

I found myself thinking of Poe—the whole tap, tap, tapping at my chamber door bit. Tabby's mother's voice was like that. It crept in like a woodpecker hammering at a piece of wood while you were trying to catch the last zzz's of the morning.

"Jimmy?" Tabby asked. "You remember my mom, Kathy."

"Of course." I reached out my hand and all I got for my trouble was a glare that made me feel like I was the dog shit on the bottom of her shoe. Nice lady. I chose to be silent about it for Tabby's sake. "Where's Isaac?"

Just hearing me speak his name, Isaac barreled from where he'd been hiding under the sofa and jumped into Tabby's arms. He was this huge darker-colored Siamese with bluish eyes. He did not look happy.

"All righty, then," I said. Poor thing. I wouldn't want to stay with that woman either. It was hard to tell what she'd done to him to make him bite her.

Tabby snorted. "Okay, Mom. I know you want him out of here, so we'll be going." With that, she turned toward the door.

Her mom grunted. I glared back at her. She did not want to get me pissed off enough that I let it all out, did she?

I held the door open for Tabby and we left. I made myself calm down before I reached the car. Her mother and the way she acted wasn't a good reason to get into an accident.

In the car, Isaac stared wide-eyed at Lucy for a minute, and then settled down into the seat beside her.

His initial uneasiness didn't do a lot to quell my fears. I hoped Lucy was benign. But beyond God coming out and saying all the badness had left with the demon, all I could do was watch. I silently hoped her obsession with horror films was just one of those things and not an instruction manual.

"Hamburgers?" Tabby asked when we were a bit down the road.

"Where do you want to stop?" I searched along the highway, but there wasn't anything yet.

"Oh, anywhere. A drive-through would be best."

"Yeah, I can't see a restaurant enjoying having 'his royal highness' come visit."

Lucy giggled from the backseat. I glanced at her in the rear view mirror. Isaac was fine. Thank God. I was being paranoid. I had enough on my plate without adding to the stress. And I needed to stop thinking about those horror films. Plenty of people watched horror films, even as kids, and came out completely normal. Right?

"Lucy, what do you think of Isaac?" I asked her.

"I don't think he likes Tabby's mommy very much."

Her insightfulness was something else. As far as I knew, she'd stayed in the car when we collected Isaac. Or maybe, she had more power than I thought.

"Why particularly?" Tabby asked.

Lucy paused. "He doesn't like how she treats you."

Tabby and I stared at each other. There was no way Lucy could have known anything about Tabby's past. And Isaac—he was a cat. I didn't want to think I was getting any crazier than I already was. Too bad it was possible.

"Does he talk to you?" I asked her.

"Kind of. It's like I look at him and these pictures appear. Like a movie or something."

I calmed down. She was a soul. It made sense that she could see other souls. Interesting that Isaac had one, though. The church taught me that animals didn't have them, and thus, couldn't be granted Heaven. One more thing the church was wrong about. I should have started keeping a list.

#

When we got back to the house, Lucy went straight into the living room and plopped down in front of the TV. I turned it on for her.

Isaac barreled through the house, his way of making the place home, but still funny having a cat run like a maniac around the place. It was kind of nice to have the house not be so quiet.

"What are we going to do now?" Tabby asked.

"What do you mean?"

"I somehow don't see Isaac participating in an exorcism."

I chuckled. "Hey, you never know. Besides, he's your familiar, right?" Of course, I knew he wasn't doing spells for her and things like that, but any animal that belonged to a witch could be considered a familiar. At least, that's what I thought.

"Well, sort of."

"Then he goes. We can get him a seat on the plane."

Tabby shook her head. "I'm not even remotely going to pretend that this isn't a dumb idea."

I shrugged. "Animals can sometimes sense stuff before we can. He might be able to help." I could see a demon screaming at Isaac's noxious fumes. They were *that* bad.

"It's your funeral," she said.

I ignored her and booted up the tablet. No sense in waiting any longer. Familiar or no familiar, we needed to get to Arizona.

#

I wasn't dumb enough to get first-class tickets. Even I couldn't have been able to justify that in my head. Isaac or not, coach it was going to be. If my legs had to stick up my butt, so be it. I wasn't going to let this company credit card thing get out of hand.

We were supposed to get into Tucson, Arizona, about 8:00 PM. I'd found a hotel that accepted animals, but I wasn't sure how long we'd be in that room. I was starting to feel like the Scooby Doo gang. I had a mystery to solve, but I didn't know what it was. I had too many pieces to put together—the strange phone call and the flask to start. Logic told me the flask was sent by the same person that made the phone call, but why? And if Tabby was right and the initials belonged to my ancestor, then that was another level to the madness.

The number hadn't shown up on my cell's call list, which was odd enough, but the call itself was the strange part. No way the guy could have known about O'Malley by getting in a database for my phone number, so that left me to believe he was telling the truth…at least about that part. Whether he needed an exorcism or not was the problem. Kind of. The possessed wasn't usually the one asking for help from the church; the family was. So that meant he was lying about who needed an exorcism.

Again, why? It made no sense to me.

One thing: I didn't like being lied to. It didn't matter if the possessed person was a real bastard or something, I'd still help. It wasn't like Lucy was nice in her possessed form. So how would this be any different?

Sometimes, I found myself wanting to dive back into doctrine and look for things, but honestly, I knew it wouldn't help. I'd had better luck with the exorcism when using the words Tabby and I had made up. Maybe there was something to that. Could it be as simple as being defrocked meaning that the church's ritual wasn't available to me, or was it all in my head?

And if doing an exorcism like a witch's ritual worked, who was I to argue?

Chapter Four

Piece of My Heart

"WHAT TIME DOES the flight leave?" Tabby asked. It was Thursday. We were flying out tomorrow. I wasn't really looking forward to it, but it was better than staying around here and wondering what might have been.

"Seven forty-five." It meant getting up at the butt-crack of dawn, but nowhere near as bad as getting there at like 2:00 AM.

"Ugh." Tabby popped her neck and lowered herself into one of the dining room chairs.

I shrugged. "At least it puts us in Arizona at a decent time."

She raised her eyebrow. "Decent for who?"

I didn't want to be mean to her, but if I could have somehow pulled a perfect flight out of my butt, I would have. It was either early going or getting in late. "What? We'll get there at eight."

"Uh. Huh. Did you get us a rental car?"

I stared at her. Shit. Of course, she'd zero in on the thing I forgot. "I'll be right back."

She snorted. I took off to the computer and added a rental car to our reservation. It wasn't like I was trying to be stupid, it just came out that way. Or, maybe, stuff in the world like to see me fail. Yeah, that sounded good.

I had to believe it would all work out; otherwise, I'd just screwed up the first assignment I had since getting marked. Great way to start a new job—mess up your first assignment. Good going, Jimmy.

After booking the rental, I plopped on the sofa and watched Tabby rush around the house. She'd gotten some stuff moved in, but it wasn't anywhere near done. If we didn't have to leave this soon, it would have been a lot easier for her. I probably could have helped with some of it, but I was comfortable on my couch.

Lucy rested on the other end of the couch, alternating between sort-of petting Isaac and watching Tabby.

"What's it going to be like?" Lucy asked.

I glanced at her. "What's what going to be like?"

"Arizona."

I thought for a bit. I had to find a way for this kid to have fun on the trip. It wouldn't be fair otherwise. "Hot, mostly. Do you feel temperature?"

She shrugged. "I don't get cold anymore."

I guess that made sense. She didn't have a body. Not one she was attached to, anyway. But a kid should be able to do stuff like play in water when it's warm. Lucy being in this state wasn't doing her any good. I just didn't know what I could do about it.

"Is Isaac going?" she asked.

I chuckled. "Yes, Isaac is going."

She beamed.

Okay, cat made her happy. Check.

#

I'd shuffled my crap together as best I could. I did manage to get a case for the iPad. Traveling with the thing exposed would be stupid, and I didn't know if I should leave it at home. It was probably better if I had it with me in case they needed to contact me or something. It was getting way too complicated.

I guessed it was connected to some cell phone or something. Yeah, they broke into the basic lock on my house without a security system. I had trouble believing they would hack my network. I didn't know enough about the thing to check to see how it was connected, though it seemed like a hell of a lot of work for something I could have done myself. I wondered if they meant for me to travel with it.

"What are you doing?" Tabby asked.

"Trying to figure out how it's linked." I searched around the house and stared out the window, but I didn't see anything unusual.

Tabby stared at me. "I've never had one, so I don't know how to check the settings. You could look it up."

Yeah, technically she was right, but I wasn't feeling like messing with the internet. Going on a jaunt was more fun anyway. "I'll just go outside."

Tabby raised an eyebrow. "Why?"

"If I walk down the street, out of range, the net connection will quit." If it was connected to my house, at least.

She shook her head and walked away.

I went outside, heading down the street. My neighborhood was one of those old housing subdivisions from the fifties. Tons of neat little houses in rows, almost as far as you could see. At one time, there had been a little supermarket settled within the grid of all the houses that had its own butcher. Way before my time.

I continued along the sidewalk. At the corner, I stopped and loaded up the tablet. It came to life just like it had in the house. I checked on the internet app and it brought up the Apple homepage.

Yeah. Okay. I was covered. Maybe. Hell, I didn't know. It would be kind of cool if the Order had its own huge server or something. More likely, the server was connected to a cell tower format, so I could just surf the net wherever there was service.

I probably should have looked up how to check the settings like Tabby said, but since the thing didn't belong to me, what business did I have messing with it?

I went back to the house. I needed to know more than I did—like usual. But even I had to admit I was probably better off not knowing.

#

Needless to say, getting on an airplane with a disembodied spirit and a cat presented quite the interesting scenario. The Isaac part wasn't too bad. I hoped there was no one on board who was allergic to cats. I wouldn't want to give someone an asthma attack or anything.

Lucy, however, stressed me out. Because she didn't have a seat, she wandered around the plane. Sometimes getting really close to people. Too close. I kept expecting for someone to sense her, but I was lucky. No one did.

I wanted to set her down and tell her to chill, but I couldn't exactly be seen as a total nutcase on a plane. Isaac even stared at me like I was mad several times. Be great if I got myself on a no-fly list.

Finally, when we landed, my heart stopped hammering in my chest.

If I couldn't calm down, I was going to need anxiety medication or something. I almost welcomed the annoying assembly line getting off the airplane.

"Are you better now?" Tabby asked as we headed toward baggage claim.

"Yeah, kinda." Maybe being enclosed with a lot of people in a septic tank had my hackles up.

"I haven't seen you that uncomfortable in a long time."

"Did you see what Lucy was doing?" My brain bounced back to Lucy staring at people, dodging the drink cart, dancing in front of the bathroom door. Yeah. The flight was not a fun time.

"Yeah?" She seemed so unconcerned. I don't know how she managed it.

"What if someone noticed?"

Tabby giggled. "I think Lucy has control over who can see her. Even I didn't see her at first."

"True." I said it, but I didn't necessarily believe it. There was always going to be someone stronger, faster, more amazing. And it was just a matter of time before we ran into one.

#

After we got into our hotel room, I allowed Isaac to take a dump in his travel litter box, and got my shoes off. That's when Lucy reappeared. Why she'd run around invisible in the airport was beyond me. I wasn't the one she had to worry about seeing her.

"Did you have fun?" I asked her.

She perched on the bed beside me. "You were funny."

The bed had one of those odd undulating wave patterns on the bedspread. At least it was blue. In pink, it would look like vomit. "You about gave me a heart attack."

"It wasn't that bad," Tabby said, coming in from the bathroom.

It amazed me. All she had to do was brush her hair and wash her face, and she'd be back to normal. Me, I'd look like shit until I got a good night's sleep.

"So you say," I replied.

Lucy stared at me. "Why were you scared?"

"What if there was someone who could see you?" I needed to put it out there. She needed to think a little more. I knew she was young, but she had different needs than a normal kid.

She stopped for a minute and then bowed her head. "I didn't think about that."

I would have liked to put my hand on her shoulder, but her not being corporeal really made that impossible. "It's okay. Just try to keep calm when we're around a lot of people."

She nodded.

"Can we let this go and get something to eat?" Tabby asked, a hint of annoyance in her voice.

"Wanna see if there's a pizza place that will deliver? I'm tired." All I wanted to do was get a shower and some sleep. I was leaning away from food. Though I'd probably wake up in the middle of the night starving to death.

Tabby went for the phone on the stand between the two beds. "Sometimes you do have good ideas." She hit the button for the front desk.

"Only sometimes?" I asked.

"Don't make me hurt you."

It was past midnight by the time Tabby fell asleep. Isaac snoozed at the foot of the bed by her feet. I had the TV volume turned down low. Lucy didn't complain. She lounged on the other bed and watched me flip channels.

In the dark, Lucy seemed sad. Her eyes lost that sparkle they usually had and there were shadows on her face I hadn't seen before. I had no way of knowing if she could tell anything about what was happening to her body or not. Who knew what God's plan was for her? Part of me wondered if it would be more humane for her to go on to Heaven instead of having to live with the pain and disfigurement her own body now had. It was probably a good thing that it wasn't my call.

#

"How do you want to handle this?" Tabby asked me after I finished getting dressed the next morning.

"To be honest, I don't know. With Lucy, I knew where I was going because Will took me. This…this is something new." Somehow, I had a feeling it wasn't going to be as easy as typing the address into the GPS.

"True, but we came here because of the package," she said.

"Yeah. Let's try that." I mean, it wasn't like I had any other plan.

First off, we had to get to our new hotel in Tombstone. I was glad I had the foresight to have us crash for a night in Tucson. Somehow, I don't think I could have driven all the way there last night.

Tabby plugged the address of the hotel into her phone's GPS, and after checking out, we were on our way. Isaac seemed a bit more nervous. I don't know if it was the recovery from the plane trip or not, but he couldn't settle down. Every time I glanced back at Lucy, she was doing nothing. If she'd been hurting Isaac, he would have made some sort of noise. All I had were sort of snorts from him. Not exactly worry-worthy.

The closer we got to Tombstone, the more my heart raced. The animal side of me was sensing something that the logical side wasn't. Logic told me I had nothing to worry about because we were simply going to look up an address. But logic wasn't exactly my best friend.

"Jesus Christ!" Tabby grabbed onto my arm.

I slammed on the brakes. The biggest badger I had ever seen stood in front of the car. He was staring like he wanted to eat our tires. The dumb thing must have weighed forty pounds.

I revved the engine. It growled and prowled the car like a lion.

"Jesus, Jimmy. Did you have to do that?" Tabby asked.

"How was I supposed to know?"

"It's getting closer." Lucy pointed from the backseat.

I rolled down the window. I had to do something. Yeah, the thing probably wasn't going to get into the car, but I'm pretty sure the rental place would have an issue with their car being totaled by a badger attack.

"Hey," I shouted.

The beast stopped and growled.

"I'm sorry I disturbed you." I motioned with my hand for the thing to continue its way across the highway. "Go ahead."

It glared at me for another minute, and then it started crossing the road.

Just as I was about to relax, it turned his head around. Almost like he was saying, "You sure you don't want a piece of this?"

I didn't move. Finally, after the creature disappeared into the sagebrush, I drove off.

"That was interesting," Tabby said.

"Is that what you want to call it? Badger attack wasn't part of the itinerary."

"Just get us to the hotel. I don't want to fight." Tabby flicked her wrist.

Who was fighting? But I said nothing. It was better to keep the peace than to wreck us because Tabby and I had a knock-down-drag-out in the car.

#

After we deposited Isaac and our stuff into our hotel room, I punched in the address of the package into the GPS on Tabby's phone. Whatever it was, it was on a street called Toughnut. That alone should have been enough to make me laugh my ass off, but the general feeling of it all wasn't funny. Dread tightened my gut. It wasn't like when I finally entered Sorrow's Point or anything, but it was there. Nineteen-seventy-three Toughnut Street turned out to be a vacant lot. Now I knew someone was fucking with me. When we pulled up to the destination, I thought the GPS had puked.

"This can't be right," Tabby said, staring at the empty space.

A few houses rested on either side of us, but nothing seemed out of the ordinary. I knew it wasn't going to be this easy. I just knew it.

Lucy stayed strangely silent.

"I guess we'll check it out."

We got out of the car. Tabby shielded her eyes from the bright sunlight. I wandered over to the house nearest the car. The number on the outside read nineteen-seventy.

I motioned to Tabby. "I think someone is playing us."

Tabby raised her eyebrow at me. "Maybe we should ask Lucy?"

I nodded and stuck my head in the car window. Lucy glanced up at me.

"Any ideas, Lucy?"

She sighed. "Someone needs your help here."

I leaned my head against the roof of the car. My patience was wearing thin. The heat from the roof soothed my forehead. "Any idea who?"

She shrugged. "Guess he'll find you when he wants you."

Not an answer I wanted. I'd rather know what I was up against so I could take care of it, leave, and go home. "What do we do until then?"

She shrugged again. "Whatever."

I don't know what I'd been expecting, but it seemed pointless to travel all the way out here for nothing. I could have found Southwestern food somewhere back home. And Lucy wasn't a lot of help.

I waved Tabby over.

"What now?" she asked.

"We find something to amuse ourselves with." Or I could find who brought me here for a fool's errand and beat the shit out of him. Either one worked for me.

"What about the address?"

"A red herring, I guess. Lucy says the guy who wants our help will find us, but I can't help to think we're going to be psychically mugged."

Tabby chuckled. "I don't think Lucy would let that happen."

"I sure as hell hope not."

#

We left Toughnut Street and found a decent place to park. Then we went down Allen Street on foot. Allen Street served as the main street in Tombstone, and part of it was where the shootout with Wyatt Earp happened. Glad I wasn't around back then. My temper combined with my general smartass behavior would have left me dead before I was twenty. I couldn't see myself bowing down to some random outlaw just because he thought he was a big shot. Yeah, I probably shouldn't hang out in Vegas either.

The old-timey look of the place was quaint. All the signs were printed with the type of font you saw on Western movies. A few people milled about in period clothes. The rest seemed like tourists. The scenery was nice, but the heat left something to be desired. Being from the east coast, I couldn't stand the intense daytime. Like walking around in an oven. Not fun at all. If this was what Hell felt like, all the more reason for me to never go there.

"Let's go in here." Tabby pointed.

It was a saloon. The place even had those old-style swinging doors.

She was probably right; a cold drink would ease our suffering. Plus, it was kind of dark inside…and cooler.

Tabby grabbed a pamphlet from a rack beside the door. "Jimmy?"

"Yeah?"

"Who told you that you were related to Doc Holliday?"

I blinked. Not something I expected to be asked today. "My mom. Why?"

"His name has two ells."

I shrugged. "I don't think that makes too much of a difference. Families alter the spelling of names all the time."

Tabby raised her eyebrow at me.

"No, really. This guy I knew in seminary had at least four different family members that changed the spelling of their last name."

"Ah ha. Do you believe you're related?"

"Probably not. It was just one of those things Mom always said." I think my mother wanted to be famous in some way. Too bad; her life was daytime movie material all right; the Lifetime movie about what happens when you're an alcoholic and your kids have to learn to cope. Not that I was bitter or anything.

She nodded. "That flask is strange."

I couldn't argue with her there. It likely would be something highly prized by a collector somewhere. Hell, I would have been fascinated had I seen it at an antiques show, but having received it at random through the mail? That was creepy. "Yeah. A lot of things are odd."

"Don't you think it's interesting that the flask has Holliday's initials on it?"

I began to chuckle. First, how would I have known Holliday's initials? And second, what did that have to do with anything? "Do I even need to mention how many name configurations could have those same initials?"

"Fuddy-duddy."

I pulled her into a hug. This trip had been hard enough for both of us. "Hey, we have enough mysteries without you creating more for us."

She pulled away and glared at me. I'd screwed up now. Yeah, I should have handled this better, but I was already annoyed enough with the false lead.

"I'm sorry," I said.

Tabby grunted and headed toward the bar. I followed behind. I guess I deserved the silent treatment, but damn she was being harsh. I'd done a lot worse than this.

"You know, you could have just checked Google Earth," she snapped. She stopped in the middle of the aisle and stared at me.

"Google Earth wouldn't have told me who sent the flask, now would it?" Yeah, I definitely shouldn't have snapped at her, but I was tired of being treated like her own personal punching bag.

"All right. Jesus, Jimmy. You're driving me crazy. I concede. Yes, there is a reason we're here. What is it?"

As I was about to answer her, a deep voice answered for me.

"That's a question we've all been asking, little lady." He was dressed in this out-of-time way with a vest and a suit coat. He had a black hat, but he was holding it in his hand. His hair, unlike his hat, was ash blond. He also sported a matching mustache.

Tabby looked like she'd swallowed a bug. Her hands shaking and she was on the verge of losing the pamphlet. What was her problem?

On a whim, I asked, "Sir, do you know anything about Toughnut Street?"

The man laughed in an awkward way. Like my question was the funniest thing he'd had in a while, but then he stopped abruptly. "Strange things on Toughnut. But nowhere near as weird as me."

I didn't doubt that. He wasn't exactly a normal guy, not with the way he was acting. But I didn't really have room to talk. I wasn't normal either.

"What is your name?" Tabby asked.

He smiled. "You can call me Doc."

Then he disappeared.

"Fuck." Tabby and I stared at each other. That was the first time I'd spoken to what was probably a real ghost. Lucy didn't count. She was a soul separated from her body. A technicality, but still.

Tabby sucked in a breath. "Maybe it isn't a man that needs an exorcism but the town."

I had this vision in my head about a circle of exorcists chanting in the town square like a scene in a movie. "Then we're going to need a lot more exorcists."

#

Seeing Doc didn't stop us. I left Tabby standing in the aisle and sauntered up to the bar. I knocked on it to get the bartender's attention. He was dressed in a white shirt with a ribbon tie around his neck. His hair was black and parted down the middle. I guessed he was told to look the part. He stopped washing glasses and came over to me.

"Whatcha need?" he asked.

"Did you see that?" I pointed toward the area Doc had been sitting.

He shrugged. "Doc is known to show himself here from time to time. He won't hurt ya."

I blinked. I wasn't used to a place where ghosts were that commonplace. "Oh, I'm not worried about that." I paused. I had more to worry about than talking to ghosts. I took a deep breath and stilled myself. It was time to get back to my real problem, figuring out who had sent that flask and why I'd been called here. "Have you heard of anyone looking for a Jimmy Holiday?"

Tabby came up behind me and put her hand on my elbow. The bartender raised his head and glanced over at her. "They got ya, did they?"

"Who? What?"

He leaned in close. "There's a lot of odd shit in this town. And we get people coming here looking for something all the time. Most, we never see again."

It was starting to sound like a bad horror movie. What was next? Being warned about the black dog that appeared only at the full moon? "Look. Someone sent me a silver flask from an address on Toughnut. No name. Empty parking lot."

"No, there wouldn't be." He leaned forward so that his nose was only inches from mine. "House there burned down a few years ago. The family wasn't real careful with their gas. Lady left a pot on the stove, flame went out, and when the furnace kicked on downstairs—boom!"

"Was everyone okay?" Tabby asked.

He nodded. "She'd gone to the store when she left the pot on the stove. Lost the whole house, though, and there was damage to the other houses around it. Took about a year to get everything set to rights."

"If the house was gone, then who sent me the flask?"

He shrugged. "Wasn't the lady that lived in that house. She left and moved to Philadelphia. No, stick around a while, and he'll find ya, but don't say I didn't warn ya."

I didn't like the idea that this bartender knew who he was talking about, but he didn't bother to tell me. It was my life that being fucked with, not his. As I was about to say something about it, the bartender put down the last glass and went into the back of the saloon.

Tabby grabbed me by the arm. "We are so screwed."

"Tell me about it."

Chapter Five

You Spin Me

SO I GUESS we did the stupid thing. I stopped getting myself worked up and Tabby calmed down. When the bartender came back, I ordered up a couple of beers and some chicken strips and fries. I knew I wouldn't be able to live with myself if I didn't at least wait for a while. The dude was supposed to show. I started wondering if this had happened before. Tabby hadn't said much at all.

I almost wished I hadn't left Lucy in the car. Who knows what could have happened if she and old Doc had gotten together? But that's something I didn't do, so no sense in worrying about it now. But it might have been something cool to see.

"Jimmy?" Tabby asked.

I glanced up from my food. "Yeah?"

"I'm sorry I was so hard on you earlier."

Holy shit. Tabby was apologizing to me. It was one of those things that like almost never happened. Ever. Maybe spotting a ghost changed her perspective on a few things.

"It's okay. I know I can be a pain in the ass sometimes. Besides, we're in this together, right?" It was the least I could do. I'd been just as much of a prick. I needed to own up to it.

She wiped her mouth with a napkin. "Right."

"I wonder when Mr. Creepy is going to show up."

"Which Mr. Creepy?"

I snorted. It was kind of sad she had to ask. We'd been through so much bizarre shit that it was an honest question. "Whatever it is we're supposed to be waiting for. Part of me hopes he looks like he's from *The Hills Have Eyes* or something. The other part of me hopes he's a normal guy, an antique collector or something."

"In your case, either one would be bad." She took a sip of her soda.

"How so?"

"Because you're an exorcist. Any of the people you encounter will likely be possessed."

Shit. She was right. Though, not everyone I encountered was possessed. I mean, her mother wasn't demonfied; she was just a bitch. "Or a pissotsky."

"What the hell is a pissotsky?"

I laughed. "It's a guy possessed by a certain type of demon. When he gets horny, he gets *horny*."

She rolled her eyes. "And what movie did you get that from?"

I grinned. "The fruit burger classic, *My Demon Lover*."

She held her head in her hands. "I sure as hell hope that the higher power knows what he's doing making you into this thing."

"Maybe it's my charm." I knew she liked me. Otherwise, she wouldn't put up with my goofy ass.

She swatted me on the arm. "You done?"

"Yeah. I give up. Let's get back to Lucy." I pushed my food away. We'd waited here long enough. I hadn't seen anyone come in to the place. It was time to cut my losses, do a little sightseeing, and go home.

I went up to the bar to pay the bill while Tabby waited for me by the door. The bartender didn't say a word to me as he settled my tab and ran my credit card. In fact, he seemed a little odd. Stiff almost. I shrugged it off as a guy being tired, but I felt that strange feeling again.

It wasn't until I got the receipt that I knew all hell was breaking loose. Instead of my total on the receipt, there was a hotel name and a room number printed. The only problem? It was my hotel, the Marian Motel, and my room number, fourteen-oh-eight. After a minute, the text changed back to what it should have been, a normal restaurant receipt.

I grasped Tabby by the arm. "We have to go."

"What the hell, Jimmy?" she asked as I dragged her over to the car. I knew I was likely hurting her arm, but she was too stubborn to just come when I needed.

"We have to get back to the room, now." Maybe it was the panic in my voice that did it. I let go of her arm and she followed me down the street.

She didn't argue anymore. We both jumped into the car and I got us to the hotel as fast as I could. It probably wasn't fast enough. I just hoped that Lucy was there and I wasn't about to find Isaac spread about the room in pieces.

We ran from the car after I parked it and dashed up to our room. I could hear Isaac yowling from within. This wasn't good. I slid the key card into the lock and the light went green. God help me if the bastard hurt the cat. I opened the door.

We headed in, Tabby bringing up the rear. Isaac was on the bed with his back hunched and his lips pulled into a snarl. He was glaring toward the window. I glanced over at the little table in front of the window. A man was there sitting in the chair, staring at us.

He was tall with these long skinny legs I could see defined by his white suit. His hair stood out as white as the suit and billowed down to his shoulders. He wore black-plastic-framed glasses.

"Close the door, if you will," he said to Tabby and motioned with his hand. The nails on his fingers were long and perfectly manicured.

Tabby complied, her eyes wide. Only, I think, because we didn't want to let the whole hotel know our dirty laundry. Though, if having a random guy break into your hotel room wasn't cause enough to create a disturbance, I don't know what was.

"Who the fuck are you?" I opened without the bullshit.

He wrung his hands together and sighed. "I had hoped things would be more civil."

Where I was from, you didn't chitchat with someone that broke into your house. You shot them. Good thing I didn't own a gun.

"Look, buddy. You broke into our room, sent Jimmy a flask from who the hell knows where, and you want us to be civil?" Tabby's eyes began to glow red. The idiot hadn't seemed to realize that she was the violent one.

I would never have come right out with the stuff about the flask. She was so flipping cool.

"I'm guessing you're the one who called me?" I asked him. I needed to get the spotlight off Tabby. She was having a hard enough time keeping her cool. At least this way, if he fucked up, she could catch him broadside.

He uncrossed his legs, stood up, and gave a strange little bow.

"Allow me to introduce myself. I am Nicholas Vespa, a spiritualist."

I nodded. He sounded more like a motor scooter salesman than a person who dabbled with the occult. I wasn't completely ignorant when it came to spiritualists. Yeah, I'd read about one with the whole Sorrow's Point mess, and I suspected she was more of a witch than a spiritualist, but whatever. If this guy was what he said he was, then I was confused as to why he was in my hotel room, and, apparently, why he sent the flask. "You said on the phone that you needed an exorcism."

He smiled like that female vampire from the old *Fright Night* movie with his mouth pulled up just a little too wide at the sides. "Not exactly. I'm not sure if an exorcism is called for, in fact. It is more of an agreed-upon possession."

Things had stopped making sense, and when stuff didn't make sense, it wasn't true. "Why did you lie?" It was a lie, after all. He'd said on the phone that he'd seen O'Malley and he'd needed an exorcism. I did not like being lied to, especially when the person lying to you thought you were stupid enough to take them at face value.

"So you're aware, lies are one of my pet peeves." I was blocking the doorway with my body. "And how the hell did you get into my room?"

Tabby moved and lay on the bed next to Isaac. The cat cuddled up to her and stayed there. It didn't escape my notice that the cat was claiming his spot. I was second place.

"Does it make a difference? I am here now. That is what matters."

This was not going to happen. I had better things to do than listen to some old dude lording it over me. "Look. There's this thing called free will, and if you piss me off, I do have the choice not to help you."

Vespa coughed. "Truly? I should think your superiors would have something to say about that."

Now what would a "possessed" guy know about the Order? "Why do I suddenly feel like I am fighting with a demon instead of a man?"

Vespa grinned. His eyes turned yellow and the pupils turned to slits. Ooh, big scary.

"Jimmy?" Lucy asked from behind me. Her voice shook a little. Not good.

"Yes?"

"He wants to take me."

I stared down at her and her body was more transparent than usual.

Fuck this shit. I was not going to let anyone mess with me a second time. I stilled myself to ready for a fight. "Foul being. Dark bearer. Hear me. You have not been invited." I put strength into my voice. "Being invited is critical. And I take great offense to those who hurt my friends."

The demon blinked. "What is it you think you can do?"

Okay, play time. The power bubbled up inside of me. I knew how to put it out there. All I had to do was speak a certain way and blammo. "You are not invited. Lucy's soul is not yours. It bears my mark. Be gone."

With every word, I could see ripples of power move through the air around me. He'd done it. Maybe it would teach him a lesson not to piss off a marker.

Suddenly, I heard a loud bang. Vespa collapsed onto the floor.

"Oh, shit." Tabby jumped off the bed. "Should we check on him?"

I eyeballed his chest. He was breathing. Good enough. "I'm not touching him. It could be a trick."

Tabby nodded. After a few minutes, Vespa woke.

"Where am I?" he asked.

"Marian Motel. My room." I leaned against the wall in front of the door. I wasn't going to let the dude run away. I had some questions.

"What am I doing here?" he asked me.

Crap. This wasn't normal.

"You don't remember?" Tabby asked.

He got up from the floor. "I get these spells where I remember nothing. Sometimes I miss entire days."

Yup. If I hadn't already seen the demon, I would have suspected he was either possessed or had some psychological disorder. But with those eyes, I was thinking possession.

"Who are you?" he asked me.

"Jimmy Holiday." Or marker extraordinaire, cool guy without a robe. I was getting ahead of myself.

"Oh, thank God. I had to be sneaky, you know?"

I blinked and felt a tension headache coming on. "Sneaky how?"

"It wouldn't let me contact you again. So I had to wait until I had the power, when he was asleep. Then I was able to send you the package."

And back to the flask we were. I ignored the fact that my brain was now thinking like the little green dude from *Star Wars.*

"What does the flask signify?" Tabby asked.

I glanced at her, then back at Vespa. Something was going on there, and Tabby being a hell of a lot more astute than I was, apparently picked up on it.

"It…belongs to a famous spirit. I knew you'd come here if I sent it." He brushed off his suit.

"What famous spirit?" I asked.

"Why, your ancestor, Doc Holliday, of course."

Fuck me.

#

Vespa left the room soon after. He did give me his cell number so that we could reach him. I'd told him I needed to think things over. The truth was, I was so pissed off about the invasion of my privacy, I wasn't sure if I wanted to help him. Demon or not, you don't saunter into someone's hotel room unannounced. It wasn't cool.

Lucy kept staring at the door, almost as if she expected him to come crashing in. I couldn't blame her. The fucker had tried to take her away. I still didn't quite understand what the marker power did, but it was able to make the bastards go somewhere else. Lucy seemed okay now, just nervous. Isaac was curled up against where Lucy's leg sort of was, asleep.

"What are you going to do?" Tabby had plopped on the bed again.

"I don't know." It was true. I wasn't even sure if I was going to bother to help the guy after all that. It would probably be best to haul our asses back to Virginia and take our chances.

Tabby rose and hugged me. "I'm not crazy about this either."

Her arms felt good, both soft and strong at the same time. I took a deep breath. "With Lucy, I cared because she was this little girl, ya know?"

Tabby stepped back. "When you were a priest, would you have done the same for all of your parishioners?"

"Not all, but most." But none of my parishioners had tried to steal the soul of a little girl, either. It did make a difference.

Tabby came over and tapped the top of the little table. "What is it about this guy that bothers you most?"

"Honestly?"

"Yes, honestly."

"That he freely invited the demon in. I don't have a problem when someone is attacked, but to make deals with these things, that's evil too." Not to mention what he'd just done. I wasn't a hundred percent sure that he wasn't aware of what the demon was doing. Lucy certainly was. She'd indicated that in the dreams I had about her at Sorrow's Point. I knew enough now not to ignore things most people would discount.

"If it really bothers you, why don't you call them?"

"Call who?"

"Your employers or whatever they are. Surely, they could send someone else."

I hunkered down on the bed. Lucy watched me. Calling the Order would be a hard thing. Telling them that I wasn't able to do this job…that would be failure almost. Maybe Tabby and Lucy should head back home and I'd stay here? No, Lucy couldn't be that far from me. Shit. That wouldn't work either.

"What do you think?" I asked her.

"You said you'd protect me."

Leave it to a kid to blatantly put it out there. "Yes, I did, and I will." That was the end of it. I had a job to do—protect Lucy. Whatever went along with it, I'd just have to deal with it.

She petted Isaac, or sort of at least. Her hand passed through his coat. Isaac opened one eye, feigned interest, and then fell back asleep. "You saw what it was doing to me. You have to send it away."

I was starting to think that Lucy was the best thing to ever happen to me. She kept my conscience straight. That was it, then. I had to deal with Vespa. "Thanks, Lucy."

She beamed.

"How are you going to do this?" Tabby asked.

Good question. I knew nothing about this type of possession. The church assumed that no one would ever want to be possessed willingly. "I guess I'd better get to know what a spiritualist actually does. After that, I'll call Vespa."

"What can I do to help?" Tabby reached for her purse.

"Find out everything you can about Doc. I want to know what the connection is. Why would a possessed man send an artifact that belonged to my ancestor to me? There has to be something there."

Tabby nodded. "I'll see what I can find."

She left the hotel room. I didn't want to do this exorcism. Of course, I hadn't wanted to do Lucy's either, but that was beside the point. The one thing I did know was that if I didn't get rid of this thing, it was going to take Lucy. That was not an option.

#

I loaded up the iPad. Immediately, I got a pop-up informing me that my forms had been received and I should get my first check in about two weeks. Yee fucking haw. I guessed that meant that I'd be getting a paycheck sometime this century. Online bill pay was going to be my friend for a while.

I pulled up the browser and searched for spiritualist information. Most of what I got was people proclaiming to do spells for money, et cetera. Definitely not what I needed. Finally, I found a site that had a lot of old photographs with ectoplasm and séances. The historical stuff. Many of the photos were debunked, but there was one that gave me chills. The guy could have been a double for Vespa: the shoulder-length white hair, the long mustache, it was all there. I saved the photo to the desktop. If Vespa was that old, that might explain the power the demon had. But with a man being possessed that long, how could there even be any of his soul left? Besides, I'd never read anywhere that a demon could prolong human life for hundreds of years. Yet again, more questions than answers.

Logic said this guy was likely a descendant, an uncanny one, but a descendant nonetheless. So that left me with one question. Who in their right mind would willingly let a demon inhabit their body? Even a normal person knew that demons weren't exactly easy to get rid of. I didn't buy the fame and fortune crap. Pride maybe. Power certainly. But money? It would be easier to rob a bank. Plus, if you got caught, you'd serve a light sentence if it was your first time doing something that bad. If you told them a demon made you do it, the judge would laugh you out of the courtroom.

Of course, the only person who could answer that for me was Vespa himself, and I wasn't in the mood to talk to him so soon. I wanted to get all of this over and done, but I wasn't about to risk anyone's well-being again. The only reason I wasn't beating myself up over Lucy is that we were all broadsided with Vespa. Now I was on the alert, and I was going to make sure nothing like that had a chance to happen.

The church would probably feel it was my duty to help him. I didn't agree. I was only helping him so nothing else bad would happen. He could shove the rest of it up his ass as far as I was concerned. It was enough that I was actually going to do this. It didn't mean I had to like it.

#

Tabby came back a few hours later with a crapload of pamphlets and a book. Her hair had escaped its bun and wafted out around her face, almost like a halo.

"Damn," I said when she dropped it all on the bed.

"Your ancestor is kind of popular, if you haven't noticed." She kicked off her shoes and walked across the room.

I chuckled. "Something tells me he wasn't like the way he's portrayed in movies."

"No one is like how they are shown in movies." Tabby sat in a chair at the table, opened the pop bottle she had in her hand, and took a swig.

I flipped through the pamphlets. "Can you imagine living back then?"

"Nope."

"Why not?"

"Because it was fucking hard. We're too used to air conditioning and buying our food at the grocery store. Hell, just to have a sandwich you had to bake the bread, butcher a pig, and then cook the ham, make the mayo if you wanted it. No, I couldn't do it."

I grinned. "Yes, you could. You can do anything."

She took another drink of her soda. "You wouldn't be much better. I can't see you riding a horse to go to the next town."

She had me. Way back when, before we'd broken up the first time, she'd tried to get me on a horse. The poor thing stood there. I couldn't get into the saddle. So I fed it carrots instead.

"Yeah…my ancestor. What do you think he was like?"

She paused for a minute. "None of these guys were sweet, Jimmy. They were total assholes. They had to be. It was survival of the fittest."

"How about Wyatt Earp?"

She chuckled. "He only took the role of marshal so he could kill the killer of his brother. Doc Holliday was a gambler. These weren't petting puppies kind of guys."

"I would love to know what my ancestor has to do with a possessed spiritualist." The link was out of my reach.

"Then maybe, just maybe, it's time for you to calm down and we'll ask him. We could meet him for dinner somewhere." Tabby raised a brow.

I stared at Lucy, but she was ignoring me and watching TV. I didn't really have any other choice. I'd exhausted all the avenues I knew of to get information. And I seriously doubted if a biography of my ancestor would have an occult section. Hell, this was the first time I'd heard of it.

"I guess that would be okay," I said.

Tabby tossed me Vespa's card. "Get on with it, then."

I dialed his number…and got voicemail. I couldn't win. Why couldn't things work out the way I needed them?

"Yeah. Mr. Vespa? This is Jimmy Holiday." I gripped the phone harder. "We'd like to meet with you for dinner. Call me back when you get the chance."

I hung up. Some days, it would be better to dig yourself into a hole in the ground.

"At least, you did all you could do," Tabby said.

"Yeah. I guess."

Part of me was upset for dragging my feet earlier. Yeah, true, I had a reason to be pissed, but once I decided to do something, I followed through. I should have told him we'd meet him later so I'd have a chance to calm down and get some of these questions out of the way. I was more concerned with keeping myself from beating his ass. Now, I hoped it wasn't too late.

"Isaac's hungry," Lucy said.

"How do you know that?" Tabby stared at my little charge.

She shrugged. "He told me."

Lucy's ability to communicate with Isaac was getting really odd. I wondered if she was putting words in his mouth or if he actually was telling her these things.

"Isaac has food." Tabby turned her attention back to a pamphlet.

"He wants fish," Lucy said.

This was getting stranger by the minute. Just what I needed, a spirit living in my house that could talk to animals. What was next, a cockroach conga line?

"There is fish in his food." Tabby glared at the cat, "Besides, he knows better."

Said cat let out a rowr in response.

"That's it. I'm losing my mind," I said. It was time I wore one of those spit hoods and drooled constantly.

Tabby chuckled. "Nope. You lost it a long time ago."

"So you say." I watched Lucy. She was back to staring at the TV and Isaac was trying to sleep.

Then my phone rang.

#

Vespa wanted to meet us at a Southwestern restaurant outside of town. I didn't care, but the farther he was from where we were staying, the more comfortable I felt. I didn't want him getting close to Lucy any more than I could help it. It was too dangerous.

"Any way you can ward our hotel room?" I asked Tabby. It wasn't a bad idea. If there was a safe place for Lucy to stay, maybe I could convince her to stay there instead of sticking to me like glue. As far as I knew, it wasn't like there was a thread connecting us. It was more like I was her marker, so thus her caretaker.

"I don't know. It's not a usual dwelling, but I can try."

"It would be a good idea, though, right? I mean, we don't need anyone or anything coming in without an invite."

Tabby sighed. "Yes, Jimmy. I know."

It was time for me to shut up. I was pushing her too far. Sometimes I rambled on and on, not letting her speak, but I wasn't sure I was being all that bad. Though her getting annoyed was probably proof enough. Maybe I needed to not be such a smartass, but it wasn't like I was trying to offend her.

"Are we there yet?" Lucy asked from the back seat.

I glanced at her through the rearview mirror. She was smiling. "Smartass."

She giggled.

Tabby spun around in the seat. "Lucy, why don't you stay in the car? I don't think it will be a good idea for you to be around the demon."

Thank God for Tabby. I had been more wrapped up in the warding of the room than what to do about things immediately. I swear, if I had a brain…

"Thanks."

She smiled. "Any time."

"I hope you get him gone soon," Lucy said.

I could hear the fear in her voice. Poor kid. She'd been through enough. I needed to step up my game. No sense in putting her through more crap than I had to. "I do too, Lucy."

By the time Tabby and I got inside, Vespa was sitting at a table toward the front of the place. The restaurant was your usual Mexican thing: dark with wooden tables and chairs. The walls were painted in murals all over the walls. On each table rested a clay pot with a lit candle in it. I guess it was supposed to give some atmosphere, but I was thinking more about what could happen with a klutz and an open flame.

"Thank you for meeting me," Vespa said when we approached the table. He stood up, nodded his head at us, and sat back down.

I pulled out a chair and draped a leg around it. Tabby followed suit.

"It isn't for you we are doing this, just so you know."

It wasn't that I was trying to be a dick or anything, but I wanted to be honest. I didn't trust Vespa, and at this point, I wasn't sure if I trusted the Order since they seemed to want this to happen. I had a hard time believing that they would knowingly put Lucy in danger. So it must be that they knew that Vespa was possessed, and that was about it.

If this exorcism didn't go right, I wasn't sure if I could handle Vespa's spirit bugging me for who knows how long. Plus, he was kind of creepy.

"I welcome the help nonetheless." Vespa seemed to curl into himself. It would take a lot for someone to accept hostile help. Interesting.

Tabby leaned forward. "How did you get yourself into this mess?"

Vespa took a sip of water and stared into the flame. "I wanted the power that my great-grandfather had. Stupid, I know."

I glared at him for a minute. "Why was the power so important to you?"

"You would have to understand my family. Spiritualism is their religion. Since my birth, I was made to study, to make contact with the dead. Unfortunately, I wasn't very good at it. To my family, that was a blight on their good name."

He reached up and began picking at his face. I had flashbacks of that scene from *Nightbreed* where the guy peels his face off. But this wasn't real. It was fake. The latex pulled off in patches. When he finally took off the white wig, I found myself facing a kid that couldn't even have been twenty years old.

I closed my eyes and counted to ten. Blowing up in a restaurant would be a bad move. "Now would be the time to come completely clean. I hate lies. And I swear, one more lie out of you, and I'll walk away."

The kid's eyes welled up. It was strange seeing a young kid with close-cropped dark hair staring back at me where an elderly man had been. They did share the same facial features, but without the wig and the latex, he was just a boy. "I thought…I thought you'd ignore me if you knew how old I was."

"Is your name at least Nicholas Vespa?" At this point, I wouldn't be surprised if his name wasn't Tom Smith or something. Jesus Christ.

He nodded. "I was named after my great-grandfather."

"All right. Let's start this again." At least I did have his name. Shit. What a mess.

The waitress came over. She stared at Vespa for a minute, noticed the wig on the table, and slightly shook her head. "What can I get you folks?"

I had to admire her professionalism. "I'll take a Coke."

Tabby asked for one too. Nicholas stuck with water. After the waitress stepped away, he stared at me.

"Get on with it." I wanted to know the story and get the hell out of there. I had better things to do than listen to lies and that seemed to be the one thing Vespa was good at.

"I was supposed to be the one." His eyes took on a faraway look.

Tabby blinked. "The one what?"

"The one who could channel great-grandpa's powers. He was the one with the real gift. The others had to resort to tricks to get similar effects, but my great-grandfather was the real thing."

Of course there wasn't anything to prove that. Too much was left for me to simply believe, and I wasn't crazy about that. Not to mention the fact that he told me he had a demon possess him so he could hopefully pull off the parlor tricks his great-grandfather did. Was this kid really that stupid? Yes, he was. "You collared a demon to take up residence so you could have 'powers'?"

"Yeah. I know it sounds bad, but my family…we're broke."

Plenty of people went and got jobs to deal with their debt. This was the first time I had ever heard of anyone asking a demon to possess him to get rid of bills. It was probably a good thing he didn't have a giant student loan hanging over his head. He'd have invoked the devil then. I guessed you would either call this kid lazy or obsessed. I wasn't sure which yet. Either way, what he'd done was far from normal, incredibly stupid, and ridiculous. Evidently, the kid never learned to grow a set and tell his family to fuck off. If that was the issue here at all. I didn't believe a word that came out of his mouth.

"Why did they think you'd be the one?" Tabby asked.

"Because I looked like him," Vespa said. "They have all these old photos of Great-grandpa from the time he was about twelve until he died."

"Genetics decided to make you look like him, so they decided you needed to have his 'gifts'?" This part kind of rang true, I had to admit. I'd seen families this fucked up before.

The waitress came back with our drinks. The poor girl was dressed in some sort of serape thing. With it being over eighty outside, I could imagine how miserable it was to work there dressed like that. I would have had heat stroke within half an hour.

"Have you decided?" she asked.

I ordered something with lots of chorizo. Needed to have my spice fix. Tabby got tacos, and the kid ordered some chicken platter. The waitress seemed to be trying to cheer us all up with her friendly demeanor, but crap was too frustrating for it to work. She picked up the menus a little sadly.

"Thanks," I said to her. I got a smile in return and she left. I kind of felt for her. She was here, working her ass off, and we weren't even playing along and trying to make this dining experience fun. Not much I could do about that. Present company put a damper on things.

"You channeled a demon? Invoked a demon? What?" Tabby asked Vespa.

"I found a spell on the internet that was supposed to bring me a demon guide."

I couldn't stop my eyes from rolling and I snorted. I couldn't help it. Vespa stared down the table and I could feel Tabby's gaze boring into me. She couldn't expect me not to laugh at that. Shit. You gotta be kidding me. "And it worked?"

"No. I ended up using a Ouija board."

Now that made sense. I knew Tabby didn't mess with them. And given her own experience with it, I didn't blame her. Bad things happened with those things.

"What did it promise you?" I asked.

"Power beyond my wildest dreams, stuff like that. I allowed it in. Now I can't get rid of it."

I exhaled. I wanted to give him a set of crayons and some paper and make him write lines like a child. Nobody did this. And with him agreeing to specific abilities, this meant there was a verbal contract of sorts. Damn. I knew nothing about this side of it. I'd never dealt with a demon contract before. It wasn't like I knew a warrior who could help me fight for people's souls or anything. Though, if they did exist, it would be damn cool.

"Can you get it out?" he asked.

Good question. It depended on what the contract actually said. "Maybe. You, doing an agreement with this thing or whatever it was, I just don't know."

"Could you mark him?" Tabby asked.

That was a very good question. I had marked Lucy's soul and that's what kept her around. But Nicholas wasn't dead and this demon seemed to be getting nothing out of living in the body. Not to mention, I didn't want to mark him if I could keep from it. I did not want him hanging around my house. Sorry.

"I don't know." I truly didn't. Of course, I wasn't exactly going out of my way to find out either.

"What? Mark what?" Nicholas asked.

"Don't worry about it." I waved it off. "One more question though. What's with all the connections to my ancestor?"

He stared straight into my eyes. "Grandfather used to channel him all the time."

I blinked. At least I sort of had an answer now. This whole thing was getting worse and worse. So we'd seen Holliday's ghost in the saloon. If Vespa's grandfather had somehow trapped my ancestor's soul here, I needed to take care of that too. Not like I didn't have a crapload on my plate or anything. "All I can tell you is that I'm going to have to research it. I don't know enough about demon contracts to know if we can even exorcise you."

He exhaled slowly. "O'Malley said you could help."

Yeah, twist my guts, why don't you? I missed my mentor. At least he died normally. A heart attack took him right after he performed his final baptism. He went out doing what he loved. But I missed him. "I'm going to try."

#

After we all got back to the hotel, Tabby took Lucy around the complex. I guess there was this gift shop. Poor kid needed something to do. TV wasn't exactly going to keep her entertained forever, and it wouldn't be a bad idea to try to educate her either. I mean, hell, the kid, if she did get reunited with her body, was going to be so behind in school that it would be ridiculous. If she were my kid, I'd homeschool her anyway. The last thing she needed was for someone to ask her about her scars or something, and then all the mess would begin.

I relaxed on the bed with Isaac lying against my leg. Having a cat that liked me enough to use me as a pillow felt kind of nice. Every so often, I'd give him a scratch behind the ears. I had the "Holy iPad" in my hands. It wasn't like they expected me to know anything. They'd said something about training, after all, but I felt bad for contacting them. I shouldn't, I suppose, but it was like I wasn't capable of doing the job. But better to look like an idiot and ask instead of majorly fucking something up.

I jotted off an email letting them know about the contract and the possible trapped soul, and questioned what I should do about either one. Then I set the machine down and spoke to Isaac. "You should be helping me."

Isaac snorted, stepped over to the pile of brochures Tabby had brought back that afternoon, and dug at them until he uncovered the one he wanted. Heh. Who knew? Maybe I should ask him for help more often. I was going to have to tell Tabby about it.

I picked up the pamphlet. It was one about a ghost tour of Tombstone. Interesting.

"You saying I should go on this?"

Isaac let out a rowr at me and laid his head down to go to sleep.

I sucked my teeth. Who knew what would be in that ghost tour, but it was at least it was a lead of some sort, and until I heard from the organization, it was the only lead I had. Plus, I couldn't exactly ignore a suggestion from a witch's familiar. That was what he was no matter what type of spin Tabby tried to put on it. I didn't know of any normal cat who could have done what he had.

Chapter Six

Creep

"WE'RE GOING ON what?" Tabby asked when I tried to tell her about Isaac. Whether the cat told me either didn't register or she didn't care. She seemed stressed out, but I had no idea why.

"There's a ghost tour of Tombstone," I reiterated. It was a hell of a lead. Maybe I could learn something about my ancestor at the very least.

Lucy kept staring at Isaac like she was talking to him with her mind. I knew I sounded crazy, but if it got me the information I needed, so be it.

Tabby placed a bag from the gift shop on the table. Her shoulders slumped as if all the wind had gone out of her sails. I didn't know what I was doing wrong.

"When does this thing start?"

Okay, maybe she was just tired. I could deal with that. I picked up the pamphlet. "Says here that tours start after dark."

Tabby closed her eyes. I could swear she was counting. "All right. Let me get my coat. It gets chilly at night in the desert."

"Better stay here, Lucy." I winked, "Don't want to accidentally scare people."

Tabby turned around. "He got in here once before, and you want to leave her here alone? I haven't tried to ward the room yet."

Eek. I'd gotten way ahead of myself. Hell, she'd been with me the whole time. What the hell was I thinking? "Crap. I forgot. Why haven't you done it yet?"

That did it. She put her hands on her hips, her eyes flashing. I swear, she was about to catch me on fire with flames from her pupils. "All day it's been, 'Tabby, go get this; Tabby, do that.' What about

'Tabby is fucking tired, it's almost ten, and you want to go to a goddamn ghost tour'?"

I'd done it. Big time. Sometimes I was so stupid. "I'm sorry. You're right. Let's do it tomorrow."

"Let's." She stomped into the bathroom.

I was so totally screwed. The last time I'd seen her this pissed was the day she left me. Not good. I waved the pamphlet at Isaac. "Too bad you aren't a dog, I could borrow your house then."

He glared at me and then closed his eyes. Great. I'd pissed him off too.

"What about you, Lucy?" I asked.

"You aren't very smart." She plopped in front of the TV.

That was putting it mildly. The best thing I could do was keep my damn mouth shut until I knew Tabby had calmed down. "I know, Lucy. I know."

#

The next morning, Tabby wasn't talking to me, so I went out to get pastries for breakfast. The less she had to do at this point, the better. And I was hoping that chocolate might improve her mood. It was worth a shot. I knew I wasn't going to get out of this easily, but maybe if I made an effort, she'd forgive me a little more quickly.

I headed for the front desk of the hotel. The lobby was this all-white thing with a big concert-style piano in front of a large curved window. Kind of fancy-looking. After a moment, the guy at the desk turned his attention to me.

"Can I help you?"

I swallowed the spit that collected in my throat. I hated being nervous. Too bad my nervousness had to do with Tabby, and this dude at the desk was probably thinking I was strange. "Is there a bakery or something nearby?"

"There's a Walmart outside of town a ways."

I nodded, thanked him, and left the building and ambled toward the car. Walmart was better than nothing. I'd been hoping for a gourmet bakery, something that would impress Tabby, but I had to take what I could get.

Lucy had stayed in the room with Tabby. Part of me was thankful for the break, but the other part was kind of jealous. I'd gotten used to my funky sidekick. It was good to know for sure that she could be places where I wasn't.

I'd just unlocked the car when my phone rang. If it was Vespa, I would chuck the damn thing down the street. I snatched it from my pocket and glanced at the screen. It was Tabby.

"What's up?" I asked.

"You need to get back to the room."

This did not sound good. There was a strange desperation in her voice. "Okay. I'll be there in a minute."

"Hurry," she said, then hung up.

I clicked the clock on the car again and ran back inside. I tapped my foot at the slow elevator, but I didn't exactly know where the steps were, so elevator it had to be. Once I got up to the room, I could hear Isaac hissing through the door. I used my hotel room key card.

I didn't know what I expected to find. Maybe blood, maybe something worse, but that wasn't what I got.

I stepped inside. "What's going…," I stopped. A huge black cloud had amassed in the corner of the room. Lucy was hiding behind Tabby, standing near the bathroom. Isaac hissed at the thing from the bed. I wanted to call to Isaac to come closer to me, but I also didn't want to antagonize the black cloud any more than necessary.

I closed the door behind me. There wasn't a foul smell like you'd have with a demon, just this freaky-looking black cloud. It could have been anything. From my limited knowledge, it meant some sort of spirit. That was all I knew. I didn't even know if it was malevolent. Black didn't have the same connotation around the world that it did in the West.

"Isaac, get away from there," I said. Antagonizing be damned. I couldn't let Tabby's cat get killed right in front of her.

Isaac turned, ogled me, and then darted off the bed in my direction. Before I had a chance to do anything else, he leapt into my arms. I held him. Poor guy was shivering. I had to keep myself from smiling that Isaac went to me when he was in danger.

"Who are you, and what do you want?" I asked the cloud thing.

Slowly, it began changing form, undulating and shifting until finally settling on the shape of a man in an old-style Western suit. I recognized him immediately. It was my ancestor.

"You could use some help, pilgrim," he said.

I blinked. Shock grabbed me, but I'd take help wherever I could get it. "Yeah, I probably could."

He sat at the table and cocked a grin at Tabby. "I always liked redheads."

She twitched and blushed a little.

Then, my ancestor turned to me. "Tell your pretty lady friend I don't bite." He winked. "Much."

Tabby stepped away from the bathroom and stood near me. "What are you here for, Mr. Holliday?"

He stroked his mustache a minute. "Guess you could say I have better things to do with my time than let my relative get screwed."

I stepped forward, put Isaac down, and plopped on the bed opposite of Doc. "You knew his great-grandfather, didn't you?"

Doc let out a belly laugh, and then got stonefaced. "Now, that would be one way to put it. He promised me immortality in exchange for gold. Preyed on a man in a weakened condition."

I knew Doc had died of tuberculosis, drowning to death because of the fluid in his lungs. Not a pretty way to go. For someone to capitalize on that was despicable. And it was further proof that a Vespa was not a person to be trusted.

"You're what, a ghost?" Tabby asked.

"If that's what you want to call it. I could have done this myself. It still burns me up that I wasted all that gold." He adjusted himself so that he had one leg crossed and his ankle resting on the knee of his other leg.

"How come you're here? You didn't die in Tombstone," I said. It was a good point. Nothing held him here, as far as I could see.

He grinned. "I go anywhere I like. Sometimes I pay the swindler's family a visit."

Ah ha, now that made sense. See, people made it so hard to get simple honest answers.

"And you're here now because of the young Vespa?" Tabby asked. She was coming forward, a little at a time.

"Nah. I'm here because your boyfriend asked for help."

Now that caught me off guard. I'd sent off a message, not verbally asked someone for help. Tabby stared at me.

"I sent an email to the organization last night, but I didn't expect this." I motioned to Doc. "Not that I'm not grateful."

Isaac hissed at him. I had to keep myself from losing it. Though I probably should have been worried that Isaac so far didn't like him. Of course, appearing first as a big black cloud didn't help matters.

"Damn things never did like me. Wyatt always said it was my sunny disposition."

I chuckled. Then, I glanced over to the bathroom. Lucy was standing there. She seemed almost frozen in place.

"She isn't right, ya know," Doc said.

"What do you mean?" My head whipped around to him.

"She ain't all there. She's not like me."

I nodded. I should have figured he would know. "She's unique all right."

Lucy came forward. She was staring at Doc like he'd just insulted her in the worst way possible. "Ever been possessed by a demon, Mr. Holliday?"

He paused for a second. I thought that was something he never expected to come out of a little girl's mouth. "No, little lady. Can't say I have."

"It changes things," Lucy replied and plopped next to me on the bed.

"Come to think of it, you ain't right either." Doc waved a hand at me.

I coughed. He was pretty damn astute. "I don't think exorcists are supposed to be normal."

"Jimmy, you weren't normal before all of this," Tabby said.

"You're going to stick around for a while?" I asked Doc. If he was, he needed to get along with Lucy. And Isaac would tell me if Doc was really bad, I thought. At least I hoped so.

"As long as you'll have me."

Later, Tabby turned on the TV for Lucy, and Lucy explained modern things to Doc. It was kind of interesting watching her accept him. He must have been okay on some level for her to do that. I tuned them out after a while.

Was I happy for the help? Yes. But I didn't know if I could trust him. Lucy accepting him said a lot, but I didn't know him. Vespa being involved didn't help matters. Tabby's earlier warning about how ruthless even the heroes of the Old West were ran through my mind. Doc wasn't *Casper the Friendly Ghost.* He was the ghost of a killer. For now, he seemed to like us, but what would happen if we pissed him off?

Letting my thoughts drift off, I finally got around to turning on the iPad. That way, I could see if I got an official reply. Doc showing up was either as a result of them, or one hell of an odd coincidence. Doc was behaving like a very strange grandpa. Lucy seemed to be happier, wearing a smile a little more often. At least, she wasn't disappearing or anything, but I was uneasy.

After the device booted up, I clicked on my email icon. I had mail all right. Too bad it was spam. I guessed I was in for a long wait. That or they wanted to see how much I could handle. I was annoyed at that thought. I mean, my test, my real test, was Lucy, wasn't it? She was still here. Kind of. If they wanted to see if I could mark someone again, they should have had me tag along with another exorcist. What did they hope I'd accomplish with this one? It almost felt like a red herring. Something felt wrong about the entire trip. The little things that kept getting added were almost like distractions to the issues at hand. Fuck.

I shut down the tablet and tossed it aside on the bed.

"Are you okay?" Tabby asked.

"Peachy."

#

Doc disappeared before lunch. I was getting testy, of course. Part of it might have been that I hadn't had my morning caffeine. And I was used to eating breakfast. I hadn't had my daily bacon fix. Believe me, bacon makes a difference.

"Where did Doc go?" Tabby asked Lucy.

Lucy turned her head away from the TV. "He said he was going to keep an eye on Mr. Vespa."

That I could live with. If he turned out to be trustworthy, it might not hurt to have a spy. And maybe the old bird figured we needed some time to get used to him hanging around. If so, he wasn't wrong.

"Want to get out of here for a while?" Tabby asked.

I glanced up. "And do what?"

"I don't know. Get out of this room; get something to eat."

I was starving. "Food sounds great. How about you, Lucy? Want to get out of here for a bit?"

Lucy raised her hand toward the TV. It shut off. I clicked my tongue against my teeth.

Okay, that was new. She was getting stronger. I took her action as affirmative.

"Maybe I can find somewhere to buy a sage bundle." Tabby tapped her finger against her chin.

"For what?" I drew a total blank. What did she need that for?

Tabby glared at me. "To ward the room?"

"Oh, yeah, right." Now I felt like a doofus. I'd made such a huge stink about it yesterday, and today, I'd screwed up again. Hopefully, Tabby was just going to take my faults for what they were. I wasn't exactly doing a very good job at changing.

After that, I kept my mouth shut. My job was to take Tabby places, be her pack horse, and make sure she got something to eat. Nothing else. The last thing I wanted to do was to stick my foot in it again. It didn't last long, though. We had just settled into a booth in the diner. Lucy had come as well. She was sitting beside me nearest to the wall. It was better that I could see her and protect her than to leave her in an unprotected room.

"Why are you so quiet?" Tabby asked after the waitress brought our drinks.

"Because I'm starting to realize which one of us is the brains in this outfit." At one time, I'd thought I was smart. Heh.

Lucy giggled.

Tabby raised an eyebrow.

"No, really." I paused and took a sip of my coffee, "I'm okay at learning stuff from a book, but apparently, I don't have common sense for shit." It was true. I really wondered how I had managed not to totally screw everything up at Sorrow's Point before Tabby got there. Then, I remembered. I had been following the Roman Ritual. No wonder that part had worked okay. I'd had a guidebook. This here, I was flying solo, sort of.

Tabby rolled her eyes. "No, you're feeling sorry for yourself. Stop it."

I lowered my head. "Yes, ma'am."

"How do you do that thing?" Lucy asked. She was staring at Tabby instead of the TV in the corner of the restaurant. In fact, the picture on the TV seemed a little fuzzy. The news channel showed some sort of unrest in the Middle East. Perfectly normal, except for the fuzziness.

"What thing?" Tabby and I asked in unison.

"What you're going to do to the room."

Tabby paused, and then inclined her chin at me for help. I shrugged. I didn't understand it much myself.

"Um. Okay." Tabby put her head in her hands. "Let's see. You've been to church, right?"

Lucy nodded.

"You know how the minister prays for people?"

"Uh-huh."

I was so glad Tabby was the one explaining this. I couldn't imagine what it was going to be like when Lucy was a teenager. I just hoped she'd be back with her parents before I had to worry about the "sex talk."

"What I'll be doing is kind of the same," Tabby said. "I'll be praying for our room to be blessed so it will be a safe place for us."

"And so Mr. Vespa can't come in again?" Lucy eyes had turned a little watery.

"Yup."

"What about Doc?" Lucy asked.

Shit. That was a good question. Doc was supposed to be helpful to us, but could Tabby direct her wards to let him in? Or could they be like they were at Sorrow's Point? In a way, if they did get set to flat-out keep away things that meant us harm, that would be proof if Doc really was on our side.

"What type of ward are you going to do?" I asked.

Tabby waited when the waitress stopped by our table. We both ordered lots of bacon on our hamburgers. Bacon was becoming a staple with us, like milk and eggs.

After the waitress left, Tabby strummed her fingers against the table. I could tell a lot of this was making her nervous, more fidgety than usual. "I'm not sure."

"Can you do something like you did in the library at Blackmoor?" I figured I should make a suggestion. She needed some of the brunt taken off her shoulders.

"Maybe. I don't know. Hotel rooms are different than being in someone's permanent residence. I don't know if it falls under the same rules."

I never knew all of this could get so complicated. "How will you know?"

"I guess when I find out if it works."

I didn't like it, but it wasn't like I could blame Tabby for it either. We both were stumbling around in the dark with a lot of this. "At least we'll know one thing if it does."

"What's that?" Tabby asked.

"We'll know if Doc is really on our side." I kind of hoped he was. I mean, Lucy had perked up so much with him being here that I'd hate to lose that. It was almost like Lucy was relieved to find someone sort of like her.

"That would be a good thing to know," Tabby said.

I took a drink. "Yeah."

#

After we finished eating, and the waitress showed up with the bill, I had a bright idea.

"Hey," I asked our waitress. Unlike the one at the Tex Mex restaurant, she seemed happy. She wore jeans and a T-shirt with the café's name on it.

"Yes, sir?" she asked me.

"Anywhere around here that sells fresh herbs and spices? We were thinking of bring a bit of Arizona back home." I figured, why not ask the locals? That way, we wouldn't be stumbling around for hours trying to find something Tabby could use.

The lady grinned. "Tombstone isn't really the place for that. Mostly, just tourist stuff here. But if I were you, I'd ask at the general store. Monti might know of a place somewhere nearby."

"Thanks." It wasn't what we were looking for, but maybe we'd get something out of it.

"Don't ya find it odd that a guy manning a general store in

Tombstone has a name like Monti?" Tabby asked.

I snorted. "It's better than Slim."

"Not much."

Later and not surprisingly, the general store turned out to be a bust. Yeah, it had that great Western look about it with flour sacks stacked in the corner, jars of penny candy, that sort of thing, but nothing really that we needed. Tabby did manage to buy a cheap container of ground sage. It would have to do. I didn't think the sage being ground up would make too much of a difference. Now, how she was going to burn it, I left that up to her. She was the witchy expert, after all.

After getting the sage, we headed back to the hotel. Our room was just as we left it. I supposed it was going to take a while before we would stop looking for Vespa—at least until this whole business was over. Isaac seemed to take it all in stride. He popped open one eye when we came in, and as soon as he saw it was us, he went back to sleep.

Tabby dug around in her suitcase until she pulled out this ceramic thing and a bag with small pieces of charcoal in it. Who carried charcoal with them on a trip? But I'd be lying if I wasn't happy she did. "You should have been a Girl Scout," I told her.

She chuckled and put a piece of charcoal into the ceramic thing. Then, using a cigarette lighter, she lit the charcoal. After she got it burning decently, she sprinkled the ground sage on top.

It stunk. Not a pleasing stink either. Hopefully, the smell would dissipate before we got charged a clean-up fee by the hotel. I could see my superiors wondering what the bad smell in my room was related to and then me having to explain to them that, no, we weren't doing drugs. That had the makings of a fun conversation.

Tabby wandered around the room, chanting and drawing symbols in the air. Like the last time I'd seen her do this, the symbols glowed green. At this point, I chalked it up to me being weird. In a way, it was kind of cool that I could see Tabby's magic. But part of me missed being normal. Though Tabby would probably say that I'd never been normal.

When Tabby finished the circuit in the bathroom, she let the charcoal burn out and then flushed it.

"When will we know it worked?" I asked.

"Same as Blackmoor. When something tries to get in that we don't want in."

I wished she had this amazing ability to have a warning beacon, like a superhero, to help me know when the bad stuff was going to happen. But she didn't. "Or has plans to harm us."

"Yeah. That too."

"I'm scared," Lucy said. Maybe Lucy was my beacon. In fact, the last two times she'd said she was scared, something happened. It was something to think about. Her senses were more finely tuned than mine, and honestly, when she got scared, my asshole got tight. Why? Because I didn't remember one time while Lucy was possessed that her spirit said that she was scared to me. All she'd done was ask for help. Not a good sign.

Out of a whim, I picked up the iPad and turned it on. Minus Vespa, the email was the only thing I was waiting to implode. I loaded the email. Something labeled urgent caught my eye. Just as I opened the email, Doc popped in.

"Trouble's coming," he said.

I heard something that sounded like the ceiling crack. "Ah, hell."

This was so many levels of not cool that I couldn't even count them.

"Here we go again," Tabby said.

Fade to Black

WIND RIPPED THROUGH the room with a roar, crashing and moaning as fierce as any cyclone. Yet, as suddenly as it began, everything stopped. The pictures on the wall swayed as the storm died. Then, someone—or something—knock at the door.

Of course, it would all be left up to me. Tabby stared at me. Lucy and Doc alternated between looking at each other and the door. I shrugged, went to the door, and spied through the peephole. I stopped myself from punching the wall. It was Vespa, all right. And his eyes had the demonic snakelike pupil thing going on again. Despite my better judgment, I opened the door…but kept the chain on.

"What do you need, Nicholas?" If he asked for my firstborn son, I was going to take him out.

"To talk."

He said that now, but as soon as I took off the chain, all hell could break loose. Tabby's ward worked enough that it kept Vespa out…so far. The wind had made it in. Not sure if I should have been worried about that or not. Should I invite him in or tell him we'd meet somewhere? It wasn't like he was all alone. He had his demon friend with him.

I glanced over at Tabby. "What should we do?"

"Tell him that we'll meet him over at the diner in twenty minutes," she whispered.

I nodded. A public place worked for me. I turned back to my visitor. "Nicholas, go to the diner near the general store. We'll meet you there in twenty minutes."

"This best not be a ruse," he said, his mouth twitching at the corners.

I couldn't tell if he was trying to control a smirk or what. Oh, yeah. The demon was speaking. The question was, did Vespa know everything the demon did when the demon was in power? I had to pay attention to see if that was the case. Asking him wouldn't work. He'd already shown himself capable of lies. "We'll be there."

He turned on a dime and sprinted down the hall toward the elevator.

I could almost feel the mood of the room lighten as he left. I closed the door and relocked it. I left the chain on as extra protection. It might not keep someone from breaking in, but the extra noise would at least get my attention.

"At least we know the ward worked," I said.

They were all staring at me. It was odd. They were acting like a giant bug was about to crawl onto my head. I glanced up. Nope, no bug. "What?"

"What are we going to do now?" Tabby asked. Isaac let out a rowr in agreement.

Seriously? Since when did I become the leader? I was the guy who could sort of save souls, not a saint. I didn't know anything about wards and magic, and basically that stuff that was Tabby's expertise.

I sighed. "We go see what he wants, I guess. I doubt this demon will do much in a public place. After all, he's not like the one that had Lucy."

Tabby nodded.

It was true. I didn't like making blanket statements, but so far, Vespa hadn't pulled out monsters to throw me across the room or anything. Plus, this demon couldn't control Nicholas at all times. The kid could be himself. Lucy's demon, Asmodeus, was a big, nasty bastard. This one had to be further down the food chain.

"The next step is the exorcism." Tabby made it a statement, not a question.

She was right. There was no doubt that Vespa was possessed and we weren't waiting around for approval from the church. But there were a few problems. One: I didn't know if there were special rules regarding doing an exorcism on a willing possessee. Two: we couldn't do an exorcism in a hotel room. And three: where would we get the stuff I needed? Yeah, I could probably look like an idiot and jump in with a super soaker filled with holy water, but I wasn't about to pull a *Lost Boys* move either. I needed to do what I knew.

All we really needed was holy water, but I didn't even know if we could get roses this time of year in Tombstone. The rum was the easy part. I was starting to think about how good my bed at home felt. But no, I couldn't give up. If I did, I would be without a paycheck again, I couldn't take that risk.

"Looks like after we meet Vespa, we'd better go shopping."

Doc snorted. "You all act like you're coming back here."

Tabby and I exchanged a look. Did Doc know something he wasn't telling us?

"What do you mean?" I asked Doc.

"Somehow, I don't think this thing is going to be as easy as you think it is." He leaned forward a little, almost as if he was emphasizing the point. I didn't need that. I knew what was at stake—at the very least, Lucy's soul, but possibly all of us.

I closed my eyes for a minute to steady myself. "It's never easy. We plan as best we can."

Doc stared at me for a minute, nodded, and then disappeared.

"Stay here, Lucy. I don't want to risk losing you." Here she had wards to protect her. Out there, she had my sheer dumb luck. Wards were better.

Her big eyes widened. "Be careful."

I could only do my best. I hoped it was good enough.

#

We got to the diner with a minute to spare. Last thing I needed was for Vespa to be more pissed off. If Tabby didn't have time to make her holy water, I could always do my old priest blessings. I knew I'd feel off doing them, but if I had no choice… Besides, I was marked by God for this after all. Somehow, I didn't think he'd mind me using his blessing.

Nothing about the diner seemed off when we entered. There were no dimmed lights, no creepy feelings on the back of the neck. I was thankful. Vespa was at a table near the back. I couldn't tell if he was still pissed or not. Tabby and I steeled ourselves and headed for him.

"Nicholas," I said. He wore a pair of sunglasses, a dark turtleneck, and a black sport coat. How he wasn't dying in the heat, I had no idea.

"Please sit," he said.

I guessed he hid his eyes for the locals. Yet I was sure that people would assume he was wearing freaking contacts for a joke. Goth kids did that stuff all the time. Kind of funny, in a way. I'd seen it a few times in crappy eighties horror comedies. It didn't even work in the movies, so why did he think it would in real life? I was starting to think that Vespa was more naive than he put on.

"What did you want to talk about?" I figured I needed to get it over with. I didn't exactly want to share a meal with him if he was going to come up with some insane idea about trading one of us in exchange for his soul or some nonsense.

"I don't appreciate you sending spies to watch me," he said.

At least he'd said it calmly, I could deal with that. I leaned back in the chair. "First, you asked for my help. It's not my fault you never checked into how I handle things. Two, if you think I have the ability to control our mutual friend, you are sadly mistaken."

The corners of Tabby's mouth jerked. At least, I hadn't lost my charm.

"I do not like being spied on," he said again. I'm not sure what he expected me to do. It had been Doc's idea, after all.

I shrugged. "Nothing I can do about it. Now, if you no longer want my help, we can head home and go our separate ways." It was best to be truthful about it. I hadn't wanted to take his case from the beginning. If I could get out of the whole thing because he wasn't happy about the way I worked, then so be it.

He took off his glasses. "I can't lose your help. My eyes won't go back now." He leaned forward, so we could see his peepers more clearly.

He had darker green eyes. I doubted if someone would notice unless they were close to him. "If you want me to help, you'll have to deal."

"*He's* not happy about it."

I did want to ask. I had to tread very carefully until I was going to do the ritual. If I didn't, the exorcism would fail for sure, and I'd be in deep doo doo. "*He's* going to be a lot worse once we begin getting him out of here."

Tabby tapped her fingers against the table. I hadn't seen her do it before this trip, but it was becoming a habit. Either she'd established a new twitch, or my job was too stressful for her. I guessed I'd have to wait and see which.

"When are we going to begin?" Vespa asked.

"I need to do more research first." I wasn't lying. I did not want to start an exorcism if there was some odd provision in the contract he'd agreed to. I wasn't going to accidentally forfeit anyone's soul, even someone as stupid as Vespa.

"Where will we do it?" Tabby cocked her head to the side.

I inclined my chin at Vespa. It was his call. He was the one who knew the area. Our hotel room wasn't going to cut it. For one, it wasn't soundproof. That, in and of itself, was important with the noises that demons tended to make.

"My house," he said. "I have my own place."

That worked. I would want to check out his house for hidden issues, but it was a place to start. "All right, then. I'll be in touch once I'm done with research."

"And it will be over?"

Sorry, buddy; it wasn't that easy. Hell, I wished it was.

Tabby spoke up next. "You should know that it might take a while."

Vespa smiled. It was unsettling with those snake eyes now that I really concentrated on them. "What, a few hours?"

I chuckled. I had a feeling he'd been watching some choice horror films. "Apparently, you've never actually read about exorcism."

His snake eyes narrowed. "No, I haven't."

That figured. Why was I not surprised? "It has been documented that some exorcisms have taken years."

He froze. "I could be like this for that long?"

Yes, idiot. You should have thought of that before making a deal with the devil. "Maybe longer. That's why people don't make pacts with demons."

Yeah, I knew I sounded like an ass, but I didn't care. He had to hear the truth sometime. I wasn't about to hold his hand and tell him it was going to be okay.

"But you'll try to get it out?"

What did he think I was here for? A vacation? I stopped myself from rolling my eyes. "Yes, I'll do what I can. I can't promise a good outcome though."

Vespa sighed. "Okay. Let me know when you know more."

"Will do." That was where I had to leave it. I couldn't comment for sure on anything until I knew what I was dealing with.

He got up and left. The waitress approached the table and asked what we'd like. I waved her off. She glared at me, but didn't say anything. I watched her walk away.

"Do something," Tabby said.

I paused for a minute, trying to see what she was getting at.

She pointed at the table.

Oh. Yeah. I dug out my wallet and put a couple of bucks on the table. We'd wasted her time. Not cool. It wasn't her fault we didn't need anything there. Not then.

Tabby and I left the restaurant. What I needed was an email.

#

I was relieved we didn't have to try to exorcise a demon in the middle of a diner. One, trying to keep people safe would be a nightmare. Two, we likely would be arrested. That would be a first, for me anyway, not for an exorcist. Sadly, there had been a few cases where exorcists had been party to the deaths of their charges. I hoped I would never ever be in that type of situation. It had been close enough with Lucy.

Speaking of Lucy, she seemed happy when we walked in. She was humming, just slightly.

"The beast didn't kill ya?" Doc asked.

"Not yet, anyway." I wandered over to the bed, picked up the iPad, and turned it on. There had been something before Vespa threw his hissy fit. I hoped it was the response I'd been waiting for.

After it finished loading, I clicked on my email. Thank God the letter was still there. It would have been my luck if the damn thing had disappeared. I forced myself not to let anything on to the others and clicked on the email. I needed it to be good news. I stared down at the screen.

Mr. Holiday,

Your request for help has been noted. We consider this a simple case, so unless there is a huge mistake, your request for help has been denied.

Fr. Johnson

"Fuck me." I couldn't stop it from coming out of my mouth. It felt like I'd been punched in the gut, sucker punched. Did they even care what happened?

"What?" Tabby asked and crossed over to me.

I turned the iPad so she could see. "I don't care that they don't want to help, but they should have answered my question. Dammit."

"Shit, Jimmy. What now?"

Back to stumbling around in the dark. I guessed the advantage of being part of the Order was the credit card and the paycheck. Woe be it that I actually need some help. "I have to find a new age store, something that might be able to give me pointers. I don't want to end up with Vespa bugging Lucy all the time."

Doc nodded. "He isn't a good one."

That was an understatement.

"Give me that thing," Tabby motioned for the iPad, "I'll see what I can find. Why don't you go get a shower? Release some tension."

It was as good an idea as any. No way did I want to leave the room again so soon. Who knew what the thing inside Vespa had in mind? I already recognized it wasn't going to go easily, and if it had the chance, it would kill me to keep its body. Not hard to figure that out.

I climbed into the shower and got the water steaming. It helped to release the tension in my muscles. Other than that, it didn't do anything. My problems remained, staring me in the face. I needed an expert.

Too bad witch schools didn't exist like the ones in books, or I'd just go and track down the dark magic teacher, but no such luck. I was hoping I wouldn't have to contact a Satanist— I'd heard that there were perfectly normal people who were Satanists, but my upbringing and my former vocation made that idea hard to stomach. How could someone who worshiped a known evil being be a good person?

Somehow, being a witch was different. Being a witch did not automatically mean evil. All you had to do was watch old movies to know that. Tabby hadn't touched dark magic in her life. And it would be kind of hypocritical for me to not accept her weird when mine was so much more strange than hers. I mean, it's not like prior to Lucy that she regularly spoke to spirits or anything. That was all me.

Man, I was pissed at the Order. I could understand them not sending someone to do the job I was meant for, fine. But to ignore my question when I, in their own words, hadn't been trained yet? Bullshit. I should have listened to Tabby more before I signed up for this, though, if I hadn't we wouldn't have made it out here. The good old boy in me was pissed Vespa was so stupid, but I couldn't not help him. Losing Lucy to this demon was not an option. Besides, God never said that dealing with this stuff was going to be fun. And he tended to protect those who couldn't help themselves.

I got out of the shower, toweled off, and dressed. I needed to do the stuff I could do here. The best thing was to stop dwelling on the Order and take care of what I was able. It was time to get the ingredients for Tabby to make me some holy water. It had worked before. No sense in messing with the system now. Apparently I was supposed to fly by the seat of my pants again. But this time, I had to do it right, or I'd be saddled with this stupid fuck. I wasn't going to let that happen. Marking be damned.

#

When I came out, Lucy was playing with Isaac, Tabby was sitting on the bed, and Doc was gone.

"Where'd he go?" I wasn't completely sold on him. He wasn't doing anything to hurt us, true, but that didn't mean that he wouldn't accidentally leave us open to something.

"Said something about going to look for information." She shrugged.

Interesting. Maybe Doc wanted to help after all. "What time is it?"

"A little after three."

I lounged beside her on the bed. The weight of everything was getting to me. I needed to stop thinking so much. I sighed. "I should have known."

She didn't need for me to say more. She put her hand on my shoulder. "It's okay. You just expected more from them than you were able to get. That's all."

"It's just...why are people such assholes?"

"I'd say that would be something to ask your boss about, but it seems kind of disrespectful."

I snorted. I knew there was a reason I loved this woman. "I wonder how happy he is with the way the Order is being run?"

"Hard to say," Tabby said. "I imagine that if they at least get the job done, he can deal with it."

I could imagine God shaking his head.

Tabby got up and stretched her back.

"Why make me a marker?" I asked. "I didn't like the church before…"

"Maybe he wants you to change things."

I thought about that for a minute. I wasn't exactly the sanest guy around. I usually chalked it up to being a product of my environment, but maybe there was more to it.

Tabby went over to the TV and turned it off. I guessed she was tired of the background noise. Lucy glanced at her, shrugged, and then lowered herself in the chair by the table that Doc had vacated.

It was kind of funny that I, a defrocked priest, was suddenly chosen to help God claim souls. Maybe it had more to do with having a good heart than status. I didn't know. And now, it seemed like there were politics in play that I didn't know understand. I swore, if I lost Lucy because of some bigwig's political move, they wouldn't like me very much. The whole thing left a sour taste in my mouth.

"Stop dwelling," Tabby admonished.

I chuckled. She knew me too well. "What should I do instead?"

She shook her head at me. "Don't look at me like that."

"Like what?" I had something in mind that we could do if Doc took Lucy somewhere for a while. I wiggled my brows at her.

"Focus, you idiot." She threw me a wicked grin.

"Yes, ma'am." It was time for me to behave. Heh.

"First, we'll see what Doc finds," she said. "Then, we'll head out and see if any of the stores I found in Tucson will be able to help us."

"We're not staying here tonight?"

Tabby stared at me. "It's three, Jimmy. We're staying here. Tucson is tomorrow."

"Oh, right." I did need to focus, but sometimes she made me feel like an idiot. Of course, it would probably help if I thought things through. My brain didn't work like that, though. I was more of a doer.

"What now?"

"We relax. Eventually get dinner and hope Doc finds something that will help us." She said it so matter-of-factly.

I didn't understand how all of this could be so easy for her to put together, and here I was, freaking the fuck out over every little change. "Looks like we'll be starting an exorcism soon, huh?"

She nodded. "It isn't like there's much else we can do."

I slouched over onto my knees. I had made the mistake of thinking I was never going to have to do this again. I knew what had happened last time, how Tabby had gotten hurt. If I had anything to do with it, there would not be a repeat performance. "I don't like doing this."

Lucy wandered over and put her head in my lap. I felt nothing, but it was sweet nonetheless. She turned her eyes up at me and gave me the ol' puppy dog look. "We need you."

I reached to pat her head, but my hand went right through her. Was it really too much to ask to be able to comfort the kid? Jesus. "I know. It's just hard."

Lucy raised her head. "He knows."

#

After dinner, Tabby and I lounged around waiting for Doc to show. I wished he was able to figure something out. Lucy read over the pamphlets Tabby had found about Doc. Isaac snored.

"This is going to be a long night," Tabby said.

"I'm glad I'm not the only one that's bored." It wasn't exactly easy waiting for the thing you wanted most. "There's only so much you can do in a hotel after a while."

"It doesn't help that this is a small town that doesn't have much of a nightlife," Tabby replied.

"Except for ghost tours." As soon as it came out of my mouth, I regretted it. I closed my eyes.

"What are those? You talked about them before," Lucy said.

Actually, we had a hell of a donnybrook about one, but that was beside the point. It was so easy to forget Lucy was only six. She seemed much older at times. The sad part was I didn't even know when her birthday was. I had no way of knowing when she would get older. I guess I could have asked, but I didn't want to remind her of her family more than I had to.

"Places that are supposed to be haunted by ghosts. Some people decided to make money off it," Tabby said. "They take people on a tour of the haunted places."

Lucy squinted her eyes just slightly. "How do they do that?"

"They walk you through a place and tell you about the people that died there, hoping that a ghost will appear," Tabby explained.

"Some of them even do fake stuff to make a place look haunted when it actually isn't," I said.

"That's not nice." Lucy crossed her arms over her chest.

"No, it isn't." I couldn't argue with her. Especially now that we knew a ghost, and Lucy wasn't all that far removed from one. If God hadn't figured out what would happen to her before I died, who knew where her soul would go then? Maybe being a soul or being a ghost were more closely related than I thought.

So a ghost tour was out. Lucy spent a good bit of time ranting about how people shouldn't be mean to Doc. I'd thought the start of the conversation had been calm, but I hadn't expected Lucy's temper. After a while, I couldn't even understand her anymore. What worried me the most was that, in her eyes, Doc had seemingly replaced her family. Being this attached to him wasn't necessarily a good thing. It wasn't that I didn't like Doc, but he didn't belong in Virginia.

Tabby finally distracted Lucy by showing her some witchy stuff. For some reason, Lucy was fascinated with Tabby's bag of rune stones. They were made of chunks of amethyst, and I thought it was the purple color that had her fascinated, but then I paid better attention. Lucy kept stroking the painted gold letters on the stones. She understood so much, and yet she never spoke about it. I had to believe she had experienced a sort of hell while the demon possessed her.

What would happen when Lucy got her body back? Could she put all of this behind her and be a normal girl? More and more I was realizing that probably wasn't going to happen. She needed therapy now, and I had no way to find a therapist for a ghost. I guessed I'd better be cracking the psychology books. At least I had done some marriage counseling, but I knew with all my heart I wasn't good enough. The best I could do was keep her alive...and that knowledge hurt.

Suddenly I had a horrid thought as an old dusty book appeared on the ground near the table. "What the hell?"

A pop sounded and Doc was there in the chair. "Howdy."

I jumped. "You are going to be the death of me."

He chuckled. "Nah. Sources say you're gonna live a mighty long time."

I wasn't sure if that was a good thing or not. Besides, "long" could mean a lot of things to a spirit as old as Doc.

"What's with the book?" I asked.

"Might be of some help. I got it from Vespa's grave."

I blinked. It took me a minute, and then I realized he was talking about the original Vespa—the one who'd stuck him on this plane. I got that creepy feeling dancing along my spine.

"Is it a grimoire?" Tabby asked.

I swallowed, but the spit stuck in my throat. My brain stayed in first gear and I couldn't stop looking at the damn thing on the floor.

Doc stared at her. "A grim-what?"

"Never mind." I shook myself out of the daze. "Do you know what this book is?"

Doc's eyes turned red. "You calling me stupid, boy?"

Oh shit, now I'd done it. I jerked back. "No, sir."

His eyes returned to normal. "That's better. What kind of foolhardy question is that? Of course I know what the book is. I never would have brought some random book to you."

He had a point. But then, I wasn't exactly known for my astute grasp of knowledge either. Sue me for asking a dumb question. I glanced at Tabby. It was probably a good thing Doc couldn't read my mind.

"What is it?" Tabby asked.

"A demon manual, near as I can tell." Doc shrugged. "Might not tell ya everything, but it sure can't hurt."

"Thanks," I said to him. And I meant it. The Order might not be willing to help, but I had Doc. At least, he was doing something. I might be creeped out by the book, but it was something tangible. He was proving to be a hell of a lot of help.

Tabby walked around the bed and picked up the book. "It's heavy." She flipped through the pages. "And it's in Latin."

I grinned. I had been a priest. Latin was part of my education. This was doable. "It's been a while, but I can't be that rusty."

Doc chuckled. "If ya talk nicely to me, I might help you."

I grinned.

"You can read Latin?" Tabby asked.

"I was a doctor, ma'am."

I glanced back and forth between them.

Tabby, somehow, wasn't getting it. "How do you know Latin?"

Doc cocked a brow.

Time for me to clear things up. With Mom's obsession with everything Doc Holliday, I knew the answer for once. "In Doc's time, you had to be fluent in Latin to read most of the medical textbooks."

Doc grunted. "Don't doctors learn it now?"

I shook my head. "The only people who learn Latin now are those studying religion and other scholars."

Doc tsked. "Seems like they made medicine worse, not better."

"In some ways, I'd agree with you," Tabby said, flipping through the pages.

I held out my hand and she passed the book to me. It would have helped if I had a Latin dictionary, but I wasn't about to ask Doc to fetch one for me from somewhere. He wasn't my servant.

I opened to the first chapter. It was time to see what the elder Vespa knew. Hopefully, there would be something that would help us with the exorcism. But I had a sinking suspicion that this wasn't going to be as easy as the Order thought.

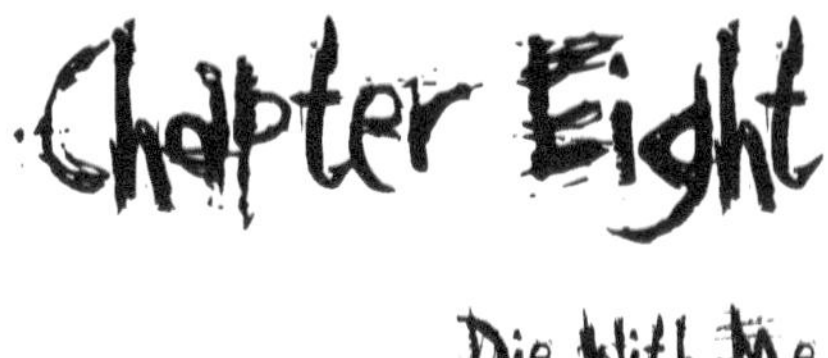

ONE THING, READING Latin wasn't exactly easy, especially when you hadn't read it in a long time. I was a hell of a lot rustier than I thought I'd be. In fact, the last time I'd done anything with Latin was when the demon spoke through Lucy during her exorcism. Speaking wasn't even using the same skill set as reading. The last time I'd read Latin? Back in seminary.

I had enough knowledge that I was able to make out a few things. Too bad it wasn't enough to know exactly what the book said. And with my limited knowledge, it was going to take me a while to work through it.

"Do you know what chapter we need?" I asked Doc. He was more of an expert on the language than me, and he had to have read part of it to know what book he'd been looking for in the first place.

"Depending on what you're wanting," he replied.

I swallowed my pride. It would be quicker to get honest help than to try to stumble through it. "Rules regarding exorcism, contracts with willing parties, stuff like that."

Doc motioned for me to put the book on the table. I complied. The pages shifted on their own, almost as if someone was flipping through them. If I hadn't been used to all the weirdness by now, I'd be seriously freaked. But it wasn't any different from Lucy doing the things she could. And in comparison to what I'd seen demons do, seeing pages in a book turn themselves was nothing extraordinary.

Tabby scratched something down on a piece of paper.

"What are you doing?" I asked.

"Trying to figure what types of herbs I'm going to need for the duration of this."

I nodded. "Might not hurt to recharge my ring."

She stared at my hand and almost seemed surprised that I still wore the ring she'd bought me. I wasn't that stupid. For me, the ring meant a couple of things. One: I was special enough to her that she was willing to do a spell to help me out—not a light thing. And two: it was a ring. Rings were about promises in our culture. She could have chosen anything, but she chose a ring. No way was I going to mess that up. I'd done enough the first time.

She scribbled some more on the paper.

"While we're up there, go ahead and get the vodka and stuff for the holy water."

"Right." She scribbled that down too. "Thank God you have that credit card. This is getting expensive."

I hoped the Order wasn't going to look at every single purchase. I mean, I could explain them all, but I didn't like being a bug under a microscope either. "At least, we don't have to worry about video cameras this time."

"Do you really think that's wise? What do you think got you off the hook with Lucy?"

She had a good point. If the exorcism hadn't been recorded, I probably would have been charged with attempted murder at the very least. Lucy's injury not being fake had something to do with it too. But I hadn't had any backing before, either. I'm sure the Order had lawyers. Besides, there was always the possibility that this exorcism would go off without a hitch. If it didn't, I could chalk it up to being my own stupid fault.

"Okay, I'll think about the video camera. Part of the reason we had it was Lucy's age." I didn't want to be accused of molesting her. I was a defrocked priest, after all. I knew what people assumed that meant.

"Yeah. And if anyone dies, there is going to be an investigation."

"That's what the Order is for." Yeah, I was probably being an idiot, but whatever. When you examined it closely, it was all out of my hands. I stared at Doc. "Find anything?"

"How do you ever get anything done?" he asked Tabby.

Tabby snorted. "What can I say? I'm used to him."

Doc grunted. "Give me some paper and a pen. I'll try to jot this down so he can stop being so impatient."

Tabby set her notepad and pen on the table.

"I'm not that bad, am I?" I asked her.

She raised her eyebrow at me.

#

I must have fallen asleep. I didn't remember anything after Doc agreeing to translate passages. If I were a more suspicious guy, I'd swear they'd figured out a way to knock me out, but since I didn't feel weird, I knew that wasn't possible. I searched the room with my gaze. Isaac and Tabby were curled up together under the covers. Doc was gone. On the table lay a stack of paper. Lucy was in front of the TV.

"Is everything okay?" I asked her as quietly as I could. I didn't want to wake Tabby.

Lucy stared back at me. "I think so."

"Okay, just checking."

She went back to watching whatever TV show her eyes were glued to. Who knew a kid would still get fascinated by a talking horse, even though the horse was in black and white. It was better than the horror films she usually watched. I could handle normal old TV.

I got out of bed, went and used the bathroom, and when I came back, I was sitting at the table. There was just enough light from the TV that I could read Doc's spidery handwriting. It was legible, but some of the letters definitely did not look like how they taught them today.

From what he translated, I had my hands full. Without knowing the full contract, I was kind of sunk. But it seemed like, for what Vespa wanted, he had likely sold his soul in some fashion. The book, near as I could tell, had nothing about "markers" in it. I didn't know if it would be as simple as my marking Vespa's forehead and rendering the contract void. Something told me it was going to be more complicated than that. But from Doc's translation, I got a better idea as to how binding the contract was. Yet I had to know the contract's specifics. Too bad there wasn't a demon-net or something I could log into to find out. If Hell was anything like Earth, the contract would be public record. I snorted. The idea of imps running around in starched white shirts sitting in cubicles was killing me.

I put down the papers and stared at the wall for a minute. I was starting to scare myself. My brain wasn't usually this colorful.

#

The next morning, Tabby and I headed for Tucson. It wasn't that big of a trip, but I didn't know how long it would take to find what we needed. She wanted to get there and look before anything else bad could happen. I guessed our goals were kind of the same, but I thought I was being a bit more chipper about it.

We took Isaac out for a walk before we left. That was an experience. He was okay with the leash, but he kept stopping and starting, and then looking back at the thing. Once we finished, we locked him in the hotel room, got Lucy in the car, and went toward our destination.

It took us about two hours to arrive. It didn't help that a cow had gotten loose from a farm somewhere and stood in the middle of the road for a bit. But when we finally made it at last, the first shop turned out to belong to this woman obsessed with angels. And when I mean obsessed, I mean really obsessed. She tried to sell Tabby a holy pillow. I could just imagine her running around after scantily clad men with white feathered angel wings, using a hoover to suck up the shed feathers.

The next store was manned by a kid who was young enough that she should have been in in school. Sixteen at the oldest. When Tabby asked to see the manager, the girl ignored her and continued texting her friends on her cell phone. The youth of America. No hope there.

When we made it to the last store, a thin Goth girl stood at the till. She too was young, but at least this one was probably eighteen.

Tabby stepped up to the counter. "I have a question?"

The girl glanced up from her book. It was one of those romance things with vampires that all the young kids liked. I didn't understand the appeal. I mean, sleeping with a vampire was technically necrophilia. Yuck.

"What can I help you with?" she asked.

Tabby took a deep breath. "A man we know was an idiot and made a pact with a demon."

The girl slammed her book shut. "I don't mess with the dark."

"You don't understand." Tabby sucked her teeth. "He wants out of the pact now. We're trying to help him."

The girl came out from behind the counter. "Sure he doesn't need an exorcist?"

I spoke up. "That's the thing. If the possessee signed up for the demon to use him freely, does that mean the exorcism will work the same way?"

The girl leaned against the counter. "That's messed up."

"Yeah. Tell me about it." I couldn't expect an eighteen-year-old to know more about this shit than I did, but hell, I'd expected to at least find someone who had some idea of what to do.

"We don't have anything like that in the shop. And I really don't know how to help," she said. She kept grasping and unclasping her hands. I couldn't tell if the subject made her nervous or if it was just us.

"Any idea how we could find out what the demon contract was?" I asked.

She paused. Then, she scratched her head with her left hand. After a minute, her eyes lit up. "It's kind of dangerous, but it might work."

I was willing to try anything, including tying a severed chicken foot around my neck.

"What's that?" Tabby asked.

"You could try a Ouija board."

#

Tabby said nothing until after we left the shop. She was walking so fast I could barely keep up with her.

"Look, I know you had bad experiences—"

She turned around and stuck her finger in my face. Shit.

"No, you look," she said, pointing her nail closer with each word. "I almost got possessed that night. I don't want a repeat performance."

I didn't want to piss her off more than I already had, but I didn't have a choice. There wasn't anything else for me to do. "How else are we going to find out?"

"We'll just ask Vespa again." Tabby opened the car door.

I grabbed her by the arm. "He said he doesn't remember. Don't you think if he knew he'd try?"

Her shoulders slumped. "It almost sounds like the demon obscured his memory."

More like she didn't want to go near a board, but I wasn't going to put it like that. I knew she had a reason to be scared. Yet this was something that had to be done. "It's a go with the Ouija board or we try to hypnotize a demon. Which do you prefer?"

"Damn it," she sucked her teeth, and then nodded.

#

I was surprised at how hard it was to find a Ouija board. Back in the day, all you had to do was go to the local toy store and grab one off the shelf. Now, not one toy store had one. I began to wonder if it was a conspiracy. But it turns out they don't carry them anymore. Who knew?

If it hadn't been for Tabby's desire to run into the bookstore, we'd have been sunk. I don't know if she sensed we could get one there, or if she had a raging desire for a book. But when she came out of the store, she was carrying a big bag. No books.

"What's that?" I'd asked.

"It's what you think it is."

I took the bag from her and riffled through the contents. She'd found one. It wasn't your usual Ouija board. It was this weird circle thing, but who cared? It was supposed to do what we needed it to do. That's all that mattered.

"Thanks."

She rolled her eyes at me. "Okay. Now that we have this fucking thing, what else do we need?"

"Just the mix for the holy water. The roses and stuff." I didn't want to be any more of a pain than I had to be. Even touching the board was putting Tabby in a worse mood. No sense in my doing something stupid and really getting into a fight.

Tabby grunted and got into the car. I waited until she had her seat belt buckled before I started the engine. Then, I put the board in the back seat.

"Be careful," Lucy said from the back.

"About what?" I asked her.

"With that thing in the bag."

"See," Tabby said. "I knew this was a bad idea."

Having two women joining forces against me wasn't what I'd bargained for. Damn. Beat the guy with a stick why don't you? "If you have any better ideas, please let me know."

Tabby grunted again. I programmed the GPS to lead us to a liquor store.

#

Tabby was silent the entire trip back to Tombstone. My stomach growled. We hadn't even stopped to eat. I probably should have tried harder to come up with another way for us to uncover the contract, but using the Ouija board was the first promising idea. Did I want to do it? No. And I sure as hell didn't even know if it was possible. I kept quiet. I was kind of pissed now, but me blowing my ass wasn't going to help the situation any. The best thing I could do was let Tabby let off some steam before I brought up the board again. I knew Tabby didn't want to do it, much more than I didn't.

I'm sure fighting a demon when you're a kid does something to you. Shit, I knew Lucy was permanently scarred and not just physically. I felt for her. But I could understand Tabby's reluctance too. It wasn't like I wanted to do this. We'd just been backed into a wall. Too bad it meant Tabby doing something she swore she'd never do again.

"Stop somewhere." Tabby threw up her hands. "I'm hungry."

The lady was hungry, finally. Her wish was my command. "Okay. Anywhere specific you want to go?"

"No."

Okay, it was going to be that way. Fine. If she got mad because she couldn't read my mind, I was going to find the nearest wall and punch it. I loved Tabby. I did. But I wished she could see it from my side too. If I didn't follow this through, Lucy was right. The demon would find a way to get her soul. The only thing standing between her and the devil's minions was me and my mark. I didn't even know if my mark would matter if I died.

Scary thought there.

We ended up back at the diner in Tombstone. By the time Tabby had decided she wanted to eat, there had been no place to stop on the way. I could tell it didn't help improve her mood. But she didn't say anything and didn't take it out on me. Thank God for small miracles.

"What can I get you folks?" the waitress asked. This one had red hair in an old lady bouffant hairdo.

We gave our drink orders and the waitress left.

"I'm getting dessert," Tabby said.

"Okay." I'm not sure why she felt she had to announce it to me. It wasn't like I had ever refused her sweets or anything.

She stared at me. "I'm ordering the biggest thing on this goddamn menu."

I didn't know what type of reaction she was looking for from me, but as far as I was concerned, she could eat a whole pie if that's what she wanted. It was a side of Tabby I'd never seen.

"Whatever you want," I said.

She brought the menu up to her face and pored over it. I set mine down on the tabletop. Finally, she lowered her menu. "Aren't you going to say anything?"

I blinked. "What do you want me to say?"

"You don't care if I eat like a pig?"

I closed my eyes for a minute, and then slowly opened them. "One, you aren't a pig. Two, if you are stressed out, I'm not going to bitch at you if you want to eat something that might make you feel better."

"Really?"

"Really."

"You don't care if I get to be over three hundred pounds?"

Okay, I could see where this was going. "I would worry about your health, but I'd love you. Weight wouldn't change that."

She slumped in her chair. Her spunk seemed to have calmed down a bit. "I'm still getting dessert."

"Whatever you want." I shrugged. What did I care if she wanted to eat a piece of pie? If she let me kiss her, her mouth would taste sweet. Yeah, better stop thinking like that now. Lucy was in the car and she didn't need to remotely see what happened when I…yeah, not going there.

I didn't bother to try to understand all of that. I knew she was stressed and pissed off, but where the weight talk came from, I was at a loss to understand. I'd never said a word about her weight to anyone. To me, she was great the way she was. Maybe she'd eventually talk to me about it. I could only hope that would be how it turned out. It seemed like something she needed to get off her chest. And if some guy had made her feel that way, I might just go and kick his ass.

#

After we got back to the hotel, I made it a point to grab the board. The least she had to touch it, the better. She didn't say a word, just grabbed up the rest of the bags. Lucy's eyes were rimmed with something that resembled water. I could tell already that this was going to be a fun evening.

Once we got into the hotel and up to our floor, Tabby opened the door to our room. Nothing was amiss. And no Doc. We set the bags on the floor near the wall. No sense in messing with them now. It wasn't like we were going to do this tonight. Isaac meowed at us. Tabby stopped to scratch him behind the ears.

I wanted to grab her and hold her, but she was being too stoic for that. I knew she liked to be the strong one, but strength had nothing to do with needing support once in a while. That made her normal.

"Want to do something fun later?" I asked.

"Like what?" She eyed me suspiciously.

"I don't know. Watch the reenactors or something?" Every day in Tombstone, reenactors performed the shoot-out at the OK Corral. While the Old West wasn't exactly my favorite thing, it was something we could do that really had nothing to do with exorcism.

"Maybe," she said.

It was better than nothing. I was at the table. Tabby lay on the bed.

"Get over here," she said.

Far be it from me to refuse her. I rose from the table and crawled into bed beside her. She curled up to me and put her head on my chest. It felt nice. Maybe she was going to let me be her comfort after all.

At some point, we both fell asleep. By the time I woke up, it was after four. Tabby was snoring softly. It felt good to know that even though she wasn't happy with me, she still wanted to curl up to me. Demon contract or not, the rest of the day was going to be about Tabby.

As far as I knew, as long as Lucy stayed in the warded room, the demon in Vespa couldn't hurt her.

Without warning, Lucy shook me from my thoughts. "I miss Mommy and Daddy."

I gently disengaged from Tabby and crawled on the floor where

Lucy was. Damn. This wasn't fair. Had she been this depressed the whole time? "I know, honey. If I could, I'd fix it."

"I know." Unshed tears swam in her eyes.

I wanted to hug her and tell her everything would be okay. I silently prayed to God that he'd figure out a way to fix this. I couldn't take much longer of not being able to actually help her and being a mere holding place for her.

"Maybe it won't be much longer," I said.

Lucy nodded. "I hope not."

What I could do was find a way to distract her. Get her thinking about something else. My choices were Isaac or Tabby. I chose the latter. "I want to do something special for Tabby. Any ideas?"

Lucy paused. "What does she like?"

"Scary movies, good food, stuff girls like." How do you answer that question for a six-year-old?

Lucy laughed. "You're silly."

"I know. Tabby tells me that all the time." I thought of myself as more of a dork, but it wasn't like there was much of a difference.

Isaac hopped off the bed and trotted over to Lucy. She began petting him, actually petting him. It was different than before. How in the hell could she pet a cat? I mean, she rubbed his ears, they moved, the whole nine yards. Her form no longer passed through him. Maybe God had answered my prayer after all.

"How do you do that?"

"Do what?" She raised a brow.

"Pet Isaac." I motioned at her hand. I wasn't sure how much deeper I should go into the situation.

She shrugged. "I don't know."

"Something is different. When you touch me or Tabby, we just feel a little coldness, but it's not like how you're petting Isaac now."

She shrugged again. "Maybe cats are different."

"Maybe." It was about the only explanation, minus the prayer, and it wasn't like I had time to explore it further right now. Besides, while I had been a man of God, I wasn't a huge believer in miracles. Sometimes things went how we wanted them to...and sometimes they didn't.

"What's going on?" Tabby asked from the bed.

Shit, we'd woken her up. "Nothing. I just noticed Lucy can pet Isaac. I mean really pet him."

"That's…," Tabby sat up and rubbed her eyes, "…interesting."

"Yeah. How are you feeling?"

"A little better." She popped her neck. "I'm hungry."

Food must be her medicine for the day. I wasn't going to say a thing, especially not with how the conversation went before. "Want to do an early dinner?"

She nodded. "Let me go get cleaned up."

I got the feeling there was something she wanted to talk about, but I wasn't about to ask. Not yet. Better to let her tell me on her own. Especially when I got the feeling it was something important. Maybe food wasn't her biggest focus. Maybe she just wanted to be away from Lucy for a while.

I got off the floor and changed my clothes.

Tabby came out of the bathroom. "Where do you want to go?"

"You pick." I pulled out the advertising stuff from the dresser drawer and handed it to her.

She took the booklet from me and flipped through it. "It's a little bit of a drive, but how does Italian sound?"

I shrugged. I'm not sure if there was anyone on Earth that would pass up lasagna. "Works for me. It's only four-thirty."

She beamed. I grabbed the keys. "Lucy, take care of Isaac. You're in charge."

"Can Doc come and play?" she asked.

Did she know how to call him? That might be a good thing to know. "Doc kind of comes and goes as he pleases. But if he comes, I don't see a problem with you making him entertain you." I winked at her.

She giggled.

Tabby and I left, making sure the door locked behind us.

"She's a good kid," Tabby said as we were heading toward the elevator.

"Yeah, she is." She deserved better than I could give her. They both did.

#

The restaurant had dim lighting and candles on every table. A series of murals of Italy encompassed the walls. I'd seen it before. Some restaurants, especially ethnic ones, liked to make you feel like you were in the country. Too bad I didn't know a lot of these scenes. The only painting I recognized was the one with the Leaning Tower of Pisa. The restaurant looked expensive with all of the decor and the crisp tablecloths. I felt seriously underdressed, but no one said anything to us. They were probably used to tourists.

"What are you going to get?" I asked after a bit.

Tabby shrugged. "Probably lasagna or something. That wasn't why I wanted to come here."

I kind of figured that, but I didn't have a clue what she wanted to talk about. "Okay…"

"We needed more garlic in our systems, and I wanted to explain a few things without Lucy being around." She arranged the napkin on her lap.

"All right." That made sense. I knew garlic had a lot of antioxidant properties and since Tabby was the witch stuff expert, I wasn't going to be upset about eating a little of it.

"I know I was being a bitch earlier." She sighed. "But it's hard."

I nodded. No sense in interrupting her. I was glad she apologized to me, but by now, it was unnecessary. Her thing at lunch proved to me there was more going on than just surface stuff. I was there for her, better and worse.

"You know the story of me with the Ouija board. I've told it to you a few times."

"Yeah, you have." She'd last spoke of it in Blackmoor. Sometimes, it felt like all of that had been a long time ago, but it was just this past November.

"What I've never told you is how it felt. It hurt, Jimmy. It was bad."

The waitress interrupted us. We gave our drink orders. Tabby continued after she left.

"Imagine feeling like something is trying to snatch what makes you the person that you are right out of your body. Then, imagine your brain being pulled out of your head through a small hole the size of pencil lead."

"Jesus Christ." That was worse than how I'd heard childbirth described—squeezing something the size of a watermelon out of a hole as small as a lemon.

"That's what it felt like. And then, bear in mind I was somehow able to have the fortitude with that pain to use the knowledge I had to fight the demon off. I'm thankful to this day it wasn't an extremely strong one."

"Me too." I could see why she didn't want to use the board. And being as sensitive to the supernatural as she was, it left her more susceptible. "I'll do it by myself."

She blinked. "Do what by yourself?"

"Use the board. That way you don't have to risk going through that again." It was time I grew a set and stopped dragging her into my stuff. She hadn't signed on for this. The least I could do was make it as easy on her as possible.

"No way, Jimmy. No fucking way. Do you have any idea how easy it is for a demon to gain purchase on this realm through one of those boards?"

"It's been done, though, right?" I blocked out what I'd seen happen in the movies. Better to think positively.

She glared at me. "Very rarely, and I wouldn't trust it. No, you and I will be talking to this thing, but it sure as hell won't be at night."

"Fine by me." Hey, if she was going to refuse to let me do it on my own, fine. But if she had nightmares over it, she'd better not blame me.

"And I never want to hear you talk about using the board by yourself again. The last thing I need is for you to be possessed."

While I had to admit that would be bad, I wasn't exactly sure a marker could even be possessed, but if it was possible, that would not be cool. "Okay. No problem. Let's stop talking about that now and do some normal stuff."

"Normal sounds very good."

#

Normal turned out to be taking a walk once we got back into Tombstone. Old Town was lit up with old-style lanterns at night. Tabby seemed a lot more carefree, for which I was thankful. The tension we added at dinner seemed to slip away and I felt almost like we were back before things went sour.

Part of me was willing to ignore what Tabby said and go ahead and use the board without her. Not smart, maybe, but I wanted to avoid causing her pain as much as I could. She was scarred by her past experience. Better to scar myself than let her add any more. I wanted to protect her from all the nastiness. Too bad my current job involved diving into hell and hoping it all worked out. Who knew what started out as a favor could turn into something this complicated? To think, at one time my life had been as simple as get up, perform mass, eat lunch, do counseling, eat dinner, relax, and then go to sleep. It was boring, but I was starting to realize how nice boring could be.

Everything was evolving, including Lucy. Her suddenly being able to pet Isaac had me nervous. I feared her body wasn't faring well. I could call Will to check on her physical form, but things had been strained to say the least after Lucy's exorcism. It probably would be the right thing to do. The kid wanted her family. Maybe, if the conversation went okay, I could let her listen to her dad talk.

"Are you okay?" Tabby asked. "You seem distracted."

"Just thinking." I didn't know if it was a good idea or not. Last thing I needed was for Lucy to shout out to her dad that she loved him and wanted to come home. Yeah. Try explaining that one.

"About what?" She looped her arm around mine.

"Lucy, actually. Her getting more solid has me worried." It did, but I also didn't want to bring the rest of it up to her. She had enough going on without my adding anything to it. But if I didn't start talking, she'd prod me until I spilled the whole bloody thing.

"How so?"

"If she's more solid here, that means she's getting stronger. Wouldn't that mean her body was giving out?" I did not want to think about Lucy dying. I couldn't think of losing her now.

"I don't know. Not necessarily. Why don't you call Will?"

"You know why." I paused. We were in front of a gift shop. In the display rested this little vase. It was exactly like one Mom had when I was growing up. Odd.

"Surely they would appreciate the call?"

"Maybe." But I didn't even know what to say to them. I mean, "How's Lucy?" seemed kind of contrite.

"What are you looking at?"

I pointed at the vase. "My mom had one just like it."

Tabby let go of my hand and stepped closer to the window for a better look. "Maybe it's a knock-off."

"Or maybe Mom was here once." Which meant that there was a possibility that she'd met Doc.

She walked back over to me. "You should call."

I sighed. She wasn't going to give up; I knew that. I needed to get it over with. I pulled out the phone and clicked on Will's name. After a few rings...

"The number you have reached—"

I disconnected the call. I wasn't surprised. Why would he want to get in touch with me? I'd been the last person to see his daughter before the accident, demon-slaying, whatever you called it. "I got a recording. Will's changed his number."

"Want me to try Tor's?" Tabby asked.

I shook my head. "Nah. I have a feeling that if they wanted to talk to us, they would have called by now."

"Yeah."

"Back to the hotel?" Our evening was ruined now anyway. I guess thinking about a sick kid will do that to ya.

Tabby brushed the hair out of her face. "Might as well."

#

Getting back to the hotel was the easy part. Finding the room trashed, however, was not what I expected.

"What the fuck?" I heard a pop and Doc appeared in from of me.

"What happened?" I asked him.

"A lady came in to steal stuff. She tried to take that thing you always fiddle with."

I almost asked what thing, then I remembered the Order's iPad. "Did she get it?"

"Nope. Lucy scared the bejeezus out of her."

I finally spied it on the floor, face down near my side of the bed.

"And where's Lucy?"

"Too tired. She has to rest before she can show herself again. What she did took a lot out of her."

I hoped it hadn't taken too much. I didn't have a great

understanding of Lucy's well-being, but her not even being able to show herself wasn't a good sign. I needed more information and the Order didn't seem to be wanting to give it.

"Isaac?" Tabby searched the room. "Shit."

I dropped the iPad on the bed and ran out of the room. "Isaac!" I dashed around the floor. No cat. So I headed down to the front desk. Maybe they'd seen him. "Anyone see a cat?"

The girl behind the desk had a stony expression on her face. "Animal control has already been called, sir."

Oh, hell no. We weren't going there. "It better fucking be canceled. Your staff broke into my room! Where's the damn cat?"

The girl stared at me like I was lying. I slammed my fist down on the counter. "I want my cat. I want to see the manager, and you'll be lucky if I don't sue your asses."

The girl behind her hopped to it and opened the door to what I guess was the copier room. Isaac snarled and hissed. I pointed at the girl who now wasn't so smug. "Cancel that goddamn call!"

She grabbed the phone and dialed. A man in a suit came out of another back room.

"Are you the manager?" He resembled a sniveling little weasel.

"Yes, sir. If you'll please take it down a notch."

"You can shove your notch up your ass. I suggest you look at the security footage in the hallway near my room." I wanted to drop kick the asshole.

"Hold on." He walked into his office. After a minute, he came back. "Sir, I apologize. It doesn't look like anything is missing."

No help from them. It was a good thing I wasn't able to shoot fire from my eyes, or I'd have burnt the whole building down by now. I guessed that's why the superheroes always were torn people— always weighing the options in any situation. Me, I'd probably make a better supervillain. "No, but my iPad was found on the floor, and if it's broken, I'll expect a replacement."

"You'd have to take that up in court, sir."

I stepped closer to the guy. Didn't he realize my fuse was almost gone? "Any idea how it will look for your hotel if I tell people how pet-friendly you really are? How you almost got my cat euthanized because some worker tried to rob my room?"

"Sir, it's standard procedure to call animal control. Especially when our staff reports being attacked."

Yeah, attacked because she tried to rob me. Fuck him. "I suggest you start paying attention to what's actually happening instead of playing solitaire on your fucking computer all day. And if Isaac is hurt, I'm holding this hotel responsible."

His mouth opened and closed a few times like a fish. "That won't be necessary, sir. Would you like him checked out by a vet?"

"Yes, dammit. That's the least you could do." I swore, if there was something wrong with Isaac, I might just let Tabby kill him.

They let me go behind the desk. As soon as Isaac saw me, he calmed down. "Let's get out of here, bud."

I untangled the rope from around the leg of the copier and off his neck. He jumped into my arms, pressing himself against me so hard. Poor thing. He was shivering.

"How long until the vet gets here?" I asked the girl.

"About half an hour. I'll send him up to your room as soon as he arrives."

I grunted and took Isaac back to Tabby. Isaac was so quiet during the elevator ride that it was starting to look like he was going to need a therapist. That was probably overkill, but whatever.

"Where have you been?" Tabby asked when I opened the door to our hotel room.

"Saving Isaac from idiots. The thief let him out. Though I guess he tore her up pretty good. They called animal control on him." I waited for that little bit of information to hit.

"Shit." She reached forward and Isaac jumped into her arms. "What the fuck was their problem? I swear, if he isn't okay—"

"They're sending over a vet to check him out." I was doing my best not to give her the full brunt of my anger. I wanted to drop-kick the manager. If I amped her up anymore, she would actually do it. But I have to admit, the stress relief of the act would do me good and probably help Tabby too.

"My poor baby," Tabby cooed at him.

I left her to Isaac, went over to the bed, and checked the iPad. The screen seemed okay. After a moment, it opened. I knew better than to count on that, so I went to a few websites and checked my email.

Everything loaded fine. I shut it down and put it on the table.

"Are they calling the police?" Tabby asked.

"Who the hell knows?"

"Want to change hotels?" She appeared concerned, but more focused on me than Isaac.

Changing wasn't an option. "This is the only 'pet-friendly' hotel in Tombstone."

"Shit."

"Yeah." Though I had a bad feeling that weasel would black-ball us at any hotel around Tombstone. We had to come up with another alternative.

"So much for a normal evening," Tabby said. She went over to the little stand in between the beds and picked up the phone. She punched a button and called down to the front desk. "Yes, this is Tabatha Settle in room one-four-oh-eight. Have the police been notified?"

"Uh-huh. Yes, we won't touch anything else...," she paused. "All right. Thank you."

I watched her hang up the phone.

"What did they say?" I asked.

"Cops are coming. Vet's coming. We are supposed to stop poking."

I sat in the chair near the table. "What a night."

"Tell me about it."

#

The cops took our statements. Tabby and I went through everything, including what we'd bought today. Not a thing was missing. I hated to think what Lucy did that scared the thief so badly and left her in such bad shape. Isaac I could imagine. Too bad Doc had once again disappeared or I'd ask him.

The vet had come and gone. Isaac was okay, but stressed. The vet suggested extra treats and plenty of water, anything to make the cat feel loved. I had to force myself not to roll my eyes. Isaac was spoiled enough as it was. This was only going to make it worse, but already Tabby was giving him extra pats.

"Guess we should ward the room again, huh?" I mean, it couldn't hurt. But it was starting to seem like the wards only worked on things connected to the supernatural. Otherwise, how would the robber have been able to come in? Unless Vespa had done something to the ward before. I didn't want to even consider that.

"Probably. I have to wonder if Vespa had anything to do with this."

Nice to know we were on the same wavelength. "Good question. I just hope Lucy's okay."

"I'm okay," she said. I couldn't see her, but at least she could communicate with us. That made me feel a little bit better.

"Is Doc with you?" Tabby asked.

"No, you are, silly. I'm here."

That was a relief. I didn't want to think she was in between worlds or something. Yet her not being able to show herself scared the crap out of me. It had been bad enough when Lucy was getting more solid. I needed to know what it all meant.

I flipped through the iPad, searching Facebook and a few other social media sites for Will, but it was like he dropped off the face of the earth. I wrote an email asking the Order if they could check on things. I loosely explained what was going on with Lucy's soul. For now, that was the best I could do.

Needless to say, getting to sleep that night wasn't easy. I woke up at any small sound, including whenever the air conditioner kicked on or off. Even though Tabby had warded the room again, I didn't feel safe. What good was a ward when it couldn't keep all the bad people out? I hoped to hell it was just a thief and not something to do with Vespa.

I was tired of the whole thing. I wanted to find out what we needed, deal with Vespa's problem, and go home to sleep in my own bed.

Tabby, somehow, slept like a log. Maybe part of it was knowing that Isaac was okay. Part of my uneasiness could have stemmed from knowing that we were going to use the board. Tabby's experience, now that I'd learned the full story, left me feeling anxious about it. If I knew of some other way to get the information, I'd have used it—even if it did mean trying to hypnotize the demon.

Chapter Nine

Bring Me to Life

"I DON'T WANT to be here when you play with that thing," Lucy said suddenly.

I could barely make her out standing by the bed. Her eyes had this wild look about them and her hands were shaking so badly that her body seemed to quiver.

"I don't know if there's anywhere to go. Do you know any way to contact Doc?" It was the best option, really. If Doc could keep her occupied, then maybe, just maybe, she'd be safe. The last thing I wanted to do was bring in another demon and have it snatch Lucy.

"I can try," she said.

"Okay. Do that. If it doesn't work, we'll come up with something else." What else, I had no idea. Maybe Tabby would have some thoughts.

Soon after, Tabby came out of the bathroom, combing her fingers through her hair.

"Any idea where Lucy can go while we do this?" I figured it was worth it to ask her. I had no more ideas.

She sighed. "No. Not really."

"She's going to try to get ahold of Doc."

Tabby walked over to her side of the bed and sat. "Okay. If she can't get ahold of Doc, then we'll have to use the damn thing somewhere else, but I don't like the idea of leaving Isaac and Lucy by themselves again."

"Me neither. I'd happily get out of this hotel if I could."

Tabby tapped her fingers on her knee. "We should only be in the hotel for a few more days anyway. We'll have to stay where we'll do the exorcism so we can make sure Vespa doesn't have a heart attack or something."

"Good point. But we're back to what to do with Lucy. Vespa's demon did something to her once before. I wouldn't put it past him to do it again."

She paused for a minute. "I could always ward the car. Lucy should be safe enough if I ward it. That way, she doesn't actually come in contact with the demon anymore."

I hugged her. Sometimes, she was so damn smart. "It's stuff like that that makes me want to marry you someday."

She pulled back. "Really?"

"Yes, really."

Suddenly, there was a pop and Doc appeared. "Don't you go getting all mushy on me."

I couldn't help but laugh. For an old-timer, he was funny. "What's up, Doc?"

Lucy giggled.

"What do you need, kid?" he asked Lucy.

"They are going to use that 'thing.'" She pointed toward the bag with the board in it.

Doc crouched down in front of her. She was a little more visible now, almost like colored cellophane.

"What do you want to do?" he asked.

I spoke up. "Lucy and I want to know if there was somewhere you could take her or if you could keep her occupied while we tried to get some information."

Doc stroked his goatee for a minute. "Don't think I can take her away from ya, but Lucy and I can find ourselves something to do."

"Thanks. I appreciate it." And I did. The sooner I could get this out of the way, the sooner we all could go home safe.

Doc nodded and went back to giving Lucy his full attention.

I turned to Tabby. "When do you want to do this?"

"Now, I guess. I want to get it over with."

I got up, grabbed the bag with the board in it, and plopped back on the bed.

Tabby shook her head. "No, let's do it on the floor. I don't want to do it where we sleep in case we end up spending another night in this place."

I got off the bed and plopped on the floor in the hallway next to the bathroom. "How's this?"

Tabby sat opposite from me. "It will have to do."

I pulled the plastic off the box and opened it. "I assume this works like it does in the movies."

"Pretty much, except in the movies they always forget to close the portal."

I didn't bother to pretend I knew what the hell she was talking about. So be it. We needed to get this done. I got the pointer thing out of the box and set it on the floor. Then I put the board down in between our knees.

"Okay, you ready?" I asked her. Would it even work with her being so reluctant?

"No, but do it anyway."

I put the pointer thing on the board. Tabby placed her index finger and middle finger of her right hand on her side of the pointer. I followed suit. "Now what?"

"We ask it things." She stared pointedly at me. "You get to ask."

Great. Thanks. I took a deep breath. "Is anyone there?"

The pointer began moving in a figure-eight pattern. Strange. "Okay. I need some information about a contract."

The pointer kept moving. I guessed I needed to dumb down my question. "Do you know Vespa?"

The pointer changed direction and moved to the yes on the board. Then, it went back to the figure-eight pattern.

"What now?" I asked Tabby.

She sighed at me. "Keep concentrating on the planchette."

"What's that?"

She rolled her eyes. "The thing that's moving."

"Oh." Now, I felt like a total dumb shit. Using one of these things was supposed to be simple. Evidently, my brain didn't get the message.

"Keep to questions it can answer with a yes or no. But like everything else, they lie. A lot."

I nodded. Got it. Remember that the demons lie. "Okay, spirit. Do you know anything about the contract Vespa made with his visitor?"

The planchette moved to yes. And that's when the lights went out. Holy shit.

I jumped up and tried the light switch on the wall. It didn't work. Rushing over to the window, I pulled the blind away so that I could see. The traffic lights outside the hotel worked.

"Fuck this," Tabby said.

I watched as she flipped the board upside down. "Goodbye," she said.

After a minute, the lights came back on. Too weird.

"See, this is why we don't mess with boards."

So much for a good idea. Not how I expected all of this to go. "Okay. Let's get rid of this thing."

"That requires burning it."

Okay, that couldn't be done in a hotel room. Good thing we were surrounded by desert. "Fine."

#

Tabby stayed at the hotel with Lucy, Doc, and Isaac. I had the board, a can of lighter fluid, and a lighter. I had to stop by a grocery store to get that stuff, but it wasn't hard.

I drove out of town into the desert. It took me a while to see nothing but sand and sagebrush. I picked a nice spot with lots of sand, pulled over, and got out of the car with all of my accouterments. Making my way down the little hill, I made sure I was away from any vegetation. No sense in starting a huge fire if I could keep from it. At least the wind wasn't blowing. I had the board in its bag along with the receipt. Best to get rid of it all so there would be no connection left.

I doused the bag with lighter fluid, stepped back, set the receipt on fire with the lighter, and then tossed it onto the bag. The whole thing torched immediately. A ball of fire whooshed into the air and then settled back down. The plastic melted first, then there was another whoosh when the cardboard box caught fire. I stood there and watched the fucker burn. Without a doubt, that was going to be my one and only experience with a Ouija board. It wasn't worth the risk, not if it meant losing my soul in the process.

Suddenly, I noticed I wasn't alone. All around me, various desert birds had formed a circle with me at the apex and around the fire. Ravens, crows, several birds I'd never seen before, and one scraggly-looking vulture surrounded me.

Not one of them made a sound. Finally, when all that was left was ash, I grabbed a nearby piece of rotten wood and scattered the ashes.

A crow cawed at me. "Thanks, guys," I said, and they all flew off. One more thing for me to chalk up in my weird file. I couldn't wait for Tabby to hear about this.

#

I got back into the car, turned around, and headed toward Tombstone. A few of the birds followed me for a bit and then, closer to town, they stopped.

"Guess I had my own personal escort."

Once back at the hotel, I parked and went to the room. In my opinion, Tabby should ward the car as soon as possible. The bird thing combined with the board and the damn break-in had me twitchy. I was going to call the Order if I had to. Enough of putting myself and Tabby in danger for an idiot. It was time I took control, and if they didn't like it, they could shove the whole thing up their asses. I was tired of trying to live by their rules. It was time I went back to my own.

Chapter Ten

Forsaken

"TABBY?" I ASKED, closing and locking the door behind me.

"What?" she called from inside the bathroom.

"Never mind. Finish what you're doing." No sense in her stopping when I could wait for a bit.

Lucy and Doc were seated at the table. The curtains were open and the sunlight streamed through both of them. They weren't doing anything, not even talking.

"How's things now?" I asked them.

"Okay," Lucy said. Isaac meowed from the bed.

I walked over and scratched him behind the ears. Then Tabby came out of the bathroom.

"I was thinking. It might be a good idea to ward the car today," I said.

"All right. I can do that."

I was glad when she didn't ask what the rush was. I wasn't sure if I should tell her about the birds or not. She was under enough stress. I grabbed the iPad off the nightstand and loaded it up. Then, I went to my email. I poured over every email I'd gotten from the Order. No contact information. No nothing. "Dammit."

"What?" Tabby asked.

"All they've left me for contact info is email."

"Okay. While I don't like it, it never seemed to bother you before."

"I didn't need to talk to them urgently before." How could I have been so stupid? I remembered a letterhead from the tax forms I signed, but those files were now mysteriously gone from the tablet. Great. Yet another thing to drive me crazy. But tax forms weren't something to worry about now.

Tabby perched next to me on the bed. "We could try to interrogate Vespa. Or maybe help him remember somehow."

"I don't think I want to interrogate a demon yet. But if we could figure out a trigger for Vespa to remember the terms of the contract, I'd be all for it." The less I had to do with the supernatural these days the better.

"You call Vespa. I'll start packing. Tell him we want to begin. And that he'll need to expect houseguests for the conceivable future."

"Works for me." It was an option and better than sleeping out in the desert. Less chance of scorpions, except for the demonic variety. I wasn't all that crazy about going to live with him, especially when we didn't know if he had anything to do with the break-in, but we needed out of a place we couldn't trust at all. I didn't want to visit a repeat of the Isaac affair.

I grabbed my phone and clicked Vespa's number. He answered on the second ring.

"Mr. Holiday. It is good to hear from you," he said.

I rolled my eyes. I wished he would stop all of the faux elegant crap. I knew that part had nothing to do with the demon, just Vespa's perception of what was high-class. "Tabby and I were thinking." I swallowed my revulsion of him. "We've done all the research we can, but now we need your help to finalize things before we begin the exorcism process."

"What did you have in mind?" he asked.

"We were thinking if we could find a trigger, something that would make you remember, it would help."

There was a pause. "I would have no issue with that."

"All right. Sounds good. Also because we plan on beginning the process as soon as we can, Tabby and I figured we could start staying with you." I hoped I didn't sound jakey slipping it in like that.

"That would be fine. I'll meet you at the diner for lunch, and then I'll lead you to my house."

I didn't want him to have to come all the way into town. "You don't have to do that. We have GPS."

"Trust me. It is easier if I help you. The back roads can get confusing. Besides, I have not had lunch."

I thought, yeah, no shit. It was only ten-thirty, but whatever. I knew he was weird, guess this was just one more thing. "All right. What time should we meet you?"

"Oh, eleven-thirty should be fine."

"Sounds good. See you there." I hung up and glanced at Tabby. "He'll meet us at the diner at eleven-thirty for lunch."

"I'm not sure this is a good idea."

"None of this is a good idea. I'm trying to find the least problematic option." And we had to stay with him during the exorcism anyway. Lucy would have to be safe enough in the car. I only hoped we could keep Doc coming and going so we'd have updates.

"Too bad it seems like we've been led this direction from the start," she said.

Tabby had a point. It wasn't like we were getting along better on this trip. We'd had several fights, when back home we'd been fine. It kept happening to us.

"Let's get packing and get the hell out of this place."

Tabby held up a hand. "Wait, speedy. I haven't even warded the car yet."

Oops. I was getting ahead of myself again. "Good point. I'll pack; you go ward the car."

"Now you make sense." She grabbed some witchy stuff and left the room.

I turned to check on Lucy. Poor kid, she'd been through enough, but there wasn't anything else to do. I knew she was going to get tired of the whole thing pretty quick. That meant I had to work harder to get it all done faster. "I hate to do this, but—Lucy, I don't want you leaving that car until Isaac says it's okay."

Now, what made me pick Isaac instead of myself, I don't know. Maybe subconsciously I was sensing that things didn't appear to be what they seemed. Everything with this trip could be described that way. And even though I hadn't heard about it, there wasn't anything that I'd read so far that said a marker couldn't be possessed. I knew a cat could not. He was the safer choice.

"What do you think, Doc?" I asked.

"I think I'll go do some spying."

"Not a bad idea." He disappeared with a pop. "Want to help me pack?" I asked Lucy.

"Nope," she said and giggled. I shook my head.

I got everything we owned into the suitcases. I'm not sure if Tabby would appreciate my packing style, but she could fix things later. I even made the bed. Lucy stayed in front of the TV almost as if she were trying to memorize as much as she could since she wouldn't be watching anything for a while. Part of me hoped this wasn't going to become the cranky young kid in the car thing. But I had my doubts. Lucy knew the ramifications of all this. Vespa scared the shit out of her. And she didn't act like she was six most of the time. I was banking on that.

Finally, Tabby came back.

"We need to get Lucy some books and toys so she'll have something to do in the car," I said. Better at least get the kid some entertainment. Asking her to do nothing for days would be cruel as hell.

Tabby dumped the little container of sage into her backpack. "I never thought. Is there anywhere in town that sells that type of stuff?"

"What about the hotel gift shop?" We didn't have time to run all the way out to the Walmart and back before we were supposed to meet Vespa.

"Good idea. We'll look while you get us checked out."

"Works for me."

We went downstairs. Tabby helped me get the suitcases to the front desk, and then she sauntered off with Lucy. It was probably better I dealt with the idiots alone anyway. Tabby had a worse temper than me.

There was a different girl at the desk than the sour-pussed one I'd dealt with before. I kind of hoped the bitch got fired, but I doubted it.

"Checking out?" she asked with a smile.

"Yup. Jimmy Holiday."

She pulled up the information and then printed something out. "Just sign here, sir."

I glanced at the paper. It was a letter of sorts stating that I was accepting restitution. Restitution for what?

"What's this?" I asked.

She peered into her computer again. "The owner requested that your bill be on us for all of your trouble."

I could tell she didn't exactly know the story. She seemed a little confused. I wasn't about to go into it. We had to get to the diner.

"All right. That does help things." I signed the paper and handed it back to her.

"Hope you have a nice day, sir," she said.

I nodded, pulled the handles up on both suitcases, and headed out to the car.

Surely, Tabby would realize where I was when she was done finding Lucy toys. If she didn't, she could text.

After I loaded the suitcases in the trunk, I got in the front and turned on the air conditioner. I was not going to miss the Arizona heat.

The car continued to smell like burnt sage. It was a smell I was starting to like. It meant safety after a fashion. And I liked not having to worry about soul-suckers killing me in my sleep, thank you very much.

Tabby came along not much later. Lucy drifted through the door of the car, while Tabby got in the front seat.

"Find anything?" I asked.

"Books and a puzzle," Lucy said.

Tabby held up the bag. "I figured when we pulled into the parking lot of the restaurant, I could unwrap the puzzle for Lucy."

Isaac let out a rowr from his cat carrier.

"You'll have more room to roam around soon, buddy. We just need to get something to eat and find our next place to stay," I said to him. I glanced at Tabby and Lucy. "We ready?"

"As far as I know," Tabby said.

There was silence from Isaac in reply. I drove to the diner, parked the car, and waited while Tabby fixed Lucy's toys in the backseat. She then poured out some water from a bottle into Isaac's travel drink thing. I made sure all the windows were down a good bit and I had parked in the shade. It wasn't quite seventy degrees in the shade, so if we didn't dawdle, Isaac should be comfortable.

When Tabby and I walked into the restaurant, we spied Vespa sitting at the table in the back. I waved off the hostess and Tabby and I headed toward the table.

"You are late," he chided.

I pulled out my cell phone and glanced at the time. We were five minutes late. Shit. "Sorry. It took us a little longer than expected."

He grunted and picked up the menu. I was tired and I didn't feel like kissing anyone's ass today. And he wasn't paying me to be his exorcist, for God's sake.

Tabby, I could tell, was getting annoyed. Her eyes were just starting to take on that blaze I knew so well.

I picked up my menu. Tabby followed suit.

After we gave our order, I turned to Vespa. "One thing I want to talk about."

"All right," he said.

"You need my help. I am not your employee." I was trying to say this as politely as possible.

"Yes."

"This means you need to pay attention to what it is we're doing and what your business relationship is."

He just stared.

"Think of me as your spiritual doctor. I have rules I must follow. You don't have to follow my advice. But you have no claim on me. I can drop you as a 'patient' at any time." And if his pompous ass blew too much more, I would drop it.

"Just as I can fire you."

I shrugged. Like I gave a shit. Go ahead, asshole. Fire me. See if I care. "Difference is, if you fire me, it doesn't affect Tabby and me at all. We'll go home. You, however, will still have a pesky demon."

"Look, I'm sorry," Vespa said. His whole demeanor changed. I wasn't talking to a man anymore; we were back to the scared teenager. His pride had become a deflated balloon.

"Just keep all of this in mind the next time you cop an attitude. I apologized for being late. We were trying to be on time." I forced myself to hold back. There was a hell of a lot more I could say, but they weren't things to be said in public.

Vespa nodded. Little did he know, had I been paying attention to the time, I wouldn't have been happy I was late. I always had this phobia about what would happen if I was late for things. It was bad enough that I was stressed from the hotel mess. Now this? I was really close to saying screw it and going back home. If it hadn't been for Lucy, I probably would have.

"I want to say something," Tabby said.

Vespa's eyes seemed to be captivated by Tabby as she spoke. I wondered if she realized he was crushing on her.

"This isn't an optimum situation. None of us are happy to be here, and we needed to stop pretending. I don't trust you." Tabby narrowed her eyes. "Your deceiving makes me not like you. But this will not stop me from helping you."

Vespa sighed. "Have I hurt you that badly?"

"Hurt, no. Pissed me off, yes." The whites around her irises began to turn red. "I don't care if you're possessed or not, there's no excuse for being a jackass."

Vespa's shoulders slumped. "I didn't mean to be a 'jackass.' I just wanted you guys to believe me."

"That's where you sold us short." I stared at him hard. It was a good thing his eyes were natural green or the elongated pupils might have shown up more prominently. "Our last case was a six-year-old kid. If we believed her, why wouldn't we believe you?"

He shrugged. "I guess I'm so used to being looked at as a suspect by my family that I assumed you'd be the same way."

"The bad part is," I began, "we look at you more closely since you deceived us. To us, you're capable of anything."

"Which we knew the minute we found out that you invited the demon into your body." Tabby crossed her arms over her chest.

I nodded to Tabby. "Yeah. People who do that are kind of divided into two categories: the evil and the stupid. Maybe stupid is too harsh a word. Naive perhaps. But since we can't take your word for what you are, you'll be suspect."

"Just so you know," Tabby added, "it partly has to do with you being possessed. You can never trust a demon; they lie."

Vespa sighed. "Yeah. I found that out… So if you are able to do this, get this thing out of me I mean, will my eyes go back to normal?"

"Probably." I thought that was the least of his worries, but said nothing.

"Just probably?" Vespa asked.

I could see he was starting to shake. He should be scared.

"I don't want to say yes when I don't know for sure. There is nothing absolute about the paranormal." I took a deep breath. "Chances are you'll go back to normal, but there's always that one percent, ya know?"

Vespa's shakes stopped. "Yeah, I know."

#

Vespa's home reminded me of the *Brady Bunch* house. A split-level thing with the outside partly a slightly muted yellow and the rest red brick. He motioned for us to pull in and park in the driveway to the left side of the house. It was connected to a single-car garage. That meant that him pulling behind me would have me blocked in.

I complied because I didn't want to piss him off, and the ground was flat. If I had to, I'd just drive on the grass and get out of there.

He pulled in behind me, but not right up on the bumper or anything. None of this seemed like Vespa to me. Part of me imagined him hanging around an old Victorian mansion somewhere, not in 1960s contemporary. His car was surprising most of all, I thought. With his age, I expected him to have some old clunker. Instead, he was driving an Infinity SUV. I guessed the demon had helped him some.

Tabby and I got out of the car. Some plant outside was making my nose itch. After sneezing a few times, I closed the car door.

"I'll get Isaac," Tabby said.

She walked around the car, opened the back driver's-side door, and grabbed him. Upon lifting the cage, water spilled everywhere.

"Shit," she said.

"It's okay. Water can't hurt anything." It wasn't like Isaac had taken a dump or something, and it was just a rental.

"Unless you like mold," Nicholas said. I'd started thinking of him as Nicholas again after he stopped acting like a dick-wad. It was like he had two separate personalities, demonic possession notwithstanding.

"I'll go get you a towel," he said and ran off toward the house.

Tabby set Isaac on the driveway. Too bad she didn't have a leash or she could have gotten him out of the now water-logged crate. Poor thing. He was sputtering and glaring at Tabby.

"I can't believe I did that." Tabby sighed.

I crept over and hugged her shoulders. "It's okay. Like I said, it's just water."

"You don't think Vespa was a little eccentric about it, do you?"

I shrugged. "Who knows? This is his part of the country, not ours."

"True."

Vespa ran back out of the house with a few white towels. He

handed Tabby one, and then went to dab out the car. That was when the trouble began.

I could see through the window that Lucy was looking at him wide-eyed. He tried to just get the towel in the car, but the invisible barrier of Tabby's wards kept him out. I wanted to cheer. At least those worked. I had visual proof of it now.

"Let me take that," I said. He handed over the towel, but kept looking back and forth between me and the car.

I leaned inside and was able to wipe up the car without a problem.

Nicholas raised a brow. "You guys are weird."

There was more to it than that. I kind of wanted to chuckle. He was the one who masqueraded as I-don't-know-how-many-great-grandfathers. But he thought we were odd. Okay. I guessed it was all in the way you looked at it.

I handed him back his soggy towel.

"Let's get everyone settled." He plastered this smile on his face that seemed too big. Too clown-like. Poor kid was trying too hard. Or maybe his messed-up family made him think he had to turn into the famous Vespa. That would make all of this not just about an exorcism, but a personality crisis issue. I wasn't a shrink. He'd have to find therapy on his own.

We followed him into his house. The front entry led to a sunken living room. It had kind of an open floor plan with the living room in front and a big dining room table toward the back. Off to the right of the living room was this big staircase. He led us through and upstairs. I swore to God if the place could have looked any more like the *Brady Bunch* house, I'd have pinched myself. All that was missing was the crazy sixties colors. He took us to a bedroom. In the TV house, we would be staying in Mike and Carol's bedroom. Funky.

"You can put your things in here. There is a bathroom across the hall. Will the cat be okay with his litter box in there?" Nicholas asked.

I blinked. "I guess so; at least when we show him where it is."

"All right." He walked out of the room. Just like that. I didn't know if we should follow him or what.

I looked at Tabby. She shrugged.

"I guess we go get the rest of our shit." Boy, the welcome mat had sure been put out for us.

"Yeah, guess so," she said.

#

Later, after we had all our stuff in the house and when Isaac was hiding under the bed in the room we'd been given, Tabby and I sat in the living room with Nicholas. He was trying to seem relaxed, but his posture was too rigid. At least he was just as uncomfortable as we were.

"Okay," Tabby began. "Where were you when you made the pact with the demon?"

Nick raised his hand and pointed at the floor. "In here. Move all the furniture out of the way and pull back the rug. I have a circle etched into the floor."

There were two sofas in the living room: a muted sage-green color and kind of modern in design. They reminded me of baby poop. The rug had these swirly designs in it and some of the things were the same green as the sofas.

"Was there anyone here with you?" I knew enough about the black arts to know that practitioners didn't necessarily have to have a coven, but with what Vespa had done, it probably would have helped. If he'd been smart, that was; I was holding out for some evidence that he had a brain.

"No, just me," he said.

It wasn't easy asking someone questions like this when we didn't even know him. If we knew him, we might have had a clue what would trigger his memory. Right now, it was a crap shoot.

"What did you eat before doing the ritual?" Tabby asked.

"Nothing. You never work with a demon on a full stomach."

That part, I knew, was probably true. Tabby had said as much before and even the official rite of exorcism recommended fasts and prayer before beginning. After seeing what Lucy's demon did before and during her exorcism, I was glad for my empty stomach.

"Before you did this, how often did you call a demon?" I had to ask. No one in their right mind would wake up one day out of the blue and say, "I think I'll give my soul to a demon today." Yeah, not going to happen.

"It took a while for me to know the process enough to get them to answer."

That made sense, sort of. I bet the demons even wanted to see if he was worth their time and bother.

"If you had to guess," Tabby said, tapping her fingers on the sofa's armrest, "how long?"

"A year. Maybe more."

Yeah. He'd been serious. And stupid. And a pain in the ass, but that was beside the point. I needed to stop dwelling on the stuff I hated about him. If I was going to manage to see this through, I needed to find something about him I liked. I knew that. Otherwise, there was no way I could work for days trying to drive out the demon. It was too hard, and when the final push came, I would need something to keep me going.

"Did you sign the contract in blood?" Hell, that's what they do in movies.

He blinked. "No, I just agreed to it."

"A verbal contract then." I couldn't believe that there wasn't some sort of demonic file reporting in Hell for all the contracts and such, but I wasn't going to go to Hell to ask either.

"In our world, a verbal contract is hard to prove in court," Tabby said.

I leaned back on the sofa. "Why do I have a feeling that Hell has scribes copying down everything a demon needs recorded?"

Nicholas giggled darkly. "You are a funny man."

I was lost on what was funny. Tabby wasn't laughing either. Social grace was not one of Nick's strong points.

"Okay. Mind explaining how this works?" I asked him.

"All I know is that when I agreed to the demon's demands, he entered my body."

That was helpful. About as helpful as saying that to make a hamburger, you need some meat. I wanted to roll my eyes.

"Do you remember how?" Tabby asked.

"Not really. Everything went black and I was out for a few hours."

Great. Things going black told me nothing. If it were me, I'd be trying to figure out anything, as far-fetched as it might sound, that could be helpful. Nick, however, seemed either not too bright, or just simple. There was the possibility that he called us out, but wasn't ready for the help, almost like an addict. If that was the case, I was going to be pissed. Being an exorcist was going to drive me to drink.

"We'll try again later," Tabby said.

Vespa nodded.

He reminded me of a bobble-head. No wonder the demon could take residence so easily.

"Now what?" It wasn't like I had anything else to do. If I could do more research, that would be different, but I couldn't look up shit until I got more information out of him. And since he was information-incompetent, I was screwed.

I missed Doc. Part of me understood why he wasn't showing himself, but it was kind of hard. I'd gotten used to his wit. And Lucy—it just about broke my heart that she was stuck out in the car, but what else could I do? It wasn't like we could trust Vespa's demon. I wasn't looking forward to this exorcism at all.

#

Later that night, after Tabby and I retired to the bedroom for the evening, Tabby set about warding the room. I was glad she was doing it. We needed one safe place to retire. And I needed a place where I could think without having to worry about everything else that could happen while we were asleep.

"When you do the exorcism, where are you going to do it?" Tabby asked.

I paused. That was a damn good question. With Lucy, I'd tried doing it in her bedroom. That didn't work. What worked was doing the exorcism in the area where she'd found the mirror the demon had been trapped in. Worked was one way to put it. More like something was accomplished. I didn't view it as a successful exorcism. If it had been successful, Lucy wouldn't be with me now. No, I just saved her soul. For some priests, that would have been enough. But it wasn't enough for me.

But Vespa hadn't been fooled by a trapped demon in an object. That made everything different. That and the fact that he called the demon to come to him. This house wasn't having quasi-haunted phenomena, so I wasn't sure if there really was a heart in this house. That meant the best option was where Vespa was comfortable. "I guess we'll do it in the living room. That's where Vespa allowed the demon in."

"But a living room?"

I shrugged. I knew it sounded dumb, but I hadn't picked Vespa's demon-working room either. "I'm not sure we have a choice."

"How are you going to secure him in there?"

Good point. The living room was one of the most open rooms in the house. "I'll just have to be creative." I steeled myself. "I doubt he has a big industrial-size freezer."

"Might be a good idea to actually plan it out, ya know? Instead of arranging it on the day you need it."

She had a point. We'd done what we did with Lucy because it was a spur-of-the-moment thing. This time, I pretty much knew where we were going to do the exorcism. I needed to know how I was going to restrain Vespa, how I was going to prepare the room. The last thing I needed was a couch thrown at my head, and what would I do if it didn't work? I needed an escape plan for Tabby and me that was better than driving the car over grass.

Maybe Tabby could make a charm that would automatically ward the front door, maybe all the doors for that matter. Something mostly to keep Vespa in, but that would let me, Tabby, and Isaac out. Now that had possibilities.

"Can a ward be an object that can move?" I asked. I wasn't sure how'd she do this, exactly.

"I never really thought about it before, but I don't see why it couldn't."

"Okay. This is what I want you to do. Make a necklace or something. It doesn't have to be fancy. And ward it to keep me out." Better to test my idea in case I was dead wrong.

She raised an eyebrow at me. "Seriously?"

"Yes! We have to know if this will work." I knew I was getting excitable again, but if she'd bear with me, this might actually work.

She didn't question me anymore. After a bit of rummaging around in her suitcase, she found a piece of ribbon. Then she held it up so I could look at it.

"Will be okay?" she asked.

"It just has to lie on the doorknob." I couldn't see why it wouldn't.

She walked over and snatched a piece of hair from my head. Then she taped it to the ribbon and did her mojo on it.

"Okay, now what?" she asked.

"I'm going to go to the bathroom. While I'm gone, put this over the doorknob." Should be easy enough to see if this was going to work.

"Oookay."

I left. Isaac didn't come out from under the bed. Poor guy, not that I blamed him. He'd been through a lot lately. I wanted to tell him we'd be home soon, but I didn't want to lie. This one had all the hallmarks of taking a hell of a long time.

After I was done in the bathroom, I walked over to the bedroom door, turned the knob and pushed. I stepped back from the door for a minute and looked at it. Then, I tried again. The door wouldn't budge. I tried rattling the knob. It shook a little in my hand but it didn't move. I took my hand off the door. Holy shit, my idea worked.

"Okay, Tabby," I said to the door.

I could hear her chuckling behind it. She opened the door, and I was then able to enter.

"It worked!"

"Yup. And watch yourself, I'm going to remember this."

What the hell had I done? I rubbed my head with my hand. No sense in worrying about it now. I looked at her. "Okay. Now, tomorrow, we need to find out how many doors there are to this place both in and around the house. When we know that, I want you to ward things that will let me, you, and Isaac out. That way, you don't have to try to steal hair from Vespa."

"Good point," she said. "I'd rather not touch him at all."

I didn't want her to have to touch him either, but during the exorcism that was going to be impossible.

#

The next morning, I woke to cat butt in my face. I guess Isaac finally felt it was okay to come out from under the bed. I was glad, don't get me wrong, but I'd rather have had the other end. At least he didn't fart. I think that would have killed me.

I sat up. The room looked like it had when I'd gone to sleep. The walls were painted a baby blue. The bed was big enough and had a white comforter on top. My stuff was stashed in the corner, and

Tabby's was on a chair. I looked over at her. She was asleep. I moved around a little, trying to pop my back. All of these strange beds were starting to get to me. I was ready to go home.I heard a soft knock on the door. I threw back the covers on my side and got up.

Nicholas stood on the other side of the door. "Do you all want to go out to breakfast? My treat."

He looked so hopeful. Honestly, I was getting tired of restaurant food, but I didn't want to hurt the kid's feelings. I glanced over to Tabby and then back to him. "Sure. Let me get Tabby up."

"Okay." He grinned and then walked down the hall.

I swear he had a skip in his step. But I knew better. It was only a matter of time before the demon popped in again. The kid was weird as hell, I'd give him that. But he was odd before the demon business. Demons did not skip, unless someone had unleashed a barrage of skipping imps I didn't know about.

Vespa's possession was so different from Lucy's. Her demon, Asmodeus, had taken complete control. Vespa's demon, however, either wasn't that strong or he hadn't gotten his claws fully into Nicholas yet. Which it was, I didn't know, but I couldn't expect this to be easy. He also didn't seem to know a whole lot of things he should. That puzzled me too. I walked back into our room. Isaac peered up at me from the bed.

"You fart on me in my sleep, don't you?" I asked.

No response from the cat. I know he did though. He looked sneaky.

I walked closer to Tabby's side of the bed and knelt down. "Tabby?"

No response.

"Hey, Tabby," I said a little louder. Again, no response. It was time to break out the big guns.

"Wake up, little rosebud, wake up!" I said in a sing-song voice.

She jerked awake. "You jerk."

I snorted. It worked every time. "Vespa wants to know if we want to eat breakfast out."

She shrugged her shoulders. "It gives us a chance to check on Lucy."

"Yeah and if Lucy heard from Doc, maybe we can get more

information on the house."

"Maybe. Let's get dressed."

I looked at Isaac. "I'm watching you."

I could swear he grinned.

#

Vespa met us downstairs with keys in hand. "You guys ready?"

"Sure," I said. With Vespa involved, anything could happen and I wasn't really ready for any of it. I needed to hire a psychic.

Tabby and I headed to the car. We'd left the doors to the bathroom and bedroom we were using open so Isaac could use his litter box. It was going to be interesting to see if he was going to roam to other parts of the house now that he calmed down. I didn't think Nick minded; at least he hadn't said he did. Isaac wasn't known to cause damage to anything except spider plants. He liked to eat those.

As we walked to the car, I couldn't see Lucy, but that didn't necessarily mean anything. My heart hammered in my chest. The closer I got to the car, the further down into it I could see. Finally, I relaxed when I saw that she was lying down on the seat looking at one of the books Tabby bought her. Reading was safe.

I pressed the button on the keys and unlocked the doors. Tabby and I got in.

I kept watching through the rearview mirror as Vespa got in his car and started backing out of the drive.

"Hey, Lucy," I said. "How are you doing?"

"I'm bored," she whined.

No doubt. She had no one to talk to all day. She couldn't go outside and run around. This was hellish for a kid.

"I'll look for more things while we're out this morning," Tabby said.

"Thanks."

I started the car and backed out of the driveway so that I was behind Vespa. There were too many things on my mind and Lucy was only one of them. I watched Vespa in his car, once he was sure I was behind him, he took off. I followed. He led me twisting and turning through various streets until we ended up at a little Mexican restaurant.

"I'll try to convince him to take us to a grocery store." I could come up with an excuse for that. And while we were there, maybe Tabby could sneak and get Lucy a few things in the toy aisle.

"That would be a good idea," she said.

"Tired of eating out?" I knew I was. Maybe if Tabby bought some stuff we could make, Vespa would let us use his kitchen.

"More like, we'll need to eat when we start exorcising him."

"I hadn't thought of that," I said.

She shook her head. "There's a lot you don't think about, Jimmy Holiday."

I laughed. Then I turned my attention to the back seat. "I missed you, Lucy."

"I missed you too. How long do I have to stay in the car?"

Dammit. Cut out my heart with a rusty knife. "I wish I had a better answer for you, but I don't know. We're trying to find out about the contract."

"It doesn't matter," she said.

I almost pulled over the car. "What?"

"The contract. It doesn't matter."

"How is that possible?" I asked Tabby.

She looked at me blankly.

I stared at Lucy in the rearview mirror. "The exorcism will be normal."

"I didn't say that."

I wanted to bang my head into the steering wheel. I noticed Vespa was standing outside his car waiting on us. Shit. "We'll talk more later, Lucy."

"Okay."

Tabby and I got out of the car. It was not easy to leave that car just when I was getting information, but I couldn't risk Vespa guessing what was keeping us in the car. I'm sure he knew on some level, but the less I made it obvious, the less chance there would be of Lucy getting hurt.

"Sorry about that," I said.

"Nothing to worry about," he said and walked into the restaurant. We followed.

Inside the restaurant, the hostess led us to a table near the front window. The walls were painted to look like fake adobe. The tables used serapes as tablecloths. With the kitchen open enough to the serving area, we could hear the cooks yammering in Spanish. Overall, a nice, homey place. Totally not what I expected from Vespa.

"Ever eat Mexican food for breakfast?" Nicholas asked.

"No, I can't say I have." Back home, Mexican places only opened for lunch; well, unless you counted fast food, and I didn't.

"It's really good," he said.

"Why don't you order for all of us then?" Tabby smiled.

Vespa blushed. I'll admit, it looked weird with his eyes. He was just about doing an evil elf thing with those snake slits.

When the waitress came over, Vespa ordered. After she left, Tabby stared at him.

"What is that migas thing you ordered?" she asked.

"It's my favorite."

God, he was trying to impress her so badly. He was so…high school about it too. I would have felt sorry for him if he wasn't hitting on what was mine.

"It's scrambled eggs with pieces of corn tortillas mixed in," he said.

Tabby grinned. "Can't wait to try them, then."

#

"Hey, before we go to the house, can we go to a grocery store?" I asked as we left the restaurant. I hadn't been this stuffed in a long time. I felt like I'd just been to someone's grandmother's house.

"We can, but why would you need to do that?" he asked.

I raised a brow. Was he afraid of the grocery store or something? "We wanted to get snacks, stuff like that."

Vespa visibly relaxed. "Uh. Okay. Yeah, sure."

He hopped into his car. Tabby and I got in ours. It was such a relief to get out of there, away from him for a bit. He made me feel almost as if I was being suffocated. Everything with him had to be a certain way. I wasn't sure how much longer I could take it.

"Is it just me, or is Nick a little intense?" Tabby asked, reading my mind.

I backed out of the spot. "More like a little control freak."

"What's a control freak?" Lucy asked from the back seat.

"It's someone who has to have everything their way," I said. It was more than that, but it wasn't exactly appropriate to put it in those terms for a kid.

"Like when Daddy says Mommy is…," she paused, thinking, "anal-retentive?"

I laughed. Never mind. I needed to remember Lucy wasn't a normal six-year-old. I kept forgetting. "Something like that."

When we got back to the house with food, Tabby conveniently left a coloring book and some crayons in the car. It was the best we could find at the grocery store. Lucy couldn't play with dolls because she couldn't hold them, so what was the point? Maybe she'd manage the crayons. Luckily, Vespa never asked about any of it. I have no idea what Tabby would have said.

It wasn't until we got to the house that I realized I'd forgotten to ask Lucy to expand on what she knew. We were already inside, putting stuff away in the kitchen, and I didn't want old Nick to know Lucy was in the car. For now, I was thankful he hadn't caught on. Even though I'm sure he guessed something was up when he wasn't able to dab out the water. But I didn't want to give him any ideas, so I couldn't go outside to ask her. I didn't want to raise suspicion any more than I already had. The ward on the car was a huge red flag. Plus, I wasn't sure he couldn't see her. With the demon in him, he probably could.

I wasn't sure if Nick was all that aware when the demon was in control of the body. And I wasn't about to lose Lucy now, not after I'd fought so hard for her. Especially since I had no way of contacting her parents. At least she was almost as opaque as she'd been when we arrived in Arizona. I couldn't imagine what I'd do if I found out that all this had killed off her body.

While Tabby was unpacking the groceries, I ran upstairs. I wanted to see if the Order had sent me anything. Like usual, there was too much I needed to know and no one had bothered to let me in on all of it. If they hadn't, I was jotting off an email about Lucy's parents. I wanted to at least know her body was alive. Surely they could understand that, right?

The iPad booted up. I opened my email. I did have an email from the Order, but not what I was expecting. It was an invitation to meet a fellow Order member in two weeks in New York. Like they expected me to have it all wrapped up in a shiny bow by then? Heh.

I dashed off a quick reply explaining that I was on a case, but I'd touch base as soon as it was over. I wondered what they were thinking. *I* knew that *they* knew some exorcisms lasted years, so why did they think I'd be done so quickly?

I got the idea that this case might be my test, not that I needed another one, but whatever. God had chosen me; the Order hadn't. So their rules were starting to piss me off. I had more important things to worry about, like saving souls, instead of hoping I passed their stupid test.

I turned off the iPad. Yeah, no job was perfect, but the church and the Order had their own special brand of bureaucracy. It was driving me crazy. I was surprised no rogue priest had gone postal yet. With the way this was being handled, I might be the first.

I wanted to get in touch with Doc, but that would have to wait until tonight. It wasn't like I could stay in the room all day. Isaac seemed content to do so. He was lounging on Tabby's pillow. But I was the one who had to protect everyone. Isaac had it lucky.

"I don't like it here either," I said to him.

He meowed.

"Yeah. I hope it won't be long too." I never thought I would be talking to a cat.

Isaac closed his eyes and went back to sleep. So much for normal conversation.

I put the iPad in my backpack and headed downstairs. I didn't like leaving Tabby alone in this place very long. Especially since Vespa seemed sweet on her. Who knew what secrets this house held? He could have a hidden basement room or something. What did we know about him? In my opinion, he was an idiot. Whether evil or not remained to be seen, but then there were different degrees of evil.

I'm sure that fucking about with conjuring up demons put you in a whole other category than the usual general sins. He was looking at thousands of years in Purgatory, at least. But depending on what he used to do the spells to bring on the demon, it might be worse than that. If he was damned, there was nothing I could do. That was, if inviting the demon in hadn't made him damned already. I could only guess. It wasn't like these things were written down specifically. At least not anywhere that I knew of.

When I made it to the kitchen, I found Vespa trying to make small talk with Tabby. It was kind of sad. He had that tone that made him come on a little too strong.

"Are you sure I can't help?" he asked.

"There's nothing for you to do." Tabby shrugged. "Everything is put away. I just need to find out what Jimmy wants to do."

She must not have noticed me enter. If I had been in a better mood, I might have tried to scare her. Not today.

"What is it I'm supposed to do?" I asked.

Tabby looked up, startled. "Mr. Vespa was wondering what we were going to do the rest of the day."

I focused on Vespa. Maybe I could trick him into some answers. "I would like to speak to Doc."

As soon as I mentioned his name, the demon's eyes began to glow bright green. "Why do you want to speak to the spy?"

I had him. Now, if I could keep him on the string, maybe I could finish my research. "One, I haven't seen him since we got here. And two, I'm trying to help your host."

He curled his mouth up and snarled. "Once I gain my strength, there won't be any more of these problems."

I was a problem, was I? I wanted to roll my eyes. Yeah, the demon was dangerous, but he was also pedantic. If he was such a big badass, he'd have made something happen by now. I exhaled slowly. "But you haven't gained your strength yet. So where's Doc?"

"If you let me in, priest, I could make you very strong indeed."

I didn't even bother asking why he turned on me. I was the stronger figure. If he was all about power, he'd want a better host. "I don't need your strength. I have my own."

Without warning, Vespa returned to normal. His eyes showed that strange look in them, but the irises were normal green. He lowered his head. Ah-ha. He was aware, somewhat at least. That would be helpful to know during the exorcism.

"I'm sorry," he said.

I sat across from him at the table. "Listen, we've been in this long enough that we know when the demon is speaking and when it's you." Might as well make him feel better. It wouldn't do either of us any good if I flat-out accused him of everything. This way, he thought of me as a friend, thus someone he could trust.

He seemed to relax a little. "I just want this thing out of me so I can go back to normal."

What was normal for him? Dealing with a screwed-up family that stressed him out until he invoked a demon? Jesus Christ.

"What about your family?" Tabby asked.

He jumped up from the table. "You know what? Fuck my family. It's their fault for making me think I had to be something I'm not."

I didn't comment. His being an emotional wreck, sure; let that blame fall to his family. His inviting a demon to possess him? That was all him. They didn't stand over him and force him to learn the rituals, for God's sake. He needed to take responsibility.

"What are you going to do if we get the demon out?" Tabby asked.

Vespa turned and stared at her. "I'm selling this house, leaving this place, and finding a different life."

That was the most intelligent thing I'd heard him say. I swore, if he'd starting talking about using the exorcism as a get-rich scheme or something, I might have crushed his head. Just a little.

"Okay, Tabby. Let's go see if we can get ahold of Doc. I want to see if he has any information for us." That was just what I needed. Let him know just enough that he wouldn't expect what I was doing. Or rather, think he had an idea of what I was doing without him knowing the full story.

Tabby nodded.

"Nick, why don't you go take a nap," I suggested. "You're under a lot of stress and it might do you some good." I meant it. He had dark circles under his eyes and he seemed paler than usual.

"Okay. Yeah. I think I will," he said.

#

I led Tabby back upstairs. I didn't want there to be any more of a connection to Lucy than necessary. If I could have, I would have snuck outside and checked on her, but there was no way. I was probably playing with fire enough by trying to get ahold of Doc. If there had been something wrong with him, Lucy would have told me in the car when we went to breakfast. Now though, she had no way to get ahold of me. I needed to remedy this if there was going to be a next time.

When we got to the bedroom, I closed the door behind Tabby.

"What's up?" she asked.

"I want to know what's going on with that statement Lucy made." I'd been stupid and I was freely admitting it.

"Why not ask Lucy?"

"Because I don't want him near her. If I go outside, you know hedl be right on my tail, asking what I was doing." I scratched my arm and lounged on the bed.

"He knows she's there. It wouldn't surprise me if he goes outside and watches her." Tabby rubbed her hands over her arms.

I blinked. Shit. "She never said anything about that."

"She didn't have to." Tabby sighed. "I can tell you haven't been around little kids."

"Why?" I was getting so confused.

"Because kids don't always come right out and tell you what's wrong. They want to be saved, but they don't know how to ask for help. And they seem a little nervous when they shouldn't be. Things like that."

Lucy had said something, I'd just been too stupid to pick up on it. She said she wanted to go home. Hell. "He's messing with Lucy?"

"Maybe. I don't know. I just felt weird."

I took a deep breath. I needed to stay on course. "Okay. More reason to ask for Doc."

Tabby stared at me hard. "What are you planning?"

"I don't know yet." I smiled. "Doc? If you can hear me, I need to talk to you." I didn't yell or anything, that would have been stupid. If he could hear me, he'd show up eventually.

Tabby lounged on the bed beside me while I stared at the ceiling.

Yeah, it was dumb, but hell, I always expected him to come from there. Maybe, because in my mind with as much of a badass as he was, he belonged in Heaven, and spirits floated down from Heaven, didn't they? The priest part of me was about to give me a lesson in true theology, but whatever.

After a few minutes, I glanced at Tabby. "Guess he isn't coming."

"Maybe he's busy," she said.

"I hope that's all it is. I don't think I can take much more excitement." And I didn't want to think about him being trapped somewhere because Vespa's demon didn't want to be spied on. If that's what had happened, it would be my fault.

Tabby got up and put her hand on my shoulder. "I know."

#

I figured Doc would get back to me when he could, if he could anyway. There was no sense in me jumping to conclusions when I hadn't heard anything yet. I never heard about him not being able to enter Vespa's house, so I doubt that was it. It left me uneasy. I'd gotten used to him being around.

Tabby and I headed back downstairs. I didn't make any noise. I'd told Vespa to get some rest, and I was going to try to make sure he got it. His room was on the first floor, somewhere in a hallway off the kitchen. I hadn't been invited, so I hadn't bothered looking for it. Tabby and I were in the living room.

"Is it me, or is everything strained here?" Tabby asked.

"Worse than dealing with a failing marriage, you mean?" I remembered how intense it had been at times when Tor and Will's marriage was falling apart in front of our eyes at Blackmoor. I thought that was bad. Somehow, Vespa and his weirdness were worse.

"Yeah. Here, I'm half-afraid to talk," she said.

"It could be the trust thing. This is the first time we've dealt with an active and productive possessed person. The demon wants to live on Earth again. It doesn't just want Vespa's soul." It was a different type of demon. He wasn't any less evil because of it, either.

"How can you tell?" she asked.

"It hasn't taken full possession of Nick. He can be himself. Lucy, however, was always demonic until her soul was separated from the demon." If all the demon had wanted was Vespa's soul, it would have killed him as soon as he'd been invited in.

"Good point. So will the exorcism be easier since Vespa isn't totally possessed?"

"A sort of logic would say yes, but I have a bad feeling that won't be the case." I needed a mentor to explain all of this stuff to me. Or a book. Or something. Flying by the seat of my pants was getting tiring.

"The contract?" she started.

"Yeah. I don't know anymore. Nothing like this is like with Lucy. He hasn't spoken in another language. He doesn't just 'know' things.

We should be trying to figure it out, but I'm lost." And then there had been what Lucy said. Maybe she was right and it didn't matter, but I wanted to know why.

Tabby stayed quiet. I didn't want to mention Lucy without being within our warded room. That kid was counting on me to protect her and I was sure as hell trying. Nick probably knew everything anyway, but I felt a lot better being inside the ward before I said or did anything to do with Lucy.

"I always thought that making a pact with Satan required a mark of some sort." I rifled through my brain, looking for some sort of answer. They had all those old movies like *The Mark of Satan* and stuff like that. It had to come from somewhere.

"Like yours?" Tabby asked.

I stared at my wrist. In a way, I almost expected the mark itself to have some sort of special powers or something, but so far, there'd been nothing. It was virtually a tattoo. Only I knew it wasn't normal. You couldn't tell by looking at it. "Yeah, I guess so. Do you think we should ask him if he has a mark?"

Tabby shrugged. "It couldn't hurt. Maybe it would give us something to research. And if we're lucky, it could give us an idea of the contract."

"Have I told you how much I love you lately?" She snickered. She really was amazing.

"Seriously, I don't think I'd make it through all of this if you weren't so smart." In fact, I knew I wouldn't. I wasn't smart enough. I needed her brain.

"You don't give yourself enough credit, you know?"

I shrugged. I didn't care what she said. She was the one who had her head on straight most of the time. I just seemed to do okay when all hell broke loose. Luckily—or unluckily— that happened more often than I liked to think about.

"How are we going to handle this?" Tabby shifted on the couch, likely trying to get comfortable.

I shrugged. "Ask him, I guess." I didn't have any better ideas. If I did, I would have done them by now.

She rubbed her eyes. "Oh, yeah, like that's gonna work. I can just see this. 'Nick, hey man. Do you have any strange markings or birthmarks?'"

"Okay, smarty-pants. How would you take care of it?"

"Simple. We figure out what to do about dinner and I'll ask you how you like my new tattoo."

I chuckled. I couldn't help it. I knew firsthand Tabby didn't have a new tattoo. She had the same one she's always had— a phoenix on her left shoulder blade. Whether Vespa's demon would tell him about the lie was another thing, but hell, it sounded better than what I would have done.

"Works for me," I said.

"Good."

#

Vespa got up about four. Tabby and I had killed time trading the iPad back and forth, reading and playing games. I'd run upstairs and gotten it out of my backpack when it seemed like Nick was going to stay asleep for a while. I never thought I'd need one, but it was coming in handy.

"Were you able to find everything okay?" Nick asked, rubbing his eyes.

"Yeah. No problems," I said.

"What did you want to do for dinner?" Tabby tapped her finger on her chin. "I could cook something."

I liked the sound of that. I'd watched her grab the ingredients she needed to make her chili at the grocery store. It had been too long since I had it.

"No!" Vespa shook himself. "No, I...I think going out is better."

"All right." Okay, I made a point to remember this. Mr. Demon did not like fire. Interesting. I glanced over at Tabby. She seemed a little shell-shocked.

"Oh, sorry." Nick rubbed the back of his neck. "I just...I don't like to cook things in the house."

Tabby nodded. "Okay, then. Guess we'll go out again."

I could hear an almost imperceptible snark in her voice. Honestly, I knew what she meant. I was tired of eating out too. It wasn't like we couldn't talk about the mark just as easily in a restaurant. That part wasn't a big deal. Vespa being a freaked-out idiot? It was becoming a bigger deal as the days wore on.

"Any Italian places around?" I asked. Yeah, we'd been to one earlier in the week, but at least it had a different taste to it. Even if it sucked, the extra garlic couldn't hurt, especially when we didn't know when we were going to start the exorcism.

Vespa nodded and walked back to his bedroom.

Tabby blew out a breath as he left. "That was strange."

"Yeah, tell me about it."

"I mean, even to do his rituals for conjuring the demon, he had to use fire."

I blinked. Okay, she would know. Now his kitchen phobia made no sense. "Really?"

She nodded. "Yeah. You have to call on the keepers, the guardians of the watchtowers: earth, air, fire, and water. Just for what he does, it's backwards."

I took a deep breath. "So the stove or the cooking thing has to be something else."

"Maybe he's afraid of being poisoned?"

"Maybe."

Chapter Eleven

Predictable

VESPA CAME OUT of his room dressed in a suit. I almost fell off the sofa. What the hell was a kid like him doing running around in a suit?

"I'm guessing this is a fancy place?" I asked.

Nick scratched his arm. "No, not really. I just think it's proper to dress for dinner." He smiled at Tabby.

The guy had almost gone cuckoo for cocoa puffs. Damn.

Tabby bit her lip. "Give us a minute, and we'll get cleaned up."

I grabbed the iPad off the sofa and followed Tabby upstairs. This was getting ridiculous. Once we were in the room, I closed the door.

"We're going to have to do something about that," I said.

"About what?"

"The way he looks at you. The way he's acting." No one on Earth could make me dress up for every meal, and even if there were someone, it sure as hell wouldn't be him.

"You think I like it?" she asked.

"No. I know I wouldn't. He needs to lay off."

She sighed. "Right now, it's harmless. Why don't we pick our battles?"

"Good point." Yeah, better not get in yet another argument. Lucy's demon had fed off that stuff. It would stand to reason Vespa's would too.

After we finished getting dressed, Tabby and I went back downstairs. I had on a dress shirt and some khaki pants—about as dressed up as I got. Tabby had on a flowery summer-type dress. It was black with blue flowers on it. I liked it on her. Made the red in her hair stand out.

Nick leaned calmly against the sofa, waiting for us. "You look nice," he said to Tabby.

"What about me?" I said as straight-faced as possible. It gave me the chance to get under his skin a little.

Nick blinked. "Uh, you look nice too."

I laughed. "Just goofing around. Tabby does look great."

She blushed and gave me a look. I could tell I was going to hear about it later.

"Shall we?" Vespa asked.

We followed him out the door. I was glad to take our rental car. I didn't trust riding with a demon. They were known to cause car accidents if they wanted to kill you. I'd read that in an old book by Malachi Martin.

Some of the stuff in the book sounded fake, but some of it had a ring of truth to it too. The car stuff felt true to me. I didn't care that he'd been eventually kicked out of the church for indiscretions. He had married the girl he'd been…having relations with. Ironically, the same thing I had been accused of that had gotten me defrocked. Conspiracy maybe?

As soon as Tabby and I got the doors closed on the car, Lucy started. "I don't like being in this car."

Uh-oh. Lucy being that blatant meant that things had gotten worse. "I know. It has to be boring." I hoped that was all it was. Please, God. I pulled out of the driveway and followed Vespa down the road.

"I'm not bored. I don't like seeing the faces," she said.

I almost slammed on the brakes. What the hell? This was the first time I heard anything about faces.

"What faces?" I asked.

"When you guys go inside, after a while, these faces look in the windows."

I didn't like hearing that at all. The kid had had enough spooky shit in her life. She didn't need any more. And here I was, forcing her to stay in a car by herself without any way to get ahold of us so we could take her away from the monsters. I was a great guy all right. Maybe it wasn't Vespa fucking with her at all.

"What do the faces look like?" Tabby asked.

"Asmodeus," Lucy said.

I almost lost control of my senses. No fucking way was I going to fight him again for Lucy's soul. I didn't give a shit. He could have Vespa for all I cared, but I knew that wasn't the case. He wasn't the one in charge of Vespa. He would have done a hell of a lot worse in the house if it had been him. No, he'd come because he wanted Lucy.

I did the only thing I knew to do. I started to pray.

Tabby did not join in. I didn't expect her to. Her religion did prayer in terms of rituals, and it wasn't like this was the time or place for that, though I'm sure she could do something small in a car. She just didn't have the stuff with her.

"Could you ward the driveway?" I asked.

"No. Probably not. It isn't a dwelling."

"Damn." It was a thought. Shame there were limitations, but I already knew that.

While we were talking about it, I figured now was the time to ask Lucy about the contract. "Remember earlier when we were talking about the demon contract?"

"Uh-huh."

"What did you mean when you said the contract didn't matter?" It was the most important thing I needed to know.

"It doesn't."

"How?" Tabby asked.

"The outcome will be the same." She was talking in that weird way that was older than she was again.

"What do you mean, Lucy?" I gripped the steering wheel hard.

She started humming. I gave up. That was all I was getting out of her today. She'd answered my question, but not as much as I'd wanted. At least we had options. The mark idea Tabby came up with. If he had one, and if he let us take a picture of it, maybe we could research the symbols.

My mark had been easy. It was the names of the archangels in their original listed languages. I'd looked up the Aramaic one, Selaphiel. The rest were in Hebrew. I wondered what was so special about old Selly, not that I'd had time to research it ever since we'd come to Arizona.

If we could catch a lucky break, maybe I could take care of this before Asmodeus made his move. Or rather, more of a move than scaring Lucy. I knew with him, there was a hell of a lot more he could do.

#

The restaurant was nice. White tablecloths, candles, but Vespa had been right. There were plenty of people dressed casually. I let Tabby take the lead. It wasn't like we could come out and ask him if he had any weird symbols or anything and she was a hell of a lot more subtle than me. I would have just tackled him at the house, stripped him, and inspected his body for a mark.

After we ordered, Tabby took a sip of water.

"Mr. Vespa. Are there any tattoo parlors around?" she asked.

Wait. She wasn't doing what she'd talked about with me. I fought myself not to say anything. It was better if I didn't mess it all up.

He blushed. "Oh, I'm…I'm sure there are, but I've never been to one."

Hmm. Satan boy didn't like tattoos. That wasn't normal. Most of these people who were obsessed with demons covered themselves in them. Not that all people with tattoos were demonics, but the demon-obsessed tended to have head-to-toe tattoos. And here, Vespa seemed squeamish of them. Go figure.

"Maybe we can check. I was thinking about getting another one," Tabby said.

"Added to your phoenix or what?" Maybe she figured it was better not to lie if she didn't have to. Probably smart.

"No. Maybe something to match your mark."

I almost choked. I was going to have to warn her to stick to the script next time. Damn.

"What mark?" Vespa asked.

I guessed it was my time to show off. "When I got involved in all this, I was granted with a mark." I unbuttoned the sleeve of my shirt and showed him my wrist.

His brows rose clear to his hairline. "Wow. That's really cool."

"Thanks," I replied. Tabby and I kept waiting for him to say something, anything, but he remained quiet.

It figured. Every time we thought we'd finally had a leg to stand on, it would be jerked out from under us. Maybe Lucy was right and we should just get on with it.

Yet, before I did something rash, I'd rather talk to Doc first. If he didn't show by bedtime, I was going to figure out how to contact him and find out what the hell was keeping him from coming when I called.

#

I didn't have to worry about it too long. On the drive back to the house, Lucy suddenly piped up.

"Doc says not to worry. He's working on something."

I blinked. Okay, good to know. "Tell him to keep the big guy away from the car."

She giggled and went back to doing whatever it was she was up to in the backseat. I couldn't exactly stop driving and look around, but she seemed happy enough.

I stole a glance at Tabby. She seemed tired. If I could, I'd let her sleep for a couple of days.

"Are you okay?" I asked.

"Not really. I thought we had it, ya know?"

She wasn't the only one disappointed. It did suck. We needed a break. "Yeah. It sucks, but what can you do?"

"He's really starting to creep me out," she said.

"Does that mean we should say screw it and start the exorcism?" I was tired. She was tired.

"No, that would be stupid."

I sighed. "I was planning on talking to Doc before I made a move."

"That's the smartest thing you've said all day."

I didn't know if I should be insulted or happy about that. I chuckled. "Thanks."

#

When we got back to the house, Tabby and I headed upstairs to change out of our good clothes. Vespa would have to deal with us not dressing every day for dinner. I knew I hadn't packed many dress clothes. It hadn't been necessary. No one wore a suit to an exorcism, except a priest, and I wasn't one anymore.

"You're too quiet," Tabby said.

"Too many places here I can't talk."

Tabby shrugged. "I'm pretty sure he knows what we've been talking about anyway. Lucy always did, even when we were in the library."

"Shit. I'd forgotten about that. It had been Asmodeus' arrogance that kept him from taking our plans seriously."

"I wish we knew what Vespa's demon was capable of."

She wasn't the only one. This thing was such a fiasco. "We know Old Ugly is involved somehow. He wouldn't be screwing with Lucy otherwise."

"I don't like that. I don't like it at all." She pulled a t-shirt over her head.

"It could be worse. At least the demon isn't coming on to you." I could just imagine this scaly thing trying to go all hubba-hubba. It was funny until my head went to what a demon's… thing looked like. I needed brain bleach again.

She rolled her eyes. "I'm not so sure about that."

"Oh, I am." Tabby had only seen a little how Lucy had been manipulated by the demon. It had been ugly. I remembered it trying to seduce me. Uggh.

Isaac mewed from the bed. I glanced at him.

"You tell her," I said.

Tabby chuckled. "You've really taken to talking to my cat."

I smiled and pulled her into a hug. "He's smart. I'm not stupid enough to ignore him."

"No wonder he likes you." She punched me on the arm. "You going to check the iPad?"

"Nah. I'll wait until we go to bed. Let's go back to playing 'let's go entertain you' with ol' Nick. Maybe he'll slip and tell us something."

#

When we got downstairs, Vespa was pouring wine into glasses. What was the special occasion?

"I thought we'd have a drink," he said.

I hoped he hadn't done anything to the glasses. I didn't want to be poisoned or anything. He hadn't yet, but I wouldn't put it past him. Not with the way that demon in him snuck around.

"Do you ever relax?" I asked.

He handed Tabby her glass and motioned for her to sit down on the sofa. Now I understood. This was another ploy to impress Tabby.

"No, not really. My family was all about appearances."

I took my glass when he offered it. At this point, a little drink would do me some good. "Since you're planning on changing your life anyway, why not start now?"

He froze. I couldn't believe he hadn't thought of this before. Kid didn't need out on his own; he needed therapy. In that, I did feel for the kid. His family wanted him to fail.

"Jimmy has a point. Why not just give it all up?" Tabby asked.

Nick sat on the other couch opposite Tabby. "You think so?"

I plopped down beside my girl. Not that she wouldn't normally hit me if I called her that, but I had a feeling that, around Nick, she wouldn't mind. He needed to get the message. Tabby was not up for grabs.

"It would be kind of silly to keep up the charade, right? You aren't eighty for Christ's sake," I said.

He winced. I wasn't sure if it was the curse or if it was my mentioning Christ. He acted like an old church lady who secretly read smut while trying to make people believe she was better than God.

"That will be so freeing," he said.

"I doubt if your 'companion' would care how you carried yourself." I smirked. It was true. I didn't think the demon would even know if a leisure suit was out of style. There was no reason Nick couldn't run around in a t-shirt and jeans.

Tabby snickered.

He needed to learn who he was, not imitate his family member. I had a feeling he'd been doing it so long he'd have trouble telling what was him and what was the persona. But he was a twenty-year-old kid. He needed to start acting like one.

He took a big gulp of his wine. "I don't know what I'd do without you guys."

I did. He'd contact other creepy shit to get revenge on his family who screwed up his life. I guess I should feel good that he thought about contacting me. I just wondered what he'd done to get O'Malley to contact him in a dream. Since it wasn't something that I directly needed to know, I didn't bother asking, but it was a good question.

"It's okay," Tabby said. "Just to try to remember you aren't him."

He swallowed loudly. "Too bad I don't know who I am."

Now that, I knew, he said for Tabby's benefit. A slight change in the tone of his voice gave him away. He was playing the sympathy card.

Tabby didn't bite, though, and said nothing. It was probably better that way. Saying nothing meant she wasn't encouraging him or hurting his feelings.

"Why is Asmodeus here?" I blurted out. Tabby froze. It was too late now. My big mouth had gotten me in trouble again. We could work it to our advantage.

His whole demeanor shifted. I knew I was speaking to the demon now. "You have something that belongs to him."

Says who? Not me. "That is under review."

The demon hissed at me. "I'll see you sleep like the dead, marker."

I fought to roll my eyes. He hadn't done anything to me yet. If he'd been able to, I would have at least been slapped, but there was just old Big Mouth over here. "What is he, your boss?"

The demon chuckled. "He is a prince of Hell. In that respect, yes, he could be my 'boss' as you say."

I nodded. That made more sense. He was some lesser demon trying to gain brownie points. "Tell your 'boss' that he'd better speak to his boss about the legalities of this. Somehow, I don't think he'd like an angel invading Hell to poke around."

It grinned. "Earth is not Heaven."

He thought he was so smart. Too bad; I was smarter. "But my marking of the soul makes the soul marked by God. You could say that your prince is trying to steal a member of Heaven."

"Semantics."

"Just so." I refused to give into him. "The rules are that God and Satan negotiate. If the soul is negotiated to go to Satan, it is up to him to decide where it goes. Not Asmodeus. Somehow, I don't think the devil will take very kindly to his ego."

The demon blinked. "You may be correct. I'll inform the light-bearer and see what he would like to do about my prince."

Yup. This demon was weak. Wouldn't even tell old Assy to get off his lawn. Had to go tattle to the big guys for it. I'd do anything to stop crap from bugging Lucy, even if it meant an interview by the devil himself.

"Sounds good," I said.

Nick slouched over. After a minute, he held his head in his hands.

"I'll be glad to get rid of him."

"We'll do what we can." Tabby patted him awkwardly on the shoulder.

He gazed up at her. "Anyone ever tell you that you look like an angel?"

Oh, Jesus. I wanted to puke. Did he ever quit?

#

About nine, Tabby and I went up to bed. The kid didn't even have a TV. Not that I'd seen, anyway. It made for some interesting conversation. Not really. I was bored out of my mind, but at least I knew that Lucy would be in the same boat in here as out in the car. I didn't feel quite as bad.

I did my evening constitutional, and then went into the bedroom.

"That was fun," Tabby said.

"About as fun as listening to a fanatic try to convert you, I guess." I plopped on the bed and took off my shoes.

"What were you playing with down there, anyway?"

"What do you mean?"

"The thing with Asmodeus." Her hands tangled through her hair. "I mean, Jesus, Jimmy. Like we don't have enough problems?"

"I'm just trying to protect Lucy." Truth was, I didn't know why I'd chosen then to ask. Maybe something else had prodded me. Something supernatural. But I didn't tell that to Tabby. She'd never believe me. Not about something like that.

"And what are you going to do if the big man himself shows up here to interview you?"

"Shit my shorts. Hell, I don't know. It's not my fault the Order expects me to do any of this without guidance." And I did have that thing where I kind of laughed in the face of danger. Maybe that made me a special kind of nuts.

She stood with her hands on her hips. "Now that was a cop-out. Before you had the Order, you lived with what you had to work with. Now it's always, 'If the Order would do this.' I'm tired of it."

I sat there silent for a minute. She had a point. I'd changed the way I saw things, and maybe that was one of my problems. I was confused as to what to do, where to turn, and before, I never worried about it.

"I need to go back to thinking they don't exist."

"Pretty much." She stared at me, and then turned away.

"Okay." I picked up the iPad and put it in my backpack. "For now, they don't exist, and they won't until we're done with all of this."

"Works for me." She left the room to freshen up before bed.

While she was gone, I refilled Isaac's food bowl. He watched me from the bed. When I was finished, he dashed over and started stuffing his face. If I were a cat, life would be so much easier.

"I'm glad somebody appreciates me."

Tabby came in a few minutes later. Her red hair glistened, wet from her shower. I loved her hair. It hung down her back in almost separate locks, it was so thick.

"Forgive me?" I asked.

"Maybe. It depends on how many demons we have to deal with by the end of all this."

"With my luck, we'll have a demon army camped out front." Leave it to me to look at the positive. I wasn't the most fortunate guy in the world. Stuff had a tendency to happen to me.

She plopped on the bed and pushed me. "Don't you even joke about that. One demon, the one in Vespa, is enough."

I agreed with her. I did. I just had a sinking suspicion. Should I have brought up all that about the hierarchy of the demons? Probably not, but it wasn't like I had much else to do. I had to stop Asmodeus from bugging Lucy somehow. I was an exorcist, a marker, not a demon slayer. And if I wanted Lucy to be safe, I had to go with what was at my disposal. Right now that meant my smartass mouth. It was probably already getting me into a lot of trouble.

Suddenly, I heard a pop.

"I hear you been looking for me," Doc said.

I almost jumped out of the bed. Thank God. "Yeah. I have."

"I'm here. Whatcha need?" he asked.

"Hell. Everything." My brain was moving faster than my mouth could. I stopped short of utter madness, got my thoughts in order, and took a deep breath. "Big demon's been terrifying Lucy. Vespa is an idiot, and I know nothing about his contract. Oh, and I might have invited the devil to come up for tea."

Doc glared at me. "What the hell you talking about, boy?"

I closed my eyes for a minute, and then told him about Asmodeus and the conversation I'd had with Vespa's demon.

"I swear. Leave you alone for a while and this is what you make of it?" He muttered to himself and paced across the room.

He glanced over at Tabby. She shrugged and the corners of her mouth were quivering, almost as if she was trying not to smile.

Traitor. I scooted from the end of the bed, making room for Doc to sit.

He took it. It wasn't like he needed to sit or anything, but hell, he was my relative and it was polite. No sense in letting the man wander around all night.

"What is it you need from me?" he asked.

"Help," Tabby answered before I could.

I added, "Some answers."

He laughed. "Maybe I can do that."

"Where were you?" Tabby asked.

"Out and around. Trying to get you people some information." He brushed some invisible dirt off his pant leg.

"And?" I prompted.

"He just doesn't quit, does he?" he asked Tabby.

"No, unfortunately," she replied.

Great. More people to team up on me. What was I, a punching bag?

"What do you want to know first?" he asked.

"The contract stuff. Lucy said something about it not mattering." That was the most important. If I knew that the contract didn't matter for sure, I could get the exorcism done and get the hell out of there.

Doc thought for a minute. "Did she say why?"

"Something about the outcome being the same anyway."

He nodded. "Near as I can tell, it's a case of where there is a contract with a demon like this, the demon can still be expelled. What will happen to the soul, however, is anyone's guess."

"So I have to mark him?" I so did not want to do that.

"Didn't say that," he chided. "The marking is only for those folks that die while you do the exorcism, right?"

"I guess. I mean, I never tried to mark someone who was alive." And there was the little matter of the training I should have had that would tell me all of this. Not that I was bitter or anything.

Doc tapped his fingers on his knee. "That would be something."

"Either way, I don't want to have Vespa with me forever. He gets on my nerves." And if he tried to get with Tabby in her sleep just because he was a spirit, I'd wrangle a soul sucker and let it eat him.

Doc shrugged. "Seems to me that it's up to you if you want to mark him."

"I don't want to."

He snorted. "Condemn the little shit to hell. He isn't exactly a pristine type."

Tabby beamed. "Doc, I like you."

He nodded to her and grinned back. "I like you too, little lady." Then he turned to me. "What else you want to know?"

It took me a minute. I probably should have made a list. "Is there anything I can do to keep Asmodeus away from Lucy?"

He adjusted himself and balanced his foot on the opposite knee. "Near as I can tell, you already did that. I stopped and saw Miss Lucy before I came in here. Kid was right as rain."

"Really?" Finally, something I did right. It would be forgotten when I screwed up again, but at least I'd helped Lucy.

"Yup," Doc said.

So the demon talk worked, but at what cost? It wasn't like any of them could be trusted, and I trusted Vespa's demon least of all. He was a sneaky bastard. And the big guy—who knew what he would do? "What if Satan decides to come investigate?"

"You'd better hope that doesn't happen." Doc wagged a finger at me. "I have no advice for that."

Of course he didn't. He was a ghost, not a paranormal specialist or anything. I was asking a lot of him. It was probably time to stop. Let him do his thing for a change instead of jumping around to my whims.

"Thanks, Doc, for all your help," I said.

"Any time. I think I'll go see what Miss Lucy's up to." He stood and nodded.

"You do that." Tabby waved.

Doc disappeared.

"I guess we gear up for the exorcism, then?" I didn't feel comfortable, but I wasn't sure if anything would make me feel better now. So much felt wrong about all of this, but I was out of ideas.

"That's what it looks like." Her eyes seemed to be assessing whether I was about to fall apart.

"I hate this part," I said.

Tabby patted me on the shoulder.

I wasn't lying. Some people might think that having permission from God to fight demons would be cool. It wasn't. Especially when everything you did, everything you fought so hard for…and the kid still died because the demon was that evil. I needed a vacation from my problems and anything that was stressful.

Doc had given me a few things to think about though. No, I hadn't tried to mark a live person, and I never would. I remembered how it all went down at Lucy's exorcism. The power that flowed through me trying to fight the demon, and then, when she was felled, instinct took me to her. The magic only worked when Lucy died, and I'd been lucky enough that I marked her in time. It seemed a small thing that her body started breathing again after her mark took. The longer this went on, though, the more it seemed like Lucy never would go back to her real body. That pissed me off. She was a sweet kid, dammit. She didn't deserve to lose her life this young.

"Why don't you try to get some sleep?" Tabby fluffed my pillow and patted it. I lay down beside her. The warmth of her body pressed close to mine felt so good. I'd missed having her next to me.

#

Part of preparing for an exorcism was getting in the mindset to be able to do it. Everything else was secondary. You had to cut off some of the emotion, force everything that could go wrong from your mind, and try to imagine that your faith was your armor.

It wasn't like you could march into the room of the possessed person with a boomstick like the guy in those movies with Bruce Campbell. I wish it were that easy.

A lot of an exorcism wasn't even physical. You had to keep your wits about you. The demon would lie and take everything it could dig up about your life and turn it on its head. Even the good things—they got distorted too. You had to be strong enough to take having your past shoved in your face and made ugly. You had to be bull-headed enough to keep after it until it was finished, no matter what happened. And above all else, you had to somehow keep your faith in God when you were handed a shit sandwich. I guess that's what made me an exorcist.

"Are you okay?" Tabby lay on her side, watching me.

I turned toward her. Trying to sleep was pointless. I wasn't going to make it. I'd been up half the night. "I guess so."

"Moping about everything?"

I snorted. "Yeah."

"Try to get your head out of the low-lying clouds. Nobody said you had to do the exorcism today, you know?"

She was right. I had no specific time frame. That was probably a good thing. But it had to be soon. "Yeah. True."

"Besides. We have to figure out how to outfit the house. Ward that large living room so Mr. Demon can't bring in furniture to hurt us."

"Why not just make a big circle around us and Vespa chained to the floor?"

She blinked. "Or that too."

Maybe my simple brain came in handy after all. "We'll have to get rid of his circle."

I wasn't looking forward to that. With the silver implanted into the floor, it was going to require manual labor.

She leaned back against the pillows. "I forgot about that."

I knew it was going to take more than ripping up the circle. There had to be some anti-magic stuff that had to be done to it too. "How would we do that? I mean, I'm sure it's going to take a hell of a lot more than a belt sander."

She shrugged. "Really, all you need is a chisel and some holy water. We damage the circle and bless it, and it will be just a floor again."

There I went again, making things harder than they needed to be. "I have a feeling we'll need to figure out how to do that under Vespa's nose. I can't see the demon lying aside while we destroy the circle."

"Okay. So relax. We have a list of stuff to do to prepare," she said.

I could tell I was driving her up the wall. My nervousness was translating into not being able to do anything, and since she shared the bedroom with me, if I wasn't getting any sleep, she wasn't either. The least I could do was be nice to her. I had Vespa to take my frustration out on. "I'm glad."

"I know you are."

#

We got dressed, gave Isaac some water, and went downstairs. There was no sense in putting off the inevitable. Vespa was sitting on the sofa with his head in his hands.

"Are you okay?" Tabby tapped him on the shoulder.

He glanced up with bloodshot eyes. "No. I didn't sleep."

At least I wasn't the only one, but what kept him up? "At all?"

"No. He wouldn't let me." He leaned back on the sofa. His skin had a kind of pasty look to it.

Uh-huh. I wasn't surprised. The whole thing was ramping up. I knew it. I'd known it all along. I'd just been a little too much of a chicken to admit it. If the demon was starting to mess with Vespa's health that meant he wanted another host. Tormenting Vespa would be enough to get under my skin.

"Let me guess. He's telling you to kill us," I said.

He stared at me in shock. "How did you know?"

"It's what they do." Asmodeus had threatened my life multiple times during my stay at Blackmoor. I kind of knew about this stuff.

"Oh, Jesus," he said.

I had a feeling that killing me wasn't what was keeping him up. I was only on his radar because I could do something for him. Really, he was upset because Mr. Demon was talking about him killing Tabby. His infatuation with her might actually be helpful. If he could keep his backbone, he might even be able to help us fight the demon. But I wasn't holding my breath.

"I don't know how much longer I can do this," he said.

Whine, whine, whine! Shit. I hated to think how he'd react if he suddenly got a serious illness. I walked over and sat beside him. "Listen, you know we are coming up with a game plan. Don't think we're here doing nothing. Everything you tell us, we catalog and use to figure out what direction everything is going to take."

"Really?" His eyes were pleading with me.

"Yup. We aren't here, all this way from home, for nothing, you know?" Though, at times, I felt like that, but I wasn't about to tell him about it.

He nodded.

I had more work to do. Exorcism was going forward. Yeah, I didn't have to do it today, but the timeframe had been sped ahead. I needed to stop thinking about me and get this done. I'd pussyfooted long enough.

"You have that look," Tabby said.

"I know."

She smiled. "I like it."

Truth was, I did too.

Chapter Twelve

How You Remind Me

"WHY DON'T WE do breakfast here today?" Tabby asked. Maybe her charm would make him change his mind about the outside dining issue.

Nick frowned at her. "I don't think that's a good idea."

Oh, good God. This was ridiculous. "Okay. I'll bite. Why don't you want food cooked in the house?"

He took a deep breath. "Because ever since the demon has been in me, any food cooked in this house turns into bugs or rats."

That made sense. Why couldn't he have just come out and said it?

"Have you tried someone else cooking it?" Tabby motioned at the kitchen.

Vespa nodded. "Yeah. My sister was over here before you came. She tried. You don't even want to know what happened to that food."

I had to wonder what it was about food that the demon didn't like. It wasn't keeping Nick from eating, or it wouldn't let him eat out. And because he wanted use of Nick's body, it made sense for it to keep him healthy. At least until I came along, that was.

"Okay, let me get my purse, and we'll go get some breakfast." Tabby sighed.

I swore, when we got home, I wasn't eating out for a month.

After she left, Nick turned to me. "I don't think I have a chance with her, do I?"

"Probably not. I mean, she and I, we're practically engaged." It was about time he asked.

"You are so lucky," he said.

"To have her, sure. But I wouldn't call myself lucky. Not with the job I have." That, and my penchant for bad luck, but who was counting?

"What's it like?" he asked. "Being an exorcist?"

I closed my eyes for a minute, trying to figure out what I was going to say. "It's hard. It's emotionally draining." I didn't want to get into specifics. Last thing I needed to do was give his demon something to use during the course of the exorcism.

"How do you do it?" Vespa leaned toward me. He was almost a little too interested.

"Perform exorcisms? Or be an exorcist?" They weren't the same thing. You could technically be an exorcist without ever having to perform an exorcism, especially if you were with the church.

"Be an exorcist," he said.

Damn. I hoped I hadn't given him a bright idea what to do with his life after I got him possession-free. He was used to faking people out by being a spiritualist. Taking on the guise of an exorcist wouldn't be far from his comfort zone. "I just do it. I'm kind of stubborn, so that helps."

Tabby came downstairs. "We ready?"

I stood up. "When you are."

#

When we got into the car, Lucy and Doc were playing a game in the back seat. It was kind of sweet, Doc finally having a kid he could call his own. I wasn't sure if he'd had kids while he was alive, but back in those days, he wasn't exactly sticking around home. He'd been out traveling the West, gambling, and participating in gunfights.

"What is the plan, boy?" Doc asked me.

I turned around in the seat a little. "We're grabbing some breakfast. Then, I have to figure out how to prepare the house for exorcism." I turned back and started the car.

Doc was quiet for a minute. "Don't forget to check the basement."

I heard a pop and looked in the rearview mirror. Doc was gone and Lucy was frowning.

"You messed up our game." She sounded so dejected.

"I'm sorry, Lucy. I'm sure he'll be back." I hadn't meant to mess up her morning, but Doc, I'm sure, had needed to do what he went off to do.

She nodded, and then started coloring in a coloring book Tabby had bought her. It was kind of strange to see a crayon move by itself, but I was used to strange by now.

"Now we have to check out a basement." Tabby tapped her fingers on the dashboard.

"Why do I have a feeling Vespa lied again?" If it hadn't been for Doc, I would have been so screwed. Another lie? I wasn't surprised. Lying seemed to be one of the things Nick did best.

"But about what?" Tabby stared out the window.

"The floor." It was all so simple. Slowly, ideas were forming in my brain.

"What floor? You aren't making any sense."

I pulled into the parking spot at the diner in Tombstone. It was weird to be coming back here, but it wasn't like I didn't miss it either. "What if the living room isn't where he does the demon stuff? I mean, wouldn't the whole house feel like the attic room at Blackmoor?"

In fact, I never felt any creepiness at all in Vespa's house. One would think the mere presence of the demon would make the whole house have a different feel, but I didn't feel a thing unless I was standing next to Nick. There had been so many lies at this point, I didn't know which end was up.

"I never thought about it, but yeah."

"Now, I don't know what that circle on the floor in the living room is for, but it sure isn't the heart of the house." I knew our time in the car was growing short. We had to get out there and deal with Nick.

"That's what Doc meant about the basement?"

I opened the car door. "Probably."

#

I'd be lying if I said I didn't want to go down to the basement right away. I needed to know the layout of the place, and get all the crap out of that room before we could start the exorcism, but that meant confronting Nick and I wasn't sure if now was the time to do it. I mean, yeah, I needed to get all of this over and done with, but I'd rather not pick a fight either.

We were on the way back to the house after breakfast, when suddenly, the car froze. Literally. Nothing moved, not the scenery, not the clock. Tabby was stuck in mid-motion of tucking her hair behind her ear. Lucy sat frozen, looking vacantly toward the back of my head. I glanced around. I didn't feel dead.

I stared outside the windshield. Vespa's car was frozen in front of me. The scenery was almost as if it were in a high-quality photograph. Even the leaves on the trees were frozen mid-sway. My stomach felt like it was being pulled in on itself. It wasn't painful, exactly. Just a strange sort of pressure.

"I understand that one of my…wards has been naughty."

I jumped and glanced in the back seat. The car heated all of a sudden. There, sitting next to Lucy, was a man. He looked to be around thirty with black hair long enough to brush his shoulders. His skin had an olive cast to it. He grinned at me. That's when I saw the fangs.

Oh, crap. I'd just landed in a whopping pile of shit. I couldn't not answer him. "If you're talking about Asmodeus, then yes."

He stayed there for a moment, not saying anything to me. Then he opened the car door and motioned for me to follow. I didn't want to, but my body did what he wanted anyway. My arm left the steering wheel and opened the door while my feet brushed the pedals and my body got out of the car on its own. I felt like a puppet.

"I have problems with that one," he said and walked over to a tree in someone's yard. He snapped off a smaller-sized branch. "Thank you for alerting me."

I nodded. This was so many levels of uncool. Getting to meet the devil was never one of my great plans in life. And there was no doubt that this was the real thing. He felt completely wrong, and yet so very polite. No wonder he was considered the great charmer.

"Now, what is it you want in return?" he asked.

I knew better than to make any requests, any agreements. If I hadn't been a stronger man, I'd have asked him to put Lucy to rights, but that was up to God, not me, and certainly, not him. "Nothing. I am just protecting my ward. I know that you and he," I said, pointing to the sky, "have a lot of negotiations to complete concerning her. Asmodeus interfering wasn't supposed to happen."

He grinned at me again. "Not all of us are quite so bad."

Oh, he was a charmer all right. The Father of Lies was a very good name for him. I had to be so careful.

"But Asmodeus is getting a bit ahead of himself. I will deal with him, permanently."

Shivers ran down my spine. Being dealt with by the devil personally was a whole other level of bad I dared not think about. Good thing I didn't have any intentions of doing something that would put me in that type of situation, but I doubt if those who were thought they would end up that way either.

Suddenly, he wrapped his hands around the little branch and fire whisked over it. Instead of a pile of ash, as I'd been expecting, there was what appeared to be a wand. Intricate swirls were charred into the wood. He handed it toward me.

"Give this to your lady friend. She may find it useful."

It was pretty almost. The charring seemed to grapevine around the wand. "No strings attached? This is not a contract of any sort?" I wanted to make sure. No way was I going to take this thing if it meant something else.

He started to laugh. It was deep and as charming as the rest of him. "No. God has his own special plans for you and your lady friend. This is a useful gift. I cannot have an outstanding debt."

Ah, because I hadn't wanted anything, he had to even up the score. Asmodeus must have had his fingers in too many cookie jars. Kind of interesting, getting a tool from the devil.

I took the wand from him. It was a lot heavier than it looked.

"I like you, Jimmy Holiday," he said. "Be careful."

He started walking away. The farther he got from me, the harder it was to see him. I got back in the car and put the wand in Tabby's lap.

Suddenly, time sped up to normal and I found myself having to step on the gas so that the car could continue moving forward.

I was scared now. Terrified, in fact. The devil telling you to be careful wasn't a good sign. It was like an explosives expert telling you that the boom was going to be a little loud.

"What's this?" Tabby asked, looking down into her lap.

"A gift." I almost choked saying it.

"Where did it come from?"

When we stopped at a red light, I closed my eyes for a minute. No way was I getting into it now. "I'll tell you back at the house."

#

Once we arrived, I told Nick I had a headache. It wasn't a lie, not exactly. The whole "meeting the devil" thing took a lot out of me. Tabby followed me upstairs. I was done worrying about what would happen once Vespa knew everything I was thinking. I mean, after all, he wasn't pulling any punches.

Upstairs, I closed and locked the door behind Tabby. The ward would keep him out.

"What is wrong with you?" Tabby asked.

I was pacing back and forth. My whole body shook. I didn't want to sit there. Part of me was afraid time would stop again. It had scared the shit out of me. For something to have that much power just wasn't right. But I knew I had to tell Tabby about it somehow.

"You know your gift?" I asked.

She tossed it on the bed like a pair of socks. "I don't know where you got that thing."

I stopped and stared. She'd just thrown that? We didn't even know what it did yet.

"That thing you just threw, it was made by the devil." I didn't need her accidentally blowing a hole through the wall or something.

She stared down her nose at me. "What?"

"Do you remember me stopping anywhere?"

She paused. "No."

"Remember me going anywhere within the last few days where I could get something like that?" I didn't have time to argue about it, but that's what we were doing.

She blinked. "What the hell, Jimmy?"

I lowered myself onto the bed. I was moving so much I was starting to make myself sick. "On the way back from the restaurant, the devil paid me a visit."

She raised her eyebrow.

"He stopped time, Tabby. You were frozen, putting your hair behind your ear. Lucy was stuck looking at the back of my head."

"If I didn't know you better, I'd say you've lost it."

"And then you'd still have a weird stick that magically appeared." Even she knew magic wands didn't appear out of nowhere.

"Where did the devil get it?"

"He made it right in front of me."

She sat beside me. Isaac meowed underneath the bed.

"See, he's hiding again. Even the cat knows." Isaac was a hell of a lot smarter than she was giving him credit for.

"Dammit, Jimmy." She grabbed a hold of my face. "Calm the fuck down!"

I stared at her. Her eyes were wild and green.

"I need you to relax, Jimmy. I can't understand you like this."

She let go of my face.

I took a few deep breaths. The fact that she was worried instead of pissed woke me up a little. "Okay. I'm all right."

"Now, run all this by me again."

I steadied myself. "The devil came to thank me for letting him know about Asmodeus."

She blinked. "What did he look like?"

"It was horrible. He was a little thinner than I am, and he wore this expensive grey suit. His hair was black, long, and kind of curly. He was dressed like a normal businessman. That is, until he smiled." Just talking about it started my hands shaking again.

"Why?"

"He had fangs, that's why. Because I wouldn't name something in return for my help, he made you that wand. Said something about how you might be able to use it."

"Do you think you should contact the Order?"

I laughed. "Why bother? They haven't answered one email asking for help. Why would they want to come in if the devil is here?"

Wimps. Oh yeah, let the defrocked one deal with it. He likes it. I rolled my eyes.

"It was just an idea, Jimmy."

I needed to stop taking it out on her. It wasn't her fault that the Order was made up of jackasses. "The sad thing is, the devil isn't what's scaring me."

She stared at me, confused. "Okay, so what has you so freaked out?"

"He told me to be careful." I let that sink in for a bit.

She whistled. "Okay. Asmodeus had soul-suckers and all types of things come after us, right?"

"Yeah." I had no idea where she was going with this.

"We survived that without knowing what we were doing."

I nodded. "Yeah, so?"

"If we made it through that okay, I don't see why this would be any different." She shrugged.

"But the devil said—"

"Did you ever think he meant to watch our backs? Besides, when did you start listening to the other side?"

She was right.

"Okay. Let's go back downstairs." I steadied my hands. "Old Nick and I are going to have a little talk."

#

I stormed downstairs. Vespa was nowhere to be found. That figured. Tabby ran down the steps after me.

"Don't do anything stupid, Jimmy," she said.

Hah. Stupid was what I did best. "Vespa! Come out here right now!"

"Oh, Jesus. Jimmy, will you just listen to yourself?" Tabby was standing there with her hands on her hips.

"Nick, goddamn it!" I was close to throwing one of those puke sofas. That would get his attention.

The boy scrambled out of his bedroom. "What's wrong?"

"Care to tell me what the fuck this is for?" I threw back the rug that covered the circle.

"I told you, it's where I conjured—"

I grabbed him by the throat and pushed him against the wall. "Listen, you little shit. I don't have time for this. Stop the lies. What the hell is going on?"

His face turned red. No sense in getting charged with murder. I let him go. He backed away from me and rubbed his neck. He actually seemed scared of me for once. Good.

He cleared his throat a few times. "This is my circle. For protection."

Uh-huh. Thanks. A lot. "Now, was that so hard? So where did you do the dirty work?"

"In the basement."

I glanced at Tabby, and then back at Vespa. He hadn't moved. I was seriously thinking about letting Doc shoot him after all of this was through.

"Well?" I motioned with my hand for him to take us to his basement.

He led us down the hallway just off the kitchen. It wasn't even noticeable from the living room. It was narrow with a wooden floor and mulberry-colored walls. We passed by his bedroom as we continued down the hall. The door to it was open and it was a mess, like a normal teenager's room. I even spied a game system. So he had a TV after all.

Tabby held my hand, I think partly because she was tired of Vespa lusting after her and partly because she was uneasy. She might have been trying to distract me enough to keep me calm. The closer we got to the door, the more a steady cold hit me. Strange for Arizona.

At the end of the hallway stood a door with an arch. No other door in the house arched like that. Vespa opened it.

"Be careful of the steps." He motioned forward.

He was right. It was almost like the place had been put together haphazardly. Somehow, the ceiling and the walls were covered in pieces of stone, almost like what you'd see in a castle, but I could spot faint cracks in the mortar. So they were basically tiles then. I had a sinking suspicion that the basement was not originally part of the house, and that Vespa had pieced this whole thing together. We'd be lucky if the ceiling didn't fall on us.

The same tile covered the steps too. I didn't even want to think about how much money he wasted doing all of this. He flipped a switch on the stairway and fake candelabras came to life with fake dancing flames. I could almost imagine the sale at the Halloween store he bought them from.

"Can you believe this shit?" Tabby whispered.

I shook my head. Vespa was showing how very young he was. A Goth would have hired a designer and some professionals, or had someone teach him how to do it properly. They would consider this a disgrace.

Finally, after a curve in the steps, we came to a large octagonal room. More of the candelabras lined the walls. Inset into the floor appeared another circle. This one was made of silver and had different markings from the first one upstairs. A five-pointed star with what was probably the head of Baphomet in the center rested inside the circle. Baphomet's eyes had red jewels. Peachy.

I forced myself not to ponder what the expense was if they were real. I had a sinking suspicion that they were. It made me sick.

"Pretty cool, huh?" Vespa asked.

I raised an eyebrow. "I think you need to reassess your views on things. A room to perform black magic isn't cool. It's dangerous."

The room felt mildly creepy, but nothing compared to the attic room at Blackmoor. Vespa was playing. Mr. Black had been adept.

"It took a lot of work," he said.

"Oh, I don't doubt that." A lot of work for an amateur so-called creepy design.

The edges of the room had a few bookcases. All filled with magic books. Some I could tell he'd bought at the local bookstore. Others were so old they were probably moments from falling apart. Those probably belonged to Nick's great-grandfather.

"How long do you think it will take you to get all of the stuff out of here?"

Vespa stared at me, puzzled. What do you mean?"

I let go of Tabby's hand and started pointing at things. "All of this. How long will it take you to make this a bare room?"

"I don't know." He shrugged. "I just don't understand why."

I stared him, dead in the eyes. "Because this is where we'll do your exorcism."

#

All in all, it took about an hour to haul all of the crap out of there. We put it in a storage room off the garage. I was happy for that extra storage room. I sure as hell would have minded all the crap going into an extra bedroom near the room Tabby and I had been using. Call me crazy, but I didn't want to be near anything a demon had used if I could help it. Stuff like that had an air about it, a sickness.

Half-way through, Vespa froze. His eyes glowed green again. "If you think this will help you, then by all means, carry on."

It was hard to tell if it was a bluff or if the demon was telling the truth. But the subtle tone in his voice led me to believe he was trying to psych me out. Bring it on, Bucky.

"I'm sorry, but I don't feel like being clobbered on the head with a knickknack," I said.

He laughed. "You are a funny one, priest."

I shrugged. "Too bad I'm not funny enough to be a comedian."

Vespa's demon stared at me oddly. "What does a comedian have to do with all of this?"

I blinked. At least my bullshit was distracting him. "You said I was funny."

"Yes."

"So?"

Suddenly, the demon went back to wherever it was when it wasn't in power of Vespa.

"You are so weird," Nick said.

"Says the kid who willingly invited a demon inside his head."

He rolled his eyes. "Now what?"

"Why don't you find out where the hardware store is? We need a chain, a hasp that can be bolted to something. And I don't know where you can get them here, but we need some handcuffs." That was all I had with Lucy. Well, except the mirror. I didn't want to think about the mirror.

He stared at me for a minute. "Do I want to know why?"

I shook my head. "Not yet. We'll hold down the fort while you're gone."

He frowned, and then went upstairs. Tabby and I didn't move until we heard the sound of him starting his car.

"Okay. We need a chisel and a hammer." I motioned toward the floor.

"Garage?" Tabby asked.

"Probably." We ran upstairs and rummaged around for tools. We found the tool chest easily enough. It was a big red case in the garage. Bad part was, it was locked.

"Shit. What do we do now?" I banged on the top.

"Silver's a soft metal, right?"

"Yeah…"

She ogled me like I'd tried to stand on one leg while doing the macarena. "Okay, get a butter knife from the kitchen," I said.

She exhaled and then left the garage. I grabbed a small piece of a two-by-four. If I didn't break my fingers, this was going to work out nicely.

I headed down to the basement. Not long after I got down there, Tabby joined me.

"All right, Mr. Fixit. What's the plan?" she asked.

"All we need to do is break the circle, right?"

"Theoretically."

"Okay." I sat on the floor in the area that seemed the thinnest. It was going to take a bit. The outer edge of the circle was over an inch wide. But since this was all I had to work with, it was going to have to do.

"Put the butter knife here." I pointed to the center of the line of the circle.

Tabby got on the floor and held it.

I raised the piece of wood I was using as a hammer and took a deep breath. "I'm going to try to be careful, but if I hurt you, I'm sorry."

"Just get on with it. We don't know how long he'll be gone." She wiggled a little to get a better balancing point on her knees.

I positioned the two-by-four over the end of the butter knife, aimed, and then I slammed the wood down on the end of the butter knife. The sound was in between a clang and a screech. Enough to give you a headache.

"Did it work?" I asked.

Tabby started laughing. "It's fake! All he did was use glue over the design and hold a piece of paper with a very thin layer of silver over it."

I couldn't believe our luck. Finally, something went our way. I probably should have known better than to think he actually had bought silver and paid to have someone make the bands to fit into the floor.

She began scratching the floor with the knife. Soon, there was a space about an inch wide that no longer had silver. Who knew it would have been that easy?

"That works. I'm glad we didn't have to pound our way through like I thought we would." With a butter knife, that would have taken hours.

She wiped the floor with her hand. The stone was a little scratched, but the circle was clearly broken.

"Put that wood away. I'll put the butter knife in the sink," Tabby said.

We both went upstairs. I went to the garage and put the two-by-four back where I found it. I wasn't stupid enough to think he wouldn't notice, but if he'd been here, we'd have had to fight the demon, it would have been a big mess, and I didn't want the bother. I'd already almost killed him anyway. No need for a repeat performance.

I met Tabby back in the living room. She was sitting on the couch and had a smirk on her face.

"What did you do?" I knew that look.

"Pick up the rug."

I walked over to the edge of the rug and lifted it up. The circle here was scratched out, down to the wood. It smelled foul.

"While I approve of being extra-careful, what's that smell?" I wanted to gag.

"Isaac decided to help."

I snorted. "Where is he now?"

"Went back upstairs. I think he'll be happy when we go back home."

No doubt. I'm sure he was tired of all of this shit too. "He's not the only one."

"One question, though."

I cocked my head to the side. "What?"

"What if he messes with the chain and stuff?"

I flopped down next to her on the sofa. "Have faith. When he brings them back, I planned on storing them in our room until we need them."

"What if he messes with them before that?"

I chuckled. "What do you think we'll be doing before we go to bed tonight?"

"You sure do know how to romance a girl."

I grinned. "You know it."

#

It took Vespa over two hours to get back. No joke. He came in through the front door, his face red and eyes exhausted. He lumbered over and set the bags down next to my feet. "You wouldn't believe how hard it is to find handcuffs if you aren't a cop."

I snorted. "Where did you have to go? Timbuktu?"

He threw himself on the opposite sofa. "Tucson. But man, you wouldn't believe the weird looks I kept getting."

Tabby giggled. "It could be worse. They could have been pink fur-lined."

He froze. "No way."

"Yes, way. So be thankful you were able to find some normal ones." She crossed her legs.

"People are weird."

"I couldn't agree more," Tabby replied.

"Out here, most folks are pretty normal." Vespa rubbed his eyes with his hands.

"Present company excluded, of course," I said. In no universe was he normal, I didn't care what bullshit he was trying to pull.

"I don't know about you, but I'm hungry," Vespa said. I swore, if I didn't know better, I would have thought he was pregnant. That's all he ever wanted to do was eat.

"Want to go get something to eat?" I asked.

"Hell, yes."

We ended up at the Mexican restaurant. I didn't care what we ate at this point. It was all starting to taste the same. Every place used some sort of southwestern rub. At first, it had been kind of nice. Now I just wanted a plain old hamburger with American cheese.

Vespa ordered enough to kill a horse. Enchiladas, burritos, a quesadilla. It was nuts.

"It's almost as if you're eating for two," Tabby said. Yup, she nailed it.

"Nope. I've always eaten like this. Used to drive Mom nuts."

I couldn't imagine being a parent to him. I guess the whole demon business clouded my perception of him, but he wasn't a good kid. I kind of felt sorry for him because his family was partly to blame, but damn. He was a baby in a man's body.

As soon as the food hit the table, he started shoveling it in. It was like watching an anteater go after a nest.

"When are we going to do this?" he asked between bites.

I leaned in closer. "What? The exorcism?"

"Yeah," he wiped his face with a napkin, "I mean, we cleaned out the room."

I relaxed in the chair. "Keep in mind it might take more than one session."

"Yeah. I know."

I took a deep breath. "We could get started as soon as we finish fixing up the room."

"How do you do that?"

"What do you think the chain and handcuffs are for?" It was getting tiresome to having to keep explaining myself. Was he that dense?

"Oh, shit." He sat back in his chair. "Are you going to keep me chained up the whole time?"

"Depends on how the demon reacts. I don't want to die," Tabby said.

Vespa nodded. It figured. To keep Tabby safe he was okay with it.

"Can I at least have a blanket?" he asked.

I almost laughed. "Of course."

"It's not us that's trying to kill you," Tabby reminded him.

What type of people did he think we were? I mean, yeah, being chained to a floor was going to suck, but it wasn't like we were doing it to be mean or anything. In the back of my head, I remembered the warning from the big guy. But that lead to a very important question: why was the devil being nice to me? I wasn't dumb enough to think that he wasn't such a bad guy. Besides, if he wasn't so bad, then why would he have demons like Asmodeus in his employ? He wanted something.

I shook those thoughts out of my head. It was best to deal with the problems I already had.

Chapter Thirteen

Coming Undone

EXORCISM. WITH A willing participant. New ground for me. "Willing" was subjective. It depended on what side I was talking to. But I had to wonder exactly how much he wanted to get rid of the demon. He seemed a little too easygoing with all of it. There had to be something I was missing.

Tabby and I went over every inch of the chain and handcuffs, looking for marks or anything that could have weakened them, but we found nothing. I'd expected something else, but what, I wasn't sure. Things were going too smoothly and I could tell that I was about to get smacked in the face with a giant clod of horse shit. It was coming. I just didn't know when.

I walked downstairs. It was time for another hardware store trip. "Nick!"

"Just a minute!" It sounded like he was in his bedroom.

I stood next to one of the sofas. Tabby was upstairs, making my holy water and trying to help me come up with a new rite of exorcism. We didn't have the one we'd used for Lucy. I'd never thought to pick it up from the attic. I never thought I'd need it again either.

Vespa came out of the kitchen. He was wearing an old t-shirt and a pair of jeans. Honestly, it was good to see him dress his age. I had to do a double-take to realize it was him.

"I forgot a couple of things we need from the hardware store," I said.

"Like what?"

A new brain for you, a piece of chocolate, and my own bed at home. Heh. "Regular bulbs for the lights in the basement. Concentrating will be hard enough without the flicker."

He stood there for a moment, almost frozen. "All right. Let me find my keys."

That was simple enough. Periodically, I could hear water running upstairs. Yep, Tabby had gotten to work. Me, I was waiting on Vespa.

Finally, he came back. "You riding with me?"

I shrugged. It didn't make a difference anymore. Not really. "Sure. Besides, I don't want to leave Tabby without transportation." That was true too.

He led me out the door and into his SUV. The floor had candy wrappers and other trash, but at least it didn't smell.

"Sorry about the mess. I haven't cleaned it out since my last trip."

I didn't ask where he'd gone. It didn't seem important. Being a spiritualist must pay okay. At least if you were one possessed by a demon, not that I was counting. But a fancy SUV covered in candy wrappers? That was a whole other type of brat. One that had been handed everything his entire life. That bothered me. "Do you keep in contact with your family?"

He glared at me from the corner of his eyes as he backed out of the driveway. "For now. I don't like them poking around in my business."

"Ah." There wasn't much else for me to say. It was a good thing we wouldn't have to worry about his family interrupting the exorcism, but something felt off. I couldn't put my finger on what, though.

We got to the hardware store in about five minutes. It was a local place. That was one thing I liked about this part of Arizona—there were plenty of non-megastores. I hadn't even come across a chain restaurant yet. It was a nice change from back home where most local businesses had been run out by big companies. Tombstone would be a good place to live if it weren't for the demon stuff.

Vespa pulled into a spot. "You don't even have to come in if you don't want to."

I knew there wasn't going to be anything to see. "You don't care?"

He shook his head. "Just bulbs for the lights downstairs, right?"

"Yeah."

He closed the car door. The bad feeling intensified and I felt myself starting to sweat. Seemed like, when we got back to the house, it would be time to fix up the basement. But I wanted a night's sleep before I did this. The lack of sleep had been doing its thing all day. Hopefully,

Tabby had time to douse both circles with holy water. It was better to be extra sure that none of the bag magic remained when I tried to do this thing.

Soon, Vespa came back to the car with a bag. He opened the door, handed it to me, and got in. I put it on the floor next to my feet.

"Want to grab some pizza?" he asked.

I blinked. We'd eaten a little over an hour ago, but whatever. Gluttony was the least of the sins I needed to worry about. "Okay."

It was almost like the demon inside him amped up his metabolism. The kid was skinny, but he ate so much. It wasn't normal. There was also the possibility that the kid had something medically wrong with him, like a thyroid disorder.

"I think I'd like to begin tomorrow," I told him.

He paused for a minute, and then glanced at me. "Yeah. I think it's about time."

He backed out of the parking place, drove a little ways down the mini-mall and then pulled into a parking spot at the pizza place. "This is my last night of freedom?"

He acted like he was going to be hanged tomorrow. Jesus. "No, don't think of it like that. Just because there have been some exorcisms that have taken years, that doesn't mean yours will."

His cat-like eyes seemed sad to me. The whole effect was kind of spoiled by those vertical slits. He was like an abused animal, wild and broken.

"I'll be back," he said and hopped out of the car.

Shit. I hadn't meant for it all to go that way. Yeah, I'd been a prick, but he'd done stuff to piss me off too. I never said I was perfect. And now, he'd taken it all to an extreme I hadn't meant. I knew this wasn't a happy thing, but hell. This kid had no idea that his possession was nothing like how bad it could be. I still woke up some nights scared to death because of Lucy. He had no idea.

When he came back, he put two pies in the backseat. "Pepperoni okay?"

"Yeah," I said. "Fine by me." I'm sure Tabby wouldn't mind the garlic either. I stayed quiet the rest of the way back to the house. There was nothing else left for me to say.

Unfortunately, the house was not quiet when we got there. A

strange car was parked haphazardly in the driveway and a group of people were screaming at the front door. The door was closed. I sat up in the seat.

Before I knew what was happening, Vespa had slammed the car in park and jumped out of the SUV. "What the hell?"

He was stalking toward the crowd at the door. I got out and followed him over to them. Something told me he was going to need backup.

"Oh, thank God. I thought that bitch had stolen your house," the woman in front said.

She was a large lady, about a foot shorter than Vespa. She was at least sixty years old and wore a black caftan with a mosaic border on the edge. She was hideous.

"Don't talk that way about her," Vespa said, his eyes starting to glow faintly.

"Baby, you know how I've always told you that women are bad for you."

Something told me that this was the type of woman that created Ed Gein. Fuck.

"Mom. Look at who is next to me." He pointed at me.

Thanks for putting me on the spot, kid. Nothing like being the target of a behemoth.

"This is my friend, Jimmy," Vespa said. "Tabby is his fiancée."

The lady put her hands on her massive hips. Two other women stood behind her, but they were bowing their heads too. Both had short-cropped grey hair. They were as skinny as Vespa's mom was fat. What the hell were they? Acolytes?

"That *whore* isn't yours?" Vespa's mom asked.

I couldn't keep my mouth shut. I didn't care if she was Vespa's mom or not, Tabby was mine, and she wasn't a whore. I cleared my throat.

She turned her hatred to me. "What are you going to do about it?"

Apparently, no one had ever just smacked the shit out of her. I didn't hit women, and I never would, but she needed someone to take her down a peg or two. I couldn't keep myself from taking up for Tabby. I stepped closer. "Be careful what you say about certain people. Unlike your son, I'm not afraid of you."

"Are you threatening me?" She pumped her head back and forth at me, almost like she was trying to mimic a snake.

I almost laughed. "No. I'm stating facts. Right now, you are out here in the yard for God and everyone to see screaming about whores. One, my fiancée is not a whore, and I think you owe her an apology. Two, you've messed your son up so badly he's going to need years of counseling. Something tells me you should be thinking more about keeping a low profile than screaming in the street."

She slapped me across the face.

I hadn't expected that. I guessed her white trash colors decided to stand out. I stood fixed even though she'd just slapped the piss out of me. If I retaliated that would make me just as bad. And if she knew what was good for her, she'd quit before I let Tabby loose on her. That reminded me—where was Tabby? I took a deep breath and glared at the peons. "I suggest you get your friend and get her the fuck out of here," I told the two women behind Vespa's mom. "Unlike Jesus, I do not turn the other cheek."

I guess I was a scary man when I was pissed off because the two women grabbed her and put her in their car. Score one for the exorcist. Zero for the battle axe.

After they drove off, Vespa turned to me. "That was so awesome."

I snorted. "I can see why you want to get away from here."

He walked over to the SUV and pulled it into the driveway behind my rental car. "Want to help get some of this?"

Tabby came out of the house. "What was that woman's problem?"

"Mom is a pain in the ass," Vespa said.

I snorted. "That's one way to describe her."

Tabby stood on the front porch while I walked back to Vespa's car. I opened the door and grabbed the bag-o-bulbs while Vespa got the pizzas.

"It's a good thing she got out of here," I said as I closed the car door.

"Dude, your hair was standing on end."

"Your face is red," Tabby said. She reached forward and touched it. It burned a little.

"Bitch slapped me." I wasn't trying to get sympathy or anything, but Vespa's mom had a hell of an arm.

We sat at the dining room table. It was this huge oblong thing that seated ten people with no problem. The pizzas were spread out in the middle of the table. We all had plates.

"Remind me to put something on it later," she said.

I nodded.

Vespa came in from the kitchen and handed us all a soda. "I'm really sorry about Mom."

I shrugged. This was the one thing that definitely wasn't his fault. "You can't help who your family is. Don't worry about it."

"What did she say to you?" he asked Tabby.

I had a feeling that if I didn't manage to get the demon out, Mrs. Vespa was going to end up one dead lady.

Tabby opened her soda and took a sip. "I finished getting stuff ready upstairs, so I came down here to wait."

I nodded.

"So," she said. "Suddenly the doorbell rang. I got up, went to the door, made sure the security thing was latched, and opened the door."

"What did Mom do?" Nick tapped his fingers against his soda can creating a tattoo.

"I asked her if I could help her, you know? And she wanted to know where you were. I told her you'd gone to the store, but then she tried to force her way into the house. I managed to get the door shut and the dead bolt on."

"Jesus," I said.

"She screamed for at least ten minutes. I kid you not."

The woman was lucky that Tabby had a long fuse. I'd seen her pissed before, way beyond how mad she'd been with me recently, and it wasn't pretty.

"Just for that, you get the first slice of pizza." Vespa grabbed her plate and loaded her with a hell of a slice. It was almost three slices worth.

"Thanks." She picked it up and took a huge bite out of it.

"Think she'll come back?" I asked. Here I'd been worried about the lighting being a distraction. The battle axe from hell was a whole other dimension.

"If she does, I'll kill her," he said.

Maybe the demon was affecting him more than I realized.

#

After pizza, Nick and I went downstairs. We needed to finish getting the room ready, and I wanted him to get used to the changes we'd made. He froze.

"What did you do?" His eyes began to glow.

"Calm down." I didn't need Mr. Demon right now; I needed Nick. "We had to break the circle. We couldn't risk anything else coming through."

His eyes started glowing full bore. Dammit. Nick was gone again.

The demon cackled. "I don't need the circle to bring more of my kind in. All I need is a little blood."

I stared down the demon. No way was I letting that happen. "It's not time for you yet. Let Nick back. Your show is tomorrow."

The demon laughed again. "I love a good exorcism in the morning."

I rolled my eyes. Either the demon was that cocky or that stupid. I hadn't decided which yet. Nick's eyes went back to normal.

"You aren't going to be doing this anymore anyway, right?" I asked him.

He exhaled slowly for a minute. "I guess not."

"Okay then." His hesitation made me uneasy. What was the point of me exorcising him if he planned to continue messing with demons? Hell if I knew. No sense in worrying about it now. "This will keep us safer. Get a drill and some screws so we can attach the hasp to the floor."

He darted upstairs. I meticulously went around the room changing out light bulbs. There had to be over a hundred. I was starting to think I should have dealt with the flicker. It would have been a lot easier, velvet Elvis setting or not.

"What do you want me to do?" Nick asked when he came back.

"Line up your drill bit with the hold on the installation plate of the hasp. Then pre-drill the holes." He was the one who'd insisted on installing that tile, so let him do the work.

Four zzzt's later and he switched to the drill. He went ahead and screwed the hasp to the floor. It had taken him like five minutes and he was done. I was still changing out light bulbs. It wasn't fair. I had no one to blame but myself; I'd give him the job.

"You guys okay down there?" Tabby yelled from upstairs.

"Yeah. Almost done," I said.

We were waiting until tomorrow for the handcuffs and the chain. I was worried about sabotage. It would be easy enough to check on the hasp in the morning before we began. And I could bless the chain and the handcuffs with holy water if I wanted.

"Want some help?" Nick asked

"Sure." I handed over the bag. The sooner I could get this done, the better off I'd be. I was done with it for the night.

Finally, we made it back upstairs. Isaac was sitting on Tabby's legs, purring. I guess now that we were going through with the exorcism, he felt it was safe enough to grace us with his presence. She was on one of the sofas. I sat next to her.

"Get it all ready?" she asked.

"As ready as we can." What wasn't ready was my brain, but that was my problem.

Vespa lounged on the opposite sofa. "I don't know if I want to do this."

Why was I not surprised? Just as we got everything ready and busted our asses, he was having second thoughts. I wasn't going to tell him one way or the other, but I was going to speak my mind. I didn't go through this whole experience for nothing. "Listen, I understand you're scared and you have every right to be. But are you going to be able to live like this the rest of your life?"

He stared at the floor. "I don't want to die."

I wanted to tell him he should have thought of that before he dragged us all the way to Arizona, but I didn't. Not wanting to die and not wanting to be possessed were two different things. "I don't think anyone does. Not really. If you decide you don't want to do this, I'll understand. But think about it before you make any decisions."

He got up and went into his room. I turned to Tabby. She shrugged.

"Guess we should go to bed," I said.

"Guess so."

#

"Is it the demon?" Tabby asked once we were safely in the bedroom. Isaac jumped out of her arms and buried himself between the pillows.

I couldn't blame the cat. "I don't know. This demon isn't like Asmodeus at all. He's quiet almost. I don't know if that's good or bad. If it wasn't for the paranormal shit we've seen, I would almost say he isn't possessed at all."

Tabby nodded. "I did get both circles blessed with holy water. And if he isn't possessed, I guess we have nothing to worry about."

I took a deep breath. That didn't sound very simple either. "And the rite?"

"I jotted down what I could from memory. I figured we could work on it."

"Sounds good." There wasn't anything else to do.

Isaac mowed from the bed. I guess he agreed too.

Later, I tried, but a good sleep was something I didn't get. As far as I knew, we had the rite as good as we could get it. We'd gone over it for a couple of hours, but I couldn't see anything that we could add that would make it better. Hell, when we'd written the one I used with Lucy, it hadn't been this much work. Part of it was that we were willing to try anything. And we'd been out of options.

This was different. Something about the whole mess left me with a bad feeling and it wasn't just the devil's warning. It could have been the lies, but I had a feeling it was that I couldn't get a handle on Vespa. One minute, he was this goofy kid, and the next, he was this weird demon. I wasn't used to dealing with a living flip-coin. I'm not sure anyone could get used to that.

I watched the sun rise. Was it smart to start an exorcism on no sleep? Probably not, but Vespa was counting on me. That was if he decided to go through with it. If he changed his mind, I'd go back to bed, get some sleep, and then book my and Tabby's flight home. I'll admit that I was kind of hoping for that option.

"Jimmy?" Tabby asked.

I glanced over at her. "Yeah?"

She picked up her cell phone off the night stand and squinted at the screen. "What are you doing up?"

I shrugged. "I never went to sleep."

She sat up in bed. "Then we'd better hope today goes smoothly."

"I think that's something we better not count on. I swear, if Nick's mother comes back, I might not be able to control myself."

"You?" She uncovered her legs. "I'm going to get my shower."

"You do that." I rubbed my neck.

Almost as soon as she left the room, Doc popped in.

"Stuff startin', huh?" he asked.

I shrugged. You could put it that way. "Vespa didn't want to go through with it last night."

Doc stroked his goatee for a minute. "I'm bettin' that today will be different."

I nodded. "We'll see. How's Lucy?"

His face broke into a smile. "She's okay. Tired of being in that car."

It was so cute. He'd become the doting grandfather. "I bet. Hell, I'm tired of being here, period."

He laughed. "Sooner you get this done, the better."

He didn't have to tell me that. "Yeah, I know. Nick's getting worse."

Doc grunted.

"What?"

He waved me off. "Let me know if you need me. I'm going to go back to Miss Lucy."

And then he disappeared.

One of these days I was going to make him stick around when all hell broke loose. "I need an easier job."

#

After I cleaned up, I got dressed in a nice shirt and some pants, dug out my purple stole, and put the bottle of holy water Tabby had prepared in my pocket. It was my uniform. Tabby grabbed the bag with the chain, the handcuffs, and a few pieces of ribbon.

"Want to make your confession now?" she asked.

"Probably. If Vespa has decided to go forward with the exorcism, I want to start right away." I took a moment to bring all the things I'd done recently to the front of my mind. Then, I nodded at her.

"Okay. What would you like to confess?" She stood in front of me with one of her hips cocked out to the side.

I sat on the bed. "I don't like Vespa. I hope we can get this over and done with and I don't want to mark him. He's a liar and a cheat, and if it were up to me, I might let the demon have him if it wasn't for the fact that I don't want to be that type of person."

"You'll mark him if you have to?" She sat beside me.

I nodded. I knew I'd been kidding myself. If it was my lot in life to be stuck with his ass, then I'd have to deal with it. But so help me God, if he tried to hurt Lucy in any way, I'd figure out how to un-mark him. Or I could give him to the devil. That might be fun.

"Okay. I think you're ready," she said.

"Thanks for the vote of confidence." Hell, I wasn't even confident in myself. This had the makings of being a very bad day.

We got up and left the room. Isaac stayed behind in the bed, asleep. Lucky shit. Tabby wrapped her ward strings around her wrist. I relaxed a little upon seeing them. At least, Vespa wouldn't be able to go everywhere we could. It was something small, but it was something for me to hold onto.

When we got downstairs, Nick was sitting in the middle of the floor with his legs crossed.

"Everything okay?" I asked. This wasn't exactly how I expected to find him.

He stared up at me. His eyes were bloodshot and slightly glowing. "I couldn't sleep."

"You aren't the only one," I said. "Have you made a decision?" I needed to know now.

He took a deep breath and then let it out slowly. "If I want to live, I have to get this thing out of me."

"Basement it is, then."

Nick smiled. "Can I get something to eat?"

Him and his stomach. "Exorcism, like magic, is best done on an empty stomach. We do this in shifts almost."

He frowned at me. "I won't be able to eat until it's all over?"

I chuckled. He never listened to me. "No. You won't be able to eat until we're done with the first session."

"Oh. Okay." He got up off the floor and led us down to the basement. I let Tabby go ahead of me. She nonchalantly slipped the ward string over the door knob. I was so damn lucky to have her. If need be, we could run. I hadn't even had that with Lucy.

Vespa sat in the center of the room. I grabbed the hasp and tested it. Then, Tabby handed me the chain and I looped it through the hasp. After I got the handcuffs attached, Vespa allowed me to cuff him.

"You comfortable?" I asked him.

"I guess. This is so bizarre."

I didn't bother mentioning how much weirder it was to conjure a demon, but whatever. I stepped back toward the other side of the room. I nodded to Tabby. She pulled out a piece of chalk. After she'd drawn a circle around us, she set down a small bottle of the holy water, a small packet of sand, a candle, and a feather.

"Hail to the guardians of the watchtowers," she said. "North, South, East, and West. Hear my call. Bless this circle and keep us safe within it. Bless Nick for the trial he's about to endure. Keep your eyes open and watch out for those that wish us harm." She folded her hands in front of her and touched her nose with her middle fingers. "So mote it be."

Then, she dropped her hands.

Suddenly, I felt a zing pass through my body. I could feel power radiating off the circle. It almost had a rainbow cast coming off it. "Damn, girl."

She blushed.

I checked on Vespa. His eyes were full-on green glow now.

"Most impressive display of power," he said.

I nodded. Yeah, sure, demon. I rely on your impression. He was right, but I wasn't about to let him know that. "Yup. Tabby's special all right."

The lighting dimmed a little. It was time.

"Wretched thing from the dark, state your purpose," I intoned.

It chuckled. "I am here to help. Nicholas Vespa invited me."

Yeah, help what? Kill us all? "Vespa does not like your agreement."

The demon chortled. "So often, they think that they can use us. Make us do their bidding. Instead, we take over the host. Change it. Mold it into something better."

The only thing I'd seen a demon do with a body was destroy it. Either his view of better was different, or there was something else wrong here. "Isn't it limiting to reside in a human body?"

"At first, but once the changes begin, it is perfect."

I blinked. Okay. Time to start with the real stuff. "What is your name?"

"You didn't think it would be that easy, did you?"

I shrugged. "Can't blame me for trying."

The demon nodded. "How much longer are you going to continue this charade?"

"It will take as long as it takes. I am in no hurry." And I wasn't. I was in this for the whole thing, even if it did take years.

Suddenly, I heard what sounded like Lucy crying. I waited. As suddenly as it started, it stopped.

"You'll have to do better than that." This demon was a lightweight compared to Asmodeus. I knew Lucy was safe.

It grinned. "Oh, I plan to."

I steadied myself. Enough chit-chat. "Begone, creature of hate. Begone, creature of lies. Go back to your world."

It laughed again.

Something was wrong. It was like my words had no power. There was none of the magic that coursed through me when I'd exorcised Lucy. Either my powers had been snatched away from me, or Vespa wasn't what he was supposed to be.

I stared down at the rest of what Tabby and I had written. Shit. Vespa, for all of his meanderings, wasn't a child of God. Not really. His inviting the demon in had created a grey area. I had to change him back.

"Vespa, listen to me. Renounce it."

The demon laughed more.

"Renounce your contract. Own up to what you've done. Confess!"

I saw a ripple move through the circle and fade on Vespa. This was not good.

"Clever. Too bad; I have him right where I want him." The demon clucked his tongue.

I pulled myself together. "What is your name?"

The demon shifted and wrapped part of the chain around Vespa's neck. "Why, Nicholas, of course."

"What are you doing?" I asked. I didn't like this. At all.

He cinched the chain together. "What would you do to save his soul?"

Dammit. He had me. The demon wanted a lot more. He wanted me. "I am doing what I was sent here to do for his soul."

"Will you mark him?" it asked.

"If it comes to that, yes." I'd made my peace with the idea. If I did have to keep him, maybe I could teach him to be a better person.

It grinned. "Will you take his place?"

Before I could even say no, the air stilled. A piece of dust floated in front of my face. It did not move from its spot.

Shit. Big bad was here and I didn't know why.

Vespa, in the center of the room, was frozen. Not even a muscle twitched. Tabby and I were normal. I could only guess it was her circle of protection that kept her from being affected.

"Is this what happened before?" she asked.

"Uh-huh." I kept searching around the room, but I didn't see anything. Not yet.

Suddenly, the wall across from us undulated. The mortar around some of the tiles cracked with the ripple. The ceiling shuddered. If this didn't get over with soon, we might well die because of the faulty construction instead of the devil. But then, his being here was causing it all anyway. So that would make him responsible. At least that's where my thoughts went. I had no time for anything else.

Loud footsteps sounded, almost like a great hoofed beast was walking across a cement floor. They echoed, but nothing appeared. A few moments later the devil walked straight through the wall.

My heart started beating in time with his footsteps, as if he held my ability to live within his hands. He did not look up at first, but a smile crept at the corners of his mouth. Oh, yes. He knew exactly what he was doing.

Dressed in a long black robe embroidered with a silver edging along the hem, he was no longer the dapper businessman. While his hair was shoulder-length, red highlights seemed to dance within it like the very flames existed within him. His eyes flashed with crimson light whenever he passed the candelabras. And then there were those fangs. He didn't bother to hide them when he looked up and grinned directly at me.

His gaze snapped to Tabby. I watched, helpless, as he stepped to the edge of the circle.

"What a powerful witch," he said, each word falling sharp as icicles.

"Only those who have discovered that pain can be sweet would be able to bear power such as this."

Tabby's eyes went wide and she swallowed hard. "Ah. Thank you."

He shot a grin of fangs and cocked his head to the side. Then, he glared out of the corner of his eyes at Vespa. "It is beginning to look like I need to reassert dominance over my subjects."

"What do you mean?" I asked. I felt stupid for asking. Interrupting him was a sign of disrespect and I had a good feeling that people had been disemboweled for a lot less.

His eyes made their way back to me, slow, deliberate movements that started a deep shiver in my blood. "What makes you think you have the power to ask?"

It wasn't like I thought I was anything. I mean, he was the devil. I was just me. "I'm just trying to understand. No disrespect was meant."

He cackled. My heartbeat started to skip beats in time with each section of his laugh. I sunk to my knees. He could kill me right there. Tabby's protective circle didn't matter. I was toast.

Tabby stared at me. Her body was shaking ever so slightly. If I could see it, the devil sure as hell could. "They should be punished."

His eyes snapped to her and my heartbeat normalized. *Fuck, Tabby. Don't let him get you too.*

"Everyone has forgotten the things I am truly capable of. Dealing with two souls, that is nothing. Marker or not, none of it matters." His eyes shot upward. "It isn't like *He* can punish me further. I have found that I am very good at my role anyway." His eyes snapped back down to Tabby. "So Tabatha, did you like your gift?"

She blinked and cleared her throat. "It is very beautiful, but I don't know what it does. It isn't like any wand I've ever held."

I don't know how she found the strength to answer him, but I was impressed.

He put his hands together. His nails draped over the tips of his fingers, so long and transparent they could have been made of glass. His face took on more shadows, making him seem more beast than human. "It is a fleshing wand. Most useful."

I frowned at Tabby. I didn't like this. I didn't like this at all.

"I'll let you research it. They are very rare." He stepped farther still, the toe of his shoe touching the edge of Tabby's circle. It sizzled and smoke rose up from it. The pain had to have been great, but he didn't even twitch.

Tabby took a step backward. "Thank you."

He nodded, and then turned his attention again to me. This time, my heart wasn't attacked.

"What do you want to do with this one?" he asked, waving his hand backwards as if to dismiss the man.

I stammered. "My plan is to get him free of his possession and then go on my way."

He shook his head. With each shake, the light in the room dimmed a little more. "Tsk, tsk. Sadly, I can't allow that to happen. You see, things are not what they seem."

I'd had my doubts. I'd never done any of the tests, never saw if he spoke in tongues or could find lost objects. I'd suspected things, sure. But I never did any of the real tests. I'd been distracted. Nicholas never could be trusted. I swiped a hand through my hair, realizing the truth. "He isn't possessed, is he?"

The devil gnashed his teeth. "I knew you were smart enough to figure it out."

I leaned back in the circle. Tabby sat quietly. I felt like I'd been punched in the gut. The demon did want me, but not in the way I assumed. We were doomed. "He can't be exorcised, if he was never possessed."

"Quite correct. I will gladly take a replacement, however."

I gulped, but found a beam of iron somewhere inside me. "I-I think since we both were deceived, he should pay the price. Not us."

The devil stared at me darkly. Images filled my mind. Of me on some torture device. Him licking the blood from my thighs. I shuddered.

"So how is he demonic?" Tabby asked.

The images disappeared. My mind was my own again.

The devil looked at Tabby like a child staring at their new puppy. "A triviality, I assure you. He is my son."

I blinked. Oh, Jesus. We'd been staying with the Antichrist. My bowels would have let loose if there had been anything in them. Once again, I was thankful for that little fasting rule before exorcisms. I was truly starting to understand nuances I never would have guessed.

The devil laughed. "You should see the look on your face. Completely priceless."

He wasn't just evil anymore. The devil was clearly insane.

"He is the Antichrist?" I asked.

He pursed his eyebrows together. "My word, no. I have many children. The Antichrist you speak of is a myth of sorts. Keep in mind, your book isn't whole."

He was right, actually. Sometime in the fourteenth century, I think it was, the Roman Catholic Church voted on what books were worthy of being in the Bible. Revelation only made it in by one vote. "Either there is no Antichrist, or all of your children are Antichrists?"

He rolled his eyes. "I can assure you that this one is not an Antichrist."

My mind jumped to Vespa's mother. I did not want to think about that woman having sex. Brain bleach on aisle twelve, please.

"You really do need to learn how to protect your mind. Don't make it so easy for me, marker." The devil laughed again. "No, I can assure you, my acolytes are nothing like that woman. Nicholas is a changeling."

Tons of old fantasy stories bounced around in my head. So fairies were of the devil? Maybe? I was starting to realize I didn't know the world as splendidly as I thought I did. Hell, I knew nothing.

"Why did your son bring us here?" That was the question. It had all been a waste of time, mine and Mr. Bad's over there. Surely, he would have something against that. Something that would save my soul.

He shook his head. This time there were no lighting theatrics. "I believe his plan was to try to steal your power. However, Yahweh and I have a very specific agreement regarding markers. You are not to be touched," he said, with an achingly horrific grin spread across his face, "at least not without cause."

I wondered about the intelligence level of his acolytes. I mean, who would want to piss him off? Then I realized: Doc was stuck here, and the original one, there was something there too. "What about Vespa? The real one?"

"There was an old charlatan who was around during the time of your relative. He had a few gifts. But Nicholas is not part of that family."

"He's half-demon?" Tabby asked. I'd almost forgotten she was there, she'd been so quiet. The devil had a way of making you pay attention to only him. I didn't like it.

He smirked. "Correct. His actual name is Arees."

"What will you do with him?" Tabby swallowed.

He shrugged. "Give him time to think about his misdeeds. Show him what happens to those who disobey me."

"Like Asmodeus?" I asked.

"Precisely." He growled and waved his hand toward the being I'd known as Nick. And Nick disappeared. "Tell Yahweh I said hello."

He began walking toward the opening in the wall. Right before stepping through, he glanced over his shoulder at me. A strange gleam lit his eyes. He said two words only with his departure: "Be careful."

Then, the devil was gone. The lighting went back to normal. The hole in the wall was no longer there, but you could see the outline of it in the cracked plaster around the tiles.

Tabby stood up and scuffed the circle with her foot.

Part of me wanted to tell her to leave it, but I'd been too late. I still wasn't quite in control of my mouth.

"Now what?" she asked.

I shoved the exorcism rite in my pocket. "We get our shit and get the hell out. Hotel sounds good."

"It sounds good to me too."

Chapter Fourteen

Always

WE ENDED UP driving all the way back to Tucson. I think we'd all seen enough of Tombstone by that point. And no way were we going back to the place that had wanted to kill Isaac.

"Pet-friendly hotel?" Tabby said.

"Pull out Mr. iPad. Try to find that one we stayed in when we first got out here."

"Jimmy?" Lucy asked from the backseat.

"Yeah?" I peered at her in the rear view mirror.

"Is everything okay again?"

"For now."

Tabby and I grabbed some food from a burger place before we arrived at the hotel. Fast food was good enough. I just wanted to sleep. I hadn't been this tired in a long time. After we got checked in and set ourselves up in the hotel room, I noticed that Lucy was staring at the corner of the room.

"Whatcha doing?" I asked her.

"Waiting for Doc."

I didn't have the heart to tell her that she'd probably never see Doc again. He was one of those ghosts that kind of stuck around a specific place, and Tucson wasn't it.

"Lucy, why don't you come with me for a while," Tabby motioned toward the door. "Let's let Jimmy get some rest."

"Okay," Lucy said.

My eyes slammed shut the minute I heard the door click closed.

I don't know how long I was asleep, but when I woke up, I felt like I'd been asleep for hours. My back hurt and my eyes felt heavy.

Doc was in the chair next to the table. The layout of the room was almost the same as our original hotel. The furniture was just different. The bed had a brown comforter and the table near the window was square instead of circular.

"What's up, Doc?" I asked, snickering.

"Funny. Very funny." He narrowed his eyes. "You and I need to have a talk."

I sat up on the bed. This didn't sound very good. "Okay. What you do need?"

"I need a favor."

#

Tabby and Lucy came back about a half an hour later. Tabby carried a bag from a toy store. I could tell right now that Lucy was going to be one spoiled little soul.

"Sleep good?" Tabby asked.

"Yeah. But I have something to talk to you about." I patted the bed beside me.

Tabby set the bag on the table and walked back to the bed. "Okay. Tell me you didn't get a call about another exorcism."

I snorted. "No. Just sit here a minute."

"Okay." She sat next to me. "What's this about?"

"How'd you like to add to our family?" I watched her for a minute. Yup, she was starting to freak. Her body grew rigid and her eyes went wide.

"No fucking way."

I started chuckling. "Not like that! Not yet anyway."

She took a deep breath. "You scared me."

"I didn't mean to." Actually I did, but she didn't need to know that.

"Okay," she said. "Back to this family stuff. What are you talking about?"

Doc popped into the chair. "How'd you feel if I stuck around for a while?"

Lucy squealed. "Oh boy!" She turned to us. "Really?"

"As far as I'm concerned, Doc can stay with us as long as he wants." Might as well make him a part of my team. Hell, it had been he who alerted me to half of Vespa's bullshit.

Lucy ran over and hugged Doc. He hugged her back hard.

"Now the house has two spirits?" Tabby asked.

Or we were making a unique family. I was for either one. "Yup."

"If you keep collecting like this, we're going to need a bigger place." She wrapped her arm around my shoulders.

I laughed. "Let's hope we can relax for a bit."

Lucy separated herself from Doc and walked over to where we'd stashed all our stuff.

"What's this?" Lucy asked, reaching for the damn wand sticking out of Tabby's backpack.

"No!" Tabby and I jumped up.

"Don't ever touch that." I snatched the wand out of her reach.

I could see the water pooling at the corners of her eyes. I handed the wand to Tabby.

I reached up and stroked her face. Wow. I could feel it. Something had gone wrong, very wrong. Lucy was no longer transparent at all. As my hand grazed her cheeks, I felt it. I felt flesh.

THE END

Book Three of the Marker Chronicles

Sorrow's Turn

Danielle DeVor

SORROW'S TURN (Book 3)

Some things are worse than demons.

Jimmy Holiday, reluctant exorcist, is finally getting the help he needs from the higher-ups. The Order of Markers is sending him to the Vatican's exorcism school. Now, he'll receive the training he should have gotten at the beginning. One problem, someone wants to sabotage him.

When his time at the school is cut short, Jimmy receives an interesting new case. It is the assignment that no one wants—a corpse has come back to life. And it isn't a zombie.

Too bad nothing goes as expected. Armed with his usual bag of tricks, Jimmy thinks everything will eventually be all right. Well, that is until his betrayer turns out to be the person he trusts most.

Chapter One

Every Little Thing She Does is Magic

IF EVER I thought stuff couldn't get any weirder in my life, boy was I wrong. Getting out of Arizona was—well, interesting to say the least. No way could we take Lucy on a plane—not without documentation or permission from her parents, which wasn't going to happen. Poor kid had it rough learning how to walk on real feet again. Then there was the airplane itself. She'd been through enough having been possessed, separated from her body, and ultimately left with me to take care of her. Now this.

How did you call up someone to ask if you could take their daughter's spirit that had just developed its own body on an airplane while they still had her real body in Virginia? It was enough to make my brain bleed.

And of course, I didn't have their new phone number, but that was beside the point.

Like I said, things had gotten a whole heap weirder.

"Are you going to help me or not?" Tabby stood behind the car, fiddling with the suitcase.

I was in trouble again. It was starting to become a trend. One of these days she would clobber me. I could see it coming. I got out of the car, took the monstrous suitcase from her, and loaded it into the trunk.

"Car rental place said we can have the car, but there's a fee," I said, closing the back hatch.

Of course there would be. It wasn't like some big organization was going to be nice or anything. Hell, I had trouble with people in general. Why would a corporation be any different?

"How much?"

I shrugged. "I didn't ask."

Thwap. My head rocked forward.

"Did you hit me?" I stared at her. Maybe being psychic was another added bonus to this marker thing. Nah, if that were the case, I wouldn't have screwed up in Arizona.

Tabby stood with her hands on her hips. Her red hair framed her face like she was some sort of pissed-off goddess. Her eyes darkened, and I was reminded of that guy on TV who kept hitting his workers on the back of the head.

"Yes, I did," she said. "Just because you love that magic black card, it doesn't mean you don't have to worry about it."

I rubbed my head. Damn, she hit hard. "If this was my sort of normal I'd be worried. But how else are we getting this menagerie home?"

"Good point."

I was glad she saw it that way because there wasn't another option. It wasn't like I had some amazing powers like flight or anything.

"Was that the last of it?" I asked. The trunk was almost full. I could maybe fit a small stuffed animal in there, but that was questionable.

"Yep."

"Okay. Let's blow this popsicle stand." I jumped behind the driver's seat and glanced in the rearview mirror. Lucy was strapped in the car seat Tabby had bought at Wally World after the fleshing rod had done its business. Doc sat next to her, showing her card tricks. I was glad for Doc. Who knew having the sentient ghost of Doc Holliday hanging around would be so useful? His relation to me was beside the point. No way was I going to complain about his help with Lucy.

I glanced at Tabby. "Ready?"

"As I'll ever be."

It took roughly three days, fourteen hours, and seventeen minutes to get back home. I knew because I counted every single minute. I probably should have let Tabby drive, but I needed something to hold, and the steering wheel served as a great source to out my frustration. My brain wouldn't stop coming up with various worst-case scenarios.

Every so often, Tabby would ask if I wanted her to drive. I refused. It was a shitty enough trip as it was. No sense in making it worse for her. I might as well keep my asshole behavior in check.

Plus, I had to get used to a child's bladder. Lucy—now that she was whole—had normal bodily functions again. Yet another thing I hadn't counted on. The next time I saw the Devil I was going to hit him with that rod. Well, not really, but it was nice to dream about.

Still, it was nice to be home. The old house with its white siding and black shutters never looked so good. It might be old, but it was mine. As soon as I stepped foot from the car, the smell of the Virginia air hit me and I smiled.

"What?" Tabby peered at me while she brushed her long hair away from her face.

"Glad to be home."

She shook her head. "We'd better get on it."

I blinked. "Get on what?"

"Get the car unpacked?"

Lucy gaped at her with wide eyes. Doc was watching the sky.

"I don't want to start anything, but I'm too tired. Let's unpack tomorrow."

Tabby glared for a minute, and then slumped her shoulders. "Okay. We can wait until tomorrow."

I hugged her. Nothing in there that couldn't wait. At least as far as I was concerned.

"Shouldn't you get your holy iPad?" Tabby asked as she unbuckled Lucy from her car seat.

Even Lucy seemed tired. Her long blond hair appeared stringy and lifeless.

"Someone probably wants to talk to you," Lucy said.

I peered at her through the car window. The kid saw right through me. "Okay. Fine."

I closed the door of the car, handed Tabby the house keys, and pulled all the crap from the trunk. I guessed it wasn't in the cards to wait until tomorrow after all. Fine. But I wasn't unpacking all the shit right that instant either.

Tabby chuckled and opened the door to the house.

As soon as I got all the crap inside, I noticed Lucy perched in her usual spot in front of the TV. Doc hovered next to her. It was kind of nice having Lucy solid. She could turn on her own TV whenever she felt like it. Eventually, I was going to have to come up with something else to entertain her. And more importantly, some sort of schooling for her.

"If you want a chair, feel free to grab one," I said to Doc. Just because he was a ghost didn't mean he shouldn't make himself comfortable. I knew he was being polite since this was the first time he'd been in my home, but I didn't want him to feel like a guest.

Doc nodded in his way. "Mighty obliged."

"I'd like you to feel at home." Since he was going to be staying with us for the unforeseeable future, he should act like family.

Isaac let out a loud meow as I put his pet carrier down and freed him from it. He sauntered over to the couch, hopped up, and promptly went to sleep.

"Yes, Your Highness." I bowed in his direction. "I swear, in my next life, I want to be a cat."

Lucy laughed.

"Jesus, Jimmy. That's just what we need," Tabby said.

I snorted. Part of me thought it would have been great to have her wait on me hand and foot, but the lack of sex would suck. I didn't even want to think about her threatening to neuter me.

"You hungry? I'm going to throw something together," Tabby said from the kitchen.

"Good luck."

#

I couldn't lie and say I wasn't happy to be in my own bed. Lucy stayed downstairs like she had before. Oddly, even though she seemed to have normal metabolic processes, she still didn't appear to be able to sleep. How this worked? I didn't know. It made me uneasy. A kid needed to sleep, and if her body didn't change to adjust, I didn't even want to think about the health problems. I needed to figure out a way to spread the worry a bit; otherwise, I was going to get high blood pressure.

"What has you so," Tabby said as she turned to me, "odd?"

I rolled over in the bed. "I'm worried about Lucy. Nothing about this seems right."

She nodded. "Did you check your email?"

"No."

Tabby rolled her eyes at me. "Didn't Lucy say that you should?"

I could have kicked myself. If I didn't get my shit together, everything was going to end up completely craptastic. "I'll be back."

I headed downstairs. Lucy was watching some documentary on the effects of uric acid on the brains of chickens. I raised an eyebrow at Doc. He shrugged. At least she was getting an education about something.

"Everything okay down here?" I asked.

Lucy glanced up from the TV. "Uh-huh."

I snatched the iPad off the table where someone had put it. I hadn't even unpacked it before I went to bed. I jogged back upstairs. Might as well leave Lucy to her chickens.

"Everything okay?" Tabby asked once I got back into bed.

"So far." I fired up the tablet. Sure enough, there was an email waiting for me. I took a deep breath and tapped it.

Mr. Holiday,

It is my pleasure to inform you that you have been accepted into the next class of Exorcism at the Vatican— Exorcismo E Preghieri Di Liberazione. We will be sending you your requirements shortly.

Fr. Martin

"Fuck me." Granted I'd been whining about wanting help, but this wasn't exactly what I had expected. Looked like the church did want me in some capacity after all.

"What?" Tabby asked.

"They are sending me to school to become an exorcist."

Tabby guffawed. Literally, guffawed. In fact she laughed so hard she fell out of bed. No joke.

"What's so funny?" I asked. Granted, I already was an exorcist, but it wasn't like I knew what the hell I was doing.

"Do you even speak Italian?"

"Well, no." Damn. She was right. The school for exorcism was at the Vatican. I was so screwed.

"Oh, God. This is going to be interesting."

I glared at her. "Okay. Yeah. But this does nothing to help with Lucy, now does it?"

I didn't mean to be a bastard, but Lucy was a hell of a lot more important than making fun of me going to exorcism school. We needed information to help the kid. The sooner the better.

Tabby got quiet. "No, it doesn't. Question is—do you want to let them know about her?"

I thought about it for a minute. I'd been Lucy's protector for so long now it would feel wrong to hand her over to someone else. And not to be mean, but she was likely to end up as some Vatican experiment. I wouldn't put anything past any of them. The Order of Markers was connected to the Vatican—not run by them. I had to be damn careful. Periodically, I found myself looking in corners of the rooms for micro-cameras or something, but I never found any. Still, since the Order had broken into my house before (when they set up the holy iPad), I knew they were watching. The question always was...how much?

"No, we aren't telling them about her." It was better that way. Maybe. If they had footage of her entering the house, they would think Lucy was a relative.

"All right then, what are we going to do?" Tabby asked.

I sighed. Sometimes, I wished she wouldn't expect me to have all the answers. I needed more of a give-and-take. "Get some sleep."

#

The next morning I got up to nothing. There was no sound. No weird events. It almost had me worried. Kind of sad I was getting so used to the unusual that when something normal happened it felt suspect.

I got up out of bed, went downstairs and found Tabby, Doc, and Lucy sitting on the sofa. They all looked like their pet rocks had died.

"What's up?" I asked.

"Something's wrong," Lucy said. She glanced at the floor. The TV wasn't even on. Bad sign where Lucy was concerned.

Nothing like those two words to scare the shit out of me.

"Wrong how?" I asked. It could be anything: a new demon, bad luck about to befall me. I began to sweat.

"I don't feel very good," she said.

Her skin had a sort of waxy appearance to it. Okay. I could work with sick. Lots of over-the-counter remedies to try. I waved at Tabby.

"Is she running a fever?" I asked.

Tabby shook her head. Doc's lips pursed together. If she was normal-sick, Doc wouldn't be acting so strangely.

"Make it stop," Lucy said suddenly. She held her head with both hands.

I patted her arm. "If I can, honey, I will."

"Any ideas, Doc?" Tabby asked.

He huffed. "All I know is that this ain't natural. And when something ain't natural, lots of bad can happen."

I ground my teeth together. It wasn't like we could take Lucy to a doctor. It was not what any of us needed right now. Not to mention the kid was in pain and I didn't know how to fix it. "We'd better look into what a fleshing rod actually does."

"Guess so," Tabby replied.

Chapter Two

Time Is on My Side

NOW, THE PROBLEM was—where the hell to get information about the damn thing. No way was I going to get another Ouija board after what happened the last time. No way in Hell. It wasn't like I could call up the Devil and ask him questions. I did not want to go down that road. Part of me did think it would be kind of cool if I could send him an email, but I didn't even want to think about the possibility of demonic computer viruses.

I also didn't want to have to explain to my neighbors the bands of birds acting weird when I destroyed it, either. No sense in imagining the same thing wouldn't happen here that happened in Arizona. There wasn't any reason at all that brand of weird wouldn't stir up again. Thank God I didn't live in a development. Somehow, I don't think me and an HOA would get along well.

I booted up my big computer, finished all the updates I missed, and started reading. Sadly, typing "fleshing rod" into a search engine only brought up a bunch of pictures of giant penises. That was something I could have gone without seeing. I was going to need to buy stock in brain bleach.

I was up a shit creek without a paddle. There were only so many options open for me now. And I was left with a pretty damn unsavory one—trying to find a person who was a true practitioner of the so-called Dark Arts. Where I would find that? Who knew.

"Here," I heard Tabby say.

I glanced up. She was holding a steaming mug toward me.

"I'm sunk," I said. She might as well know.

"Sunk how?"

"You don't even want to see what I've been looking at." In fact, if I had to look at it again I was going to need a stiff drink. Stiff. Heh.

She laughed. "Anything useful?"

"Not a thing. That's why I'm stuck." The information I needed was probably hidden in some ancient tome somewhere.

She sat down at the table beside me and threw her hair over her shoulder. "Want to talk about it?"

"Not yet." I didn't want to unload all of my fears onto her. It wasn't necessary. Especially since I didn't exactly know what I was talking about yet. My brain was latching onto random shit to worry about.

"Well, we still need to go to the store, or do you want me to do it?"

I shook my head. I wasn't accomplishing anything anyway. I might as well get off my ass and do something. "No, I'll go. Keep an eye on Lucy. Maybe I'll come up with an awesome idea."

"It would be different if she'd just gotten sick or something."

I nodded. If it wasn't for Doc's reaction, I would be thinking it was the flu or something. But his comments about the unnatural made me definitely feel it was not an illness. And, well, Lucy wasn't actually supposed to have a body to begin with. She already had one. "Tell me about it. Not with the way Doc is acting; that isn't it at all."

"I know."

I grabbed my car keys from the dining room table. "We need to return that rental car."

Tabby sighed. "Okay. I'll follow you—keep Lucy in the car with me. We can get rid of that thing and then you can drop us back by the house."

"That works." Plus that way someone living had their eyes on Lucy. I wasn't too sure what else we could do. Maybe she'd get over whatever this was.

#

It didn't take long to drop off the car. Luckily, there wasn't any damage to it. They still stuck me with the drop off fee, but I'd been expecting that. Now we could go about our business and not have to deal with anything left over from Arizona. At least, anything physical anyway. The rest of it was a work in progress.

Lucy still looked horrible. Her skin appeared waxy, like it was fake, and she seemed to get paler by the minute. And she wasn't talking. At all. I think that bothered me most. Hell, it wasn't even demonic Lucy. This was something new. Usually, she would at least chuckle at stuff Tabby and I said, but there was nothing. The silence seemed so wrong.

I dropped the horde back at the house. I paused before turning off the car. Then, I glanced over at Tabby. "I'll be back as soon as I can."

"Okay. Be careful," Tabby replied.

I nodded. "I will."

I got out of the car, walked up to the house, opened the front door, and waited for Tabby to unbuckle Lucy from the car seat and carry her to the house. I opened the front door for her and waited until she and Lucy were safely inside. Then, I closed the door. As soon as I knew everything was okay, I left.

The irony did not escape me that even though I was at a complete and utter loss, I ended up doing something with food. I was starting to think that Tor's food obsession had somehow rubbed off on me. Lucy's mother had a real obsession with food. I'm sure a shrink would have a field day with that. Of course, the dude probably wouldn't believe in exorcism either and that's where the real trouble would begin.

I pulled into the parking lot of the mega-mart. As usual there was nowhere to park except Timbuktu. At least it wasn't hot like it had been in Arizona. Spring was still nippy here back East. I had to appreciate the little things. If I didn't, I would start to get cynical and that wasn't going to help a damn.

I wandered the aisles without paying too much attention. Stuff landed in the cart almost by osmosis. Needless to say, I was preoccupied by the Lucy problem. Spirits didn't get sick, did they? Not like that. I mean, Lucy had faded when she expended a lot of energy before, and it was the same way with Doc. But they never seemed to feel ill or in pain. That damn rod had caused us a nest of problems.

And since Lucy already had a body, a real one, my mind could only rest on one thing. Her spirit was rejecting this body. It was not conscious. If it were, Lucy would stop it because it was hurting her. This was completely out of her control.

I didn't even know what that meant for her. As far as I knew, her real form was still on a machine in Virginia. The Order had directed me to cease trying to contact them. But the Order wasn't aware of this latest development. At least, I didn't think they were. Something told me that Lucy would already be with them if that were the case. Their all-seeing eye had limitations.

All of this stuff with spirits and rules was making my head spin. I took my haul out to the car and headed back home. Maybe Tabby would have another idea, but I figured that my suspicion was right. Doc had alluded to this very idea. And if my hunch was correct there was no telling what it meant for Lucy.

When I got home, Lucy was laid out on the couch—breathing heavily. Tabby seemed scared to death with her eyes wide and her hair all messed up. Strands were falling out of her ponytail and whorled around her head like a red cloud.

"I take it she got worse?" I asked. At that moment, I felt completely helpless. I wanted to jump in and save the day, but I knew nothing to fix this.

Tabby nodded. "Doc left to see if he could figure out something."

I dumped the bags onto the floor and pulled her into my arms. "This sucks."

"What if the Devil won?" she asked. Her head angled toward me, her eyes brimming with tears.

It wasn't supposed to happen like this. The Devil didn't win. That was the whole point of everything. I sighed. This was not something I wanted to mull over. "I don't think that's it. If he had, he'd come and take her and let old Asmodeus have his way. There's something else afoot here."

She sighed and leaned her head against my chest. "Could the higher power be calling her home?"

I shook my head. "Keep in mind it was that damn rod that gave her another body in the first place. I think she's rejecting it."

Tabby leaned back. "Like some organ transplant?"

"Something like that."

"What can we do?" Tabby stepped back from me and wiped her hand through her hair.

"Nothing. I don't think anyone has made anti-rejection medicine for this." I wished God would tell me what to do, but, as usual, I was left on my own. Shit.

"What about her real body?" Tabby asked.

I sighed. Sometimes, it was helpful to bounce ideas off her, but now it wasn't helping. Her fears put a voice to my own, and I just wanted to bury my head in the covers upstairs. "Alive as far as I know. I think someone would tell us, don't you?"

She nodded. "I hope they would. So what do we do?"

I began picking up bags off the floor. "Make her as comfortable as possible."

I wished I had some light bulb moment, but I had nothing. This was one of those times when I wished that Tabby's witchery worked like it did on TV, but this was reality.

Tabby sighed. "I don't know if I can do this."

I didn't know if I could either, but I couldn't tell her that. I needed to buck up and get my shit together. It was time I stopped thinking about myself and my reaction to crap alone. "If you want to, go upstairs until it's over. I'll understand."

Tabby closed her eyes for a minute. "No, I can't do that to her. It wouldn't be right."

"I'll put this stuff away, then." I was at a loss as to what else I could do.

"All right."

#

I brought Tabby in a soda and sat down on the floor beside her. Every so often, she would stroke Lucy's head. Isaac perched on the back of the sofa, watching intently. The expression on his face was a mix of anger and sadness. I knew exactly how he felt.

Lucy's breathing was getting more and more labored, and her skin didn't look quite real anymore. It was starting to take on a plastic quality that reminded me of the creatures in that bad vampire movie based on Matheson's *I Am Legend.* I wondered how many times this kid was going to have to experience death. Once had been bad enough.

Suddenly, there was a bang. I jerked up. Doc was standing next to me. He watched Lucy and shook his head.

"Might be better if you didn't see this," he said.

I felt like my stomach had fallen down and bounced off my asshole. It wasn't fucking fair. I glanced up at him. "That bad?"

His eyes went dark and sad. He nodded.

That decided it. I turned my attention to Tabby and tapped her on the shoulder. I wanted to remember Lucy as herself, not as whatever she was going to become in the next few minutes. "Doc is going to care for her now. We need to go."

Tabby's eyes flashed. "Go where?"

For once, I wished she wouldn't question me. And if Doc felt we shouldn't witness it, it was pretty damn bad. I didn't want her to have this pain. She needed to learn to trust me once in a while. "Just leave the room. Doc said we'd better not see what's coming."

"How dare you," she said in a hushed voice. "I am not going to leave this little girl." Her eyes were on fire, and if her powers worked that way, I would be about to find myself melted into a pile of red goo. There was that red-headed temper I knew and loved. But this was not the time for it.

I sighed.

Doc cleared his throat. "Ma'am. Some stuff is better left unseen. I am the doctor, after all."

She peered at him for a minute, her bravado gone. Then, she stood up. "You really think this is for the best?"

Doc nodded. "Yup."

Tabby took a shaky breath and grabbed me by the hand. "Come on, Jimmy."

I hopped off the floor and guided her upstairs to our bedroom. At least we knew Lucy was in good hands. If there was anyone who would want to make her hurt less, it would be Doc. Heck, if he knew of some way to make this painless, he would do it. She was basically his grandchild, after all.

Once we got upstairs, I closed the door to the bedroom behind us and sat her down on the bed. She shook all over.

"None of this should be happening. If it wasn't for that stupid stick," she said. She moved her head.

I glanced over at where she was looking. The fleshing rod was still sticking out of her backpack. I had my doubts that the Devil meant for this to happen, but considering who he was, there was no way to know for sure. Still, though, if he meant for it to happen, that would have been against the agreement he had with the big guy upstairs. Or maybe not. Hell, this was confusing.

"Well," I said. "He did say to be careful with it." I wasn't trying to take up for him, but, obviously, putting it in a backpack was not careful enough.

Tabby glared at me. "I'd rather get rid of the fucking thing."

I sat on the bed beside her. I wasn't ready to let it go yet. There was some motive the Devil hadn't revealed as to why he'd given it to her. I wanted to find out the purpose. "I don't think that would be a good idea. It was given to you for a reason. Best not to mess with that."

"Well, we'd better figure out a fucking case for that thing. I don't want any more mistakes." She hunched over and hugged her knees to her chest.

"Me either." She was right. There needed to be something to protect people from the effects of it. Otherwise, we may have more mistakes than just what happened with Lucy. And if it kept happening, stuff could get a whole lot worse.

Suddenly, there was an odd howling sound from downstairs.

Tabby let go of her knees and jumped off the bed. I grabbed hold of her arm before she could get very far.

"If Doc wanted us to come down there, he would call for us," I said.

She glared at me and snatched her arm out of my hand. "I still don't have to like it."

"No, you don't."

#

It felt like hours. Tabby and I sat on the bed, gaping at the wall. TV would have reminded us too much of Lucy, and we weren't doing all that great a job of talking to each other, so staring at the wall it was. At least then we weren't fighting. I didn't bother looking at the clock. It would have made me more uneasy. Better I didn't know how much time had passed. It would only make my frustration and fear worse.

Finally, after what seemed like a very long time, Doc popped in.

"You all can come downstairs now. But just to warn ya, there's some weird afoot." His face was almost unreadable. None of the earlier sadness remained. Just a matter-of-fact expression.

"Is Lucy okay?" Tabby asked.

He nodded. "Better. Going to take her a little bit to adapt." He glowered at the rod in the backpack. "Better get that thing out of reach."

"We're way ahead of you. But for now…." I hopped up, walked across the room, and grabbed the rod from the backpack. Why it had no effect on me, I didn't know. Maybe because my soul was connected to my body? Of course, it didn't do anything to Tabby either when she touched it. It had to be the spirit. It was called a fleshing rod, after all. Jesus, I needed a manual.

I shoved it on the shelf in the top of my closet. At least it was out of the way of prying eyes, and, hopefully, that would prevent Lucy from even thinking to look in the closet for it. Though I suspected that she probably would never touch the damn thing again. 'There. That should do for now."

"And later?" Doc asked.

I sighed. Sometimes, it seemed like nothing I ever did was good enough. "Tabby and I are working on that."

We headed downstairs. I couldn't help but shake the feeling that this wasn't so different from when it all began at Sorrow's Point. We were trying to get the demon out of her then and it hadn't all gone well. I felt the creepy-crawlies dancing up and down my spine. Something was off. I smelled something bad…like rotten meat.

I took the lead. No sense in making Tabby see things if they were truly awful. I tried not to psych myself out. I drew in a deep breath, stepped off the staircase, and peered into the living room. At first, nothing seemed amiss. I saw Lucy in spirit form standing very still. She was back in her little white dress. That was okay. More normal than not. But then my eyes drifted downward and I saw it. A pile of skin lay on the floor. She had been wearing a meat suit. Blood and mucus pooled around the little pile of skin. It was sad, disgusting, and…wrong. I forced myself not to gag.

"Is it bad?" Tabby asked.

I closed my eyes and didn't answer. This was going to take some doing. I didn't want to make it seem like a walk in the park, but I had to think of the kid's feelings too. This wasn't Lucy's fault. I needed to be strong for her. I stilled and then stepped forward. "It could be a lot worse."

I focused on Lucy. "Are you okay?"

Lucy shifted her head toward me very slowly. Her mouth quivered as if she were about to cry. I opened my arms. Her little spirit body rushed to me. I felt a bit of coldness. I reached up and tried to pat her head, but my hand passed right through her. This sucked. "I'm sorry, honey."

I could hear her sobs, but no wetness emerged. Nothing. Poor thing. It was one of those times when something so cruel happened that you never would have even imagined or thought about it, unless you'd seen it with your own eyes.

"You've still got us," Tabby said from in front of me. I hadn't even noticed that she'd come over. I smiled at her.

Lucy glared at her. "Don't let that happen to me again."

Chapter Three

Every Rose Has Its Thorn

NEEDLESS TO SAY, our day was shot. Boxes littered the place. Tabby and I hadn't had the chance to unpack yet. I sent Tabby and Doc upstairs with Lucy to keep her occupied while I got rid of the mess. No sense in traumatizing the kid more than she already had been.

Isaac was trotting around the mess, being ever so careful not to step in any of the goo. That would have been yet one more disaster to add to the list. Yeah, gooey, bloody kitty pawprints all over the house. Yuck.

"Thanks for the help," I said to him.

He chirped back at me, seemed to glare in fact, which gave me the impression that he would roll his eyes at me if he could. Then, he turned his tail and walked into the kitchen. I could almost swear that animal was reincarnated from someone. Jesus.

"Thanks a lot," I said. I gaped at the mess. The goo had soaked into the carpet. I was so screwed. Where was the paranormal cleanup company when you needed them?

I went into the kitchen and got one of those big black lawn and leaf bags. I also grabbed an oven mitt. The less contact I had with it all, the better. I made a mental note to keep around some of those rubber gloves that people use to do dishes by hand. That is, if I could find any to fit my big mitts.

I headed to the living room with my goodies. Taking a shallow breath, I tried to ignore the smell, which was a combination of unwashed ass and rotting flesh.

"Okay. Let's do this." I tried to amp myself up. It wasn't working.

I shook the trash bag and set it outside the goo. After that, I gloved up my right hand with the oven mitt, grabbed what had once been

Lucy's physical head, and adjusted the mouth of the bag. I held my breath and got the sack of skin into the bag as fast as I could. It was drippy, wet, and plain gross.

I stared at the floor. It was going to take a hell of a lot more than OxiClean to get rid of the mass of mucous and blood. It was going to have to be me to fix it. I needed a damn assistant.

"Shit." I went back for paper towels and started the disgusting task of soaking up all the fluid. It sort of helped, but it was like herding snot.

All in all, it took two rolls of paper towels to get it all up and I was still left with a giant ugly fucking stain. Nothing like old mustard-colored carpet with a giant reddish-brown stain in the middle. Sure, no one would notice that at all. I sighed. Hopefully, the carpet-cleaning crap would prevent it from stinking. I'd about had enough.

"Tabby!"

"What?" she yelled from upstairs.

"Can you come down here for a minute?"

Soon, I heard the pitter-patter of her feet on the stairs. Not that her feet were all that small, but she had a way of carrying herself that made her sound lighter than she was. Maybe it was all those years of ballet training.

"What do you need?" she asked as soon as she hopped off the stairs.

"How do I take care of this?" I pointed at the stain. It now seemed kind of brown. Technically, it still should have been red, but nothing about this was normal.

"Shit. I don't know. I'm not a magical cleaning fairy, you know."

I tapped my foot for a minute. "Got any of that anti-pee stuff for felines?"

She laughed. "You mean that pet smell stuff?"

"Yeah."

"Somewhere, but you need to do more than that." She leaned over, peered at the stain more closely, straightened up, and shook her head.

I sighed. "So any ideas?"

She tapped her fingers against her leg. "I'd get one of those industrial carpet cleaners you can rent from the store."

It was a damn good thing I had money in my account again. No way did I want to put this on the Order's credit card. It would cause too many questions.

"Okay," I said. "Don't let Lucy down here until I get this all cleaned up."

Tabby nodded. "Buy spot remover too. I have a feeling this is going to be a multi-step process."

"Great." I tied off the bag. No way would I let that sit in my garbage all week. I needed to find a dumpster. "Tabby, is it illegal to use someone's dumpster without asking?"

She shrugged. "I have no idea. Probably. I mean, the business has to pay for the trash removal, and since you're dumping your trash without paying them for it, it's almost like theft."

'That's what I figured. Shit. Looks like I'm going to have to be creative." Which is what I normally did, but that was beside the point.

She laughed. "Aren't you always?"

"Thanks a lot." She didn't have to agree with me.

She went back upstairs and I surveyed the damage. All I could do was hope that the garbage can outside Wally World was empty. That, and that the Order was out to lunch.

#

Driving in the car with that bag was worse than smelling a dead deer rotting alongside of a roadway in the heart of summer. Even though it was only forty degrees, I drove with the windows down. It was that disgusting. Part of me wished I still had the rental, but logically I knew this stench would cause a hell of a fee. The last thing I needed was to have to answer more questions for the Order.

I got a parking place as close to the front door as possible. Sadly, this meant roughly in the middle of the lot, but it wasn't like I had much choice. I carried that gnarly garbage bag as best as I could up to the trash bin. I did not want to get any of that crap on my hands. At least the bag wasn't leaking—yet.

The can was one of those that had the spring-loaded top. Lovely. I probably should have expected it. But it would have been nice for luck to me on my side for once. The dumpsters were nowhere in sight, probably to prevent exactly what I was doing.

I shoved the bag in, top first. Still, nasty liquid squelched out onto my hands through the small opening that was left after I tied off the bag. I gagged. But I got the damn thing in the garbage. I felt sorry for the guy who was going to have to take care of that later.

I looked around frantically for the disinfectant wipes they kept out front—and I was in luck; the container was full. I scrubbed up my hands and arms. I got a few odd looks, but I ignored them. No way was I going to have that crap on me any longer. Let them deal with the shit I'd been through the last few months. Finally, I tossed the wipes in the receptacle and headed into the store.

I almost felt like I was readying myself for the zombie apocalypse instead of going after cleaning supplies. This was what my life had become.

When I arrived back at the house and got the carpet cleaner hauled in, the odor assaulted my nose again. I had almost lost all trace of it from the car, thank God. But now, here it was. If all of this didn't work, I was going to be in a real mess. I guessed I'd have to completely re-carpet the living room and hope that took care of the smell. Now I wondered what serial killers did to keep from getting caught for so long.

Part of me expected for the cops to show up at the house at any minute for dumping body parts. It would be my luck, after all. I did have the argument that I didn't dump body parts, just a pile of skin, but somehow I didn't think that they would be very sympathetic.

The Order probably had it all on video somewhere. I'd considered it before, but now, it seemed a plausible idea. They'd been in my house, after all, to deliver the tablet. Yet I doubted my house was bugged—simply because I couldn't imagine them leaving Lucy alone, but there was part of me that wondered if they wanted to see how long it would take for me to hang myself. Then again, with the Devil popping in for chats, I seriously doubted they had the stuff inside the house. No way would they pay me if they knew that. They seemed just as uptight as the Vatican.

I should have buried everything in the back yard and hoped for the best. Nah. Then I'd end up with some old, gnarly, blood-dripping tree like in that version of *Sleepy Hollow* with Johnny Depp. Man, I was losing it.

I hooked up the carpet cleaner as fast as I could. It wasn't hard to get the solution going or anything. I wanted it all to be done and over with. Soon, the noise of the machine blotted out everything else. Maybe there was something to the "white noise" machines. When I had the time, I was going to have to look into one. My sanity could use a breather.

By the time I was done, most of the stain was gone. It was still dark in the middle, but now, at least, it didn't look like someone had been murdered on my carpet. I would have to see about the smell.

I switched off the machine. "I think everyone can come downstairs now."

I said it loud enough for them all to hear upstairs. It wasn't long before both Lucy and Doc popped right in front of me. Doc was his usual self. Lucy's eyes, however, brimmed with tears.

"I am so sorry," Lucy said.

Dammit. I needed her to calm down. It was an old carpet. Shit. I shook my head. "Don't worry about it, kiddo."

Tabby came downstairs. "What do we need to do now?"

I stared at her. "Wait until the carpet dries and see what else we need to do."

She nodded. "I guess we still have research to do."

Might as well. Standing here watching the carpet dry wasn't going to help us with anything. "I guess so."

We needed to know the implication of the rod. We sure now knew what it was capable of, but we needed to know a lot more. Thinking about it gave me chills, but it wasn't like that ever stopped me before.

"Who would know about stuff like this?" I asked. I couldn't go to the Order about it. And ordinary people wouldn't have a clue.

Doc cleared his throat. "You ain't gonna find anything 'cept probably at the Vatican."

I blinked. He'd been able to find out information before, so I wondered what made this so different.

"What do you mean?" Tabby asked.

"No low-rent Devil-worshipper is going to get one of those. It's the real deal." He scratched at his chin for a minute.

"He has a point," I said.

"What do we do?" Tabby asked.

I took a deep breath. Sometimes it would have been easier if she could have read my thoughts, but she wasn't that type of witch. "We do what we were going to do before—get a case for it. Then, maybe when I'm all in research mode, I can dig through the library over there and see what I can come up with."

"Wow. That sounds like an actual plan," Tabby said.

I laughed. "Smart-ass."

She didn't have to seem so damn smug about it.

"Can we talk about something else now?" Lucy asked. Her voice sounded nervous and I didn't like it. We needed to pay attention more to how all of this was affecting the kid.

I sucked at this whole parenting thing. I crouched down. "Whatever you want."

#

We ended up going out to a fast food restaurant. Even though she couldn't eat it anymore, Lucy wanted to watch us eat. It was such a small request that I didn't think much of it. Hell, I'd have probably bought her anything under the sun if I thought it would do any good.

As it was, there wasn't much at all I could do for the kid and it broke my heart. At least she had Doc, but she needed more and I didn't know how to get it for her.

"Get a chocolate milkshake," Lucy said to me after I shoved a French fry into my mouth.

If I was going to start eating for Lucy, too, I was going to have to do some road work or some type of exercise to offset the extra calories. I needed a stiff drink. "Okay."

I laughed. Who was I kidding? There was no way I had time for road work. Granted, an exorcism was a hell of an ordeal, but I was hoping I didn't have to perform those all that often.

She smiled slightly.

I got out of my seat and walked to the counter. There was a girl with black hair and a lot of piercings manning the register. She couldn't have been more than twenty.

"I'd like a chocolate shake," I said.

"How'd you end up with her?" the girl asked and motioned with her chin toward where we'd been sitting.

I glanced over. Tabby wasn't there. Maybe she'd gone to the

bathroom. Lucy was staring out the window, watching kids play on the playground. I glanced back at the girl. Now I was really confused.

"The ghost?" she asked.

I almost choked. I'd never met anyone else who could see Lucy like that. Even Tabby had had to work at it. "It's a long story."

The girl nodded. "You've got her happy though. That's hard to do."

I leaned closer. "Just how many have you seen?"

"Enough. I've always been able to see them." She headed to the back and I heard the mixer whirring to make my shake. She came out again and handed it to me.

"Here," she said.

"How much do I owe you?" I asked.

"Nothing. It's on me."

I'll admit it; there was part of me that wondered if she'd put something bad in my drink, but I didn't get that type of vibe from her. I smiled. "Okay. Thanks."

Her eyes grew sad. "No, thank you."

I walked to our table in sort of a daze. I wasn't sure if she was a marker, or even if she knew what we were, but she sure as hell was what people tended to call "sensitive." Yet another thing I was going to have to look out for.

Tabby was standing there with her hands on her hips. She did not look happy. "Who was that?"

I stepped forward and leaned in close to her ear. "She could see Lucy."

Tabby blinked. "Well, at least Doc went off to do God knows what. I can't imagine what she would have thought of him."

I laughed this time. "I'm not sure. She gave me the impression that she sees a lot of ghosts."

Tabby shrugged, and then looked over at Lucy. After a minute she motioned toward Lucy with her chin. "I feel so bad for her. I think she got her hopes up."

I put my hand on Tabby's shoulder. "Yeah. I wish I could make everything right."

"Me too," she said.

#

By the time we got home, Doc had returned. He was sitting on the sofa, watching Isaac chase a catnip ball. Luckily, he didn't seem worse for wear or anything. Just pensive.

"Everything okay?" I asked him.

He cleared his throat. "Depends. I got some information for you."

That could be good, or it could be very bad. Either way, I was nervous as hell. "All right. Let me get everything settled and then we'll talk."

He nodded.

I deposited Lucy in front of the TV. Well, more like I switched the TV on for her and she sat down in front of it. Her having been flesh and its rejection seemed to have weakened Lucy a bit. In Arizona, she'd been able to control the TV a little herself. Now, not so much.

I paused inside the kitchen doorway and motioned to Doc. Tabby headed toward me and Doc followed. Soon, all three of us were sitting around the small table.

"Whatcha got?" I asked quietly. It wasn't like Lucy wasn't eventually going to find out, but it was better if she focused on the TV for now.

He kept his voice lowered. "That stick is pretty highly prized. Throughout history, they have been used to give flesh to demons. Let them invade our world."

The words "holy" and "shit" struck notes in my head.

"And Lucy?" Tabby asked.

Doc shrugged. "I'm going to guess it didn't stick because she isn't demonic. Though the Devil was right about one thing—they are useful."

"How?" I asked. In the wrong hands, every evil entity in the world could be made flesh. But that was of no help to me at all. And that seemed too easy somehow. Why would the Devil want Tabby to have that power?

"Since you're the owner of the rod, the demon you could give flesh to would be beholden to you. In other words, you would own him. He would be your servant. That's what the legends say, of course. Not sure how much stock you can put in it."

I leaned back in the chair. Now, that was interesting. He was wrong about one thing–the rod belonged to Tabby, so all the demons would be her servants, not mine. But it made me wonder if it would make it easier to dispatch them if they were controlled. I wasn't sure if I wanted to find out. Since the rod wasn't mine, none of these thoughts mattered that much. Big Red had made it for Tabby. Again, I had to wonder what his agenda was for giving her this power.

"Where did you get the information?" Tabby asked.

Doc smiled, then disappeared.

"Son of a bitch!" Tabby crossed her arms.

"Guess I don't have to research *that* at the Vatican."

Her eyes flashed for a second, and then she laughed. "Small favors, right?"

"Why do you think Big Red wanted you to have that rod?"

She shrugged. "Maybe he likes me."

I rolled my eyes. "Smart-ass."

She swatted me on the arm. "Since there is nothing going on for half a minute around here, help me finish unpacking."

I saluted her. "Yes, ma'am."

#

I slept like the dead. Dreams flitted in and out of my subconscious until finally, my inner self landed in a black expanse. My brain evidently wasn't big on sitting still. Kind of interesting. There was nothing as far as the eye could see but sheer darkness, and yet my feet felt solid on a floor. I was reminded of this book I'd read once about a haunted house that had more space inside than out. Suddenly, I heard a voice. I looked up and there he was, dressed in his red regalia. Maybe it was the Devil that didn't care about the setting.

"So life has been interesting has it, Mr. Holiday?" the Devil asked. His fangs glinted in an unseen light. Whole place was odd. Maybe I was actually in part of his domain and not in my head.

"You could call it interesting. Stressful, too," I said. This had "wanting something" written all over it. The question was, besides the obvious, what?

He smiled. "Things are in flux, changing. Whatever you do, keep my gift safe. It wouldn't do for it to fall into the wrong hands."

I gulped. With what Doc had told me, and with what I already suspected, I knew the rod was major bad news. "No, I guess it wouldn't."

"And your messenger should check his sources a little better."

I blinked. Did this mean that Doc was wrong? "What are you talking about?"

He laughed. "My gift isn't so easily explained."

He disappeared from in front of me, and very faintly, I heard his disembodied voice say, "Beware."

As soon as it faded to nothingness, my eyes popped open. I was alone in the bed and the sun was shining. I need sleeping pills.

"Holy shit."

Things connecting with me in my sleep made me uneasy. It was the second time it had happened. The first had been Lucy at Sorrow's Point. But the Devil doing it was not cool. Maybe a sleeping pill wouldn't be a good idea. What if it trapped me wherever the dream was occurring?

I got up and headed downstairs. The house seemed almost too quiet. There, on the carpet, was the mess. The blood and glop was back, as well as the smell. I glanced around for Lucy's spirit. It was nowhere to be found. I got that odd feeling spread through the nerves in my body, like I'd bitten down on a piece of foil while having an aluminum filling.

Not cool.

I spun around and there was the meat suit, standing there looking at me with those empty eye sockets. The eye sockets dripped with blood. It reached toward me and I screamed. I closed my eyes and screamed some more. I felt its hands on me. Shaking me. I wanted the fucking thing off me. I lashed out, but it seemed like I wasn't hitting anything. Still I felt the touch of it.

"Please, stop." I kicked and screamed.

Something slapped me across the face.

"Goddamnit, Jimmy. Wake the fuck up!"

My eyes popped open again. Doc and Lucy stood in the doorway to the bedroom. Tabby was on her knees in the bed, waiting to give me another shot if I needed it. Fuck.

"Jesus Christ." I sat up. I was going to have to do something about these dreams if they continued. This was starting to verge on night terrors. Maybe stuff was affecting me after all, but I didn't show it all that well when I was awake.

“What the hell is wrong with you?” Tabby asked.

I scanned the room. Nothing was weird. Everything was fine. I shrugged. “Bad dream.”

“He came to see you, didn’t he?” Lucy asked.

I blinked. The way she could sometimes sense things caught me off guard. I glanced over at her and nodded.

“Who?” Tabby asked.

“Big Red,” I said. “Told me not to let anyone else have the rod. Also, said something about not believing the stuff Doc found out about it.” I scratched my arm and thought about it all some more. Maybe, Big Red wanted Tabby to have it because he planned to use her for something. The question was what.

Doc glared. Then huffed.

“I know. Believe me.”

“Just remember you can’t trust the Devil,” he said.

“Well, it’s not like you tell us where you go on these information expeditions Jimmy sends you out on,” Tabby said.

Doc snorted. “I go to the places that make the most sense. Come on, Lucy. Let’s go where we’re wanted.”

He winked at me, then led Lucy out of the room.

I chuckled. “Yeah. Though sometimes I wonder if what Doc goes after is as reliable as I’ve been thinking it is. I rely on him too much.”

Tabby sighed. “It isn’t like you have any other choice. Not really. Besides, has he led us wrong yet?”

I scratched my eyes with the back of my hand. She, as usual, was right. “No. It could be more like the Devil has more information—which is entirely possible.”

“Exactly.”

“And apparently, we are to keep the damn thing out of the wrong hands.” I watched for her reaction. Her eyes went from wide to narrow.

“How are you supposed to know whose are the right hands?” Tabby asked.

That was a damn good question and one for which I had no answer.

Chapter Four

Black Hole Sun

NONE OF US got much sleep. Doc, Lucy, and Tabby all settled in with me in the bedroom. I couldn't help but be reminded of the library of Blackmoor, but this time, it was not the house that was haunted, it was me. I was going to have to figure out how to fix it, but for now, I had other problems.

About seven thirty, when the sun rose, we all headed downstairs. The light from the living room window was highlighting *the* part of the floor. The carpet was stained, but the chemicals had done their job pretty well. No smell. Thank God. At least my dream hadn't come to life.

"We can try the OxiClean today," I said. It couldn't hurt. Maybe it would do something.

"What?" Tabby asked from behind me.

"On the floor." I pointed.

"Oh. Yeah. Sure." She stepped around me and wandered into the kitchen. She had pulled her hair up in a loose bun today. I preferred it flowing down her back.

"She needs her coffee real bad this morning," Lucy said.

I looked at her and laughed, then sat on a chair at the dining room table. I patted the chair next to me. Lucy climbed up. The poor kid was still wearing the white nightgown I'd always seen her in. Well, prior to the fleshing. When that had happened, we had gotten her some clothes, but her spirit seemed stuck in the clothing she had been in when she ended up in this state. It was sad. I doubted she could change it. Doc hadn't.

"How are you doing, kiddo?" I asked her.

She shrugged. "At least it doesn't hurt anymore."

"That's good." I wanted to give her more, but there was nothing. Just about the only thing I could do was make her feel loved and I was trying to do that.

"Here," Tabby said, handing a steaming mug toward me.

What did I do to deserve her? Damn. I took it. The caffeine would do me some good.

"Sit down," I told her. "We've all had a rough night."

I didn't have to tell her twice. She plopped in the chair opposite me. She looked exactly like I felt—completely exhausted and tired of all the bullshit. Her hair was flying around her head after having escaped her bun.

"Damn, Jimmy," she said.

"What?" It wasn't that I didn't want to say the same thing, but her meaning behind it could be completely different, and I could come out of this looking like a total jackass again.

"If you have any more dreams like that, I swear."

I snorted. Well, sort of what I was thinking, but not exactly. I'd been right not to assume. "What are you going to do?"

"Probably beat you with my broom."

I laughed. "Just don't pee on my head and use it as a coconut."

"What?" Doc asked. His eyebrows were raised up so high on his head I thought they might pop off.

Tabby turned to him. "Old Voudou saying. To get evil spirits out of your home, you take a fine coconut, place it on the floor. Then, open the doorway to your house. You squat and pee all over the coconut. After that, in the most forceful voice you can muster, you scream, 'Get the fuck out of my house!' And you kick the coconut out into the street."

Doc scratched his hand through his hair. His hat he held in his other hand. Rarely did he even set it down. I wondered if it had some power of its own, but so far, I hadn't seen anything out of the ordinary pertaining to it. It was probably because, long ago, men wore hats all the time and you never wanted to lose yours since they cost money. It would be like me leaving behind something that made me, well, me. Maybe the hat was the 1800's version of the cell phone. He could never leave it alone or put it down.

Lucy laughed. I mean really laughed. If she had a body, her belly would hurt.

"That's one of the weirdest things I've ever heard and I've been around a while," Doc said.

Tabby chuckled. "I never tried it myself, but it is unique."

Isaac hopped up on the table and head-butted me. Hard.

"Ow." I glared at Tabby. "You feed him yet?"

Tabby laughed. "No, I forgot."

That figured. Ack. I glanced back at that cat. "Okay, Mr. Man. Come on."

#

After breakfast, I attacked the carpet again.

"I'm sorry," Lucy said.

I glanced up. Poor kid seemed like she was going to cry. It was a fucking carpet. If she didn't get over it soon, I was going to go crazy. Even if I had been poor, the worst that would happen would be that I would tear the damn thing up and live with the subfloor until I could afford to replace it. "Don't worry about it. It was an old carpet anyway. When stuff calms down, we'll get a new one."

"Okay," she said, still looking sad.

"Here, come help me," I said. She needed a distraction and fast. Good thing I was good at coming up with stupid shit.

"Do what?" she asked.

I motioned for her to follow me. I walked into the kitchen and dumped the OxiClean out of the squirt bottle into the sink. Then I rinsed it out really good. After that was done, I peered down at Lucy. "Want to have some fun?"

She nodded her head slowly. Her eyes were as wide as dinner plates. This was going to be a blast.

I filled the bottle with water. Then I crouched down. "Okay. I'm going to hide right behind the edge of the doorway here." I pointed to the doorway of the kitchen. "Now, what I need you to do is to go get Tabby and tell her that you really need to show her something. Then lead her down here."

Lucy giggled and jumped up and down.

I loved hearing her laugh. "Okay. Ready?"

She nodded, almost quivering in anticipation. I couldn't stop myself from grinning. "Go!"

She disappeared in a pop. Was Tabby going to be pissed? Probably. But it was worth it to cheer up Lucy. Besides, it wasn't like this was going to hurt anyone. And the worst that could happen would be for Tabby to beat my ass. I could handle that. In fact, that might be kind of fun too—in a twisted kind of way.

Soon, I heard footsteps coming down the stairs. I waited until I saw her arm, and when I was about to strike, the doorbell rang. I shoved the bottle on the table and stepped out of the kitchen as Tabby opened the door. Plan foiled yet again.

"Yes?" she asked when she opened the door.

The postman handed her a thick envelope and walked away. Damn, I was starting to think there was something sinister about getting mail. Especially after getting the flask from Arizona that led me to Vespa and his fake possession.

I looked over her shoulder. "What's that?"

I watched her analyze the address.

"It's for you," she said, handing the envelope to me.

It was from the Vatican. If that wasn't enough to make my asshole grow tight, I didn't think anything would. Images of being carted away in an old black sedan filled my head. It was all nonsense, but my brain went there.

I flipped the envelope around in my hands. I knew what it was. I let the breath I'd been holding out. "These are my acceptance papers."

I walked over to the dining room table and opened the envelope. There was a letter and some sort of guide. I chose to read the letter first.

Mr. Holiday,

We are pleased to invite you to our school of Exorcism. Your class will start on 1 May, 2015. An interpreter will be provided for you.

Enclosed you will find the booklet. Please pay careful attention to the rules.

Fr. Luca Rossi.

"I start May first," I said. That gave me a little time to prepare. For that, I was thankful.

Lucy crawled up beside me in a chair. "Can I come?"

I glanced over at her and smiled. "I don't know how I'd leave you behind."

It was true. She was tied to me. It was one thing to leave her at the house while I went to the store. Another thing entirely for me to be a whole continent away.

"What was it you wanted to show me, Lucy?" Tabby asked.

"Never mind," she said in a sing-song voice.

#

Later that evening, after dinner, I sat at the dining room table looking over the class stuff. Most of it was the regular church info. The rules were something else. I was almost reminded of that movie with Brad Pitt and Ed Norton. "First rule: never talk about fight club."

I'll admit it, there was a big part of me that wanted to waltz in there like John Bender from *The Breakfast Club,* smoking a cigarette and wearing old ripped-up doo rags on my boots. But I couldn't. It would be an insult to God. Granted, the church did a lot of shit that wasn't cool, but it wouldn't do any good for me to do something that was an honest affront. I was better than that. Plus, there were plenty of places where I could get my Bender on. Heh.

I refocused on the class. One thing: I had to dig into my old work clothes. Because I was no longer a priest, I didn't have to wear the uniform, but I was expected to present myself in a certain way. I guessed khakis and a nice shirt were good enough for the Lord. The most important thing I knew was that I was going to have to keep my mouth shut. It wasn't going to be easy. A lot of the stuff I'd learned since starting all of this was probably not with the program. And having an exorcism ritual written by a witch was definitely not on the Vatican's list of crap to do. But maybe, if I was lucky, they could teach me something. If I could be a good boy, that was. That part was questionable.

I could almost head the bass line of "Inna Gadda Da Vida" in my head. My ability to be humble to an authority figure kind of went out the window when I was kicked out of the church. Being surrounded by muckety-mucks all day was a recipe for disaster. I needed to keep it all tamped down though. Especially since this trip wasn't cheap and the Order was trying to help me for once.

I wasn't even a church employee at all anymore, so their politics meant nothing to me. I simply needed to be respectful. Just as long as no one was an asshole, stuff would be fine. I hoped the Order knew what they were doing. Of course, with the way crap had been, so far they'd let me fly by the seat of my pants. That could be the biggest mistake of their lives.

"What are you thinking?" Tabby asked me.

"That this is going to be an epic fail." I knew I was eventually going to fuck this up. The only question was how bad. Maybe I could hope that my "issues" would not present themselves until I was back from Italy.

"How do you know that?" she asked.

I sighed. "Because I won't be able to stop myself from speaking. I don't have the patience anymore. I'm not sure I ever did."

She patted me on the arm. "Just keep in mind that it isn't these people who chose for you to be a marker."

She had a very good point. God had given me the ability to mark the souls of the possessed before they died during the course of an exorcism. The only one who had the ability to take any of that power away was God. Screw all the rest. If I could deal with demons, I could manage to keep my mouth shut long enough to make it through the class. The insides of my cheeks were going to be bloody, but so be it.

"So I've got to be on my best behavior," I said. "What are you going to do?"

Tabby leaned back in her chair. "How long is this class again?"

"Six weeks."

"If it wasn't for the fact that I know you very well, I'd go back to school. But something is going to happen."

I rolled my eyes. "Thanks for the vote of confidence. Anyway, why don't you do something with your Mom?"

She shrugged. "Maybe. More than likely, I'll just get this house in order."

"You could get the carpet replaced." It was an idea. And something that was easy. She could go pick it out and pay to have it installed.

She laughed. "I could."

"That settles it then." Suddenly, I got this feeling I couldn't shake. Before I knew it, my mouth was moving faster than my brain. "When I get done with all this shit, will you marry me?"

Tabby looked at me for a minute like I'd grown another head. Hell, I was shocked myself.

"You're serious?" she asked.

"As a heart attack." And I was. No other person on this Earth was going to be willing to put up with my weird bullshit.

"Okay," she said.

I almost swooned. Seriously.

#

Later that night, I sat up in bed, looking at the packet again. I figured I might as well memorize the damn thing. At least, then I'd know what rules I'd be breaking. I knew me too well. If I behaved like I normally did, I'd break every one of them. Most of the time without meaning to. I did have a tendency to bumble through life that way. Hell, if I was honest, I'd been bumbling through the exorcisms I had performed too.

"You know you've looked at that same page for ten minutes," Tabby said as she rubbed lotion on her elbows.

I shrugged. "I don't want to do this."

It was true. I had no real desire to set foot in the ruling paths of the church again. Going to Mass once in a while was fine. Dealing with bureaucracy was not. Hopefully, I could avoid most of it as much as possible.

She started laughing. "All you've been doing since you started this was bitch because you didn't know what you were doing. And now that they are actually going to train you, the only thing you can do is complain about that too? You amaze me."

I shrugged my shoulders.

.She had a point. Every exorcism I'd had to do, I'd performed with instinct, mistakes, and a lot of luck. I was a novice at best. It was time I manned up. I was getting what I had asked for. I needed to remember that, in the future, it would be best if I were careful in what I wished for.

"What, you aren't going to say anything?" she asked.

"Nope." Why would I? She'd nailed the whole thing.

"Why not?"

I leaned over and kissed her on the forehead. "Because you're right."

She sat back, eyes wide. "Are you sure you're okay?"

I laughed. "Yes."

"Did you ever get back in touch with that other priest who wanted to meet up with you?"

"Yeah, told him the meet-up would have to wait. Too busy."

She nodded

"Now, why don't we try to get some sleep?"

She glared at me sideways. "If you say so."

#

The next morning, I made myself get up at a decent hour. There was so much to do. I had to find out who was handling my reservation for the school. Honestly, I hoped they were going to do it because I didn't know a damn thing in Italian. If I had to make my own reservations, I'd probably end up in the slums or something.

It was 6:30 a.m. and Tabby was snoring softly next to me. Her long red hair was scattered all over her face in a tangled mess. Part of me wanted to move it, but I was afraid I would wake her up. Still, I couldn't imagine being comfortable with hair all over my face, but maybe that was me.

"Jimmy," I heard someone whisper.

I glanced up and Lucy was there in the doorway with her finger over her lips. I crept out of bed and followed her. She led me downstairs.

I couldn't imagine what this could be about, but since she didn't seem upset, I tried not to worry.

"Look," she said once my feet hit the living room floor. She was pointing at the spot where the stain had been, but it looked like it had never happened.

I closed my eyes and then peered again. The stain was still gone. No way in the world was this natural. "How did this happen?"

Lucy shrugged. "I don't know. I was watching TV and I heard this weird noise. When I went to look, it was gone."

It took me a minute to make sense of what she said. I looked down at the floor. Even the bleaching was gone. I'd been involved with this shit long enough to know that something like that was reason to worry. There was more to it than a noise. A lot more to it.

I glanced back at Lucy. "And all you heard was that sound?"

"Uh-huh."

There was something about what she was saying that left me feeling like she was holding back. Almost like a little kid lying about something they'd done that they knew I wouldn't be happy with. I wasn't about to accuse her of anything though without more proof. "Well, put a call out for Doc. I'm not liking this at all."

Lucy nodded. "It didn't feel bad, though."

Well, that was something at least. Every time she felt bad before, there was something for me to deal with. Her not feeling something bad…well…it could be that she was still weak, or that whatever took away the stain wasn't malevolent. Kind or not, I wanted to know what was helping me and what it wanted in return. If there was a spirit helping us, that was. Nothing in return would be way too damn easy. I was pretty sure she'd done something, but I still didn't want to create resentment.

With nothing else to do, I headed into the kitchen and began making breakfast. Tabby was going to have to check her wards. Somehow, whatever this was had gotten through, and I wanted to know why. If Lucy did have something to do with it, she was going to get a hell of a talking to.

I pulled out the eggs and began scrambling them in a pan with a little butter. It wasn't long before I heard footsteps. I smiled. Nothing like the smell of food to wake people out of a deep sleep.

"Making breakfast?" Tabby asked from behind me.

"Yep. See the living room?" I asked.

She froze. "What do you mean?"

She must have been tired. That, or she wasn't as obsessed with the stain as I was.

"Go look at the floor," I said. It was easier for her to see it than for me to describe it. Plus, I wanted to find out if her reaction was the same as mine.

She turned around and backed away. Soon, she ran back into the kitchen. "How?"

"That's the problem. I don't know. Lucy came to me this morning and told me about it." I proceeded to tell her exactly what Lucy had said about the strange sound. I still wasn't buying that there wasn't more to it, but Tabby's reaction confirmed my suspicion that this was very wrong.

"So," I said. "You'd better check your wards."

Tabby walked over to the back door, stood in front of it for a minute, and glanced at me. "They're fine. Remember, I set the wards to only let in things that meant us no harm."

I paused. Meaning harm and paying a price were two entirely different ideas. I was still uneasy. "Still doesn't explain what did it."

"No, but at least it did something helpful."

"I guess." Granted, it might not be a bad idea to think positively about all of this, but I'd had too much bad shit go down to not be suspicious.

She came up to me and hugged me. "You worry too much."

"No, I don't like things in my house I don't know about."

Tabby laughed. "You'd better get used to it. The other world knows who you are. It makes perfect sense for them to seek you out."

"So very comforting."

She punched me on the arm. "Finish breakfast. I'm going to get a shower."

I saluted her. "Yes, ma'am."

Man in the Box

AS SOON AS I set all the breakfast food on the table, Lucy trotted up and crawled up in a chair. Isaac followed her and sat on the floor next to Lucy's chair. I don't know if Isaac knew she'd killed her own cat or not, but I still found myself watching Lucy now and then to make sure she wasn't going to do something like that again. I did give her the benefit of the doubt because she'd been possessed at the time, but once a demon puts its claws in you, nothing is certain.

"What are you guys doing today?" I asked Lucy.

"Isaac says you shouldn't be so nervous," she replied.

I raised an eyebrow, and then stared down at the cat. Isaac was licking his balls. I glanced back at Lucy. I seriously doubted he'd said that just then.

"Does Isaac know what fixed the carpet?" It was an odd hunch. I had no explanation for it. Of course, I had hunches about a lot of shit. It didn't mean any of them were right.

Lucy nodded.

"So?" I asked.

She fidgeted. "He said something about horses with gifts."

It was times like this, when she messed up a phrase, that I remembered she was only six. I had a feeling that she was grafting what she was telling me onto Isaac, when she really wanted to let me in on everything. "Tell him that isn't good enough. I need to know."

Lucy laughed. "Isaac isn't just a cat, you know."

I plopped in the chair opposite from her. This was different. "What do you mean?"

"What's going on?" Tabby asked from behind me.

I jumped. "Jesus Christ!"

Lucy snickered behind her hand.

"Damn, Jimmy. I didn't mean to scare you." Tabby parked herself in the chair to my left and began spooning eggs on a plate. "You didn't used to be this jumpy."

"I also didn't used to be an exorcist." I chuckled. "It's okay. You caught me off guard."

"So go on," Tabby said.

I shoveled some eggs onto my plate. "Lucy was explaining to me that apparently Isaac has something to do with the clean floor."

Tabby froze. "Like what?"

I looked at her. "She won't say."

Tabby pointed a fork at Lucy. "Okay. Time to spill it."

Lucy shook her head. "Uh-uh. He won't let me."

"Wait," I said. It felt like the temperature in the room had dropped several degrees. "Who won't let you?"

Her eyes got serious. "You know."

Then she hopped off the chair and ran upstairs.

Tabby looked at me. "What did that mean?"

"I honestly have no idea." And I didn't. There were probably about forty million possibilities. I was guessing, but as far as I knew, there was no way to document every single demon that existed throughout history. Was there?

#

As I got my shower, my thoughts drifted to Isaac. I'd always known he was Tabby's familiar, but I guessed that meant more than him being just a cat who wasn't afraid of magic. I still figured the crap she was telling me about the floor wasn't from the cat's mind. As far as I knew, Isaac didn't actually help Tabby's magic at all. She'd done plenty of it without him around. More so, I think he kept watch over things and, if he thought something should be done about it, he acted. I still remembered in Arizona when he tried to get me to go on the ghost tour. Thinking back on how things ended up, I probably should have listened.

Yet, someone telling Lucy she couldn't tell anyone about the whole thing—that sat wrong. If it was Isaac, I could handle it, but I had a sinking suspicion that Big Red had his hands in more than one cookie jar and I didn't like it. Granted, again, there were lots of possibilities, but with the weird visit-dream from Mr. Man, that put him in the running for the number one culprit. And I'd rather not tell Tabby about that yet. It was better for me to wait until I was sure. No sense in making problems where there weren't any. It wasn't like I was going to march down to Hell and demand an answer, so I was stuck.

Best to concentrate on the things I could fix, like figuring out how I was going to get to Italy. Too much dwelling on all of this crap was going to drive me bonkers.

After I got dressed, I went into the bedroom and grabbed the iPad. I went ahead and plugged it in so it would have a good charge; then I powered it up. I jotted off a message to the email address of the Order and asked about flights, etc. Hopefully, they would get back to me soon. If the shit that had happened in Arizona was any indication, they seemed to reply when they felt like it. I had a feeling that it might take a while for me to get an answer, which was why it was so important to contact them now. I didn't want to leave any of this until the last minute.

I shut down the tablet and left it on the bed to charge. Then I headed downstairs to try to make some sense of everything and make sure we had a decent day for a change.

#

We'd spent the day finishing up all the unpacking that needed to get done before I left for Italy. We were all tired, but it was a good tired. Nothing weird happened, and in my book, that was a plus. After dinner, and after all the trash was taken to the garage, Tabby and I sat on the sofa and watched TV with Lucy for a while. It was some survival show. I could deal with that compared to her love of horror films. Maybe she wanted mindless stuff too. "Why do you think she likes TV so much?" Tabby asked suddenly.

I shrugged. "You'd have to ask her."

"What?" Lucy asked as she turned around to face us.

"Why do you like TV so much?" Tabby asked her.

I almost expected some sort of bizarre story dealing with the space-time continuum and Isaac's love for tuna fish.

Lucy paused for a minute. Her eyebrows scrunched together. After a bit, they relaxed. "It lets me see things I never see when I'm here."

"And the scary movies?" I asked.

"Oh, those are fun because they are so fake."

I laughed. I should have smacked myself. She did have the mind of a six-year-old. I don't know what the hell I was expecting. "Guess you'd know."

Lucy's eyes darkened. "We all would."

Sadly, she was right.

Doc popped in. "Seems to me that life is easier without all those thingamagigs."

He was holding his hat in his hand and grinning.

"You're probably right," I said to him.

He sat effortlessly at the dining room table and set his hat on the table top.

Lucy walked over and hopped up on Doc's lap. "I feel so much safer when you're here."

In a way, it was kind of sweet, but it also made me feel like chopped liver. I had to wonder exactly how much she remembered about being possessed. If she remembered a bunch, God help me. I still had nightmares about Lucy propositioning me back at Sorrow's Point. I had to hope that, over time, the memories would fade. That was, if she was stuck like this for a while. Hopefully, she didn't remember that much, though my funky detector said otherwise.

Suddenly, my phone rang. The timing could not have been better. I picked it up. There was a string of numbers I did not recognize. I shrugged and answered it, getting ready to use my telemarketer spiel.

"Hello?" I asked.

"Mr. Holiday. This is Father John." His voice was deep, but not quite baritone.

I paused. I'd never heard of him before. He hadn't even been mentioned in any of the emails. "Okay."

"I am with the Order of Markers," he said.

"Oh, okay." Glad we cleared that up. I rolled my eyes. "Is this about my email?"

Ol' Johnny Boy coughed. "I'm afraid not. This is about something more… unsettling."

I paused. It did not sound good. I had a feeling I was in deep shit.

"Okay."

"The girl who was part of your first experience, Lucy Andersen?" he asked.

My heart started hammering in my chest. "Yes?"

"We received word that she left this life very early this morning."

My eyes darted over to Lucy, sitting in front of the TV. She seemed fine. My stomach felt very heavy, like I'd swallowed something made of cast iron.

"Is there a way I can pay my respects?" I asked.

He cleared his throat. "We never provide that information. Just know that her family is upset, but doing well. They've had a long time to adjust."

I couldn't even imagine what all Will and Tor had been through. The time had been hard on them. There had been so many times I'd wished I could give them an update. Something. But I'd never been able to make contact. The Order, apparently, had made sure of that. "That's true," I said. "Thanks for calling."

"Yes, we thought you should know," he said, and then he hung up.

I set my phone on the dining room table and glanced at Tabby. I needed to talk about this. Part of me felt like my soul was breaking. "Will you come upstairs with me for a minute?"

Tabby gawked at me, puzzled.

Dammit. I didn't want to have to explain anything in front of Lucy. I pleaded with her using my eyes.

Then I glanced at Doc. "Don't let Lucy watch any scary movies."

Doc chuckled.

"I'm sure we can find something to do, can't we, Lucy?" Doc asked her.

She giggled.

I motioned for Tabby to follow me. Then, I led her upstairs into our bedroom, and once we both were inside, I closed the door.

"What is this about?" She stood there, hands on her hips.

I practically fell onto the bed and patted the mattress beside me. She joined me.

"Lucy's dead," I said.

"What?" Her eyes were wide and I watched as her body started to shake slightly.

"That was the Order. I guess her poor body finally gave out." I could feel the wetness creeping into my eyes.

She took a deep breath and stopped shaking. "Do you think she knows?"

I shrugged. "I think with what happened this morning she does know, but maybe God put it in such a way that it didn't upset her."

It was the best I had. Anything else was going to have to come from other sources. Just about the only thing I had in mind was a stiff drink.

"So the weird sound?" Tabby asked.

That was the question, wasn't it? Was it just a magically cleaning spirit, or was it something more? The fact that Lucy hadn't been bothered about it still left me feeling a bit odd. There were so many possibilities that I found my head swimming.

"I think it was what was left of her soul leaving her real body," I said finally. It was the only thing that kind of made sense. For the sound anyway, not the carpet cleaning.

OUR EVENING WAS pretty much ruined by that point. I couldn't make myself pretend everything was fine when it wasn't. I suppose part of me had figured that, as long as Lucy's real body was still alive, she'd be fine. But I'd been wrong. I felt like an epic failure. No kid should have to die that way. And fuck, Lucy had died twice.

At least Lucy was still here though. Her soul was safe. I'd done something right. Not that it had happened because of anything I'd done specifically. I had a feeling that the Good Guy was a lot more active than he let on. Didn't mean I wanted visits from him either. Still would be better than visits from Big Red.

Too bad that wasn't very comforting at the moment.

Tabby poked me with her fingernail. "You know you are going to have to talk about it eventually."

I sighed. "Yeah, but I want her to have at least one more normal night."

Tabby shook her head. "We already figured out that she knows. I don't think she's ever had one normal night around us."

On the normal part, she was probably right. But having to prod Lucy about her feelings? It could wait. Tabby's prodding nature was one thing that drove me crazy about her. She could never let stuff rest. I'd rather have all my teeth pulled from my mouth with a rusty set of pliers than talk about this, but I could tell I wasn't going to get an opinion.

I went downstairs and paused in the doorway. Doc and Lucy were watching a nature show on TV. It was interesting that he was such a good influence on her. Doc wasn't exactly known for being a nice guy. He'd been a gunman in the Old West, for Christ's sake.

I took a deep breath. "Lucy?"

She spun her head around to face me. "Yeah?"

"Come here a second." I motioned her over with my hands. This would all be so much easier if I could hug her. Dammit.

She got up from the floor and walked over to me. Doc watched her, glanced at me, and nodded.

When she was next to my leg, I began. "You know that phone call I had a while ago?"

She nodded her head.

I looked into those innocent blue eyes and silently cursed Tabby for making me do this. I was going to get my revenge…somehow. "You didn't lose your fake body."

She ogled at me for a minute, and then blinked. "I know."

I shook myself. I felt like someone had pulled the emergency brake on the roller coaster ride. "What?"

"My real body died when I got rid of the fake one. They just didn't realize it with all of the machines." She shrugged.

Tabby had put me through this for nothing. I was so confused. If she died when the meat suit did, then the weird noise and subsequent cleaning wasn't connected to it at all. It was like I'd thought before—something else I didn't want in my house. Great.

"What about the weird noise? Was it Isaac?" I asked.

She laughed. "No silly. Isaac can do a lot, but not that."

Like what? Dress in drag and do the hula? Well, I would have liked to see that, but oh well. I needed to focus. "Then who?"

Her face got very serious then. "I already told you, I can't tell you."

I decided to leave it alone for now. No sense in upsetting her for no apparent reason. Nothing bad had happened here. Not yet anyway. But I wasn't willing to press my luck either. "Okay, Lucy."

I could let it go for now. I was back to having that funky feeling. Even though whatever it was meant no harm, the Devil hadn't exactly meant for Lucy to have her accident either. I was so fucking confused. If all this shit weren't happening, I would spend some time in the dark cave of my bedroom eating chocolate and hiding from the world. But that wasn't an option.

#

Later that night, while I was lying in bed, and Tabby was in the bathroom getting ready for the night, Doc suddenly popped in with a serious expression on his face. Doc being serious was starting to feel like the times when Lucy had a bad feeling. I needed a drink.

I sat up in bed. "What's wrong?"

Doc came a bit closer. He floated. I didn't even think his "feet" were touching the ground. Usually, he gave the impression that he was walking. This time, however, he didn't bother. "I think Lucy made a deal."

"With who?" I asked.

Doc rested on the bed. "It might not be a deal per se, but I think she felt so bad about your carpet that she asked for help from someone you don't use for help."

I put my head in my hands. This was it. Dammit. I'd suspected it before, but the fact that Doc was here talking to me, well, that kind of pointed toward it. If it looked like a duck, walked like a duck, and quacked like a duck, it was probably a duck. "Please don't be telling me she made a deal with the Devil."

He nodded. "That's exactly what I think. Now, I don't think the death of her body had anything to do with it. But there's something there. I'm sure of it. What he wants, that's the question."

"Shit." I scratched my head. Then, glanced back at him. "Thanks for letting me know. Kind of explains the feeling I've had about all of it."

Doc nodded. "I'm going back to her now. I'm going to try to stick to her like glue for now on."

"I appreciate it." I was kind of sad that Lucy needed a full-time sitter and not for the usual kid stuff either. I couldn't help but imagine what her parents would think about all of this. Tor, Lucy's mom, would probably have a heart attack.

"Who are you talking to?" Tabby asked as she walked out of the bathroom. She had on this pair of pajamas that had ducks on them. I almost laughed.

I looked up. "Doc."

She sat on the bed and threw the covers over her feet. "What did he have to say?"

I sighed. "Oh, nothing. Just that Lucy made a deal with the Devil."

"What?" Tabby gaped at me. Then she opened her mouth as wide as a bass.

"For the fucking carpet." Who would have thought that a stupid old carpet would be this much trouble. Had I known that, I would have put down hardwood. Jesus Christ.

"Oh, no." Tabby slumped her shoulders. "What are we going to do?"

"I guess I have to figure out what the hell the terms of their agreement are. Doc said he isn't going to leave her alone again." I hoped she hadn't promised something stupid. If she had, my head was going to explode.

Tabby nodded. "That's probably a good thing."

"Yeah. So any ideas how to contact the Devil?" I was partly joking, but not really. I needed to get to the bottom of this and fast.

Tabby laughed nervously. "Not anything without risk."

"Shit." Nothing with the supernatural was without risk. I needed to get drunk. It wouldn't solve anything, but it would be a hell of a lot more fun.

"Yeah." Tabby leaned into me and gave me a hug.

I needed that.

#

It probably wasn't hard to figure out that I had a hell of a time getting to sleep. The only thing I could be thankful for was that what dreams I had were normal stress dreams and nothing supernatural. It was a nice change of pace, and I'd had enough stress for one day. I guessed the beasties felt I had too. Nah. They weren't paying attention. For all I knew, they were hanging out in a bar in Hell. Heh.

I spent most of the night tossing and turning. Just trying to find a comfortable spot. But as soon as I moved, my brain started rolling again. I eventually fell asleep because by the time I woke up, Tabby was gone from the bed.

I got up and shuffled downstairs. I found Tabby in the dining room with Lucy beside her looking at Tabby's laptop. Not exactly what I expected to see, but I could take it. It was something normal for once.

"What are you guys doing?" I asked.

"I thought Lucy might like her own room," Tabby said.

Lucy grinned.

I sat in the chair opposite from Tabby. She had a point. Now that Lucy was going to be living with us…well…for a while, she might as well settle in. If I was honest with myself, I should have done it sooner. A little girl has toys and stuff. I could have made her feel at home. I was an idiot.

"You're going to paint?" I asked.

Lucy nodded. "I get to pick the color."

I grinned. It was so awesome to see her happy about something. Granted, there were still issues, but it was nice to see her smiling.

"Besides, we need a good project while you're gone," Tabby said.

I didn't even bother to ask where the money was going to come from. The paycheck I was getting from the Order was more than I'd ever had in my entire life. I knew I needed to start saving away retirement funds and crap, but I hadn't exactly had time to breathe either. Yet another thing that needed to be put on the list of crap I had to do. Maybe the Order would have someone I could go to about setting up an IRA or something.

"Do you think we should make Doc a room too?" I asked. I mean, shit. If Lucy was going to have one, it was only right. I wasn't about to start playing the spirit favorites game.

"I don't need nothing like that," Doc said suddenly from behind me. "I got a whole house to roam around in."

Lucy laughed.

Part of me felt for Doc. At least I didn't have to worry about playing favorites now. He seemed happy enough. Of course, before we'd gotten in contact with him, he'd just been hanging around Tombstone watching Vespa. At least now we gave him something to do. Our lives were anything but boring.

I thought that, if Lucy weren't a kid, this would all be a lot easier. But in a weird sort of way, she was my kid now. That changed stuff a little. She was going to have whatever she wanted—within reason, of course.

"I'm going to make breakfast." I stood up. They were too busy staring at the computer. I shook my head and headed into the kitchen. Let them do fun stuff. It didn't bother me at all.

As soon as I pulled the eggs out of the refrigerator, I had a weird feeling again. The leaves of the trees outside the window were frozen in place. Fuck. He was here. I set the eggs on the kitchen table and waited. Soon he walked into the kitchen.

Today, the Devil was back to wearing his black suit and a blood-red tie. Nice way to seem non-threatening—not. I wanted to kick him right square in the ass for making a pact with Lucy. I kind of wondered if that was against the rules somehow. Then again, it would help if I knew what all the rules were in the first place, but the higher powers hadn't provided me with those either.

"What do you want?" I needed to find out what the hell he had planned.

He paused in front of me, pulled out a chair at the table, and sat. "To talk."

Now, I was really uneasy. There was never "just talk" in a situation like this. Everything had meaning with him and I wasn't stupid enough to fall for it.

I pulled out the other chair and sat too. No telling how long this was going to take. "What do you want to talk about?"

He looked up at me. His eyes flashed red for a minute, then settled on dark brown. "I have a warning for you."

I raised an eyebrow. This was different. I'd expected it to have something to do with Lucy. Evidently, I was wrong. "Okay."

"Things are coming that will not be easy. Things that you will not like." His voice was steady, not too deep, and definitely not high-pitched. And yet, it had this creepiness to it. Not what you'd expect, but not nice either.

Again, the demons were under his control, so if they were the threat, then he was behind it. I wasn't that easily deceived.

"Again, I have to ask, what is it you want?" I wasn't about to assume a damn thing.

He laughed. "You can't blame me for trying."

I nodded my head. At least I'd gotten something honest out of him. "True."

Isaac popped his head in the doorway. One look at Big Red and his eyes narrowed as he hissed, and then he darted away. How in the hell he wasn't stuck in the Devil's thrall, I had no idea. Maybe Lucy was right. I didn't understand all of the things that cat could do. And maybe

Tabby didn't even know what her familiar was capable of. Not that it really mattered, but Isaac was definitely more than a pet.

"I've always liked animals," the Devil said.

I laughed. "They sure like you."

He smiled, coldly. "They simply do not know me better. Not yet."

I felt a chill travel up my spine. Yeah, best not to forget who I was talking to. "So what did you do to Lucy?"

His smile waned. "Nothing. It was not my intention that the fleshing rod be used on her."

That made me pause. I'd expected something much more sinister. More stuff was afoot than I realized. "What is your intention for it?"

He adjusted himself in the chair. "As I told you, it is for your safekeeping. Or rather, your safekeeping as well as use by your witch. Little Lucy was an accident, so I made it up to her."

"For what price?" This was it. I was going to get the rub.

"None. It was I who owed her." His odd morality set me on edge. It was almost as if he was more predator than anything else. Maybe that was why he was so hard to understand.

"You aren't any closer to collecting her soul?" I could almost kick myself for asking such a thing.

He laughed. "Oh, I'm not worried about that. I'll collect hers when I collect yours."

My asshole snapped shut. "What?"

He disappeared in a loud whoosh.

That figured. My life had gotten more fucked up than I thought was possible. And leave it to me to ask the questions that could very well make it all worse.

#

"I thought you were going to make breakfast?" Tabby asked from the doorway. I was still sitting there, stunned.

"Something came up," I said. Granted, that was an understatement, but whatever. I was tired of having to explain.

"Obviously." Her hands were on her hips and she was giving me that look.

I peered up at her. "He was here again."

"Who?"

Did I have to whack her over the head with a stick? Who else came to visit and left me all discombobulated? Jesus Christ.

"Who do you think?" I asked.

She glared at me. "There is no sense in being like that."

Great. I did not want to start an argument on top of everything else. This was getting worse and worse. I got up from the table and pulled her into my arms. "You're right. Forgive me?"

"Maybe."

I nuzzled her for a minute. I was lucky she let me.

"What did he have to say?" she asked.

I let go of her and swallowed. "He fixed the carpet because he 'owed' Lucy."

"What?" Her eyes seemed like they were going to pop out of her head.

"Yeah. Because he hadn't meant for her to use the rod," I said. That part still felt wrong. Like usual, there was more to it than that.

Tabby scratched at her head. "That makes some sense, I guess."

"I asked him if it put him further to claiming Lucy's soul, and you know what he said?"

Tabby shook her head.

"He said he wasn't worried about it because he'd be claiming her soul when he claimed mine." That still had me freaked out and it probably always would. If I kept my cool and played by the rules I knew were right, I should be okay. That was, if my brain wasn't trying to trick me or anything.

Tabby glared at me. "What have you been doing?"

"That's just it. I haven't done anything." Well, except do exorcisms and flounder around in my usual fashion. Nothing damnable there. I was actually a pretty decent guy.

She tapped her fingers against her hips. "He could be trying to get your goat, you know?"

"It's possible. Before I even asked about Lucy, he had an answer waiting for me." It was almost as if he could read my mind, but I didn't even want to think about that too much. It wasn't like I had special powers or anything to stop him if he did.

"About what?" Tabby asked.

"Just that things were changing." I suppose I should have been grateful that he warned me, but the fact that he was behind the changes kind of negated the kindness of the whole thing. I was probably overthinking everything.

She shrugged. "Guess we'll find out."

"Guess so."

#

A few hours later, Tabby, Doc, Lucy, and I were in the car. The house had started to feel too closed in, so we figured we would get out for a while. It would probably do us all some good.

"Where are we going?" Lucy asked.

"To Tamarack," I said. "It's an artist colony with shops and stuff. I thought we could look for some stuff for your room." I glanced at her in the rearview mirror. She was grinning. Score. I needed to do crap like this more often.

I drummed my fingers against the steering wheel. "Well, they have all those quilts, right?"

Tabby leaned across the car and hugged me. "I love you."

I chuckled. "For what?"

She shook her head and settled back into her seat. This had the makings of being a good day after all.

"You folks done with all the lovey-dovey stuff?" Doc asked.

I laughed.

Lucy giggled. "Yeah. No kissing."

I smiled. Part of me wondered if this was how she was with Will and Tor before Blackmoor. It didn't seem fair somehow. They were left with a broken heart and I ended up with their daughter. Not fair at all. Still, I was viewing it as the gift it was. Unless something changed drastically, I would not be having kids of my own. Maybe Lucy was my chance.

Be Like That

QUILT PROCURED, WE ended up going to a Waffle House to grab a late lunch. Tabby had a hankering for pancakes. I didn't care. Food was just food at this point. It was all tasting the same to me. I needed to start getting off my ass and making something.

It pained me to see Lucy sitting in the car with Doc, but it was the most humane thing to do. I mean, how kind would it be if Tabby and I ate in front of her like that? Especially something sweet? I supposed that she'd eventually adapt again, but for now, since it had been so short a time since she'd eaten normally, I wasn't going to put her through it. At least Doc was in the same state, so she had someone to complain to who could understand.

"What are you getting?" Tabby asked.

We were sitting at a booth near one of the windows. We could see my car from there. Doc was talking to Lucy about something. Neither one of them was smiling. Not good.

"I don't know." I picked up my menu and glanced at it. I didn't feel like eating. I wanted to go home and hide in my closet for a while. It wouldn't solve anything, but maybe it would make me feel better. Sort of, anyway. That was, until the closet monster came out of his hiding place. Now I was being stupid.

The waitress came over and took our orders. Tabby got her pancakes. I ordered a breakfast sandwich.

"You need to snap out of this," Tabby said.

I looked up. "How am I supposed to do that?"

She rolled her eyes. "You could at least fake it."

"Like Lucy wouldn't see through that in two seconds." It was true. That kid was more astute than most adults.

She crossed her arms. "Don't you think you'd be better off killing the pity party? It isn't like you don't have a lot to do."

I sighed. "I know. I have to prepare for Italy."

Since Lucy was going with me, she would be taken out of the house and the stuff that seemed to be happening there would be over soon enough.

"Do you even know where your passport is?" she asked.

I laughed. "I'm not that stupid. It's in my desk drawer. I renewed it a couple of years ago."

"Okay. Okay." She waved her hands as if to admit defeat. "You just seem to have your head up your ass."

I raised an eyebrow. Maybe she was lashing out because of what had happened to Lucy, but I didn't want to start an argument in the middle of the restaurant. Best to do it at home where no one was watching. My eyes darted back to Lucy and Doc in the car. Yeah. Right.

"Fine," I said. "So it isn't okay for me to grieve for Lucy?"

She gaped out the window. "That wasn't what I meant."

The waitress arrived with our food. Nothing like timing. Damn, I needed some hobbies. Maybe then I would have something else to talk about.

"Anything else?" she asked. She was dressed in a brown uniform and had this silly hat on her head. I felt sorry for her. These companies needed to think about the shit they were making their employees wear. Jesus.

"No, this is great," I said. No sense in dumping all of my crap on her. She didn't do it. I wanted to give Tabby a piece of my mind, but my desire to not make a scene outweighed that urge for the moment.

The waitress nodded and left.

Tabby dug into her food without saying anything. I didn't bother to try to insert conversation. Things had gone badly as it was. No sense in making it worse. Maybe by the time we got back home, the stress would have calmed down and the fight wouldn't happen. I had to hope for something. I needed a vacation from my problems.

I picked at my sandwich. Part of me was daring her to say something, but she didn't. Frankly, I knew Tabby was more adult than me, even though I was almost ten years older than her. Still though, I was used to fighting for what I wanted, and believed, so it was hard to stop—even when it was over something fucking stupid.

Needless to say, it wasn't long until we were climbing back into the car. Amazing how lack of conversation can make a meal pass quickly.

"Ready to go home?" I asked Lucy and Doc.

"Yeah," Lucy said.

I nodded, put the car into reverse, and backed from the parking lot.

Tabby kept quiet. This was turning out to be a fun day. I should have known not to be optimistic. Maybe one day I'd know better.

#

When we got home, Tabby went upstairs. Fine. She could be that way. I did have better crap to do than spend the day being all pissed off. Frankly, now she was the one being childish, though I wasn't stupid enough to tell her that.

I settled on the couch and watched TV with Lucy and Doc for a while. Nothing like mind-numbing entertainment to help me block out everything else. Maybe that's why Lucy liked watching TV so much. It was something to think about.

About an hour later, Tabby came downstairs. Her hair was wet. She sat on the couch beside me, grabbed my arm, and wrapped it around her. Maybe I was misjudging her again. I needed to stop assuming shit and just take in the facts.

"You okay?" I asked.

She snuggled into my chest. "Are you going to check on your trip tomorrow?"

I stroked her hair. "I'll power up the email tonight before I go to bed to see if I got a reply yet."

"Okay," she replied.

Lucy spun away from the TV and looked at us for a minute, then she went back to the TV.

"Everything okay, Lucy?" I asked.

She spun toward me. "Yeah. I'm just kind of bored."

She didn't admit that often, so I knew it was really bad. Time to try to fix it. "Anything you'd like to do?"

"Can we play a game?" she asked.

I smiled. "We can play any game you want."

She scooted closer on the floor. Tabby sat up.

"Any game?" Lucy asked.

From the mischievous look on her face, it was starting to seem like not so good of an idea.

"What do you have in mind?" Tabby asked her.

"We all can tell a story about something that scared us most. The one that is the scariest wins."

Okay, now I wasn't liking that at all. One, Lucy had made a deal with the Devil, even if it was loosely formed. Two, after dealing with the demonic this long, there was no way I was going to vocalize what scared me most. So I was caught. Did I tell her no and make her choose another game? Or did I lie? It was a conundrum.

Technically, I could lie about the thing that scared me most, but that wouldn't be fair to Lucy. Plus, I didn't lie lightly. It was one of my pet peeves.

"What if we choose whether to tell a scary story or a funny story?" Tabby asked.

Leave it to Tabby to step in. I wanted to hug her so hard.

"Okay," Lucy said.

I could tell she wasn't happy about it by how rigid her body went, but she didn't vocalize it. Maybe the poor kid was happy we agreed to play a game with her at all. Kind of sad. We needed to include Lucy more instead of having her tag along. This sudden parenthood business wasn't doing any of us any favors.

Doc cleared his throat. He'd been sitting in the chair on the other side of the sofa. Lucy and Tabby gaped at him. Kind of amazing he could get them to listen by clearing his throat. Me? I was chopped liver. I guessed you had to have a presence or something.

"I think there's a reason Miss Lucy wants to know what you're afraid of," he said.

Okay. I'd bite. It wasn't like I had anything better to do. "Okay, Lucy. Are you afraid of something?"

She nodded her head very slowly.

Sometimes getting information from her was like pulling the teeth out of a cat. "Okay. What are you afraid of?"

She adjusted and sat cross-legged. "I don't want to lose you."

It was really fucking sweet. I nodded at Tabby and looked back at Lucy. "We aren't going anywhere."

Lucy blinked. "What about when they decide where I'm going?"

There was no way I could see her either place unless I was dead too. And there wasn't anything I could do about that. It was out of my hands to make any decisions with that much importance behind them. I didn't want to lie to her, so I presented it in the only way I could. "Lucy, all we can do is the best we can. Who even knows when we'll have to worry about that. It might be a very long time."

"Okay," she said.

That was all it took. I thought it was going to be a hell of a lot harder than that. "Next time, just tell us if something is upsetting you, okay?"

She got up, ran over to me, and hugged me. I felt a slight bit of pressure this time. Maybe all the stress was getting to her too. I wished there was some way to make all of this a lot easier on everybody.

"I love you," she said.

I smiled into where her hair would be. "Love you too, kiddo."

#

Later that night, I peered at the iPad. Still no word from the Order. Hell, it was possible I wouldn't even be told until the last minute. With the way they'd done everything else, it wasn't out of the question. Yet, I wasn't too worried. It was on their dime after all. If it had been coming out of my pocket, I'd have been throwing a shit storm.

"What are you doing?" I asked Tabby. She seemed to be staring off into space.

"Thinking," she said.

Okay. Now I was interested. There was a lot of stuff I loved about Tabby and a big one was her brain. "About what?"

"Coffee."

Jesus Christ. Here I thought she was having some sort of major epiphany. I rolled my eyes. She had this unhealthy obsession with those crappuccino things. "You know those are bad for you, right?"

She looked at me and rolled her eyes. "Like bacon isn't?"

I laughed. "Hey, bacon is wonder-food."

She laughed back at me. "If you say so."

I shrugged. No way was I going to back down from that one. Meat had nutritional content. Besides, my father had eaten it every day of his life along with his morning oatmeal and his cholesterol was great.

"What are we going to do tomorrow?" Tabby asked.

I noticed how she was slyly trying to change the subject, but I chose not to call her on it. "Well, I think I'd better check the airline rules and crap so I can make sure I have everything I need, just in case they tell me at the last minute."

She flopped over on her side, facing me. "That's actually not a bad idea."

"Thank you so much for your faith in me." Sometimes I wondered if she thought I deserved to walk upright.

She smacked me on the arm. "That's not what I meant and you know it."

I grinned at her. "We still need to find a box or something for el rod-o."

"Any ideas?"

My brain bounced around about fourteen different items at once. Most of them from old movies I'd seen. "We could go old-school Mafia-style and get a violin case."

Tabby laughed. "You are interesting, you know that?"

I chuckled. "You have to admit, that would be interesting to go through security with. Here's a violin case. They put it through the x-ray machine and it is not a violin. So they open the case for further examination and–dum dum dum–find a stick!"

She shook her head. "What am I going to do with you?"

I shrugged. "Keep me around, I guess."

"Turn off the light," she said and reached toward me.

"Yes, ma'am."

#

The next morning, I didn't wake up until eleven. Part of me was happy for the sleep. The other part was afraid that I'd wasted too much of the day. I needed to start setting an alarm or something so I wouldn't waste so much damn time. Not having regular hours was fucking up my system. The old body needed more rest.

I got up out of bed, grabbed a quick shower, and then lumbered downstairs.

I heard nothing, which was odd. Usually, the TV was on and I could hear voices.

I peeked into the living room and the place was spotless. It was so wrong. I knew Tabby had to have been the one picking up. It sure as hell hadn't been my lazy ass. When I'd been by myself, the house had been lucky to get cleaned like once a week.

I went into the kitchen. The only evidence that anyone had been there was the dishcloth draped over the sink. It was wet. At least I knew they hadn't been gone that long.

I stared out the window.

Tabby was sitting cross-legged in the middle of the backyard. Her eyes were closed and she was in what I called her "meditation pose." Lucy was copying the same pose, but the only difference was that she was hovering in mid-air. Doc was leaning against a tree, watching them. Probably a good thing that very few people could see them. Otherwise, our street would become the haven for rash car crashes in the area. That, or misinformed Goths trying to connect with their inner supernatural. Were there even Goths anymore?

I opened the back door and walked over to Doc. The grass felt cool against my feet.

"How are they?" I asked him.

"Okay, for now. They decided you needed some rest."

I laughed. Maybe I'd been crankier than I realized. "They did, did they?"

Doc chuckled. "Mentioned something about you being entirely too grumpy."

Suddenly I felt something warm and furry land on my foot. I looked down and Isaac stared up at me. That damn cat.

"Guess this is your version of man time?" I asked him. He meowed back.

I looked back up at Tabby. Her eyes were still closed and it was almost as if the sunlight was bursting from the highlights in her hair. Damn, she was beautiful like that. With the sun glowing around her, I could almost see her special powers.

"You got yourself a mighty fine filly," Doc said.

I blushed. It was ridiculous, but I did. "Yeah. She's something else."

Doc grunted. "Better take good care of her."

"That's the plan."

Hell, I'd been doing better this time than I had before. We didn't fight as much. I wasn't sure if it was because I was older, or if I had mellowed out any. Or, maybe, Tabby and I just had the ability to deal with each other better.

"Jimmy!" Lucy floated across the yard toward me.

I waved. "Hey, there."

"Tabby's been teaching me to…to…medi-something."

I grinned. I couldn't help it. She was so damn cute sometimes. "I see."

"Remember what I said about rule #1?" Tabby asked. Her eyes were still closed. The corners of her mouth were quivering like she was trying not to laugh. I wondered how long it was going to be until she gave up.

Lucy stilled. "Be very, very quiet."

Tabby opened her eyes and grinned. "That's right."

I snickered. It was so great watching them interact. I could almost imagine Tabby actually being Lucy's mom.

Tabby put her finger in front of her lips, got up from the ground, and walked over to the rest of us.

"Finally decided to get up, did ya?" she asked me.

I laughed. "Guess so. I haven't slept that well in a while."

It was true. Maybe we all needed to talk about crap more instead of jumping in and trying to fix everything. And I knew I was one of the worst culprits of this, but we all needed to take a step back.

She nodded. "That's why I let you sleep."

I plucked a strand of her hair out of her face. "Want to grab some lunch, then hit the antique shops?"

"Sounds good to me."

"What are we going there for?" Lucy asked.

I glanced at her. "To find a protective case for the rod."

She stood on the ground and stopped hovering. "I promise I'll never touch it again."

Her lips were quivering, and I could almost see tears forming in her eyes.

Dammit. Either she was too sensitive, or I was a fucking idiot. Frankly, the jury was still out. I needed a manual or something. "No! We know you didn't mean it. It was an accident. We're just going to get a box for it so that doesn't happen to anyone else."

Her eyes were so large, looking at me like that. "Really?"

"Yup. Besides, we have to keep it safe, don't we?"

She nodded again.

I waved my hand toward the back door. "Okay, everybody inside. Let's get ready for the road trip."

They followed me like a herd of geese.

#

I was getting tired of driving, but hopefully, after this trip, I wouldn't be doing any traveling until I had to leave for Italy. If everyone wanted to do something, we'd do it closer to home. That, or I'd have Tabby drive, though I would imagine even she was getting tired of spending so much time in the car.

I don't know what possessed me to go to antique stores. One—who knew there were this many in southern West Virginia? I lived right on the border, right past Bluefield into Virginia. Not much was there on the Virginia side, so West Virginia it was. Two—everything was overpriced. And three—no one had any violin cases. I was ready to give up. I should have gone to the local music store, but I hadn't been thinking. And apparently, Tabby hadn't either. I wasn't blaming her or anything. It was just something we both normally would have caught. I think we both needed some more rest.

We were sitting in the car outside the last store. Doc and Lucy were in the back seat as usual. They'd stopped going into the stores after the third one. I didn't blame them. This sucked lime-green donkey balls. I didn't even mention the music store. Frankly, I didn't want to pay two hundred dollars for a good hard case.

I glanced at Tabby. "Got any other ideas?"

She leaned against the headrest. "Does it have to be a violin case?"

"No," I said. "Not really. Just would have been cool." Hell, at this point I would take something made out of duct tape. Well, not really, but I was tired.

"Well, all you want is something that can be secure, right?" Tabby asked.

"Yeah."

She stared out the window for a minute, and then suddenly turned to look at me. "What about a gun case?"

I paused. It was a pretty good idea. You could get them in various sizes. People would know whatever was inside was dangerous. Better yet, the hard cases locked.

"Any idea how much they cost?" I asked.

"Around a hundred dollars for a good one," Tabby said. She adjusted herself in the seat.

That was better than the violin. I put the car in gear. "Okay. Sporting goods store here we come."

I didn't go to one all the way down there. I drove us back home first. No sense in waiting to get rid of the long drive when we had sporting goods shops close to the house. It was Virginia, after all. Hunting was huge here.

Once I got there, Doc and Lucy stayed where they were. In fact, Tabby did too. That shocked me.

"You aren't coming in with me?" I asked Tabby.

She shook her head. "I'm feeling kind of tired."

Welcome to the club. But whatever. It wasn't like this wasn't something I could do myself. "Okay. I'll be back as quick as I can."

I closed the car door and walked into the store. It was your usual chain sporting-goods store. Helpful clerks standing here and there—mostly looking bored. I didn't bother taking any of them away from their cell phones. It took me a little bit to find the cases. But soon I found what we needed. It was a hard black case with silver metal clasps. It was designed to let you carry your gun broken down. It was a little wide, but the length left enough room on each end to keep the rod safe. Best of all, it was on sale.

The clerk didn't even look at me twice on the way out. She was more interested in staring at the clock. After a while, I could imagine how mind-numbing her job was. Made me thankful for the one I had—and that's kind of sad.

I walked out the store and held up the bag. I was about to show Tabby the prize when I realized she seemed a little too still. Oh, shit.

I ran over to the car and threw open the door. It was like everything alive had been sucked out of the car. Even the air inside it smelled stale. Doc gaped at me and tried to speak, but I couldn't hear a word he was saying. His mouth moved, but nothing was coming out. Not good.

Next thing I knew, everything went black. And the bag with the case in it? It was gone from my hand.

#

"You didn't think it would be so easy, did you?"

The voice was tenor. Not bad and not good. Just there. I opened my eyes. The place I was in felt wrong. Like it was a little too hot. The walls were a red color. I wasn't sure if this could get more cliché or not. I was starting to feel like Scrooge felt in that 1970's musical.

I looked around. Standing over me was the man himself. Big Red wore flowing black robes that seemed to undulate between lightness and darkness. Just one problem. The voice wasn't exactly how I remembered Big Red's to be. That was a big problem. Something was off.

"What did I think was going to be easy?" I asked him.

"Your debt."

Now I was confused. I had made no deal with him at all. In fact, I hadn't done anything. Plus, he'd said himself that Lucy didn't owe him anything, so this wasn't making any sense.

"I believe you are mistaken," I said.

He laughed. Heartily. "How easily you mortals forget."

I sat up on the floor. My head was spinning. This seemed like Big Red, but his mannerisms were different. His voice was different. Either the man I knew as Big Red was a hoax, or this one was. I suspected the latter.

"Who are you?" I asked.

"Now, why would I tell an exorcist my real name?" he said.

Big Red wouldn't have worried about it. When he'd been around me, he'd shown no fear at all. Well, that's because he was a bucky badass and didn't have anything to prove. This idiot…yeah.

"Well, that makes a lot of sense," I said. "You might as well drop the façade. I know you aren't who you are pretending to be."

It laughed. The face slowly changed shape. It almost undulated like something from an old werewolf movie. Soon, the transformation was complete.

His hair had turned white. I don't mean blond either; I mean white. His eyebrows and eyelashes were white too. His eyes had the odd red hue that many albinos possessed. His ears were pointed like an elf. No wonder he was such a pissant.

"You're one of his sons, aren't you?" I wasn't sure how I knew that, but it fit. Especially since the last dealing I'd had with one of the sons had been so great.

He smiled. His teeth were pointed, like his father's.

"What debt do I owe to you?" I knew that there wasn't any damn debt, but I needed to know what the hell he was claiming before I could counter it.

He walked over and sat on a great marble throne that randomly appeared out of nowhere. "You were young at the time, but any age will do."

"I still don't know what you are talking about," I said. Also, his ability to randomly have stuff be suddenly there made me think this wasn't the actual place per se. More like he'd taken my soul somewhere or he was somewhere in my own mind. No matter what, though, I didn't like it. I should have control over my own damn soul, thank you very much.

"The man who hurt your sister. You damned him to Hell, did you not?"

I stood up. Oh, hell, no. He was not taking this there. If there was one thing that was going to piss me off, it was trying to blame shit on what happened with my sister. He'd run into a fucking buzz saw. "First, how do you expect me to remember something I said when I was a kid? And second, plenty of people damn others to Hell and they don't owe a thing."

He leaned forward and sneered at me. "Those people are not markers."

"And third, preying on something that makes me rather emotional was a big fucking mistake." I was tired of this shit. "There is no contract because I didn't even know I was a marker. I had no way of knowing that. Besides, I didn't even have the power back then, so I suggest you try to fool someone else."

"Not knowing makes no difference. A pact is a pact."

"That makes no difference? I'll show you a difference in a minute." I was gearing up to beat his ass, but then I thought better of it. I didn't know if I even had any powers where we were, so it was better if I played it cool. "No, send me back or I will alert your father."

He smirked again. "And how do you expect to do that?"

I reached down and held out my mark. I began strumming my fingers over the top of it as if I were playing a harp. Shit, I didn't know if that did anything, but the important part was that neither did he.

"Dare me," I said.

In a flash, I was sitting on the concrete in the parking lot. Tabby was screaming at me. Doc and Lucy were hovering nearby. The bag with the case in it was sprawled at my feet.

I glared up at Tabby. "I'm okay now, but someone has a hell of a lot of questions to answer."

Tabby wiped her forehead with the back of her hand. "Who?"

"I need to invoke the Devil."

Chapter Eight

Witchy Woman

TABBY GOT ME loaded into the passenger seat of the car. Apparently, I had only been unconscious a few minutes, but it felt a lot longer than that. She was probably right that I wasn't fit to drive. I didn't argue with her either.

She loaded the case in the trunk and then sat in the driver's seat. The whole time, she didn't say one word.

"You can't be serious," she said finally. She put the car in gear and headed toward the house.

I didn't want to fight with her, but apparently I had no choice. "I am perfectly serious. No way in hell am I letting some bratty devil kid get the best of me."

"I agree with Tabby. This sure doesn't sound like a good idea," Lucy said.

I spun around in my seat and looked at her. I was going to get nowhere if I made the kid cry again.

"Have any better ideas?" I asked Tabby.

"You could research demons, you know? Try to find out who it is that way."

I glared at her. "How did you know this was what this was about?"

She slammed on the brakes and turned to me. Her eyes grew wide. "I don't care."

"Okay. Let's get the fuck home. We'll figure out what to do then." If she wasn't going to help me—fine. I would figure out how to do it myself.

"And I am blessing this car," she said a bit too loud.

"Okay."

#

To be honest, maybe carrying the meat suit in the car had something to do with it, but nothing bad had happened and it had been a couple of days. Not to mention that we were still using that car. For the car to be cursed, it was pretty fucking light. Hell, we'd even taken some road trips. Granted, this last one had ended in disaster, but not by way of an accident or anything.

As soon as we got home, Doc and Lucy got out of the car, and I went around to the back to get the case.

Tabby stepped up and put her hand on the back hatch of the car. "No, leave it. I'm blessing that fucker too."

"Okay…?" If she thought it would help, then by all means.

"You were handling it before you went down. That smells fishy to me," she said.

Okay. We were back to being concerned. All right. I held up my hands. "You're the expert."

I went inside and laid on the couch. It didn't take long before she was heading back outside. Why was I going to interrupt her now? It was better to let her get it done; then, we could talk about what we were going to do. That was if I felt like running it by her. She was overreacting in my opinion. But then maybe demons were a lot scarier to her than they were to me.

I didn't think that the car was haunted at all, but if blessing it made her feel better, so be it. Now, the gun case could possibly be compromised—possibly. But I had my doubts about that too. It was probably just the son having more powers than he needed. And going behind Daddy's back. I had my doubts that Big Red would operate that way. He'd snatch what he wanted, not mess around with all of this bullshit. He had better things to do.

I knew better. Demons, if they wanted to have dealings with you, they'd just come. They didn't need a special invitation like a vampire. All they had to do was get you open enough to notice them. And of course, I could see them, which meant they could see me too.

Whatever; maybe having the case for the rod blessed would make it less noticeable or something. It couldn't hurt.

#

By the time Tabby came back inside, it was me, Doc, and Lucy sitting side-by-side on the couch—waiting. I don't think any of us expected her to lose it like this. Though, in her defense, it wasn't every day I threatened to invoke the Devil either.

I had to wonder—was that a sin? It was possible. But the fact that it wasn't for a bad reason somehow made me think it wasn't. I wasn't exactly operating on church rules anyway. Whether that was a good or bad thing remained to be seen.

I shrugged it off. No sense in worrying about it. If I already had a mark on my head—however tremulous, I needed to know how to get rid of it. And the Devil needed to rein in his children. Unless driving me crazy was his plan all along. I knew God and the Devil were playing a giant game of chess. The question was what piece was I standing in for?

"I want you to know I don't like this," Tabby said as she came inside carrying the gun case.

Well, at least she wasn't going all batshit-crazy on my ass now. That was improvement. I still felt a little loopy, so when she caught me off guard, I almost fell off the couch.

She set the case on the floor and crouched down next to me. "You really aren't okay, are you?"

I rubbed my head. "This time? I guess not."

"Do you think the demon did something to you?" She was parting my hair with her fingers, almost as if checking for bugs.

I shrugged. It was hard to say. It could be the stress of being pulled down to Hell, then sent back that left me like that. Or him being in my head. I still wasn't entirely sure what had happened. All I knew was that I had a whopper of a headache.

"Well, we need to do something," Tabby said.

I nodded. "Which is why I need to invoke Big Red. He has the answers. It's his kids who keep fucking with me. I think it's time to stop it all."

Tabby sighed. "Are you even in any shape to do this?"

"Nope, but that never stopped me before." It was true. So far, bumbling through all of this shit worked out okay. I had no reason to think that this would be any different. It was my talent.

"Sadly, I know that's true." Tabby pulled her hand away from my head and stared at me.

"So," I said. "How does one invoke the Devil?"

Tabby shook her head. "I have no idea. That's not something I even ever wanted to touch."

I leaned on the sofa and scratched my head. I did what I always did when I was left with something I didn't know. I winged it. "Hey, you! Dude. Devil man. Guy that gave me that nifty present—or rather gave it to Tabby! I have some questions for you."

Tabby gaped at me in shock. "Jesus Christ, Jimmy. Warn me next time you decide to do that."

I laughed.

Suddenly, there was a thunderclap. Big Red stood in the middle of the living room dressed in another suit. His tie was dark green. I had to admit that he was a snazzy dresser. Isaac darted underneath the sofa. I didn't blame him.

"I come out of sheer curiosity, Mr. Holiday. I believe that was one of the most ridiculous incantations I have ever heard. And for your personal information, in order to invoke a demon, you need to use their true name." He smiled quickly and flashed his teeth at me.

"Well, it got you here, didn't it?" One thing I noticed about this time was that no one was frozen. Maybe it was because I instigated this visit. Or maybe he just didn't bother. It was hard to tell.

"What is it that you need?" he asked.

I sat up on the couch straighter. "A few questions answered."

The Devil motioned toward one of the dining room table chairs. It glided over to him and he sat. "Begin."

"One—is there a mark on my soul?"

The Devil laughed. "Of course there is. Everyone has them. What do you think allows God to measure how many sins you've performed in your lifetime?"

Okay, that wasn't exactly comforting. But I wasn't about to stop now. "Oh," I said. "What about marks that *mean* something? Have I ever made a contract with one of your sons?"

The Devil sighed. "Is Leviathan trying that business again? I do not have a son that is more power-hungry than he."

I blinked. If this was his opinion, he needed to pull rank and fast. I had a sneaking suspicion that he wanted this stuff to happen. It put him in contact with me after all.

"So he has no contract with me?" I asked.

The Devil shook his head. "If he did, you would have a mark bearing his name. You do not."

I knew the Devil was the father of lies, but that rang true to me, so I relaxed. Some.

"Okay," I said. "Did he do anything to me?"

The Devil glared at me. Then, he stood. "Do you mind if I try to find out?"

"Go ahead, but no funny business." Hell, if he could fix it and it wouldn't cost me anything, then why not?

He laughed and held his hands over me. Soon, I felt warmth, as if I were standing under a heat lamp spreading warmth throughout my body, and then it stopped. The Devil backed away.

"Do you feel extremely tired?" he asked.

I nodded. "Yeah. And a little dizzy."

He nodded. "A weaker person would be under his thrall. Consider yourself fortunate, Jimmy Holiday."

"He didn't do anything?" With the pain in my head, I was kind of surprised.

"Not because he didn't want to. He tried and he failed."

I guessed my hard head was good for something after all. "Will he try again?"

"Most certainly. But he will come at you from a different direction."

"Why not just stop him?" Tabby asked.

He turned to her and laughed. "Now, why would I do that? The world is ever so much more interesting when the lot of you are scrambling."

"Gee, thanks a lot." Though at least I knew I was appreciated.

Big Red winked at Tabby. Then he disappeared. Like usual.

Tabby rubbed her arms. "Do me a favor? Never ever do that again."

I glanced up at her. "I'll try not to."

#

"I miss pizza," Lucy said long about dinnertime. Every time I turned around, she broke my heart. The hits kept on coming. It was a good thing I was a stubborn bastard or I would have needed therapy by now.

She was in her usual spot in front of the TV. Poor kid. I wished we had hidden the rod or something, but that wasn't exactly something we could have prepared for. We still didn't even know what it did. Not really. It took Lucy touching the damn thing to figure it out.

"I know, Luce," I said. "If I could fix it, I would."

Doc started making a sound like he was clacking his teeth together. "I have an idea."

I raised an eyebrow at him. "Okay. I'll bite."

"Sometimes, I can smell very strong smells. It's almost as if they drift through what's left of me," he said.

"Okay…?" I had no idea where this was going, but whatever. If he knew of some way to make all this shit better, then by all means.

"Maybe if we put down some food and Lucy stands right over top of it. Maybe, just maybe, she could at least smell it." He scratched his head, and then smiled.

I didn't know if that would be crueler or not but, shit, it was worth a try. The kid needed something to hold onto. "What do you think, Lucy?"

She hopped up. "I would like to try."

"Okay. That's settled."

Isaac came from under the couch and rubbed against Doc's leg, or rather where Doc's leg should be. The man reached down and scratched the cat on the head for a minute.

If it weren't for the fact you could see Isaac's fur through the tips of Doc's fingers, it would have been kind of cute. But instead, it was weird as shit. That's what it was. I was still trying to get used to seeing all this crap on a regular basis, and I wasn't doing a very good job of it. Every time I tried to make a difference, something new would happen.

"I'll go let Tabby know what we're doing for dinner," I said.

Doc looked up. "Good idea."

#

I went upstairs to our bedroom. Tabby was sitting on the floor with the fleshing rod nearby, a bunch of her witchy stuff around it, and the case. I did love watching her work. It was amazing what she could make from a few herbs.

"What are you doing?" I asked.

"Warding the case so that only you and I can open it," she said.

I took a deep breath. Granted, it was a good idea. I was just uneasy about being one of the keepers for that damn thing. But I was stuck with it. Shit, even the Devil felt the thing was co-owned by Tabby and me. I was seriously fucked. Though, honestly, I couldn't think of anyone else better suited to keep the damn thing. Also, I had to wonder if the Devil had actually made it for Tabby for a reason other than safekeeping. That didn't make a lot of sense. Why make it at all, then? There had to be a reason. Still, no sense in rambling about it all now. I had more important stuff to attend to.

"Lucy wants pizza for dinner," I said. I didn't mean to blurt it out like that, but it could have been worse. Besides, pizza was the least of our worries.

Tabby tilted her head to the side like a dog.

Was I really being that weird lately? I didn't feel any stranger than usual. "Doc thinks he's come up with a way for her to at least smell it."

She leaned back a little and blinked. "Okay. That's fine by me."

"How much longer are you going to be witchy?"

She shrugged. "Not long. Why?"

"Want to go with me to pick up the pizza?" I thought we needed some alone time. Maybe it would give us a chance to calm down some.

"Why not? I'll be down when I'm finished."

I saluted her. "Okay. Take your time."

#

Doc and Lucy played a game with Isaac while I waited. Doc would make a light glow on the wall, Isaac would jump up and try to catch it, and Lucy would giggle. They did it over and over. It was amazing what types of things could entertain a kid for hours. I wished I had that ability now. The best I could do was read a story in a silly voice. The ability to make something glow was a much better superpower.

It felt good to hear her laugh. My mind drifted back to the girl at the fast food restaurant talking about how I was doing a good job—that Lucy was happy. My question was: compared to what? Lucy was going to be seven eventually, and even though her body couldn't show it, all the crap she has had to put up with had to weigh on her. She was never going to be a normal kid and she could partly thank me for that. The fact that I managed to give her some sort of home counted for something, but there was only so much I could not erase.

Tabby came downstairs and grabbed her purse. "You want to order or should I?"

"Go ahead. I didn't do it because I didn't know how long you were going to be," I said. I also didn't want to make a mistake and order the wrong type or something. Granted, the standard was pepperoni and sausage, but she might want something different.

"Okay." She pulled out her cell phone and headed into the kitchen. Lucy and Doc continued their game.

As I watched them, I thought about my sister and how the room always seemed to light up for me when she smiled. I knew that when she was happy, everything was going to be okay. I missed her. Candy had been my protector when I was little. She was the one I wanted to be, not Dad. Dad couldn't keep his head out of a bottle long enough for me to get to know the real him.

But Candy, she kept it all going. Had I known that asshole down the street was attacking her, I would have killed him myself. Leviathan's claim that I'd called to him and damned the man to Hell was false. The bastard had damned himself.

Though I did find it interesting that as many of the Devil's children were after me. Ares had wasted most of my time. Granted, I'd known him as Vespa for the most part, and still thought of him that way, but his father had been the one to expose his true motive. I still had to thank him for teaching me something though—don't get cocky. Investigate everything. And ask all the questions. I wasn't about to make those mistakes again. At least I learned something, which was probably counter-productive to what they had intended.

"You ready?" Tabby asked from the kitchen doorway.

"Yep." I glanced at Doc and Lucy. "You guys be good while we're gone."

Doc nodded. Lucy ignored me.

I let Tabby go first. I closed and locked the door behind us. I had a feeling that this was going to be an interesting evening.

#

Tabby insisted on driving. I think she was afraid I'd have a fit or something, but I was honestly starting to feel better. Maybe the Devil had done something to me to lessen the effects. It was possible. He didn't seem to want me taken over by one of his sons, and that's exactly what Leviathan had tried to do. He'd tried to possess me. Good thing I was as goofy as I was.

"Are you sure you're okay?" Tabby asked.

I patted her hand. "I'm fine, so okay per se. Takes more than a Devil visit to take me out."

She rolled her eyes. "Sometimes, that's what I'm afraid of."

"You think Lucy is going to be okay?" I asked. What happened to me didn't matter so much now that the crisis was over. Time to go back to thinking about what was important.

"Of course."

It kind of made me uncomfortable that she was so nonchalant about it. "How do you know?"

Tabby glanced at me from the corner of her eye. "Because she has to be. What good would it do her to be a mess forever? Even we don't know how long she'll be in limbo."

She did have a point, but Lucy was still six. She always would be. Spirits didn't age. "Yeah…Just been trying to figure out how to make it better for her."

Tabby pulled into the parking lot of the pizza place. It was this little mom and pop shop that would even put prosciutto on it if you asked for it. It cost a lot extra, though, so we usually skipped that part.

"That's what we're doing right now," Tabby said.

"It seems like so little." And it was. It was a fucking pizza for Christ's sake, and that was all we were doing to make a kid happy. It verged on ridiculous.

She sighed. "To us, maybe, but to her, we're giving her everything we have the ability to give. For a child that's more than enough."

Sometimes she was so damn smart. I needed to stop overthinking things.

"Stay here," she said and started crawling out of the car.

"Come on; I can at least pay for pizza." I was starting to feel a little worthless.

She finished getting out and leaned into the car to look at me. "Nope. Jimmy, let me take care of you for once."

I sighed. "Oh, all right."

She grinned and closed the door.

This was going to be a lot harder than I thought it would be.

#

Back at home, Tabby did at least let me carry the pies into the house. I guessed I'd proven to her that I wasn't going to fall down every two seconds. I let her open the door for me and I walked inside.

Doc and Lucy were back to watching TV. I needed to come up with some stuff that would get Lucy away from the TV. It wasn't healthy.

"Get the plates," I told Tabby as she passed me. She saluted.

"Smartass," I said.

I walked into the living room and set the pizzas on the floor. Lucy crawled over near the pies. The TV was on yet another bad horror film.

Doc floated down from his perch on the recliner.

Tabby came in and sat on the floor, plates in hand. I lumbered to the floor and felt my knee pop. I was getting too old for this. If I kept this up, I could see myself in a wheelchair doing exorcisms and swatting at demons with my cane. I was destined to be crotchety.

I opened the box and put a slice on a paper plate Tabby handed me. Then, I set it on the floor in front of Lucy. This was the moment of truth.

"Okay, kid. Give it a try," I said. It was going to be weird as shit, but whatever. Weird had been the norm around here for a long time.

She stood up and positioned herself right overtop the plate. At first, she seemed kind of confused. Then, suddenly, her eyes lit up with light. "I can smell it!"

Tabby, Doc, and I all clapped. Ectoplasmic tears of joy ran down Lucy's face.

"Congratulations, kid," I said. It was bizarre, but who cared.

She darted across and grabbed me in a huge hug. I could feel her denser now. More real. It was nice to feel that again. I'd missed it.

"Thank you, Jimmy," she said.

I smiled. "You're welcome, Lucy."

Thank heaven for small favors.

Chapter Nine

Fly Like a Bird

WHEN WE WENT upstairs to bed, the first thing I did was turn on the iPad. I'd almost gotten out of the habit of checking it and that was probably a bad thing. Especially since there was a note waiting for me. Whoops.

Mr. Holiday,

Please review the following visa forms to make sure that they are correct. We will be making all reservations for you. Relax.

Fr. Martin

At least, it was an answer this time. Maybe they were getting used to me and my way of doing stuff. Although this was also a new guy. I was starting to wonder if their secretarial staff cycled around that much or if I was being considered a "special snowflake."

"Tabby?" I asked.

She popped her head from the bathroom door. "What?"

"Do you have any experience with visa forms?" It was something out of my league. I'd never done anything outside of the country besides vacation.

"Credit cards?" she asked.

"No, immigration stuff." I sighed. Nothing like paperwork to put a damper on things. I'd known it was coming, but I'd been avoiding thinking about it like the plague. And I'd been kind of preoccupied.

She stepped out of the bathroom. "No, not really. Why?"

"The Order sent the forms that I have to have filed to stay in Italy for the length of the course."

She shrugged. "Oh. Well, print them out and we'll find someone to look at them tomorrow."

Leave it to her to simplify everything and make it seem manageable. I needed to calm the fuck down. "Good idea."

I forwarded the email to my usual address. I had no way of accessing my Order email any way except on the iPad, and since I'd never figured out how to link my tablet up to the printer, emailing the file was a lot easier. And I had to admit, I was sort of lazy. It was easier to climb the stairs than fuck with networking.

I got up, ran downstairs, and started booting up my laptop. The spirits were in their usual spots: Doc in the chair and Lucy on the floor in front of the TV.

"Everything all right?" Doc asked.

"Yep. Got some paper from the Order I gotta print out," I said.

He grunted and went back to watching TV. Lucy was focused on some old 1980's sitcom. I could handle that a lot better than her unhealthy obsession with scary movies. It wasn't that I had a thing against scary movies, or even against kids watching them. It was that she'd lived through enough horror, so why add to it? But if she liked them, and wasn't afraid of them, there wasn't much else for me to do. Maybe she was just a weird kid. Hell, I certainly wasn't anything you could call normal.

I got the files printed and flipped everything off. Then I went back upstairs.

Tabby was in bed, flipping through a magazine. She glanced up when I entered the room.

"That could have waited until tomorrow, you know," she said.

I nodded. "Technically, yes. But if I didn't get it done, I would drive myself crazy thinking about it all night."

She shook her head. "You really are an odd duck."

I laughed. "And you're normal?"

She smacked me with her magazine. "Normaler than you."

I crawled into bed, put my hands behind my head, and lay down. "It's weird how fast your life can change."

Tabby stared at me. "If we'd be honest, we were destined for this, though."

I couldn't deny that. My life was steamrolling ahead and I wasn't sure when it was going to stop. "Ever think about what it would have been like if we'd never split up the first time?"

She put down her magazine and glanced toward me. "We probably would hate each other."

Thinking back to how it was…she was right. I hadn't been willing to believe in her, not her religion anyway. Now, I had a hell of a lot more open mind. Encountering the demonic had a tendency to do that.

I leaned over and switched off the lamp on my side of the bed.

"It's only ten," Tabby said.

"Go ahead and stay up. I'm tired."

I felt her adjust in the bed. "Are you sure you're okay?"

I nodded. "Yes. I'm just tired. Can I go to sleep?"

She sighed. "Go ahead."

#

I almost expected to have a weird sort of dream, but there were none. I got up and looked at my cell phone. It was after seven. At least I hadn't slept the day away. I needed to do something about my stress level though. And, well, the crap my brain picked to worry about wasn't helping either.

I glanced over and Tabby was still snoring softly. No sense in waking her up. She deserved to sleep in once in a while. Especially with my crazy ass driving her up the wall.

I crept out of bed and made my way downstairs.

Lucy was perched at the dining room table. Isaac sat near the doorway to the kitchen. I was honestly surprised that she wasn't watching TV. I didn't know where Doc had wandered off to.

"Where's Doc?" I asked.

"When he heard you get up, he said he had to go take care of something," she said.

I shrugged. It wasn't like I owned Doc or anything. He was with us because he wanted to be, not because I had any hold on him. Still, I felt a little uneasy not knowing what all the man was involved in, even thought I was probably better off not knowing. He'd promised to keep an eye on Lucy for me. Granted, I hadn't been awake all that long, but I would have rather he waited until I was downstairs. Oh well.

"Lucy, what do you want to do today?" I asked.

She shrugged. "Maybe just have a normal day."

I plopped down beside her. One thing was sure: she was going to have to come with me to Italy. I wasn't sure if this meant Doc, too, but I had a feeling I could only be away from her for so long before the bad stuff happened. If that was worse than what happened when I was with her, then I didn't know what I would do. She would have to get used to hanging out with me again.

"How do you feel about going away with me?" I asked.

Her eyes got big. "Go where?"

"The Order wants me to take exorcist classes. And the only school is in Italy." I watched her expression very closely. She didn't seem upset or anything.

"Is Tabby coming?" she asked.

"No." I shook my head. "She will be staying here."

Lucy's face kind of drooped. Damn. Had I thought about it earlier, I might have been able to do something, but I never would have guessed that Tabby staying home would be a problem.

"Can Doc come?" she asked. Her face was a little brighter.

I shrugged. "I don't know. You'd have to ask him."

It was true. I had no idea if his ghost was somehow tied to somewhere and had a certain reach or not. I knew he'd said something about recharging once in a while, but I wasn't entirely sure if he meant what I thought he did. I had read a couple of ghost-hunting books where the entities followed the people, but I couldn't remember if any moved that far away and still had experiences. It was one more thing to add to the list of stuff I needed to research. Good thing that, as far as I knew, I'd be a marker for life. So there should be plenty of time for research.

"Jimmy?" Tabby asked from upstairs.

"Yeah?"

"Want to go out for breakfast?"

"Sure." I was getting tired of eating out, but I didn't feel like cooking either. So laziness won.

Lucy crawled off the chair and sat in front of the TV.

I went upstairs to grab a shower. I still didn't know how Lucy felt about the whole thing. She hadn't told me. But then, I hadn't given her the chance, either. I was going to have to be more thoughtful when it came to her.

#

"You got everything?" Tabby asked next to the front door. Doc still hadn't returned. Lucy was standing next to Tabby.

"I think so," I said. Surely we could make it to breakfast and back without any bad shit happening. At least I hoped it would be that way. I needed a spiritual bodyguard.

"Even your papers?"

"Oh, shit." I swear, I was starting to wonder how I even functioned when Tabby wasn't around. I probably was more alert because it was always my own ass in a sling.

I went over to the desk, grabbed them, and shoved them in a folder. "Now, can we go?"

My stomach was starting to make enough noise that I thought it was going to eat itself. The pull of food was strong.

Tabby opened the door and we all piled into the car.

"Where do you want to get breakfast?" I asked.

"IHOP," Tabby said.

I was surprised she let me behind the wheel, but I guessed I must have seemed normal enough now. "What do you want, Lucy?"

"I can have something in the restaurant?" she asked.

I shrugged. "I don't see why not. Not many people can see you anyway. You tell me what you want and I'll order it."

"Yay!" She was grinning so wide I thought her mouth might split.

Tabby glanced over at me and smiled. I nodded back. Maybe I wasn't such a bad parent after all.

#

We didn't make it back to the house until around noon. We'd taken my papers over to the university to talk to their travel coordinator. She said everything was in order. I was glad to have at least that part done. Now, all I had to do was reply to the email. It was nice to have something simple work out. All it had taken me was a little time.

As soon as I got close to the front door, I knew something was wrong. I heard Isaac yowling. My brain went to the idea that some sort of demon was in our house again. Or someone was trying to hurt him, like what happened in Arizona. I looked around for a weapon, but there was nothing. I was going to have to use my fists and hope for the best.

I threw open the door and saw nothing. I heard Isaac's yowling, but I couldn't see him. That wasn't good.

"Oh, Jesus Christ." Tabby ran past me and up the stairs. At the top, there was a little bit of railing where the steps angled around. Isaac had his head stuck between the railing and the wall.

I let loose the breath I'd been holding. It was sad that I was relieved that his distress was from a normal problem. I still felt sorry for him, but the lack of the supernatural was a welcome surprise.

"Dammit," Tabby said. She reached for Isaac's head and he tried to bite her.

"A little help would be nice," she called down the stairs.

I dropped the keys onto the table and walked up. Time for me to come to the rescue. I hoped I was up to the challenge.

He was wedged all right. "How in the hell did you do this?" I asked him.

He made an angry chirp at me.

"He was chasing a cricket earlier," Doc said.

I looked up. He walked toward me from the room that was going to be Lucy's. Shame he couldn't have prevented the damn cat from doing something this stupid, but oh well.

I turned my attention back to Isaac. "Okay. Let me help you."

Isaac stilled.

At least he listened. I gently took hold of his head. "Now, move with my hands. Don't struggle." I twisted his head sideways and pushed it through. Isaac shook himself and sauntered off. He didn't even stop to thank me. Cats.

"I swear, that cat," Tabby said.

"What are you talking about? I thought we had another demon." There was a pause where laughter would normally be inserted, but neither one of us felt like laughing. Things were getting way too strained. We went back downstairs.

"Is Isaac okay?" Lucy asked. She was still in her usual spot.

"Yep. Just got himself caught in the railing," I said.

Lucy shook her head. Doc came down the stairs and Lucy squealed. Again, I had to remind myself how old she was, but damn. I was not used to squeals in my house.

"Doc, where did you go, if you don't mind me asking?" I asked.

"Had to recharge. Nothing interesting," he replied.

I didn't poke further. I had a feeling that there was more to it than that. I imagined part of it he didn't want Lucy to know. The other part, well, it technically wasn't any of my business. Perhaps, in the future, he'd let me in on his secret. But it seemed awfully quick for him to go and come back if he really was recharging.

"Don't you have an email to write?" Tabby asked.

Good thing she was keeping me on schedule or I would have been totally screwed. "Yeah. Right."

I left them all to whatever it was they were going to do, went upstairs, and flipped on the iPad. A bright red alert popped up. I tapped on it and a video played. A video of me dumping Lucy's skin at Walmart. Fuck. Suddenly, I was staring at another priest. This dude had gray hair.

"So, Mr. Holiday," he said. "What is this?"

I didn't even want to think about how long he'd been sitting there, waiting for me to turn the thing on. It was not a good feeling. My asshole was so tight I didn't think anyone could even drive a nail into it.

"I was getting rid of trash," I said. Might as well call it that. It was better than saying it was the skin sack from the spirit of a six-year-old.

"Soupy, foul-smelling, organic matter is not normal trash," he said.

I shrugged. There wasn't a damn thing I could say to counter that. He was right. "No, it's not."

"Mind explaining what the substance was in the bag?" he asked.

Evidently, the skin melted into something else. What, I was not sure exactly. It was a boon for me. I could keep Lucy safe. No sense in giving away more information than needed.

"Gosh. Um. Ectoplasm would be part of it," I said. "Not sure what else. All I know is that it was gross."

The priest nodded. "And how did you come by it?"

That was the tricky part. I couldn't very well lie to the man. It would be so wrong on so many levels. "It was in my house. My living room to be exact. Had to rent a rug doctor to get the rest of it out of the carpet."

I knew he could look and see that was true. My own conscience felt better because I didn't bullshit him. Leaving out stuff wasn't lying. At least in my book.

"You are very lucky that humans do not normally know what ectoplasm is made of. From the stench, they thought you'd thrown away a body." Then he chuckled.

I felt so damn uncomfortable. "Is that all you wanted to know?"

"Yes, that will about cover it. Allow me to introduce myself. I am Father Nicholas Martin, your assigned adviser."

Apparently, they'd passed the buck enough that he'd gotten stuck with the problem case. I kind of felt sorry for him. "Nice to meet you, Father. Oh, and I got those visa papers looked at. Seems fine to me."

He nodded. "Good. I'll have them sent to the proper channels. One more thing, Mr. Holiday."

"Yes?"

"Remember–we're always watching."

The screen blinked out. Great. It's hard to tell what all they had footage of. Probably a lot of me talking to myself. They could look at that as much as they wanted. Hell, I'd talked to myself long before becoming an exorcist. Still, though, I didn't like being told how extensively they were following my every move. But I did now have complete proof that they were not filming inside the house. If they had that, I would have been shown it. Still though.

"Motherfuck."

I should have known that Big Brother was watching, but I'd allowed myself to be lulled into a false sense of security. I needed to reexamine how I felt about all of this next time. Being a marker was hard enough without all of this going on as well. Besides, what business was it of theirs what I did in my private time?

I put the device away and went back downstairs. My mood was betrayed by my look because Tabby started in right away.

"What's wrong?" she asked.

I sighed. No sense in hiding it now. "Let's just say that we weren't as discreet as we thought we were and leave it at that."

"Eek. Are we in trouble?" Her eyes grew wide.

I shook my head. "No, we're both lucky I am full of bullshit."

She leaned back on the sofa. "Now what?"

"We relax. The guy that read me the riot act was apparently my 'case worker.' So he's the dude I had to tell about the visa anyway." I sat down next to her on the couch.

"I swear. Every time we relax, something happens," Tabby said.

She had a good point. We needed to change the way we did stuff.

"You know how to solve that, right?" I asked.

"How?"

"We never relax."

Chapter Ten

Give It to Me

WITH THE FEELING that I was being watched hovering over me, I kept looking over my shoulder, almost expecting a priest to be there shaking his finger at me. Of course, no one was there. It was completely psychosomatic, but I couldn't help it. I probably should have been more worried about the demons…I wasn't.

"I need to do something to get my mind off all of this," I said.

Tabby tossed me the remote. "Watch a movie?"

I threw myself back into the sofa. "Like what?"

"I know! I know!" Lucy jumped up.

Her excitement had me worried. If this were a normal kid, we'd be watching pink princesses or something. But this was Lucy. I'd better prepare for something monstrous. "Okay, Lucy. What movie?"

"On the pay-for channel thing, there's a new movie," she said.

I could almost imagine what type of movie it would be. Something bloody and gory and completely inappropriate. I wasn't complaining. It kind of fit my mood. "What movie?"

"Turn on the thing and I'll tell you. The name is too big. I can't remember it." She stared at the TV screen.

"Okay." I grabbed the remote off the coffee table and hit the button for the pay stuff. I entered the movie section.

"Click on the scary movies," Lucy said.

I rolled my eyes. I knew it. Maybe seeing the fake stuff comforted her. I entered the horror section. It was my fault anyway. If I wanted to watch something else, I should have picked it.

"I think it starts with an 'e.'"

I followed Lucy's directions and started scrolling.

Tabby was watching me, and every so often, she would smile. I wasn't sure what amused her more, Lucy or me dealing with Lucy. Probably both.

"Stop," Lucy said.

I obliged. "This one?"

It was highlighting a movie called, "The Exorcism of Annelise." Great.

"Are you sure you want to watch this?" I asked her.

She nodded.

I glanced at Tabby. "What do you think?"

Tabby spoke to Lucy. "Do you find any of these movies scary?"

Lucy shook her head.

Tabby turned to me and shrugged.

With that resounding endorsement, I bought the movie. So much for getting my mind off all of this shit. It wasn't going to do a thing to stop me from thinking about everything. I already knew how the movie ended. Or a close approximation at least.

Annelise Michel was a young girl from a farming community in Germany. Her folks were devout Catholics. When they didn't believe their daughter's problem was epilepsy, they brought in the local priest who pronounced her possessed. Her bout of exorcism lasted for several years until she died.

I couldn't help but think about the similarities between her and Lucy. Part of me was now afraid that the authorities were crazy. Annelise could have been possessed. And maybe the priests who were working with her were not strong enough.

It was something to ask about at the Vatican school.

I turned my attention back to Lucy. She was enthralled. I watched the movie for a while, but there was so much wrong with it or flat-out stupid that I ended up watching Lucy instead. Sometimes, she was captivated. Other times, she smiled or rolled her eyes. Not once did she seem afraid. It was something, at least.

After the movie was over, I said, "What did you think of the movie?"

"It was okay. Some of it was really silly."

I nodded. "Why do you like scary movies so much?"

She shrugged. "They're fun. And I keep hoping someone will get it right."

"Wouldn't that scare you?" I would have thought there would be some sort of residual PTSD or something.

She shrugged again. "I don't know."

I motioned for her to go on her way and sunk into the sofa. Did I believe that her watching scary movies would set her up for possession again? No. If it were that simple, there would be millions of people walking around possessed. It still left me uneasy. Her parents had never mentioned her love of scary stories. All they talked about was the cat they'd had and how much Lucy had loved it. Before she killed it.

I feared her being possessed had changed her in a way no one suspected. Technically, I could have asked her. But there was something telling me not to and I wasn't sure what it was.

The next morning, I came downstairs about five. I needed some alone time, or at least as alone as I could get, and that meant Lucy watching TV with Doc while Tabby slept. No sense in driving anyone crazy but myself.

I'd made a decision right before going to sleep. I was going to try to find Will, Lucy's dad. If I had a kid, and she died yet was still around in some way, I'd want to know about it. I hoped he wouldn't want to kill me. It felt like the right thing to do. I didn't care if I got in trouble or not. It was about time I was proactive about something.

I switched on my laptop and typed Will Andersen into the search engine. I didn't know why I had stopped at social media listings before, except that I knew that while part of Lucy was alive, he'd want nothing to do with me. The search engine came up with a good number of listings for Will. But the latest thing I could find was from 2011. It was like he'd dropped off the face of the Earth.

Just for fun, I pulled my cell phone out of my pocket and searched there too. It was possible they'd added something to my computer, but my phone would be harder. Granted it'd searched before, but it had been in the middle of Arizona, and I could have missed something.

I typed his name into the phone and got the same results.

"What are they, the holy witness protection program?" I was tempted to throw something. If this kept up, I was going to need a heavy punching bag. I needed something to relieve my tension.

"What?" Lucy asked from the other side of the room.

I shook my head. "Never mind."

"Okay."

I didn't like this. Not at all. I couldn't imagine Will abandoning his entire life, his career. His ego had been too big for that. I had a big feeling that the Order had done something to him. The question was what.

Still, I was left with nothing. For now, I'd file it all away for the future. I was going to get some answers. Even if I had to force them out of somebody.

#

By the time Tabby came downstairs, I had mopped the kitchen floor and dusted and vacuumed the living room. It was amazing what all I could get done when I was annoyed. I probably needed to get annoyed more often…well that or be less lazy, but whatever.

"To what do I owe the extra help?" Tabby asked.

I chuckled and put the sweeper away in the closet. "I couldn't sleep and after what I found this morning, I couldn't sit still."

"Explain?" She sat at the dining room table.

"There is nothing online about Will at all past 2011."

She shrugged. "I thought you researched that before."

"Sort of. But it isn't right. There wasn't even an obituary for Lucy."

Tabby's eyes grew wide then. "That is a little odd, but maybe they're going to wait a while. That happens sometimes."

I sat beside her. "Do you really think Will could abandon all of his accolades?"

She drummed her fingers against her knee. "Okay. I'll admit that seems a little fishy."

"I just want to know what's going on." I didn't care about the Order's need-to-know basis. I needed to know.

She paused for a minute. "You know, before this, we had never heard of the markers or the Order."

"True." That in and of itself wasn't all that bothersome—mostly because anything supernatural was kind of hidden. I was used to how the church worked.

"There's one thing that would make Will abandon everything," Tabby said as she set a glass for me to dry.

"And what's that?" I asked.

"Money."

It was possible, but it didn't feel right somehow. "I'm not sure I'd buy that."

"Think about it. All of their money was tied up in that damn house. Will had nothing. Everything belonged to Tor."

The more I thought about it, the more it seemed probable. "You know, you have a point."

"Ever try searching about Blackmoor?"

I froze. Then I checked my phone again. "Not since we left it behind."

I entered Blackmoor into the search engine and waited. After a little bit, I knew why. "Hey, Tabby. Look at this."

It was an article dated roughly around the time we left for Arizona. "Fire Demolishes Historic Home."

"Maybe he did buy his freedom," I said.

"Though it's kind of nice to know that damned place is gone," she said.

"Well, as long as someone doesn't build on the site." I had visions of countless ghost movies rolling through my head.

Tabby swatted me on the arm. "You had to say that, didn't you?"

"Well, it's true. That place had enough bad for forty houses, let alone one." Hell, all it took in *Poltergeist* was a graveyard that hadn't been moved. Blackmoor had way more bad mojo.

"What do we do?" Tabby asked.

"Nothing. There isn't anything we can do. It's yet another place where the supernatural can get in."

She patted my shoulder. "Still sucks."

"Hey, there's always the chance that the fire cleansed the ground and got rid of the badness." I was trying for hopeful, but I knew it didn't even come close.

"Gotta love that wishful thinking."

#

"Why do you worry so much?" Lucy asked.

I glanced up from the book about the Centralia Mine Fire I'd been reading. I'd figured it would be better for me to read about something that had nothing to do with what was happening now. It wasn't working very well. "I just do. Tabby always said I think too much."

Centralia was the loose basis for the old video game and movie, "Silent Hill." Basically, the town burned up and the government allowed it because it was cheaper to cause cancer and screw the residents than to fix it and not give the government officials raises. While nothing supernatural happened there, plenty of real-life devastation occurred.

"Oh," Lucy said. "Doc thought it was something else."

I glanced at Doc. He seemed a bit tired, which wasn't normal for a ghost. It was yet more proof that he hadn't been truthful with me. Still, I wasn't sure if I had the right to know what he was doing every waking minute. If he wanted to tell me, he would.

"What's up, Doc?" I asked.

"I think you have to worry in order to keep everything together," he said.

"That's possible." I didn't think I'd ever made it two weeks without worrying about something.

"But that's not what I wanted to talk about." He adjusted his hat in his hands.

I nodded and put my book on the coffee table. "I thought not."

"I figured I might go home once you and Lucy head off," he said.

"Any reason why?"

"I forgot how much energy a kid takes. Wouldn't hurt to fully recharge. What I've been doing has been in fits and starts, and it truly isn't enough. Besides, I can't go across the pond."

"And your 'recharge' was what exactly?" I asked.

"Something you need not trouble with. But the fact now remains that I have to do it whether I like it or not."

Lucy was staring at him. "Why?"

He crouched down in front of her. "You are different, Lucy. Your soul is tied to a human. That means you can go where he goes. I'm tied to a place. And while I've gotten strong enough I can wander, there's only so far I can go."

Lucy sighed. "Will I ever see you again?"

Doc laughed. "Course. I'll be able to sense when you're close enough. Then I'll come back."

She turned to me. "How long are we going to be gone?"

I sighed. "Over six weeks."

I knew it was a while, but it couldn't be helped.

"But that's like forever."

I forced myself not to laugh. Six weeks was a while, but it wasn't that bad. I'd forgotten how kids view time. They had no ability to see how fast it truly traveled. "Look at it this way: after this, I shouldn't have to go there again."

She frowned. "I hope not."

"Come. Let's go play a game," Doc said and took her by the shoulder. They went upstairs, I supposed to the room that Tabby was making Lucy's.

I hoped I hadn't lied to the kid. Some days, I couldn't do a damn thing right.

#

"What are you brooding about?" Tabby asked that night in bed.

"Everything." I needed for my brain to shut down for a while, but it wouldn't comply. I needed a "sleep" button.

"I take it," Tabby said.

"It's this whole thing sucks. First, Lucy dies here, and then her body dies. Now Doc's leaving and I can't find her parents." I needed to figure out a way to let myself off the hook when shit didn't work out, but I couldn't help it. It was kind of like if I thought it should happen and I failed at getting it done, then all I'd done was waste everyone's time.

"But all of that is out of your control." Tabby untucked the blanket from around her legs.

I punched my pillow. "Doesn't seem like it."

Tabby scooted closer. "Keep in mind that if you were doing a bad job, Lucy wouldn't like you."

Isaac hopped up on the bed and took the space between Tabby and me.

"Guess with him the jury's still out," I said.

Isaac meowed.

Tabby laughed. "Tomorrow, I don't want you leaving this bed until I'm ready to get up."

"And when is that?"

"You and lack of sleep doesn't mix. If you don't start resting, you're going to drive yourself crazier than you already are." She pushed my head down onto my pillow.

"Okay. I'll stay in bed," I said.

"Besides, there might be a very good reason for you to stay in bed," she said and wiggled her eyebrows.

I playfully bopped her on the nose. "You are something, you know that?"

She grinned. "Yup."

Chapter Eleven

One Thing

I DIDN'T HAVE to worry about beating her out of bed. I slept until half-past ten. I crawled out of bed and popped my back. Then, I shuffled downstairs. One of these days, I was going to fall down the stairs with all of my shuffling, but oh well.

I heard them before I saw them.

"Can we, please?" I heard Lucy ask.

"For the umpteenth time, let's wait for Jimmy," Tabby said.

I chuckled and stepped into the living room.

"Wait for me for what?" I asked.

"I made the mistake of mentioning to Doc that Blackmoor had burned down," Tabby said.

I blinked. "Why?"

"Because Lucy was talking about it and I remembered hearing something about it somewhere. And now, Lucy wants to go check it out."

The giant hole in my stomach made its presence known again. Kill me now. This was not what I wanted to wake up to. "I don't think that's a very good idea."

Lucy blinked. "Why not?"

I crouched down in front of her. "Because I'm afraid too. I don't know what will happen, and I'd rather not risk losing you."

"I don't think that would happen," she said.

I fought not to roll my eyes. Kids always thought the bad stuff would never happen to them…again.

"Why don't we compromise?" Tabby said. "We could have Doc go and make sure everything's okay."

I watched Tabby. While I liked that idea a lot better than me taking

Lucy, I worried about what would happen when a powerful spirit like Doc got around that place. Would it absorb him or would it change him? I didn't want to find out.

"Where is this place?" Doc asked.

"Down in Sorrow's Point, Virginia. Blackmoor was the huge mansion house of the coal baron who lived there," Tabby said.

He nodded.

I gritted my teeth together and rubbed my arms. I still didn't even like to think about that place. "Be careful."

Doc tipped his hat to me. "Always am."

Then, he disappeared.

"What are we going to do if this turns out to be a giant epic fail?" I asked. Maybe I'd seen too many horror films too, but my brain was full of evil demigods trying to take over the world. And, well, if it was possible for a spirit to absorb another spirit, we were all seriously fucked.

Tabby shrugged. "We'll deal with it like we always do."

Lucy shut off the TV.

Shit. I knew the kid wanted some connection to home, but that was one place I wished I could forget. Hell, I wished she would forget it. Maybe I was being too pessimistic.

Suddenly, my phone chimed. I picked it from my pocket and glanced at it. It said I had email, but the notification wasn't my usual email notification. They'd been in my phone too now. The notice contained an icon that looked suspiciously like my mark.

"I'll be back," I said.

"What's wrong?" Tabby asked.

No sense in hiding it. "The Order."

I ran upstairs and powered up the iPad. The email notification popped up immediately and I opened my inbox. It was my travel itinerary. I took a deep breath.

Mr. Holiday,

I hope to find you well. Attached is your travel itinerary, flight information, and hotel reservation. Please inform us if something does not meet your expectations. I'll look forward to meeting you—in person this time.

Fr. Martin

I was leaving in two weeks. This was actually happening. Holy shit. I took the tablet with me and ran back downstairs. I needed to get this crap printed as soon as possible.

"What's up?" Tabby asked.

"Got my deets."

She raised an eyebrow at me.

I laughed. "I'm leaving for Italy in two weeks."

Tabby grunted. "Better find that passport."

I grinned at her. "I'm on it."

#

Finding it wasn't as easy as I thought it was going to be. I tore my desk apart, dug through my bookcases, and even cleaned my kitchen junk drawer. It was that bad. I checked my personal safe just in case I put it there. But I had to dig that out of the closet first, and it was covered in dust. Needless to say, the passport was not in the safe.

I started digging through my desk again. I knew if I didn't find it, I'd have to file an emergency rush or something like that, and then hope it would turn up in time. After rooting around in the drawer, I grabbed a plain white envelope. My passport was inside. I glanced around the room. It looked like a tornado had passed through it.

"You know you are going to clean this up, right?" Tabby asked.

I raised up and shuffled the envelope in my hands. "I hadn't actually thought that far ahead, to be honest."

She laughed. "Give me that."

She motioned for me to hand her my passport. I did.

"Before you put it somewhere stupid, I'm making you a trip folder," she said.

I snorted. "You act like I couldn't function when you weren't around."

She stopped. "Well, I didn't mean it like that."

I took a deep breath. "Let's just start over. It isn't going to do any of us any good to get into a fight." I could so see this becoming a huge thing that could result in something neither of us wanted. It was a good thing I wasn't quite as hot-headed as usual.

"Okay," she said. She quietly walked from the room.

"You look like you need a hug," Lucy said.

I smiled at her. "I'd love one."

She wrapped her arms around me as best she could. I could feel her cold energy wash over me. It felt good in an odd sort of way. At least somebody loved me.

"You're a good kid, you know that?" I asked.

She stepped back and grinned. "Wanna see what I taught Isaac to do?"

"I'd love to."

#

At least it wasn't something freaky. It looked like she'd had Tabby draw a piano keyboard. Interesting. Then she pointed to it and Isaac walked over and sat down.

He meowed.

I was reminded of the funny pet tricks that happened on late night TV.

"Now, Isaac," Lucy said.

The cat glared at her. And if I hadn't been there myself, I wouldn't have believed it.

He chirped out, "Fuck you."

I lost it. What the hell it had to do with a piano, I had no idea, but it was funny as shit. "Next thing I know, you'll have him flipping the bird."

She giggled.

"But," I said, "keep this between us. We have enough eyes already."

She put her hands on her hips and stuck out her tongue. "Uh. Duh."

I held up my hands in defeat. "Just trying to help."

I could imagine Lucy somehow making herself visible and performing this trick to some unsuspecting neighbor…and us ending up with a visit from child protective services.

"Okay," Lucy said.

"You know who is going to love that?" I asked.

"Who?"

"Doc."

She sighed. "I hope he comes back soon."

"So do I, kiddo. So do I." I wanted to reach out and pat her on the head, but her being incorporeal sucked sometimes.

#

As soon as Tabby came back from wherever she'd gone with my passport, she headed straight for the kitchen and I heard pots and pans on the stove. My ears pricked. This could be a very good thing.

I left Lucy playing with Isaac and went into the kitchen.

"What are you making?" I asked as I looked over the top of the pot she was stirring.

"Fudge. I want some fudge."

I wasn't about to argue with that. We'd had so much crap happen that something sweet wasn't a bad thing. "Mind if I sit here and keep you company?"

"You can if you want."

It was a lot better than being told, "Fuck, no." I was still treading lightly. I didn't want to leave for Italy with stuff being all weird between us. If I did that, I'd probably come home to an empty house. Besides, I was better than that.

"If you want, when you're done, I'll do the dishes," I said.

She shook her head and turned around. "Stop. Okay. Just stop. What I said was shitty. Now you're here acting apologetic, and I should be the one apologizing. Just let it go."

I blinked. Wow. That was different. "I'm sorry…but I still want to help."

She took a deep breath. "Okay. You can stir."

#

Having fudge for dinner was kind of fun. Granted, it was probably the worst thing in the world in terms of nutrition, but who cared. Heck, some of my favorite dinners as a kid were when my sister, Candy, would announce that we were having ice cream for dinner.

"Mommy never made candy for dinner," Lucy said.

"Well," Tabby said. "Your Mommy is a hell of a cook."

"Oh, I don't know, I think you're pretty damn good too," I said, thinking about her chili made my mouth water.

Tabby smiled shyly.

"When's Doc going to be back?" Lucy asked.

Tabby's face fell. "I don't know, honey."

Lucy stared at the carpet.

Had I known it was going to take this long, I wouldn't have even recommended he go and would have come up with something else to distract Lucy. Damn. "Hey," I said. "I bet he's just researching things really good."

Lucy shook her head. "It didn't feel like this before."

She wasn't the only one who was worried, but there was nothing else to do about it. If he didn't come back after a few days, I was going to have to make a trip.

"Well, all we can do is wait. Hopefully, we'll know soon," Tabby said.

"Keep in mind that Doc is crafty. He might even be cooking something up. After all, we don't know what he's into when he isn't with us." I reached down and scratched Isaac behind the ears. He meowed.

I needed to be positive for Lucy. Hell, I needed to stop coming up with worst-case scenarios about everything.

"That's true," Lucy said.

"Why don't you see if you can find another movie?" Tabby asked.

Lucy grinned and walked over to the TV.

"If he doesn't come back, I don't know if I'll be able to forgive myself," Tabby whispered.

"No sense in inviting trouble where there isn't any. Try not to freak out until we know something." Even though I said it, I didn't believe it. Most of the time, Hell was coming. It was only a matter of when.

"But it's so hard. "

I nodded. "I know."

#

I kept waking up all night long in the hopes that any little sound I heard was Doc coming back, but it was just the house settling. If Doc didn't show up soon, I'd have to concede defeat. Granted, I'd probably try to rescue him, but how does one rescue a ghost? I guessed I'd do what I normally did, get me a supply of holy water and hope for the best, but I wished I had something to help me out.

Around five, I gave up and went to the bathroom. When I got out, I heard someone saying my name very softly. I glanced around the bedroom, but there was nothing there. Then I peered into the hallway.

I could faintly see Doc's outline. Not good.

"Are you okay?" I asked.

"I've been better. Gotta go recharge early. I already told Lucy." I couldn't even make out his face. That's how weak he was.

"Okay. Thanks for letting me know," I said.

"Not a problem, but that isn't why I'm here."

"Okay?" He grunted. "Don't ever say I never gave you anything." A small piece of paper fluttered to the floor and Doc disappeared. I picked it up. In Doc's spidery handwriting, two items were written:

Will Andersen

Crazy88@xxorder.xx

"Holy shit."

I crept back into my bedroom and grabbed the iPad off my nightstand. I stared at Tabby for a minute to make sure I hadn't woken her up. Luckily, I hadn't. Then, I went into the hall and sat on the top step.

I fired it up, opened the browser, and loaded my personal email account. I took a deep breath and started typing.

Will,

I had to write when I found out Lucy passed. I am so very sorry. I may be able to help though. Feel free to give a call.

555-778-4213

Jimmy

It was the only thing I could do. In a way, I would have rather gotten the story about Blackmoor from Doc, but this was the right thing—even if the Order didn't view it that way. I was pretty much done with living my life inside a bubble. I should have the choice whether I wanted to contact an old client or not, dammit.

I heard a chime. I looked down. Will had replied.

Is this a joke?

I didn't know if he thought it was a dummy account or what. I didn't blame him. As far as he knew, I'd dropped off the face of the earth.

No joke. Had to jump through some hoops to get your email address.

I waited. After a few minutes, he replied again. It seemed like his sleeping patterns were matching mine.

I'll call in five.

I hopped up, almost dropped the iPad, ran into the bedroom, and grabbed my phone. Then I closed the door to the bedroom and sat on the step again. I put the tablet on the floor. In a way, it was kind of funny, sitting there, holding my phone like a school-girl waiting for the boy she liked to call. I couldn't help but be excited. There was so much that had happened.

Finally, my phone rang.

"Hello," I said.

"Jimmy."

His voice sounded gruffer than I remembered. Sadder too. "Hi, Will. I'm glad you called."

"Maybe I can get some answers for once. Those people you work for have made living hard."

I could only imagine, with the way he'd had to put himself under the radar. Hell, he was probably living under an assumed name now. I felt sorry for him. I took a breath. Might as well give him everything I had.

"What would you say if I told you that I might be able to let you talk to Lucy?"

It was silent on the other end for a long time.

"So it's true…what they told me?"

"Depending on what that was. I have no idea what they told you," I said. How could I? I hadn't been there, and it wasn't like the Order was great at giving me info.

"That you were special. That you made sure Lucy was safe."

Okay. I could live with that. It certainly didn't tell the whole story, but there was time for that now. "That's true. I'm also the keeper of her soul. For now, anyway."

He was silent again. He cleared his throat. "A few short months ago and I'd think you'd gone crazy."

"And now?" I asked.

"Now, I'm scared."

Damn. I wanted to give him a beer and tell him to relax. "If it helps at all, Lucy is her old self."

He started sobbing. "If only Tor had known."

I froze. "What are you talking about?"

He hiccuped. "Tor killed herself. She couldn't take knowing Lucy was gone."

"Jesus, Will. I'm so sorry." I felt like such a fucking heel.

He took another deep breath. "You said I could talk to her?"

It was worth a shot. I mean, I could hear her and Tabby could. I hadn't tried it with anyone else. "I'm going to try. Listening to her is a little different."

"That's okay."

"Okay, Will. Hold on." I went downstairs and found Lucy in her usual spot in front of the TV. I grabbed the remote and muted it. Then, I put the phone on speaker.

"Lucy?" I said. "Your dad would like to talk to you."

She ran over. Her eyes sparkled. "Daddy?" She asked the phone.

"Oh, my God. Lucy, baby, it's so good to hear your voice."

She twisted her body back and forth, almost like she was about to spin around. "I miss you, Daddy."

He sobbed again. "Oh, honey, I miss you too."

She bowed her head over the phone. "Don't cry. Jimmy and Tabby are real nice."

He chuckled a little. "Yes, they are."

Then, she sauntered away. I shook my head.

"I guess she's done," I said. I would have thought that she would have wanted to talk to him longer, but I was wrong. I was wrong about a lot.

Will laughed. "She never did like talking on the phone. Can I call again sometime?"

"Any time you want. I'll be going to Italy in a couple of weeks and Lucy has to go with me. Might be a little hard, but you can call and Tabby will keep you updated."

"Jimmy?" he asked.

"Yeah?"

"Thanks."

And he hung up.

"Daddy shouldn't be so upset about Mommy. She knows I'm fine now." Lucy was perched in front of the TV again.

My eyes grew wide. "Lucy, you never cease to amaze me."

She grinned. "I know."

Then she turned the sound back on the TV with a flick of her hand. I had a feeling there was a lot I needed to learn about Lucy.

Chapter Twelve

Awake

TABBY CAME DOWNSTAIRS a couple of hours later. Her hair was wet from her shower. I was watching some home improvement show on TV. Lucy and Isaac were lying on the floor in front of it.

"How are you all today?" Tabby asked.

"Okay. Doc's gone," I said. I still hated he'd drained himself so much to get details for me, but at least it seemed like Lucy was going to be better for it.

She paused. "What do you mean?"

"He came back last night to say that he was leaving for home early. Something happened that had to do with Blackmoor, but I don't know what. Only that Doc had a present for me that turned out to be Will's email address."

Tabby pulled out a chair from the dining room table and sat facing me. "So what happened?"

I shrugged. "I emailed him. He got back with me almost immediately."

Lucy turned her head. "Yeah. Daddy's upset that Mommy died."

Tabby stared at me questioningly. "I gave Will my phone number and when he called last night, I let him speak to Lucy. Tor took her own life after Lucy's body passed away."

Tabby glanced at Lucy who had gone back to watching TV. Sometimes, I wondered if everything affected Lucy as little as it seemed, or if the kid was good at hiding it. If it was the hiding, we were going to have to try to figure out something to get her to open up. Spirit or not, it wasn't good to hold in that much stuff.

"Damn," she said.

"Yeah. So when Lucy and I go to Italy, keep my phone charged. I told Will he could call you for updates."

"Okay. That makes sense. What else do you need to do for your trip?" she asked.

"Little toiletries, a power converter. That will get me started at least. Anything else I need, I can either buy or have you ship it to me." I wasn't fretting about it too much. I'd traveled before.

"Where will you be staying?"

I shrugged. "I forget. I need to print all that and figure out how to print from the iPad."

Tabby laughed. "It can't be that hard."

I got off my ass and powered up my computer. Then I searched it. The problem was that it used a wireless printer which I did not have. Oh, well; it wasn't that big of a deal to email shit to myself.

"Well, that takes care of that," I said as I leaned back in the chair.

"What?" Tabby asked.

"I'm stuck forever emailing this stuff to myself. Or, well, until I decide to upgrade everything." And I was too lazy to do that—especially when everything was still working.

"Yay! One more thing I can get done while you're gone."

I could almost imagine her clapping her hands. Jesus. I got up and walked over to her. Then I kissed her on the head.

"Update the whole house for all I care," I said. "But don't touch my refrigerator."

She laughed. "Most men have a favorite chair. You have a refrigerator."

I shrugged. "Where else would I keep my bacon?"

She swatted me on the ass. "Go get your shower. We aren't going to stay inside all day."

#

Days passed. Tabby, Lucy, and I fell into a sort of routine. I helped Tabby pick paint colors for the entire house. Lucy finalized everything for her room. Doc did not come back. At least, this time, as far as I knew he was fine. There was no danger of him going home.

The night before the trip to Italy, I pulled Lucy aside. Well, sort of. I asked her to step outside with me.

She followed me into the backyard without a word.

I closed the door behind us and turned to look at her. "I know it is going to be hard to do this, but while we're in Italy, you'll have to be quiet."

"Why?" she asked. Her eyes were wide as she stared at me. It kind of gave me the heebie jeebies.

"We don't know who will or won't be able to see you or hear you. I want to draw the least amount of attention to you as possible. If it wasn't for the fact that I don't trust the safety of hotel rooms, I'd just have you stay there."

"Because of Arizona?"

I nodded. "You'll be going to class with me. It is going to be hard, but maybe you can help by watching for stuff you find unusual."

"I have to be quiet all the time?"

I shook my head. "Only when we are in class or at the school or around anyone we don't know. So in restaurants and at the hotel, everything should be fine. There's so much noise in those places that no one should notice."

"I'll miss Isaac."

I sighed. No way would I get away with taking a cat with me. He would probably have to be quarantined and everything else. "I know, but he'll be waiting for you when you get back."

She wiped at her nose. "Why didn't you want Tabby to hear this?"

"Because she worries too much." Granted, she didn't vocalize it, but I noticed the dark circles under her eyes that weren't going away. My bullshit was getting to her. Maybe me going away for a while would be a good thing.

"That's why you are letting her fix up the house?" Lucy asked.

"Yup."

Suddenly, Tabby opened the door. "What are you two doing out here?"

"Preparing for Italy," I said. She didn't need to know much more than that.

She grunted.

I held up my hands. "I swear, it was nothing bad."

She laughed. "Okay. Okay. Hurry it up, though, because I'm bored."

I laughed, then turned to Lucy. "You ready to go inside?"

"Yeah."

I herded Tabby and Lucy back into the house. Now that that was out of the way, I could concentrate on getting my shit ready to go.

#

The airport was crazy. Somehow, it seemed more hectic than when we went to Arizona. Maybe because Tabby wasn't there. She kept me grounded. Now, I was on my own.

"I think the gate is over there," Lucy said, pointing.

I followed her finger and there it was. Maybe it was a girl thing. I wasn't quite ready to admit that I couldn't handle this without them, but I'd sure be a lot more bumbling about it.

"Thanks, Luce." I headed toward the gate and Lucy trotted behind me. I sat in a chair to wait and set my carry-on bag in front of the chair next to me so Lucy could sit down.

"I like airplanes," Lucy said.

I inwardly groaned. The last time had been a stressful mess for me. On our way to Arizona, she flitted about the place like a bumblebee. I kept expecting disaster to strike, but it never did. But ever since that girl at the fast food restaurant admitted to seeing Lucy, I'd been pretty uneasy.

I could only imagine the types of shit she could get into on a transatlantic flight. It could be an epic disaster.

"Lucy," I said out of the side of my mouth. "Remember not to do anything crazy on the flight, okay?"

"Uh-huh." She was looking out the window at the big plane coming in.

This was going to get interesting.

#

I was surprised. As far as plane rides went, Lucy mostly sat at my feet. I was thankful for the little bit of legroom. Maybe she was as nervous about it as I was. It was still nice to know that she was listening to me finally. I knew it wasn't an easy thing for her to do, but the minute I got the chance, I was going to do something special for her. I didn't know what. Hopefully, inspiration would strike.

The first thing I did when we get to the hotel room was check for bedbugs. Tabby had given me a checklist of stuff to watch and that was at the top of the list. Luckily, it didn't have any. I brought my suitcase into the main part of the room and sat on the bed to relax. All I wanted to do was sleep, but it wasn't happening yet.

"We're staying here for six weeks?" Lucy asked.

"Yep." The room was one of those hotel apartments. It had a single bed, a small table with two chairs, and a kitchenette. The bathroom was serviceable, and I was thankful we were staying in a place where there wasn't a communal bathroom for the entire floor. Those were common all over Europe. I wasn't ready to get that close with other people.

It was fancier than the room I'd had in seminary, but it wasn't luxurious either. The most important part? I could work with it.

"Where's the TV?" Lucy asked.

I looked around. She was right. I guessed either the Order didn't feel it was important or TV in a hotel room wasn't a necessity in Italy. Either way, Lucy was going to have to figure out something else to do. Shit. More and more I was starting to wish I could have left her at home. This was not going to be a fun trip for her.

"Guess we don't get one. I'm sorry," I said.

She shrugged. "It's better than staying in a car for days."

In Arizona, we'd been left without a choice as far as that went. The supposedly possessed dude had forced us into staying with him. It hadn't been pretty. Plus, since he was actively contacting and dealing with demons, it wasn't good to have Lucy there. So Tabby had warded the car and Lucy had stayed in it with Doc.

"I'll get you some books and anything else you might want tomorrow when we go out. Right now, I need to get some sleep." My eyelids were starting to close on their own and even blinking a lot wasn't stopping them.

"Okay," she said.

I lay back on the bed and my eyes slammed shut almost as soon as my head hit the pillow.

#

I didn't wake up until almost noon local time. Starting tomorrow, I was getting up at seven. According to my packet, the classes for Exorcismo E Preghieri Di Liberasione started at nine. I was thankful they brought me over a few days beforehand. Otherwise, this exercise would be a disaster.

It was Friday morning. Class started Monday. I crawled out of bed and went to the bathroom. When I came back, I sat down at the little table and peered outside. Lucy was sitting opposite me, very still.

"What are you looking at?" I asked.

"Nothing. Everything. It's almost as good as TV."

I chuckled. "Well, that's good. I'm going to get a shower. Then, you and I are going shopping."

She turned to me, grinning. "Okay."

It was the least I could do. Maybe I would find her some toys or games to help her occupy the time.

#

The first thing I did was to buy myself a cell phone and minutes to use while I was there. If I ran out of minutes, all I needed to do was buy a new SIM card. So much easier than in the States. If it wasn't for the fact that I was used to the way stuff was in America, I would consider relocating. But I wasn't sure if Europe could stand that much of me.

Lucy and I sat at a little café. I was programming Tabby's number into the phone when Lucy gasped.

I glanced up. "What?"

"He's gone now, but there was a guy that looked like Mr. Black."

I peered in all directions, but there was no one there. I sighed. Chances were it was a fluke, but I knew better than to count on stuff to go the way I wanted them too. "Well, keep your eyes open. If you see him again, let me know," I said.

"Okay."

The waiter came and took my order. I got a cappuccino and had to stop myself from calling it a crappuccino. I also ordered a breakfast pastry platter the waiter recommended. And people complained about Americans being obsessed with sugar. I wanted to laugh.

After he walked away, I stared at Lucy. "Want to talk to Tabby?"

She shook her head. "Not today."

"Okay." I shrugged. I guessed Will was right about Lucy and phones. Oh, well. I dialed Tabby's number.

"Hello?" I heard her answer.

"Hey, wanted to make sure you got my number while I'm here," I said.

"How's Lucy?" she asked.

"She's okay. No TV in the hotel room, so after breakfast, I'm going to get her some books and toys."

I heard her sigh. "This house feels too empty."

I was starting to feel sorry for her. I'd figured she'd be happy to have the house to herself. I assumed wrong yet again. "At least you know the date we'll be back."

"True. And I'm counting on it."

The last bit, the way she said it, was almost angry. Not like Tabby at all. Maybe she was having a bad day.

"I'll let you go now, looks like the guy's coming with my food." The waiter had a tray piled high.

"Okay. Love you."

"Love you, too." I hung up.

The waiter deposited my pastries in front of me. "Anything else?" he asked in halting English.

I shook my head. "No, thanks."

#

After a few misunderstandings, I found how to get to a bookstore that was close by. I bought Lucy several picture books and as many coloring books as I could find. They even had these cute little bird dolls and I bought her one of those too. It wasn't TV, but it was something at least.

We caught a cab back to the hotel room. As soon as we were up in the room, Lucy visibly relaxed.

"It is really hard to not say stuff," she said.

I wanted to ruffle her hair. Poor kid. This was sucking for everyone. "I know. I wish it wasn't so bad."

She nodded.

"Want me to set up your books here on the table?"

"Yeah."

I got all of her stuff organized. Then I set myself up on the bed. I'd brought along both my Bible and my copy of the Roman Ritual for the sole purpose of brushing up on information before class on Monday. I imagined that they would be referring to both often. At least that's how everything in seminary had been. No reason to think this class would be any different.

It had been quite a while since I'd read either one. And well, this was the Roman Catholic Church. They didn't do too well with unconventional. I could imagine how well me and Tabby's ritual would go over with them. The fact that it worked would only make them more pissed.

"Jimmy?" Lucy asked.

"Yeah?"

"What are we going to do if they can sense me?"

I stared at her. Dammit. She shouldn't be fretting so much. "Who?"

"The people in the class."

I sighed. And they all wondered why I worried about stuff so much? There was no guarantee; I'd already learned that. "We'll deal with that if we have to. God wouldn't have put you in my hands for no reason at all. Try not to worry."

She sighed. "Okay."

#

Getting to class Monday wasn't as easy as I thought. Rome had all of these twisty, turny streets with names I had no way of remembering. I thought about using the GPS on the phone, but who knew if I even had enough data for that. Best to be frugal and try something else.

I ended up getting the directions via the iPad. I honestly wasn't surprised at all to find that it worked there. So far, the Order's network seemed to be everywhere. In a way, that was unsettling, but now, it made it all a lot easier. I was going to have to start being thankful for the little things.

Lucy almost floated behind me as I rushed through the streets. Just getting to the bus stop was an adventure with the morning thrall. I hated the traffic, and unlike the States, most of it was people walking every damn place. It was complete chaos.

Eventually, I found my way to the school. It was the campus of the American Catholic University, but the exorcism class was part of their offerings. I stopped at the big map located near the elevators and found the classroom.

I hopped onto the elevator and rode silently up to the proper floor. Lucy was being good and quiet. I wished that there was something else I could do for her, but there was nothing. The only consolation was that I was probably going to be as bored as she was.

I got to the classroom with about a half an hour to spare. There were a few students waiting there already. Among the mix were priests, a nun, and one man dressed in a suit. Good to know I wasn't the only oddball in the class. Or at least the only one dressed in regular clothes. I was probably the weirdest person there no matter what.

As the minutes ticked by, more and more students crowded around. On a good note, not one of them appeared to notice Lucy. That made one less thing to worry about. And if Lucy got bored and wanted to make silly faces, she could. In fact, I would have to try to encourage it.

My imagination wandered and, suddenly, I found myself wondering what would happen if someone dropped a giant pack of fireworks in the middle of the hallway. I had to keep from smiling. These people were entirely too formal. I could almost see one of the nuns pulling out a ruler to smack me.

I mean, granted, this was a class about how to do an official exorcism, but shit, even the demons laughed. Looking at the stoic faces around me, I had to doubt if they'd even seen a demon. I, however, probably had too much experience with them at this point. I should have been given this class as soon as I was "welcomed to the family." Not now when I had already performed exorcisms, discussed evil with the Devil, and dealt with a fucked-up changeling.

Soon, a man dressed in a black robe came and opened the door with a large set of jingling keys. I chose a seat in the back. No sense in drawing more attention to myself and, well, maybe I could whisper to Lucy now and then from up there. Surely, the teacher wouldn't be looking in the back all the time?

The dude in the black robes went to the front of the classroom, and began turning on lights and firing up computers. It was kind of nice to see the Vatican was high-tech. I should have known, though. The Order certainly had plenty of fancy doo-dads.

He said something in Italian. I raised my hand. I needed to see about the translator they had said I would have. I hadn't seen him anywhere. It was possible one of the guys dressed like a businessman was my translator and hadn't been given my picture or anything.

"Che cosa?" he asked.

I cleared my throat. "What about my translator?"

"Lo non parlo inglese," he said.

I figured that meant he couldn't speak English. Great. This was going to be fun.

I pulled my iPad out from my bag and held up my hand with my index finger up. I hoped he'd recognize I was wanting him to wait. As soon as it loaded, I pulled up a translation app and had it say, "Traduttore."

The guy paused for a minute, then said, "No."

Well, at least I had confirmation. Either the Order had lied, or there was a fuck-up. I let the guy ramble on. He started passing out papers. I sent off an email to Father Martin about my lack-o-translator. Hopefully, they could get it sorted out as soon as possible.

There wasn't anything else I could do. I leaned back in the chair and let him drone. Every so often, he'd put up a picture that was supposed to be scary, but since it had no meaning to me, it didn't touch me. None of the photos were very graphic either. I had the American insensitivity in my favor.

I finally got my piece of paper passed up to me. It was in Italian. I could get it translated, but there was a big part of me wondering why should I bother. If I couldn't understand the lecture, the notes from it wouldn't help all that much.

Every so often, I thought I understood something because it was similar to Latin, but I couldn't be sure.

#

After class, Lucy and I hit a café nearby for lunch. I needed something good after that fiasco.

"How are you supposed to learn anything if you don't understand?" Lucy asked.

I shrugged. "My point exactly. I mean, they could have set me up with some of those headphones they use at the UN or something at least, but no. I got squat."

"Can your thing do it?" She pointed at my bag.

I blinked. "What, the iPad?"

She nodded.

"Well, it could if he was close to me, but being that far away, even if I sat in the first row, it wouldn't work. I honestly can't see them hooking him up with a microphone for one student."

Lucy twirled the ends of her hair in her fingertips. "That sucks."

"Yeah. Even worse, I know the Order isn't going to be getting back to me all that quickly. This isn't an emergency."

She sighed. "I think they need a 911 instead of this silly email thing."

I laughed. "I'll be sure to tell them that."

We went back to the hotel after that. There wasn't any reason to stay near the school. Lucy went to her coloring books. I plopped on the bed to try to translate the damn paper. I hadn't bothered to look at it too closely before.

After a bit, I realized what it was—a syllabus. But the second page made my asshole grow tight. There were, from what I could tell, a list of dates of the class, and there were a hell of a lot more than six. More like ten. Either this was yet another fuck-up or the Order only wanted me to take part of the class. I wouldn't know anything until they got off their asses to talk to me. Great.

I pulled out the phone and called Tabby. She answered on the third ring.

"Jimmy."

"Hey, how is stuff going back there?" I tried to keep my voice upbeat, but it was damn hard.

"Okay," she said, sighing. "I got everything moved out of the living room. I plan on painting that tomorrow."

"That's good." I drummed my fingers against the bed.

She was fiddling with paper or something. I could hear rustling.

"How was the first class?" she asked.

"I have no idea. The translator is nonexistent." No sense in lying about it.

"Oh, no! What did they say?"

I sighed. "No response from the Order yet. I swear. One of these days I'm getting a phone number."

She groaned. "That is if they'd answer your calls."

"Yeah. True."

"What are you going to do?"

That was the question. "Hell if I know. Even their estimate was wrong. The syllabus says ten classes."

"Maybe the Order only had a few classes they want you to go to."

I was reminded of how much Tabby and I thought alike at times. But I wasn't about to jump to conclusions. "At this point, a clerical error seems more and more possible."

"When's the next class?" she asked.

"Next week. Each class is like four hours long."

"Shit."

I heard some thumping.

"Yeah. It isn't just Lucy who is going to be going crazy from boredom." I made a couple of faces at Lucy. She smiled slightly.

"Don't be stupid. There are so many cool things to do in Italy. So do them."

I laughed. "Okay. Okay. I will."

"Good." She hung up.

She was right. Why spend the entire trip in the damn hotel room? It was time Lucy and I explored Rome.

#

Exploring Rome with a spirit was interesting. Everything was fine until we ran into one of those little carnivals. Lucy forgot to be quiet and kept begging me to let her ride. It was partly my fault because I had told her that restaurants were okay to talk in, and there was food at the carnival, but this was a disaster. I kept trying to motion for her to shut up, but she wasn't having it.

"No," I said quietly. If I tried to buy her a ticket, I'd be carted off to the nuthouse.

"I want to ride!"

Shit. Her scream exploded the guy's iPhone next to me. I jumped back. Glass sprayed out like mist from an aerosol can. The man dropped what was left of the phone onto the pavement. Blood ran down his face and cheek.

I stared at him, not even knowing how to ask if he needed an ambulance, but luckily none of the blood seemed to be coming from his eye. I dug in my bag and handed him a handkerchief. He nodded his thanks. A few other people came up to help.

I took a deep breath.

Car alarms were going off. Motherfuck.

Lucy's eyes went as wide as snowballs. I walked away as soon as I was sure the guy was okay.

It was best to get the hell out of Dodge. As soon as we were several streets away and no one was around, I turned and glared at Lucy. "Do you see why you have to be quiet, goddammit? What if you killed someone? Hell, you hurt that guy. Was it really worth it?"

Her eyes welled up and her chin quivered. "But I didn't mean it."

"That's all well and good, but we talked about it. You are going to have to start thinking a bit. And I'd like to know how I'm supposed to buy a ticket for a ghost?" I hadn't meant to be so damn mean about it, but she needed to learn. Being nice wasn't working.

She started to cry. "I'm not a ghost."

"Yes, you are. That's what you became when your body died." I knew it was a shitty thing to say, but I had to do it. I hunkered down, my anger gone. "Here, even more than America, you have to be careful. People believe in the supernatural in this part of the world. The last thing I want is for us to be hounded by some fanatics."

"What's that?"

"What's what?" I crossed my arms over my chest.

"The Fat. Fant. Thing?"

"A fanatic?"

She nodded.

I was going to teach her how to read as soon as I could. She needed to learn more of these words. Shit. "A person who uses their religion or a religion to hide their own crazy beliefs. Like the Jihaddists in the Middle East."

"Who are they?"

I kept forgetting that I was being faced with her six-year-old brain and it was difficult. I was getting ready to give up. "They are the guys who were behind the two thousand and one bombings in New York."

"The twin towers?"

"Yes."

She bowed her head and shuffled her feet. "Why do people have to be mean?"

I sighed. "I have no idea. Let's go back to the hotel, okay?"

"Okay."

One thing was for sure, there would be no more exploring with Lucy in Rome. It was shitty, but I couldn't risk it.

#

Once we got back to the hotel, Lucy was quiet. I hadn't meant to yell at her like that, but shit. What she did wasn't cool. It made me uneasy as all hell. It was one thing for electronics to stop working, but another thing entirely to blow them up and hurt someone. Six or not, she was going to have to grow up before her special powers killed us. It was almost like being the guardian of Godzilla.

"I think room service would be a good idea for dinner," I said once we were back in the room.

Lucy ignored me, sat in her chair at the table, and peered out the window.

I shrugged. She could pout all she wanted, but I was not going to give in. What she'd done had been wrong.

I never thought about having kids, and what it was like to make them atone for their actions, but now that I was having to do it, I didn't like it. It wasn't the punishment part. It was the fact that her childishness could have hurt someone way worse than she had and her little kid brain didn't fully process it. She felt worse about my damn carpet at home than she did about this—probably because she didn't get what she wanted. And that didn't sit well with me at all.

I didn't have the patience for it. I could see now why my parents had spanked me when I was a kid. Today, that would get you brought up on abuse charges, but I had to admit, corporal punishment made sense to me. Whether I felt it was right or not, it didn't matter. There was no way to spank a ghost. My hand would go right through her.

"Do you want to talk about anything?" I asked.

She turned around and glared at me. "No."

"Well, I think we should."

She rolled her eyes.

"Do you understand why I was mad?"

She shrugged.

"Don't you care that you hurt someone with your stunt?" I felt my blood pressure rising.

"But you wouldn't listen to me."

It was taking everything I had not to blow up. "I was listening fine. I just said no. You are not always going to get what you want."

She frowned. "But I never get what I want."

I sighed. "What is it you want?" I held up my hand stopping her from speaking. "And don't say to be alive because that ship has sailed. Hell, it sailed when you were no longer connected to your body. So before you speak, think about it."

She frowned some more. "Okay. I didn't want Doc to go away."

"I didn't either, but he had to recharge like you've had to before. I'm sure he'll be back."

"I wish Isaac were here."

I nodded. "If Tabby could have come, that could probably have been done, but with that class, and since this was only for me, there wasn't much I could do."

"Guess I have to get used to forever being like this," she said.

"Pretty much."

"Are you still mad at me?" she asked.

"A little, but I think you understand better now." I was calming down too. Though I was starting to think that Tabby better be the disciplinarian from now on. My tendency to get really mad wasn't a good thing.

"Can we call Tabby?"

It was a little request, and if I needed another SIM card, I would get one. "Yes, we can."

I set the phone to speaker and left it in the bathroom. I figured Lucy would want some privacy. As far as I was concerned, she could talk to Tabby as long as she wanted.

"Go ahead in. I have it dialing. Just let me know when you're done," I said to Lucy.

She hopped off her chair and went into the bathroom. The door closed by itself behind her. It still took some getting used to, seeing stuff like that. It was the stuff of horror films. But it was my life. Good thing I'd never been the type of person who got easily scared.

I loaded the iPad to see if there was any response to the email. Unfortunately, there was none. At least the next class wasn't until the following Monday so there was time for them to rectify the problem.

But the longer I was here, the more I had a bad feeling about the whole thing.

Chapter Thirteen

On the Dark Side

THE NEXT MORNING, I woke up grumpy. Maybe it was the way stuff had turned out the day before or maybe it was the fact that the class was four weeks longer than I was told it would be. Hell, grumpy didn't even cover it. I was a bear.

Even Lucy wasn't as opaque as she'd been the day before. Most likely, it was because she'd had that fit. I got all my stuff together and paused by the door. "You coming?"

"Where are you going?" Lucy asked.

"Library."

She got off her chair and followed me out. It probably wasn't a great idea taking her anywhere now, but I couldn't leave her by herself either.

On the way to the library, I simply watched the people meandering around the sidewalks. I was heading to the NAC or the North American College. I knew it had a good library and I hoped to read up on some stuff about exorcism I hadn't been able to find back in the States.

The building was massive, but you'd never have known it was a college by looking at the outside of it. All that betrayed its purpose was a small bronze plaque beside the front door.

As soon as we walked inside, Lucy moved slower.

"What's wrong?" I whispered from the corner of my mouth.

"Feels funny here," she said.

I looked around, but nothing seemed amiss to me. I felt nothing, but she was a heck of a lot more sensitive than I was, so I left it at that. There was no sense in getting caught talking to thin air.

Luckily, since this was an American college, the signs were written both in English and Italian, so I had no trouble at all finding the library. The biggest advantage? This library had the largest number of English books in Italy. If I couldn't find what I was looking for here, it probably didn't exist.

I walked up to the circulation desk. "Where can I find the books on exorcism?"

She was this older lady who looked like she could have been my grandma. I could only assume that she was a nun. While a lot of the nuns in Italy still wore habits, not all of them did. The church, it was changing.

"Are you in the class?" she asked.

I nodded.

"Wait right here. I'll get them." She slowly got up from her chair, grabbed a little cart, and left. I couldn't help but be reminded of the library at Sorrow's Point where the only one who had the balls to tell the secrets of Blackmoor was that old librarian. At least this one didn't look at me with disdain or anything. But she worked for the church too. A priest wasn't anything out of the ordinary.

Lucy stood quietly beside me. For that, I was grateful.

After a few minutes, the librarian came back with a full cart.

"This is all we have. Some of it is in Italian, but if you need a translation, I can help you find someone who would be willing to translate for you."

I smiled. "Thank you so much for the help."

She smiled back at me and went behind the desk. I took the little cart and rolled it over to a large study table.

"I wish Doc was here," Lucy whispered.

I pulled out a chair slightly so she could crawl up and sit down.

Then I grabbed the first book.

#

I sat there for hours reading. It was a shame that I couldn't check out the books to take back to the hotel, but I understood why I. Some of those texts were irreplaceable. Every book was covered in a special plastic cover that I was sure was paper-friendly. A few of the books had been rebound. But I knew the rare books were probably in a vault somewhere and my grubby mitts wouldn't be allowed anywhere near them.

Instead, I took as many notes as I could on the iPad. In a way, scanning would have been better, but I didn't want to mess up the bindings any worse than they already were. There were specific mentions of different rituals and strange items that appeared during exorcisms. Even mention of cases with famous people. It was fascinating. Almost like being in a guarded society for once.

I had to hand it to Lucy. She sat there and kept quiet. Every time I'd look at her out of the corner of my eye, she was simply watching the people that walked by. I could handle that. Maybe the talk yesterday had helped.

Finally, I made it through the last book written in English and popped my back.

"You ready to go?" I whispered.

She nodded.

I loaded the books back on the cart and I wheeled them up to the desk.

"Thanks," I said to the librarian. This was a different one from this morning, younger.

She smiled and took the cart. I led Lucy out of the building and into a little sandwich shop. I hadn't noticed how hungry I was until I walked in.

#

"Are we going to do that again tomorrow?" Lucy asked.

We were back home in the hotel room. I'd been smart and ordered an extra sandwich so I wouldn't have to go back out. It was currently sitting over the top of a cup with some ice in it to keep it cool.

I stared at her. "No. That was probably a one-time thing."

"Good."

This was the first time I'd seen her react so strongly about a place. Not a good sign.

"What's wrong?" I asked.

She shivered. "I don't know. There's just something I don't like about that place."

"Is where the class is okay?"

She nodded.

"Okay. Well, I'll do my best not to go back to the other place." And since I didn't know what was in the Italian books, there was no way I would miss it. I had enough notes to last me for a while. Worse came to worst, I could always see if the Order had their own library.

She smiled.

#

Later that night, I jerked awake. I glanced up and there was a long black shadow on the wall. It was deeper than the shadows I had been used to seeing from the window. Every so often, it would move slightly. Herky-jerky, like a stutter. I looked around the room, but there was nothing I saw that could be causing the shadow.

"What the fuck is that?" I asked Lucy.

Lucy stared at the shadow and had her back pressed into her chair. Her being scared was not good at all.

"I told you I didn't like that place." She slowly moved her head and stared at me in the dark. Then she shook her head.

I crept out of bed. The shadow moved toward me. Looming, almost as if it wanted to swallow me. I glared at it for a moment then pointed with my hand—showing that on the inside of my wrist I had the mark. "Go. You have not been invited."

The ripples of magic from my voice stilled the air and the shadow somehow disintegrated.

I exhaled slowly. "Well, that was interesting."

"I think there are entities or whatever you want to call them here. Stuff that is way stronger than back home."

She wasn't kidding. "Sure seems that way."

"Are you doing to tell somebody?" she asked.

I shrugged. "Who? The annoying email monster?"

Lucy giggled.

"That reminds me." I grabbed the iPad and powered it up. After a little, the email notification popped up. I got excited. Maybe something would get done at last.

Mr. Holiday,

We hope that you find Rome a fascinating place. I'm sure that the class is most helpful. Please, feel free to contact me with any problems.

Fr. Joseph Hardy

"You've got to be shitting me!" I almost threw the damn thing across the room. Again, this was proof that the left didn't know what the right was doing and it was bullshit. Then they wondered why people had such high stress levels.

I calmly turned off the tablet and set it on the nightstand and went back to sleep. There was nothing else for me to do.

#

I goofed off the rest of the week. I knew I shouldn't have, but if they didn't care, why should I? Besides, the one time when I tried to be proactive, I ended up with something in my room—so there.

Lucy and I went a lot of places: the Sistine Chapel, the Leaning Tower of Pisa, a real Italian pizzeria. I tried to make sure that everywhere we went, there was something she could do. I was hoping that would stave off any desire to make more scenes and maybe, she learned her lesson.

We had no more incidences like at the NAC. The more imaginative part of my brain took that as a sign. The problem was, I still didn't know of what.

The tone of the day had been gradually going downhill. I didn't have to ask why—the class was tomorrow. I was not looking forward to it.

Every so often, I'd pull up my email, but there was nothing. I didn't relish sitting for another four hours looking at pictures and not having subtitles. I was going to recommend that either they make an American version of the class, or make sure every marker being sent to learn at the exorcism school have a crash course in Italian.

It was no wonder the people that moved to the US from other countries tried to learn some of the language before they moved. I couldn't imagine much worse than this and I at least knew some Latin.

"You should get Tabby a present," Lucy said out of the blue.

I looked up at her. "What type of gift?"

She shrugged. "Something pretty."

I nodded. "We'll have to go tomorrow. People are in church today."

"Why? Because they are in church? Why can't we shop?" she asked.

"People are more religious here. Restaurants and grocery stores close early on Sundays and open late. Most people go to church here."

"Oh."

"We'll have better luck finding her something after class."

She sighed. "Okay."

"Don't feel bad. I'm getting bored too."

"Those people need to treat you better."

"Who?" I was lost.

"Your bosses."

"The Order?"

She nodded.

"Yeah, I agree. Believe me. Next time I actually get to talk to someone, I'm getting a phone number." And anything else I could get my hands on.

"You'd better or Tabby is going to kill you."

I laughed. Sadly, she was probably right.

#

The next morning, I dutifully packed my bag and headed off to class, but I didn't like it. There was some small part of me that hoped that I was wrong and that there would be a translator waiting for me. That would be a nice change of pace. But I knew I was pressing my luck.

Lucy followed me through the Regina Ateneo Pontificio Regina Apostolarum to the classroom. This time, I arrived late enough that the door was already open. I chose the chair I had sat in at the last class. I saw no translator, or any teacher for that matter. At least I wasn't late.

I took my Bible and my Roman Ritual out of my bag and laid them on the table along with my iPad. I watched everyone that came in carefully—just in case they could be my translator–but there was no one different.

Finally, someone with some purpose entered into the room and went to the lectern. He wasn't the same guy as last time. Maybe each class was going to have a different teacher. In a way, that was kind of nice…of course, if I could understand them.

He started firing off in rapid-fire Italian. Soon, I lost interest. Lucy was sitting on the floor next to me. She even rolled her eyes and I had to force myself not to doze off.

As the guy in front droned on and on, I felt my attention slip. I didn't care anymore.

I doodled on pieces of paper and made origami animals out of my notebook for Lucy. I even had the animals stage a mock battle on the chair next to me. Granted it was stupid, but it was also kind of fun. Better than staring at the wall anyway.

"And Mr. Pig-bottom had to go away forever and ever," I whispered.

Suddenly, I realized the room had gotten very quiet. I glanced up and the teacher was glaring at me from his lectern at the bottom of the classroom. Then he launched back into class. I shrugged. I couldn't have been that distracting. His voice was damn loud. One of the other students must have complained or something. Oh well.

I stared down at Lucy. She seemed more bored than ever. I felt for her. I did. This trip had sucked donkey dicks and there wasn't a damn thing I could do about it. Since the paper animals were out, I needed to find something else to entertain her. Too bad this wasn't a day when they could dim the lights. I could have done shadow puppets.

"No, after the other disaster, we don't need any more of those," I mumbled.

The teacher continued to drone on and on. It seemed like everyone but me was paying attention. Good for them.

Finally, a light-halo went off in my head. I grabbed the Bible and the Roman Ritual and placed them so that the pages were facing each other roughly six-inches apart. Then, I grabbed some pages and put my thumbs between them in each book. I now had hand puppets. Heh.

Lucy looked up and stared—ready to watch.

I started moving the "mouths" along with Mr. Blowhard at the front of the class. Yeah, technically what I was doing was definitely one hell of a no-no, but I didn't care anymore. Entertaining Lucy was a lot more fun.

The teacher put on a bit of audio that was again some other dude speaking in Italian. I continued with my "puppets." Lucy was trying very hard not to laugh.

And then, her eyes got as wide as dinner plates. I followed her gaze—into the eyes of Mr. Blowhard.

Oh, shit. I'd done it now.

"Cio che nel mondo pensi che stai facendo?"

"What?" I asked.

His face turned red and his eyes seemed like they were going to pop right out of his head.

"Ive!" he pointed with his finger toward the entrance to the classroom. I didn't stall. I didn't even need a translation for that. I showed all my shit into my bag and ran out of the room.

"I am so fucked," I said as I rushed down the hall.

Lucy giggled as we walked from the building. "Good one, Grace."

"Where did you hear that?"

"TV."

I laughed. "Well, seeing that I'm probably kicked out of the Order, want to get some ice cream?"

"Yeah!"

At least that was something both of us could use to put smiles on our faces.

#

I'll admit it. That ice cream tasted better than anything I'd had in a long time. Maybe it was because I was my own man again? Or it could have been that it was Italian and didn't have the crappy chemicals that get added to everything in the US.

None of that mattered though. Now, I had more problems than I knew what to do with. We went back to the hotel. I started pacing and shit. I wasn't so stupid as to think I'd be given another chance. Old Blowhard would make sure of that. I would be damn lucky if I got to keep my job. The old resume was going to need a brush-up.

My phone rang. It was a number I did not recognize. Maybe it would be a wrong number. It was possible. Especially since this wasn't my regular phone.

"Hello?"

"Mr. Holiday. I don't think I have to tell you how disappointed we are in you." He had the tone of an elementary school principal. It was ridiculous. I'd long since outgrown that, no matter how childish I seemed.

"That's a bit of the pot and the kettle, isn't it?" I couldn't help it. I was tired of holding back.

"I do not understand," he said.

"It doesn't matter. But maybe this wouldn't have happened if I'd been given the translator I'd been promised." It was bullshit and I wasn't going to take flack for that. If he wanted to yell at me about what I'd done in the class, fine, but it wasn't all me either.

He was quiet for a minute. I suspected this was Martin again, but I wasn't totally sure. I'd only heard his voice once, so it wasn't like I was all that familiar with it. It didn't matter who it was, so long as they were from the Order.

"According to my notes, you refused the translator," he said.

"What? I can tell you that's a damn lie. Why would I put myself through four-hour classes of sitting and twiddling my thumbs for nothing?" They sure knew how to piss me off about right.

He sighed. "It is certainly something to look into. For now, you'll return to America. I will look into this personally."

"Oh, and Martin?" I was pretty damn sure it was him now.

"Yes?"

"I want a phone number where I can reach you. Now. No more of this email bullshit." I wasn't about to let him get away with it this time.

He cleared his throat and rattled off the number. "Yes, with this new development, this is probably best."

"How long do I have before I'm fired?" I figured I might as well ask. It wasn't like being an exorcist offered unemployment.

"I don't know. I honestly don't know," he said.

He hung up then. I finished pacing. I didn't even have the chance to tell Tabby about what had happened. One thing was sure—there was too much to do. My life was, once again, a mess. I was starting to think I liked it that way. Otherwise, I would be quiet and wouldn't cause myself any more undue chaos.

#

I used the iPad to buy a ridiculously expensive ticket back to the US. Almost three thousand dollars, but it couldn't be helped. At least

I'd been smart enough to bring the Order's card along with my own. If I was kicked out of the markers, or at least the organization, the paycheck would be gone and I'd have to jump through some serious hoops. There was no way I was going to ask Tabby to get a job. I was still able to work. She'd go back to school. She needed to finish anyway.

The flight was set to leave at ten in the evening local time. I knew I'd better get out of the hotel before anything else was added to the bill. Lucy and I left the room and I checked out. Then, we went to a restaurant to get something to eat so I wouldn't have to shell out any money on the plane. Besides, plane food kind of sucked.

Once we were seated, I called Tabby.

"Hello?" she asked.

"Hey, can you pick me up at the airport tomorrow?"

"Wait. What?" There was some sort of deepness emanating from her voice I hadn't heard before.

Maybe she had a cold. I sighed. "It's a long story. Can you do it?"

"Sure. What time?"

"I think I should be landing in Charleston about two. I've got a layover in NYC."

"Okay. Keep me posted," she said.

"Will do."

I didn't bother to mention that she had my cell phone, but surely someone or somewhere at JFK would let me send a text. A payphone was probably nonexistent. I hadn't seen one of those in years.

"What are you going to do now?" Lucy asked when I hung up the phone.

"Probably hold my asshole tight. I'll have to find a job if they fire me. It's not like I can sue an organization that isn't supposed to exist. They aren't even part of the Vatican." I set my phone down on the table. It was the truth. Even if I had to take a job at a restaurant or something, that was what I was going to have to do.

"Maybe Doc will be back when we get home," Lucy said.

"I hope so. He's good at ferreting out information." And maybe he could figure out who had sabotaged me in the Order. Fucker.

I ate quickly, and then called a cab. I knew getting through customs was going to take a while. This wasn't like America. Here, they made you open everything. Thank God the only things I'd bought were some stuff for Lucy. Never did get around to buying Tabby something.

Still, it wasn't my fault that I didn't learn anything from the class. Hopefully, Father Martin would be able to find out what had happened and be able to do something about it. Then, at least, I could maybe save my job.

I wasn't denying that I shouldn't have done what I'd done. I'd been stupid. An adult would have sat there quietly and let the class go. I didn't have the attention span for that. I knew I could be out doing something constructive instead of wasting my time. I'd wanted the class originally, but now that I knew it was worthless, I was wondering why the Order didn't have their own class. It was odd.

I'd already performed exorcisms. Granted they weren't exactly successful, but the experienced exorcists couldn't swear theirs would be either. Nobody could.

I hunkered down in the security line to wait. It was going to be a long flight.

#

As I wandered through the JFK airport, I found myself humming the old Quiet Riot song, *Bang Your Head.* It fit my mood. Though it was probably ironic that an exorcist listened to rock music, but I was so far off the grid at this point it didn't matter.

Hell, I had a witch as a sidekick—though she'd probably kick my ass for calling her that, but oh well. It wouldn't be the first time. In fact, she was kind of sexy when she got angry. I'd been away from her for too long.

Was someone on the inside of the Order working with Big Red or his offspring? What had happened in Rome was too ridiculous. I could see, sure, no translator for the first class. But for someone to mark down that I said I didn't need one? Bullshit. Especially when I had filled out the form in pen. They had had to make an effort to change it.

There was a stink in the woodpile and I had to figure out what it was.

#

By the time I landed in Charleston, I was sleeping on my feet. Hell, if it hadn't been for Lucy guiding me where to go, I would have gotten lost for sure. I probably should have tried harder to sleep on the flight, but I couldn't stop thinking about it all. It was way worse than usual.

I spotted Tabby in baggage claim. I ran over and picked her up off her feet. Shit, it was good to see her. Tired or not, I needed to feel her.

She pulled away from me a little. Maybe I'd grabbed her too hard.

"Damn," she said.

I kissed her. "What can I say? I missed you."

Her face stilled, but then she laughed. "Obviously."

I put her down.

"Are you hungry?" she asked. "I could stop somewhere on the way home to get something to eat."

"Nah. All I want is the bed. Food comes later."

Tabby grunted. "I thought you would have missed me more than that."

Kind of odd for her to say that with the way she'd acted a bit ago, but whatever. I laughed. "More than you'll ever know."

She wandered over to the luggage carousel and got my bag. Then we were on our way.

#

Truth was, I fell asleep in the car. I didn't even make it out of the parking lot. Lucy had been saying something about Doc, and I was out. If I hadn't been so tired, I would have felt bad about it.

It was a bump that woke me up. Tabby was still driving on the interstate.

"Everything okay?" I asked.

"Just a pothole."

She was staring intently at the road. She didn't even turn her head to look at me.

"Ahh," I said.

"You were snoring really loud," Lucy said from the back seat.

I laughed. "Proof as to how tired I was."

"Still sleepy, or do you want food?" Tabby asked.

"Food would be good, but let's wait till we're closer to home." I wanted to get to the point where I didn't have to travel for a while.

"I can do that," she said. "Now, want to explain what's going on?"

I took a deep breath. "I may or may not be fired."

She made a weird noise that was almost the cross between one of

Isaac's sounds and a groan. "Okay…I'm confused already. You either are, or you aren't."

"It's complicated." As if nothing wasn't complicated with me, but whatever.

"Obviously."

I sighed. "Apparently, some joker wrote down that I had refused the interpreter, which I didn't. So that's part of it. The puppets were all me."

"The what?" Her eyes grew wide and the corners of her mouth were moving up and down like she was trying not to laugh.

Lucy giggled.

Tabby might as well let it rip. I still thought it was funny.

"These classes were like four hours long," I said. "Think about it. The dude was too far away for the translation thing on the tablet to work, so here's Lucy and me with four hours of droning. Every so often, the teacher would display a picture or play an audio clip, but other than that, it was like watching a foreign film without subtitles."

"Okay. But puppets?" Tabby asked.

I chuckled. "It started out as doodling in my notebook. And, well, you can only do that for so long. Then, I made all these origami animals and was putting on a little play for Lucy when it all got quiet. I kind of got bawled out for being loud. I don't think he could see the animals. Someone had to have ratted me out."

"Oh, Jimmy." She snickered.

"It gets worse."

I watched her roll her eyes.

"How?" she asked.

Lucy laughed.

"Well, when the class got back to normal, I knew I couldn't do animals again, so I pretended my Bible and the Roman Ritual were puppets."

She laughed. Hard. "Oh, Jimmy. You didn't."

"Yep. Soon, Mr. Blowhard had book equivalents. I was totally doing the whole Parkay vs. butter routine. Lucy found it hilarious. I'm not sure how the teacher found out. Could be he noticed something odd from my desk. It wasn't long before he came up there and caught me making my little tableau."

Tabby snorted.

"Needless to say, he kicked me out of class. When I got back to the hotel, I got the phone call that my job was in jeopardy."

"I'm honestly not surprised and neither are you." She laughed again. "So now what?"

I shrugged. "Father Martin is going to see who's been messing with my file. In the meantime, I go home. Don't know anything else yet."

"When will you know?"

I shook my head. "No idea."

Chapter Fourteen

Livin' on a Prayer

AS SOON AS we stepped into the house, Isaac leaped into my arms. I was more used to him reacting this way with Tabby, but I guessed he missed me.

I chuckled. "It's good to see you too, buddy."

He meowed, then hopped down. I took a look at the living room. It was brighter with the paler white on the walls. The sofa and my chair had green slipcovers on them. The carpet was still the same old tan.

"You've been busy," I said to Tabby.

She shrugged. "Kind of. Got Lucy's room done, too."

"Really?" Lucy asked.

"Uh-huh," Tabby replied, smiling down at Lucy.

Lucy took off up the stairs. I shook my head.

"Any problem with her while you were gone?" Tabby asked.

I nodded. "Some, but I'll tell you about it later."

Lucy came back downstairs and gave Tabby a huge hug.

"Thank you. Thank you. Thank you!" Lucy buried her head into Tabby's legs.

"I take it she likes it?" I asked.

Tabby laughed. "Now, you don't have to stay all the way down here at night. You can watch TV in your room."

Lucy appeared to hug her harder, and then let go.

Isaac walked over, looked up at Lucy, and meowed at her. She jumped down on the floor and hugged him too.

Then, she jumped up. "Jimmy, come, you gotta see it!"

I laughed. "Okay.

She led me upstairs. The kid wasn't even walking up the stairs in any fashion. She floated above them as quickly as she could. No way could I keep up with her, but it was damn cute.

She led me down the hallway and into her new room. The walls were a pale lavender color. There was a twin bed with a white bedspread and purple flowers on it. A painting of a unicorn was on the wall. In the corner of the room was a TV on a stand.

Lucy was grinning so hard, if she hadn't been a spirit, I would have been afraid that her mouth would split open.

It was so good to be home.

#

Later that night, after we'd gone to bed, Tabby brought up the thing I'd been trying to avoid again.

"No, seriously. What happened to Lucy?" she asked.

I sighed. I knew this was one of those cases where Tabby wasn't going to let up. No sense in dragging it out further. She needed to know anyway. "This one day after we'd gone to class or the library or something, we were exploring around town. Well, we came upon this little carnival and it had a fun kid's ride. Lucy wanted to ride and when I told her no, she threw a fit."

Tabby shrugged. "Well, a tantrum was bound to happen."

I shook my head. I let my brain wander back to the memory. I still felt chills from it. "Not like this. She screamed so loud that regular people heard it. The screen on this dude's iPhone cracked. Busted part of his face. It was like nothing I'd ever seen, but that wasn't the worst part."

Tabby waited. She seemed like she was trying not to object.

"She couldn't understand what she did was wrong. It took me several times before I got her to understand that she actually hurt someone."

Tabby pursed her lips together. "I'm not sure I'd call that odd."

I shrugged. "You kind of had to be there."

"Guess so."

After that, I arranged my pillow and lay down to get to sleep. I couldn't shake the feeling that something worse was coming and Lucy might or might not be part of it.

#

The next morning, the house was quiet. I stretched. It felt so good to be in my own bed. Nothing against Italy, but it was too formal. Here, I could run around in fuzzy slippers and most people wouldn't care. There, well, they probably wouldn't care, but I'd get more odd looks.

I got up and went downstairs. Tabby, Lucy, and Isaac were watching TV.

"I take it no phone calls?" I asked.

"Not yet," Tabby said.

"Doc said he'd be back tomorrow," Lucy said suddenly.

I stared at her for a minute. Her eyes were glued to the TV. I guessed spirits had their own sort of communication system or something. She was so focused on the TV that I didn't bother asking her. It wasn't like I had to know right now. Probably best I didn't in this case. It was something a demon could possibly exploit.

"Looks like everything will be mostly back to normal," I mumbled.

I plopped on the couch next to Tabby.

"Did Will call while we were gone?" I asked.

"A couple of times," Tabby said. "I told him what I knew at the time."

I nodded. "Makes sense. Hopefully, the next time he calls, I won't have to lie about why we're back."

Tabby sighed. "I think you worry too much."

"Probably."

Truth was, I was worrying more than she thought. Lucy acting the way she had in Italy had made me uneasy. Then, the fits. Me almost getting fired. Now, Tabby acting a little weird. It was too fucking coincidental. If I had to bet, all of this was coming from the one person I'd pissed off recently and that would be the being known as Leviathan. The fact that he could have a goon in the Order was pretty damn scary.

And then, there was something about me that Big Red wanted. What it was, I didn't know, but it evidently was important enough for the Devil and his children to try to do something to me to get it. And Asmodeus had to have been the first demon to recognize it. Too bad; I'd gotten him in trouble twice. But I did wonder if I was going to have to beat my way through all of the Devil's children. That would royally suck.

The way things stood, I was at a loss. All that was left was for me to wait on Father Martin and hope for the best. If I had any luck at all, it wouldn't be long.

#

"Jimmy. Lunch," Tabby said from the kitchen.

I got up from the sofa and went into the kitchen.

"Well, you look cheery," she said.

I shrugged. "Just worried."

She handed me a plate. "I know."

"I think the biggest problem is the not knowing." Granted, that could be for anything, but I wasn't the most patient person in the world.

She pulled out a chair at the kitchen table and made me sit down. "I would tell you not to worry, but I know it's pointless."

I took a bite of my sandwich. "Could be worse, I guess."

"Exactly. It can always be worse."

I finished my grilled cheese in silence. Tabby looked at me every so often. I could tell I was worrying her, but I couldn't stop. I wasn't going to calm down until I knew for sure what I had to do next.

Would it be so bad if I was fired? To me, I would figure out how to muddle through somehow. I very well could be fired by the Order, but not fired by God. That left a lump in my stomach. Could I turn my back on that? I'd be, what, a rogue exorcist? Maybe? I'd still have to have a full-time job. Just the thought of charging for my services made me sick to my stomach.

"Stupid," Tabby said suddenly.

"What?"

"This mooning. There is no need to invite problems."

I sighed. She was right. All the dwelling I'd been doing was wasting my time. "Okay. Distract me. What should we do instead?"

"Kill a llama? How should I know?" She stole my last bite of sandwich and popped it into her mouth.

I laughed. "Come on. Let's go sit outside. Maybe Lucy would like some sun."

"Now that sounds like the best idea you've had all day."

#

The sun was so bright that I wished I'd brought out my sunglasses, but I was too lazy to go back inside to get them. The patented "hand shield" would have to do.

Lucy and Isaac were playing in the grass. He'd chase a bug and leap. Lucy would leap behind him and then it would start all over again.

"Who would have thought that a cat and a spirit would play their own version of leapfrog?" I asked.

"What can I say? It's Isaac," Tabby said.

I laughed. "He's special all right."

"What are you going to do when he starts talking?" I heard a deep voice ask.

I jumped and looked behind me. Doc laughed. Lucy ran over and gave Doc a huge hug. I felt the stress leave my shoulders. Even I had to admit I felt more relaxed that he was back.

"How is everything?" he asked.

I exhaled. "Screwed up. Like usual."

He laughed. "Anything I can do to fix it?"

I shook my head. "Not right now. Maybe when we know more."

He nodded, then stared down at Lucy. "I have a feeling you've been busy."

She looked up at him and grinned. "I scared Jimmy."

He stared at her wide-eyed for a moment. "Well, come over here and tell me all about it."

I watched him walk into the shade and sit on the ground. Lucy followed suit.

I wondered if the sunlight depleted his energy or something, but I didn't ask. He had his own activities to do with Lucy. My silly questions could wait.

Tabby took a deep breath. "Why do I have a feeling we're gearing up for something big?"

"Because we usually are and you are usually right."

"I'm going to hold you to that," she said, grinning.

I laughed. "I didn't say all the time."

She snorted.

Isaac walked over and hopped up into her lap. He fidgeted for a minute before settling down.

"Any idea what's coming besides insanity?"

She shrugged. "You were abducted by a demon and kicked out of exorcism school. I don't even want to imagine what the third could be."

"Bad crap does always come in threes. I don't know how you put up with me," I said.

"Because I love you, ya goof."

#

I checked the iPad throughout the day, but there were no emails. In a way, that was good because it meant that I hadn't been fired—yet. But I would have rather had all of this resolved. My mind kept going back to the possible sabotage and then to Leviathan. Could he really have a minion in the Order? Or was it a simple clerical mistake that had me overreacting? If I learned anything from all of this it was that I had to always expect the worst. And if it came out better, so be it.

"I'm starting to think that you are going to drive yourself into the hospital with all of this," Tabby said.

I was sitting at my desk in front of my computer. My tablet was off to the side, sitting there, calling to me. I sighed. "I'm not trying to drive you crazy too, you know?"

"It isn't me you're driving crazy; it's yourself."

I could have tried to argue about it, but there wasn't any point. I was more nervous than I'd been when I got kicked out of the church. And that was saying something. "Can't you do a spell or something to make this all go faster?"

She laughed. "If I had that type of power, I'd already have my Ph.D. and not be on leave of absence, remember?"

"Oh, yeah." One of these days, I was going to figure out how to increase her power. Somehow.

She patted me on the arm. "One of these days you'll get it. I have faith in you."

"I'm glad somebody does." I sure as hell was starting to doubt myself.

She growled. "Jesus Christ. Stop with all the whining already."

I shut up. She had a point. I'd been so wrapped up in worrying that all I'd done was be a pain in the ass. It was time to get my butt in gear.

"I'm sorry," I said. "I promise to do better."

She grunted. "No sense in making a promise you can't keep. Just get your shit together and go back to being you."

I saluted her. "Yes, ma'am."

Chapter Fifteen

Gone With the Sin

AT ONE TIME, night was a time of relaxation and quiet. Ever since Sorrow's Point, I kept expecting something to happen as soon as the sun went down. I don't know what you'd call it exactly, PTSD maybe. But I knew it was an irrational fear. Lots of things had happened in the daylight too. Yet not being able to see the horrors somehow made it worse. I liked seeing the monsters I had to fight. It gave me a little bit of knowledge as to what I had to face.

I rolled over and stared at the back of Tabby's head. At least someone was getting some sleep. I gave up and raised myself to a sitting position. The TV was turned to some cooking show. I crawled out of bed and went downstairs. There was no light. Lucy was in her room now, so there was no reason for the downstairs TV to be on, but it felt lonely. I'd gotten used to seeing her whenever I got up when everyone else was asleep.

I flipped on the light, walked over, and started booting up my computer. Then, I started searching for information about Leviathan.

I should have done it sooner, but I'd had my head up my ass. According to the search engine, Leviathan was the demon of envy. I paused to let that sink in. Was I envious of anyone? Not really. Not any more than the average person. So that left another hole. Back to why he would target me.

It wouldn't surprise me if he hadn't been given the task of pestering me. I was going to wind up fighting all of Big Red's offspring before this was finished. Though I figured the seemingly benevolent version of the Devil I'd been shown was gone too. I hadn't fallen for the trap. So that meant a different type of attack.

The problem was I had no idea what type of attack it would be. Be prepared. Check.

And what was going on with Lucy? Intuitively, I'd been afraid that she's kept some of the badness of the being that had possessed her. But now? I didn't know if it was that or what. The Devil, he'd said she'd made a pact with him. If it wasn't for Doc's confirmation, I would have said he'd lied to me. Now, I was worried about whether it was what the pact entailed that he lied about.

Unless Lucy fessed up to something different, I couldn't know that either. Still, she was changing and not for the better.

My life was shit.

#

The next morning, Doc seemed fidgety. Every time I glanced over at him, he was fiddling with his hands or bouncing his knee. Something was clearly going on.

Finally, it was Tabby who asked. "Okay. I've had enough," she said. "What's going on, Doc?"

He shook his head. "Don't know for sure. I can feel the badness setting in."

"Does it have to do with Blackmoor?" I asked.

"Nah. That place is a burned-out shell."

That was a relief at least. One less thing to have nightmares about.

"Where'd you get the number for Lucy's dad?" Tabby asked.

Doc laughed. "Real estate office. There was a file on his desk, so…well…you know."

Lucy spun around from the TV to look at us. "How is Daddy?"

"Last time I talked to him, he was okay. Kind of sad, but he's all right," Tabby said.

Lucy nodded, then turned back to the TV.

Her not liking the telephone much was kind of interesting. The only person she'd asked to speak to had been Tabby. She'd barely spoken to her father for five minutes on it.

Doc was scowling. That wasn't a good sign. Every so often, he'd look at Lucy and shake his head.

I motioned for him to follow me and I went outside. I closed the door behind Doc and walked under the tree in the backyard so we could have a little privacy.

"What you want me out here for?" Doc asked.

"Lucy. What the hell is wrong with her?"

He stared at the ground and shook his head. "I don't think there's anything wrong with her per se. She didn't live long enough to be human."

I raised my eyebrow. "What?"

"Do you know how long she was possessed?" he asked.

I exhaled slowly. "Months. Not sure exactly, but I know she was sick for a long time."

"And her age at the time of the exorcism?"

"Six." It didn't escape me that part of her problem was that she was going to be like that little vampire girl in those Anne Rice books. Forever a child, but the brain of someone much older. There were only a certain number of years before it would really hit home.

"To a child, a few days can seem like forever. Her last tie to her old life went away when it died," Doc said.

I blinked. "So she's what? Evil?"

"Nope. Didn't say that. Just she has no idea of right and wrong really, and with the stuff she'd been exposed to, it's more extreme."

"Her body dying made that much of a difference?"

Doc coughed. "I think she used to go to it when you were asleep. Not visit it in person, but let her mind drift. Could have been imagination of sorts. Now that her body is dead, her last bit of hope of going home is gone."

That made some sense. "She's like the grumpy old man who's been kicked out of his house by a big corporation?"

Doc shrugged. "She's angry. All she wants to be is a little girl and she can't be that anymore."

"So what do I do?"

"What you been doing. Keep teaching her when she does something you don't like. Don't be afraid to get mad right back."

I nodded. "I take it she told you everything about Italy."

"I'm guessing. Even then, she was surprised I didn't find what she did right. I'm thinking that maybe she'll believe me better because I'm almost like her."

"We'd best figure out a way for you to charge up here, or for you to take her with you."

He chuckled. "Only one way to do that, Jimmy. Next time, you'll have to come along."

"I had a feeling you were going to say that. Let's hope I still have a job and can afford the trip."

Doc crossed his fingers and smiled.

#

Being a parent wasn't going to be as easy as I thought it would be. I never would have imagined that Lucy wouldn't be human anymore. I'd heard, too, that angels weren't human at all—not in appearance and not in the way they were emotionally. And yet they were considered benevolent beings. Maybe that was something I could teach her.

As long as Doc made sure to watch Lucy like a hawk, everything should be okay. I was going to have to step up to the plate, too. It wouldn't be fair to make him do all the hard work. Besides, Lucy was my charge.

My cell phone rang. I grabbed it out of my pocket. The number was one I recognized. This was it. I took a deep breath and swiped my phone screen.

"Father Martin?" I asked.

"Mr. Holiday."

I swallowed. "I'm assuming you have some news for me."

I almost didn't want to hear. The waiting sucked, but now that I was getting an answer, I wanted to go back to ignorant bliss.

He cleared his throat. "It is most strange. I have your paperwork that you submitted in my hands, and, of course, nowhere do you state that you do not want a translator."

"Yeah." At least he'd found the proof. That was score one in my favor.

I heard some rustling. "For that, I am quite sorry," he said. "Though even more strange is the fact that there was no one logged into the servers at the time the network states that the refusal was posted."

I rocked back on my heels. This was something new. "Wow."

Maybe someone inside the Order hadn't tried to screw me after all. Maybe Big Red was involved.

"Because the powers of the supernatural are involved, you are not dismissed, but suffice it to say that the senior members are not happy with you."

Yeah, stuffed shirts wouldn't be. "That makes sense," I said. "I freely admit that I was an idiot."

He laughed. "I must say it is nice that you admit it." I heard some more papers rustling in the background. "You are not welcome back to the school. This means that you will receive no more training in regards to exorcism." He chuckled again. "Not that the standard way seems to be your forte. In any event, you either sink or swim. God will decide what to do with you."

Since that was kind of what I wanted in the first place, I wasn't all that unhappy about it. I would have been better off working with a mentor, teaching me the ropes. Evidently, it wasn't in the cards. "That seems fair."

"You may be able to find some…." He cleared his throat. "…willing partner in terms of mentors. I am going to make sure you have access to the Order's marker list."

Something useful at last. It was close enough that I was starting to think he could read my mind. "I appreciate that."

"I will make sure it is sent to you sometime soon. But I'm not sure you'll thank me after this," he said.

Here it was. The catch. "What?"

"The seniors feel that you should be punished for your antics. So you are to be given the case that no one wants."

I laughed. "I thought that was every case."

"You do have a point. Also, this one isn't so far from you. It is in Kitzmiller."

I'd never even heard of it. "Where's that?"

"Close to Maryland. I'll be sending word so that they will be expecting you."

"No more information?" They were hanging me out to dry.

"I think it's best to hear from those who have witnessed the phenomenon. It isn't something we've heard before and I'd like a fresh mind on the matter."

That wasn't as bad as I thought, but still not great. "So I'll be able to call you during this case?"

"From now on, I hope you will keep in touch rather frequently.

Certain avenues cannot be trusted."

This might be a man I could actually work with. "Okay, then. I'll leave tomorrow."

"Tell your witch friend good luck."

I choked and he hung up.

What the fuck did he mean by that? No sense in worrying about it now. I had to pack. Unless I royally screwed this up, my job was safe. I finally relaxed.

I headed into the living room.

"Well?" Tabby asked.

She probably had heard me talking.

"I'm not fired," I said.

She blinked. "That's good."

I nodded. "And we have a case."

"Where this time?" she asked.

"Kitzmiller."

Her face fell. "Oh, shit."

"What do you mean by that?" Apparently, she'd been there. Her reaction wasn't good.

She shook her head. "It's better for you to see it for yourself."

"Why do I have a feeling that this is going to be the trend with this case?"

She laughed. "Guess we need to pack, right?"

"You guessed correctly, madam."

Packing was the easy part. Well, sort of. Isaac kept lying down inside the suitcase. Silly shit. Granted, he was going too, but I planned for him to have a better ride than that. No way would I ever do that to an animal. A demon, however…they could ride in my dirty gym sock.

"Listen, you. We're taking you along. Now, get out of there," I said to him.

He meowed at me, got up, stretched, then farted.

"Oh, Jesus Christ. Thanks, Isaac." I fanned the air in front of my face. That cat had worse gas than any other creature I'd smelled in my life.

He trotted nonchalantly out of the room.

"I take it you pissed him off," Tabby said.

I ran into the bathroom and sprayed down the room with Lysol. "I swear. That cat's ass gets worse and worse."

Tabby giggled. "I could almost swear that he had a special compartment for these occasions."

"You may be onto something. Shame we can't market it."

"Now that would be the end of the world."

I laughed. "Probably."

#

The next morning, we all piled in the car early. Isaac was in his pet carrier in the backseat with Lucy and Doc. I'd been smart enough to call in advance and find a hotel. It was a plain old Best Western. They made me add on a pet deposit, but at this point, I didn't care. As long as no one tried to break into the room, like in Arizona, we'd be in good shape.

Tabby had made sure to bring plenty of warding materials, so I knew what her first task was going to be.

"I can't believe we are going to Kitzmiller," Tabby said.

"Why the hate?" I asked.

"Because there's nothing there. It's just grass and trees and rocks and a general store."

I rolled my eyes. "There's got to be more than that."

"If you say so."

Doc snorted from the back.

"Hey, no comments from the peanut gallery," I said, looking in the rearview mirror.

He chuckled.

"I think there's something weird about this…Kitz-…place," Lucy said.

"Do you have a bad feeling?" I wanted to ask what else she had a bad feeling about, but I was probably pushing my luck.

"Maybe. I'm not sure. It's just weird." She crossed her arms.

"Okay. I'll keep my eyes open."

Lucy stared out the window.

"Did the Order give you any indication as to what this case is about?" Tabby asked.

"You know what they told me. I guess whoever we need to meet will get in touch with us. Martin said he'd let them know we're coming."

'That's ever so comforting," Tabby said.

'Tell me about it. I'm already having flashbacks of Arizona."

"Ever notice how we always refer to the last case we dealt with?" Tabby asked.

"What do you mean?"

"Well, in Arizona, everything was like Sorrow's Point. Now, everything is like Arizona."

I laughed. "God help us if next time everything is like Kitzmiller."

"I have a feeling that, if that's the case, we'll have done nothing wrong."

"Or something fantastic." Hey. Might as well be positive.

"That too."

"How much longer do we have to do this?" Lucy asked.

"What, drive?" I asked.

"Yeah."

"Still a few hours left," I said.

"I've decided I don't like car rides," Lucy said.

I laughed. The classic kid mantra.

"Why not?" Tabby asked.

"Because they're long."

I chuckled. She was killing me today. "Well, want to play a game?"

"Like what?"

"A color game. My dad used to play it with us when I was a kid." One of the few happy memories from my childhood I had, but I wasn't about to lay that on her.

"Okay. How does it work?"

Woot. I had her attention. "It can be the color of something in the car that we all can see. Then, once you've chosen the thing, you say, 'Willy, Willy, I, Dee, Dee. I see something you don't see and the color is—whatever the color of your thing is. Then, we all have to guess."

"Okay!" Lucy said.

At least she wasn't bored anymore.

#

We decided to stop in Morgantown for lunch. At least they had lots of places to go. It was still springtime, so I didn't have to worry about leaving Isaac in a hot car.

"Any suggestions?" I asked as I pulled into town.

"Well, the Indian restaurant went downhill when I was here last." She drummed her fingers on the dashboard. "Want Italian?"

"Fine with me. Where?"

"Go to the town center. There's one up there," Tabby said.

"You're cleansing us," I said. I remembered that when she'd come to Sorrow's Point, she'd smelled like garlic. Tricky witch.

She shrugged. "Sort of. It's not like I meant for it to happen exactly."

I nodded. "I'm not mad. I find it interesting that you do it even without thinking about it."

"Guess I'm used to it."

"It was easy in Arizona with Vespa's love of pizza." I'd never eaten so much damn pizza in my life.

Tabby laughed. "That it was."

"Anything else we can be doing?"

She smirked. "Nothing legal."

Doc snorted.

"I don't think I'm even going to ask," I said.

"That's probably a good idea," Tabby said, then got an evil glint in her eye.

#

After lunch, we headed to Oakland, Maryland. That was the closest town to Kitzmiller. The scenery was already changing. There were a lot more trees. The green leaves were still that lighter green they were after they first budded.

Checking in happened without a glitch. As I was unloading the car at the hotel, my phone rang. I almost dropped my suitcase.

I fumbled with my pocket and finally retrieved my phone.

"Hello?" I asked after I swiped the screen and put the phone to my ear.

"You the marker?" he asked.

His voice was gruff and countrified. Okay. One, I wasn't used to people calling me that. Two, I wanted to know their ulterior motive.

"Who's calling?" I asked.

"Name's Sam Moore. Got your number through your boss."

Well, that part checked out.

"How'd you know I was here?" It wasn't like I had a special GPS tracker or anything. Or, at least, I knew the Order hadn't given him one. They might be accessing my phone. At this point, I didn't put anything past them.

"What are you talking about?" he asked.

Maybe I was getting way too paranoid. "Never mind. We just got here."

"All right. Call me back when you're ready to meet."

"Okay. Sounds good."

"Yup."

Then he hung up. I was starting to wonder what happened to normal telephone etiquette.

I hauled the suitcase and Tabby's large witchy bag up to the hotel room, then knocked on the door.

She opened it soon after. "What took you so long?"

I hauled the luggage inside and set it on the bed. "Our contact got in touch already."

"Damn. That's fast."

Glad it wasn't only me that felt it was odd. "Tell me about it. Makes me feel kind of weird."

Isaac meowed from his carrier.

Tabby rushed over and let him out. He leaped free and darted under the table Doc had settled at.

'That doesn't look good," I said.

"Do we have time for me to ward the room?" Tabby asked.

"Looks to me like we'd better make time." I wasn't going to take any unnecessary risks.

Tabby grabbed her witchy stuff. I snatched the remote from the nightstand and turned the TV on for Lucy. No sense in her being without it when she didn't have to be.

"Thanks, Jimmy," she said.

"No problem, kid."

I sat on the bed and watched Tabby go through her routine. She used sage and a few other herbs, wound together in a stick and lit one end. Then, she went to all the heating vents, windows, and doors to the room and drew symbols with holy water. Each symbol glowed green like it usually did.

Tabby's magic always looked green to me. I wasn't sure why. Maybe it had something to do with the type of magic she did. Since I had no one to ask, I shrugged it off and put it on the "to be answered" list. That list was getting pretty damn long.

I'd seen other colors come out of her magic before, but the predominant color was green. It reminded me of nature. That was probably a good thing.

It didn't take her long. Maybe twenty minutes and then she extinguished the herb bundle. The smell was pungent, but not horrible. Just herby and burnt.

"That should do it," she said.

"I love watching you work."

She paused, then blushed. "You're crazy."

"Nope. Really. It's cool watching you do what you do." Hell, I wished I could do it.

She shook her head. "Well, thanks, I guess."

"Should I call the guy?" I asked.

"Might as well." She sat on the bed beside me.

I pulled my cell phone free and dialed the number.

"Mr. Holiday?" the guy asked.

"Yup. Where do you want to meet?" I was hoping it was going to be a decent place and not some hole in the wall.

"Where are you staying?"

"The Best Western in Oakland."

Tabby was making odd faces at me.

I rolled my eyes. She could be such a dork.

He paused for a minute. "There's a diner down the road. I forget the name, but it's only a couple of places from the hotel. How 'bout I meet you there in a half-hour?"

"Works for me. My assistant and I will see you there." I wasn't ready to eat again, but whatever.

"All right." And the guy hung up again.

"Must be a cultural thing," I mumbled to myself.

"What?" Tabby asked.

"Never mind. We're to meet at a diner nearby in a half an hour."

"Guess we're officially involved then."

"Guess so."

"Do we have to go?" Lucy asked.

"No. You and Doc are staying here I think." There wasn't a reason at all for them to come along. "If someone breaks in, do what you did in Italy."

She grinned at me. "Okay."

What was I getting myself into?

Possession

TABBY AND I headed down to the lobby. I stopped at the front desk. After a minute, a young girl with long brown hair came over.

"Can I help you, sir?" she asked.

"How do we get to the local diner?" I asked her. It was much easier than checking online. Besides, Sam hadn't even told us the name of the place.

"Turn right at the parking lot. It's a couple of places down. Look for the sign that says, 'Mabel's.'"

"Okay. Thanks." If I'd been wearing a hat, I would have tipped it to her. Maybe Doc was rubbing off on me.

When we got to the car, Tabby paused. "Are you ready for this?"

I shrugged. "It's not like that part matters, does it? I have to do this, or you and I are going to have to get very creative about our finances."

Tabby got into the car and I crawled into the driver's seat. What I wanted to do was spend the rest of the day hiding in the hotel room, but that wasn't going to happen.

"I'm thinking we'd better start saving more anyway," Tabby said as I pulled out of the parking lot.

"For what?"

"So you aren't beholden to the Order forever."

I didn't answer. In a way, she was probably right, but this wasn't the time for that conversation. I had to stay focused. Demon time was upon us.

I spied the Mabel's sign about two seconds later and had to slam on the brakes not to miss it. It was an older, smallish sign with "Mabel's" spelled out in cursive writing.

"Jesus Christ," Tabby said.

"Sorry. The oaf can't handle doing more than one thing at a time." I pulled into a parking spot.

Tabby waited until we were about going into the restaurant. "You are not an oaf."

She stepped past me and entered the restaurant.

I had to smile. I got that goofy feeling in my gut. My girl loved me.

It was an old-timey-looking place with chintz curtains. I stepped over to the "Please Wait to Be Seated" sign, but then Tabby poked me on the arm. I stared at her. She was pointing at a guy dressed in a plaid shirt that was unbuttoned. He was waving us over.

I followed Tabby's lead.

The guy stood up from the table and held his hand out to me. I noticed he had sidestepped Tabby. That, I wasn't too crazy about. Countrified or not, being a dick wasn't going to get you on my good side.

I took it and shook.

"Mr. Holiday. I'm glad you could make it," he said.

I nodded and sat down. Tabby sat beside me.

I pointed to her. "This is Tabby. My assistant."

"Sam Moore. Nice to meet ya, ma'am."

She smiled. "Nice to meet you, too."

She was good at hiding her real feelings. I had to give her that. I knew, in a different situation, she would have kicked his ass.

Sam turned back to me. His eyebrows were bushy. I was tempted to get out a weed whacker to trim them.

"I thought we'd get somethin' to eat while I explain this mess."

The food made sense. These were country people. If you didn't share a meal with them, they figured you couldn't be trusted. "Sounds good to me."

In general, food was a good way to make a connection with people. Granted, it had only been a few hours since we ate, but a little discomfort was a small price to pay for creating a sense of ease. Maybe we'd get some solid information.

A waitress came over and took our drink orders. When she stepped away, Sam leaned forward. "I don't think I have to tell you that there are some weird things going on here."

"Weird seems to be the norm with this type of thing," I said. I glanced at Tabby. "Tabby and I have seen a lot."

Sam nodded. "Might as well get it all over with. It all started with Mikey Fisher's funeral."

I nodded.

The waitress came back with our drinks, then took our food order. I got a hamburger. Tabby got a club sandwich.

As soon as she left, Sam continued, "The thing you have to understand about Mikey is that he never did anything. I mean nothing. His mother was his slave."

He picked up his soda and took a drink. "You can imagine what his health was like. Every so often, you'd see them come into town, but Mikey couldn't walk very fast. If he did, he'd get out of breath so bad you'd think he was going to drop dead in the street. 'Long about three weeks ago, he up and died."

Tabby exhaled slowly. I had to admit, I was interested too. But I still had no idea how this had anything to do with exorcism. Hell, if that was the case, I could solve the obesity problem systematically.

"They had to cut a hole in the side of the house to get his body out."

"That's so sad," Tabby said.

Sam nodded. "He did it himself, but still don't change how horrible it was. Anyway, they had to use a stretcher that would be used for a large wild animal. His mother was hysterical of course."

He took another drink of his soda. "We all went to the funeral. Not many of us left in town, so we kind of stick together. It was awful. Not so much because it was a funeral home, but because of the stink."

"What stink?" I knew morticians washed bodies and stuff, so there shouldn't have been any smell.

"Mikey's family are kind of backwoods believers. They don't believe in having a body formaldehyded or whatever you call it. Even had an autopsy refused in the will. Cited religious reasons, I think. So it's spring. And around Mikey's funeral, we had a warm spell. The smell wasn't pleasant and here we all were hoping the minister would get on with it."

"If they aren't Catholic, how did we get involved?" Tabby asked.

Sam chuckled. "Impatient, aren't you? I'll be getting to that in a minute."

The waitress came with our food and set it all down in front of us. We were all quiet for a few minutes while we ate. Kind of said something about what we had gotten used to. Talking about a funeral stink hadn't affected our appetites. Sam's either. It was almost as if Sam couldn't stop himself.

He wiped his mouth with a napkin. "So we were all there, listening to this fire-and-brimstone preacher, when old Mikey sat right up in his coffin. We all freaked out. Women screamed. He turned his head, looked at us all, and laughed. I don't have to tell you, I hauled ass outta there."

He shoved a French fry into his mouth. At least he chewed with his mouth closed.

"Were they sure he was dead?" I asked.

Sam nodded and swallowed. "By the time I had the funeral, his body was all bloated like a fish. Even green and black in places. He was right dead."

"I have to say, that's different." I scratched my head. I hadn't ever heard anything like it.

"But that ain't all," he said. "Ol' Mikey went back home. I shit you not. He was totally different though. First thing he did was fix the hole in the wall of the house. In days, his mama's house was a hell of a lot better than it ever had been. He was still discolored in spots, but it was like all that excess fat melted away."

I froze. I *had* heard of that before. "That almost sounds like an old episode of *The Twilight Zone*."

Sam laughed. "Believe me, I wish that was the case." He pushed his plate away. "Every day, Mikey changes more. He don't even smell anymore."

Now, I had to admit, that was weird. "How did we get notified?"

"I guess the church got people who look for stuff like this. Our local newspaper published an article about it. A few priests tried to talk to ol' Mikey, but he run them off with a shotgun."

"He looks normal now?" Tabby asked.

"Yep. Fit as a fiddle. Nothing like what he was in life. Only thing is his eyes."

"What about his eyes?" I asked.

"Milky-white dead. Ugly they is, but nothing to help that."

"Yuck," Tabby said.

I rolled my eyes at her. "Guess that's why I was put on this."

"What do you mean?" Sam asked.

I stared at him. "I tend to get the weird cases. Weirder than usual, I mean. This is the first time I've heard of a dead body being possessed."

"Might be the first time you've heard about it, but the Jews have a legend about it," Tabby said.

I stared at her. This was news to me. "Really?"

She nodded. "It was in this movie I saw a few years ago. Let me think about it and I'll try to see what I can find out."

"Sounds good to me." I turned to Simon. "Looks like we have some research to do."

He nodded. "I feel better knowing you all are gonna try to make this right."

"We'll do our best," Tabby said.

"We'll give you a call when we're ready to meet Mikey," I said.

"Fair enough," Sam replied.

#

"I gotta say I didn't expect that," I said when I got in the car.

Tabby slapped her hand on the dashboard. "I remember what it's called now. A dybbuk."

I started the car. "And those entities can possess dead bodies?"

"According to the movies they could."

"It's a starting point at least." I had a feeling that I needed to start reading more books dealing with the occult when we got home. There was too much I didn't know and watching movies didn't cut it. Too much stuff was changed to be more dramatic.

"Yes, it is." As soon as we got back to the hotel room, I pulled out the iPad from the suitcase.

"I take it you got a hell of a case," Doc said.

"Know anything about dybbuks?" I asked him.

"Duh—what?" He raised his eyebrow.

"Never mind." Maybe they were called by other things by different cultures.

Isaac hopped up on the bed beside me and watched me fiddle with the tablet. That cat was something else. One day, I was going to wake up and find him searching for kitty porn or something.

Lucy got up from the floor, came over, and sat on Doc's knee.

"I don't like this," she said.

"I know if you feel bad about it, it's going to be bad, but I have to try."

She nodded. "I still don't like it."

"Duly noted."

Tabby sat on the bed beside me and started flipping channels. One of us might as well relax.

I typed "dybbuk" into a search engine and got a bunch of hits.

"Aha!" Tabby said suddenly. She was on a movie channel. Some scary movie was playing.

"What?" I asked.

"This is it. It's called *The Unborn.*"

I set the iPad down on the bed. Not exactly the best way to research, but hell, maybe it was better than nothing. Better than general descriptions I was finding online anyway. I needed to start creating my own occult library. This was getting to be ridiculous.

#

Was the movie any help? Not really. I'd dealt enough with demons to recognize when someone could be faking. I already knew that there was some truth to it or the Order of Markers wouldn't have brought me in. I wasn't going to make the same mistake as last time, either. I would still do all the tests. Whether alive or dead, this was a possession. I didn't know by what. Whether that mattered remained to be seen.

Even odder was that I felt more at home in this hotel room than I did in my own house. Maybe because home was now soiled by what happened to Lucy. When I got home, I needed to fix that. I hadn't felt it so much before Italy, but after, the house felt almost suffocating.

I knew Tabby wanted to save money, but I thought the proper thing to do was get rid of that fucking carpet and pad. At least then all vestiges of what the fleshing rod had done to Lucy would be gone. If nothing else, it would make me feel better.

"You think too much," Doc said from his spot at the table.

I laughed. "I'm that bad, eh?"

If Doc noticed it, I needed to reassess what the hell I was doing when I wasn't working on stuff. Shit.

"Yup," he said. "Gotta let all that go. You need to focus on the task at hand."

He was right. As usual. "What would you suggest?"

"Does it really matter what this thing acts like? You fight demons with a mish-mash of witchcraft and discombobulated Christianity."

"Yeah."

"Point is—why concentrate on the type of thing it is? I can see the little gears in your head rolling round and round—mostly getting stuck on the religious aspect of the thing. That part doesn't matter in the way you think it does. Do what works for you."

"You know, you are really wise sometimes."

Doc laughed. "You know better than that."

"Okay. Okay. I'll stop."

I stared at Tabby asleep beside me in the bed. It was her words that had kept me going. Her attitude, too. Doc was right.

"I promise," I said. "I'll listen to you more often."

He laughed. "Don't make promises you can't keep, boy."

"So again, what do I do now?"

"Tomorrow, I'd call your boss, see if they gathered any evidence about the case, and if the men sent here ran away like little chickenshits."

I snorted. "Okay. That's a good a place to start as any."

"Whatever answer he gives you, you'll know what you have to do."

I exhaled. "This is going to be a weird one."

Doc shrugged. "Just when you think you've seen it all, something worse comes in to take its place."

"Ain't that the truth," I said.

Chapter Seventeen

I'll Follow You

I TOSSED AND turned all night. My brain wouldn't stop working. I knew, because of the last time, that whether they had investigated or not, the best thing to do would be for me to investigate myself. Other information might give me extra stuff to look for, but it wasn't a replacement for me seeing it with my own eyes.

I got up about five, went down to the hotel's conference room, and grabbed some pastries and coffee. Then, I carted it all back to the room.

Tabby sat up as soon as I walked inside and closed the door.

"What are you doing?" she asked, rubbing her eyes.

"Couldn't sleep, so I come bearing coffee and breakfast."

She forced herself into a sitting position. Then she grabbed her cell phone off the nightstand and stared at the screen.

"Do you know how early it is?"

I laughed. "Sadly, yes."

I handed her a cup of coffee and set the plate of pastries on the bed. Then I went to my side of the bed and sat.

"Figure out what we're doing?" she asked.

"I'm going to call Father Martin. Find out what the other priests knew, if anything. After that, I'll call Sam and see about going to see our subject."

She nodded. "And Doc and Lucy?"

"They can come along and stay in the car. I'd rather Mikey not see them if he is possessed. They would be close enough if we need their help. All I plan on is a meeting. Maybe do an investigation. Nothing more."

"You do realize that your plan is destined to fail," Doc said after he popped into his chair.

I looked at him. "Why?"

Lucy got up from the floor in front of the TV and walked over to me. "Because your plans never work."

I laughed. "What is this, Gang Up on Jimmy Day?"

Tabby snickered. "No, I think we all know enough by now to expect all hell to break loose."

"Okay, fine. But if I don't plan, I'll never get anything done."

Tabby patted me on the shoulder. "Do your best. So when are you going to call?"

I took a sip of my coffee and grimaced. It tasted like black tar. "Probably at least eight. I hope I can catch him before Mass."

"All right."

#

I tried to call, but all I got was voicemail. As usual, the others were right. Still, it didn't prevent me from moving on with my day. I could do my own thing. So I called Sam.

"Hello," he said.

"Yeah. This is Jimmy. I wanted to know if you could set it up for me to meet Mikey."

"Don't know about that. One, he doesn't have a phone. And two, don't know how I feel about just going over there."

That was a bunch of help. No wonder this case was such a clusterfuck. "Well, if I'm going to do anything about this, I have to meet him sometime."

"I wish there was some way to let him know we don't mean him no harm."

I sighed. I was starting to get irritated. "That's the problem. We do mean it harm. That spirit needs to go back from where it came from."

Sam tsked into the phone. "It ain't gonna like that."

I started laughing. "You know, you are something."

"How?"

"You are all hell-bent on telling me about this guy, but the minute I choose to do something, you turn chickenshit and run." I knew I was adopting Doc's term, but shit. It fit. If I was willing to risk my rosy-red ass, he could too.

"Hey, nobody said anything about me having to get involved more than I already am."

"Fine." I rolled my eyes. "What's his address?"

"1473 Turnbill Road, Kitzmiller, WV. You need the zip?"

"Nope. Got GPS."

"All right then." And he hung up.

"Sonofabitch!"

"What?" Tabby asked.

"Old Sammy boy is too much of a pussy to even show us where the home is." No wonder this was the case no one else wanted. Jesus Christ.

"Seriously?"

"Yep. I'm not kidding." I wished I were.

"All right. I'll go get my shower. We might as well try to go out there."

I nodded. "My thought exactly."

#

As soon as I got off the phone, Tabby and I packed up our tools and got ready to leave. One problem: Isaac was standing near the door.

"Where do you think you're going?" Tabby asked.

Isaac meowed at her and stared at her with wide eyes.

She crouched down. "I know you are my familiar, and while I don't exactly know what all it is that you can do, I'm not about to put you directly in the path of danger. Stay here and protect the room."

Isaac huffed and stomped off into the bathroom. I made sure his water bowl was full and shut him inside where he couldn't cause too much damage. At least I knew for sure where he was. Worrying about Lucy was enough. I didn't need to add another thing to my list.

We left the hotel and went downstairs. We all piled into the car as fast as we could. No sense in holding back now. I got the car started and set up the GPS.

"How far is it from here?" Tabby asked.

I glanced at the GPS. "Says about five miles."

All we saw were lots of trees and old homes that probably needed to be torn down. Every once in a while, we'd spy a decent looking house. I kind of worried about that nice house next to all the desolation.

"Does everyone around here have fourteen dogs?" Tabby asked.

I knew she was exaggerating, but almost any house we passed had a bunch of them. "Probably crime."

"It's a shame. This was an old mining town. You can tell from the row houses."

"What are row houses?" Lucy asked from the back seat.

"Back in the old days," I said. "Each coal mine would build housing for the miners. They paid a certain amount of rent to the mine company out of their paycheck."

"Wow. That's weird," she said.

I nodded. "The mine companies controlled everything for the miners. They even gave them their own type of money so the miners could only shop at the company store."

"That's so wrong."

"They don't do it anymore. Laws were written against it," Tabby said. She turned in her seat. "Were the gold miners out West the same way?"

Doc shook his head. "Gold miners were mostly independent. If a seam of gold was found, the miners worked until it was gone. There wasn't enough to support something like that."

"That makes sense," Tabby said. "If there'd been that much gold, nobody in this country would have to work."

I laughed. "Nah. One lucky bastard would have it all and the rest of us would still be scrimping and saving."

"My, aren't you a ray of sunshine today," Tabby said.

Doc laughed. "Ain't he always?"

Lucy giggled.

At least someone found this funny.

#

Mikey's house was bad. There were tatters of plastic hanging in between the support beams of the porch. The wooden siding was gray from years of weather beating away at it. The porch seemed like it would break off the house if someone stepped onto it.

I didn't even make it to the porch. A man barreled out of the house holding a shotgun. "Whatcha want?" he asked, harshly.

I held my hands palm up. "To talk. Am I speaking to Mikey?"

He spat a wad of tobacco juice at my feet. "Mebbe."

His coal-black hair was flying around his head in the wind, but it was clean. His skin was pale and his eyes were blue. If this was Mikey, either Sam had been lying or the transformation was complete.

"I heard about what happened from Sam. I'm here to investigate."

His eyes narrowed. "Investigate what?"

"Your possession." I figured there was no sense in lying.

He started laughing hard. "All right. You and your lady friend can come in, but don't touch nuthin'."

I motioned for Tabby to get out of the car. She followed me up the steps.

As soon as I got close to Mikey, I smelled it. There was still a faint scent of death. It wasn't enough to make me gag, but it was there. Sam hadn't been lying.

"Thanks for talking to us," I said to him.

He chuckled. "You're the first one that's shown up here with some sense."

"How did the others act?" Tabby asked.

He guided us into the house. In the front room, there was a sofa, a rocking chair, and a recliner. An elderly woman sat in the recliner.

"Ma," Mikey said. "We got company."

She turned her head up to look at us. "What are you nice folks doing here?"

"We came to talk to you and your son," Tabby said.

Tabby and I sat on the couch. It smelled strongly of body odor, but I forced myself not to make a face. I seriously doubted the old woman could manage to even buy a new couch, so there was no sense in making her feel bad.

Mikey leaned the shotgun against the wall and sat in the rocking chair.

Mikey's mom turned to us. "Would you folks care for something to drink?"

There it was–the country test again. If we refused something when it was offered to us, it made us out to be untrustworthy. Tabby didn't miss a beat.

"That would be great," she said.

The old woman smiled. "I have water and I can make coffee if you don't mind sitting a spell."

"No need to trouble yourself with us," I said. "Water is fine."

"You sure?" she asked.

I nodded. "Thank you."

Mikey spit another wad of juice into a cup. "Momma don't get a lot of visitors no more."

"That's a shame," Tabby said.

Mikey nodded. "Ain't her fault I come back from the dead. Not like it's catching or anything."

"In general, people are idiots," I said. I was thinking of old chickenshit Sam.

Mikey laughed. "Ain't that the truth. Them priests they sent before, didn't take much to scare 'em."

Mikey's mom came back with the drinks and handed each of us one. The glasses had painted yellow flowers on them and they were clean.

"Thank you," I said.

She settled herself back down in her recliner with a grunt.

"How long have you lived here?" Tabby asked.

"Lived in Kitzmiller my whole life. Don't imagine I'll live long enough to go anywhere else," Ma said.

Mikey spat in the jar again. "Don't say that, Ma. If I got anything to do with it, you ain't leavin' this Earth anytime soon."

"I don't want you messin' with that book again. Look what it got you."

"What book?" I asked. I had visions of the book from those demon movies with Bruce Campbell.

"Found it in the woods out behind the house," Mikey said. "Went back there 'cause I heard something, but I wasn't fast, so I missed whatever left it."

He reached into his overalls and pulled out a stained volume. It had a wine leather cover. "I did a spell in it and it kept me from bein' dead for good."

"Wow. Must be an amazing book," Tabby said. "May I see it?"

He spit more chaw into the jar. "You promise to give it back?"

"I promise."

He handed it to her.

I leaned over and started looking. It was written in Latin. No way was I going to be insulting and mention how odd it was he could read Latin. Besides, at this point, I wasn't all that great at reading it myself. Kudos for him.

Tabby flipped through the pages. Periodically, there would be a passage I could kind of understand. Hell, it was a good thing I'd boned up on it when I was in Italy, but I was far from fluent. From what I could read, there were a lot of animal sacrifices.

Tabby closed the book gently and handed it back to him. "It must be very old."

"Guess so," he said. "Don't find a lot of books in Latin no more."

I wasn't sure if that could account for knowing a language a person shouldn't know, since it happened before he died. I'd be more inclined to say Mikey was a smart kid. Shame he'd been stuck here.

"Where did you learn Latin?" Tabby asked.

Inwardly, I cringed.

"My poppa. He was always reading something. Was even educated at college." He watched Tabby carefully, but she didn't give any expression at all. That, in and of itself, was weird.

Ma started to laugh. "Then he fell for me, and since I wouldn't leave the holler, he dealt with it. Been gone fifteen years this December."

"Sorry to hear that," I said.

Ma nodded. "Why are you really here?"

It was time to come clean. No sense in lying. They'd know anyway. "I'm an exorcist. I'm here to see if I can help Mikey."

"Help me with what?" He glared at me.

"Help you be in the place you are supposed to be. That is, if you are possessed," I said.

He laughed. "They send you all the way out here for that?"

I shrugged. "Well, you did scare those priests."

His eyes flashed yellow so fast, I wasn't sure if it happened or not. "Now, that was something to see."

His voice was different. Darker. It almost sounded like more than one person had spoken. I knew his real soul was gone, but this…this was doing a hell of a good job hiding. I needed to remember that.

He stopped and glared at me. "You're a priest too."

"Sort of. I was defrocked by the church."

He laughed then. "So they sent the outcast to deal with little-ole-me. I love it."

Ma cleared her throat. "See. He ain't my little boy no more. Roses die when he touches 'em. I had rose bushes all around the outside of the house until he came back from the dead."

I glanced at her. She was about the only sane person I'd met in investigating this mess. Well, normal, anyway. "What is it that you want?"

She shook her head slowly. "If it weren't for that damn book…I don't tarry with things that are unnatural."

"Oh, not this again," Mikey said in the demonic voice.

I didn't think there was any doubt about him being what everyone said he was, but I still needed more proof.

"It's true. Somethin' here ain't right. It's against the Lord."

He gnashed his teeth and angled his head toward the wall.

I stared at Ma. "You want him back to the ground?"

"It's only what's right."

I looked at Tabby, then back at Ma. "We need to look some things up, but we'll be back."

Mikey snarled. "I don't like it, but I can't go against Ma."

I didn't know what that was about, but I wasn't going to question why he deferred to her either—not if it got us back in the house. His choices were his own and I wasn't about to say a word about it.

"We will be back after we figure out a few things," Tabby said to her.

I nodded at Mikey and we left.

#

We got in the car almost as fast as we could. Just because Mikey was listening to his mother didn't mean that he couldn't do something to us out of her sight. Besides, now that I was pretty damn sure a demon or something was involved, I didn't want Doc or Lucy anywhere near the place again.

"I'm guessing it didn't go too well," Doc said.

"Oh, I wouldn't say that. We just have to find out where the courthouse is," I replied.

"What for?" Lucy asked.

"I want to look at Mikey's death certificate," I said. It would be nice to know what he died of. And if he'd been declared dead. He could have had the smell because he rubbed a dead squirrel on himself. I wasn't about to believe anything.

"Who's Mikey?" Lucy asked.

"Our case. I want to look at his death certificate."

"Oh," Lucy said. "To find out if he really was dead?"

"Uh-huh. Gotta look at everything." I steered the car back onto the main road.

Now, where the court house was, I had no idea. Best thing to do was go back to the hotel and use the holy iPad. Then, if we could find out in time, maybe it wouldn't be such a big deal. And if I couldn't get a copy. I would have Doc use some of his swarthy talents and get a copy that way.

"I think I'd like to get some lunch first," Tabby said.

I glanced at the clock on the dash. It was just after eleven thirty.

"All right, madam. Where would you like to eat?"

"Anywhere, kind sir, just as long as the food is warm and the drinks are cold."

Lucy giggled. "You guys are silly."

Tabby and I smiled at each other.

As a team, we worked pretty damn well together.

Chapter Eighteen

Bodies

WE GOT TO the hotel room around twelve thirty. Part of me wanted to lay down on the bed and grab some sleep. The other part knew that I didn't have that luxury. I'd have time to sleep when I was dead. I picked up the tablet and started looking at rules about death certificates in West Virginia.

"Shit."

"What?" Tabby asked.

"I can't get a copy of the death certificate." Again, I found myself wanting to swat whoever abandoned this case. It was the biggest pain in the ass I'd encountered in a while. I almost preferred sitting in that class in Italy. Almost.

She wrung her hands together for a minute. "I was afraid of that."

I stared up at Doc. "Looks like I'll need you to do your magic."

He laughed. "Gotta wait until tonight. Won't be good for people to see a piece of paper traveling through an office on its own."

I laughed. "A big part of me would love to see that, though."

Tabby cuffed me on the arm lightly. "You are so bad."

"Jimmy isn't bad," Lucy said.

I laughed and patted the bed beside me. She walked over and hopped up.

"Since we can't do anything else today, what would you like to do?" I asked her.

"Can we take Isaac for a walk?" Lucy asked.

I glanced at Tabby, and then back at Lucy. "I think we can do that. That is, if Isaac will put on his leash."

"I'll take care of it," Lucy said.

Tabby and I looked at each other again and watched as Lucy

crawled onto the floor. Isaac trotted over to her. She crouched down and whispered something in his ear. He licked his lips and sat up on his haunches as if someone had asked him to look pretty, but there had been nothing.

"Isaac says, 'okay,'" Lucy said.

Tabby laughed. "Okay."

#

I wouldn't have believed it if I hadn't watched it. Usually, when Tabby pulled out the leash, Isaac would have a fit. Thus, the whole reason we use the pet carrier in the first place. This time, when Tabby pulled out the leash, he just sat there. She attached the harness to him and then clasped the leash to it. He didn't bat a paw. Leave it to Lucy to be the ghostly animal whisperer.

So that's how we were outside when my phone rang. I looked at the caller ID. It was Father Martin.

"Hello," I said.

"Mr. Holiday. How can I help you?"

At least he sounded jovial for once, and I had to be happy he was finally returning my call. It seemed like ages ago. Too much had happened in the meantime. "I was wondering if the other priests had managed to investigate Mikey at all."

The father cleared his throat. "Unfortunately, they did not get close enough to perform an honest investigation."

I laughed. I couldn't help it. They must have sent eighteen-year-old novices. Jesus Christ. "Did they get to look at the death certificate?"

I heard him typing on a keyboard. After a minute, the typing stopped. "It appears that they simply abandoned the project."

"Okay, at least I know where I stand." Right where I started. In a way, that was better.

"I take it he did not scare you off?" Martin asked.

"No." I cleared my throat. "There's something weird going on between him and his mother. He seems to not to want to do anything she objects to—except things to do with spellwork."

"That does seem odd. Be careful."

"I will."

Then he hung up.

"Well?" Tabby asked.

"Nothing. The other guys were too wimpy." And, honestly, that made me scratch my head. Being a priest, you had to deal with some stuff that wasn't pretty. The Last Rites for one. I couldn't reconcile these guys running away from Mikey, then being put out into the world to perform all of the rituals priests needed to do. If this was what the priesthood was becoming, the Catholic church was in a sorry state.

"I thought exorcists were supposed to be brave?" Tabby stared at me.

I shrugged. "No one said that they were exorcists, just that they were priests sent to investigate. But still, damn."

"Hmm. That may make a difference."

"At least you know you're doing the right thing," Doc said.

"I hope so," I replied.

I had to get my head screwed on straight. Okay. The other priests had done jack and shit. The only thing that meant was that I had to start at the beginning, which wasn't a bad thing. Doc could get me a copy of the death certificate as soon as he could.

For the rest of it, I needed to go back to the old rules of exorcism. I needed Mikey to speak in a language he could not know, tell me the location of a lost or hidden object, and display powers of some sort that were not of this world. All of these things were not easy to get. The demons liked to hide their power. If they were blatant with it, they would be easier to discover, and thus, easier to expel.

I had a feeling witnessing all of these things was going to be tricky. I guessed his voice sounding the way it had when Tabby and I were there would loosely be considered an out-of-this-world power, but I was looking for something more.

Then there was this weird say his mother held over him. I'd never even heard of a demon not doing something because its last wish can't go against his mommy. It didn't make any sense. The only thing that made sense to me was if the old woman was a practitioner not unlike Tabby, but I'd seen no evidence of that. It was strange.

We'd gone back to the room after the walk with Isaac. I felt tired all of a sudden. "I think we'll find out where the nearest delivery place is and order some pizza for tonight."

"Yay," Lucy said.

I laughed. Kids and pizza.

"Fine with me," Tabby said. "I wanted to look at what the town has to offer anyway."

I raised an eyebrow. "Are you looking at the same town I am? Granted, yes, there are some pretty farms, but there is nothing here."

She laughed. "I was talking about the guide here in the hotel room to try to find a pizza place."

I blushed. "Oh."

Tabby walked over to the dresser, started ruffling through papers, and looking in binders. "Aha!"

"I take it you found it?"

"Yup." She walked over to the bed and sat down.

I picked up the iPad and checked my email. Nothing. It was kind of interesting that, ever since I had gotten a phone number for Father Martin, it was no longer as important that I had an email address. Of course, my stuff wasn't being passed to the general clerics anymore either. And with the results I'd had with them, I was kind of glad. Still no list of Markers, but there was time. It wasn't like I needed it for this case or anything.

Lucy was staring at the TV again. We were going to have to do something about that. Spirit form or not, she needed to learn something not from TV. I shook my head. When all of this calmed down, maybe Tabby could try to homeschool her somehow. I wouldn't even know where to start beyond handing her books she didn't know how to read.

Doc cleared his throat. "I'll be off for a while now. Can't say when I'll be back. Though I'm hoping this won't take long."

I nodded. "Good luck. If it proves too hard or puts you in danger, just forget it."

He tipped his hat at me and disappeared.

"This whole thing seems somehow more complicated, doesn't it?" Tabby asked.

"Yeah. And I'm not sure I like it either."

#

Hours ticked by. As each one passed, the more nervous I got. It wasn't like the local courthouse should be hard to find. That meant that Doc had encountered something that made his task difficult. I was starting to think it was a bad idea to send him out. Granted, he got results, but I didn't think I could live with myself if he somehow got hurt.

With so many weird things going on, I wouldn't be surprised if someone hadn't created a ghost catcher. But if they had, how would they have targeted Doc?

What made more sense was the possibility that Mikey could see Lucy and Doc. I would be surprised at this point if he couldn't. It was possible, with that infernal book, he could have done a spell on anything connected to him—not that I knew enough about magic to know how that would work. But anything was possible.

The person I could ask was asleep. She'd passed out about ten. I didn't want to wake her up because I got another shiny new idea. And, well, Doc being gone left me uneasy.

"What's taking so long?" Lucy asked me.

I shrugged. "I don't know, honey. I'm hoping it's as simple as a computer problem."

I didn't say that I didn't think that was it.

She nodded slowly. "If he doesn't come back?"

'That's simple. I'll go look for him."

That seemed to calm her down. But she went and sat in his chair instead of plopping in front of the TV like usual. Isaac snored at Tabby's feet.

'Long about twelve-thirty, Doc popped in. He was slightly less opaque than before, but seemed no worse for wear. He dropped a piece of paper on the table.

"What happened?" I asked.

Doc shook his head. "Nothing interesting. Some kid they hired to clean pissed around more than anyone I'd ever seen. I thought he was never going to finish. Finally, he moved onto a different floor and I was able to get your paper.

"Thanks. Hate that it was so much trouble," I said.

He shooed Lucy out of his chair. She giggled, then sat in the other chair.

He took his seat and sighed. "If it was too much longer, I was going to forget it, but dammit, I didn't want to fail because of some stupid pipsqueak."

I got off the bed and picked the death certificate up from the table. Yep. Mikey Frazier, age thirty-four, died on April nineteenth. There it was in black and white.

"Thanks again, Doc," I said.

"If it helps ya, I don't mind doing it."

In a way, it would be nice to have a coroner's report, but I didn't think it was all that necessary. Sam hadn't lied about Mikey's death, so why would he lie about how he died? It didn't make sense. And if it didn't make sense, it wasn't true.

"Well, guess tomorrow it begins," I said.

"Can I come?" Lucy asked.

I shook my head. "After the way I felt in there, I think you and Doc better keep Isaac company. Anyway, the only thing I plan on doing is investigating for the exorcism. I'm going through the whole thing this time."

"Like you did with me?" Lucy asked.

I nodded. "I am assuming nothing. That's what got me into trouble last time."

I wouldn't admit it to her, but I wondered if I would have ended up meeting the Devil anyway if I hadn't been so damn dumb. There was a chance he wouldn't have been involved because I would have backed out. The deep part of my brain knew that it probably wouldn't have mattered, but I still felt guilty for the fleshing of Lucy. And if I had anything to do with it, I was going to make it up to her—somehow.

Chapter Nineteen

Private Eyes

THE NEXT MORNING, I had a notebook, a pen, and a vial of holy water sitting together on the table next to Doc. An aversion to religious objects was also a sign of possession, but I didn't want to use it if I didn't have to. It tended to piss the demons off.

"Are we going to get breakfast first, or are we heading out?" Tabby asked.

"Better to go ahead. I think fasting would be the right thing, don't you?"

She shrugged. "The exorcism, for sure, but I don't think we fasted before you did any of these tests. At Blackmoor, Tor was always cooking something."

I paused for a minute. She was right. Every time you turned around, Tor was cooking things. So that meant I couldn't have fasted. Especially when I did the investigation thinking I would not be the one to do the exorcism. It made me sad to think that she was gone from this world.

"So breakfast?" I asked.

"Where do you want to go?"

I shrugged. "I guess back to the diner. It's closer."

"All right."

I didn't talk much while we were eating. I think between what had happened in Italy and the thing with Lucy, I was getting burned out. If I survived this latest round, I was going on a vacation whether they liked it or not.

I was dealing with the case no one else wanted, punishment be damned. If I resolved the fucking thing, I deserved a treat.

"Boy, you are in a mood this morning," Tabby said.

"Why?" I asked.

She threw her napkin down on her plate. "You won't look at me. You griped about even having breakfast. Frankly, Jimmy, you're being a dick."

I stared at her for a minute. "Shit. I didn't realize. I guess I want to get all of this over so bad that everything else has been pushed off to the side."

She sighed. "I understand that. I do. But us going in there half-cocked is not only sloppy, but stupid."

I nodded. "You're right. Okay. So how do you want to handle this?"

"It would make the most sense to decide what test you're doing today."

I blinked. "It doesn't necessarily work like that. Sometimes, you can get proof of a few things at once."

She shook her head. "Well, that's fine, but you still need to know how you want to start."

"The first things to come up are usually the language thing and the shying away from holy objects, but I'd rather not do that one." Mikey did have that shotgun. He didn't need to pull anything supernatural to hurt me.

Tabby nodded. "Yeah. Let's not piss off Mikey until we have some protection."

She paused. "We could go ahead and hide something of yours."

I nodded. "That will work. What do you want to use?"

Tabby laughed. "Never you mind. It is a test after all."

"Okay, ole wise one. I'll defer to your grandiose knowledge."

"Smartass."

#

We got on the road about ten. At least we shouldn't run the risk of disturbing Mikey's mother at that hour. She'd seemed so little and frail that I was half afraid that she couldn't take the stress of her son's exorcism. Of course, him coming back from the dead hadn't helped either.

The road was as twisty-turvy as it had been the day before. It was warm enough to drive with the windows down. Forsythia bloomed along the roadway. All that yellow hid the ugliness of the place. It was pretty until you ran across a run-down old house.

I pulled into the driveway at Mikey's place. Mikey stood on the front porch—watching. At least he wasn't holding his gun this time.

I got out of the car.

"You couldn't get information?" he asked.

I laughed. "Guess not. Mind if Tabby and I come in?"

"Suit yourself."

He turned around and walked into the house without giving us another look.

I stared at Tabby. She shrugged. Then I walked to the house and opened the door. Ma was seated in her chair, fiddling with some yarn.

"Come on in, folks. I'm mighty interested in hearin' what you have to say," she said.

Tabby closed the screen door softly behind her. We walked over and sat back on the couch.

"How are you doing today, Mrs. Frazier?" Tabby asked.

She waved her hand at Tabby. "Don't be calling me by no formal names. Ma's just fine."

Tabby smiled. "Okay. How are you feeling today, Ma?"

She smiled back. "Been better. Been worse. Just another day."

Mikey walked into the room and sat in the rocking chair. "Might as well do them things you want to do to me."

I blinked. It wasn't proof enough, though. He could have been operating off what he knew about possession. I didn't see a TV, but that didn't mean he'd never seen a movie about it or anything. We hadn't exactly seen the entire house.

It wasn't that I didn't believe he was possessed, but I wanted to see if his demon operated on the same rules. If it didn't, I wasn't sure what I was going to do.

"What's in my bag that belongs to Jimmy?" Tabby asked suddenly.

I stared at her. I hadn't quite been ready to leap into that, but whatever. I knew, at least, that this would be the real thing. Tabby wouldn't fake something like this.

He stared at Tabby for a minute, then smiled. "Dunno if I be wanting to do parlor tricks all day."

Tabby smiled back. "Just a few. Your case interests us."

He nodded then. "His wallet is in your bag."

Wait a minute. I felt around to my back pocket. Holy shit. She'd pickpocketed me. I wrote it down in my notebook. Add that to yet another thing Tabby could do.

He chuckled and leaned forward toward Tabby. "He's pretty easy, ain't he?"

Tabby laughed. "Yep."

"Hey, um, sitting here, ya know," I said. Granted, she was creating a rapport with the guy, but I didn't feel like having my ego trampled either.

Ma started cackling so hard I thought she was going to keel over at any second. "You people are so funny. Just a laugh riot."

I liked Ma. It wasn't her fault her son was such a fuckup. I was kind of glad I was entertaining to her. She needed to laugh.

"What the hell else ya need?" Mikey asked me.

I shrugged. "Do you have any special talents?"

"Like what?"

I sighed. He was making this as difficult as possible. "Moving objects with your mind, being able to fly, do something that's supposed to be impossible?"

He leaned back in the rocking chair, then looked at Ma. "I don't know. Can I do anything like that?"

She shook her head. "I'd say coming back from the dead is pretty impossible."

Mike turned to me. "There ya go."

Now things were going to get ugly. I could feel it. "See, the thing is, I gotta witness it."

The room grew so silent you could have heard a pin drop. "Don't know what to tell ya 'cept I ain't leavin' this body."

I figured this was where it was going to go. "Ever ask what Ma wants?"

It was a whim, yeah, but it was worth a try. With that weird co-dependency that was going on, I might as well exploit it if it helped me out.

"Don't go rilin' him up none, ya hear? Last time took three days for them eyes to stop a-glowin'," Ma said.

While interesting, it was not what I needed, so I dropped the testing for the moment.

"Do you have any pictures of Mikey from before?" I asked.

Ma stared at Mikey. "Bring out the album."

"Yes, Ma."

Again, I was flummoxed. I'd never seen a possessed person defer to the living before. There was something I was missing. But I didn't know what.

Mikey left the room for a minute and came back with an old photo album. He quickly handed it to me.

"Thanks," I said.

He grunted and sat back in his chair.

Tabby and I started at the beginning. There was Ma's wedding day. Pictures of her looking carefree amongst a passel of dogs, and then there was Mikey.

As a baby, he was like any other critter, but as he got older, he got bigger and bigger. By the time we were looking at the end of the album, Mikey had to have been seven hundred pounds or more. From the photos, it looked like he lived on the couch we were sitting on. I was honestly surprised it was still holding together. His father had to have reinforced it with extra wood or something. Damn.

I stared at him, then back to the last photo in the book. The likeness was there, right around the eyes. Unless there had been two boys, this was definitely Mikey.

"How quickly did he lose the weight?" Tabby asked.

"You mean after the funeral?" Ma asked.

"Uh-huh," Tabby said.

"Right about two weeks, give or take. Skin was loose for a while, but it all seemed to go back where it oughta."

"How did you do it?" I asked Mikey.

He grinned evilly. "Magic." Then he winked.

Not wanting to stir stuff up more than I had, I figured we'd overstayed our welcome for the day. We'd gotten some answers anyway.

"How about we come back tomorrow? Give things time to calm down," I said.

"That there might be a good idea," Ma said. "Maybe Mikey won't be as cantankerous tomorrow."

I stood up and Tabby got up beside me.

"See you tomorrow," Mikey said. Then he began to laugh.

I nodded to him and Tabby and I left.

#

"I'm not sure if I like this," Tabby said after we were out of sight of the house.

"You aren't the only one. He's like a regular demon, but not. There haven't been any of the theatrics presented by Lucy, or, hell, even Vespa."

"Maybe he's trying to lull you into a false sense of security?" Tabby asked.

I shook my head. "I don't know."

"Was it just me, or did Ma seem a little weaker than yesterday?" Tabby asked.

"I don't know. She has white hair and a face with a road map of wrinkles. I'm not sure how much weaker she can get."

Tabby tapped her fingers on her leg. "She still seemed more frail to me."

"I'll take your word for it, then."

"What do we do now?"

I sighed. "I'd better ask Father Martin if he knows a thing about dybbuks."

"Fun stuff."

"Yeah."

#

By the time we got back to the hotel, Tabby and I were more quiet than we had been that morning. There wasn't much more to say. We had gotten physical proof of one item. The photos, while real-looking, could have been doctored, but it was beyond me how they could afford something like that. With the house falling in, I couldn't imagine there being a computer in that house. Hell, they didn't even have a phone. These were mountain people.

Tabby opened the door to the hotel room and Isaac jumped into her arms.

"Whoa," I said.

I closed the door behind me and stepped into the room. Everything was fine. But I remembered putting Isaac inside the bathroom. Maybe Lucy learned more tricks.

"What's going on?" Tabby asked Lucy.

"Almost the whole time you were gone, we could hear something scratching at the window, but Doc and I couldn't see anything," Lucy said.

I stared at Tabby. "Looks like Mikey isn't as beholden to his mother as we thought."

Tabby set Isaac down on the floor. "I'm glad the wards held."

"Me too." I did walk through the room in case I smelled something foul or strong, but there was nothing.

"How powerful would you say he is?" I asked Doc.

He scratched at his chin for a minute. "Outwardly, not all that strong, but he's hiding something."

I nodded. "And the hidden part is what has me worried."

"Why not ask Levi?" Lucy asked.

I blinked. "Who's Levi?"

"My friend. He's really nice. Too bad he doesn't like you very much though."

I froze. A normal little kid having an imaginary friend was one thing, but this? This was scary on a whole other level. My asshole grew tight and I hoped this wasn't going the way I thought it was.

"How long have you known Levi?" Tabby asked.

"Before we went to Italy."

I glanced at Doc. "Do you know who she's talking about?"

He shook his head slowly. "But I'll keep an eye out."

"Thanks."

Chapter Twenty

Within You, Without You

IT HAD BEEN a long time since I felt this freaked out. Little things, like how Lucy knew to contact the Devil to clean the carpet and what she'd done in Italy, now made a whole lot of sense. I had my suspicions about who Levi was, but I wasn't about to jump to any conclusions. I'd thought it before, but I needed proof before I jumped in with it. Mostly because, if they weren't the same entity, I could leave myself open for some bad shit.

Something demonic was influencing Lucy and it was something hugely powerful.

I wasn't so obtuse that the name Levi didn't automatically make me think of Leviathan. It was so easy. I now wanted to know how he got past Tabby's wards. That is, unless he was careful not to even want to cause us direct harm. It was something to ask about for sure.

"Hey, Tabby," I said.

"Yes?"

"When you ward the house or this room, do you tell it to protect us from any harm?" Granted, I had been in here when she did it, but I tended to pay attention to the magic I could see more than the words coming out of her mouth.

"Yeah, pretty much. Why?" Tabby asked.

"What if there's a loophole?"

She blinked. "Explain."

"Okay. If the spell is being interpreted as direct harm, then isn't it possible that someone could, say, have someone cause us harm and yet still enter because they themselves did not mean us harm?"

"What?"

"I mean, like, if some creature-thing hired a hit man or something."

She stared at me like I'd turned into a giant platypus. "This is why spellwork is so damn tricky. Shit."

"Believe me, I wish I could think of this shit a hell of a lot sooner too," I said.

She got up and started digging through her witchy stuff bag. "So they want to play hardball, do they?"

I scooted back on the bed. This was a witch on a mission and I was staying out of her way.

'Those fucking bastards," she mumbled under her breath. "If they think they can enter *my* house."

She frantically began drawing symbols in the air. This time, the color of her magic was red—and only red.

From someone who usually glowed green, this was not good. I had no idea what it meant, but I hoped it was just her being mad.

After about twenty minutes, she collapsed in a heap at the foot of the bed.

"There."

"Are you okay?" I asked.

"As okay as I'm going to be. Now, anyway. No one or no thing can enter this room without your or my permission. So right now, that is Isaac, Doc, Lucy, and you and me, of course."

"I take it, when we get home, you'll do that to the house?"

"You betcha."

#

As soon as it grew dark, the scratching on the window began again. I got close enough to see that there wasn't any person or thing close by to be causing the phenomenon. Compared to the stuff Lucy had pulled, a little scratching was nothing. Though the little voice inside my mind reminded me that this was how it started with Lucy, too. All Mikey needed to do was get a little stronger.

I forced myself to stop dwelling on it.

I texted Father Martin and asked him if the Order had any books on dybbuks I could use. His reply was a simple "no." I was on my own with this thing. It wasn't all that different than usual, but I didn't like it. Not with that book I couldn't read. There was too much that was unknown involved.

"If there was something you could change about all of this, what would it be?" Doc asked.

I stared at him. "I'd get hold of Mikey's book and, after finding out everything it said, I would destroy it."

"Do you know where he keeps the book?" Doc asked.

"No. Don't you dare," Tabby said. "If you do this, Doc Holliday, I'll never speak to you again."

He laughed. "Yes, you would and you know it."

He glanced over at me. "One book coming up."

"No," I yelled. But it was too late. He was gone. "Shit."

Lucy stared at me, her eyes brimming with tears. "Why does he keep going away?"

I crouched down to her level. "Because he wants to help, no matter what it costs him."

My phone interrupted the moment. I looked at the caller ID. It was Will. I hit speaker.

"Hello, Will. How are you holding up?" I asked.

A gnarled voice answered. "Will won't be talking any time soon."

"No!" Lucy cried.

"See you tomorrow, Jimmy boy."

Then the line went dead.

I took a deep breath. Lucy was nearly hyperventilating.

"Tabby, do me a favor and call Will using your phone," I said. While I hadn't seen this type of thing before, I'd heard about it.

Tabby took my phone and typed Will's number into hers, then called.

"Will? Oh, Thank God. We had a scare."

She paused. "No, Lucy is fine. Just a case we're working on has...some new tricks...Yes, of course."

She cropped the phone down to her side. "Lucy, honey, do you want to speak to your daddy?"

"Uh-huh."

The little ghost drifted over and Tabby held her phone so that she and Will could talk.

"It's either the speaker phone or just my phone," I said quietly.

"I'd say it was speaker. My phone has been in that house as long and as many times as yours."

"At least we got Lucy calmed down."

Tabby nodded. "And now we know how tricky he can be."

"That too."

#

"What do you want to do for dinner?" I asked.

"Well, I'm not feeling pizza again," Tabby said.

"I say we find a place besides the diner and Lucy can come into the restaurant with us." Kid needed something fun. And, well, this was the only thing we'd discovered that made her excited.

"That works," Tabby said.

We all climbed into the car and I plugged the place into the GPS on Tabby's phone. We left and started following the directions. Suddenly, I realized, it was not taking us to the restaurant at all. We were heading in the direction of Mikey's house. I stopped and turned around in the driveway of a construction business. Interesting that Mikey's prowess was connected to technology.

Tabby turned her phone off completely.

"I'll admit it. We should have just stayed there. That was stupid." I wanted to kick myself. We knew better than to leave the protected area when a demonic attack was going on. Hell, I was starting to wonder if Mikey was affecting our brains too.

Tabby sighed. "It is almost like someone or something is messing with our minds."

"You know who it is, don't you?" Lucy asked.

"Who?"

"The one. The light bringer. It's he who wants it."

"Well, he's not gonna get it. Hear that?!" I belted out. "You can't get me that way."

Then time stopped. Tabby was frozen beside me. Lucy was still in the back seat. The Devil, back in his business suit, sat on the other side of Lucy. I was getting tired of him invading my space.

"What is it with you and cars?" I asked.

He laughed. "Every day, someone always dies in a car accident."

"That's sick."

"I am. Isn't it marvelous?"

"What is it you want?" I knew he wasn't here for bizarre chitchat.

"Your soul, of course," he said.

"Oh, there's more to it than that. This isn't your usual thing."

He grinned. "That is what I love about you, Jimmy Holiday. You are so astute. It is ever so refreshing." He leaned against the seat. "Think of this as a job opportunity of sorts."

"Why me?"

"Because, don't you know, you're the most powerful one he has. That's why your paperwork was altered. That's why you never get any help. They are all jealous."

"Wait. Isn't envy a sin?" I *knew* it was Leviathan's expertise, but the Devil was master of them all.

When he laughed this time, ripples of power shook the car. "I want you, Jimmy Holiday."

It dawned on me then, not the part about me being most powerful or not. This was the Devil, after all. He could well be lying about that. But it did make more sense regarding the paperwork. I didn't think a human had any part in that. It was all a part of his grand design. Suddenly, I realized what it was.

"You want your own marker," I said.

He dropped his smile. "Of course I do. No reason for him to always have the upper hand."

"Well, I'll beg to differ, but you figured that."

"Which is precisely why it must be you. You are not afraid. Think about it."

And he disappeared. I sat there staring out the window. Of all the job offers I've ever gotten, that one I wasn't going to accept.

"Are we ever going to go, Jimmy?" Tabby asked.

"After I get my bearings straight," I said.

She paused. "He came again, didn't he?"

I nodded. "He wants me to be his marker."

I put the car in gear.

"Fuck."

"Yeah."

"What are you going to do?"

I swallowed. Hard. "I'll do what I always do. I'll prod on."

#

On the way back to the hotel, we stopped by a mini-mart and grabbed some cereal, candy, and chips. It wasn't healthy, but it was food. I had no plans to go out after dark at all until this case was resolved.

The only good thing was that I knew not everything that had happened had to do with Mikey and that took a bit of a weight off my shoulders. I wasn't going to underestimate him, though. He was still dangerous, but it was like comparing a rattlesnake to a black mamba.

Isaac meowed when we got back into the room.

"I know," I said to him. "Next time, speak up."

He ignored me and started licking his balls.

"Are you going to help me with this?" I heard Tabby ask.

I spun around. Tabby had all of the bags from the mini-mart.

"Shit. I'm sorry." I grabbed some of the bags and set them on the table.

"Doc's not back," Lucy said.

I sighed. "No, he isn't, but remember last time. He wasn't back for hours."

"Yeah." She settled down in front of the TV.

I ripped open a bag of chips with my teeth. "Find us something to watch, Lucy."

"Okay."

#

Tabby fell asleep around ten like usual. I stayed up with Lucy to wait for Doc. I sure as hell hoped he made it back. If he didn't, I knew Lucy would never forgive me.

I wasn't planning on doing the exorcism the next day, but it felt like I was going to. With every hour that passed, I suspected more and more I was going to have to rescue Doc. I didn't like that at all.

'Round about four, I was putting together a kit to prepare for battle when Doc popped in. He was holding the infernal book.

"Here," he said. "Put it in with your Bible. That should prevent him from knowing where it is."

I did as I was told. After the visit from the Devil, reading the book could wait.

"Are you okay?" Lucy asked.

"Was close there," Doc said. "I had to hide and make sure he didn't see me. Eventually, he went to sleep."

"Won't he know the book is gone?" I asked.

"I replaced the inside. The book he's holding is a collection of Donne's poems."

"All right. That works." I tapped my finger on my leg.

"Don't tell no one. Keep it completely to yourself. You don't know what he was digging out of someone's head."

I nodded. "Like last time, you and Lucy are staying here. I don't want to have to worry about you."

Doc returned my nod. "I think we all can work with that."

I grabbed items to do an exorcism. No sense in putting it off. This was coming. In my pack I put in the hotel's Gideon Bible. My Bible stayed where it was next to the evil book.

"I might as well write my ritual," I said.

"If you did it on that thing, you wouldn't have to write it every time," Lucy said, pointing at the iPad.

I laughed. "One of these days, I'll do that. For now, though, I think I'd feel safer with my own paper and pen."

#

Tabby cracked open an eye at first light. "What are you doing?"

I looked up. I was sitting in Doc's chair staring at the sunrise. He and Lucy were on the floor watching some TV show. I didn't know what it was. I hadn't been paying attention.

"Getting ready to do an exorcism," I said.

"This soon?" She sat up in bed.

"After the night we had, it's time to end this." I meant it too. I wasn't willing to have each day amp up more and more until Mikey gained enough power to truly fuck with us.

She nodded slowly. "Would you like to confess your sins?"

"I'm glad I don't have to worry about marking this one. His soul is already gone where it was supposed to go. I hate secrets. I don't like keeping stuff from you, but sometimes it can't be helped. And I'm horny, but that doesn't seem appropriate on the morning of an exorcism."

Tabby snorted. "If that doesn't take care of it, nothing will. So we're fasting?"

I nodded. "After this is over, I'm going to buy the biggest steak I can find and eat the whole damn thing."

Tabby chuckled. "I'll go grab a bath."

"Take your time. We actually do have all day." It was six-thirty in the morning. We had nine hours until nightfall.

Chapter Twenty-One

Suspended in Dusk

NO WAY IN hell was I going to do this exorcism at night. I hoped I would be home by then, too. It would be stupid—somewhat like going to stake a vampire right before he's ready to have dinner.

Doc and Lucy were leaving me alone. It was probably better that way. My eyes kept drifting over to the giant-size bag of Hershey's Kisses one of us had bought last night during the junk food run.

Maybe it was me who got grumpy being forced to not have chocolate instead of Tabby. It was something to ponder.

"Jimmy?" Tabby asked from the bathroom doorway.

I glanced up. "Yeah?"

"Have you put any thought into how we are going to create a safe place for the exorcism?"

I stopped. Shit. That place was full of objects that could be used as weapons. Around the outside, there were numerous old rusty cars, flat tires, and tons of various metal junk. Inside the house, well, it was full of old stinky furniture, Ma's knickknacks, and whatever the fuck Mikey had in his bedroom.

"Can you do an exorcism in a bathroom?" I asked.

Tabby choked. "It would be a little small, wouldn't it?"

I blew air through my mouth and wiggled my lips. "This sucks."

"Tell me about it."

I glanced around. Technically, the hotel room was exactly what we needed, but no way was I doing that either. Too many potential witnesses.

"Do you have to do the exorcism today?" Tabby asked.

I nodded. "I mean, it isn't like someone is holding a gun to my head or anything, but I feel like this is it. I can't explain it."

"If that's the case, then we don't have a choice," she said. "Let's prepare for battle."

I laughed. "I guess we'll see if there is a room we can clean out and hope for the best."

"If he even lets us do that."

"That's the other thing."

#

I almost expected some magnetic source to keep us driving in circles, but that didn't happen. The Devil would have thought that was funny. Perhaps there was something to this case that he wanted taken care of as well. I had a funny feeling that God and the Devil were using me. Otherwise, my exorcisms would be a hell of a lot more by the book.

Tabby had her witchy bag in the back seat. I had my holy water in my pocket and the Roman Ritual, the Gideon Bible, and my scribbles on the seat behind me.

The closer we got to Mikey's, the more nervous I became. I'd now seen a bit more of what he was capable of last night, and I didn't like it.

"What are we going to do with Ma?" Tabby asked.

I shrugged. "She'll go into the protective circle with us. I don't think she has anywhere else to go."

Tabby sighed. "Let's hope she doesn't bean you over the head or something."

I shook my head. "That would suck."

We made it to Mikey's around eight. It was easy and I almost expected them all to be asleep, but as soon as I parked, Ma shuffled out of the house.

"You come to make things right," she said.

I held my hand up to shield the sunlight from my eyes. "I'm going to try."

She nodded. "That's all I ask. He's in his room."

She shuffled back inside the house and Tabby and I followed behind her after we grabbed our stuff from the car.

"Is there a place where it would be best to do this, Ma?" Tabby asked.

"Basement's where he does all that foolishness," she said.

My asshole grew tight. I didn't even know this place had a basement. Shit. Note to self: start getting a tour of the house before getting involved in the exorcism process. The tours had happened organically the last two times. I needed to stop assuming shit.

Ma shuffled through the house and led us down the steps. They were rickety and moved with every step you took. The basement itself had a dirt floor. On one side, there were shelves and shelves of canned goods. On the other, there was a bunch of old rusty tools. Just ducky.

"Mikey's stuff is in there." She pointed to a wooden door that had a new padlock on it. Of course it was locked.

"How are we going to get in there?" Tabby asked.

Ma cackled, shuffled over to the workbench, and came up with an old crowbar. "Step aside, children."

She jammed that crowbar up under the hasp and in no time at all, the padlock was pried loose from the door. The nails Mikey used to attach it were bent off to the side.

"Wow," I said.

Ma smiled. "I know. I'm stronger than I look."

"I'll say," I said. Her being as frail as she was, well, that show of strength was odd. Since Ma had never threatened us, I had no reason to believe she would now. But maybe the hold she had over Mikey was somehow connected to the magic. I still didn't know how.

She pushed open the door and Tabby and I stepped inside. The smell was foul—like rotten goat's milk. All over the walls, symbols were painted in what seemed suspiciously like blood.

"Did Mikey do any of this before he died?" I asked.

Ma chuckled. "Hell, before he died, he couldn't even get off that couch upstairs."

The light bulb went off in my head. That old stinky couch was the true heart of the home. This room was a decoy.

"I think it would be best if we go back upstairs," I said.

Tabby stared at me strangely.

Ma shrugged.

"It's better to take everything from where it started," I said.

Ma's eyes twinkled. "Living room it is, then."

We all shuffled back up the stairs and through the kitchen. Right before we entered the living room, Mikey stepped into the doorway.

"Help you with something?" he asked.

His eyes were dark. I could almost feel the hate radiate off him.

"Your mother was giving us the grand tour," Tabby said.

Ma swatted at Mikey. "Get yourself somewhere useful, boy."

He stepped away. Again, I'd never seen anything like that. I almost wondered if it shouldn't be her that performed the exorcism.

Mikey loomed, but he did not touch us.

"Go on and sit down," Ma said to Mikey. He complied and sat in his rocking chair.

I glanced at Tabby. "I guess we wing it."

"I guess so," she said.

Tabby set her bag on the floor and started rifling through it. Soon she had a piece of chalk in her hand as well as a few other items.

"Just go ahead and relax, Ma," I said. "We'll do this with your chair inside."

Ma laughed, then sat down. Mikey was giving us all the stinkeye.

I forced myself not to stick my tongue out at him, but was I tempted.

Tabby drew a lopsided circle around Ma's chair. Unfortunately, there was nothing to tie Mikey down with, and since he wasn't going to be cooperative, he'd have to run loose. Well, sort of.

Tabby left a part of the circle open, went around the house with ribbons, and tied them to the windows and doors. That little trick was coming in handy. Mikey watched her closely, but did not say a word.

Then she stepped back into the circle and closed it with her piece of chalk.

"Hail to the guardians of North, South, East, and West—Earth, air, fire, and water. Hear my call. Aid us in our struggle. Keep us safe from harm within this circle. So mote it be."

When she touched the edges of the circle with her finger, the whole thing grew up into a faint green-colored bubble. I was kind of relieved to see the color of her magic go back to normal.

Tabby stood up and whispered into my ear, "He's bound to the living room, kitchen, and hallway. I put a ribbon on every door."

"Good girl."

I stared at Mikey. "Now, I know you've fought long and hard to become part of this world, but you do not belong here. It is time for you to go back home."

Mikey laughed. It seemed to echo around the house.

"You didn't think it would be that easy, did you?" He gnashed his teeth together. His eyes turned back to sickly white and his skin took on a lovely greenish purple hue. This was his true face.

The ceiling over my head cracked and plaster floated down onto my head.

I took a deep breath. "Evil being from a distant place, you have no purpose here. Be gone from this place."

Mikey, well, it laughed again. "If you tell me where my book is, I might let you in on a little secret."

Ah. So he'd discovered the ruse after all. I kind of figured that it wouldn't take all that much time for him to figure it out.

"Be good and get gone," Ma said.

Whoa. Okay. Note to self: parents as part of exorcism aren't necessarily a good idea. I got my focus back.

He was smiling. Suddenly, the wall separating the kitchen from the living room buckled. The house groaned.

"Who gave you that book?" I asked him, operating on a hunch. I had to keep focused. If the house collapsed around us, so be it. I didn't know what else to do.

He narrowed his eyes. "I found it in the woods, like I said."

"No way." I held myself ramrod straight. "You couldn't get up off that couch."

He stopped smiling.

"Now, tell me the name of the person who gave you that book. Or rather, tell me your name." I said it with that special voice. The power rippled through the air, outside of the bubble, and into him.

The body convulsed. He angled those milky-white eyes on me and snarled.

"Sit in your place, heathen." I pointed to the couch. "That is where it began."

It laughed. "You know, I find it hilarious that you are giving me orders from behind a protective circle. Hilarious."

I blinked. I knew it was only trying to bait me, but damn it was annoying. "What is your name?"

"Can't you think of anything else to say?"

I closed my eyes and prayed to God. "Please, Heavenly Father. Help me return this body to the earth. Help Ma get some peace in her last days. And help this thing go back to Hell."

I opened my eyes. "Tell me your name."

That time, I felt something extra. I couldn't explain it exactly, but it felt strong.

Mikey's body flopped out of the rocking chair and onto the floor. A pool of green liquid seeped onto the floor.

"Levi," he said in a grunt.

I glowered at him. "Your full name."

His eyes glowed yellow. "Leviathan."

Now, knowing what I knew about this stuff, a demon might be the actual demon or an emissary. This was not Leviathan. I knew better. Nothing about this dude had the power of a Prince of Hell.

"Give me *your* name."

It choked and sputtered. "Grandier."

Tabby gasped.

I whipped around and stared at her. "What?"

"That's the name of the priest who made a pact with several demons to possess nuns in Loudin, France."

I blinked. "Okay. Be quiet."

Jesus Christ. We were all acting like amateurs.

I stepped forward to the edge of the circle. "Grandier, I command you to take your rightful place in Hell. Leave this world and give back this body to the earth."

His body convulsed once more, then settled. There was a smell. A rotten smell. The skin on the body burst open and turned black.

"Thank you, dear ones," Ma said. Then she literally slumped over dead.

"Motherfuck!"

I smudged my foot against the circle and stepped out to look at the room. Sunlight shone dimly through the window, which was odd since it was noon. It should have been brighter. Something was not right.

I heard deep laughter. I peered at Tabby. She was grinning and her eyes were glowing yellow. "You never answered me whether you wanted to know the secret."

I backed up against the wall. I was staring at my worst nightmare.

Her face had become almost reptilian, complete with scales. "Shit."

"Like my new look?" She licked her lips seductively.

All I wanted to do was puke. How in the hell did Tabby become possessed?

She floated out of the circle and grabbed me around the throat. She wasn't squeezing. Not yet.

"I do not bargain with demons," I choked.

It laughed. Tabby's skin began to crack around her mouth and the skin was turning a bit purplish. It was almost as if the deadness was coming to her.

I had to pull myself together and fast. "Stop it!"

The Tabby-thing threw me against the opposite wall. I landed on Mikey's corpse. The rotten mess smashed underneath me and I got some of it in my mouth. I coughed and heaved, but nothing, not even saliva, came out of my mouth. The taste was like breathing in the ashes from a charnel house.

"You see. We are much stronger than you are. Give in. Join your queen."

I ogled the creature I was in love with. The travesty that she'd become. "In the name of God and all that guard the Watchtowers, I command you to stop!"

She backed away, sidestepped Mikey's corpse, and sat on the sofa. It was so nonchalant, I almost forgot I was dealing with a demon.

"Tricky witchy got bit by the great big bug," it said. It chuckled and pulled a chunk of hair from her head. There was some blood.

Jesus. I wasn't sure how much longer I could deal with this. "You can tell Asmodeus to go fuck himself for me."

It grinned. "I'd be glad to, but he is indisposed."

So Big Red had stepped in. Good to know, but that did not help me here at all. And if Big Red was my "friend," then why would my fiancée be sitting in front of me all possessed? Screw this shit.

"What is it you want?"

It blinked. "Your soul, amongst other items."

"I don't think he is going to let that happen when he wants it for himself." Then I paused. It all began to make sense to me now. "All of this for a book?"

It chuckled.

"That's what you are concerned about, isn't it?"

It got quiet. "The book is very important to me."

I closed my eyes. None of this had gone like the other times. I started thinking back to Tabby's magic going red. Her seeming less sure of herself. The house feeling off. He'd been strong enough to hide very, very well.

"You aren't the same demon, are you?"

It cackled and clapped its hands. "You are ever so smart."

"How long have you been with her?" I asked.

"You were in Italy, I believe. Poor Tabby was all alone."

It was coming together now. The time frame. The look. Lucy's sudden new friend. Her pact with the Devil.

"You're Levi," I said.

It nodded.

"Or, shall I say, we meet again, Leviathan."

He sidestepped out of Tabby. Literally. Her body fell to the floor beside Mikey's.

"You didn't kill her, did you?" I ran over and felt for a pulse. It was weak, but it was there.

He slowly shook his head. "She'll come to after a few of my playthings have their way with her."

"You sonofabitch!" I darted over to Tabby's bag and started digging.

He kept watching me, as if amused.

Suddenly, my hand fell upon something I could not believe. It wasn't in its protective case either.

"If I give you your book, will you bring Tabby back?" I kept staring at the bag, trying not to let on what I was doing.

"That would be ever so nice, but if that's the way you want it, I can oblige."

I took a deep breath and launched myself at him. This was it. My only shot.

He stared at me as if I'd turned myself into a flying squirrel. But it worked. I whipped up my hand and held the fleshing rod to his head.

He howled and sunk to the ground. Flesh began growing on him.

I dropped the rod and watched the magic work. Right before his body was fully formed, I licked my finger and made the sign of the cross on his forehead.

"You belong to God now," I said.

There was an electric jolt. It was flung across the room into the wall.

"No!" he screamed.

The flesh melted off him in a great puddle. Even what was left was sinking into the floor.

"What is that smell?" I heard Tabby ask.

I crawled over to her and held her head in my hands. "Are you okay?"

"Now I am." She glanced around the room. "What did you do?"

I shrugged my shoulders. "Caused havoc. Got my point across. You know. The usual."

She shook her head. "What am I going to do with you?"

"Love me."

"I already do."

"How do we take care of all of this?" Tabby motioned around the room.

I laughed. "I think it's time to give old Sam a call, don't you?"

#

I waited until Tabby had the fleshing rod hidden back in the car. I wasn't going to risk anyone's hands getting on it. But I had to admit, if it hadn't been there, I would have been sunk. Maybe I was going to become the Devil's boogeyman. He sure liked having me correct his children.

"Did you remember putting it in the bag?" I asked.

She shook her head then she walked back into the house. "I remember most of what happened after he was in me. He wasn't there all the time like with Lucy. I honestly thought I was just getting depressed."

I nodded. "So if you didn't put it there and Lucy or Doc didn't, that means this is another one of those things."

Chapter Twenty-Two

Paint It Black

"ALL RIGHT. YOU have my attention," the sheriff said. Sam had told me he was calling him in. Tabby and I were at the police station. It was so small it was just a little set of offices behind the jail.

Tabby was in another room.

"I am an exorcist and I was called in to help with the Michael Fisher situation."

The sheriff was this older guy. Kind of reminded me of this old actor, Wilford Brimley. He was balding and overweight with short white hair, and he sported a mustache.

"How'd this all happen?" he asked.

I took a deep breath. "We made sure Ma was behind us. Mikey was sitting in the rocking chair. There must have been some odd connection between the two of them because when the dyubbuk, spirit, whatever-it-was left, Ma died."

The sheriff shook his head. "Hopefully, she won't sit up in her coffin."

I sighed. "Believe me. I hope she doesn't either. I just want to go home and relax."

He nodded. "Is it as bad as they say?"

"What?"

"Performing an exorcism."

"The best I can tell you is that the movies don't give it justice."

He sat in his chair. "If we ever have something like this come up again, can we call you?"

I shrugged. "Why not? It isn't like there are all that many people around who can do my line of work."

#

"This was so messed up," Tabby said.

I was driving home. Or rather, driving back to the hotel room. It was too late to head back for the day. Not if we wanted to drive in daylight.

"When we get back to the hotel, do one of those cleansing baths."

"You know those wards on the hotel room and the house are worthless right?"

I shrugged. "You can redo them. It's going to be okay."

She slumped in her seat. She still hadn't told me what part of Hell she'd seen, but she had plenty of time. I wasn't going anywhere.

Doc and Lucy jumped up when we walked in. Isaac meowed at us. It felt good.

"Get it taken care of?" Doc asked.

"Yup. Tabby's going to get a bath and then I'm going to find a place to get a big steak."

Tabby laughed. "Men and their steaks."

"Hey, meat is good."

She walked into the bathroom.

I wandered over to the dresser and grabbed one of the drinking glasses. I unwrapped it and threw the wrapper in the trash. Then, I grabbed that bag of Hershey Kisses, unwrapped a bunch of them and put them into the water glass. I upended it into my mouth. It was heaven.

My cheeks were stretched out like a chipmunk's.

Tabby walked back in and froze. "I thought we were getting steak?"

I grinned around the chocolate. "Appetizer."

THE END

Thank you for reading! Find book four in the Marker Chronicles, SORROW'S LIE, in 2017!

Please sign up for the City Owl Press newsletter for chances to win special subscriber-only contests and giveaways as well as receiving information on upcoming releases and special excerpts.

www.danielledevor.com

@sammyig

All reviews are welcome and appreciated. Please consider leaving one on your favorite social media and book buying sites.

For books in the world of romance and speculative fiction that embody Innovation, Creativity, and Affordability, check out City Owl Press at www.cityowlpress.com.

About the Publisher

City Owl Press is a cutting edge indie publishing company, bringing the world of romance and speculative fiction to discerning readers.

www.cityowlpress.com

ACKNOWLEDGEMENTS

So many people I want to thank. First and foremost, Tina Moss. Without her, Jimmy would not have a home and look as amazing as he does. Josh Devor, for being the most amazing cousin ever. Kristin Dutt, for helping get the word out about Jimmy. Tabatha Barber, for giving me cat stories. Charles and Linda DeVor, for allowing me to be as weird as I want to be. Em Shotwell, for having an amazing marketing mind. All of the rest of the crew at City Owl Press, for being amazing. And, finally, the fans. You are the one's keeping Jimmy's heart beating.

ABOUT THE AUTHOR

Named one of the Examiner's Women in Horror: 93 Horror Authors You Need to Read Right Now, Danielle DeVor has been spinning the spider webs, or rather, the keyboard for more frights and oddities. She spent her early years fantasizing about vampires and watching "Salem's Lot" far too many times. When not writing and reading about weird things, you will find her hanging out at the nearest coffee shop, enjoying a mocha frappuccino.

www.danielledevor.com

www.ingramcontent.com/pod-product-compliance
Lightning Source LLC
Chambersburg PA
CBHW030813310726
48980CB00006B/483/J

* 9 7 8 1 9 4 4 7 2 8 4 7 2 *